THE
SMOKE
AT
DAWN

THE
SMOKE
AT
DAWN

A NOVEL
OF THE CIVIL WAR

JEFF SHAARA

RANDOM HOUSE
LARGE PRINT

Copyright © 2014 by Jeffrey M. Shaara

Published in the United States of America by Random House Large Print in association with Ballantine Books, New York. Distributed by Random House LLC, New York, a Penguin Random House Company.

Jacket image: From the original painting by Mort Künstler, **Battle Above the Clouds** © 1992 Mort Künstler

The Library of Congress has established a Cataloging-in-Publication record for this title.

ISBN: 978-0-8041-9442-6

www.randomhouse.com/largeprint

FIRST LARGE PRINT EDITION

Printed in the United States of America

10 9 8 7 6 5 4 3 2 1

This Large Print edition published in accord with the standards of the N.A.V.H.

CONTENTS

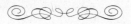

TO THE READER

This novel is the third in what will become a four-book set, taking place in the "Western" theater of the Civil War. As with the first two in this series, I follow several historical figures by telling you the story through their eyes, from their own points of view. Though the history is accurate, and every event happened as portrayed, because there are thoughts and dialogue, this has to be described as fiction.

This story deals with the critical campaign around Chattanooga in the fall of 1863. Consistent throughout this entire series is the voice of Union general William T. Sherman. Here, as well, are Ulysses S. Grant and George Thomas. On the Confederate side are two widely different personalities: Confederate commanding general Braxton Bragg, and Major General Patrick Cleburne. Also in this story is a voice I introduced in the first two books, that of Private Fritz "Dutchie" Bauer. I have come to accept that no story like this can be told effectively without focusing on the man with the musket, who truly determines if the decisions of the generals will succeed or fail.

In every case my research takes me back to this time, to the thought processes of the characters themselves. I am often asked about my research, and many times I've been asked **"How do you write the dialogue?"** There is no easy answer to that. The Acknowledgments section in this book offers a glimpse into the original sources, including diaries, memoirs, and collections of letters that offer enormous assistance in my efforts to find out just who these people are, to hear the "voices." My job then is to tell you what I hear. That might sound a little "mystical" (or a little schizophrenic), and I don't believe I'm either. The goal, ultimately, is to put words in the mouths of memorable and historically important people. If those words are not accurate to who that person was, either by deed or personality, the dialogue will come across as counterfeit— first to me, and most certainly to you. That's the magic of the research, and, I hope, the magic of the writing process.

It has been extremely gratifying to hear from so many readers, either through my website or on the road throughout my book-signing tours, who might have had no real interest in this particular topic (not everyone is a Civil War buff), but who have been drawn into these stories. One point I emphasize to every audience I speak to is that this is not a history book, nothing like what you were required to read in high school. My father, Michael Shaara, taught his creative writing students at Florida State that if you have any interest in writing a story, you must start and end with exactly that: the story. That's a lesson I've taken to heart for the past twenty years. I am under no illusions that if my father were still alive, many of the books I've written would have been his stories to tell. His masterpiece, **The Killer Angels,** is now forty years old, and is currently in its 112th printing. He died in 1988, having no idea what he had left behind.

The 150th anniversary of the Civil War has already been commemorated in all fifty states. I'm honored to have been a part of many of those events. Unfortunately, this four-year anniversary has overshadowed other milestones from our history, notably the bicentennial of the War of 1812, and, in 2014, the centennial of the start of World War I. With all due respect to those whose interests lie outside of the Civil War, the attention this particular anniversary has received is, to me, a sign of the power that the Civil War still holds over us. There are enormous numbers of descendants of the veterans of that war who still honor their ancestry in very graphic and impressive ways. (I have been caught completely off guard by the extraordinary emotions that pour through many events involving both the Sons of Union and Sons of Confederate veterans.) But even those with no personal connection at all continue to be drawn to the great fields where the war was fought, most notably Gettysburg. I was amazed how many visitors to the 150th anniversary events in July 2013 were making the trip to Gettysburg for the first time—and how many of those insisted they would return. I am a rabid supporter of battlefield preservation, and that kind of ongoing interest and passion is reassuring. As entertaining or enlightening as any battlefield might be, for me, **the ground** is an essential part of the research. As I mention in the introduction to my nonfiction **Battlefields** book, as the zoo is not the jungle, so the museum is not the battlefield. If any of these stories and characters are appealing to you, I implore you to see these places for yourself. You might find, as I did many years ago, that you are captured by what happened there. And perhaps you might sit down and write a book.

JEFF SHAARA

MAY 2014

LIST OF MAPS

ACKNOWLEDGMENTS

I am frequently asked about the sources for research for these stories. The following is a **partial** list of the original voices whose firsthand accounts were of considerable help in completing this story.

Lucius W. Barber, 15th Illinois Infantry
John Beatty, CSA
Ira Blanchard, 20th Illinois Infantry
Cyrus F. Boyd, 15th Iowa Infantry
Braxton Bragg, CSA
Irving A. Buck, CSA
Sylvanus Cadwallader
Joshua K. Callaway, 28th Alabama Infantry
Augustus Louis Chetlain, USA
Dr. James B. Cowan, CSA
Charles Dana
Thomas D. Duncan, CSA
Ulysses S. Grant, USA

William J. Hardee, CSA
William B. Hazen, USA
Joseph E. Johnston, CSA
St. John Liddell, CSA
James Longstreet, CSA
Arthur M. Manigault, CSA
Jacob B. Ritner, 1st Iowa Infantry
William T. Sherman, USA
Moxley Sorrel, CSA
Leander Stillwell, 61st Illinois Infantry
Sam R. Watkins, 1st Tennessee Infantry

My deepest appreciation to the following, who contributed invaluable information and assistance:

John Belfrage, Pierce, Colorado
Patrick Falci, Rosedale, New York
Colonel Keith Gibson, Virginia Military Institute
Kilwin's Ice Cream Parlor, Gettysburg,
    Pennsylvania
Charles F. Larimer, Chicago, Illinois
Stephanie Lower, Gettysburg, Pennsylvania
Emma McSherry, Gettysburg, Pennsylvania
Lee Millar, Collierville, Tennessee
Irene Wood Stewart, Jarrettsville, Maryland
Terrence Winschel, Chief Historian (Ret.),
    Vicksburg National Military Park

My sincerest thanks to the following historians whose published works proved extremely useful in the telling of this story:

Benson Bobrick
Captain H. R. Brinkerhoff, 15th U.S. Infantry
First Lieutenant Charles H. Cabaniss, Jr., 18th U.S.
  Infantry
Colonel Vincent J. Esposito, USA
Judith Lee Hallock
Captain J. Harvey Mathes
James Lee McDonough
Grady McWhiney
Don C. Seitz
Matt Spruill
Wiley Sword
Craig L. Symonds
Jeffry D. Wert
Brian Steel Wills

INTRODUCTION

By mid-1863, the Civil War has turned decidedly in favor of the Union. In July of that year, Federal forces win two monumental victories, at Gettysburg, Pennsylvania, and Vicksburg, Mississippi. Gettysburg is far closer to the great media centers of the day, including Washington, Baltimore, Philadelphia, and Richmond. Thus, most of the public's attention is drawn to the events there, including the astounding casualty count. More than fifty thousand soldiers are killed, wounded, or missing, after a three-day fight that many now believe will prevent Southern forces under Robert E. Lee from ever again challenging any Union army for dominance on the field. With so much newspaper and photographic coverage of Gettysburg, overlooked by many is what the capture of the Mississippi River town of Vicksburg has done to Southern fortunes. Whereas Gettysburg crushes Lee's hopes to end the war by posing a threat to Washington, D.C., the North's victory at Vicksburg accomplishes three things that in the long term have a far greater impact. With unobstructed control of the Mississippi River, Federal armies can now travel freely from the great cities of the North and Midwest directly to the Gulf of Mexico. Supplies and equipment can be fed to Federal forces now in nearly every part of the South, and there is very little that Confederate armies can do about it. Worse for the Confederacy, they lose the enormously valuable lifeline of men and resources from those states beyond the river, including Texas, Arkansas, and most of Louisiana. But there is another notable story told at Vicksburg, as important to the outcome of the war as the battle itself. It is the ascendancy of the Federal commander there, Ulysses S. Grant.

For two miserable years, Abraham Lincoln has struggled to find a general, **any** general, with the ability to confront his Confederate counterparts, and **win.** Though the Northern armies have on occasion been victorious, none of the Federal commanders can drive home those successes in a way that brings the war to an end. Some, especially in the East, fall flat on their faces, in stunning defeats where Federal forces greatly outman and outgun their adversaries.

West of the Appalachian Mountains, it is a different story. The enormously superior resources of the Union overpower what the Confederacy can put in the field. So far removed from Richmond, the Confederate commanders are often given second-class status by their leadership, denied supplies and manpower adequate to hold the Federal armies away.

For much of the war, both sides are concerned with a game of "capture the flag," as though by either capturing or preserving the Confederate capital of Richmond, Virginia, the war will be won or lost. In the West, the conflict rarely involves major cities at all. In 1862, the bloodiest battle yet fought on American soil takes place at Shiloh, in southern Tennessee, where no real town even exists. The crucial city of Nashville, Tennessee, is surrendered by the Confederates without a fight, and Memphis and New Orleans fall into Federal hands by the superior strategies and maneuvers of the Federal navy. At first, President Lincoln is no more impressed by the Federal commanders out west than he is by McClellan, Burnside, Pope, and Hooker. Early in the war, the Federal armies west of the mountains are commanded by Henry Halleck, and despite several victories, Halleck proves unable to press home his successes, allowing Confederate forces to rally and rally again. Lincoln recognizes that Halleck, though a capable administrator, is not a warrior. In mid-1862, after Halleck squanders the enormous Federal victory at Shiloh, he is called to Washington to serve as Lincoln's chief adjutant general, a role that seems far more suited to his talents. After his success at Shiloh, Ulysses Grant is elevated in Halleck's place. The next twelve months prove to Lincoln that his decision is the right one. Grant's star continues to shine, reaching a pinnacle after the fall of Vicksburg, where Grant accepts the surrender of thirty thousand Confederate troops.

In the cities of the North, the twin victories in mid-1863 produce a euphoria that the end of the war is a simple inevitability, that Southern hopes have been crushed. But dangerous Confederate armies still roam the great middle ground between the mountains and the Mississippi.

Grant's authority does not extend into eastern Tennessee. That command rests in the hands of Major General William Starke Rosecrans. During the 1840s, while most of his West Point contemporaries earn valuable combat experience in the Mexican War, Old Rosy, as his troops call him, pursues a career in academia, becoming a professor of engineering at the United States Military Academy. But his reputation is sound, and at the start of the war he immediately goes into service as subordinate to George McClellan. Rising through the ranks, Rosecrans is given command of the Army of the Cumberland, following a poor performance by Don Carlos Buell. Rosecrans now commands an area that includes eastern Tennessee, and parts of Alabama and Mississippi. But Rosecrans is a man who studies details better than he relates to his fellow officers. His unfortunate temperament makes enemies, including Grant, and Rosecrans never receives the attention, nor the respect, he feels he deserves.

His adversary is Confederate lieutenant general Braxton Bragg, who has risen to command following the death of his superior, Albert Sidney Johnston, killed at Shiloh. Bragg's reputation has been built upon a solid foundation of discipline, and his own troops learn to fear the severity of his punishment for offenses common to any army. But the Confederate troops benefit enormously from Bragg's discipline, and become an effective fighting force, easily capable of handling itself in the face of any Federal army. Still, he is never embraced by his officers, and survives in his position only because of his friendship with Confederate president Jefferson Davis. Like Rosecrans, Bragg is difficult at best, and is quick to pass negative judgment on his colleagues, which damages his ability to supply his army or gain preferential treatment when his campaigns require it. That kind of dismissal only adds to Bragg's hostility toward the ranking commanders throughout other theaters of the war.

Rosecrans faces off against Bragg at the Battle of Stones River, near Murfreesboro, Tennessee, over the New Year 1863. The battle is one of the bloodiest of the war, and though Rosecrans claims victory, neither side dominates the other. The victory in many ways is handed to Rosecrans, as Bragg chooses to retreat southward, though Confederate

forces prove superior in many of the battle's engagements. For the next six months, neither man
makes an aggressive move, inspiring vigorous protests from their respective governments.

In June 1863, Rosecrans finally moves, and engineers a tactically brilliant deception around
Bragg's army that causes Bragg to abandon the city
of Chattanooga. But Rosecrans's great triumph
is severely overshadowed in the press and among
Northern civilians by the twin victories at Gettysburg and Vicksburg. Rosecrans takes advantage
of the momentum he has been given, and flush
with confidence, he pursues Bragg into Georgia.
Both armies now stumble into confused maneuvering and inept positioning, caused by incompetence among commanders, as well as the difficult
mountainous terrain. By September 1863, the two
armies settle down to face each other west of
Dalton, Georgia, along Chickamauga Creek. The
resulting bloodbath severely weakens both armies,
but when Rosecrans makes a catastrophic blunder
in repositioning his lines, Bragg's field commanders, notably James Longstreet, take advantage. The
result is the complete collapse of the main Federal
position, and a stampeding retreat back toward
Chattanooga. Bragg refuses to grasp the magnitude
of his victory, and thus does not order a full-on
pursuit. Though Rosecrans is swept away by the
panicked retreat, the Federal troops make good
their escape in part by the solid wall of defenses put

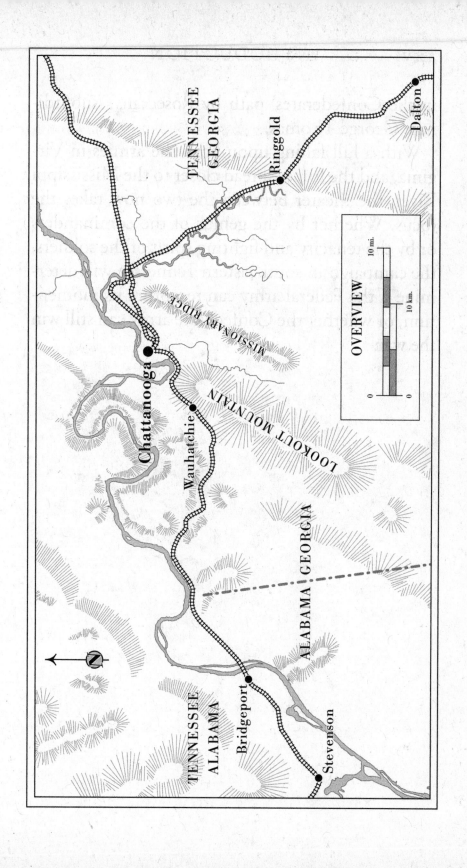

OVERVIEW

10 mi.

10 km.

TENNESSEE
GEORGIA

Dalton

Ringgold

MISSIONARY RIDGE

Chattanooga

Wauhatchie

LOOKOUT MOUNTAIN

ALABAMA GEORGIA

TENNESSEE
ALABAMA

Bridgeport

Stevenson

N

in the Confederates' path by Rosecrans's subordinate George Thomas.

With a lull falling upon both the armies in Virginia, and the forces spread closer to the Mississippi River, the theater between the two now takes the focus. Whether by the genius of the commanders or by the tenacity and fighting spirit of the soldiers, the campaign in southeastern Tennessee will determine if the Federal army can recapture its momentum, or whether the Confederate army can still win the war.

PART ONE

RECOIL

AND

REPOSITION

CHAPTER ONE

FORREST

NEAR ROSSVILLE, GEORGIA— SEPTEMBER 21, 1863

The prisoners were marched away under guard of only a few of his men. It was clear to Forrest, and to anyone in his command, that these Federal troops were not frightened, seemed instead to be relieved to be out of the fight. He moved the horse past them, stared up along the muddy road, and beyond, to a wide ridgeline. There were Yankees there, too, some in the road, many more just lying flat in the grass, some seated against a scattering of timber. They were stragglers, no weapons, their equipment no doubt part of the scattered heaps alongside the road. He watched for any sign of aggression, his own instinct, a hint of danger from these enemy troops. But there was only the despair, the paralysis that comes from defeat, most of the Yankees with no energy for escape, for anything at all. His horsemen were gathering them up, forming them into uneven columns just off the road, and Forrest could see the exhaustion, filthy, ragged men, torn shirts, remnants of blue uniforms. The horsemen had dismounted, rough shouts to the new prisoners of what would happen to them, useless threats, the ridiculous boasting Forrest tried to ignore. He glanced back to an aide.

"Gather 'em up, send 'em to the rear. And tell my boys to keep that nonsense to themselves."

"Yes, sir."

Forrest sat high on the horse, spoke out toward a group of a dozen men, the prisoners closest to him, most too tired to stand.

"You boys get to your feet. The march is back that ways. There's food, water. Get going."

The Federal troops seemed to recognize his authority, something in his voice, the uniform, and they began to obey, rising up with slow, automatic movement. Forrest had no idea if there was food anywhere behind him, but to these men, it didn't matter. Any promise was better than what they had now.

The air was damp and cool, and he thought back to the early morning, climbing into the saddle, the anticipation, pure excitement over what might come. The fight that had consumed this countryside for most of two days was over completely, nothing at all happening anywhere near

Chickamauga Creek. But the Federals had left a rear guard behind, several squads of cavalry, protecting the troops whose retreat was absolute. From the reports of his own advance scouts, Forrest knew that through every mountain pass the Yankees were flowing away with the kind of panic that makes men vulnerable. But not all the Yankees were in disarray. He knew of General Thomas, the tough fight the afternoon before that required too many deadly attacks from most of the Confederate forces on the field. Forrest wouldn't know anything yet of the army's casualty counts. That would come later, all those official reports, commanders trying to elevate themselves above the bloodletting, that no matter the confusion, the mistakes, the loss of so many good men, the generals could, after all, claim **victory.** He thought of Thomas, the Virginian who went north. Thomas had gathered up what he could, hunkered them down on a broad hill, good high ground, beating back every assault. Now Thomas and his Yankees were gone, pulling what remained of the Federal forces northward with as much order as those men could muster, protecting the rabble, the rest of the Union army, from being annihilated.

With the dawn, Forrest had gathered a force of some four hundred cavalrymen, had pushed out hard into the misty daylight, slogging through the mud and rain, driving hard to find the Federal position, if there was one to find. He had to believe, as they all did, that Thomas had given the Federal army the enormous benefit of time, that the Yankees might make good their escape through the mountain passes, a desperate drive toward the defensive lines around Chattanooga. If Forrest could cut them off, even a piece of that army, it would be a marvelous success. What he saw now was a hollow victory, his men finding only the basest remains of the Federal infantry. The cavalry was still out there, more of the Federal rear guard, but it was a toothless threat, a final effort to protect the men in blue slogging their way over the mountains.

He glanced back again, a larger column of his troopers gathering closer, coming together, re-forming after the latest skirmish, and called out, "Push on! No pause. Rest will come later. Care for your mounts, but we've got an opportunity here. I mean to make the most of it. Major Harvey."

The officer moved closer, and Forrest could see the man's weariness, felt it himself.

"Major, take fifty men, move out through those scattered trees. There's Yankees scampering away on every path, every trail. Round up what you can. Be sharp, keep your eyes out for a skirmish line, for any sign of an ambush. But I'm betting the Yankee cavalry's mostly gone. If we'd have started sooner, pushed them harder . . ."

He let the words trail away, stared back down the muddy road, over the heads of his men. He knew they were exhausted, that their mounts were in worse shape than the men, little time for forage, for water, for rest at all. He felt the soaking wetness from the rain, magnifying his own weariness, adding to his frustration. This is our chance, he thought. Our best chance in months. And by God, we're letting them get away.

He looked again up the long slope, saw past the debris in the road, the hill cresting in a scattering of timber.

"Forward!"

He spurred the horse, felt the unfamiliar gait, the uncomfortable rhythm, had a sudden flash of sadness. His own horse had gone down with a fatal wound not an hour before, another brief skirmish with Yankee cavalry that had gone his way. The Yankees had gotten the worst of it, again, but the wound to the horse had given him a jolt. He had seen that before, many times, the great obedient beasts standing tall in the storm of shot, absorbing the musket fire as though it were just part of their duty. Some horses could suffer a half-dozen wounds, yet still move forward, seemingly oblivious to agony or pain, determined only to serve. But his own mount had been hit in some vulnerable place, a horrible spurt of blood, which Forrest had tried to stop with his own hand. The animal had staggered, and even as his men drove the Yankees away, Forrest had dismounted, focusing on the beast, had spoken to it, soothing words, as though it might help. But the wound was deep, the blood unstoppable, and within short minutes the horse had collapsed, one more casualty. There were other horses there, of course, but the unfamiliar mount was the cavalryman's curse, suddenly astride a stranger, no bond between them, no rhythm to the ride. Forrest tried to ignore that, had driven the fresh animal to the head of the column, resuming the pursuit. He reached down and slapped the horse's neck.

"Let's go to work, old boy. This is a glorious day. You'll see that for yourself."

He crested the hill, saw a larger hill to the front, a long, high ridge that spread out to the north, speckled with a scattering of trees. To the left, westward, was the vast hulk of Lookout Mountain, rising up into heavy mist, the crown of the enormous rock disguised by a layer of fog. He glanced that way, nothing to see, pushed the horse beyond the ridge, rode down into a low bowl, the timber closing in on the road. Careful, he thought. One coward, trying to be a hero, taking his last shot at some officer on a horse. Not how I want to die. Stand up and face me, bluebelly. Let's see who the better man might be.

Beside him, one of his officers moved close, the man's voice, Captain Seeley.

"Sir, that's the big ridge. Mission Ridge. The enemy's likely to make a stand there. Good defensive position."

"Nope. They're not making a stand anywhere, not today. You see all that equipment along the road?

They're whipped. We keep pushing them hard, we'll haul in the whole Army of the Cumberland. About time, too. I want to see the faces of all those bluebellies who thought they could shove their way anyplace they saw fit. We handed them Tennessee. But not Georgia." He paused. "Let's get to the top, see what kind of view we have of Chattanooga. If the fog's not low in the valley, I'm wagering you'll see just how right I am."

He raised his hand, pointed toward the long ridge, spurred the horse to a trot. The climb was long and steady, and he knew the young captain would be alert, wouldn't just take Forrest's word for it. Good, he thought. I'm not certain, either. He doesn't need to know that. My job's simple: Convince them they can whip the entire Yankee nation. This past couple of days, that's just what we did. If I have my way, we'll finish the job.

He reached the wide crest, another glance at the enormity of Lookout Mountain, but the fog was high, the valley that spread out below clear, bathed by patches of late morning sunlight.

"Sir!"

He saw his men, and Major Harvey, farther along the ridge, a gathering near a small cluster of trees, the men surrounding a pair of bluecoats. The major was waving to him, a beaming smile, and Forrest rode that way, his men spreading out just behind the ridge, good training. They would know how visible they might be, the ridgeline mostly open.

Any thick mass of cavalry could be a perfect target for enemy artillery. Harvey was still waving, excited energy, and Forrest obliged him, kept his eyes on the two Yankees. He saw the signal flag, heard a whoop high in the tree, looked up, saw one of his own men sitting on a fat branch.

"What you have here, Major?"

"Two prisoners, sir. Signalmen. Good place for 'em to be, sir. They were up in the trees, waving them flags like they was calling out for Heavenly Deliverance. Guess it didn't work."

Forrest looked at the two men, both staring up at him, curious. He focused on the younger man, hoped to see fear, but the man was stoic, defiant. Forrest leaned out closer, said, "What's your name, son?"

"Kirkman. I'm from Illinois. Not telling you nothing else."

"Don't much care if you do, Mr. Kirkman from Illinois. What I want from you is right there." Forrest pointed to the man's chest, the field glasses hanging on a thin leather strap. There was no protest, the man sliding the strap over his head.

"Here you go, rebel. I reckon you captured these, too."

"Yep, that I did. Major, call your man down from that tree. I'd fancy my own look."

The trooper slipped down quickly, no order required, and Forrest dismounted, took the field glasses from the Yankee's hand.

"Thank you, Mr. Kirkman. Now, I'll just be taking a look at what your army is up to."

Forrest moved to the tallest tree, saw the limbs trimmed, a perfect ladder upward. He draped the field glasses over his neck, climbed, felt the ache. He had taken yet another wound in the fighting the day before, a nagging slice across his back, soothed by the constant motion from the horse. But he felt it now, stiffening, a burning stab. He tried to ignore the pain, moved up higher, one limb at a time. He reached the platform the Yankees had used, their observation point, the last sturdy limb where the thinner branches had been cleared away. He stood gingerly, one hand on the tree, steadied himself, now saw why the signalmen were there. Below him the valley stretched for miles, north and west, and far out in front, the looping meanders of the Tennessee River. Just this side of the river was the city of Chattanooga, lined with stout earthworks and lines of cut timber, most of that work done by Confederates a month or more before. Even at this distance he could make out the flow of humanity, pouring through the mountain passes, across the flat plain, masses of men in blue.

On every road, in every open field, Federal troops were on the move toward the town. But there was little order, nothing to resemble a march at all. He wanted to shout, felt a great flood of joy, could see what remained of the Federal Army of the Cumberland, a distant swarm of blue insects, a massive

ant bed stirred up by the Hand of God. He looked
to the left, the near side of the river that wound
past the base of Lookout Mountain. There was blue
there as well, wagons, teamsters making use of the
good road that ran westward along the river, salvaging whatever they could carry, some no doubt hauling the wounded, a great many wounded. Yes, by
God, we whipped them. Anyone who has a horse is
making his way out of those hills quick as the horse
will take him. The whole army . . . they've got their
minds set on one thing: getting out of this place
completely. If we push them hard enough, quick
enough, we'll shove them right out of Chattanooga,
back north, maybe all the way to Nashville.

He looked down, called out.

"Captain, I need to send a message to General
Polk. I want to make sure General Bragg sees it as
well. These are strict orders, you understand?"

He saw Captain Seeley, the young man motioning for a courier, a piece of paper emerging from
the man's coat.

"What's the message, sir?"

Forrest stared out again across the open valley,
could feel the desperation in the enemy soldiers
even now, miles away, could sense the panic he
knew he had to exploit. He scanned the ridgelines
to the south and west, hoping to see more columns
of Bragg's men, the victorious army driving their
pursuit with lustful energy, completing the great
victory. But there was only the fog, thick timber

hiding the roads, no signs of movement from Bragg's army at all. Surely, he thought. Surely he knows. They must come. It is so . . . simple.

He thought of the words, knew that Polk might hesitate, and so Bragg must be told as well. They despise each other, he thought. Two cackling hens. Well, today it's time to be soldiers. Your enemy is right out there, beaten and disorganized and they know what it feels like to be routed from the field. In fear there is opportunity. Our opportunity.

"Tell him . . . our position, our strength. We do not have the numbers up here to do much more. The army must come up. We must push them . . . hit them. Tell the general . . . we must press forward as rapidly as possible."

He thought of climbing down, saw Seeley writing furiously, but Forrest felt frozen, the pain in his back, the exhaustion holding him in place. We must keep them scared, he thought. Drive them wherever we can, let them know we're right behind them. Demons, chasing them to hell. We have you, he thought. We have you in our hands. And now we will crush you.

For most of the day, Forrest had waited atop Missionary Ridge with pulsing frustration, continued to send couriers back to the places where the generals were supposed to be. By late afternoon, he had grown sick of his impotence, unable to do anything more than watch from his perfect vantage point as the flood of Yankees drifted across the wide plain into Chattanooga. With no instructions, no words of encouragement from the commanders, he made the decision to leave his horsemen up on the ridgeline, while he and a small number of troopers rode back southward to face the generals himself.

BRAGG'S HEADQUARTERS— NEAR CHICKAMAUGA CREEK— SEPTEMBER 21, 1863

The room was hot, a roaring wood fire from a wide stone hearth, the thick air intoxicating, sleep inducing, Bragg's aides supporting themselves in small camp chairs or leaning against the crude walls. The wetness in Forrest's uniform had turned to sweat, both from the heat in the headquarters and Forrest's manic pacing. He thumped his boot heels into the wooden floor, turned, made the short march back the other way, waited for Bragg to complete some detail, jotting notes on a piece of paper, reading, then rereading, what seemed to Forrest to be a deliberate effort to hold the horseman back.

A new burst of pain drove through Forrest, and the words came now, his weariness and the agony of the wound breaking down his discipline.

"Sir! Please! I was told you received my dispatches."

Bragg looked up, blinked, as though fighting back sleep. "Yes. Calm yourself, General."

Forrest could wait no more. "General Bragg, the enemy is filling the defenses at Chattanooga. I have seen it myself. I have sent messages back here, imploring this army to take advantage of the opportunity the enemy is providing us. That opportunity will not last, if we allow him to find the full protection of the barricades in the city. I firmly believe that a swift and decisive push against those works will convince the enemy he cannot remain, that Chattanooga is no safe haven. He is inclined still to retreat. He is beaten, a whipped dog that needs only a sharp strike from us. He will either surrender, or he will scamper away."

Forrest was running out of words, nothing coming yet from Bragg. He had little respect for Bragg as a leader, had already experienced Bragg's tendency to make battlefield decisions based on personality clashes with his own subordinates rather than whatever the enemy might be doing. If Bragg had one characteristic Forrest respected, it was a fierce dedication to discipline. Bragg might shoot a miscreant soldier just to prove a point.

But there was nothing fierce in Bragg's demeanor now.

"General Forrest, I appreciate your zeal for combat. I share it, as you must certainly know. There is great honor in besting the enemy. I am told we bested him right here. My ranking generals seem convinced we handed General Rosecrans a crushing blow. It puzzles me why officers who are supposed to know something of battles can be so misled by first impressions."

Forrest stopped moving, tried to decipher whatever message Bragg was giving him.

"Sir, do you not believe the enemy was swept away from this field? Every officer I have spoken to insists we secured a major victory along Chickamauga Creek. Is that not what . . . you believe?"

"General Polk sent one of his commanders . . . Maney, I believe . . . sent him forward to observe the mountain passes. He reports much the same as you. But General Polk has not performed to my expectations, to my orders. I am examining even now a path of corrective action. And so, place yourself in my position, Mr. Forrest. Polk has been derelict, and yet I am to believe everything he tells me. I have thus far no complaint against you. And yet I am to act solely upon your observations. I can most reliably depend upon those things I can see for myself, General. Have you ridden across these fields, these wood lots, these patches of forest? I can rarely recall such carnage, such a human tragedy. The dead and severely wounded of both sides lie mingled in a horror that no general can accept lightly, that no civilian can ever understand. The mothers and wives of our fallen men will find no comfort in this so-called victory."

Forrest stared, a glance at one of the aides, a young captain, who avoided his eyes.

"General Bragg, is not the duty of my cavalry to offer you reliable information? You said yourself we have performed well."

"You fought well, yes. I have not heard any reports of your men failing to carry out their orders. But with all respects to your accomplishments and your reputation, I learned long ago to distrust cavalry. There is a great deal of **romance** in your service, is there not? All that professed gallantry can lead to carelessness, more time spent impressing the ladies along the way than accuracy in locating the enemy. With respects to you, Mr. Forrest, I must accept your reports with a measure of skepticism."

Forrest felt a boiling anger sprout in his brain, the insult more than casual. But still . . . Bragg was in command. And every officer in the army had been insulted by Bragg more than once. He took a long breath, tried to calm the instinctive response, unclenched a tight fist, a weapon that one part of him wanted to plant squarely across Bragg's chin.

"Sir, I can only offer you what I saw myself. The enemy is in full retreat away from here. He has made a frantic withdrawal through the mountains. I made every attempt to engage him, push a fight against the obstacles he put in our path. His rear guard did little more than delay us. Every observation I made tells me that right now, there is no fight in the Federal army. We must drive General Rosecrans from the sanctuary they seek in Chattanooga. He is defeated. He is inclined toward further retreat. We must see it so. We must not allow him the false confidence of believing us too weak to crush him."

Bragg shook his head, stared down at the desk. "I wish this entire army shared your passion, Mr. Forrest. But we are in no condition to drive forward with any conviction. We must recover our wounded, regroup, sort out the units. Entire regiments are jumbled about, their officers confused, stumbling about seeking their commands."

"Sir, I am told that General Longstreet is prepared to move forward, that he has gathered a sizable force. . . ."

Bragg sniffed loudly, and Forrest saw something awaken in the man, the familiar fury he had seen before, that every officer in the army had seen before.

"Do not speak to me of General Longstreet. The man marches his troops into my command intending to conquer all that lies before him, as though he has been anointed with superior genius, superior forces. Am I to believe that his mission here is simply to assist me? For reasons I do not understand, the president and General Lee believe I require his help in order to succeed. The newspapers trumpet Longstreet's name as though he alone can save our cause! Are we so inept, so consumed with misdeeds and errors that only a man from the East can deliver us? I will entertain no such notions, General. It is of no interest to me what General Longstreet believes possible, or what he intends to do. I am in command of this army, and I shall make the decisions as to how it is used. We must regroup, we must reorganize, we must replenish. We have been bloodied. We have endured severe losses."

"What of the enemy's losses? The enemy has abandoned this field to us. He is fleeing in a panic. Or . . . he was. I fear now we have granted him a full day to calm his demons. Every moment we delay is worth a thousand men."

"Too many thousands of men lie out there, never to return. General Forrest, I have allowed you to speak your mind, because I know your horsemen have performed ably, and with honor. Please return to your command, and extend my deepest appreciation for their service. We shall reevaluate our situation in the morning, when this army has regained a portion of its strength. Then we will decide how best to deal with the enemy. If what I am told is accurate, and mind you, I still have my doubts, then isn't it possible that General Rosecrans is already preparing to march away from here completely, abandoning Chattanooga, and perhaps all of Tennessee? Is not that what a great victory will grant us?"

Forrest felt the responses erupting inside of him, the heat in the room dizzying him.

Bragg rubbed a hand through his beard, seemed

satisfied by Forrest's lack of protest. "Yes, you see? I am well aware of our options. Now, I can see you are tired. It is very late, after all. We are all drained by what has happened here. Be assured, this command recognizes your good work. Get a good night's rest. I will have orders for you tomorrow, or soon after."

Orders to do what? Forrest kept the question to himself, saw Bragg's eyes drift shut, a perfect symbol of the day's end. Forrest wanted to say more, tried to ignite the protests again, but on one point Bragg was right. It was very late, close to midnight, and Forrest had been in the saddle nearly all day, and two days before that. The helplessness was overwhelming him, the anger and frustration pulling away. Nothing he could say to Bragg would change the man's resolve to simply . . . do nothing. He does not believe the enemy is crushed, does not accept what I saw with my own eyes. There is nothing more for me to do here.

Bragg seemed to come awake again, said, "A night's rest, General. Do you a great deal of good."

Forrest said nothing, turned to the open door, felt the cool wet breeze flooding the heat in the firelit room. He moved out through the door, thought, There will be no rest for the men **over there.** In Chattanooga, the enemy is doing his own regrouping, reorganizing. He is fortifying those works, and gathering himself for what he must believe is our inevitable attack. But there is nothing . . . inevitable. Except perhaps . . . that those dead men General Bragg so mourns will have died for no good reason.

He moved out into the chilling mist, the darkness giving way to the light from a single lantern. His staff was mounting their horses, and Forrest took the reins from an orderly, climbed up into the saddle, sharp pain in his back, a small grunt he tried to keep silent. He looked at the others, saw Captain Seeley watching him, questioning, expectant, the enthusiasm of the young.

"Orders, sir? Is General Bragg going after them?"

Forrest shook his head, looked down, the horse moving uneasily beneath him.

"Captain . . . I cannot imagine what General Bragg is going to do. I only wonder . . . if he does not see the value in what we have accomplished here, does not understand the magnitude of our success, the opportunity that we were given. If he has so little faith that we can win victories . . . then why does he fight battles?"

CHAPTER TWO

BRAGG

BRAGG'S HEADQUARTERS—
NEAR CHICKAMAUGA CREEK—
SEPTEMBER 22, 1863

The breakfast was already sour in his stomach, the ailment that never seemed to leave him.

"Take this away. Are there any rations to be found in this army that are suitable for consumption?"

The aide did not respond, the china plate whisked away. Bragg put a hand on his stomach, probed the discomfort, shook his head.

"What must I endure, Mr. Mackall?"

His chief of staff sat across the long narrow table from him, swallowed quickly, and said, "Sir, I will order the commissary to find something more to your liking. Can you offer me some suggestion what that might be?"

"Better commanders, General. Men who follow orders." He paused. "Victories."

Mackall took another bite, and Bragg avoided watching the man eat, stared away, his mind reeling with thoughts of the report he had still to compose, giving Richmond, and especially President Davis, his official accounting of what took place along the Chickamauga. He could hear Mackall chewing the food, the sounds grating, fueling more of the turmoil in his own stomach, and Mackall seemed to understand, had been through this before.

"Sir, I shall retire, if you wish. My presence here is an annoyance."

"No, certainly not. My stomach problems are my own. One more curse of command. Enjoy your breakfast."

Mackall had stopped eating, sat back. "Sir, allow me to suggest . . . this could prove to be a glorious day. Your mood could be heightened considerably if the reports are as accurate as their authors claim. The enemy is most certainly on the run. Or at the very least he is disorganized, and vulnerable to attack."

Bragg heard the emphasis . . . authors. There had been a consensus among his highest-ranking generals that finally Bragg could not ignore. No matter what he still feared, it seemed as though the Federal army had in fact conceded defeat, had withdrawn completely from their camps west and north of Chickamauga Creek. He felt a hard knot growing in his throat, the burning from his gut rising up with Mackall's optimism.

"You as well? Am I thus to accept that by majority rule, I may claim the fight at Chickamauga Creek to be my magnificent victory? If everyone insists it is so, then who am I to dispute that? I have seen no evidence of anything but a mutual slaughter, but if my generals and my chief of staff insist, well, then it must be so. So, you and half the officers in this army must agree that the next course should be to march this battered army straight to Chattanooga, to provide all the excuse General Rosecrans would need to scamper away. We survived this fight by the grace of God, not by the abilities of my generals. They seek any opportunity to exercise independent commands, to ignore my orders, to belittle my position at every turn. Now they create reasons why my judgment must be questioned. Charge ahead, with no regard for military protocol, or the care of the men." Bragg sagged in the chair, tried to control his breathing, searched Mackall's expression again, but Mackall seemed content to wait patiently for his time to speak. Bragg slapped one hand on the table, said, "So tell me, what is our effective strength?"

Mackall seemed to weigh if Bragg's question was serious. "I'm not entirely certain, sir. Our losses have been significant. The reports are still arriving. But there is much confusion."

"Yes, by God, there is. One of the most confusing problems seems to be just who commands this army.

Before I can engage our effective forces in any kind of campaign, I must know what those forces are, and which generals I may depend upon. I am not certain of any of them. Did you not hear me? Since the president placed me in this command, I have been more heavily assaulted by my own generals than I have by the enemy. Ambition and subterfuge infect them at every turn. I walk among the men, and I hear cheers, adulation, the proper amount of respect due my station. But when I meet with my officers there is silence and intrigue. Every one of them is engulfed by a disease of promotion, thinking more of his own elevation than the well-being of the troops in his care. I will not tolerate this any longer. The president favors **me** in this chair, and I will do what is necessary to justify the president's confidence. One mistake I will **not** make is to rely on the exaggerated boasting of commanders who campaign on the basis of hope, rather than our true tactical situation."

Mackall stared at him, still expressionless, said nothing. Bragg looked at the man's plate, a half-eaten slab of hard bread.

"You intend to discard that?"

Mackall glanced down, pushed the plate toward Bragg. "By all means, sir. You must eat."

Bragg took the bread, bit off one corner, the churning in his stomach calming a bit. He fought to swallow, tried to read Mackall, the man keeping his thoughts hidden away.

William Mackall was a year older than Bragg's forty-seven, had graduated from West Point in the same class of 1837. They had served together in the Seminole Wars and Mexico, and Bragg had gained respect for Mackall from their service together the year before, when they were both subordinate to Albert Sidney Johnston. Before Johnston's death at Shiloh in April 1862, Mackall had earned respect as a staff officer, but more so, Bragg knew what Johnston knew, that Mackall could lead troops in the field. That spring, Johnston had appointed him to lead the desperate defense of Island Number Ten, on the Mississippi River, an inevitable defeat for which Mackall could not be blamed. Though captured, Mackall was quickly exchanged, and resumed his good work both in the field and through diligent administration of various commands in the West. Mackall was one of the few general officers in Bragg's department whom Bragg believed he could trust.

"Your suggestions are welcome, Mr. Mackall. You know that. Is there some flaw in my thinking? You cannot deny that there has been discussion as to how others might usurp my authority. I am not without my sources, you know."

Mackall seemed to hesitate, then said, "I cannot report what I have not witnessed, sir. I agree that you cannot lead this entire army by yourself. But I am not aware that every officer seeks to rise to your

position, and I do not believe every officer is as ambitious as you say. With all respects, sir."

"You will make a fine politician one day." He had
no real reason to be angry with Mackall, felt a sudden twinge of guilt. "I return your respects, Mr.
Mackall, but I must suggest that until you occupy
this chair, you cannot understand the pressures
I must endure. Think about what has happened.
Barely three months ago, this nation was forced
to swallow two enormous catastrophes. I admit to
having little faith in General Pemberton's efforts
to hold Vicksburg. But I did not anticipate General Lee could be so utterly defeated, certainly not
in such an advantageous position on the enemy's
own soil. And now, I find it no coincidence that of
all the troops that could have been sent to our assistance here, the president and General Lee chose
General Longstreet. I am not fooled by Longstreet's
strutting arrogance. There is something of punishment in his being sent here, I feel certain of that.
Lee removed him for a reason. I walk this path with
great care, General. The people of the Confederacy
have been battered by the failure of their generals.
There is despair throughout this nation. My duty
is clear: Turn the tide back in our favor. And yet, all
the while the president expects me to be our savior, I am to regain all that is lost with subordinate
officers who have shown me little respect, and on
occasion, outright disobedience. Now, am I to feel

blessed that the great Longstreet performs his tricks in my part of this war? I am already hearing talk, General, that this fight at Chickamauga Creek was won by Longstreet alone. The newspapers back east will embrace that, no doubt. So, regardless of what I have seen on this ground, regardless of the destruction of this army, I am to move out in pursuit of a dangerous enemy solely because **Longstreet** leads the way?"

Mackall shook his head slowly, stared down at his empty plate. "I would suggest, sir, that you lead this army against the enemy because it is the right thing to do. If the Federal army is inclined to retreat, as General Forrest and others have suggested, that is an opportunity we must explore."

Bragg rubbed his aching stomach again. "Forrest is a raider, a pirate, nothing more. He is celebrated with tactics that amount to little more than a mad rush into some weakly defended place, causing terror among the helpless. He steals horses and burns a few houses and then scampers away again. For that he is a hero. And that is the kind of man whose observations I should rely upon? No simple cavalryman can appreciate the necessity for strategy, for care, for diligence. If the Federals have retreated into Chattanooga, then the correct strategy is to sweep around their flanks, maneuver to the northwest, cut Rosecrans off from any supply line, before he can make good his escape. General Forrest tells me that with just a minor push, the

Federal army will be inclined to do just that. He is certain of it. And then, in the same moment, he tells me the enemy is perhaps not yet retreating, but in fact could be gathering, regrouping behind the defenses at Chattanooga. Which is it? Is Rosecrans leaving? Or is he preparing to receive an attack? If we attempt to flank him now, spread our forces out in the mountain passes, we could be vulnerable to an attack from **him.** If we drive straight into Chattanooga, and he does not simply melt away, we might find ourselves crushed against a strong defensive position. General Rosecrans is no doubt receiving urgent orders from Washington, Lincoln's minions screaming at him for his failures in Georgia. The Northern people are spoiled by their recent successes. If Rosecrans has indeed been defeated here, there will be little patience for that in Washington. He is also a man of ambition, is he not? If he wishes to hold on to his command, he must satisfy those loud voices behind him. And so, he will strengthen and resupply. Or he will leave Chattanooga behind him, and seek the protection of the Tennessee River. Or even the Duck River. We might very well fight him again at Stones River, or Tullahoma, or Murfreesboro. How am I to decide such things when I cannot rely on the information my own generals are providing me?"

Bragg tried to inhale, fought the tightness in his throat, the agonizing pains in his gut, and Mackall took advantage of the pause, said, "Sir, the best way we can know what General Rosecrans is doing is to see for ourselves. If you do not rely on the reports of your scouts, your cavalry, your senior officers, then perhaps we should ride out there ourselves."

Bragg soaked up the simple logic. "Yes. I had thought of that. Very well. We shall continue to receive the reports as they come in here. Send word to the commanders that if they do not find the enemy in strength, they may push their people closer to Chattanooga. Be sure General Longstreet receives that order with perfect clarity. Be certain he understands whose authority he answers to here. And communicate to every division commander that there must be no significant confrontation with the enemy. We cannot withstand another general engagement. No one in this army can convince me we are ready for another sharp fight. If all goes well today, then in the morning, order the aides to prepare the horses, and we shall ride out there ourselves, you and me. We will advance toward Chattanooga, as far as the enemy allows. If there is to be an honest victory here, if we are to inform Richmond of great success, I suppose I should get the facts for myself."

MISSIONARY RIDGE—
SEPTEMBER 23, 1863

The rains had stopped, but the mud still swallowed the horses' hooves, slowing the movement of artil-

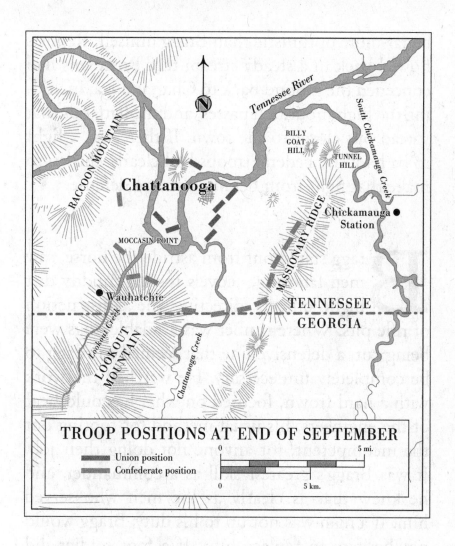

TROOP POSITIONS AT END OF SEPTEMBER

Union position
Confederate position

0   5 mi.

0   5 km.

lery. As Bragg had ordered, the troops had pushed
north and west, but the observations of the lead
units continued to confirm what Bragg had been
hearing for two days.

Rosecrans had withdrawn at least as far as Chattanooga, though whether or not the Federal forces
were in a panic to evacuate the town, no one could
be certain. Most of Bragg's generals continued to

be far more optimistic than Bragg himself. Reports flowed back in a steady stream that Rosecrans had conceded the ground back to Chattanooga, including the high mountain passes, and the flatlands that spread out closer to the town. If there was a fight to be had, the Federal troops had clearly chosen to make that fight from behind a strong defense.

B ragg stared out from astride the horse, saw men laboring, shovels tossing muddy dirt high, officers directing the construction of rifle pits. Where timber was available, logs were being cut, a defensive line that seemed to Bragg to be completely unnecessary. He watched the work with a hard frown, focused on what he could hear of the engineers, his usual method for rooting out the incompetent, for anyone not doing their job. It was Bragg's greatest skill as a commander, and he knew that as clearly as the men who served him. If a man was not up to his duty, Bragg would not hesitate to replace him. If a foot soldier did not perform, Bragg would make certain the man paid some kind of price, whether confinement in a stockade or worse. Discussion and explanation, if Bragg would hear that at all, could come later.

Mackall had ridden down below the crest of the hill, and Bragg saw others there as well, a cluster of officers on horseback, a scattering of regimental flags. Bragg tried to clear the stale air from his lungs, jabbed a spur into the horse's flank, moved along the crest, his aides trailing behind. He could see all across the face of the ridge, men laboring in a long line that bisected a slope that was hundreds of feet high, nearly all of them preparing defensive positions. He felt the stab of the headache, almost always there, made worse now by his annoyance at his engineers, who had convinced his generals that trench lines and earthworks were worth the effort from so many troops. Bragg had always believed that such defenses only demoralized the men, planting them in ground they might begin to see as their own graves. But here we are, he thought, digging holes, while the enemy is . . . where? Behind entrenchments of their own? I am advised to attack him, and all the while, my generals insist we plan for defense. How am I to command this army in such a storm of confusion?

He halted the horse, ignored the gathering aides behind him, saw his men spread out as far as he could see. It surprised him that his men were on the heights in such numbers, that the probing advance had been made virtually without opposition. All through the night and into the early morning the reports continued to come, infuriating contradictions as to just what Rosecrans was doing. Many of the scouts insisted the Yankees were indeed gathering up strength in Chattanooga, digging in, improving the existing defenses, pulling artillery into organized batteries, their commands no doubt coming back together. Yet others reported pontoon bridges being laid across the Tennessee River, that men were continuing to scramble away beyond the river, an unorganized mob, still reeling from their bloody defeat. The pontoons were a clear sign that Rosecrans was intending to leave, and yet Bragg could see for himself now that the blue mass was still in Chattanooga, the view from the great ridge absolute. He raised field glasses, no strength in his arms, let them drop.

"Don't need the cursed things anyway."

"Sir?"

"Do we have the first notion if the enemy is in those trees? Has anyone tried to find out if all these earthworks are a waste of time?"

"Not certain of that, sir. General Mackall is down that path. . . ."

"Yes, I see him. Keep close behind me, in case I require your service."

"Certainly, sir."

Bragg stepped the horse carefully down the path, didn't look back to see if the aides were obeying him at all. He moved toward Mackall, who saw him now, turned his own horse to face him.

Bragg spoke first. "What is happening? Is the enemy on the move? I see smoke from the town. Are they burning the place? Since my generals have halted this army on this high ground, there must be the opinion that we are to be attacked. The message I am receiving is clear, gentlemen. There is confusion here. Am I correct? Are my generals in consultation somewhere on this hill, planning our next move? Might someone advise me what that might be?"

Mackall glanced at the others, said, "Sir, the infantry on the ridgeline here belong to Harvey Hill's division, with General Cleburne's men farther to the north. General Wheeler's cavalry secured the ridge all the way to its most northerly point, with no enemy opposition. General Longstreet has occupied the high ground to the west, including the summit of Lookout Mountain. I had been led to believe that Chattanooga was being abandoned . . . the smoke, as you say, sir. But now . . . the forward scouts report a great deal of labor ongoing. There are enemy stragglers still scattered about, but any organized force has settled into Chattanooga." Mackall paused, and Bragg rubbed at the headache, the image of Rosecrans in his mind. Mackall pointed up toward Lookout Mountain. "Sir, it is something of a surprise to me, and to others as well. The enemy made no effort to block the mountain passes. We were able to advance to this position with only a few brief skirmishes. There is some retreat across the river, but from my own observations, and that of General Hill, the enemy is most definitely in force in the town. General Longstreet reports that the enemy has placed several pontoon bridges to the rear of the town, and wagons have been observed crossing. But there is no sign of a significant retreat. The wagons could be ferrying wounded."

Bragg stared up to the left, the mass of Lookout Mountain. "The enemy made no effort to hold that eminence? It is a superior vantage point."

"Sir, General Longstreet is moving his people onto that peak right now. The enemy offered little resistance."

Bragg felt a nervousness, an uneasy nagging that he was being led into a trap. He pulled the horse back, moved uphill, Mackall and the aides following. He crested the hill, looked to the north, where hundreds of his men continued their work, saw artillery pieces coming up on various trails, supply wagons gathering down below, the east side of the ridge. He halted the horse, the words coming out in a low whisper. "He gave us this ground?"

"Sir?"

Bragg looked at Mackall, shook his head. "I am baffled by the Federal strategy, General. They could have kept us back from here with little effort. If he intends to remain in the town, he has afforded us this perfect place for observation, for placement of artillery, for gathering supplies. He is inviting us to attack him."

"Perhaps, sir. If I may suggest . . . that might not be wise."

Bragg looked again toward the distant town, the winding sweep of the river. "No. You are correct. That would not be wise at all. There is considerable open ground between the base of this hill and those defensive works. Their artillery would sweep us away should we make the attempt to march across. To the west . . . the river runs close to the mountains. There is no assault to be made there. Not even Longstreet would attempt such foolishness. The enemy is surely in force directly across the river from that mountain. We do not have bridging material. Am I correct?"

"No, sir. We have no pontoons close at hand."

Bragg felt a sudden burst of elation, the headache fading. "Oh, my, yes. The president will be greatly pleased."

"Sir?"

"General Mackall, order the cavalry . . . Forrest and Wheeler . . . order them to make every effort to cut that town off from the north and west, from any route of supply." He paused, thought a moment, had festered over what he now saw as arrogance in Forrest's report. "Send word to the famous General Forrest. I want him to transfer a significant portion of his strength to the command of General Wheeler. We do not require more than one romantic cavalier sweeping through this countryside causing heart flutters among the female population. General Wheeler has not displayed as much arrogance as Bedford Forrest, and for that he should be rewarded. If General Rosecrans has a supply train, it must be well to the rear, beyond the river. I want General Wheeler to use the cavalry the way it was

intended, and destroy the enemy's means of supply. If Rosecrans intends to hole himself up behind
those marvelous earthworks, we shall oblige him.
In fact, it would suit me if the Yankees remained
there all winter."

Mackall moved up closer, lowered his voice, as
though keeping his words from other ears. "You
mean . . . we will lay siege?"

Bragg slapped his thigh, made a fist, shook it
toward the town. "I mean to starve him. I mean to
force Rosecrans to become so weak that he must
crawl his way into our lines begging for sustenance,
for relief, for the proper opportunity to surrender
his army. I shall have his sword, I shall have every
sword of every officer in the Army of the Cumberland. You hear me, Mr. Mackall? **Here** is where we
shall find the victory. Here is where my generals will
learn why the president has such faith in this command. Here is where I shall earn their obedience."

CHAPTER THREE

THOMAS

CHATTANOOGA—
SEPTEMBER 24, 1863

"They're growing stronger. But they are still not coming."

The staff officers behind him stared out as he did, none of them with the benefit of field glasses. Thomas didn't need the others to agree, had already seen for himself how the rebels had followed his retreat, what could have been a dangerous maneuver made relatively simple by the lack of a vigorous pursuit. Now they seemed content to occupy the higher ground on two sides of Chattanooga, as though satisfied with the position that Rosecrans had ceded to them. Have to be a cheerful bunch, he thought. They know sure as rain that they whipped us pretty bad. But they could have done so much more. We might have given them the field, but they bled on that ground as much as we did. We hurt them, no doubt about that. So they're gonna sit up on those heights until . . . what? We do something stupid? Old Rosy could have kept them off those hills, but he couldn't make up his mind what he wanted me to do. Or rather, he made up his mind in every direction at once. I could have held them back, until he ordered me not to. By the time he thought better of that, it was too late. This isn't good. Not good at all. He'll pay a price for that. Maybe . . . we all will. But mistakes are not confined to generals in blue. Bragg might have made a big one, not taking advantage of the mess we left behind. Mistakes and more mistakes. Seems like that's the way this war's being fought all over the place. Good men doing idiotic things. Hopefully, every now and then, one of us will do something right.

Already praise was coming Thomas's way, the few reporters who fluttered about the camp sending dispatches to their papers how Thomas's vigorous defense had saved the day at Chickamauga. Even Rosecrans's own staff were speaking of it, how Thomas had rescued so much of the army as the scattered units had found their way back to the defenses around Chattanooga. He wouldn't listen to any of that, wouldn't give the reporters what they hoped to hear, the breathtaking tale of a fight to the last, a heroic stand against the rebel hordes. Garbage, he thought. It was the men, men I had never seen before, men from units scattered all over the field who knew where the fight was, who came ready to show the rebels that this army wasn't going to collapse just because we had one break in our lines. And now we're here, and very soon we'll be strong again, ready for anything they have. Bragg's mistake.

He had ridden past the leading edge of the Federal defensive position, had been given charge of strengthening those defenses, the vast improvement to the earth and log works left behind by the rebels weeks before, the prelude to what had pulled Rosecrans and his Federal forces down into Georgia. Though the bulk of the army was now safely behind their barricades, Thomas was seeing something in Rosecrans he hoped never to see. It was clear even to Rosecrans's own staff, the men most loyal, that with the collapse of the Federal center at Chickamauga, with the desperate retreat that Rosecrans had led himself, that no matter the lack of pursuit, Rosecrans had found none of the renewed energy of his men. Instead, Thomas had seen clear signs that their commanding general was falling apart.

Thomas stared through the glasses at the signal flags on the crest of Missionary Ridge, rebels talking to one another. He knew that artillery had been pulled up on the heights as well, the shelling coming toward the Federal lines in inconsistent waves, scattered and haphazard. They're trying to scare us, he thought. They must believe we're ready to scamper out of here completely, that if they drop a few explosives into our lines, that's all it'll take. Not now. Not anymore. Yes, show us how strong you are, all that great power up in those hills, waiting to rush down here and sweep us away. That's what you want us to believe, isn't it, Mr. Bragg? Sorry, old friend, but I'm not convinced. We spent two days toe-to-toe with you, beating each other's brains out, and if you thought your great victory was going to be overwhelming and perfect, my men changed your mind. We held the last piece of good ground, and made you pay for every step you made. How many times did you send those boys against us? Ten? More? And how many of those boys are still out there, lying on those fields? By now, they've told you the numbers. It's what you're good at. And your burial parties are working still.

Thomas lowered the field glasses, stared out to the larger mountain to the right, but he had seen all he needed to. He thought of Bragg, impetuous, quick to anger, and yet, for more than fifteen years, Bragg had been a good friend. Mexico had been a triumph for both of them, as it had been for so many of the fresh-faced officers who had risen now to command in both these armies. It had been difficult for many of those young men, coming home from their first taste of combat with all the images of horror tempered by the unexpectedly one-sided victory, a job well done. After Mexico, many of the officers had found peacetime to be painfully monotonous, some, like Thomas Jackson and Ulysses

Grant, leaving the army completely. But there was opportunity still for a man willing to endure the brutal conditions out west, Texas mostly, newly organized cavalry regiments waging a new kind of war against the Indians. There was adventure in that for certain, and opportunities for promotion, if a man could tolerate the living conditions, and the sheer misery of chasing Comanches through their own territory. It was Bragg who had been selected for a new position with the cavalry, but Bragg had instead recommended Thomas for the assignment. It was an amazingly generous gesture, driven mostly by Bragg's respect for Thomas's service in Mexico, as well as their time together in Florida, another kind of misery for the soldiers who fought the Seminoles. It wasn't because he liked me, Thomas thought. I don't think he ever **liked** anybody. Probably doesn't like anybody up on those hills, either. And I assume the feeling is mutual. But I'll hand it to you, Braxton. You might be the most cantankerous man I ever met. But along the Chickamauga, you licked us good. We made more mistakes than you did, and you stuck us for it.

Thomas knew what a few of the men closest to Rosecrans were tossing about, that the blame for the catastrophe at Chickamauga lay squarely at the feet of their commanding general. That opinion was shared by most of the higher-ranking commanders, some of those showing undisguised relief that Rosecrans might be the scapegoat, someone besides them to absorb the blame. Thomas didn't want to hear that kind of talk, or the talk about how he had saved the entire campaign, as though any one man could be responsible for either the failure or the salvation of this army. Whether he was a hero or not was hardly what mattered. A large part of the Army of the Cumberland had been brought back from their disaster, had been allowed to retreat back to Chattanooga because Thomas had commanded a defensive position that the rebels couldn't break through. It was good ground, he thought. The better ground. Bragg sent his people against a superior defensive position, and the **logical** happened. No genius in that. We had rocks and timber and they had an uphill climb. If we'd have had more ammunition, we could have beaten them back for days.

Several of the brigade and division commanders had come to him privately, as though keeping some dark secret, that Thomas had saved Rosecrans's career, along with the entire army. He wouldn't hear that, either. The casualty count at Chickamauga had been catastrophic long before Thomas's men made their final stand. So much of that battlefield was cloaked in forest, he thought, entire brigades marching right up to their enemy before they knew what was happening. You fight like that, a few yards apart, and you don't need marksmen. Just . . . numbers. Well, it's certainly not like that here. Nobody's confused about where we are now. And from everything I can see, Bragg's army is just sitting up there, happy to watch us. A man gets a broken nose, he's not so much in a hurry for another one. I wish Old Rosy appreciated that. I wish he understood how badly we hurt them, how good this position is around Chattanooga. Bragg knows it, for sure. He loves his paperwork, numbers and organization, so he'll find out what kind of strength he has, and he'll play with that, tweak it, nudge things around, scream at a few people for being stupid. And when he thinks he's ready, maybe he'll come down here and try us. But right now, Bragg's got the good ground, and he's not real comfortable giving that up just so there'll be a fair fight. Loves his men too much. That just might be his greatest weakness. Bragg doesn't think anybody can run that show over there as good as he can, and so he doesn't trust his generals to do anything unless he's perfectly sure it will work. And, marching down off those hills right into a hundred artillery pieces, walking those men across all this open ground . . . nope. That's not going to work, old friend.

He turned slightly, stared at the base of Lookout Mountain. He could barely make out the flow of the river, winding close beneath the massive rock walls, the waterway any riverboat would have to take to bring supplies directly into Chattanooga. Already, rebel artillery was tossing shells across that part of the river, rebel sharpshooters settling down close, taking aim at any careless soldier who dared to strut out along the river's edge. That part of the river is useless, he thought. And so, if we want supplies to get in here, they'll have to halt well back of us, come the rest of the way overland.

He looked back, saw his staff alert, waiting for his instructions, and said, "Did we get confirmation from General Rosecrans what kind of supplies we have?"

Colonel Hough rode up close to him, said, "I spoke with General Garfield this morning. He believes that the first estimates are correct. We can hold out here for about ten days without assistance."

Thomas stared out again, nodded slowly. "Alfred, we're in a serious pickle here."

"Yes, sir. General Rosecrans seems convinced of that."

Alfred Hough had been Thomas's friend long before the war, served now as a staff officer with no real authority beyond what Thomas required of him. But Hough brought the kind of loyalty Thomas appreciated, an effective sounding board, unafraid to give Thomas his honest opinion. Even more, Thomas knew that any conversation between them would remain theirs alone. It was dismaying to Thomas that throughout the command of the Army of the Cumberland, few secrets were kept, too many seeming to delight in gossip. Even now, as rumors flowed out as to Rosecrans's uncertain state of mind, Rosecrans's own staff seemed far too willing to reveal those things a commander had to keep private. Old Rosy's not being served well, if those boys can't keep their mouths shut.

"It'll be cold tonight. Let's ride back along that last defensive line. I want to be sure the engineers know what they're doing. There might still be a fight here."

He moved the horse, Hough still beside him, the half-dozen aides spreading out in file behind him. Hough said, "You don't think we're in trouble . . . that the men won't run again?"

Thomas didn't look at his friend, said, "The men? Nope."

"What about General Rosecrans? There's talk he's planning on retreating, pulling us out of here completely."

"You keep that kind of **talk** to yourself, Alfred. Old Rosy is a man of the Catholic faith, devout, as dedicated to his religion as any man I've ever seen. Every day he's been here, he's asked for divine strength. Let's just hope he finds it. As long as he doesn't decide to . . . **run,** these boys won't, either."

THOMAS'S HEADQUARTERS— ARMY OF THE CUMBERLAND— CHATTANOOGA— SEPTEMBER 26, 1863

Charles Dana had arrived at Rosecrans's headquarters a few days before the great confrontation at

Chickamauga, and Thomas knew only that he was the assistant secretary of war, a lofty title that meant he answered only to Edwin Stanton, in Washington. Rosecrans assumed Dana's purpose for being there was to report back to the War Department just how Rosecrans was managing the Army of the Cumberland. That alone would have put the entire command on edge, but the failure at Chickamauga only made Rosecrans's suspicions of Dana more intense. Dana had made every effort to reassure Rosecrans that his purpose was simply to observe. There was no subterfuge, no hidden agenda, no urgency to put someone else in Rosecrans's place. But that was before the disastrous rout on September 20. Dana was no soldier, had reacted to the terrifying stampede by firing off numerous telegrams to Washington, graphic descriptions of just how bad the chaos had been, and how completely the Army of the Cumberland had been crushed by Bragg's forces. Once Dana had spent a full day in the safety of the Chattanooga defenses, the telegrams had grown more tempered, and thus more accurate. But Rosecrans was still not convinced that Dana wasn't there to find a replacement more agreeable to Stanton, or even to President Lincoln. Thomas could see for himself that, regardless of Dana's motives, Rosecrans was doing nothing to help his own cause. No matter how secure the army might now be in Chattanooga, Rosecrans continued to show signs of instability and a complete lack of confidence. His own messages to Washington seemed to emphasize a disturbing lack of faith in the army, and much more certainty that whatever happened next was a product of God's will. It was not the kind of message Washington wanted to hear.

Thomas had no real animosity toward Dana, saw him as a reasonable man, sent out to do a job that didn't include a chaotic pursuit by a deadly enemy. If it had taken Dana a couple of days behind the army's defenses at Chattanooga to find his composure, this was no surprise to Thomas. He knew there were fighting men in this army who still weren't finding much sleep, knowing that every maneuver they might make was being clearly observed from at least two directions. If that made Dana nervous as well, it just meant he was paying attention.

"I apologize for the intrusion, General. Your Colonel Hough allowed me to pass. Please don't find fault with him. I was rather insistent."

"If Colonel Hough knew I wished to be alone, you would not be here. No matter, Mr. Dana. I can tell . . . there's something on your mind."

Dana looked toward a small chair, and Thomas pointed.

"Yes, sit."

"Thank you, sir."

Dana paused, seemed to gather his thoughts, and

Thomas said, "It's late, sir. Have you something to say?"

Dana nodded, still hesitated. "Sir, as you know, I am in regular contact with the secretary of war. He is insistent on that point. I must mention that this camp, this command is a very different . . . er . . . beast than what I encountered with General Grant."

Thomas knew that Dana had first come west to accompany Ulysses Grant's campaign through Mississippi, a campaign that had concluded with the complete success at Vicksburg.

"Mr. Dana, there will be no talk of competition between this army and the command of General Grant. Grant's success in Mississippi was a sterling achievement. This army has accomplished much as well, though not the kinds of victories that make for attractive headlines."

Dana had been a newspaperman before the war, a fact no one took for granted. Thomas assumed, as did many, that Dana's correspondence with Washington would most always carry a flair for the dramatic.

Dana seemed to appreciate the insinuation, nodded, a slight smile. "General Grant is an interesting study, sir. His response to my presence was hostile, certainly. But he was at least polite about it. I went to great lengths to assure him that whatever campaign anyone in Washington might be waging against him, whoever his detractors might be, none of that was of concern to me. By the time the Vicksburg campaign concluded, I'm certain he believed me. General Sherman . . . well, I'm not so certain. He has a striking dislike of newspaper reporters."

"So do I."

"Yes, I have heard that. I am not here to offer headlines to anyone, General. Not at all."

The room was small, low ceilinged, the headquarters a fairly nondescript house, the hearth part of a crude kitchen. Thomas enjoyed the warmth of the fire, a soothing balm to the ever-present pains in his back. He shifted in the chair, adjusted a pillow beneath him, and Dana said, "I understand you were injured. Before the war."

"A newspaperman, yes, Mr. Dana? Observant, catching every detail."

Dana looked down, said, "Yes, quite so, I'm afraid. One is taught to notice the trivial, that great messages lie in those things most people might miss."

"Makes you good at your job. Yes, I understand. Injured myself around the time the war began. Was a passenger on a train, heading to one of my early assignments. Train halted, I took a walk, slipped down a hill. Bad fall. Colonel Hough refers to it as my personal train wreck. I'm supposed to find humor in that. Nothing humorous about pain, Mr. Dana. In two years, there has been little relief."

"Very sorry, sir. I would never make light of such a thing. Nor would I make casual remarks about a man's chosen loyalties."

Thomas was becoming annoyed, the pains in his back sapping his patience. "If you mean to question my upbringing, sir, and the hostilities I have endured from my own family, save that for another time. Yes, I am a Virginian. As is, I might add, General Winfield Scott. There are others in this army whose place of birth is in the South, who considered their oath of allegiance to the United States to be paramount. I believe even a newspaperman would consider that a sign of honor."

Dana put a hand on his face, rubbed slowly. "I do not wish to agitate you, sir. Forgive me for straying from the point. I am here because I must seek your counsel."

"For you, or for Stanton?"

"Oh, this is my own journey, sir. But certainly, the secretary is seeking some input from me about a matter of utmost urgency. Two matters, actually."

"Get to it, Mr. Dana."

"Yes. There is a consensus in this camp that the army can be maintained here as long as necessary, if we can bring in supplies in a consistent manner. As you know, sir, the quartermaster general, Mr. Meigs, arrived here only a few days ago with a most pessimistic forecast, that the route the supply trains must travel is difficult at best. His report inspired considerable despair from our commanding general. The supplies are out there, no question, a lengthy wagon train, so I've been told."

"Yes. It's no secret. Eight hundred wagons, at

least. Just beyond the mountains to the west. That should give us time, sir, and more trains will be forthcoming. The high command of the Federal army is not forsaking us, no matter what rumors you might hear. Or, you might originate."

Thomas regretted the insult, could see the wound in Dana's expression. "Please, General, I am here only to observe. I hoped you would confirm what I have heard from your staff. Washington will certainly do what General Meigs requires of them to sustain this army."

"Yes. The second matter?"

Thomas saw the hesitation again. He adjusted his back in the chair, but there was gravity in Dana's expression, and Thomas put off his impatience. After a long pause, Dana looked at him, said, "Sir, I am of the opinion that it is no longer appropriate that General Rosecrans remain in command of this army. Mind you, I have no personal animosity toward the man. But I have observed . . . things."

"I do not wish to hear your observations. I know Rosy well, and I will not entertain disparagement against an honorable man."

Dana lowered his head, then looked up at Thomas with a slight nod. "As you wish, General. But you are not deaf, dumb, or blind. Your loyalty to your commander is admirable. But my loyalty is to events as I see them. General Rosecrans is demonstrating a lack of fitness for command. You may not enjoy hearing that. But the secretary has already heard it, believes it, and the president is in agreement with him. A decision has to be made."

"I wish no part of that discussion. I am his subordinate, after all."

"You also outrank him. I have done my research, sir."

"Are you suggesting . . . are you intending to report to Washington that my name should be considered—"

Dana held up a hand. "Let's not go that far. I can offer suggestions, certainly. But I have no influence on what is decided in Washington."

Thomas felt something turn over in his stomach, the cold reality that Rosecrans might truly be relieved of command. "I will not be a part of a conspiracy, sir. I will not campaign for a position I have not earned, not at the expense of my commanding officer."

"Very honorable. Events are in motion already, General, events that neither of us control. General Grant has been called upon for reinforcements, and orders have been given to Sherman's command for troops to march this way. General Burnside has been given those same orders. And, let us not forget, sir, there is an enemy out there who might make his own contributions to our . . . **decisions.** I just thought it important you know what kinds of considerations are being made. My reports must continue, and your name is mentioned with some frequency. If that's more than you wish to hear, I will abide by that. If General Rosecrans shows himself to be in control of our situation here, if he regains the confidence of the War Department by his actions, then so be it. I will report that as well."

There was a sharp knock at the door, a voice: "General? Are you awake, sir?"

He knew the voice, one of his aides, Lieutenant Ramsey.

"What is it, Roger? You may enter."

Ramsey ducked through the low doorway, seemed surprised to see Dana, made a short bow toward him, said, "Um, sir . . . we received word . . . General Rosecrans is considerably agitated, sir. His aide, Captain Stiles—"

Another voice burst through from outside the room.

"Where is he? Thomas? You in here?"

Thomas was surprised to see Rosecrans, the man bursting in, pushing aside the young lieutenant. Thomas pulled himself out of the chair, saw the wild glare from Rosecrans, the man's eyes darting about, as though searching for something. He seemed to notice Dana now, pointed a finger at him.

"You might as well go to your precious telegraph. Washington will be utterly delighted with today's events. Delighted."

Thomas knew Rosecrans was being sarcastic, said, "What has happened? The enemy isn't moving from those heights. I have heard nothing. . . ."

"You weren't outside. We heard it, a while ago,

didn't know what it meant at first. Artillery fire to the west, carried on the breeze, I suppose. A long way off." He sat heavily in Dana's chair, leaned his hands on his knees, stared at the floor. "We're in a serious way, George. A serious way. Riders came in a short time ago. That artillery came from rebel cavalry. We knew they had sent horsemen out north of the river, tried to keep an eye on them. But they had a purpose, one purpose. They hit the wagon train. Riders say we lost most everything. Rations, ammunition. Most of the train was burned, men captured." He paused, put his head down in his hands. "We are in a serious way, George. That train . . . was our salvation."

Thomas looked at Dana, said, "You will report none of this until we confirm what has happened. Panicked men bring rumors, exaggeration. Until we know what the rebels did . . ."

Rosecrans looked up, and Thomas was shocked to see tears on the man's face.

"They have us, George. There is nothing we can do."

"There is never **nothing we can do.** It was a cavalry raid. We have cavalry of our own. Gather them up, push them out along the supply routes."

Rosecrans shook his head. "They're scattered. I've sent out word, but it could take days to bring them together, rest them, put them back into the field. I just wasn't certain where the rebels would hit us, thought they might try to get between us and Knoxville, so I ordered our horsemen to watch over most of the river crossings up that way."

Thomas felt sick, thought, The wagon train was a ripe target. Did you not think of that? He said nothing, knew the rebel raiders would be long gone, their mission completed.

"Are we certain they did that much damage to the wagon train?"

"Four couriers made it out, George. Four. Same report. The smoke from what they left behind was visible on the ridges to the west. What do we do now? How do we feed the men? I will order three-quarter rations in the morning. That will help. Or perhaps half rations. I must speak to General Meigs. He might know of some means of securing another train. Surely there will be more supplies."

Dana said softly, "And more rebel cavalry."

Dana moved to the door, looked back at Thomas. "I will do as you ask, sir. I will send nothing of this on the wire yet. By morning we will know our situation with more clarity."

Thomas nodded, waved him away, the pains in his back pulling Thomas down into the soft chair. He looked at Rosecrans, the man's face in his hands again, heard words, soft, pleading. It was a prayer. Thomas looked toward the fire, thought, Yes, pray all you must, Rosy. I'm quite sure that somewhere out there, Bragg is saying a prayer of his own.

CHAPTER FOUR

BRAGG

Bragg's dislike and distrust of his subordinates had begun to boil over. No one disputed that Chickamauga had been a resounding Confederate victory, but Bragg was hearing a growling sentiment throughout his command that another victory had been squandered, the enemy allowed to turn the tide, or escape from what might have become complete destruction. Bragg had known of that criticism as far back as the vicious fight at Murfreesboro the first of the year, noisy rebukes drifting toward him from several of his generals, Leonidas Polk in particular. Polk had been outspoken in the extreme against Bragg, a lack of respect that Bragg took as outright defiance. As the voices flowed back to Bragg's headquarters,

Polk's voice seemed most grating of all. But Bragg finally found a way of striking back. On September 20, the climactic day's fight at Chickamauga, Polk had failed to push forward the attack as Bragg had ordered. On September 29, after Polk had failed to adequately respond to Bragg's criticisms, Bragg ordered him suspended from command. Polk was ordered to remove himself from the army and retire to Atlanta.

Leonidas Polk was an Episcopal bishop from Louisiana, held the respect of nearly every commander in the army, and had been a special favorite of Albert Sidney Johnston. Worse for Bragg, Polk was extremely close to Jefferson Davis. Davis responded to Bragg's order by pointing out to Bragg that suspending Polk meant that Polk would have to be tried for the alleged crimes Bragg had accused him of, a process that the president made clear he was not likely to pursue. Bragg had to be satisfied merely to have Polk elsewhere. But there had to be a replacement, someone of equivalent rank and experience, and the most logical choice was General William Hardee, who had served alongside Bragg at Shiloh. Hardee was highly respected as a battlefield commander, even more so than Polk. Bragg could not dispute the logic of Hardee's selection, despite the fact that Bragg despised Hardee almost as much as he did Polk. To Bragg, President Davis's "solution" was a poor compromise, but one he had to accept.

Polk had no choice but to obey Bragg's order, and he immediately relocated his headquarters to Atlanta, but his own campaign against Bragg continued. There were vitriolic letters to his friend Davis, to others in Richmond, and an ongoing communication between Polk and several of the other senior officers now entrenched around Chattanooga, including Longstreet. Though Bragg had purged his army of one significant enemy, a tempest continued to build around him.

"NAIL HOUSE"— BRAGG'S HEADQUARTERS— MISSIONARY RIDGE— OCTOBER 4, 1863

"I do not have a copy of the petition, sir. It would have been unwise for me to attempt to procure one, not having affixed my own signature. But its meaning requires no special interpretation. Please understand, sir, that I come here knowing that it is inappropriate for an officer of my subordinate rank to bypass my own commanding officer."

Bragg waited for more, had heard only fragments of gossip about the document General Liddell was now revealing to him. He didn't completely trust Liddell, knew that Liddell had been one of those noisy annoyances from the field, speaking out against Bragg's decisions during several engagements. Bragg had little regard for brigade commanders who assumed to know more than their commanding general. But still . . . Liddell was here now. And the message he was offering to Bragg might be placing Liddell in a compromised situation within his own command. At the very least, Bragg was intrigued by the courage, or the backhandedness required for Liddell to address him at all.

"Is it not true, Mr. Liddell, that you have been a critic of mine in the past? Have you not done your own share of spouting out? Now you tell me others are doing the same, and you come here . . . why? From a sense of outrage?"

Liddell seemed to understand his predicament, chose his words carefully. "Sir, I admit that I have often disagreed with your command decisions, or your methods of maneuver. I have however been discreet within the bounds of my station. My concern is that others . . . including many who outrank me . . . are not so discreet. There are boundaries of protocol. Those boundaries are being grossly violated."

Bragg stared at Liddell with a hard scowl, waited for more, could see that the man was extremely uncomfortable. "You said a petition. Who signed it?"

Liddell looked down. "I did not, sir."

"I assumed that you are not both indiscreet and stupid, General. If your signature was on that petition, you wouldn't be here, correct? You'd be out there, scurrying about your headquarters like the other rats who claim to support this **vessel** of an army, all the while abandoning it."

"I cannot recall every name, sir. Numerous officers were present. Most all outranked me, though there were some regimental commanders who signed as well."

"Longstreet?"

"Yes, sir. Most definitely."

That was no surprise to Bragg. Any petition condemning Bragg that was being circulated through his command would most likely originate with Longstreet.

"What does it say, precisely? As precisely as you can recall."

"I . . . prefer not to attempt to quote such seditiousness, sir. Suffice to say that a dozen or more general officers in this army have petitioned President Davis to remove you from command. Your abilities are being soundly dismissed. Must I say more?"

"Hill? Buckner? Breckinridge?"

Liddell took a long breath. "I believe so, sir. Cleburne, Randall, Preston. No, not Breckinridge."

"No, of course not. Ever the politician. One's name on a piece of paper can't be so easily denied should that piece of paper one day become inconvenient. But, General, tell me, why is your signature not on that piece of paper? I am well aware of your lack of respect for this chair."

Liddell seemed to ponder the question. "Sir, I have revealed to you the details of a subject which has caused me, and will cause this entire army, considerable anxiety. My own feelings are well known within my own camp, and no further. Two weeks ago, the fruits of victory were right before us. All we had to do was grab them. I believe an opportunity was lost. But I would not voice that opinion to any public forum. It is unbecoming an officer. I was outraged that these men would be so blatant in their efforts to remove you from command. It is no less than an act of mutiny."

"And by that you are outraged. And you would perform an act of indiscretion by approaching me directly to let me know just how outraged you are. You, who have been quick to question my decisions, who may perhaps believe with those others, that I am not fit to command this army."

"I would not sign, sir. I would not go so far as to question your abilities for command."

"Go as far as you wish, General Liddell. By signing this ridiculous petition, my enemies have made themselves known to me. They have revealed their cards, as it were. But I am not concerned by this. Not at all. For every critic, I have a voice of authority who speaks out on my behalf. Already I have received the heartiest congratulations for my success from Joe Johnston, from General Lee, from a great many of those loyal to me in Richmond. This kind of chicanery cannot be tolerated, and it will not be tolerated. Leave me, General. The pretense of your loyalty is noted, as is your lack of decorum, and your unwillingness to document what you say."

Liddell hesitated, said, "Sir, before I leave this office, I must mention that there are others who would not be a party to this scheme. Not every general officer in this army is so eager to express their disloyalty, or demonstrate such flagrant disrespect. It would be an error on your part to assume such."

"It is a little late for you to kneel down, General."

"Sir, I only . . ."

Liddell stopped, seemed to run out of words. He made a short bow, marched noisily from the office. Bragg felt his heart racing, ran the names through his head, the faces of Longstreet, Buckner, Cleburne, thought, They would test my resolve? They would urge the president to remove me, after such successes as we have had? They have made a serious tactical error, one that will cost them dearly.

Mackall was in the doorway, said, "Excuse me, sir. It was impossible not to hear General Liddell's report. If I may inquire, sir, what are you going to do?"

Bragg felt energized, the familiar ailments swept away. He looked out toward the open ground beyond the Nail House, the rain blowing past in a steady torrent, several days of that now. He heard a distant thump of thunder, and Mackall looked that way, said, "It is just the storm, sir. There is no movement, no activity."

"Oh, there is activity aplenty. They wish a war, they shall have a war."

Mackall started to protest, then stopped, seemed to understand what Bragg was saying. "Sir, if I might offer, with deepest respects—"

"Later. There is much to be done. Plans to be made, correspondence to be sent. Have the secretary prepared with pen and paper. I must think about this, put into words the best strategy."

"You are not speaking of the Yankees."

Bragg made a small laugh, as much joviality as he permitted himself. "I am speaking of the **enemy**, Mr. Mackall. We have a war, and I mean to fight it. President Davis will expect something from me very quickly. I must not hesitate."

Mackall said nothing, stared at him for a long moment.

"Be selective with your comments, Mr. Mackall. I might assume you to be among the conspirators."

Mackall waited, then said softly, "Does this affair, this confrontation with your subordinates . . . bring you joy?"

Bragg was surprised by the question, thought a moment. "There is never joy in disloyalty. I did not ask for this controversy, but I will confront it. Those who dismiss my willingness to fight shall pay for their mistake."

"I know of no one in this army who questions your fight, sir."

"I suppose I should thank you for your blindness.

No good, Mr. Mackall. I am like the serpent who has been tread upon. I will rise up and smite my enemies."

"You're referring to your own commanders, sir. No one is your enemy. They are critical, they have different opinions of what we must do. They are impatient. They seek to correct errors. If we devote too much energy to this kind of squabble, it can only harm us, harm our cause."

"This is far from a squabble. There is great danger from those who oppose this command, who would seek to remove me from this office at the moment of a great triumph." Bragg tilted his head, examined Mackall's stoic expression, had grown weary of that. "Have you nothing to add, Mr. Mackall? Do you not see opportunity here? Finally, I may rid the army of those who seek to defeat us."

Mackall turned away, then paused, stood in the doorway, said in a soft voice, "What of the Yankees? We must put our attentions there."

"The Yankees are of little concern right now. This rain could last for days, and with every creek overflowing and every road a sea of mud, there will be little activity on the front lines. Would you at least agree with that?"

"They have thus far shown no activity in our direction, sir."

"And they will not. Not while we have the good ground. They are content to cower behind their defenses, and even now, they must be contemplating their own starvation."

Mackall looked his way again. "If that is true, surely we can expect them to act. They will not just sit still while they exhaust their rations."

"Then they will leave. Either way, our victory is secure. Do not talk to me of such details, Mr. Mackall. You may choose to support my efforts, or you may resign from my service. Those are your options."

Mackall looked down, and Bragg saw a glimmer of despair on the man's face, felt a surge of relief from that. Yes, he is loyal. He does not stand up like some rooster and defy me. "Go on, Mr. Mackall. You have your duty."

Mackall nodded. "I shall bring the secretary . . . when you order it."

Word of Joe Wheeler's October 3 cavalry raid on the Federal wagon train had come back to Bragg's headquarters in a rush of celebration. With a long stretch of the Tennessee River useless to Federal boat traffic, the only supply route that Rosecrans's commissary officers could use came over the mountains, the kind of ragged narrow passageway that was difficult for horses and wagons even in good weather. If his siege was not a complete encirclement of the Federal camps, Bragg had confidence that this single lifeline left to the enemy was woefully inadequate to supply their needs. Wheeler's resounding success in crushing the Federal supply train seemed to Bragg to be one more nail in Rosecrans's coffin. More important to Wheeler, who had a simmering dislike of the more flamboyant Nathan Bedford Forrest, Bragg allowed himself to be convinced that Forrest was simply ineffective, Wheeler persuading Bragg that Forrest should be ordered to give up most of his strength, and transfer those horsemen directly to Wheeler. In effect, Bragg had elevated Joe Wheeler to overall command of the cavalry throughout this entire theater of the war.

Bragg expected this powerful force of horsemen to fight off any confrontation with Federal troopers, allowing Wheeler to maintain a strong force in the Federal rear that would crush any attempt to resupply the Federal troops in the town. But Wheeler had overplayed his hand.

The plan was to reinforce Wheeler by additional cavalry units under the commands of Stephen D. Lee and Phillip Roddey, who were ordered to join Wheeler from their bases in Alabama and Mississippi. But Wheeler's impatience pushed him into action before Lee and Roddey could reach him. Undermanned for such an ambitious raid, Wheeler was now in danger from rapidly gathering Federal cavalry. His only choice was escape, which meant a retreat back across the Tennessee River. As gleefully as Bragg had received word of the blow to the

Federal supply train, his own prejudice against the vainglory and haphazard efforts of cavalry blossomed once more. What he did not expect was that one of those men, Nathan Bedford Forrest, would not meekly accept the order to strip himself of manpower just to fuel the ambitions of Joe Wheeler.

NAIL HOUSE—
BRAGG'S HEADQUARTERS—
MISSIONARY RIDGE—
OCTOBER 7, 1863

Bragg heard the commotion outside, saw Mackall backing into the room, pushed by heavy boot steps, the man now pushing past him. It was Forrest.

Bragg sat motionless, saw a look he had seen before, a red fury, but this time, Forrest's anger wasn't directed at any Yankee. Forrest spun toward him, ignored the pair of aides who stood back to one side, papers in their hands. Bragg tried to avoid Forrest's glare, stood, said, "General Forrest . . . it is late."

Another man scrambled in behind Forrest, and Mackall said something, a hesitant greeting, the man unfamiliar to Bragg. He moved up close behind Forrest, put a hand on Forrest's shoulder. Forrest shook the hand away, and the man looked at Bragg with obvious concern, made a short bow, quick, soft words.

"Sir, I am Dr. James Cowan, General Forrest's surgeon. We regret the sudden intrusion."

Bragg made a brief nod to Cowan, his eyes still on Forrest, a quick glance toward the pistol at Forrest's side. "Doctor, is it? Welcome to my headquarters. General Forrest . . ."

Bragg held out a hand, as though Forrest should take it, but it was a gesture born of fear, nothing friendly in Bragg's mind. Forrest ignored the hand, stared hard at him, no ebb in the man's temper. Bragg sat down again, felt pushed backward by Forrest's anger, and Forrest spoke now, slow and deliberate, his words slicing the air between them like the blade of a knife.

"You have pursued a cowardly and contemptible persecution of me since Shiloh, and you have kept up such behavior ever since. You take me to be your foe because after every fight, my reports contain facts, while you only tell Richmond damned lies. You have robbed me of my command before, and now you do it again. I have trained and equipped my men from the spoils we have gained against the enemy, and because I will not fawn upon you as so many others have done, you offer me only revenge and spite. You have made every attempt to ruin my career, and now you are doing so again. I command a brigade of men who have never been bested, men who have sacrificed themselves, men who have won a reputation for successful fighting second to none in this army. You take advantage of your position as

commanding general, and in order to further hu-
miliate me, you take these brave men from me. I
have stood your meanness as long as I intend to.
You have played the part of a damned scoundrel
and are a coward, and if you were any part a man
I would slap your jaws and force you to resent it.
You may as well not issue any more orders to me,
for I will not obey them, and I will hold you personally responsible for any further indignities you
endeavor to inflict upon me. You have threatened
to arrest me for not obeying your orders promptly.
I dare you to do it! And I say to you that if you ever
again try to interfere with me or cross my path it
will be at the peril of your life!"

Forrest turned quickly, marched from the
room, the doctor taking a last hesitating glance
at Bragg. Then he, too, was gone, and Mackall
stared toward the doorway, his mouth slightly
open.

"What . . . should I do, sir?"

Bragg felt frozen in his chair, realized his uniform
was soaked with his sweat. He tried to speak, his
voice held by the tightness in his throat, and he
coughed, forced a response. "You will do nothing."

"Sir, he . . . that was . . . he risked his life saying
such things. He threatened you!"

"You will do nothing, do you hear?"

Bragg felt his hands shaking, worked the cold
out of his fingers, sat straight, fought to breathe.
He wanted to stand, to show Mackall he had the

strength, but there was no power in his legs. He heard the hoofbeats, Forrest riding away, and Mackall said, "It was unwise of him to bring a witness . . . or to speak such things in our presence, in the presence of your aides."

Bragg felt a bolt of fire through him, stood now, his fists on the small desk, looked at the other two men, young, standing silently with wide eyes, their backs pressed against the wall.

"You will say nothing about this! Nothing! Do you understand?" He fought to stay upright, the cold deep in his gut, his hands steadying on the rough wood of the desk. He forced the words out slowly, the fear subsiding, the image of Forrest's glare fading. "Nothing more. It is merely . . . the solution I have searched for. General Forrest has done us a service. He knew certainly that his days in this army were few. No doubt he will remove himself from this command. That is . . . a convenience. Think nothing more of it."

Mackall made a silent gesture, ordering the aides away, the two men responding gratefully, a quick exit. Mackall sat on a small camp stool, still stared at the open doorway. More aides were there now, word spreading through the headquarters, and Mackall said, "Away! All of you! There is nothing of concern here!"

The men obeyed, quick glances at Bragg, who sat back, his hands still quivering. He planted them in his lap, tried still to calm himself, said to Mackall,

"There is work to be done, yes? The staff shall be kept busy. Do your duty, General. In the morning . . . the sun shall rise on this army, and it shall be a new day. We shall put our minds to work on solving what troubles us. Nothing further will be heard from General Forrest. And so, I am confident that this one . . . **trouble** . . . has been handled quite nicely."

CHAPTER FIVE

BAUER

NEAR NATCHEZ, MISSISSIPPI—
SEPTEMBER 25, 1863

He had never been so bored in his life. The daily walks had become a drudgery, and he forced the pains from his legs, shoved through the weakness, pushed air in and out of his lungs, fighting the temptation to stop, to rest on some moldy tree stump. For all the boredom, he knew better than to complain, accepted easily that doing anything out of doors was far more satisfying than more dismal conversation with the doctors. And in their insistence that he take the lengthy walks, Bauer understood the message the doctors were giving him: After several agonizing weeks, he was finally healing.

The illness had come to him at the end of July, and Bauer was one of many. It had to do with the swamps, the summer heat, the lack of clean drinking water from the lack of rain. The army seemed to plant the troops in a place guaranteed to create sickness. In Bauer's case, what had seemed to be dysentery had turned even uglier. A fever spread through the entire brigade, long nights of drenching sweat, his joints stiff and swollen, which seemed to mystify the doctors. And there were deaths, Bauer absorbing the unavoidable sadness of a man beside him suddenly taken away, the tearful reaction of silent nurses, the dull stares from overworked stretcher bearers. The glorious mansions around Natchez had become crushingly depressing places, the finest homes now pressed into service as hospitals. To some, the death of the man beside you was welcome, a silent farewell as the man was taken away, the most devout reassuring themselves that one more man was now in that "better place," their suffering ended. To Bauer, it just meant that, once again, death had missed **him.**

The route was laid out, a wide path that carried him through the most dismal wood and swamp bottoms he had ever seen. If he needed some boost of enthusiasm, something to ease the monotony, it was first, that he was alive at all, and second, the aches and agonies from his illness were noticeably diminished.

The orderly who followed him was there for discipline, to keep Bauer honest, a task that Bauer had to believe was as boring as his own. He glanced back from time to time, the orderly nowhere in sight, hanging back, he thought, to perhaps catch him in some improper disregard for the doctor's instructions. Bauer had begun to imagine that the orderly might be back there performing some indiscreet act of his own, probably with a flask of spirits. It was speculation that offered Bauer at least some kind of break from the fog that still filled his head, what the doctor assured him was only the aftereffects of the drugs they had given him.

He stared into a deep hole in the woods, a cavelike tunnel through dense brush over a carpet of black water. There was too much of that, too many places that reminded him of the endless swamps that seemed to fill every low place in this part of the world. Any soldier who had served this long close to the Mississippi River had seen for himself that such places held terrifying and dangerous creatures: alligators, snakes, other critters that belched out groans and shrieks that had inspired numerous legends. Even now, the talk in the hospital was of some man-ape creature, who slogged his way through the deepest mud holes, silent, efficient, sure to attack anyone foolish enough to tread too near the swampy bottoms. His brain tried to focus, the talk even from the doctors of that demon of the deep woods, and Bauer wondered now if the tale had begun from the imaginations of the medical men, to keep anyone, patient or orderly, from slipping off on some indiscreet mission that had nothing to do with medicine. This was, after all, Natchez, and many of the troops had found that the gentility of this Southern community masked the availability of a different kind of creature, one who smelled of perfume. Bauer stopped, looked back, saw the man now, coming around the curve behind him. No, he's too efficient. Takes his orders too seriously. Bauer began to move again, the stiffness in one knee tormenting him. A man-beast, he thought. A great hairy ape. That kind of tale is good for tormenting new recruits, give them a healthy fear of these swamps. Most of the fresh-faced boys tried to laugh it off, just some fairy tale, but Bauer knew that several of them slept with their muskets.

He saw another gap in the thickets to one side, more black water, thought, No shortcut that way. I've seen at least one alligator in that hole, and I know full well there are snakes out here big enough to swallow me right up to my neck. That doctor knew just where he was sending me. If I tried to slice off a mile or two from this hike, I might never be heard from again. They'd find me when some gator spit out my bones. Or maybe I'd come out the other end. Either way, Fritz, stay on the road. Damn it all anyway. My legs are doing just fine.

He winced, the strain in his calves giving the lie to his attempt at bravado. His lungs ached as well, but the pungent stench of the swampy water was far better than what waited for him at the hospital. Okay, just keep walking. Can't be too much more of this. Your gut's doing okay, for now. That's a good thing, for certain. A man ain't built for permanent squatting. I've hugged my knees so much, they're rougher 'n my pants legs.

The trail curved around a muddy water hole, and the smell curled his nose, as it always did. That's gotta be where they get our rations from, he thought. Fill the canteens with something you can't even see through.

He knew it hadn't really been like that in Natchez, and not for a long time anywhere else. The food had improved considerably since the long marches had stopped, their supplies coming in regularly from upriver. Some men still griped, always griped, but he knew better, had heard plenty of stories from the rebels they had captured at Vicksburg, many of those men, and the civilians along with them, enduring Grant's siege by drinking water straight from the Mississippi River. Bauer had experienced that misery back before Shiloh, the soldiers often forced to drink right out of the Tennessee. There was sickness then, too, dysentery, or something close enough, sweeping through the regiment. Bauer had dodged that one, one of those pieces of good fortune that some insisted on labeling **fate.** Bauer didn't have much faith in that, believed instead that he had just been lucky, or that by sheer strength of will, he had kept the diseases away. The inspiration for anyone to stay healthy came from any visit to a field hospital, miserable bloody places that no one wanted to see, sick or not. But his luck had run out. At least the hospital's a big damn house, he thought. Mansion. Some rich rebel long gone, figuring us nasty old Yankees are gonna burn his place, or tear everything to shreds. Good. Keep outta the way, let us do our business. My business is to get this affliction outta my body and get strong enough so the doctor'll send me back to the regiment. Mansion or not, right now, a tent would be a whole lot nicer than big rooms full of puking soldiers.

He emerged from the woods, the trail intersecting a wide road, could see the first of the grand houses. To one side, the regimental camps spread out through what had been a massive cornfield, white tents in rows that stretched as far as he could see. The regiment had been sent southward from Vicksburg soon after the surrender of Pemberton's Confederates, most of the army going into garrison duty in several of the cities that lined the river. The only contact with rebels had come from a few brief skirmishes, most of the rebels gone completely from this part of the war.

He still didn't know how far he had walked, had thought at first it had been a dozen miles. But even through weak legs, he knew better. There had been too many of those twenty-mile excursions in the past, toting his various equipment. He had pushed hard at those memories, keeping away what would certainly be the worst experiences of his life. And his brain had obliged him. Now those days seemed forever in the past, unexpectedly fading into faint memory. What emerged instead was a strange kind of nostalgia, vivid recollections of the exhilaration that came after the bloody successes at Shiloh and Vicksburg. The worst surprise was that no matter how awful those fights had been, for all his terror, the horrific sights and sounds and smells that could still inspire nightmares, he was engulfed now in a different kind of nightmare, something he never expected. He had **nothing** to do. There was no fight anywhere close, no marching, no enemy, no screams, no terror. Even through the long days confined to a bed, his brain pondered the possibilities, wondering just what they would ask him to do now. More marching? Where? Why?

He was surprised to feel the itch he had heard of from some of the veterans. There was no challenge in camp life, and so some of the men reacted with a different kind of aggression. There were fistfights nearly every night, some men finding liquor, and so, drunken brawls, even a deadly knife fight. The result was usually a trip to the stockade. But some men made a more radical escape. The army still called them **deserters,** and when they were caught, the results could be gruesome and heartwrenching. He had seen one execution, the entire regiment gathered into formation to witness a man shot down by a firing squad, tumbling into a grave he had dug himself. Bauer had known the man, a fearsome soldier. But when the guns went silent, the man did not, and if there were no rebels nearby, the man seemed intent on finding them himself. The army didn't seem to care if he had run away just to go home, or if he was still soldiering, off on a rebel hunt. It was a lesson Bauer found difficult to digest, but he understood discipline. Even in garrison duty, the army had its rules.

Not all of the veterans festered over the inactivity. Many spoke about going home, undisciplined chatter that they weren't going to fight, no matter who gave the orders, no matter how many rebels there were. Bauer rarely responded to that, and not because it was dangerous talk, something to land a man time in the stockade. His first reaction was outrage, that anyone would claim to be a part of his army, to stand beside him and face the enemy, only to make the purposeful decision just to run away.

The new men were very different, fresh volunteers full of enthusiasm for the unknown, seeking out the stories, which the veterans supplied with exaggerated vigor. Bauer had learned to despise the mouthy recruits, knew that when the shooting started, they were the most unpredictable. Some had risen up to heroics in the most unlikely ways, while others, especially the biggest talkers, would most certainly disappear when the fight grew hot. During the great horror of Shiloh, Bauer had been among the latter. That haunted him still, not the bloody memories as much as what he had done, how he had reacted to his first confrontation with the rebels. His courage, his sense of honor and duty had simply collapsed and he had joined a manic stampede away from the fight until his legs and his lungs gave out. But Shiloh was a very long time ago now, and since then, the other great fight had been at Vicksburg, where most of the veterans stood tall and did the job they had to do. The satisfaction of that victory wiped away the stains of Bauer's own shame; and any thoughts of escape, of scampering away from the firing line, had dissolved completely. He was a soldier now, had accepted that with perfect certainty. He had been wounded only once, a small slice along his arm, not deep enough to cause alarm. He knew that others kept a healthy fear that somewhere, sometime, there was an inevitability that one musket ball or one piece of shrapnel was meant only for you, would find you no matter what safe place you tried to find. Bauer believed now that when a man accepted the certainty of his own death, he became a better soldier. If God had decided your destiny, running away had no point. But Bauer had also drawn inspiration from watching the good soldiers around him. He believed now, more than ever, that he was fighting for them, that the man beside you expected you to do your job, and the man who led you expected you to follow. It was as simple as that, what he assumed the army meant by **duty.**

He didn't feel any great hatred for the rebels, had killed several of them with the keen eye of the sharpshooter, a talent that surprised him. But through all of that, he had grown to love the men around him, the men he served beside, something he could never admit out loud. He had served with two different regiments, the 16th and now the 17th Wisconsin, and in both places, the men he fought with, fought for, had become the most important thing in his life. He would never commit any act of shame, would never display cowardice in front of those men. He had no idea if anyone else felt that way. The only real displays of affection and camaraderie seemed to erupt when one of the men was struck down. You were allowed tears then, and men shed them without embarrassment. But when the guns stopped, and the campfires lit the night, you didn't speak of fallen comrades. The talk returned to the mundane, bragging rights, skills with the musket, the knife, talk of women and home. Some didn't at all, settling for card playing and letter writing. Some kept to their Bibles; some, like Bauer, spent long hours staring into the night sky, wrapped in the privacy of their own thoughts. Those thoughts had once been about home, going back to the world he grew up in, Milwaukee, his father's business. But that ended a year before, the death of both his parents, a sudden, crushing blow that ripped away any desire for going **home.** For nearly two years now, his home had been a tent, or a bed of leaves, a night sky, or a mud-slop march. His Sunday dinner had been stale crackers and sour beef, raw bacon and foul water, and if it had ever been any other way, his memory wouldn't take him there, wouldn't allow him to sit at the family's table with china plates and steaming bowls and the voice of his mother.

He could see the magnificent house that was his own hospital, saw other soldiers emerging, some accompanied by orderlies, or walking in pairs. He felt the same relief as the doctors, that more men were regaining their strength, that the number of new patients was decreasing, the number of deaths falling off dramatically. He knew that some of the men had grown stronger far more quickly than he had, and by mid-September, with a slight break in the torrid summer heat, some of those men were being returned to duty. As much as he despised the hospital, Bauer had no particular desire to jump back into the ranks, knew that the daily routine for the healthy wasn't much more interesting than it was for the sick.

Garrison duty meant marching, formations, bugle calls, inspections, and, worst of all, speeches. The victory in July at Vicksburg seemed to rouse official Washington to a mass travel schedule that brought all manner of politician and orator to the Mississippi River, each one seeking to bathe in the army's glory. Throughout August, as Bauer suffered in his hospital bed, the railroad tracks anywhere near an army post were kept hot by the steady traffic of enthusiastic civilians, and though some made it to the hospitals, the speechmakers quickly learned that the best audience was one that didn't smell of death and disease.

With the return of his strength came a curiosity for just what was happening with the men he had fought with, the Irishmen who populated the 17th. Some of those had taken the time to visit him, cautiously peering in on him, keeping their distance. As grateful as Bauer was for the hesitant company, it was one man's absence that now affected him most of all.

Sammie Willis had visited him often, had shown none of the hesitation of the others, had sat on Bauer's bedside, scolding him for what Willis claimed was Bauer's clear dereliction of duty. Bauer knew better. Willis had come into the regiment with Bauer at its formation, and both men had endured the worst fights the army in the West had experienced. Willis had become Bauer's best friend, but more, Willis had a knack for being a soldier, had taught Bauer how to find the courage, how to stand tall when it mattered. And how to kill. Willis also had a talent for leadership, and very soon, someone besides Bauer had recognized that. Willis had been given a commission, had served through the siege of Vicksburg as a second lieutenant, a platoon commander. By the end of that extraordinary success, he had been promoted again to first lieutenant. And now, Willis had been promoted again to captain. With that rank came new assignments, command of an entire company, and Bauer had been devastated to learn that Willis would no longer be part of the 17th Wisconsin. Willis was still the same quiet, intense man, short, thick, and stocky, who had led his platoon with plainspoken discipline that the men instinctively knew to follow. Now the lieutenant who led a dozen men into fire at Vicksburg would be the man who would lead several times that many in the next fight. But the worst news for Bauer was that Willis had made the jump away from the volunteers, and enlisted in the regular army, leaving the Wisconsin men behind.

With Bauer confined to his bed, there had been little time for conversation, a quick goodbye, a brief handshake. Willis had left him claiming that the orders had come more quickly than expected. Only later did Bauer learn that Willis had started this process weeks before, a trail of army paperwork pushed hard by Willis for much longer than he admitted to Bauer. Bauer had to admit that the move was completely in character. But without Willis in the regiment, Bauer felt a gaping hole, a hint of the old panic returning, that no fight would be as glorious or as successful without his friend to lead the way.

Willis had a wife, and a child he had never seen, and sometime in the aftermath of Shiloh the year before, Willis had revealed to his friend that his wife had ended their marriage by running off with someone Willis wouldn't speak of, but a man he certainly knew. Bauer couldn't help nursing a volcanic sense of revenge for any man who would steal away anyone's wife. But Bauer couldn't probe that wound, Willis always shutting down. To the men who didn't know Willis's humor, his good-natured jabs at Bauer, who only saw the officer, that change barely mattered. To the men who followed him, Willis was just the "good soldier," the man who stood up in the storm of musket fire and never flinched. Willis even seemed to **enjoy** it, had stood up to the rush of the enemy, had led charges into places that few should survive. And yet, survive he did, prepared, even eager, to do it all again.

HEADQUARTERS, 17TH WISCONSIN, NEAR NATCHEZ, MISSISSIPPI— SEPTEMBER 27, 1863

"Good to have you back in the ranks, Private. You're a lucky man. This miserable sickness has affected the whole division."

"Yes, sir. Thank you. Um, sir, I have a request. Lieutenant O'Brady said I could speak to you directly, that maybe your office could help me."

The officer sat back, said, "You're Captain Willis's friend, right?"

Bauer was surprised. "Yes, sir. Sammie's my best friend. Well, hard to think of him as an officer, begging your pardon, sir. Sammie . . . Captain Willis and I go back to the beginning, the formation of the 16th Regiment. He was transferred over here last year, brought me with him. Still not certain how he managed to do that."

The lieutenant laughed. "It's war, Private. It's the army. I remember now. Colonel Malloy had me do some checking, asking around to the other Wisconsin regiments. We needed a couple lieutenants, and your colonel over there owed me something. Once Willis got here, Colonel Malloy and I saw something we didn't expect. Frankly, he scared us a little. And his company commander agreed. Some of these low-grade officers assume they're on track to make general, think Abe Lincoln's gonna pick them out to run this whole show. Not Willis. He made it pretty clear he would much rather be out front. No surprise then, when he went straight to Colonel Malloy and asked for a discharge, insisted he wanted to sign up for the regulars. We've had a few do that. First time it was an officer, though. Hated to lose him, but the regulars need good officers, too. We sent him on his way. But I guess you know all this."

"Yes, sir. Sammie . . . Captain Willis . . . he's given me a fright sometimes. Never seen a man who loves hearing the musket balls whiz by." Bauer paused. "Well, sir, as I said, I have a request."

"What is it?"

"Sir, please don't get me wrong. I love Wisconsin, love everything about it. It's my home, and I reckon one day I'll end up back there again. Right now, the doctors are sending me back to the camp, saying I'm pretty well fixed up. I hear we're likely gonna be in garrison duty for a while, and Lieutenant O'Brady says we're not figuring to go much of anyplace any-time soon. Sir, Sammie taught me something. At Shiloh, I was more scared than I've ever been, ran away from the enemy like a pure coward. Found my wits only because Sammie made me. If there's another fight, I want to be in his feetprints, sir. He's the only reason I'm still in this army, and not in the stockade, or in a box back home."

The lieutenant leaned forward on the desk, his hands folded under his chin. "You telling me you want to be discharged, so you can enlist in the"—he looked down, shuffled a paper—"the Eighteenth United States Regulars?"

Bauer had no idea which regiment Sammie had joined, saw a hint of a smile on the officer's face. Bauer took a breath, had spent a sleepless night pondering this moment, what the adjutant might say, if anyone would grant him anything at all. And if they did, would Bauer still jump at the chance to become a regular soldier? He wasn't even sure what that meant, just how different the regular army was from the men who volunteered. But he had to try. He had to do anything he could to stay close to his friend.

"Yes, sir. With all respects, sir, and all respects to Colonel Malloy, it is my desire to become a regular soldier. Sir, if I may be frank . . . there's no other place feels like home anymore. I have no place else to go."

The lieutenant shook his head, examined him, questioning. "You're not homesick? I get every kind of request in here for some fellow to go back home, misses his mama, misses his children. Makes sense. None of us like being off in some Southern pigpen. You've no tie back home, no gal?"

"No, sir. Sir, I lost my parents last year. I settled all the affairs. I love Milwaukee, but not sure I have anything waiting for me there. I gotta say, sir . . . I like the army."

"So do I, Private, but not sure I want to spend the rest of my life here, or even the rest of this war. Not sure how long this'll take. None of us do. But when the fight's done, one way or the other, the army might not need **you.**"

Bauer hadn't thought of that, that the army might toss him out whether he liked it or not. He tried to imagine Willis's response to that. "Not sure how that would be, sir. But right now, it's the only thing I want to do. There's just no other place I wanna be, sir."

The lieutenant looked down, picked up another piece of paper. "Private, this just came in today. Your name is on a list of those in Company A to be considered for sergeant. It's about time you moved up in rank. Better pay, you know."

Bauer pondered that, another surprise, glanced at his own sleeve, imagined chevrons. "I appreciate that, sir. But, like you said, I'm just a private. I learned how to carry a musket by watching Sammie, following him. I'm hoping, with your permission, sir, I can do that again."

"Can't guarantee you'll end up in the Eighteenth. There's battalions of regulars all over this army, scattered in different commands."

"I thought of that, sir. I was wondering if you could put in some kind of recommendation, maybe to Captain Willis's commander. Since, begging your pardon, sir, I'm willing to let go of a sergeant's stripes, maybe you can do me this favor?"

The lieutenant laughed again. "All right, Private Bauer. I'm only Colonel Malloy's adjutant, and my job is to get the papers ready. But the colonel is a reasonable man, and he'll go along with my recommendation. I'll contact General McPherson's adjutant, too. Can't ever hurt to break the door down at high headquarters. Make some noise. Army seems to respect that." He paused, the smile slipping away. "Private, I know you've been laid up a good bit."

"Yes, sir. More than a month."

"You heard about the fight?"

Bauer felt a stir inside him, gravity in the man's words. "What fight, sir?"

The lieutenant sat back again. "Hell of a scrap . . .

well, no. It was worse than that. The toughest lick-
ing this army has experienced since Chancellorsville. We took a hell of a beating, Private."

Bauer felt a cold stab, said, "Where, sir? Doesn't
make sense that I wouldn't hear . . ."

"Well east of here, in north Georgia. They're calling it Chickamauga, for some river there. We got
busted up pretty bad, lost ground, lost a lot of good
men. The whole army's getting its back up. Word
is that General Grant might be sending some of his
people thataway to help out. We figure that'll be
Sherman. He's Grant's favorite, most experienced.
General McPherson's too fresh to command. That's
just . . . well, it's opinion, Private. No need to start
rumors."

"No, sir, certainly not."

"Point is, the Army of the Cumberland is hurt
pretty bad. That's where your Eighteenth Regulars
are now. Not sure what kind of shape they're in, but
I would bet they're needing some replacements. You
want your chance, Private, the damn rebels might
have given it to you."

"Any word, sir . . . the Eighteenth . . ."

He felt stupid asking the question, knew that a
regimental adjutant wouldn't know any more than
he already said.

"You mean . . . is your friend all right? No idea.
If the papers go through, you'll find out everything
when you get there. If you get there. Don't be in
such a hurry, Private. There's time enough to die."

CHAPTER SIX

SHERMAN

GAYOSO HOTEL— MEMPHIS, TENNESSEE— OCTOBER 4, 1863

He looked again at the paper, couldn't focus, the faint light of the lantern not helping, the blur of the ink more from the tears in his eyes. He tried to hold back the sounds, wouldn't wake anyone with his own grief, wouldn't let the staff see what they already knew to be the worst tragedy of his life.

The boy was only nine, had begged and cajoled to accompany his father as much as the boy's mother would permit, and so the boy's parents had compromised, Sherman taking him along in those places where the enemy was not. The ride through the camps, past lines of drilling soldiers, had been pure joy for the boy, the father very aware that the men responded with an extra bit of precision, making the best show they could for the oldest son of the commanding general. Sherman's personal guard, a battalion of the 13th Regulars, had adopted young Willie as something of a mascot, which only heightened the boy's rampant enthusiasm for spending time among soldiers. It had been curious to Sherman how much the troops accepted the boy's presence, even encouraged it. He had seen that with Grant of course. Fred Grant was three years older than Willie, and so was able to ride a horse with a hint of expertise. With both boys, the most formidable obstacle to rides with their fathers had of course been their mothers, and Sherman thought of Ellen, all that protest for its own sake. Compromise or not, Sherman knew she had given in more than he had, crumbling in the face of so much enthusiasm from her son. But the wink from her had been clue enough that Ellen was only doing what a mother was supposed to do, acting as the Protector, while her husband, the soldier, would teach the boy just how to be a man. The soldiers seemed to understand that as well, allowing Willie to participate in all manner of camp life, though Sherman had to draw the line when it came to firing a musket. At nine, the boy was simply too small, and Sherman knew that Ellen's tolerance would draw shut if the boy's shoulder erupted in a massive bruise.

The typhoid fever had come on gradually, the boy weakening in that horrible way a father can see, the eager smile disappearing, the brightness in young eyes fading. Sherman had sought out the best doctor available, a surgeon from the 55th Illinois, but by the time any help could be found, any medicines procured, it was too late. On October 2, with Ellen and their other three children close by, Willie died.

He sat back in the chair, stared at the lantern, blinked through the wetness, wiped his face. They loved him, he thought. The whole battalion. He'd have joined them one day, no doubt about that. Another argument with Ellen, that he would be too young. He'd insist on it as soon as he was old enough to shoulder the musket, and then we'd have had a brawl about it. Sixteen? No, I wouldn't have that. Eighteen at least. But she would insist on twenty-five. Or perhaps . . . never. Now . . . it will never be. The other three children . . . Tom is my only boy now, and Ellen will grab on to him like a small piece of treasure. And I cannot object. Ever.

He scanned the room, something to occupy his mind. You cannot just brood, he thought. But how can a father have so little power, so little control over what might happen, what God might do to his children? And why? Is it my sins? Is it punishment for my . . . what? Cowardice? My fears and lack of faith? Is it the killing?

He pushed through those thoughts, knew there would be no answers, and no one he could ask. He glanced down at his uniform, thought, A general can command anything he wishes, can move thousands of men and kill everyone who stands in his way. And with all that authority, all the **official power,** I could do nothing for a nine-year-old boy. **My** boy. And now, I must let him go. He will never be a soldier now, and there is no satisfaction for his mother in that. Not this way. The other three children were there, by his side. A blessing in that. They will remember him, no matter how small they are now. I will make sure they remember every detail. They will grow up knowing a wonderful child was taken away, from all of them. And from me.

He shifted in the hard chair, the piece of paper on the desk in front of him. He thought of the soldiers, one, Captain Smith, the battalion commander, the man sobbing out loud, as full of grief for the loss of the boy as Sherman's own family. They all felt that way, he thought, the men in the ranks. So very generous of them. Remember that, Sherman. Next time you order them to charge the enemy, to face death because you think perhaps it is the right thing to do . . . remember that they loved your son.

He stood, slammed his hands down on the desk. Stop this! You cannot do this, you cannot spread your grief around like some miserable shroud over your army. It is enough that Ellen bear this, and Minnie and Lizzie and Tom. This is our own burden, not the army's.

He paced the small hotel room, glanced down at the sheet of white paper, stopped, let out a breath. Nine years old. They loved him. They made him a sergeant, for God's sake. Grandest smile I ever saw, that I will ever see.

He sat again, moved the lantern closer, illuminating the paper, picked up the pen, dipped it in the inkwell. He stared at it, had written only the heading.

Captain C. C. Smith, Commanding, Battalion Thirteenth United States Regulars.

He thought a moment, blinked again through the wetness, put the pen to the paper, began to write.

"My Dear Friend: I cannot sleep tonight till I record an expression of the deep feelings of my heart to you, and to the officers and soldiers of the battalion, for their kind behavior to my poor child. . . ."

He stopped, stared ahead to the blank wall. **Nine years old.** He continued writing, long minutes, then finished the note, his signature at the bottom, then read it over, one line digging into him.

"On, on I must go, to meet a soldier's fate. . . ."

The captain will understand that. We have no choice. And now . . . it's time to go.

ON THE RAILROAD—NEAR COLLIERVILLE, TENNESSEE— OCTOBER 11, 1863

The order had come within two days of the disaster at Chickamauga, handed him by Grant, passed along from General Halleck in Washington. Sherman had wondered about Rosecrans, if the defeat in north Georgia would just erase the man from the army, condemn Rosecrans to permanent shame. But that judgment would be made by others, and right now, Sherman had no other concerns but the single order. The Army of the Cumberland required immediate assistance, Halleck giving Grant the call to mobilize a significant portion of his army, those men mostly in garrison duty along the Mississippi River. It was no surprise to Sherman that Grant would come to him. If there was a single piece of Grant's army that would move as Grant expected, and Washington would demand, it would be Sherman's.

They would move by rail, but the rail lines had been wrecked continuously by rebel cavalry patrols, and any movement at all would require repairs. It was infuriating to Sherman that there could be no rapid march, no quick transport. Instead his divisions could only move eastward as rapidly as the tracks were replaced. By the ninth of October, two divisions were on the move, but Sherman would move faster, would push himself and his small guard of regulars to explore for himself just how bad a situation Rosecrans had created for himself. Halleck's orders still came, the tenor somewhat hysterical, warning of impending doom for the entire Army of the Cumberland, something Sherman doubted. He knew Halleck well, an old friend even before Mexico, knew how excitable the man could be. But then, rumors had flown westward that Robert E. Lee himself was headed toward Chattanooga, and whether or not that was true, he knew that Halleck's hysteria would only grow. If Lee was indeed moving that way, Rosecrans was in serious trouble, and so, for now, Sherman understood that his mission was one of rescue.

As the train passed through Germantown, a few miles outside Memphis, he had stopped his work in the railcar, stared out toward the roadway near the tracks, where his own Fourth Division was marching. He stepped outside, stood in swirling mist on the small rear platform of the last railcar. It was all for show, a demonstration to his men that their commanding general was aware of their misery on the march. At the very least, seeing him salute them might inspire a small boost in morale for men who, so far, had to use their feet. He watched them for a while, the train rocking precariously on freshly laid track. There were men on horseback, a cluster of officers, and they watched him with calm respect, obviously aware who he was. He returned their salutes, but studied the road more than the men, saw deepening mud, the infantry's blue pants legs soaked to the knees. That will get worse, he thought. Hell of a way to move an army. Rivers of mud and busted-up rail lines. Could take us a month to get across this damn state, and I don't think Rosecrans can wait that long.

He slipped back into the car, wiped rainwater off his sleeves, removed his hat, slapped it dry against his leg. Behind him, the familiar helpfulness of Colonel McCoy.

"Get you some coffee, sir? They say it's not near what we had in Memphis, but beats nothing at all."

Sherman tossed the hat to one side, sat, felt the damp chill in his coat. "Yeah, I guess. Make sure it's strong. Some aide brought me a cup of something looked like horse pee. You threaten those fellows with a flogging, they do that again."

McCoy smiled, knew Sherman too well, turned to leave, and Sherman felt the train slowing, heard shouts, a flurry of motion outside, men in blue, horses. He leaned down, peered through the glass, saw officers, a frantic waving of arms.

The train lurched to a stop and Sherman said, "What the hell's going on?"

McCoy had no response, and Sherman pushed back out to the rear of the train, hopped down from the small deck, his feet splashing into thick mud. A horseman moved close to him, familiar, the man reining up, calling out, "General! Colonel Dewitt Anthony, Sixty-sixth Indiana. You have to stop this train!"

"I know you, Colonel. What's the delay?"

Anthony was clearly agitated, looked toward the front of the train, and Sherman heard it now, a short rattle of musket fire.

"Sir, I command the garrison at the depot here . . .

Collierville. We were hit hard by rebel cavalry . . . drove in my picket line, captured some men, some wagons. There's a pile of 'em, sir!"

"Easy, Colonel. I've got a battalion of regulars on board. Better than two hundred men. We'll hold off any cavalry raid."

"Sir, it's more than a raid! Looked to be at least several regiments! My men are in position to receive an assault, but we have no artillery, and our position isn't strong. We'll do what we can, sir!"

Sherman looked back down the empty track, shook his head.

"All right, we'll back up this damn train. If the rebs are cavalry, we won't get off too far anyway. Listen, Colonel. Calm yourself down, and do your job!" He turned now, saw McCoy, wide eyes, staring out toward the musket fire, saw to one side, a long knoll, a spur of higher ground. "Colonel, order the troops off the train, position them along that knoll. I want to know just what Colonel Anthony considers to be a **pile** of rebels."

"Sir!"

McCoy disappeared into the railcar, the troops already jumping down, orders going out from officers who had heard the muskets. An officer ran alongside the train toward him, Captain Smith, the man who received Sherman's letter.

"General! There's word we're in for a scrap! That knoll looks like a good—"

"Already there, Captain. Place your men with

care, get them ready. Not sure yet what's out there, but I suspect we're close to finding out."

Sherman followed the officers on foot, Smith pulling the men off the train quickly, McCoy and Sherman's other aides moving among them, repeating the order. Sherman climbed the knoll, saw a wide cornfield to the south of the track, woodlands beyond. The muskets were silent now, and he stared at the distant woods, a flicker of motion catching his eye.

McCoy called out to him, "Sir! A rider!"

"I see him. Keep moving. Get these men into position."

Anthony was beside him, still on the horse, said, "Sir, there's a unit of Illinois cavalry up behind the town. I've sent word. . . . I'm sure they heard the ruckus. My men are pulling back into our stockade at the depot. We've got other men positioned inside the depot itself. If your regulars link up with our flank—"

"They know what to do, Colonel. I'm wondering what **that** fellow wants."

Anthony followed Sherman's gaze, other officers moving up, staring out. The man was in plain sight now, moving through the cornfield, a rebel officer's uniform, a white flag above his head, riding with caution, eyeing the Federal troops who were most certainly eyeing him. He seemed to be aiming for Anthony's horse, understood where the authority might be, rode closer, slowing, and Sherman leaned up toward the horse, said to Anthony, "This is your command. Don't call me by name. You understand? Get out there and meet him, but keep him away from me." Sherman glanced back to his own staff, saw Dayton, waiting for instructions. "Colonel, go with Colonel Anthony. This man wants a parley. Give him one. A slow one. Delay him, you understand? Colonel Anthony, leave your horse here. If they have sharpshooters in those far trees, white flag or not, somebody might take you for a tempting target."

Anthony didn't hesitate, jumped down from the horse, Dayton moving up next to him, both men walking out toward the horseman at a quick pace. Sherman slipped back up onto the railcar, hid himself slightly, strained to hear. The rebel was walking the horse slowly now, the white flag held higher still. Sherman saw the man's fear, quick glances at the muskets now lining the low ridge. He saw no weapon in the man's belt, thought, He believes in the power of that white cloth. All right, so do I. For now.

The two blue-coated officers moved out into the horse's path, stood side by side, a symbolic attempt to block the man's way, and Sherman could hear the man speak, a high-pitched shake to his voice.

"I am Captain Fraley, adjutant to General Chalmers. The general offers his respects to the officer commanding this post, and suggests in the strongest terms that you avoid the slaughter of your men, and surrender this position without incident. The general assures you of fair terms."

The officers responded, forced conversation, a chatter of nothing pouring back to the man, social banter, the rebel seeming to take the bait, still nervously eyeing the Federal muskets. Sherman backed away from the window, leaned out the other way, could see Anthony's makeshift fort just ahead, and beyond, the rounded brick walls of the Collierville depot. His mind was churning, feverish, the old fear rising up, the panic of the unknown. Is it a bluff? Chalmers. He's a Forrest man. Probably wrecked this track himself, came back to do it again. Do we believe him? Damn it all, how many men is a **pile**? He looked back out to the ongoing parley, saw Dayton moving toward him, purposeful slowness, the man's expression carrying a message. Sherman moved back to the rear of the train, and Dayton was there now, said, "Sir, he expects us—"

"I heard him, Colonel."

Sherman felt the heartbeats thundering in his chest, thought of Chalmers, good reputation. Damn rebel cavalry all over this place, and we can't round 'em up worth a damn. But we aren't giving up several hundred men right here without a good accounting for it. I did that, Grant would have me whipped.

"Offer our kindest respects to General Chalmers, but tell that fellow we're not surrendering a damn thing. You can be polite about it. Tell him the government pays us to fight, not to surrender. Then we'll see what they're bringing to this party. But take your damn time about it."

Dayton moved off at a casual pace, obeying Sherman's order. Sherman looked toward McCoy now, said, "You wait until that rebel chap gets tired of all our **parleying** and as soon as he rides off, you hightail it to the telegraph office at the depot, and get a wire back to Germantown. The Fourth Division's sashaying through the mud back there, and I want a fire torched under their backsides. Tell them anything you want, but get those fellows up that road as quick as they can move."

RAIL DEPOT—
COLLIERVILLE, TENNESSEE—
OCTOBER 11, 1863—MIDDAY

He had reached the stockade, stout walls of logs and dirt, and knew that beyond, the brick depot was a far stronger position. But here he was anchored between his own men and Anthony's Indianans, could send orders out in either direction. He could see now, gaps cut through the logs, crude rifle ports for his men to return fire. All around him, smoke boiled past, the destruction of whatever houses were nearby. It was Sherman's order that if the rebels were coming at them, any structures the rebels could use for cover would be burned. Even now, men with torches scrambled down a small street to the rear of the stockade, another house erupting in flames.

He stood up high on the makeshift parapet, no need for field glasses, all of it laid out right in front of him. The cornfield was below the rail tracks, the train sitting out to the right, silent, still, the only passengers, one car of the horses. He cursed now, thought of his own, Dolly, his favorite, thought, Nothing I can do about that now. Damn you, McCoy, you should have opened that up, let them all out. But he couldn't fault his aides, the men doing efficient work putting the troops together, gathering them up to the best position they had. He looked over the men inside the stockade, the Indiana men, tried to recall if he had ever used them before, if they had seen action, taken fire. Well, you're going to take some now. You'll learn to appreciate fat logs.

The regular troops were in place outside the walls of the stockade, some in small rifle pits near the knoll, the narrow stretch of high ground that gave the men a good view of anything around them. Anthony's Indiana troops were scattered beyond the stockade as well, more rifle pits, the men who dug them now appreciating their labor. Sherman had made a rough count, using Anthony's numbers, his own, knew he had barely six hundred men close at hand. All he knew yet was that Chalmers had a **pile.**

The men were positioned all along the south wall of the stockade, muskets up in the ragged openings of the logs, more men standing close behind, loaded muskets ready. Sherman dropped down to the hard ground, peered out through one of the holes. Good place, he thought. Tough to get an accurate shot at anyone in here. We may need that, any advantage we can get. He glanced back, saw his staff coming together, their work mostly done, the men spreading out behind him, waiting for orders. He knew they were nervous, had rarely been under direct fire. He glanced at Dayton, thought of the parley, the rebel cavalry officer, thought, Was it all a bluff? They grabbed a few wagons, and might have been content with that. Hell, I'd have tried to push a little bit, done exactly what this Chalmers fellow did. Threaten to kill every damn one of you, unless you surrender right now. See if the commanding officer of the outpost here has anything down his pants. Not sure what Anthony thought he could do here, but I don't think he'd have given this place up that easy. Chalmers probably figured that out by now. Sorry there, friend. As long as the cartridges hold out, you'll wish it was a bluff after all.

He could see the cornfield clearly, well within musket range, heard a single drummer, far distant, looked out to a low ridgeline behind the field, a thick line of gray forming along its crest. Six hundred yards, he thought. Not yet. Nobody get anxious. Above him, men began to shout out, the expected warnings, obvious and unnecessary.

"Here they come!"

Now, to one side, another call.

"They're at the train! They're coming in on our flank!"

"Both flanks! Cavalry coming along the tracks to the east!"

Sherman moved to one side, stared at the train, the horsemen dismounted, moving in slowly, testing. He slapped a man on the back, said, "Smaller targets. Too bad. But it doesn't matter. Just aim low."

He slipped quickly back to the south wall, found his opening, peered out, could see the rebels moving down into the cornfield, a heavy line, far heavier than he had hoped to see. He scanned as much as he could, saw a scattering of flags, the colors, thought, A couple thousand . . . maybe more. Yep. That's a **pile.**

The musket fire started outside the walls, a skirmish erupting along the tracks near the train. But the men inside were holding fire, waiting, good discipline, though Sherman knew it wouldn't last. The first musket fired above him, then a half dozen more, and now the first massive volley from the troops in the field, smacks of lead against the dense wooden walls. Sherman backed away from the hole, a rifleman stepping forward, filling his place, and Sherman watched him, the man peering out, slow and precise, aiming. Sherman waited for the shot, the man, keeping his calm, was saying something, low words, a curse of his own, and Sherman tried to see past him, the hole just wide enough to see the flicker of color beyond, the line of rebels coming up through the cornfield. The yells came now, high shrieks, and Sherman felt the stirring in his gut, the sound he knew well, had heard in so many places before. The man in front of him had chosen his target, and fired the musket.

The musket fire came at the stockade from three directions. Most of the rebel cavalry had dismounted, had pushed completely through the cornfield, were dueling now with the men on the knoll, the men in the stockade, small fights ongoing around the depot itself. Out both sides of the log structure, the rebels pressed forward as well, seeking some kind of vulnerability, an opening to drive through. But the Indiana men kept up the fire, choosing targets, the muskets reloaded, passed forward with a steady rhythm. Sherman stayed back from the wall, could only listen, the skirmishes to both sides steady, but keeping in place. He knew the regulars would hold their ground, would give the rebels a problem, possibly a surprise by their sheer tenacity. He could hear the musket balls still peppering the timbers, wanted to climb up again, a better view of the fight. But his place was back, behind, watching, preparing whatever order might be needed, and right now, there was nothing else he could do.

After long minutes, the musket fire seemed to slow, shifting direction, the fight growing near the train, and he thought of his horse, the rest of them, helpless, useless. Cavalry, he thought. At least . . . the rebs'll know what to do with 'em. If it comes to that. He scanned the wall, watched the riflemen, the others still loading the spent muskets. There were boxes of cartridges by their feet, and he clenched his fists at that, yes! Someone made sure they were prepared. Colonel Anthony did that, had to. Good man. Remember that. Might never have seen a damn rebel before, but now he's staring down a few thousand of 'em. He could see Anthony now, scurrying along the wall, pistol in hand, doing his job. Sherman called out, "Colonel!"

Anthony looked at him, fire in the man's eyes, something Sherman never took for granted.

"How's your ammunition?"

"Good enough, sir! The magazine's down those steps, back that way. Good supply!"

Sherman glanced behind him, saw the quartermaster storehouse, steps leading down, was surprised to see one of his aides coming up the stairs carrying a box of cartridges. The man approached him, breathless, his hat whisked away, and Sherman said, "Lieutenant James, you look a fright. You intending to fight this war with these infantry?"

"Yes, sir! I've armed the orderlies and kitchen staff. There's plenty of muskets down belowground. Boxes of cartridges. I put them to work, sir. They're out the backside of this place, figuring out how to shoot rebels. Sir, there's a passel of rebs in a thicket of woods out that way. They're in good cover, taking shots at our boys. Most annoying, sir. With your permission, sir, I'd like to rally these men and make a charge. They keep telling me they want to be soldiers. I figure, maybe we should let 'em. We can clean out those woods, give us some relief."

Sherman saw youth, blind enthusiasm, knew that James had never been in any kind of fight before.

"You may do so, Lieutenant, but only if the enemy appears to be drawing closer. But take good care. Our enemy outnumbers us by a good measure. The best time to strike is when they aren't expecting it. They line up in a formation for advance, strike them before they can prepare. Then you may make your sally."

"Thank you, sir!"

The young man hurried away, and Sherman smiled at his enthusiasm, thought, Yes, cooks and nursemaids had better know how to fight the enemy. Right now, we don't have much else to offer. He faced forward again, saw men watching him, dirty faces, blackened eyes. Sherman fought through the overwhelming smell of the powder, felt a hard thump, close behind, then more, saw shattering timbers, the impact of solid shot. Men were staggering back, sprayed with splinters from their own protection, one man down, bloody face, pulled away quickly, others stepping forward, manning a

smoking breach in the wall, muskets up, answering.
Sherman stood in the center of the compound, had
nowhere else to go, could hear the artillery shells
coming in pairs, thought, One battery to our front.
They'll be more to the flanks. And we have . . . none.
Damn! Where's the Fourth Division? At least, their
artillery teams could be moving up quick. I assume
they know the meaning of **urgent.**

The smoke rolled through the stockade, thick
white, stinking sulfur from the musket fire, and
Sherman fought to breathe, the men around him
dropping down, kneeling, finding their wind. The
artillery shells whistled overhead, impacts behind
the stockade, and Sherman could see them, thumping into the timbers from above, more splitting
logs to his front. But the solid shot was small, a
single round ball rolling past him on the ground,
spent, useless. He stared at that for a long second,
thought, Two inch? That's what they've got? Surely
there're bigger pieces moving into position. These
logs won't hold up under too much more.

The men were mostly silent, the muskets moving
back and forth, fired, reloaded, then fired again.
But the rebels were close, close enough so Sherman could hear the screams, the orders, pieces of
the rebel yell. He held his ground, motionless, felt
his hands starting to shake, the cold in his chest,
shouted out inside himself. The feeling was raw,
fresh, the horror of collapse, of panic, desperate

flight to safety. It had happened at Bull Run, had nearly happened at Shiloh. But that was long past, too many good fights since. He closed his eyes, cursing hard to himself, pulling himself out of that awful place, those terrible days, those fights when the enemy was too good, too fast, too strong. Or, like now, too many. He opened his eyes, the smoke thick around him, flashes of fire, the muskets inside the stockade still answering, the men still fighting back. He felt utterly powerless, no orders to give, the men fighting for survival, all of them knowing that if the rebels got inside, it was over. He thought of his guard, the battalion of regulars keeping up their fight outside the protection of the timber. Barely more than two hundred men, but they were professionals, men willing to die rather than surrender. They'll give the rebels all they have, he thought. It might not be enough. Movement caught his eye, Anthony again, still up high, shouting orders, rallying his men, and Sherman thought of the young Captain Smith, outside, knew he would be doing the same.

More artillery came in, piercing the timbers, and now a single whistle, high scream of the iron, and the ground to one side erupted in a fiery blast, the magazine underground seeming to rise up in a single surge. He felt the shock of that, the ground shivering beneath him, more men down to that side, his brain focusing, the magazine. They hit the damn magazine! He saw fire, but not much, the rebel artillery still only the small-bore solid shot. Thank God for that, he thought. A twelve-pounder might have blasted us all to pieces. The iron blew through the timbers in front of him, another volley from the rebel battery, one man screaming, shredded by the splinters, direct hit from the iron ball, blood on dirty blue. Sherman tried not to see that, his mind still clinging to the thought of the good men, one in particular, the young captain Smith, always the smile, until that one day, a week ago, the shock of the man's unsheathed grief, the flood of tears. And Willie would have been with me, Sherman thought. On the train. He would have been . . . **here.** Nine years old.

The thought of his son in this place made him shudder, and he shoved that away, forced himself to look again at the men still making the strong fight, trading volleys with more rebels than they had ever seen, smoke and fire, screams and curses, orders flowing out from their officers, the men with pistols raised. Sherman stood alone, silent, still, the war raging inside of him, panic and terror and furious hatred for the men outside, the rebel cavalry, their haphazard raid now billowing up into a full-blown battle. Through it all, one image pushed through, forced itself into his brain. **Thank God my son is not here.**

The fight lasted for nearly four hours, Sherman's men holding off a force close to five times their own. With the afternoon passing, the sun starting to set, the rebels began to pull away. The men from Indiana were as surprised as the regulars, watching as the dismounted cavalry returned to their horses, pulling back into formation, then simply riding away. Most expected a return, that the rebels were just regrouping, taking stock, refilling ammunition boxes. At first Sherman had agreed with the men around him, that it could not just . . . end. Surely, he had thought, the rebels would know they had the numbers, the maneuverability, that if they kept up the assault, the Federal troops would eventually have to surrender. But the rebels didn't return, had done what good cavalry does, had simply melted away. For their trouble, and their losses in men, the rebels had succeeded in capturing a few wagons and damaging the train, their artillery putting a scattering of holes through the engine, a portion of the train put to the torch. Sherman had made his own appraisal of the train's engine, too many holes to repair, had sent a wire back to Memphis for a replacement, assurances already coming back to him that the new machine was on its way, that there would be no delay in his journey beyond this one day.

The greatest loss besides the casualties to the men was in horses, including Sherman's own. But one casualty in particular punched him, and he lowered his head, had seen the young Lieutenant James, the man and his impetuously ridiculous charge, leading men who had no business in a fight at all. Amazingly, James had done the job, had cleared the patch of woods, the rebels choosing retreat rather than engaging what Sherman had to believe was a motley assortment of overweight old men, with one deranged boy at their head. But none of that mattered now. Sherman saw the stretcher, the bearers hauling it into the stockade, calling to Sherman, James with a splatter of blood on his chest. They took him away, the doctor offering Sherman a hint of optimism that the wound was not mortal. But Sherman had seen those kinds of wounds before, knew that a musket ball did terrible things inside a man's chest. He thought, I told him to go. If I hadn't, he might have gone anyway. There was too much happening, too many dangerous places. The stupidity of the very young. That thought dug at him, stirred up an angry response. No, it isn't like that at all. I can't lead every charge, every attack. It's their job, and if they happen to be young, it's just . . . how it is. They're volunteers, after all. Stop treating them like they're being punished for something. The only punishment comes to the generals, when they fail to do the job. He looked to the soldiers inside the stockade, the Indiana men working to make some use of the broken timbers, gathering ammunition, preparing for what might still come. He saw Anthony, issuing orders, the man's staff attentive, spreading out as he instructed them. That's what makes up for youth, he thought. Leadership. Anthony did a hell of a good job here. We might have been wiped out. Maybe should have been. These . . . boys learned something today, something about themselves. If they had any doubts, they know now that they're soldiers. Lieutenant James . . . he learned that his place was close to me, not out leading some fool attack.

He stood up high in the wooden stockade, looked beyond the walls, where men in blue moved out through the field, along the tracks, gathering up the wounded, picking up muskets, scavenging for anything still usable. Their own wounded had been gathered up inside the fort, the doctors from Indiana doing their work, the cries of the men sifting through the calm. His own staff did their work as well, the telegraph wire singing again, a different message going back to Memphis, Sherman's brief report to Grant, nervous staff officers relating his version of the fight, what he knew had been an amazingly close call.

Sherman heard a voice, one of his aides, the man pointing to the west down the tracks. Sherman looked that way, could see horses, flags, the lead elements of his Fourth Division. He understood now. That's why the rebels scattered out of here, he thought. They knew help was coming, and they were about to have a fair fight.

He didn't know James Chalmers, knew only that

a general officer who rode under Nathan Bedford Forrest could be expected to show a stubbornness that would usually bring victories. Sherman stood with his hands on his hips, fixed his gaze far behind the train. He could hear a hint of drums now, the column closing in, men moving with quick steps, expecting a fight, expecting to be heroes. Not today, he thought. There'll be time for that; sure enough. He looked out toward the trampled cornfield, thought of the rebels, of James Chalmers. If your scouts told you reinforcements were coming, then you did exactly what I'd figured you to do: Get the hell out of here. But I know one thing you don't, and I hope like hell that one day I have the chance to meet you face-to-face, so I can tell you exactly what you missed here, maybe the best opportunity you'll ever have. If you'd have known, you wouldn't have been in such a hurry to leave just because you might have gotten your nose bloodied. Sherman smiled through gritted teeth, stared at the darkening horizon. You had no idea who was standing in the middle of this pile of timber. No idea at all. If you knew, you'd have poured every artillery shell you had into this stockade, sent every carbine and every saber you had . . . right here. Well, old fellow, you rebel son of a bitch . . . maybe next time.

CHAPTER SEVEN

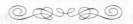

BRAGG

The train left Richmond on October 6, its most prominent passenger bearing a sheaf of letters from the men he had charged with winning this war. The journey was one of necessity, a crisis of command. He believed he had chosen his generals on their merits, and the whispers around him in the capital had been mostly ignored, how too many of the commanders kept their posts only because he favored them, their friendship and loyalty a far more valuable asset than good strategic skills. The most notable exception thus far had been Robert E. Lee. Davis wasn't ever sure of Lee's feelings, the man keeping them mostly to himself, but that really didn't matter to Davis. That train ran on a single track. From the earliest days of the war,

Davis had suffered his critics, the men who blamed him for the failings of men like Albert Sidney Johnston, or even Lee himself. The loudest outcries yet had come in the aftermath of the fall of Vicksburg, when another Davis acolyte, John C. Pemberton, was widely blamed for a collapse of command that even Davis couldn't ignore. Pemberton was now on Davis's informal staff, and accompanied him on this journey westward. Everyone in Richmond knew that Pemberton ached for another command, and that Davis was sliding through the Confederate hierarchy trying to find him one.

Davis had seen the belligerence toward Bragg in the Richmond newspapers, and more recently, had received the letters from the generals themselves, primarily Polk and Longstreet, who echoed what too many of the other commanders in Tennessee were spouting out, lengthy pleadings with Davis that he order Robert E. Lee to travel west, that Lee might be the only man in the Confederacy to carry the army to victory in Tennessee. Davis had approached Lee, feeling out Lee's thoughts on the matter, but Lee had been adamant. His place was with the Army of Northern Virginia, a battered and bloodied force still reeling from the disaster at Gettysburg. Davis hadn't tried to persuade Lee to go to Tennessee, knew as well as Lee did that the army closest to the northern borders near the large cities had to be rebuilt. The Federal congress was gleefully expectant that their armies, so victorious during the summer, would once again resume their drive into Southern territory, with yet another eye toward Richmond. Davis accepted Lee's reasoning for remaining in Virginia, tried his best to ignore the chatter from those who did not understand, as he did, how best to manage this war. But the tide of hostility toward Braxton Bragg had gone far beyond what Davis had ever expected. Bragg could be difficult, had certainly made enemies, especially with his penchant for military discipline. Davis had no problem with that at all. Bragg had risen well under Albert Sidney Johnston, had been used effectively by Johnston to mold an effective fighting army out of a rabble of undisciplined volunteers. But the voices against Bragg had turned far more ugly. The complaints were no longer aimed at the man's harsh treatment of the men. Now the focus was on Bragg's lack of leadership, lack of action, failures to follow up successes in the field. For an army desperate for victories, a passive leader was utterly unacceptable. Davis found it hard to fathom that Bragg would have fallen into that kind of lethargy, believed instinctively that men of ambition were seeking to push Bragg aside, serving their own cause. He suspected that of Longstreet, certainly. Longstreet was no better at making friends than Bragg, and there had been talk around Richmond that Longstreet's failures had been the army's failures at Gettysburg. Davis had to abide by Lee's view on that, Lee of course doing the honorable thing, accepting blame himself. Bragg had done the same after the defeats in Kentucky and central Tennessee earlier that year, suggesting that if his generals had lost confidence in his command, Davis should replace him. Davis had rejected that out of hand, as he had rejected Lee's offer to stand down. In Davis's mind, there was simply no one more qualified to replace either man. There were experienced generals of course, Joe Johnston and Pierre Beauregard in particular, men who outranked Bragg. But Davis had dismissed them from his thoughts at every turn. He knew, as did everyone else, that neither of those men respected Davis, or regarded their president with the kind of loyalty Davis believed was his due. If they would not show proper deference to him, he certainly wouldn't reward them with a significant command.

The lack of activity after Chickamauga was puzzling to many, Davis included. The letters that flowed out of Tennessee had become venomous, violations of military courtesy and protocol that Davis could not merely address with his pen. If his generals needed to know what kind of support Braxton Bragg was receiving from their president, he would communicate that firsthand. Davis had no doubts at all that Bragg would perform, and perform well, as long as his subordinates fell in line behind him.

If Bragg's generals had grievances, he would hear them, certainly. As he drew closer to Chickamauga

Station, Davis had settled the arguments in his mind, knew that his mission to Tennessee would be one of reason, of reconciliation, that with the proper amount of convincing, even the most cantankerous generals would come to understand that their faith in Bragg should be as strong as his own. To suggest that any one of them could do Bragg's job any better than Bragg himself was not a question Davis would even consider. After Lee, Joe Johnston, Beauregard, or Pemberton, the primary alternatives would probably be Longstreet or William Hardee. But both seemed to make enemies too easily, demonstrating a level of ambition that didn't suit their president. As long as Bragg continued to demonstrate complete dedication to Davis's authority, he simply would not be replaced. All Davis had to do was make that point with perfect clarity.

As the train lurched to a stop, Davis stepped down absolutely certain that his mission would be a simple one.

NAIL HOUSE— BRAGG'S HEADQUARTERS— MISSIONARY RIDGE— OCTOBER 10, 1863

They arrived after the evening meal, and as each man entered his headquarters, Bragg felt the strain, the forced politeness. The collective staffs remained outside, Mackall as well, some of the men already engaged in low conversation. There were few secrets in the camp, every soldier in the army aware that President Davis had come, every staff officer understanding that his arrival carried far more meaning than some glad-handing social visit.

Bragg welcomed each man with the same perfunctory handshake, no one rejecting his hand, as Forrest had done, none likely to make such a blatant show of disrespect in the presence of Jefferson Davis.

Longstreet had arrived first, and Bragg watched him now, felt a grinding dislike for the man, knew Longstreet felt the same way about him. Bragg felt disgusted by Longstreet's demeanor, the large man sitting sloppily in a chair to one side of the room, close to the hearth, a small pipe clamped in his teeth. Simon Buckner had arrived shortly after Longstreet, Harvey Hill and Benjamin Cheatham close behind. The four were Bragg's most senior commanders, but no one mistook the evening to be anything about glad tidings.

Bragg remained standing, Davis sitting at the desk, and Bragg felt the sweat on his skin, the deep rumblings in his stomach, nothing unusual about that. Davis smiled, a brief formal greeting to each man, pleasant instructions for each to take a chair. There was typical formality to that, Davis not given to friendly banter, the useless small talk that some politicians seemed to enjoy. Bragg appreciated that, shifted his weight from one foot to the other, impatient, still sweating, tried to avoid looking at Longstreet, Longstreet watching him, seeming to taunt him. Bragg felt the man's smugness, infuriating, Bragg still wondering if Longstreet believed himself to be so far above the rest of them, that his service to Robert E. Lee had somehow imbued the man with angelic powers. Bragg sniffed, tried to erase the thought, looked at Buckner, who nodded toward him, watching Bragg carefully. The stare made Bragg even more uncomfortable, thoughts racing through his brain. What does he know? He has been loyal to me, at least when he served my staff. But give a man power over others . . . He stifled that, blinked through stinging sweat in his eyes, the heat from the fire at one end of the room beginning to suffocate him.

Benjamin Cheatham was the only one of the four generals who had not been to West Point, but his skills as a leader in the field had put him in position as the man Bragg had suggested to replace Leonidas Polk. Cheatham seemed more nervous than Bragg, glanced around the room, as though searching for something. Bragg winced at that, thought, Liquor? Is it so true then? It was the one black mark against Cheatham, the rumors that Bragg could never quite confirm, that Cheatham had a tendency toward drunkenness when his leadership was needed the most. Those rumors had extended through the fight at Chickamauga, but Bragg had no direct evidence of that, and so, no real reason to distrust the man. Of the most senior commanders, Cheatham, like Breckinridge, had not placed his signature on the petition calling for Bragg's ouster. Breckinridge was a politician, his motives simple to dissect. Cheatham's motives were more of a mystery, whether he had kept his name off the petition as an act of loyalty to Bragg, or whether he was simply too cowardly to document his feelings. Bragg had no idea which.

Simon Bolivar Buckner was the youngest of the group, but certainly not the least experienced. It was Buckner who had surrendered his forces to Ulysses Grant at Fort Donelson early the year before, the first in a series of battlefield disasters that allowed the Federal army to occupy most of Tennessee. But Buckner carried no stain for that particular defeat, no disgrace. The surrender had been ordered by his commanding general there, John Floyd, who had put Buckner in charge of handling the surrender, while Floyd himself slipped away. The outrage against Floyd had been absolute, and Davis had responded by removing Floyd from command. That had cost Floyd more than pride, the man's health failing rapidly, his death coming just a few weeks prior to the fight at Chickamauga. For a while, Bragg had appointed Buckner to his staff, but Buckner's experience in the field made him too valuable to keep that close to headquarters. The inevitability of losing Buckner to field command had annoyed

Bragg, but now, knowing Buckner had put his signature on the petition, Bragg had forced himself to
forget any good service the man had done. He was
simply one more enemy.

Daniel Harvey Hill had come west after the fight
at Gettysburg, though he had not served under Lee
for several months. Bragg had already experienced
Hill's disagreeable nature, a penchant for bitter sarcasm, and a surly personality that had tested the
patience and the tolerant spirit of Robert E. Lee,
as well as several of Lee's commanders. Prone to
feuding, Hill had been received by Bragg as a form
of punishment, as though Hill's inability to get
along with anyone had caused Davis to force him
on Bragg. Though Hill had served well in Mexico,
and led troops in the field up through the Battle of
Fredericksburg, Bragg had to wonder if Hill had
advanced to the rank of general for any other reason than his being the brother-in-law of the late
Stonewall Jackson.

The silence in the room was complete now, the
greetings past, Bragg's nervousness growing, his
fists clenched by his side. He caught the continuing look from Longstreet, saw a hint of a smile,
but there was no friendliness to that, Longstreet
staring at him with more of a smirk. Bragg tried
to look away, couldn't avoid Longstreet's show of
slovenliness, the man showing a kind of relaxed
confidence, as though something had been decided,
some secret that only Longstreet knew. Bragg waited

for Davis, who said, "Please, General Bragg. Be seated. It is my honor to be among such an illustrious group of commanders, distinguished as you all have been. There are two purposes for my visit here. I should like to address the presence in this camp of a man you all certainly know, in the hope that the charitable hearts among you should find a place for him at your councils. I refer of course to General Pemberton. I have asked the general to remain away from this meeting, so as not to cause him any undue embarrassment. I had thought we could discuss an opportunity for returning him to the field, at the head of a corps perhaps. Every army must make use of experience where it is found, and John Pemberton is certainly a man of experience at leading troops in the field. I defer to General Bragg of course, as to what, if any position there might be here. General?"

Bragg blinked sweat out of his eyes, had suspected this was coming. He had met briefly with Pemberton when Davis first arrived, a formal, awkward conversation about nothing at all. Pemberton's eagerness to find a place in Bragg's army was painfully apparent, but Bragg had done nothing to encourage the man. Now Davis was asking for a formal response to a question that most of the Confederacy already answered. There was no confusion as to who carried the blame for the catastrophic failure at Vicksburg.

Bragg shifted his weight in the chair, glanced at

the others, saw nothing pleasant in their expressions, thought, Yes, it's good Pemberton isn't sitting here. This could be most humiliating.

"Your Excellency, with all respects to General Pemberton and yourself, I do not feel there is an appropriate place for General Pemberton in this army. I have given this a great deal of thought, and I do not believe anyone here would disagree, though of course I will not speak for these men. But, in my opinion, sir, if General Pemberton was given command of a corps, or even a single division, there would be a mass protest that might very well result in a great many desertions from this army. No man from Mississippi would serve under him, I assure you."

Davis seemed annoyed, and Bragg felt he had tripped over Davis's foot. Surely, he thought, he does not believe Pemberton will be accepted. Davis shrugged, another surprise.

"Yes, well, I defer to your judgment, General. I continue to believe that General Pemberton will yet serve this nation in some excellent capacity. His zeal for our cause is unquestioned."

Bragg looked at the others, Cheatham shaking his head, Hill and Buckner staring down, Longstreet chewing on the pipe with irritating disinterest. Bragg said, "Does anyone wish to comment? Does anyone here feel that General Pemberton would serve well beside you?"

Longstreet said, "Nope."

Cheatham shook his head again, said, "I regret to say that no soldier from Tennessee would serve under him."

The others kept silent, and Davis said, "Well, then, I shall explain to General Pemberton that his place shall remain with me. Any disappointment in that regard shall remain private. Let us move past that. I did not make this disagreeable train ride solely to find a command for a friend. I am hoping to understand why, in the Army of Tennessee, there has been so much . . . well, turmoil. General Bragg has won a truly marvelous victory against our enemies. I for one am greatly pleased with his leadership. But there is discord here. I have been informed that the victory at Chickamauga is regarded by some as an empty one, a triumph for which we gained nothing. I do not agree with that. Not at all. I am hoping that this gathering shall convince me that you do not believe that, either. I intend to put a halt to the loose talk I have heard coming from this place. You can assist me by offering your absolute support and loyalty to your commanding general. I should like to hear from each of you. I should like to know your feelings about General Bragg, and I would like you to offer a constructive view as to how this army can move forward with General Bragg at its head. General Longstreet, as ranking officer here, will you lead the way?"

Longstreet looked at Bragg, shook his head. "I have not been in the service of the Army of Tennessee for sufficient tenure for me to offer any opinion. With all respects, sir, I should not be called upon to offer one."

Bragg looked at Davis, saw a hard stare toward Longstreet. Davis said, "I insist, General. Your observations carry great weight in this army, no matter your tenure here."

Longstreet slipped the pipe into his pocket, rubbed a hand on his beard, and Bragg waited for the stare again, but Longstreet looked only at Davis.

"If you require me to speak, sir, then I shall obey. My estimate of General Bragg's abilities is not high. The little experience I have had under his command has not changed that opinion. I believe, sir, that General Bragg could be of far better service to this nation in some other position than by leading the Army of Tennessee."

Davis seemed surprised, and Bragg saw a quiver in Davis's hand, the man flexing his fingers for a long moment. Davis said, "General Longstreet, I had hoped . . ." He stopped, looked down at the desk, and after a pause, said, "General Buckner, will you offer a word of support for General Bragg?"

Bragg looked at Buckner, saw his head slowly shake.

"I am sorry, Your Excellency. I cannot. General Longstreet's views . . . are my own. General Bragg is not the man to lead this army."

Davis did not look up, seemed to close his eyes. "General Hill, will you offer your view?"

Hill did not hesitate, his voice clear and distinct, louder than Bragg wanted to hear. "The others have spoken. I can offer nothing to distract or contradict their words. I would prefer that some other commander be elevated by you, sir, to head this army. The men in my command have little confidence that General Bragg will lead us to victory. As you all are aware, I served as honorably as was in my power under General Lee. In that army, the spirit of the men remains high, even in times of trial. The men there rally to their commanding officer. Such is not the case here, and I do not believe that, unless there is a change . . . it will ever be."

Bragg felt a rush of heat, steadied himself in the chair, his face flushed, the sweat soaking his shirt, running down his back. He could feel the familiar fury rising up, the need to shout them down, to strike back at their words. But Davis looked at him now with a hard stare, a silent command, **quiet.** Bragg felt the energy drained from him, Davis still watching him through tired eyes.

After a pause, Davis said, "General Cheatham, your comments?"

Cheatham hesitated, no surprise to Bragg, the man most new to his command. And perhaps, Bragg thought, he will set them right. He will not be so quick to push me aside. Cheatham cleared his throat, said slowly, "Your Excellency, as you know, I did not add my name to the disgraceful document that was either inspired by or authored by, I would assume, someone in this room. I do not feel it serves our cause, or this army, to embrace such discord as we now suffer."

Bragg looked at Cheatham, felt his heart racing, felt grateful for the courage it required to speak out against the others. But Cheatham would not look back at him, stared ahead, seemed to fumble for words.

"Though that was my feeling when presented with the petition that I must believe is the reason you have come here . . . I must now agree with the sentiments expressed. I do not feel General Bragg is the best man to lead this army. I am hopeful that Your Excellency will name a substitute, who shall inspire the confidence of the men, and my fellow officers."

NAIL HOUSE—
BRAGG'S HEADQUARTERS—
MISSIONARY RIDGE—
OCTOBER 11, 1863

The rains continued, Bragg staring out the small window, engulfed by the dreary gloom that washed over the men of both armies. He had begun a letter to his wife, a few lines of writing on the paper behind him, had stood, turning away from the desk, still holding the pen in his hand. There were just no words. He watched a horseman move past the house, mud splashing high, a flood of rainwater running off the man's coat, the man's head down, enduring the misery as he passed. *What mission is so important . . . or are you just parading past my window for a good show?*

He glanced back toward the desk, thought, *My dear wife, my dear Elise. She would feel this, as I do. She would know I am betrayed, I am insulted, I have been shamed before the men whose respect I have done so much to earn.*

Elise had become a prolific letter writer, had stood tall defending his honor to many of the men who sought to disgrace him, mainly the politicians and newspapermen in Richmond. He enjoyed her letters, angry protests to the War Department, though he had to wonder if anyone there even read them. *Do they take her seriously, or do they merely gather around in mockery of her, making light of the angry rants of a general's wife? I treasure her every word,* he thought, *no matter her occasional lapse of . . . well, manners, I suppose. I hope there is at least respect due to the wife of a commanding general, that she is not regarded as a fountain of blather. We shall be vindicated, in the end. You may speak out how you wish, dear wife, since it is sometimes best if I hold my tongue. For now, anyway. I know . . . I know I have the confidence of the president. But those others . . . if they sway him.* He turned, looked at the letter, said aloud, "No. Not today. I shall not burden you with my disgust. There is no justice on God's earth if I am to be so . . . cast aside. I am not, after all, John Pemberton."

"Sir?"

The voice was Mackall's, peering in through the door, but Bragg had no desire for company.

"Nothing, General. Go about your duties."

"Yes, sir. The president has returned, sir. He wishes to speak with you."

Bragg closed his eyes, felt unsteady, one hand on the back of the chair. "Yes, by all means. There must be a reckoning."

Davis had spoken to him at length immediately after his arrival, well before the meeting with the senior commanders. Bragg had been gratified by what seemed to be Davis's ongoing friendship, the president offering him no real hint that Bragg's command was in jeopardy. But it was painfully obvious that if Davis had not been at all surprised by the outright rejection of Pemberton, he had been stunned by the outpouring of negativity toward Bragg, the amazing frankness of the four men to lay blame for the army's problems squarely at the feet of its commanding general. Bragg had heard rumors that the petition against him had been written by Buckner, though Bragg couldn't shake the intense feeling that Longstreet's hand was there as well. Now the president had had a full night to absorb what had been so brazenly offered directly to his face. Bragg had suffered a night of his own with

the usual sleeplessness, made worse by the fear that
Davis would turn against him. How can the presi-
dent stand tall against such . . . influence? How am
I to lead men such as these?

"This way, please, Your Excellency . . ."

Mackall opened the door, stood aside, and Davis
stepped in slowly, dripping wet, Mackall removing
the president's raincoat.

"It is good you have this prominent piece of
ground, General. Noah himself would find this rain
a challenge. Perhaps if we wait a few more days, the
Tennessee River shall flood its banks, and wash
the enemy away."

Bragg did not respond, saw no smile from Davis
at his own joke. He knew Davis suffered from a
variety of ailments, as Bragg did, the constant nagging of some pain somewhere, the stomach distress,
the lack of sleep. Davis looked worn, moved slowly
to a chair, sat, leaned his head back, closed his eyes.
Mackall said, "If you allow, General Bragg, I shall
retire. As you said, I have . . . duties."

Bragg nodded, said nothing, felt too weak to
speak. He sat heavily in his own chair, pushed the
unfinished letter aside. After a long silence, Davis
said, "It has been suggested, back east, that General
Lee be ordered to this command. General Longstreet seems to prefer that, though I suspect General
Longstreet has ambitions of his own. Regardless,
General Lee insists his place, for now, is in Virginia,

caring for his men. It is hard to argue with a man of such . . . dedication."

"So, if I may ask, do you feel General Longstreet is the man for this position?"

Davis seemed to wake up, looked at him. "Of course not. I have given you my confidence, my assurances. You have served this nation well, and I have no doubts that you will continue to do so. This command is yours. Do you doubt that?"

Bragg absorbed Davis's words, said, "Actually, yes, sir. I have been pushed into doubting that. It is apparent that the officers under my command—"

"Bah! This is your command, and that's all there is to it. I care nothing for such blatant dissension from men who should know better, who seem to forget what **obedience** means. You have done nothing to shake my resolve, you have committed no crime, you have made no great blunder. You have given me no cause to remove you from this post. Have you?"

Bragg gripped the edge of the desk, his heart beating faster. "I most certainly have not."

"I would suggest, however, that you remove yourself from any controversy regarding General Polk. There is nothing to be gained there."

Bragg felt confused, said, "But, I was very clear in my complaints—"

"Nothing to be gained! They will serve this nation yet, in great capacity. Do not concern yourself with their station. It most certainly will be pleasing to you if I remove them from your theater. Leave it at that."

Bragg felt energized, thought, That is the compromise. That is how he justifies ignoring the others. He is, after all, loyal to Polk. As he is loyal to me.

"Your Excellency, are you telling me that if I devote my attentions . . . closer to home, as it were, that you will allow me to resume my campaigns, in my own fashion?"

"I didn't say that, precisely. But you're close. I have no reason to restrict what you do. I would not dare to instruct my generals how to manage their actions."

Bragg knew better, let the words slide by. He stood now, took a few steps, turned, paced back through the small room, looked again at Davis.

"I must ask . . . I must know. Am I to be allowed to determine who my most capable commanders are?"

Davis tilted his head, nodded slowly. "This is your army, General Bragg. The command decisions are yours to make. Your recommendations as to promotions will be given highest priority, as they always have been."

"I was not thinking of promotions. . . ."

He regretted saying the words out loud, but Davis smiled, surprising him.

"General Bragg, if there is anyone in your service

who is not performing to your high standards, it is of course your prerogative to take appropriate action. But, use some reason, General. You cannot cast out everyone in this army who dares to disagree with you. Certainly not. Put your men to the best use you see fit. That is after all what a commanding officer must do."

There was a finality to Davis's words, no explanation required. Bragg paced again, the pains gone, the fire in his brain taking over, and he pounded a fist into his open hand, did it again. Now they will know their places, he thought. There will be no discussion, no dissent, no obscene **petitions.** I have the authority, the command, the power. Deliver me from mine enemies, O Lord . . . or I shall do it myself.

CHAPTER EIGHT

CLEBURNE

MISSIONARY RIDGE— OCTOBER 13, 1863

The rains had slowed, a light mist, but everywhere Cleburne rode, the mud holes were deep enough to break a horse's leg. He moved the animal carefully, pushed slowly past one of the camps, Arkansas men, some of his own, familiar faces. But few were cheering him, few noticing him at all. They tended mostly to laboring over the makeshift shelters of leaves and branches, the only thing they had to pass for tents. There was smoke, someone's dismal attempt at a campfire, but most didn't bother, nothing anywhere near them that would burn. He shivered, as his men did, pulled at the rubber raincoat that few others had, felt that pang of guilt, always, never took for granted that just by the formality of his gray uniform, a division commander **deserved** the luxuries. In this weather, a dry shirt might be as much luxury as his men would hope for. That, and something more than a single ear of corn for a day's rations.

He looked back, saw Captain Buck leaning low from his saddle, speaking to an officer. Cleburne pulled at the reins, halting the horse, watched, wondered if there was some business that required his attention. The officer acknowledged him with a quick salute, said something else to Buck, then pointed, and Cleburne looked that way. Through a foggy mist he saw more of his men, a few horses, but there was movement, more men emerging from the crude shelters, the crowd increasing. Buck moved up alongside him now, his breath coming in short bursts of fog.

"Sir, there's some kind of ruckus over thataway, some visitor that's got the men all churned up."

Cleburne had no interest in a show of graciousness toward some dignitary.

"Did that lieutenant have any idea who it is?"

"No, sir. Just said there was a hoot and holler about somebody special."

"Let's hope for a commissary officer. That would put a bounce in their step."

"Just don't know, sir. That lieutenant just said . . . a bunch of horses, some bigwig, maybe some kinda speech."

Cleburne slumped in the saddle. "Perfectly charmin', eh, Captain? The men are eatin' little more than mashed-up dirt, and some Richmond political types decide they'll bring us a morale boost. Unless they brought a wagon full of corn or a passel of blankets, I doubt the boys'll pay much mind."

The crowd was growing, a few shouts, hands in the air, and Cleburne heard a cheer, thought, Must be a decent speaker. Those boys don't have piss else to cheer for.

"Tell you what, Captain. We'll ease over that way, see what's up. Not likely some high-faloot chap will know who I am all bundled up in this raincoat. If we know him, we'll have a word. Pay our respects, as it were. If it's not worth soaking up any more rain, we'll slip on by."

"As you wish, General."

He led Buck past a gaping mud puddle, saw a nearby battery, the gunners leaving their post, a quartet of brass twelve-pounders, barrels glistening in the rain. The artillerymen recognized him, friendly waves through the mud-soaked shirts, a few of those men fortunate enough to have coats. Cleburne felt a tug in his chest, knew how badly the men were suffering, that there was nothing he could give them, no supply wagons of any kind for several days now. And still, something had their attention. If it's not a few ears of corn, maybe it's General Bragg, telling us all we can go home.

He moved close to the wide sea of men, saw the speaker on horseback, others back behind him, and now he heard the words, ". . . as you shall bring honor to our nation and our cause. The commanding general of the Army of Tennessee has my full support and admiration. With the help of good Southern men such as yourselves, we shall prevail. I must ask you all to endure, strengthened by the knowledge that our entire nation is behind you with utmost enthusiasm. This rain is a misery unto itself, but there is misery aplenty out there, in the camps of the enemy. The Yankees will suffer God's own wrath for their invasion of our soil, and it is you men, the cream of our manhood, that shall add mightily to that suffering, until every last one of those blue-coated vermin has been driven from our sacred land. God bless you men. God bless you all!"

The cheers went up again, men pushing past Cleburne to catch a better look at the speaker. Cleburne could see clearly now. It was Jefferson Davis.

"I must say, General, your performance in the field has earned you the respect of your men, and of every officer with whom I have spoken. You are to be commended for that. It is not always so in this army. Though, when respect is called for, we should pay heed. Perhaps you should consider that the performance of the commanding general in this very army is worthy of **your** respect."

Davis kept the tone of his words pleasant, but Cleburne heard the scolding.

"Your Excellency, I regret the unpleasantness that has embroiled us here. I will certainly do what I can to inspire men to move forward, putting any dissent behind us. If I may offer, sir, your words to my troops have put me to shame. I am no orator. Any time you wish to add some fire to the spirit of my soldiers, you are most welcome." Davis didn't react, seemed occupied with the cup of coffee in his hand, a brew whose parts Cleburne knew the mess sergeant best keep to himself. "Very sorry about the taste of the coffee, sir. We are making do with what the commissary can supply."

Davis kept his stare into the cup, took another sip, a noticeable curl gripping his face. "Yes, well, we shall endure. I have every expectation that the enemy's coffee is no better than this."

Cleburne was puzzled by Davis's presence, knew only that the president had ridden along the ridge, speaking to many of the camps. But Cleburne hadn't expected Davis to linger, didn't know if Davis even understood just how many men were spread out all along the crest of Missionary Ridge, or to the south and west, through the valley that led to the much larger prominence of Lookout Mountain. Does he intend to speak to everyone? Cleburne felt more anxious now, glanced around the tent, an awkward pause, Davis preoccupied, still fingering the coffee cup. He noticed the wetness in Davis's coat, the man's face pale, drawn, thought, He can't enjoy riding all over hell and gone in this weather. But, I suppose, it's his job. After another long moment, Cleburne said, "Yes, sir. We're doing all we can to keep the Yankees in their pen. Um . . . is there anything else I can get you?"

Davis looked at him now, studying, said, "Irish. Knew that. Some of the best officers in this army came to us from the Emerald Isle."

Cleburne was self-conscious about the slight hint of his lingering accent, but whatever embarrassment he felt was tempered by his pride in the fact that Davis was right. Throughout the army there were the telltale accents, entire companies of Irish and Scots.

"Yes, sir. County Cork."

Davis nodded idly, stared into the side of the tent, and Cleburne wondered if the president even heard him. Davis didn't look toward him, said, "A great many Catholics in the army. They do good work, for the most part. Our adversary over there, General Rosecrans, he's Catholic, you know."

"Sir, begging your pardon, but my family wasn't Catholic. We're Episcopal."

Davis looked at him now, a glimmer of surprise. "Eh? Don't say? Hmm. Well, I guess that's possible. Haven't studied much about what goes on over there. Pretty nasty business, though. Always some trouble brewing, wars and revolutions and whatnot. Knew some Irishmen marched with us back in Mexico. Turned coat on us. San Patricios, they were called. Another nasty business. A man pledges his loyalty to his nation, then runs off and picks up a musket and shoots at his own. Outrageous. We hanged a bunch of those fellows. Winfield Scott not a man to give much slack to traitors." Davis paused. "I've seen Northern newspapers that claim the same thing of us, that the Confederacy is just a bunch of treasonous ne'er-do-wells, common criminals. So tired of that nonsense. But that's what newspapers do: Talk nonsense. This army . . . well, you know the job we have to do. We make our point with the bayonet, shove a few Northern newspapermen against a wall, and that kind of talk will stop. It's coming, inevitable, like the sunrise. We've come so close. And we will again, and this time, the Almighty will allow us to prevail. Inevitable. Those who fail to understand us . . . the meaning, the importance of what we're fighting for . . . well, I can't see how the Yankees can keep up the fight. We have the passion for it, General. The passion, the commitment, the dedication. No different than George Washington, Sam Adams. Independence, pure and simple. Break the chains. Much more at stake here than those people out there seem to realize. **Much** more. You agree, don't you?"

"Certainly, sir. A great many similarities between the Union's efforts and what the British have done to the Irish people."

He dreaded the subject, hoped Davis wouldn't pursue it. Cleburne understood Irish politics, but had little fire for political debate.

"All that history behind you, prepared you well for what's happening here, I suspect. When did your family come over?"

Cleburne was relieved, recognized Davis's attempt at polite conversation, though he was still mystified why Davis was there at all.

"Not quite fifteen years ago, sir."

"Hmm. I've heard you were a soldier in the British army. Good stock, that. Maybe you can persuade some of your former comrades to follow your example. Could use some help with the Cause, you know. The British officials don't listen much to me. Oh, they come by my office, great ceremony in all those official visits, wearing expensive suits made from Southern cotton, smoking Southern tobacco, their women oh so anxious for the grand ballrooms, all of them bursting with good cheer. And every day, they offer promises to us that none of them intend to keep. Maybe take a man like you, go over there and have a council with your generals. Convince them to leave the ball gowns at home. Bring a few brigades over."

Cleburne was increasingly uncomfortable, had never had a conversation with the president at all. Now he had to correct an obvious misimpression. "With all respects, sir, I was only a corporal when I left British service. I don't think there's many generals in the Empire who would pay me much heed."

Davis focused on him through clear eyes, as

though for the first time. "Corporal? Hmph. You made good in **this** army. Maybe those fellows missed an opportunity letting you go."

"Perhaps, sir. Thank you."

"I suppose, if you had been an officer, with all that tradition and all, you'd have seen the foolishness of putting in with these renegades on this mountainside who spoke out so inappropriately, so distressingly against General Bragg. No protocol, no deportment in that. Weakness of character."

Cleburne had feared this, hoped Davis might not recall just whose signatures had been on the petition calling for Bragg's removal.

"I regret that Your Excellency should have had to address this personally. There are times when a division commander reacts in tune with his peers, especially superior officers . . . men of influence. . . ."

"Don't try to be a politician, General. If you knew politics at all, you'd know that it is most often unwise for a man of influence to inform the world of his views. You're subordinate to John Breckinridge. Pay attention to his . . . methods. Says a great many things, none of which anyone can recall. That's why President Buchanan picked him to be his vice president. I made him a general, and even in a uniform, he's still at it. But I give him credit for not signing some fool piece of paper."

"Yes, sir. Perhaps I made an unwise decision. I'm just a soldier."

"Well, a soldier follows orders, respects his superiors, and supports the wishes of his president. Wouldn't you agree?"

Cleburne felt the weight of the question, understood now that Davis's visit had a purpose.

"Absolutely, sir."

Davis seemed to energize, stared at him, mustering strength. "Well, **absolutely,** a man in your position understands that Braxton Bragg commands this army. A man in your position understands that if your commanding general calls upon you in time of crisis, that it is your duty **absolutely** to respond and perform with all the abilities that took you from that boat from Ireland and put a general's stars on your collar."

Davis crossed his arms, the same cold stare directly at Cleburne now. Cleburne stood, straightened, stared ahead.

"Yes, sir. Absolutely."

Throughout Davis's weeklong visit, the president passed through most of his army, reassuring anyone who might doubt that Braxton Bragg was firmly in command. Davis spoke mainly to the troops, hoping to boost their flagging morale, a president's attempt to bolster the spirits of miserable men who suffered a want of supplies, who had few tents, and miserably poor rations. The senior officers learned quickly what had taken place in Bragg's headquarters, the emphasis placed

on Davis's support in a way no one could ignore. If
any of the senior officers had counted on a change of
command, they knew to keep their disappointment
to themselves.

Within a day of Davis's formal endorsement of
Bragg's position, Bragg acted by reorganizing the
army. In Richmond, the War Department acqui-
esced to Bragg's strong recommendation that Nathan Bedford Forrest be sent farther west, possibly
even an independent command, though Bragg
didn't suggest where. Within days, the appointment was made. Whether or not Forrest appreciated the gesture, Bragg received the order with a
sigh of barely disguised relief.

Bragg moved swiftly in other directions as well.
With Davis's approval, Bragg ordered the removal
of Simon Bolivar Buckner and Daniel Harvey Hill
from the Army of Tennessee. Rumors had sifted
through the headquarters that Buckner had indeed
authored the infamous petition, reason enough for
his dismissal. Hill had been pointed out specifically
as the cause for the costly delay in the final day's
fighting at Chickamauga, a charge leveled at him
by Leonidas Polk. Whether Polk was seeking to de-
flect any further criticism of himself, Bragg simply
didn't care. With such a charge, Bragg had no other
need to justify removing a man who most agreed
could be a thorn in a commander's side.

With Bragg accepting Davis's solution to the
"Polk problem," more reorganizing took place, di-

visions shifted from one commander to another, Cheatham's temporary command of Polk's corps now passing into the hands of the newly arriving William Hardee. Cleburne's own division was re- moved from Breckinridge's command, and put under Hardee's umbrella of authority, a change that delighted Cleburne. If Hardee was well respected by many of his peers, he was admired enormously by Cleburne. Their connection had gone back to 1861, when Hardee was appointed to command a barely organized brigade in Cleburne's home state of Arkansas. As a Georgian, Hardee's authority was questioned by many who had no concept that an army's command might cross state boundaries. Cleburne commanded the 1st Arkansas Regiment, and had done as much as he could to convince his own men that Hardee was a professional soldier of a stripe that inexperienced men should follow.

Hardee's army career had begun well before the Mexican War, and his rise in rank was attributed not only to success on the battlefield, but to his studious understanding of infantry tactics and strategies. In the mid-1850s, Hardee had authored a text on drill and maneuver that was still used at West Point, but with the outbreak of the war, Hardee chose loyalty to his home state of Georgia. He had served alongside Braxton Bragg at Shiloh, and later, throughout the campaigns in Kentucky, as Bragg's subordinate. But Bragg had tired of Hardee's willingness to impart his own expertise, and, like so many others under

Bragg's command, Hardee found himself on Bragg's list of enemies. By July 1863, while most of the nation reeled from the twin disasters at Vicksburg and Gettysburg, Bragg had made the move that sent Hardee away, the War Department replacing him with Harvey Hill. But Jefferson Davis saw past the clash of personalities, knew that Hardee brought more experience to the front lines than any other corps commander in this theater of the war. Bragg's grumbling protests notwithstanding, Hardee was back under Bragg's authority.

MISSIONARY RIDGE— OCTOBER 16, 1863

"They moving out there at all?"

Cleburne knew that Hardee would already have a clear idea what was happening across the wide valley below, that he would never ride out to the lines without complete knowledge of what he would face. The question was simply good manners.

"Not a whit, sir. Rain solid most of the past two weeks. Nobody's going anywhere anytime soon. Only my opinion, of course."

Hardee lowered the field glasses, looked at him with a smile. "Of course." He nodded, still smiled. "Really good to see you, Patrick. Hard to sit tight in some backwater, while the action's happening somewhere else. I heard nothing but good things about your division. Took some heavy losses. Not sure if that would have been different, if I'd have been here. You know what to do when it gets hot."

Cleburne nodded, didn't respond. He had taken serious losses before, all the way back to Shiloh, through the fight at Tullahoma, to the brutal day at Chickamauga. And, in every case, the casualties had grown beyond anything Cleburne expected because of the orders that came to him from Braxton Bragg.

Hardee looked back toward the others, his own staff, a pair of Cleburne's aides. "Gentlemen, I recall when your commanding officer ran his regiment by himself. They promoted him to brigadier, and he found out that entitled him to a staff. Never saw an officer so reluctant to have somebody do his chores for him." He looked again at Cleburne. "Now, Major General Cleburne, I see you've accepted your responsibility to delegate a few things. I saw Lucius Polk this morning. Full of vinegar about what Bragg did to his uncle. But he kept it brief. Knows he's your man, and wants to keep the job. He'll keep his mouth closed. I see you've brought along your own counselor." Hardee looked back again. "Lieutenant Mangum, you have ambitions to join General Cleburne at the top? Some catching up to do. His horse left you behind."

Mangum smiled in return, said, "Yes, sir. He'll stumble, I'll be there to pick him up. Always been that way."

Learned Mangum had been Cleburne's law partner in Little Rock, and, like Lucius Polk, had been
a good friend of Cleburne well before the war.
Now they wore the uniform, and Cleburne still
had a difficult time giving them orders, accepting
that he had the power to tell them what to do, anytime, anywhere.

Cleburne stared out across the misty valley,
said, "I use the whip once in a while. They're get-
tin' it."

Hardee moved the horse forward a step, a sign
Cleburne understood. The banter with the staff
was over for now, Hardee staring again through the
field glasses.

"Bragg thinks they're starving to death, that we've
got 'em right where he wants. What do you think?"

Cleburne knew better than to give Hardee an
opinion of strategy. "I think the commanding general gives orders, and I follow them."

Hardee didn't laugh, sniffed, lowered the glasses
again, said in a low voice, "Not a good thing,
Patrick. Not at all. This army's in tatters, and I
don't just mean the shirts on the men's backs.
Longstreet's up there on Lookout Mountain like he
owns the whole place, and he's made it pretty clear
he isn't paying much attention to the **orders** coming from our commanding general. Dangerous,
stupid. Feuds have no place in a high command,
and we've got feuds in every direction. Bragg thinks
he's done himself good by sending away all his de-

tractors. But now, it's going to get worse. You hear about Knoxville?"

"Only that the Yankees have the place in hand."

"Burnside's sitting up there, wondering when we're going to hit him. I expected Burnside to strengthen Rosecrans right here. Scouts reported all kinds of jabbering between those two. Even the Federal War Department is pushing Burnside up his rear end to move down here. Could have turned the tables on you at Chickamauga. But Burnside is Burnside. Unless there's a superior shouting right into his ear, he's going to move slow. Right now he may not move at all. In his mind, he conquered Knoxville, so I expect he'll enjoy that for a while. Rosecrans is still screaming for reinforcements, but so is Burnside. Whoever screams louder keeps Washington's attention." He looked at Cleburne now, still no smile. "There's stupidity on both sides, Patrick. And so, your division will again suffer a long casualty list before it's over with."

Cleburne wondered how Hardee had so much information, had to assume that Hardee had cavalry scouts and perhaps even spies scattered all around the Federal armies. He had been commandant of cadets at West Point for several years just prior to the war, and surely, Cleburne thought, he has young men out there who are still willing to do him favors, no matter what uniform they're wearing.

After a long moment Hardee said, "So, how are you handling Liddell?"

Cleburne absorbed the question, shrugged. "He's not happy being back in brigade command. Can't really speak to that. General Bragg put him in command of his own division, then took it away. Not sure what that was about, but Liddell understands he's my subordinate again."

"Keep an eye on him, Patrick. St. John Liddell has serious ambition. He was on my staff, you know, first part of the war. Decent staff officer, decent field officer, to a point. But he thinks he ought to have more, a great deal more. Your other brigades shouldn't be a problem. Good men, veterans. They'll do what you tell 'em to. Liddell might try to make a name for himself, do something . . . independent."

"I've had some conversation with him about General Bragg. We both sided with General Longstreet, the others. But Liddell seemed to back away from that, insisted General Bragg might be the best we have. Challenged me to name someone else to step into the position. I thought of you, of course."

"Never. Leave my name out of it."

"Oh, yes, sir. I would never have suggested something like that. Not my place."

"Yes, but you signed that blamed petition, didn't you?" Cleburne lowered his head. "This isn't a democracy, Patrick. You throw in with men who spout off about Bragg, it can't end well for you."

"Yes, sir. President Davis told me as much."

"I know. That was a good sign for you. If Davis didn't think you were worth the bother, he'd have ignored you, let Bragg toss you in the latrine. You and Polk and Buckner, Hill and Hindman, whoever else he chooses, you could all sit around some parlor in Atlanta and moan about injustice, while Bragg fights this war with lapdog subordinates. You're not a good enough politician to take sides in a pissing match."

Cleburne nodded. "That's what the president said, in a manner of speaking."

"Good. Just do your job. If we're to win this thing, we need Bragg to do his. Not sure that's going to happen, not with Longstreet on top of that mountain tossing spit at him."

Cleburne glanced up that way, the crown of Lookout Mountain hidden in a veil of fog.

Hardee said, "Bragg thinks he has the good ground. Thinks the enemy is penned up like so many chickens. That's going to change, before long. This weather breaks, we're in for a fight."

"You think we'll go down there, hit 'em straight on? They've strengthened the defenses. They don't want us in there, it'll be a tough go. General Bragg thinks they'll give up without a fight."

"They won't give up at all if they get reinforcements. Washington's not just going to let Rosecrans hang himself out here. Chattanooga's too important. They want those railroads as bad as we do, as bad as we need 'em. There's already buzzing all over the telegraph lines about orders out west, putting people into motion."

Cleburne wasn't sure what Hardee meant. "Out west? Who? Maybe they'll figure Burnside needs help, too, hanging on to Knoxville."

"We're not a threat to Burnside. Not yet anyway. But out along the Mississippi River, there's a whole flock of Federals with not a lot to do. I'm guessing you'll hear word that Sherman's been ordered to march this way, maybe McPherson. We've got time, but not a lot of it. If this weather hangs across this place, there won't be any serious fighting. All we can do is sit and wait. The longer we wait, the closer those Yankees will get. I'm betting it's Sherman."

Cleburne hadn't thought of Sherman at all. "He's . . . where? Memphis?"

"For now. But we've got cavalry watching him. That's where I spent most of the summer, remember? The railroad's pretty torn up, but the Yankees have more engineers than we do, and whatever slaves they've gathered up will fall in line, help with the labor. One thing we don't have up here is a wealth of labor. You don't feed the men decent rations, you can't expect them to do any serious work. Not sure why Bragg hasn't pushed hard to get the commissary wagons out here where we need 'em. I'll jab him about that. He won't like it, but he knows I'm right."

Cleburne looked out to the side, along the wide

ridgeline, saw men working with shovels, more men down below, toward the flatter ground. "We're trying, making do. My men are pretty sore about the lack of rations. But General Bragg, his staff officers, they keep pushing the men with how much the Yankees are suffering. If General Bragg's right, we're in a lot better shape than they are. Time ought to be on our side."

Hardee looked at him. "When was the last time you knew General Bragg to be **right**? No, don't answer that. You got yourself in enough Dutch already. He's our commanding general, and we'll follow him straight to the gates of hell, if he tells us to." Hardee paused. "That's what I'm supposed to say, anyway. But if Bragg's wrong about how long it'll take those Yankees to starve to death . . . well, the gates of hell might not be too far from where we're sitting right now."

CHAPTER NINE

GRANT

INDIANAPOLIS, INDIANA— OCTOBER 17, 1863

The leg was killing him, a relentless ache that had kept him on crutches now for weeks. The fall had come at New Orleans, a nasty horse someone had loaned him, the animal doing its best to show Grant who was really in charge. The fall had been brutal, knocking him unconscious, his only real memory of that a gathering of scowling doctors hovering over his bed. He hated the crutches, his underarms as sore as the lingering effects of the bruise all along his side. But Julia insisted, backed up by the orders from the doctors. No matter Grant's rank or authority over a hundred thousand men, he knew better than to disobey his wife.

He hobbled his way along the corridor of the

railcar, flinched with every step, reached his compartment, the door closed, heard her voice, some conversation about hotel rooms. He rapped one end of the crutch against the door, announcing himself, the door opening quickly, the efficiency of his chief of staff, John Rawlins.

"Welcome back, General. Were you able to . . . manage?"

"If I ever require you to assist me in the latrine, Mr. Rawlins, you shall know before anyone else." He saw Julia now, caught her glare of disapproval. Grant let out a breath, said, "My apologies. My patience is at a low ebb these days."

"Apologies not necessary, sir. Mrs. Grant and I were just discussing the accommodations we are expecting to find in Louisville."

Grant shrugged. "The telegram said the Galt House. I'm sure whatever they offer us will be fine. If there's a bed, I'm happy."

"Now, Ulyss," Julia said, "you be gracious to General Rawlins. He goes to great lengths to look after you. Someone has to, when I'm not about. Just look at you. Your shirt is dirty."

Grant nodded in resignation, saw Rawlins step forward, a brief hesitation, then a quick wipe at a smudge on his collar.

"Get away from me! When I feel the need to change uniforms, I shall inform you. Should I do it in the latrine, you can have double duty."

"Ulyss!"

He knew her tone, that there would be a stern lecture now, once Rawlins had retired. Rawlins seemed to know it as well, made a short bow.

"I shall leave you, with your permission, sir. Anything you require . . ."

"Yes, I know. I'll belch in your general direction."

"Ulysses S. Grant!"

He closed his eyes, his mind filling with apologies, knew what it meant when she used his full name. There would be little peace anywhere she made her headquarters. Rawlins was slipping out the doorway, stopped, expecting Grant to require something else. It was Rawlins's way, always had been, the man ever anxious to sweep through any task that surrounded Grant's command. Grant hobbled toward the bench seat, said, "Leave, Mr. Rawlins. There's a storm brewing here, and I shall absorb the brunt of it."

"As you wish, sir."

Rawlins was quickly out, closed the compartment door behind Grant.

"Ulyss, why must you be so disagreeable? He is only doing his job, and you need his every effort. Just look at you . . . your hands are dirty. Even your crutches . . ."

"Yes, dear. It has been a tiresome day. And once we reach Louisville, it will be tiresome still."

"Do you know yet who we are meeting?"

The **we** caught his attention, Julia always hoping that any gathering he was called upon to attend would be more of a social affair than something military. He turned, leaned on the crutches, dropped himself down to the seat with a dull groan. She stood with her hands on her hips, shook her head.

"I could help you, you know. If you weren't so stubborn."

"My dear, I don't need your help, really. As for General Rawlins, he provides me all the assistance anyone could ask for, and a good deal more that I don't ask for. He's my mother, your mother, and you, all in one."

He knew immediately he had made a mistake. She turned away in cold silence, her arms crossed, stared out the train window. He struggled to say something that would help, had learned long ago that the effort would likely make matters worse. He tried to soften his voice, add a lilt of affection.

"My dear, I don't know who is meeting with us. All I know is what Halleck's telegram said. They want me in Louisville to meet with an officer of the War Department. Things are . . . messy these days. I have to assume they want me to help clean it up."

"They should be using you more efficiently. Memphis is horrid, a terrible place. No better than Vicksburg. And Cairo . . . my word, Ulyss, could anyone ever suggest you make your headquarters in such a place?"

He knew better, that every hint the War Department had given pointed to some place for him much closer to the crisis in Tennessee. He kept his silence, felt the train slowing, and he could see buildings, homes, a general store. He peered out past her, said, "Indianapolis. Train will take on water, or wood, or whatever trains require. No one ever said I should command a railroad."

He heard shouts from the platform, could see movement, a man rushing through the small crowd. In a few seconds, there was a hard rap on the door. Julia turned, moved that way, and Grant felt a stab of alarm, held up his hand, "**No.**" It was a signal she understood, a sternness to his voice when the army got in the way. Grant pulled one crutch close to him, a potential weapon, and she watched him, her face reflecting his concern. "Stand away from the door, please, Julia. I'm not expecting a visitor."

He forced himself up from the padded bench, the rap on the door coming again, more insistent, and now a voice, Rawlins.

"Sir! Most urgent, sir!"

Grant felt relief, knew Rawlins wouldn't be there unless it was necessary. "You may enter, General."

The door opened, to Rawlins and another man, nervous, out of breath, a civilian. Rawlins seemed annoyed, said, "Sir, this man says he is from the War Department, and that it is imperative the train hold here at the station."

Grant looked at the man and said, "I'd like to hear it from you, sir. You have something for me?"

The man was young, short, small frame, held a

hat in both hands. He made a short bow toward Julia, then said, "Sir, if I may speak in front of . . . um . . . the lady."

"Speak, sir. What is it?"

"General Grant, I am to inform you that another train, a special train, is just now arriving at the station here. You are to await its passenger. He shall meet with you presently, and possibly accompany you on your journey to Louisville."

Rawlins stepped in, as though shielding Grant from the man's intrusion.

"This man knows details of your itinerary, sir. It is possible that he is telling the truth. However, I wouldn't take him solely at his word. Should he be found to carry false information, I shall have him detained."

Grant sagged. "General, I detect no subversion here. Sir, in the interest of relieving my chief of staff's concerns, are you a spy? An assassin perhaps?"

The man's eyes widened, and Grant saw far more indignation than fear. The young man seemed to puff up, a distinct air of haughtiness.

"Most certainly not, sir. My name is Heathcliff Baker. I am here under official orders, with the full authority of the secretary of war."

"I know a government man when I hear one, Colonel. So, might I ask, Mr. Baker, just what official of the War Department I am to meet here?"

The man kept his lofty attitude, a slight sneer toward Rawlins. "Sir, I just told you. The secretary of war. Surely you know him, sir. Mr. Edwin Stanton."

Grant had never met Stanton before, though the two had passed lengthy telegraph messages back and forth, with Henry Halleck's missives spread throughout. During the Vicksburg campaign, Grant had gone to great lengths to keep telegraph wires far from his headquarters, preventing official Washington from meddling in his day-to-day business. His explanation to official Washington was an easy one for a general in the field, no matter how exaggerated the reasons: He was just too heavily engaged in mortal combat to keep the War Department informed of his every move. Keeping a telegraph operator out of his camp made that explanation easier to enforce. Winning victories over rebel armies, especially significant ones, helped as well. He had never gotten along with General Halleck, knew that any collapse Grant might suffer against the rebels could give Halleck the justification to remove Grant from his command, something Halleck had done once before. But Halleck's temperament had shown itself too clumsily, Grant dismissed from command after his victory at Fort Donelson. Halleck's personal animosity toward Grant hadn't been a sufficient reason for the president or Secretary Stanton to accept Halleck's strange logic that a winning general had no place under Halleck's authority. Halleck had grudgingly agreed, putting Grant back in command of the next campaign, which resulted in another, far more bloody victory at Shiloh. Now, with his success at Vicksburg, Grant had to believe that the hearty congratulations he had received from Washington were genuine. It had been Sherman who was quick to point out that Grant's star was clearly on the rise. Grant paid little heed to that, though he had become confident that Halleck's personal dislike of Grant would not become a problem again, unless of course Grant suffered a mammoth defeat. Lincoln had suffered too much ineptitude in the East, the morale of the entire Union crushed under the weight of Generals Pope, Burnside, and Hooker, each man handing Robert E. Lee monumental victories that might have ended the war in the South's favor. It had been the triumphs in July, George Meade's enormous success at Gettysburg, coupled with Grant's at Vicksburg, that had swept away the defeatism that poured out from Northern newspapers. But that euphoria was short-lived, and Grant knew that the gift Rosecrans had given the South at Chickamauga had to be answered for. From the smell of the messages that came to him from Washington, Grant assumed that Rosecrans's hold on command of the Army of the Cumberland was in serious jeopardy.

The telegram from Halleck had reached Grant at Cairo, Illinois, that morning, explicit instructions for Grant to take a train to Louisville. Halleck had only hinted to Grant that it might be necessary for Grant to travel to Nashville, where he might assist in reinforcing the Army of the Cumberland, guiding supplies and men to ease the dangerous burden Rosecrans was facing. Grant had no expectation of going to Chattanooga himself, assumed that if Rosecrans was to be removed, the job might be offered to someone else, perhaps George Meade. But Grant also knew that Meade was too fresh in command, and some around Grant's army, Sherman in particular, were assuming that Meade had wandered into a victory in Pennsylvania by pure good fortune, that the fight had been won more on the backs of men like John Reynolds and Winfield Hancock. But Reynolds was dead and Hancock badly wounded. Even Julia seemed to believe that Grant was being singled out as the best man to take charge of the Army of the Cumberland. That Grant had little desire for a complete change of scenery didn't seem to matter to any one of them. But he was realistic about his alternatives to anything the War Department wanted him to do. There were none.

E dwin Stanton was everything Grant expected, a loud voice, heavy handshake, and a man who put his cards directly on the table.

"General, it is good to finally lay eyes on you. I admit to being curious about your demeanor, your methods. General Halleck has his ways, and I am well aware that there was conflict between the two of you. I assure you that any such disagreements are in the past. The president is mightily impressed by your accomplishments, sir, as am I."

The words flowed over Grant in a fog of cigar smoke, inspiring Grant to retrieve his own from his coat pocket. Stanton struck a match, obliging Grant, a show of politeness that made Grant cautious. He leaned forward, his eyes on Stanton still, the small flame rocking with the sudden movement of the train. Stanton returned the stare, Grant averting his eyes, laboring to keep his balance as the train gained speed.

"Mr. Secretary, I am honored by your making this journey. I assume you had other business to attend to in this part of the war, and that this meeting is a matter of convenience. We should be in Louisville by tonight."

Stanton laughed, shook his head. "Sit down, General, before this confounded railroad causes you further injury. Pleasantries wore out a long time ago in Washington. The president sees through such things, as do I. You're wondering if I came all the way out here just to see you. I did just that. There are important matters for us to address, General. Highly important." Stanton waited for Grant to tumble into his seat, his attempt at decorum failing miserably. "Are you fit to ride, General?"

Grant was curious about the question. "Am I to leave the train, sir?"

"I am merely concerned about your mobility, General. Trains can be tempting targets for enemy raiders. I'm sure General Sherman understands that, if he didn't before."

"Yes, sir, I'm certain General Sherman will take better precautions on his travels."

"Can't have that, General, can't have senior officers putting themselves at risk."

"Sir, it is the job. If I sought a lack of risk, I would have hoped for assignment in Washington."

Stanton ignored the joke, and Grant was instantly relieved, had no talent for small talk, scolded himself. Just answer his questions, for God's sake. Stanton reached into a leather case, produced a sheaf of papers. He sifted through, then pulled two from the rest, held one in each hand.

"General Grant, I wish you to read both of these. They are mostly identical, but there is one significant difference. I wish you to choose the one you find most acceptable."

Grant took the papers, more curious now, read through the first, stopped partway, read the second. Both began the same way. Grant paused, looked at Stanton, who sat back, clearly pleased with the drama of the moment.

"Sir, does this mean I am being promoted?"

"It means that your sphere of authority is being expanded. The president has approved placing you in command of the newly created Military Division of the Mississippi, which will encompass the Departments of the Ohio, the Cumberland, and the Tennessee. I suppose you could refer to that as a promotion, though your rank remains major general. But you will now be superior in rank to the commanders of all three departments."

"Sir, I am presently commander of the Department of the Tennessee. I now outrank myself?"

Stanton studied him, and Grant felt he was being examined, thought, He's trying to figure out if I'm especially thickheaded. Just answer his questions.

Stanton rubbed one hand on his stomach, peered at Grant through his small spectacles. "It has been decided, General, that you should choose a successor to command the Department of the Tennessee. Obviously."

Grant nodded, silent, realized that there was nothing lighthearted about Stanton or the purpose for this meeting. There was only one name that poured into Grant's mind, the only man Grant had the confidence in to move up to take his own command.

"If I may be allowed to suggest, sir, General Sherman is the most suited for that command."

"We assumed such. You'll get no objections from Washington, as long as you can assure us that General Sherman's . . . um . . . unfortunate tendencies are in the past."

Grant hated the assumption that Sherman still had to be watched over, like some errant child. "I have full confidence in General Sherman, sir."

"Yes, well, most in Washington would agree with you. But don't be hasty in your decision. There is time. Sherman is still on the march, is he not?"

"Yes, sir. Two divisions are en route to Chattanooga. Additional troops are preparing to follow. Their progress has been delayed somewhat by General Halleck's order that Sherman repair the railroad along the way. Given the state of crisis at Chattanooga, it seems more efficient for Sherman to move his people more quickly. If I'm not exceeding my authority, sir."

"See to it. You'll need every railroad you can get, I would imagine. But you're probably right. You need Sherman's troops even more." Stanton pointed to the papers still in Grant's hands. "Finish reading, please."

Grant complied, read silently, saw now the difference between the two orders. He looked up at Stanton, bit down hard on the butt of his cigar.

"You are leaving this decision up to me?"

"You're the commanding general. You know who inspires confidence in the field and who does not. This is no time for avoiding hurt feelings, General."

Grant had little affection for William Rosecrans, the two men dueling over authority and Washington's attentions well before now. It was a common thread that ran through the entire Federal military, competing spheres, army versus navy, the Army of the Potomac versus the Army of the Ohio, on and on, each commander trying to make himself heard above the din, the effort to gain priority for supplies and reinforcements. But now, the order given him by Stanton had elevated him to full authority over any force west of the Appalachian Mountains, all the way to the Mississippi River. And the orders were clear and to the point. One called for Grant to assume command over Rosecrans, and handle the situation at Chattanooga by assisting Rosecrans in holding the rebels away. The other called for Rosecrans's outright removal, with command of the Army of the Cumberland to fall upon George Thomas. Grant stared at the papers, felt the weight of what Stanton was doing.

Stanton seemed to enjoy himself, smiled, said, "It's the very thing you generals crow about the most. Washington keeping its nose out of your affairs, Washington permitting you to run your commands the way you see fit. I've been hearing that since the first weeks of the war. George McClellan spent every waking hour badgering the War Department, insisting we round up a half-million volunteers to fight off a scourge that would otherwise engulf the entire Union. In return, he expected Washington, and especially the president, to keep out of his way. No questions, no suggestions. Unfortunately, there were also no victories. As well, McClellan was prone to exaggeration. I do not believe that affliction applies to you." Stanton paused, still enjoying the moment. "Well, General, this time, you are getting what I assume to be your greatest desire. You may choose your subordinates. The War Department is confident you will choose wisely. So, which is it? Which order do you accept?"

Grant thought again of Rosecrans, the man's successes in the scattering of fights through Tennessee and Kentucky, his accomplishments against Braxton Bragg throughout the past year, especially the slick maneuver that summer, drawing Bragg out of Chattanooga. It was the kind of campaigning that earned promotions, that inspired newspapers to trumpet your name, and politicians to hold fast to your support. But, then there was Chickamauga, the kind of tragedy that would erase memories of any success, the kind of failure the North could no longer tolerate. Grant was far removed from the swirling tornado of politics, just how Washington intended to respond to that defeat. But there were plenty of voices in and around the army, speaking out about the mood of the citizenry. The jubilation over Vicksburg and Gettysburg had been swept away, the hourglass emptying again, draining away the country's patience for this war that seemed never to end.

Grant held up one hand. "Sir, I choose this one. If you require explanation, I shall provide it."

Stanton took the paper from him, a quick glance, showed no surprise at Grant's decision. "As you wish, sir. The decision is yours, thus, so is the need to communicate the order to your subordinates. I would suggest you not leave General Rosecrans hanging too long. The Army of the Cumberland is standing in the face of the enemy. A change of command should be rapid and efficient."

"Of course, sir. I will see to it."

Stanton pulled himself to his feet, steadied himself against the rocking motion of the railcar. He peered low through the train's windows.

"Beautiful country hereabouts. Don't get out this way often enough." He looked at Grant now, a narrow squint to his eyes, nothing pleasant in his words.

"General Grant, you have a job to do. Mr. Lincoln is sincerely concerned about next year's elections, that if the people are not pleased with their army, they will inflict their feelings on the president. That would be an intolerable situation. For all of us. You are being given a task of utmost importance. The War Department and the president are risking a great deal by choosing you as the man least likely to fail us. You will not fail us, will you, sir?"

"Sir, I will do my best."

"Then we shall learn just what your **best** is, won't we, General?"

THE GALT HOUSE HOTEL— LOUISVILLE, KENTUCKY— OCTOBER 17, 1863

They had ridden the carriage through a miserable storm, sloshing mud that had soiled the hem of her dress, his own boots caked with a sloppy goo. He moved to one side of the room, sat slowly, still unsteady with the crutches, removed the boots, wiped the mud from his hands with an already dirty handkerchief. He felt the aching need for a cigar, glanced around the spacious room, admiring.

"They provided us very nice accommodations, I think."

Julia was fussing over the stains on her dress, said, "Very nice, I suppose. Very nice weather they provided you, as well. I have never seen such a flood."

The dinner had gone very well, a gathering of relatives who lived near Louisville, a family Grant had not seen in some years. He watched as Julia moved to her leather trunk, sifting through her clothing, the room choked with the essence of her perfume. Grant was used to that, but the ache for the cigar only grew. He glanced at his pocket watch, after eleven, stared out the window through the driving rain. The lights of the city spread out in several directions, a scattering of carriages still moving past, the streets rivers of mud. Who in the world, he thought, would be out on such a night? Well, you were. People have business, war or no war. Families must eat, young people must court. You wouldn't know there is a war at all. Who would care anything of the task I have been given? So much of this country is so far removed from the duty I must oversee. There will be another fight, perhaps very soon, and if we are successful, these very people will rejoice. And if the army fails, they will condemn us all. Well, no. They will condemn **me.** That's the point, after all. Stanton knows that. The president has just concerns for his election, but my concerns must fall on the men who march to the fight. I may remove a general who no longer performs, who shows failing abilities. But I cannot scold an army if we are beaten in a fight. Stanton is right. If my best is not sufficient . . . we could lose this war.

Grant gave in to the temptation, lit a cigar, erasing Julia's flowery scent, stared again into the rain. What have you done, Grant? You have traveled to the center of the storm. The secretary will return to Washington knowing he has cleansed himself of responsibility for what happens next. It is the game they play. He gives me **command** . . . but what do I really control?

The rap on the door was loud, something else he was becoming accustomed to. He turned, saw Julia cover her garments with a blanket. He pulled the crutches close to him, lifted himself upward. Julia looked toward him, said, "The hour! What on earth . . . ?"

Grant said nothing, stared at the door, waited a long second, said, "Enter."

The door opened slowly, Rawlins, rapidly buttoning his uniform shirt. Behind him, another man, a look of desperate relief on his face. The man didn't wait for Rawlins, said, "General! Secretary Stanton has been seeking your whereabouts. Thank God you have returned, sir. The secretary requires your presence immediately!"

"Immediately?"

The word came from Julia, who moved up close beside Grant, Rawlins responding to her with a short bow. Grant said, "General, assist me with my coat. Sir, you may lead the way."

Stanton was in his nightclothes, showed no embarrassment for that, and Grant watched as he paced the floor of his room.

"I have great respect for Mr. Dana, General. He has been extremely useful, extremely observant in those places where my own eyes cannot be." Stanton stopped now, looked at Grant. "Yes, well, you know that, don't you?"

Grant said nothing, thought, Yes, Sherman was right all along. As was I. Charles Dana was sent to Mississippi as a spy. I hope he saw what he needed to see.

Stanton seemed to read him. "He's the reason you're here, General. It's no secret he was reporting directly to me on a number of issues in your department, as he is doing so right now in Chattanooga."

Grant nodded, thought, It's no secret now.

"Yes, sir. I appreciate the assistant secretary's vigilance."

"Yes, well, that vigilance is now being tested every minute of every day. I received a telegram earlier this evening. Conditions in Chattanooga are deteriorating rapidly. So rapidly in fact that General Rosecrans is contemplating an immediate retreat. Mr. Dana informs me that such a retreat will sacrifice a great number of artillery pieces, and many of the stores we have tried to gather for the welfare of the men. That job has gone badly, General, badly indeed. Mr. Dana tells me that horses are starving en masse, and that it is possible the men are next. We must relieve those conditions, or the catastrophe will be felt across the entire country. Do you understand?"

Grant felt Stanton's concern, detected a hint of panic. "Sir, I understand that Chattanooga must not be abandoned. Recapturing such a valuable rail hub could be costly."

Stanton stopped pacing again, looked at him. "General, you are master of the understatement. What do you intend to do?"

"I will issue an immediate order to General Rosecrans, that he not retreat. I have also penned the order to my adjutant relieving General Rosecrans of command, replacing him with General Thomas."

"Good."

Stanton seemed to wait for more, and Grant knew what had to follow, that such a crisis would require more from him than a comfortable headquarters in Nashville.

"And, sir, I will make immediate arrangements to journey to Chattanooga."

CHAPTER TEN

GRANT

NEAR STEVENSON, ALABAMA— OCTOBER 21, 1863

At Secretary Stanton's insistence, the War Department's official order had been transmitted from Washington as quickly as possible, Special Order #337, relieving Rosecrans of command of the Army of the Cumberland, and naming his replacement, General George Thomas. Grant had issued a duplicate under his own name, exercising the authority Stanton had given him, communicating to both Rosecrans and Thomas that Grant was now in overall command of the entire theater. Grant had no idea how Rosecrans had responded to his dismissal, might never know. He fully expected that Rosecrans would accept the order with decorum, would vacate his post as quickly as possible, with a minimum of acrimony or protest, or, more important, with little disruption to the army's already hazardous situation.

Grant's train had left Nashville early that morning, a lurching, unsteady journey along tracks the rebels had made a constant target. He left behind a lengthy list of progress reports, communicated to Washington, his details for the gathering of an immense army, the enormous effort focused now on the most immediate crisis of the war, the impending difficulties at Chattanooga. Grant knew of Sherman's progress through Mississippi, but he couldn't avoid thinking of the near catastrophe at Collierville. Grant had absorbed Sherman's report on the incident with well-disguised alarm, wouldn't allow anyone around him to know how the possibility of losing Sherman would affect him. Sherman was more than a good subordinate. He was the man Grant knew he could depend on in any circumstance, that despite Sherman's failings, his quick temper and tendency to talk too much, without Sherman, the great campaigns Grant had led in the West could have had very different outcomes. Grant knew from Sherman's telegram that a crucial lesson had been learned at Collierville, that an army commander should know just where he was going, long before he actually arrived there. Now Sherman was making far better progress, the War Department finally backing away from the absurd order that Sherman's people waste enormous amounts of time repairing the railroad line along the way. Grant knew that every day of decent weather meant that Sherman was that much closer to Chattanooga.

To the east, Ambrose Burnside was anchoring his forces around Knoxville, and despite urgent instructions from Halleck that Burnside move his people much closer to Chattanooga, Burnside continued to offer reasons why the move just couldn't happen. Grant knew enough of Burnside to expect delay, and he expected it now. But Grant understood what the War Department did not, that Burnside's forces were valuable right where they were, a juggernaut that Braxton Bragg could not just ignore. With Knoxville secure in Federal hands, the rebels had to consider the possibility that Burnside might suddenly shove his troops toward Bragg's northern flank on Missionary Ridge, making convenient use of the available railroads and the Tennessee River, which could suddenly put Bragg in serious trouble. Grant's best hope was that Bragg had a healthy fear of what Burnside might do, whether or not that fear was ever justified.

Grant's short stay in Nashville had been tiresome, the annoyance of official protocol, meeting with the military governor there, Andrew Johnson, shaking hands with numerous dignitaries, suffering lengthy speeches, all meant to bolster Grant's spirits, as though only these civilians understood the challenges that lay ahead. Grant had learned to endure that kind of suffering, especially when he had no control over the surroundings. During the Vicksburg campaign, Grant had made it a point to keep most of the politicians and civilian orators at bay, a silent luxury he never took for granted. As he suffered in Nashville through the lengthy orations, one thought had crept into his brain. Julia had not accompanied him. It was never an argument between them, that when Grant moved toward the front lines, her place was elsewhere. With the speeches droning past him, he couldn't avoid a hidden smile, that had she been there, all the dignitaries, the grand reception, would have made for a glorious time for her.

Stevenson, Alabama, was the southernmost termination point of the Federally controlled rail line, and Grant knew it would be necessary to resume the journey toward Chattanooga by boat, as far as the riverside town of Bridgeport. There, safe passage on the river ended, and the journey would be completed on horseback, a thought that gave Grant no comfort at all. The injured leg continued to annoy him, and Rawlins had insisted on a cavalcade of doctors, had gone out on his own seeking a blend of concoctions, salves, or potions meant to soothe Grant's agony. Grant began to suspect that Rawlins was doing business with an African witch doctor.

Rawlins had been a close friend of Grant before

the war, and Grant knew that Rawlins's political influence in Illinois had done much to secure Grant's
first command in an army that Grant had once
left behind. That resignation had come in 1854,
Grant avoiding a career-crushing court-martial. It
was the most miserable time of his life, stationed
in a post without his family, immersed in the tur-
bulent decadence of gold-rush San Francisco. The
despair of life so far removed from his family had
pushed Grant to the liquor bottle, a balm that only
numbed the brain, but never could cure his aching loneliness. He understood the ramifications,
that the army couldn't tolerate so many bouts of
drunkenness, but through the generosity of his
commanding officer, Grant had been offered the
option of resigning his commission rather than be
publicly humiliated. The humiliation would come
later, from Julia, harsh and accurate, that Grant
would only keep his family by keeping sober. Julia
had of course been backed up by her father, an arrogant, dismissive man, who had never approved
of his daughter marrying a soldier. It was an easy
conclusion for Frederick Dent to believe that
Grant had soiled his reputation for all time, one
more reason for Dent to scold his daughter for her
ill-advised choice of a husband. Dent was a loud,
opinionated man, who did nothing to hide the
most glaring point of contention between them.
Julia's father was a slaveholder, and even now, Grant
had little patience for discussions of politics or just

what a Northern victory would mean to his father-in-law.

Whether or not Dent approved of a blue uniform, the outbreak of the war had offered Grant the escape he desperately needed from his numerous failures as a civilian. That escape came courtesy of John Rawlins. In early 1861, Rawlins had gained considerable influence in Illinois politics, had helped persuade Congressman Elihu Washburne, a strong supporter and friend to Abraham Lincoln, that Grant was still fit for an officer's commission. Grant gratefully accepted the opportunity to begin anew in the army, and from Grant's first days as a regimental commander from Illinois, Rawlins had volunteered his services. The army seemed to recognize Rawlins's value not just to Grant, but to the entire command, and Rawlins had been officially promoted to captain, rising through the ranks until, in August 1863, he was promoted to brigadier general, a rank befitting the post he occupied alongside Grant. Grant appreciated the army's respect for Rawlins's competence, even if the man's fierce loyalty could be somewhat smothering. But there was more to Rawlins's affection for Grant. Shortly after the outbreak of the war, Rawlins's wife had died of tuberculosis. Both men kept their emotions well hidden, and so their conversations kept mostly to the business of the army. But Grant had to suspect that Rawlins's pure dedication, no matter how annoying he might be, came partly because he had no one else in his life.

G rant felt the train lurching to a stop, pulled himself awake from a fitful nap. He stared out through the glass, saw lantern light reflecting across a depot, a dozen armed soldiers coming into formation, others mingling behind, no doubt aware just who had arrived. Grant pulled out his pocket watch, just after eight o'clock, thought, Long day, indeed. He felt a stuffy rumbling in his stomach, the aftereffects of his dinner, some kind of vegetable Grant had never seen before, one of those odd species that seemed only to grow for rebel farmers. He sat up, heard the commotion beyond his quarters, knew the staff would already be handling the baggage, making preparation for the next part of the trip. I can't imagine the Tennessee River will treat me any worse than this train, he thought. At least water is . . . soft. Later, the horse . . . well, don't think about that now.

The knock came, expected, the voice of his aide, Henry Dixon. "Sir, we have arrived in Stevenson. This is as far as we can travel by train."

Grant shook his head, bleary-eyed patience. "I know where we are, Lieutenant. I shall be prepared to move in a moment. Is General Rawlins in contact with the boat's commander?"

The door opened abruptly, Rawlins breathing

heavily, pushing past the wide-eyed lieutenant. Rawlins motioned the young aide away, closed the door with a self-conscious flourish. He leaned low toward Grant, and Grant could feel the man's breaths, had rarely seen Rawlins looking . . . nervous.

"John, are you all right?"

"Sir! It is something of a surprise. Fate, as it were. Perhaps. Not certain of that, of course. But, it is curious, nonetheless." Grant reached for the crutches, and Rawlins held up a hand, his words coming in a quick, jabbering flood. "No, sir. Perhaps not just yet. We should remain here. The train."

"Why? What's happening out there?" He thought of Sherman now, the amazing close call at Collierville. "Is there a problem?"

Rawlins tried to gather himself, took a deep breath. "Not really certain of that, sir. I've heard of duels being fought over this sort of happpenstance. There could be a serious issue of pride at stake."

"What is it, John?"

Grant's tone left no room for maneuver, and Rawlins snapped himself together, his formal demeanor returning.

"Sir, I must report to you that in a stroke of coincidence, another train has arrived in this station. It seems that General Rosecrans is . . . here, sir. Or rather, right across the way . . . there. Should I post a guard?"

Grant looked out to the darkness, nothing to see but the glimpse of the men standing guard on the platform. He rubbed his chin, reached for a cigar, took his time lighting it, thought of Rosecrans. He would fight a duel?

"John, I have a better idea. Offer my respects to General Rosecrans, and escort him to my car. I just terminated the man's career. The least I can do is talk to him."

Grant studied Rosecrans carefully, felt idiotic believing Rawlins's suggestion that Rosecrans might actually attack him. Rawlins stood back, outside the entrance of Grant's private car, one of Rosecrans's aides beside him. Grant ignored them, said, "I assure you, General, this rendezvous was not planned. I do not expect you to regard me with any more pleasantness than you ever did before. Perhaps less, considering."

Rosecrans still stood at attention, obviously uncomfortable, a feeling Grant shared. Grant had forgotten how much larger the man was, several inches taller than Grant, a thick chest, tall forehead, a handsome man by any standards.

"I am pleased to meet with you, General Grant. I have always held a high respect for your abilities, and your authority."

Grant pointed to the bench seat across from him. "I doubt that. Sit down. You stand like that, you're making my leg hurt."

Rosecrans obeyed with a crisp formality, kept his

back straight, looked at Grant's leg, a hint of curiosity. Grant responded to the unspoken question.

"Happened in New Orleans. Some horse that didn't share your respect for my authority. It'll heal one of these days."

"You look fit otherwise, General. Much like West Point, I'd say."

The strain in Rosecrans's compliment dug at Grant, and Grant was curious now if it carried an insult. Grant glanced down at his dingy greatcoat, the wrinkled shirt. Rosecrans was in full finery, what seemed to be a new uniform. Grant looked at the gold braid on the man's hat, saw his own, even that detail a striking contrast between new and old. Beyond his appearance, the entire Federal command was aware that Rosecrans had graduated fifth in his class at the Point, a year before Grant's graduation far down the middle of the pack.

"Don't really need to discuss the Academy, General. Is it proper I call you William?"

Rosecrans didn't flinch, gave Grant no opening. "By your authority, you may address me as you please. I shall address you accordingly, sir."

Grant was beginning to regret the decision to bring Rosecrans aboard the train, pulled a long draw from his cigar, the smoke drifting upward. "All right, **General.** Tell me about Chattanooga."

Rosecrans seemed surprised at the question, the first break in his demeanor. "I have made considerable effort to bring in supplies for the men, and I will state with pride that elaborate plans have been devised to turn the enemy away. Conditions in the town and in our camps are most difficult. We have lost most of the livestock."

"Horses? Cattle?"

"Horses and mules. Cattle are making their way in, but their condition is extremely poor, near starvation. There is no forage. The men are using their ingenuity for survival, a trait I hoped to inspire. The enemy's sharpshooters along the river prevent us from gathering much-needed lumber, either for structures or for fire. There is one route of supply, over the mountains. A most difficult passage, which I just traveled myself. It is the route by which you shall reach your . . . new command." He paused. "Sir, I believe the enemy can be removed with the resources that have been sent our way. Excuse me, sir. **Your** way. With the reinforcements certain to arrive with General Sherman, with the additional strength from General Hooker's corps, and General Burnside's forces at Knoxville, I do not believe Bragg's noose can be tightened any further. I have spoken at length with General Smith, whose engineers are awaiting instruction to open additional routes of supply, possibly driving the enemy back from the river so that the waterway will serve us far more effectively. It is possible a vigorous campaign may be waged to drive the enemy off the heights that threaten our position. I had hoped to be allowed the time to put some kind of strategy into our overall planning, both to relieve the suffering of the men, and to continue our campaign."

The words came toward Grant in a flood, but Rosecrans's energy was weakening, and Grant could see that whatever fire Rosecrans had tried to bring was now flickering.

Grant waited for more, but Rosecrans seemed content, as though making his case by carefully stopping short of any suggestion that the War Department, or Grant, should reconsider their orders. Grant said, "I wish you to know, General, that the order removing you from command did not originate with me."

Rosecrans looked down, shrugged. "Does it matter? I am aware how the War Department functions. Past successes do not compensate for recent failure. After Chickamauga, I was hoping to be allowed to right our wrongs. I have devised what I believe to be several excellent options to reverse our fortunes."

The question rose up in Grant's mind now. Options? All this talk of such good plans? Why did you not carry them out? How much time did you require? And how many horses will die waiting for some . . . plan?

Rosecrans was fidgeting, and Grant could see that the man was anxious to leave.

"Where will you travel now?"

Rosecrans spoke slowly, still nothing friendly in

his words. "By rail, to Cincinnati. After that, I will await orders. If orders should come."

"Well, I am certain your usefulness to this army has not concluded."

"Are you?"

The question surprised Grant, and Rosecrans stood now, made a gesture of brushing away dust from his clean uniform. Old habits, Grant thought. But now, there are new habits in this man, and they are not positive. He has learned that men will die in his command in a fight that he will lose. What has that taken away from the man?

"General Rosecrans, I thank you for meeting with me. Travel safely. Perhaps we will serve together in some future campaign."

Rosecrans looked at him now, soft, sad eyes. "With all respects, General Grant, I do not believe that will happen. I do hope that the men in the Army of the Cumberland fare better under your command, and the command of General Thomas, than they did with me. If I may be allowed to continue my journey?"

Grant sifted questions through his mind, any other detail Rosecrans could offer him. But Rosecrans seemed drained, and Grant reached for the crutches, would stand, the only respectful gesture he could make. Rosecrans didn't wait, turned, moved quickly past his aide, the man staring at Grant with a hint of hostility. Rawlins said something to the aide, who saluted, moved away, following Rosecrans. Grant released the crutches, relaxed again on the seat, Rawlins watching him. Grant stared out, saw Rosecrans and the aide on the platform, passing through the formation of guards, disappearing into the darkness. Grant retrieved another cigar, stared at it for a long moment, then looked at Rawlins.

"He was a brilliant man. A year ahead of me at the Academy. Big fat reputation. One of those men you talk about, **the chosen one,** the great certain future. I doubt he recalls me at all. Just one of the crowd."

Rawlins bent low, a brief glance outside. "He didn't do the job, sir. Failure has its price."

Grant shook his head. "He has failings, yes. But he also won fights. He bested the enemy far more than he failed this army."

"Do you think the War Department made a mistake, removing him?"

Grant considered the question, the cigar smoke drifting up around his face. "He knew what he was supposed to do. Still does. But he didn't **do** it. That's all it takes, John. This war is a close thing, no matter what the newspapers say. Any of us falls on our face, the cost is too high. And sometimes . . . it's time for a change, time for a commander to just go away. Remember that. None of us is infallible. Not Sherman, not Thomas, not Bragg or Lee or Beauregard or Meade. It's so rarely about military genius, who the greater tactician might be, who sat higher in his class at West Point. It's about mistakes, some of them unavoidable, some of them purely stupid. My job is to make fewer mistakes than the enemy, and to ensure that Thomas and Sherman and Burnside don't pull us into some kind of abyss we can't escape. It's that simple."

Grant saw a question on Rawlins's face.

"What is it?"

"Sir, just thinking. What of General Thomas? He served under General Rosecrans. Will he be up to the job?"

Grant finished the cigar, ground the stub into an ashtray. "I suppose we'll find out."

CHAPTER ELEVEN

GRANT

WALDRON'S RIDGE—
WEST OF CHATTANOOGA—
OCTOBER 22, 1863

The death of the animals had always been harder for him to accept than the death of soldiers. The animals after all had no choice. None of them had volunteered for this duty, none ever protested the lack of food, none had any concept why their bodies had grown weak, none understood why their legs would no longer climb, why the labor of pulling the wagons had become too much to bear. None understood why, finally, they simply could not move, collapsing alongside the muddy trail, until death swept away the last glimmer of sight, of sound, of feeling.

"Dumb beasts," he had heard, teamsters and supply officers sometimes abusing the animals, but if they did that in Grant's presence, they never did it again. He had loved horses even before Mexico, had become an expert rider, a surprise to many in a man of his small stature. Some insisted it took brawn, sheer muscle to control the great beasts, but Grant had his own way, held the reins loosely, seemed clumsy at first, helpless, inspiring laughter from the other troops as he rode away. But he never lost control, never let the horse know he was afraid, and very soon the horse seemed to know that the rider was not simply a burden, but his partner, the ride over any kind of terrain an equal challenge for both of them. Grant loved the gracefulness, the ease in climbing rocky hills, no trail too narrow, no hill too steep. It was a marvel to him that the horses could absorb the sounds that terrified so many of the men, the shock of the artillery blasts, musket fire inches away, rarely any reaction at all. The artillerymen knew that of course, shared his respect for their mounts, understood that in the worst fights, the men would lose their nerve long before the beasts. They were targets, certainly, far larger than the men who rode them, and so in every great attack, the horses went down more quickly than the lines of men who marched beside them. It was something he had come to accept, as the cavalrymen did, that you could love the beast, but you could not expect to keep it, not if you rode into the fight at the head of your men. Even then, the horses could absorb far more punishment than any man, and Grant had seen mounts with a dozen wounds in the most vulnerable places, the animal still charging forward, until the legs gave way and the blood ran dry.

The horse beneath him now was called Kangaroo, had been abandoned by a rebel in Mississippi. The animal inspired jeers among the men who found him, a horse of odd coloring, a slightly misshapen face, none of the handsomeness that any cavalry commander would insist on. But Grant knew fine stock, knew the horse was a thoroughbred, even if his own staff joked behind his back that the animal was far too ugly to serve the commanding general. Very soon, Grant and Kangaroo had reached that understanding common to good horsemen, and as they left the riverside town of Bridgeport, pushing through the sixty miles of ragged mountainous terrain, the horse seemed to know of Grant's injury, kept the gait slow, rhythmic, no lurching bumps. Grant returned the favor with a gentle hand, steadying himself on the slippery roads by leaning more on the horse's neck rather than jerking back on the reins. If the weather and the muddy conditions made the journey a challenge in itself, Grant had not been prepared for the horror that met him along the way, the grisly sight of so much carnage, so many carcasses of fallen horses.

There were hundreds of them, alongside the rivers of mud the men were forced to travel. He had expected some of this, Rosecrans at least sharing the difficulties of crossing the mountains, what it had cost the men and their animals. It was, after all, the only supply route open to the army. But nothing could prepare Grant for the smell. As they moved farther away from the river, onto higher ground, the trails became more treacherous, steep and rocky, made narrow by deep gullies and sharp ravines, and in every open place, near the muddy road or just beyond, in the holes and across the patches of wet grass, the remains of dead horses and mules were unending, hundreds becoming thousands.

Some of the animals had been there for days, empty shells of bare ribs, stripped clean by the scavengers that even now circled overhead. Some had died within a day of Grant's ride, stiffened animals with legs stretched taut, empty eyes and bare teeth, skin stretched tight over rib cages that showed just how poor the animals had been. There were cattle as well, what remained of the small herds driven toward Chattanooga, the weakest animals tumbling over into low places, shoved aside like the horses and mules, too wet to burn, too many to bury.

Up ahead, the narrow trail forced the men to ride in single file, many with their heads down, shielded by the thick misty rain, trying to avoid the stink they couldn't escape. Others were more curious, or equally horrified, scanning the animals as well as the debris they had left behind. Grant saw that as well, the shattered remnants of wagons, cracked wheels, piles of broken timber. There were aban-

doned artillery pieces, but not many, and he studied what seemed to be a twelve-pounder, far below
in a muddy hole, the roadside too soft to keep the
cannon from slipping away, the carriage tumbling
down into cracked pieces.

A man rode toward him, water dripping from his
hat, a quick wipe of a soggy handkerchief across
his face.

"Sir, the road just past that rise is washed out
completely. With all respects, sir, I would prefer
you not make any attempt to cross. We can take
care of it, sir."

Grant knew this routine all too well. Back at
Bridgeport, Grant could barely climb the horse at
all, so Rawlins had ordered the aides to lift Grant
up like some sack of flour, placing him on the horse
as though he might require a tie-down. Grant held
his complaints to himself, knew it was the only way.
As they climbed farther into the hills, the mud had
grown worse, the narrow roadway often impassable
without dismounting. Through it all, Rawlins had
been there, the men lowering Grant from the horse,
carrying him across some absurd pool of slop, then
hoisting him up one more time onto the horse.
Now, it would happen again.

He saw the apology on the young man's face,
said, "No matter, Captain. We'll do what we must.
When this is over, I will offer my appreciations to
the entire staff."

Grant halted the horse, patted the wet hair on

the mane, reached back, retrieved the crutches from behind him, handed them to an aide, then swung the uninjured leg over the horse's back. He waited while the hands came up, supporting him, easing him down, Rawlins there now, always the terse command, "Don't drop him, by God."

From Stevenson, the boat ride to Bridgeport was uneventful, but it was nothing of a rest for Grant or his staff. The wires were reaching him, details of conditions in Chattanooga, of the progress along the march from the other commanders, Sherman in particular. At the town of Bridgeport, he had been surprised to find General Oliver Howard, whose Eleventh Corps had marched westward under Joe Hooker, part of the grand effort to add to the strength of the forces now facing Braxton Bragg. Howard had been as surprised to see Grant, and Grant had passed through the brief meeting with formal respect, though he knew well that Howard's men had borne the brunt of the disgrace for the disaster at Chancellorsville, the spring before. That disgrace fell on Hooker as well. Grant knew, as did most of the officers in the army, that President Lincoln had put Hooker in command of the Army of the Potomac with a bit of desperation. There had been too many failures by Hooker's predecessors, too many losses on too many battlefields so close to Washington. But Hooker had done no better, and so the War Department had sent him to the usual backwater, the same punishment handed out to Ambrose Burnside for his dismal showing at Fredericksburg. But Burnside showed no fire for redeeming himself, more excuses why the Army of the Ohio was mired in their camps around Knoxville. Hooker at least had made a good show of the long journey, his men now in place for the final leg that would take them directly into Chattanooga. The bulk of Hooker's forces, Oliver Howard's corps included, was stopping short of the town as ordered at first by William Rosecrans. That order was backed up now by George Thomas, and Grant understood the wisdom of that, keeping Hooker's thousands of troops back where the supplies could still reach them. The dismal conditions in Chattanooga were growing more dangerous every day, the single supply line that Grant now traveled hardly suitable for hauling any substantial rations or equipment into the town. The rebels held a strong line all along the south side of the river, completely eliminating that route for supply boats, as well as the wide, flat roads that ran alongside the waterway, which had been so easily passable for wagon trains.

At Bridgeport, the talk had centered on the frustration of the commissary officers, excuses pouring out where none were needed. The men now holding their place in Chattanooga were calling the lone supply route the **Cracker Line,** and Grant thought of that even as he traveled the same trail, that the

few wagons that had survived the treacherous journey would likely have added little to anyone's relief,
even if all the men expected was . . . crackers.

CHATTANOOGA—
OCTOBER 23, 1863

The trail sloped downward, the hills now behind
them. The last leg of the route had offered Grant
a panoramic view of the Tennessee River, the great
hills beyond, where Bragg's army seemed only to
wait. Once they reached the river itself, far downstream from the rebel sharpshooters, Grant had
been relieved to find a pontoon bridge, the last
part of the journey that now took Grant straight
into the town. There, escorts had joined his staff,
guards leading him through the streets. There was
no escaping the mud, just as deep here as it had
been in the hills, and Grant focused more on what
remained of the buildings, homes and businesses
now reduced to skeletons, some of the structures
only a rocky foundation. He expected that, knew
from the reports reaching Bridgeport that the soldiers had made use of the only lumber available,
adding to the defensive positions, creating shelters
for themselves at the expense of the civilians. What
wasn't used for shelter went up in flames, the grim
necessity of keeping men warm. The few homes still
standing held the distinct odor of hospitals, and

Grant passed by one, saw a row of graves, crude wooden headstones, the resting place for men who might have survived Chickamauga, carried back here in ambulances, only to die behind the safety of Rosecrans's defensive lines. There were men outside every hospital, some just sitting in the rain, ragged coats pulled over their heads, others with barely a shirt. By their faces alone, Grant knew they were the sick, whatever plague had spread through the Army of the Cumberland, brought on by a lack of food, of clean water, of clean anything at all. There were civilians as well, small gatherings who watched him pass, none recognizing him, few with any expression beyond the faint hope that what remained of their homes would not be swept away in a firestorm of battle. A few spoke out to him, a counterfeit salute, or a plea for some kind of help. But he knew they saw him as only one more Yankee officer, and Grant ignored that, could do nothing for these people at all. The first priority was his army, the soldiers here, now, who had to be fed. The dead horses were here, too, dragged into piles, still too wet to burn. And once more, with the beasts came the smells, the rain doing nothing to disguise the horror of so many swollen carcasses.

His escort led him down a side street, a wider square, another hospital to one side, more soldiers huddled together on a sheltered porch. They saw him, but still there was no recognition, just another officer moving past, mud covered, soaked through with the misery of the rain.

One man called out to him, "Hey! You got crackers? I'll give you a dollar for an ear of corn!"

The aides moved up beside Grant, as though shielding him from some potential danger, and Grant ignored that, too, knew if that man was hungry, so were they all. He glanced again at Lookout Mountain, invisible in the blackening sky, no sign of Missionary Ridge in the deepening darkness to the east. He thought of Bragg, wondered how many rebels there were, what kind of strength Bragg still brought to the fight. You must be weak, he thought. Or, you have made a mistake, by taking your time. You thought these men would just starve, and then we would simply surrender. No, sir. If there was ever a chance of that, or a chance that this army would run away from you again, there is no chance of that now.

He understood his first priority, saw it in the soldiers who watched him as he passed. I will find the way to feed you, he thought. Give you back the strength. There will be more horses, more guns, more ammunition, and most of all, there will be a great many more troops. He ran through those numbers in his mind, the great strength he commanded, the combined forces Stanton had given him. Bragg had these men licked, he thought. But he gave us the magnificent gift of time. We will not starve. We will rebuild and replenish and reinforce.

If you keep to those heights, if you are content to merely suffer the rain and watch us, you will see it for yourself. And you will have made a far greater mistake. And with God and these men as my witness, I shall make you pay.

He moved into the parlor of the house, a larger room ahead, the heat of the fireplace drawing him closer. In the larger room, officers were mostly standing, their talk growing silent, and he saw one older man, leaning on one end of the mantel, gray in his beard, hard eyes, staring silently at Grant. Grant moved to a chair, sat heavily, felt the relief of the leg relaxing, the fire now close in front of him. The silence was odd, uncomfortable, and Grant looked at the older man now, could see his mass, much taller, taller than Rosecrans, wide and stout, every sign of the man in command.

"General Thomas."

"Yes, sir."

Grant glanced around the room, faces lit by firelight, all watching him, no smiles, no words at all.

"I am here to assume command of this campaign. I trust you are aware of that."

"Yes, sir."

Grant wanted to say more, no one else offering any kind of conversation, no pleasantries, no formal greetings to the man who now commanded them

all. He glanced down, saw a puddle of water forming beneath the chair, welcomed the fire even more,
set the crutches aside, held out his hands, soaking
in the warmth. But the response from the men
made him supremely uncomfortable, as though he
had stomped the life out of some kind of joyous
party. He stared at the fire, stretched his aching leg
out, water dripping from his boots. He considered
who these men were, what they had done, what
they expected of Rosecrans. Unhappy men, to be
sure. Probably loved him, and probably hated what
happened to their army. Now, they have me. Not
sure what I'm supposed to say about that.

He saw one officer to the side, a cigar clamped in
the man's mouth, thought, Yes, a wonderful idea.
He reached in his pocket, saw the mud now on his
hands, a thick smear on his coat, realized there was
mud on every part of his uniform.

"Does someone have a dry cloth?"

Thomas responded with a quick glance to the
side, an aide moving away. But the others kept
their silence, and Rawlins moved up beside him,
knelt low, looked at him with a hint of confusion.
Grant waved him back, said to Thomas, "The decision to remove General Rosecrans did not originate with me. By chance, we were able to meet in
Stevenson. I believe he understands the necessity
for the change."

Thomas nodded slowly, said nothing. Grant
looked at the others, saw the deference to Thomas,

his authority holding everyone to silence. Grant felt the need to stand up now, to say something **meaningful.** But the leg was throbbing, the fire too comforting, and he settled into a boiling annoyance, thought, Is that how this army is to receive my authority? Will they even listen to my orders?

The door opened with a clatter, a gust of chilly wind rippling the fire, and Grant turned in the chair, saw his staff officer, Wilson, and a civilian, realized it was Charles Dana. Wilson surged forward, saluted Grant, then seemed to absorb the odd demeanor of the room, said something to Rawlins, quiet words Grant couldn't hear. Rawlins responded in a whisper, as though even Grant's chief of staff was unable to break the room's strange frigidity. Wilson stepped toward the fire now, said to Thomas, "Sir, General Grant and his escorts are most certainly tired, hungry, and wet. General Grant is in pain. His wagons and equipage are no doubt far behind. Can you not offer the general some dry clothes, socks or slippers perhaps, and can your officers not provide some supper?"

Thomas seemed to come alive, as though the thought had never occurred to him.

"Yes, of course." He looked to one side, to his own aide. "Lieutenant, see to it. There are rations in the cellar. I should have prepared something. I do not know of a suitable house that is yet appropriate for a headquarters, but General Grant is most welcome to bed here."

Grant saw the surge of activity around him, looked up at Wilson, saw a quick nod. He watched as Thomas moved away, taking charge, and Grant began to understand, thought, He's as awkward as I am. Never been in this situation before. Well, me neither. I guess it never occurred to him to be anything more than . . . polite.

Grant looked toward Dana now, the man easing up close to the fire, his hands extended toward the warmth.

"General, it is good to see you again. We have much to discuss."

Grant nodded slowly, couldn't escape Sherman's description of the man from his days in Vicksburg: Stanton's spy. But Grant was here now, had been promoted to this command because Dana had lit that fire. Grant studied the man, saw no subterfuge, no hint of deceit, just a pleasant smile. Dana moved toward him, extended a hand, which Grant accepted, a brief, firm shake.

"Mr. Dana, Secretary Stanton was most gracious to journey out of Washington to meet with me."

"Yes, sir, I am aware. Washington continues to be fully apprised of our situation here. There is great anticipation that your new authority will have a most positive influence."

Dana seemed suddenly self-conscious, looked back toward Thomas, who returned to the mantel, staring ahead, nothing to say. The mood of the room was seeping through Grant now, and he began to see it in the faces, in Thomas himself, the others who gathered to greet Grant by not greeting him at all. Grant stared at the fire again, thought, What did you expect? They're taking a hard look at you, Grant, figuring out just what kind of general you'll make, what you'll expect from them, what kind of changes will come. They know Sherman's coming, they know Hooker's already close, and they can't be too happy that they couldn't get out of this mess by themselves. Not much I can say to that. We'll worry about what happens next . . . tomorrow.

Behind him, men were in motion, a trunk of clothing spread open, Rawlins taking charge, a formal discussion over just what articles were appropriate. Grant knew better than to interfere, made a quick look at Thomas, who was still looking at him. Grant turned again to the fire, suddenly remembered: He outranked me a while back. Now he doesn't. Maybe he thought he should have more, this whole theater. He'll obey orders, but he won't like me giving them. Until I earn his respect. Shouldn't have to do any of that foolishness. Stanton's respect is what matters here. He looked toward Dana again, saw the cordial smile, so very different from Thomas.

"Yes, Mr. Dana. It seems there is much to discuss."

CHAPTER TWELVE

THOMAS

THOMAS'S HEADQUARTERS— CHATTANOOGA— OCTOBER 23, 1863

He hadn't known what to expect of Grant at all. Their only meeting he could recall had come in the aftermath at Shiloh, when Thomas's superior, Don Carlos Buell, had rescued Grant's army from the near destruction they had suffered at the hands of the massive rebel surprise attack. Thomas knew what many were saying, that Buell had done no rescue at all, that after a full day of vicious combat, Grant's army had regained their courage, the officers gathering up their men into some kind of effective fighting force, so that by the second day, victory over the confused and disorganized Confederates was inevitable. That argument had never ceased, those commanders loyal to Grant insisting Buell was simply late to the party, picking up the pieces. Buell and Thomas had a very different take, had chafed mightily under what was becoming the official version of events, the War Department giving the public an unsatisfying blend of the two sides, as though Edwin Stanton, and possibly Abraham Lincoln, chose to walk the fence, neither offending nor glorifying either Grant or Buell. But now Buell was gone, sitting in some office in Indianapolis, "awaiting orders," a sentence imposed on him by Washington for what the public perceived as a string of failures against Braxton Bragg in Tennessee and Kentucky. As Buell fell out of favor in Washington, his command had been offered to Thomas, an opportunity Thomas had refused. He respected Buell, but Thomas had more respect for William Rosecrans, believed that he was the better man for that job. And now Rosecrans was suffering the same fate as Buell, shoved into an official closet, while Washington sought out the next general to toss into the fire. Thomas knew his name was trumpeted about Washington, though he never campaigned for anything beyond the care of his men. But newspapers fueled public opinion, and Thomas wasn't naïve, knew that the War Department might bend to the pressure of all that shouting about Thomas's army-saving stand at Chickamauga. He still downplayed that, hated the nickname now floating about, many of the newspapers hanging the moniker on him of the **Rock of Chickamauga.** The men loved that, of course, saluted him with heavy compliments everywhere he went, more so now that he had been called upon to slip into Rosecrans's shoes. But Secretary Stanton had been praising Thomas a little too loudly for Thomas's comfort, hints that much more was in store for Thomas, should he perform more successfully than his predecessor. What Thomas did not expect was that Grant would get that nod instead, and Thomas couldn't help wondering if Stanton's flowery praise was designed to soften the blow of Grant's promotion, that Thomas had never really been considered for any higher post than he had now. It was the kind of duplicity Thomas had become accustomed to, that every general had his champion in Washington, until he fell on his face, or a better general could be found. Thomas just didn't expect that man to be Grant.

Thomas welcomed the word that serious numbers of reinforcements were pouring toward Chattanooga. The rebel siege had impacted the Federal forces far more drastically than Rosecrans seemed able to handle. Thomas had acted under Rosecrans's orders, had strengthened the defenses close to Chattanooga into an impregnable line, manned by troops who seemed to accept the despair of Bragg's siege with a spirit that surprised even Thomas. Officially the men were on quarter rations, but that was fantasy. Throughout the town, and out on the lone trail that brought the meager supplies, soldiers gathered in hordes, raiding those few wagons that

carried corn for the animals, scrounging the roadway for anything edible that might have jostled off
the wagons into the mud. Some of the teamsters
had hauled their wagons away for good, too frightened by the drawn faces and fierce hunger of the
men who took matters into their own hands, vio-
lently pirating a wagon for themselves, no matter
the cargo. Feeding the army was the highest priority, and Thomas had gone much further than
Rosecrans, working late nights to devise some plan
to relieve the suffering of the men by opening up
a channel, either by water or land, where supplies
might reach them.

There was danger as well from Bragg, a threat
that had seemed to push Rosecrans further into
a state of panic. Bragg's army was holding their
ground on the ridges, on Lookout Mountain, but
Thomas understood that Bragg might move after
all, and not toward Chattanooga. Rosecrans's greatest accomplishment had been the sly maneuver that
had tricked Bragg into abandoning Chattanooga
months before, the feints and jabs that convinced
Bragg that unless he pulled away from the town, and
backed his army into Georgia, Rosecrans was likely
to surround him. The maneuver worked, which
only added to the impact of the failure at Chickamauga, Bragg righting his own ship, shoving the Federal army back to Chattanooga. Now Thomas had
to fear that Bragg would make the same maneuver,
driving his army westward perhaps, beyond Look-

out Mountain, circling up to the west and north of Chattanooga, cutting off the Army of the Cumberland from any supply line at all. Thomas knew the possibilities, that Bragg might also shift northward, threatening Chattanooga from above. Rumors still, birthed by the grandiose claims of rebel deserters that Robert E. Lee himself was on the way, or at least a huge portion of his army, crossing the Appalachian Mountains in a thrust that would obliterate Thomas's command. That panic erupted from the War Department as well, Henry Halleck playing straight into the hands of the rebels by believing the rumor was true. Thomas knew that panic was his worst enemy, that all around him, men were hungry, low on ammunition, burning houses for firewood. No matter how many hordes of rebels might be descending on his camps, if the men couldn't find rations, and quickly, none of that would matter.

Grant's arrival had been a surprise, and not because of the man's new authority. Thomas had watched Grant's entrance with curiosity, his slovenly appearance, crutches and all. There was no dress uniform, no grand show of military formality. In front of the great warm fireplace, Thomas had waited for the ceremony, one of Grant's aides reading some official order, telling Thomas exactly where he ranked, as though Thomas needed to be reminded. He had been caught off guard by Grant's silence, couldn't avoid feeling impressed by Grant's commitment, riding to Chattanooga as quickly as he could, taking the only route open to the Federal forces, and braving the miserable ride with a crippled leg. But the awkwardness had been just that. His reception for Grant and his staff wasn't rooted in disrespect. Thomas simply didn't know what to do.

For the rest of that evening, Thomas and his senior officers had done only what Grant seemed to want, had laid out the specifics of the crisis that surrounded the Army of the Cumberland. Thomas had hoped for more input from Grant himself, what he expected of them, and more, what Grant was adding to this fight. For a long hour, Grant had sat expressionless, and Thomas began to feel a nervous itch, that perhaps Grant was overwhelmed by the task at hand, that what the officers were telling him was just too much for him to absorb. But then there was a change. The officer who stepped up was "Baldy" Smith, the Army of the Cumberland's chief engineer. Smith had offered Grant details of a possible assault on rebel forces that might accomplish two enormous objectives. One would be to push the rebels away from a lengthy portion of the Tennessee River, allowing boat traffic to resume on a route much closer to Chattanooga than they could safely travel now. The second had surprised even Thomas. Smith was convinced that if the Federal strike was energetic enough, it could shove the rebels back far enough from the river to give the men in blue a bridgehead on the far side of the river. It might create the opening they would need, not only to expand the Cracker Line, but to break out of Chattanooga altogether. Then came the greatest surprise of all for Thomas. Grant's entire demeanor abruptly changed, and with each of Thomas's officers completing their reports, Grant suddenly turned inquisitor, ripping through the room with questions, clearly absorbing every detail offered him. If Thomas suspected that Grant's appointment might be little more than a political reward for success at Vicksburg, by the end of the evening, Thomas began to feel that Grant might actually know what he was doing.

NEAR BROWN'S FERRY, ON THE TENNESSEE RIVER— OCTOBER 24, 1863

They eased along on foot, Thomas following up behind Grant, who hobbled close behind Baldy Smith. The staffs had spread out in all directions, alerting the skirmishers who held position on the Federal side of the river. Thomas had done this before, knew the ground, knew that as the engineer, Smith had covered every foot of shoreline along the river, seeking the opportunity to exploit any weakness in the rebel positions.

The rains had mostly stopped, but the mud was

deep and cumbersome, and Thomas watched as Grant struggled, a step at a time, soft grunts from Grant that he most certainly tried to hide. Up ahead, Smith stopped, waited with jumpy impatience, the mind of the engineer already working, designing, picturing what might happen now. Thomas liked Smith, appreciated brilliance when a man knew how to put it to good use. Smith was doing so now. The greatest challenge might be to convince Grant that any plan would work.

William "Baldy" Smith had graduated from West Point two years after Grant, and five after Thomas, and his accomplishments at the Academy had surpassed either one. Smith had graduated fourth in a class of forty-one, had excelled at engineering, immediately earning a position as a professor at West Point, teaching not only engineering but mathematics. In the aftermath of the Federal army's bloody failure at Fredericksburg, Smith's outrage had been equal to anyone who observed Ambrose Burnside's disastrous handling of the battle, but his public calls for Burnside's dismissal had caught the ear of too many in Washington. After Gettysburg, he assisted George Meade's pursuit of Lee's beaten army, but the War Department continued to believe that Smith's tendency toward criticism of his superiors wasn't appropriate. Smith fell back on his considerable talent for engineering, and secured an appointment as the chief engineer for the Army of the Cumberland. Thomas had no real feelings for Smith's temperament one way or the other, but he welcomed the man's expertise. If the Army of the Cumberland were to break Bragg's siege, Thomas was confident that Smith would find the way.

Thomas stepped up close to Smith, only feet from the riverbank, Grant settling into position on the other side. Smith was animated, looked out in both directions, as though searching for something. He pointed straight across the river.

"That's the best place, by far. The gap between Lookout Creek and Raccoon Mountain. The enemy is all over the big mountain, and is probably in force on Raccoon, with people strung out through the valley in between. If we're quick about it, and hit them hard, I believe we can cut off a sizable portion of whoever's troops are on Raccoon. They'll have to withdraw, and take their artillery with them. Once that's accomplished, this entire section of the river, all the way back to Bridgeport, will be in our control."

The man's enthusiasm was usually infectious, but Thomas watched Grant, saw little reaction. Grant smoked a cigar, stared out from under his slouching hat, toward the far side of the river. Behind them, a burst of noise rose up from a low wooded area, something Thomas had heard before. Grant looked that way, said, "What in blazes is that?"

Smith seemed to inflate, pointed back to the thicket behind them. "Sawmill, sir. I made use of a steam engine from a factory in the town, had the men haul it out here, and now, we're cutting planks. It's how we were able to construct the pontoon bridge at the town. We're also in the process of constructing a riverboat. It is expected that the boat could be put to considerable use once this line of passage is opened."

Grant focused on the trees, nothing to see, and Thomas said, "Keeps that whole thing hidden. Rebels may hear it, but they can't tell their artillery where to find it. Doubt they care enough anyway. Nothing dangerous about a sawmill. I've suggested that the captain of the skirmish detachment keep up their chatter about it, maybe inform any curious rebel that the thing is run by civilians. We're so generous, we let Southern workers go about their business. Seems to have worked. So far, no artillery has targeted the place."

He waited for a response from Grant, felt the nagging annoyance again, that Grant was simply observing, no real concept of just what Smith was trying to do. Thomas had his doubts as well, but Smith's enthusiasm for his evolving plan had convinced Thomas that it might be their best hope to open some passageway for feeding the men. If it didn't work, they would be no worse off than they were now. Grant surprised Thomas, pulled a small roll of paper from his pocket, studied it. It was a map, and Smith jumped in, more energy still.

"Excellent, yes. Sir, we're standing . . . here. Western base of a large loop in the river, the loop that encloses Moccasin Point. Downriver, there is a much larger loop that surrounds Raccoon Mountain. The rebels there are penned in even more so than we are here. I have a larger map back at the horse, if you wish to see more detail."

Grant made a small gesture with the cigar. "Nah. I can see just fine. Moccasin Point's to the left. Raccoon Mountain across the way. Rebs all over the place, right?"

Thomas was intrigued again, more curious just what Grant was thinking. After a long moment, Grant said, "How many rebels up there? You sure you're just going to cut them off without somebody over there raising one big ruckus in your direction?"

Smith puffed up again, clearly pleased with himself, looked at Thomas, as though seeking some kind of confirmation. Thomas hesitated, then said, "Well, sir, that's the part of the plan I was hoping you'd agree with. Joe Hooker's downstream, far side of Raccoon Mountain with ten thousand men or more. It was my intention to have him cross the river out that way, march south of the river, move around south of Raccoon Mountain, and make real damn sure those rebels are cut off. If we try to bring Hooker straight in by the same route you took . . . well, I think you know why that might be a bad idea. Could take them two months to get here."

Grant looked at him, the cigar hard in his teeth. "This Rosecrans's idea?"

Thomas was surprised, appreciated that Grant

had at least a flicker of respect for what Rosecrans was trying to do. "Somewhat. He had his hands full with other problems. There was considerable anxiety that Bragg was going to smack us where we sit. I won't apologize for him, sir. Chickamauga changed him. I'd rather not muddy his name any more than Mr. Dana has done already. General Rosecrans didn't deserve to be this army's only scapegoat."

Grant tilted his head. "Your loyalty is admirable, General. I saw all I needed to see in Rosecrans. I do respect the man. Sometimes that isn't enough. And you know, it wasn't solely my decision." Grant looked at the map again, then across the river. "Nope, this operation was your idea. Both of you. Rosecrans didn't say anything about this plan to me, and he would have. General Smith, tell me more."

Smith seemed to dance in place, clearly excited by Grant's willingness to listen. "Sir, if you see that sweep of the river . . . with the enemy removed from Raccoon Mountain, we'll have a clear passage all the way to Kelley's Ford, and from there, it's easy transit to Bridgeport. It means crossing the river three times, but when you study the narrow loops this river makes, pontoon bridges are a far simpler way of drawing a straight line, from our supply depots in Alabama, straight to Chattanooga. Right now, the enemy has guns trained on the river well to the west of here, right up to . . . this point, and probably, sir, right on our position here. Find that rather entertaining, if I may say, sir. Some artillery observer up on that hill is no doubt watching us through his field glasses, wondering why three officers are having this little conversation."

Thomas glanced at Grant's uniform, the unbuttoned coat, still muddy from his long ride. Well, he thought, two officers, anyway. Doubt they'd know who this short fellow is.

Grant pointed the cigar across the river. "Guess those fellows are curious, too."

Thomas could see them clearly now, a squad of rebel skirmishers, maybe two dozen, most just standing in the open, staring back at them. Thomas felt a surge of uneasiness, was suddenly grateful for Grant's lack of pomp with his uniform. He understood now: Crutches or no crutches, this was why Smith insisted they leave the horses behind.

A voice came toward them now, from a cluster of brush a few yards off the riverbank.

"It's all right, sirs. They're just Alabama boys, out for a look-see. All part of the agreement."

Thomas moved back away from the river's edge, saw a hollowed-out opening in the brush, occupied by a man in a dirty blue uniform, his hat cocked to one side.

"So, you think it's good to listen in on what generals have to say? Or are you assuming to be our bodyguard?"

The man seemed impressed at the word, smiled. "Well, that would be mighty fine, sir, but you'uns don't really need nothing of the sort out here. We got what you call a peace treaty with those boys. We don't shoot them, they don't shoot us. Now, if you'uns were to send a whole mess of blue up here, well then, things would change mighty quick. Same goes for them rebs. We see a few dozen scattered about, nobody complains. They do prize our newspapers, and they do smoke some mighty decent tobacco. That's more of our **treaty.** We've done worked us out good swapping arrangements. As long as they don't try to swim a whole bunch of Johnnies over here, we'll keep doing business with 'em. They feel the same way about us."

Thomas saw more of the skirmishers now, specks of blue spread out through the brush line, some peering up from their carefully constructed hiding places. He saw a sergeant farther away, who glanced at Thomas with disinterest, more concerned with lighting his pipe.

Thomas looked to the closest man again, pointed toward the river. "You keep a pretty close watch on them, then?"

"Like I said, sir, they want our newspapers real bad. Must not be no printing presses in Georgia. Our lieutenant does have a partiality for tobacco, so we makes sure he gets his, then we get the rest. So, yes, sir, we watch 'em. Don't quite trust 'em, and sure as the dickens they don't trust us. But, business is business."

Thomas looked back toward Smith and Grant,

Grant studying the map, Smith still offering details. Thomas saw Grant look up, toward the heights across the river, asking questions in a low voice. Thomas looked again at the small gathering of rebels across the river, saw one man waving, a boisterous call.

"Hi yo, bluebelly! You all got any corn over thataway? Maybe some more of that Yankee coffee?"

The man from the bushes emerged now, walked out past Thomas, shouted back to the rebel, "Hey, Josephus! You mind your manners! You want coffee, you talk to me! These boys here got business to do. You know how them officers is!"

Thomas cringed, moved back quickly to the riverbank, as though to grab Grant, pull him away if the musket fire came.

"Nothing to be scared of, sir. A deal's a deal. Unless you're planning to bring a whole passel of our boys out here to stir things up, we'll just go on about our business." The man paused, looked at the other two, seemed more impressed with Thomas. "Um, you fellows wouldn't happen to bring some rations with you? Those boys across the way say they're in just as much of a hurt as we are. A few ears of corn would go a long way in trade, though we might like to keep that for ourselves. We'uns is all mighty parched, sir. Two crackers at dawn. That's all they give us. Maybe you brought along some good old Tennessee corn liquor?"

Thomas looked back to the staff officers, a hand-

ful of them easing forward. He knew they were eyeing the man, all of them knowing how to discipline
a soldier so casual with his commander. But Thomas
caught the eye of his adjutant, Lieutenant Ramsey,
said, "At least one of you has something stronger
in your canteen. Give it to this man." Thomas
looked again to the soldier. "You be generous with
your friends, won't you? We expect you to keep
up your vigilance."

The man looked back at Thomas's staff, a beaming smile. "Yes, sir, that we will do. I always said
you was a real prince, General."

Thomas felt the punch of alarm again, said, "You
know who I am?"

"Oh, yes, sir. General Smith's been out here for
a few days now, drawing up all kinds of maps and
such. I'd be mighty honored if you'd tell me when
it's all gonna blow up."

Thomas felt a strange urge to confide in the man,
something disarming about his words. But the
temptation passed, one eye still watching Grant's
keen interest in what Smith was telling him.
Thomas shook his head.

"We're just out here doing some . . . scouting,
Private. Don't give it another thought."

Ramsey returned now, on foot, the canteen held
gingerly, a hint of regret on Ramsey's face. "Not
sure who this one belongs to, sir. The others . . .
just water, sir. This one must have been a mistake,
for certain."

Thomas ignored the man's embarrassment, said, "We'll discuss that later, Lieutenant. Since I doubt any one of you will lay claim to these spirits, you will give it to this man here. He has an unenviable duty, and deserves our gratitude."

The soldier took the canteen with a quick grateful bow, then looked again at Thomas. "I knew it. Dang it all, I knew it. Much obliged, sir, but I know what this means. You'd a not paid a bit of attention to us'ns out here if it weren't about to get hot. Trouble afoot, that's for sure."

Thomas felt the need to pull away from this man, pointed to the brush. "You go on and share that with your friends, Private. And keep your eyes sharp."

The man made a quick short bow, no salute, backed away to the other skirmishers, who were gathering quickly, aware of their good fortune. Thomas moved closer to Grant, who kept his stare across the river. Grant glanced at Thomas, kept his voice low.

"We can discuss details tonight. But I like this plan a great deal. Mighty risky, if the rebels don't cooperate."

Thomas looked at Smith, who held tight to his broad smile. Grant rolled the map up, stuffed it in his coat, and Smith said, "Pontoon bridge will go right here, sir. Already got the lumber cut. That gap in those far hills, as you can see, is straight across. Should make for easy going."

Grant looked at Thomas, tossed the stub of his cigar into the river, said, "No such thing, General. General Thomas, I wish to go over your thoughts on the specifics of this operation. Clearly, this is not the place for a council, unless you think we should engage some ideas with your skirmishers, or perhaps those fellows across the way?"

Thomas studied Grant's expression, a hint of a smile, something he had never seen before. "By all means, sir. General Smith has been most thorough. He can go over the smallest details at my headquarters."

Grant looked again to the river, hoisted the crutches up under his arms. "Yes, by all means. General Smith, I understand your theory that supplies travel best when hauled in straight lines. I commend you." He looked at Thomas now, another hint of a smile. "Engineers do love their straight lines."

Grant began to hobble back toward the staffs, and Thomas waited for him to move away, Smith trailing close behind Grant, still with bouncing enthusiasm. Thomas looked again to the river, the hills beyond, the brush lines where the men on both sides had turned this war into some kind of game. He moved away from the water's edge, saw the man with the canteen, the cluster of blue shirts emerging farther along the brush line. The sergeant was in charge now, making certain each man received his fair share of the precious liquor. Thomas moved past them, the horses gathered farther back in the trees, saw Grant's aides preparing to hoist him up to the saddle. Thomas couldn't ignore the skirmisher, the lack of discipline, so many men completely honest about their casual contact with the enemy. There should be discipline for such things, he thought. Well, perhaps another time. The skirmisher's words rolled into him now, **trouble afoot.** Yes, young man, I'm afraid so. But if you want something more than a pair of crackers for your breakfast, a push right here, across this river, might open the door.

CHAPTER THIRTEEN

BRAGG

"I think I ought to go . . ."
(General William Mackall, to his wife,
October 1863)

Bragg was shocked when Mackall resigned, the man he believed most faithful to him suddenly announcing that he could no longer serve as Bragg's chief of staff. There had been little hint that Mackall was discontented, but Bragg could see from the carefully laid out protocol that Mackall's decision had been planned for some time. On October 16, Mackall himself informed Bragg that he had sought, and been granted, a transfer, and had accepted a new position on the staff of Bragg's superior, Joseph Johnston. There had been no communication from Johnston about the matter, something that punched hard at Bragg, one more senior commander who seemed to enjoy adding to Bragg's torment. As much as Bragg had been surprised by Mackall leaving him, he could not be all that surprised that Mackall's next move was higher up the chain of command.

But the more Bragg pondered Mackall's decision, the more convinced he became that Mackall had planned this maneuver to coincide with the plot the field generals had hatched, to toss Bragg from his command. Bragg conceded that Mackall was a clever, intelligent man, and by distancing himself from the conspirators, Mackall might have believed that Bragg would never suspect his true motives. Now that Jefferson Davis had so completely endorsed Bragg, and crushed the obvious conspiracy, Bragg convinced himself that Mackall had no choice but to quietly slip away, thus keeping his reputation intact.

The staff officers around Bragg seemed to share serious regrets about Mackall's decision. But Bragg took that for duplicity, that Mackall's absence had created a vacancy that every staff officer would strive to fill, the honored place as Bragg's chief of staff. Bragg pondered that decision carefully, sifting through the qualifications, and especially the loyalties, of the men, most prominent among them Colonel George Brent, a lawyer and well-known Virginia politician. Bragg had seen little to fear from Brent, studied the man carefully for any hints that Brent might be yet another conspirator in Bragg's command. The primary difference between Mackall and Brent was experience in the field leading troops. Brent had very little. Though Brent would assume many of Mackall's duties, Bragg stopped short of promoting the man to chief of staff. After Mackall's sudden departure, Bragg made the decision to do without a chief of staff at all.

The fear of another uprising against his authority wound through Bragg's daily routine, aggravated by the physical ailments that continued to plague him. For several weeks after Chickamauga, Bragg had kept his morale high by touring the camps of the men in the field. Their occasional cheers energized him, eased the burdens of a command that called for more attention to his own generals than any problems caused by the Yankees.

MISSIONARY RIDGE— OCTOBER 25, 1863

He rode over the crest of the ridge seeking a remedy for the twisting torment in his stomach, would move past the various camps, seeking some kind of positive response from the troops, the boisterous salutes that inspired him, erased the fears of what kinds of conversations were happening in the various headquarters. He passed through Hardee's corps, had no interest in meeting with Hardee, or any of his commanders. He had come for what he saw now, dozens of campfires spread out just back of the ridgeline. Men were in clusters around each fire, the chill of the breezy morning drawing them to the warm places. He pulled himself taller in the saddle, his aides strung out behind him, made a cursory inspection of an artillery battery, the same big guns in the same dug-out hollows he had seen before. Along the crest of the ridge, men were at work, shovels tossing muddy dirt to the front, strengthening still the lines of rifle pits Bragg believed they would never need. But the labor kept the men busy, constructive work overseen by the engineers. Down below, on the steep hillside that faced Chattanooga, the same kind of work went on, rifle pits and barricades that made the great ridge an impregnable natural fortress. At the base of the hill, more work, more rifle pits, and he moved the horse down that way, halted, peered over a stout rock outcropping, could see the activity far below. Excellent, he thought. This will inspire them, far more than parade ground drills. This is labor that strengthens the men as it strengthens this entire army.

He glanced upward, a blanket of thick gray clouds, but the rains had stopped, the fog lifting, even the peak of Lookout Mountain clearly visible. He marveled at that, the natural formation that added so much to the invincibility of his army. He thought of Hardee, glanced back up along the ridge, dreaded seeing him, but he couldn't avoid respect for the man's tactical skills. Hardee's textbook was used even now by officers on both sides, and

Bragg stared again at Lookout Mountain, thought, Not even an expert like Hardee would ever hope to have such ground as this. And the foolishness of the enemy who handed it to us . . . that requires no textbook to appreciate the magnitude of such a mistake. By God, we ripped every advantage away from those boys in that town. Now we shall wait with patience and vigilance. And if those fellows don't run away, then we shall bag them up and ship them off wrapped by a neat ribbon, a gift for the prison camps of the Confederacy, courtesy of Braxton Bragg.

He waved his hand, the signal to the aides to follow as he pushed the horse back up to the top of the ridge, then over, away from Chattanooga. He could smell the smoke from the fires, a gray haze that drifted past him, lingering in the tops of the few remaining trees. There were stumps scattered about, the men taking down most of the timber for whatever they required, most likely serving as the crude shelters he could see now. The sight dug at him for a long moment, the utter lack of tents, no more than one or two per regiment, manned by their most senior commands. He led the aides through a boggy mud hole, toward a cluster of campfires, thought, It is one more cross we must bear. The enemy can have their canvas. We have the strength of our cause. Nothing in Hardee's textbook can defeat a soldier who loves his bayonet. And that is why we will prevail. And that is why I have been granted the power to remove those who would block our way.

He couldn't keep the anger away, the churn in his stomach rolling over, fueled by the nagging controversies that still poured toward him from his generals. Most all of the key participants in the plot against him were gone, assigned officially to new posts. The infuriating exception was Longstreet, who had been assigned to the peak of Lookout Mountain.

He rode near the largest campfire, saw a dozen men huddled close, passing around what seemed to be the very emaciated carcass of a chicken. They barely acknowledged him, not what he expected, and he stopped the horse, waited for the usual recognition. One man caught his eye, a dirty face, rags of a coat, the man struggling to chew whatever it was they were eating.

"Afternoon, General. I'd ask you to join in with us here, but there ain't much to go around."

Bragg kept to the horse, saw the others turning toward him, a few casual nods. "What exactly is that?"

The first man spoke, held up a small bone. "That'd be goose, sir."

Bragg turned toward his aides, pointed to the man. "I do not recall the commissary issuing goose meat to these men." He spoke to them all now. "Who is your company commander?"

The men continued to eat, one man speaking up

through whatever remained in his mouth. "Today, sir, I'd say it's Captain Bird."

"And does Captain Bird approve of you men plundering the local farms for your rations?" Bragg was angry now, said to his closest aide, "Find this Bird fellow. Report him to his regimental commander. I won't have this."

"Uh, sir?" The voice came from closer to him, the near side of the fire. "I'm Corporal Keene. Captain Bird is . . . uh . . . presently unavailable. Not sure when he'll be around again."

There was a low laugh through the crowd of men, and Bragg didn't get the joke, but their insubordination was punching his anger to a raw boil.

"On your feet! You will address your commanding general with a proper military attitude! You men were trained by your officers, and are most certainly veterans. On your feet now!"

The group complied, some of them still chewing, moving together, forming a crooked line.

Bragg saw more men in the distance, another fire, his voice carrying, those men rising, an officer emerging from a leafy shelter, moving quickly toward him. Bragg held tight to the horse's reins, the horse protesting, a slow turning dance, and Bragg felt unsteady, realized the horse might stumble. He swung one leg over, leapt down, his boots sinking into soft mud. He wiped furiously, the mud only worse, in full temper now, and the officer was there, stopped, threw up a crisp salute.

"Sir! Captain Winkler, Company D."

Bragg ignored the salute, saw more officers coming toward him, more dugouts and shelters farther away. He suddenly felt enormously satisfied, his anger inspiring men to their discipline as soldiers. He stood with his hands on his hips, waited for the handful of officers to gather close, then said to them all, "I am witness to the depraved disregard for those good Southern civilians who, by no fault of their own, are in proximity to this conflict. It is very clear to me that these men here have availed themselves of some farmer's private property, by killing a goose that most certainly is not a part of our commissary. I will not tolerate raiding and plundering of the innocent. I would like an explanation. Where is Captain Bird?"

There was a ripple of giggles along the line of men, and Bragg saw questions on the faces of the officers. One of them stepped forward, another young captain.

"Sir, I am not aware of a Captain Bird in this regiment."

Bragg saw the scattered bones around the fire, heard the low laughter, saw the men looking away, suddenly got the joke.

"I believe you are correct. These men find it amusing to demonstrate their lack of respect for this command by toying with their commanding general. I will not tolerate this. So now, two offenses have been committed here. Captain, other than the remains of some poor farmer's personal property here, who might be the true commander of this company?"

The first captain spoke up now. "That would be myself, sir. Captain Herman Winkler."

Bragg looked at the man, older, a scar on his cheek, the sleeve of his coat ripped at the elbow. Bragg studied him, saw a grim stare, the hard look of a man who has seen the fight.

"Captain Winkler, since I was elevated to command of this department last year, it has been my singular goal to rid this army of malcontents and ne'er-do-wells. In the past, this army suffered often from a complete lack of discipline, and it seems, that curse has not been lifted. Despite my most dedicated intentions, these men feel no hesitation in stealing from the citizens they are here to protect. I must assume their behavior is even worse than that, since of course, a commanding general only sees his men in two instances: when they fight, and when they rest. Since there is no fighting at present, and these unceasing rains have made rest difficult for us all, I must therefore conclude that these men are engaged in nefarious activity, beyond the scope of my orders."

"Sir, these men—"

"I did not ask you to respond, Captain."

From the line of soldiers, one man spoke up. "Sir, with all respects, sir, we ain't had so much as a corncob in the last two days."

"What are you talking about?"

The captain waved the man into silence, took a step toward Bragg. "Sir, you may remove me from this command if you wish it, but it is the God's honest truth. If this army's got any commissary wagons at all, we haven't seen them up here. Major White told me that the kitchens are all set up well behind the lines, and by the time any of that food gets anywhere close to this hill, it's grabbed up. Begging your pardon, sir, but I have to agree with the major. He heard the same from our brigade commander, General Manigault. Someone's not paying much mind to these boys who are out here looking right down on the enemy. If it weren't for the good flow of a spring back down in those woods there, we wouldn't even have decent water to drink."

Bragg pressed his hands hard into his hips, fought to keep his composure, wanted to launch a fist at this man. "I did not grant you permission to speak with such disregard for officers over which you have no control, commissary or otherwise. I shall speak with General Manigault myself about this. But you had best tell Major White to use his mouth to positive effect, instead of passing along that kind of injurious lie. This army is well fed, and well equipped. Any sacrifice we make up on this line will be made worthwhile by the inevitable victory we shall enjoy over the enemy. Captain, I know miscreants when I see them. These men . . . **your** men have ignored my regulations, and have stolen private property. Do I punish them . . . or you?"

"Sir, with all respects to you, it is no lie. There are no rations to speak of on this ridgeline, at least in this position. The last we saw of anything from the commissary, they sent us spoiled beef and meal rife with worms. But even then, sir, there wasn't enough for a half pound per man. If other units have sufficient rations, then someone has chosen this one unit for starvation. I cannot speak for any other command, sir, but I do not believe that is the case. These are good South Carolina men, and they've never run from a fight. If you must inflict punishment on this particular company, I will accept the responsibility for feeding my men."

Bragg looked at the faces watching him, no smiles now, no one else speaking out. He looked back to his aides, saw the young Lieutenant Scruggs, said, "Lieutenant, you will determine just how much a goose should be worth, and have Captain Winkler make restitution to the farmer."

"Yes, sir."

Bragg mounted the horse, saw another salute from the captain, the man's eyes looking away. Bragg pulled on the horse's reins, the horse turning clumsily in the mud, and he called back to his aides.

"I have had enough of this. We shall return to my headquarters. Next time I wish to ride among the men, find me a unit who understands respect."

NAIL HOUSE—
BRAGG'S HEADQUARTERS—
MISSIONARY RIDGE—
OCTOBER 26, 1863

"I'm afraid it's true, sir. The commissary reports that rations are being issued with all due efficiency, but that the preparation areas are well to the rear."

"Who's responsible for that?"

Brent seemed nervous, looked to the man beside him, neither man willing to speak out. Bragg sat back, nodded.

"Yes, so I see. You do not wish to incriminate General Mackall. I have seen many details that are lacking since Mr. Mackall's departure. Certainly he knew of his shortcomings, and chose to leave this post before his perfidy was discovered. Well, gentlemen, this matter shall be handled straight from this office. I have struggled mightily with Colonel Northrup, who holds court over his commissary supply from some glorious palace in Richmond. Not even the president seems able to contradict Northrup's treasonous lack of concern for this army. All I hear about is General Lee, about the most pressing requirements of the Army of Northern Virginia. Lee requires cattle, Lee requires railcars, Lee must have the corn. And for what? Lee sacrifices his army in the worst defeat this nation has suffered since the start of the war, and so he engenders sympathy. Here, we achieve victories, and are ignored!"

Brent pointed to a paper on Bragg's desk. "Sir, that letter from Major Cummings convinces me that your assessment is accurate. There are stores aplenty in the warehouses in Atlanta, but Major Cummings answers directly to Colonel Northrup, and the orders coming from Richmond are unequivocal. The majority of the supply trains are being sent to Virginia. And no order from this department seems to change that."

"I should like to meet Colonel Northrup on the field of battle. Two sabers. It would be a brief affair. Major Cummings has informed me of his frustrations. I do not expect him to remain at that post much longer. I have written directly to the adjutant general, Mr. Cooper, explaining our predicament, and thus far, even General Cooper seems to fear the almighty authority of Colonel Northrup. If I did not believe my presence was essential here, I would go to Richmond myself." Bragg pondered that for a moment. "Might do so anyway. Someone is keeping the president in the dark on this matter, and no one in Richmond seems immune from the magnificent charms of General Lee. Well, there is a good way, the only way to gain their attention. We shall destroy the enemy in Chattanooga." He glanced at the lone window that faced Lookout Mountain. "It would be most useful to our cause if we did not have General Lee's **favorite boy** sitting out there seeking to steal a portion of that glory."

Bragg stood, fought through a searing headache

that had plagued him since that morning. He moved to a map pinned to the wall, a broad sketch of eastern Tennessee.

"What have we heard from Knoxville?"

Brent moved up beside him, pointed. "Sir, General Stevenson is en route, and very soon, he should sit astride any good route that Burnside could use to inconvenience us."

"But Stevenson is not strong enough to clear the enemy out of Tennessee."

Brent glanced at the other aides, no one disagreeing with Bragg. "No, sir. Most likely not. He can hope to slow the enemy's progress, should General Burnside attempt to move this way."

"Then, that is a situation we must confront with vigor. And the solution to our difficulties is right in front of us. Or rather, just to the west of us. I will prepare a letter to the president, expressing in the most definite terms, that the enemy's presence in Knoxville is a threat we cannot ignore. I will suggest that as rapidly as they can be put to the march, that General Longstreet's corps strengthen the meager forces now protecting us from the enemy's position in Knoxville."

The others kept silent, and Bragg was suddenly overjoyed, moved to the view of the great mountain. Marvelous, he thought. This is a victory for everyone concerned, even the president.

Brent spoke slowly, choosing his words. "Sir, General Longstreet commands a sizable portion of our strength. If he is sent off, we will be forced to thin our position, spreading the remaining troops across to Lookout Creek. We could become vulnerable to any sudden move by the enemy."

"What kind of move? The only activity we have seen over there is a change of command. I doubt very seriously that General Thomas, so new to his post, is in any position to launch offensive action in this direction. If anything, he is contemplating a retreat. Should that occur, we can strike his flanks with cavalry, and possibly cut him off on the road to Nashville. General Wheeler is fully capable of striking the enemy as required. We do **not** require General Longstreet." He returned to the chair, the headache blissfully erased. "Leave me now. I must write the president."

The officers obeyed, filing out of his room. He turned again toward Lookout Mountain, a hint of fog settling across the center of the great rocky mass, as though separating it in two great pieces.

He was certain of the information they had received from a handful of prisoners. Rosecrans was gone and George Thomas was now in his place. Thomas's stout defense at Chickamauga had inspired talk not only among the Federals, but in Bragg's army as well. He is a good tactician, Bragg thought. But he has one fatal flaw, a disability that he cannot overcome. He is after all, a Virginian, and so, in his heart, he knows he has betrayed his cause. It is no different than John Pemberton, another foolish man who believes he can pledge his loyalty as easily as he would choose which shirt he will wear. Pemberton's heart was not in his fight at Vicksburg, and Thomas will be no different. No, he will not strike us. He will defend, he will maneuver, and very soon, he will bend to pressure from Washington, and he will save his army by attempting to withdraw. And when he abandons his carefully strengthened earthworks, and strings his forces out on every road to the north, we shall crush him piecemeal.

He turned in the chair, retrieved a blank piece of paper from a drawer to one side. He began to think, forming the words, a knock on his door breaking through his thoughts.

"By God, what is it?"

Brent was trailed by a rough-looking cavalryman, an officer Bragg didn't know. The horseman followed Brent into the office without hesitation, and Bragg was annoyed, sputtered a curse, but Brent spoke up, his hands out in front of him.

"Sir! This is Lieutenant Garland, of General Wheeler's first brigade. Lieutenant, make your report."

There was an authority to Brent's words that pushed Bragg back in the chair, a gravity to the horseman that Bragg couldn't help respecting.

"Sir, my men have been in position keeping watch on the enemy's supply route across Waldron's Ridge. I have observed personally the overland march of a significant squad of horsemen, a battalion of guards escorting a man that, by all reckoning, sir, we believe to be General Grant."

"Grant? Grant has come here?"

"Yes, sir. With all respects, sir, we have men posted near the Yankee depot at Stevenson, and near the water at Bridgeport. The talk there is considerable, and I do not believe the enemy is attempting to mislead us in any way. They are claiming that General Grant has been given command of this theater, and that he is now in Chattanooga. We do know that General Sherman is en route through northern Mississippi with a considerable force."

The man was breathing heavily, aware of the gravity of his report. Brent said, "Sir, I do not wish to dismiss this man's word, but how can we be certain that Grant has come?"

Bragg was smiling now, felt rejuvenated, a surge of excitement he had not felt in a very long time. "I do not doubt you, Lieutenant. Not at all. It is perfectly reasonable. Washington understands the value of Chattanooga, as they understand the force now threatening their precious Army of the Cumberland."

"But, sir, we should seek further confirmation."

The horseman seemed to bristle at Brent, said, "Sir, I witnessed the man from no more than a hundred yards' distance."

Bragg rubbed his chin. "Fancy dress uniform? Brass band following close behind him?"

The man seemed puzzled. "No, sir. Nothing

like that. He was barely in a uniform at all. Plain dressed, no band, certainly. His staff was carrying him through the worst holes, 'cause of his leg. He was injured, it appeared."

Bragg smiled now, looked at Brent. "This man knows what he saw, Colonel. And so do I. Grant hasn't changed since Shiloh, and it makes perfect sense that those biddies in Washington would send him here." Brent was puzzled, and Bragg kept the smile. "Don't you see? I expected this. The enemy has only told us what we already believed. This is the place where they are most afraid. What we do here could turn this war completely in our favor. A great victory here could be the first step in driving the enemy completely out of Tennessee, cutting him off in Alabama and Mississippi, leaving him a single option. They will be forced to retreat to the Gulf Coast. I can imagine that with perfect clarity, Colonel. They will scramble in panic on board their great warships, desperate to survive, as we rid this country of their noxious stain."

He saw Brent's stare, the man still not seeming to understand the magnitude of the lieutenant's report.

"Sir, will you still be writing the president? Certainly, Richmond should be informed of this turn of events."

For a single moment, Bragg had forgotten the itching torment, the aggravation driven into him every day by the presence of James Longstreet.

"Oh yes, Colonel. Richmond shall know exactly what I intend to do, and exactly who faces us across the way. But what we do here, we will do with this army alone. Longstreet came riding down here with every expectation that he would assume full command, **my** command, or that he would be independent of any authority. Well, on that I shall oblige him. Once he marches away from here, and assumes his new position at Knoxville, he may perform exactly as he wishes. And he will no longer be my problem."

CHAPTER FOURTEEN

BAUER

BRIDGEPORT, ALABAMA—
OCTOBER 26, 1863

"You see him? Right above that rock."

Bauer didn't answer, felt his hands shaking, shouted silently at himself to calm down. The target was moving in every direction. The musket was jiggling in his hands, his grip sweaty.

"You got him?"

"Yes."

He said nothing else, could feel the small crowd of men behind him, eyes following his, small voices distracting him, whispers and taunts. He kept his eye focused down the barrel of the musket, knew some of the men had bet against him, were trying to break his concentration, while the others, the ones who dared to risk a dime or a dollar, were only adding tension to his aim. He closed his eyes, tried to relax, opened again, blinked, focusing, the target still dancing through the iron sights, but slower now, less movement; his hands were more settled. He blocked out the sounds behind him, had done this so many times, his careful routine, strengthening and narrowing his focus. He slid the musket back and forth a few inches along the soft padding of the leather cushion. His hands pulled the musket tighter against his shoulder, anchoring it firmly, but not too firmly. The voices still engulfed him, men cheering him on with intense nervousness, a part of the game. They were testing him, after all, no surprise to Bauer. He was the outsider, the stranger, the only man among all these Pennsylvanians who was no longer a part of the volunteers.

"Come on, boy, take him down!"

The voice came from the sergeant, close behind him, Bauer catching the hint of whiskey on the man's breath. He didn't respond, kept his stare down the long barrel of the musket, found the target again, a wide gray hat, the man's head and chest clearly visible, something small and black blocking the man's face. Field glasses. Looking at what? Me?

His own voice took command now, calming him from inside, soft, intense, erasing the chatter from the others, his eyes and his brain settling onto the one place that mattered, on the head and the chest of the man in gray. He eased his finger into the trigger guard, then slowly, carefully wrapped his finger around the trigger, a minuscule space between his skin and the steel, putting no pressure on the trigger at all. His cheek rested on the smooth wood, and now he was alone, nothing else around him, staring out toward a far distant speck of color. Just me, just you. He spoke silently to the man in the distance, too far to see details of the man's face, assumed from the uniform it had to be an officer. The field glasses appeared to drop, the man jostling just a bit, and Bauer hesitated, thought, A horse. He's sitting on a horse. Definitely an officer. The black spot came up again, the field glasses obscuring the man's head completely, nothing visible but the hat, the small patch of gray, the man's upper body. Half hidden, he thought. Thinks he's safe, protected by rocks. Thinks he's **clever.**

Bauer centered himself on his own breathing, slow, steady, pushed his shoulders downward, a slight adjustment, to raise the iron sights, just above the man's head. Four hundred yards, he thought. At least. Raise it a bit more. He was aiming higher now, two feet, three feet above the hat, and the voice in his brain grew quiet, no other sound reaching him, everything coming together into his eyes, and again, the slight touch of cold steel at the tip of his finger, his lungs emptying slowly, no movement at all.

The musket fired now, surprising him, as it always should. The smoke blew out in a thick white cloud, and Bauer let out the rest of the deep breath, didn't move, felt the jarring shock in his shoulder, his cheek. It was the worst moment, always, the agonizing seconds when you couldn't see anything, but behind him, the others were scattered out beyond the smoke, one man with field glasses of his own, the smoke now giving way.

"Hooeee! You see that? He fell like a sack of flour!"

The men were shouting now, moving in close, a hard slap on Bauer's back, and he closed his eyes, another piece of his routine, a quick, silent **Thank you.** He didn't have to see the target to know what he had done. The sights hadn't moved. The musket was aimed perfectly; the ball should have thumped straight into the man's chest. And it did.

"Dangdest shootin' I ever seen! I give it to you, Dutchman. Didn't think anybody'd be that dang good."

The others joined in the grand congratulations, more slaps, Bauer opening his eyes now, the smell of the powder lingering. He rolled over, sat up, allowed himself to enjoy this part of it, the approval of the others, all the blue coats, smiling faces, shaking heads. Back behind the men was a cluster of officers he hadn't noticed before, observing silently. Nearby, a handful of men were paying off their bets to the winners, those who believed in him, happier still. He rested his arms across his knees, said to the man with the field glasses, "Keep a good watch. They might have somebody out there send a ball this way. There's some good shooters among those boys."

The sergeant stood over him, stared out toward the distant rocky hill. "Not like you, Dutchman. Ain't never seen a reb could take a man down at that distance. They's cavalry, anyway. Do their work with a saber, all that whoopin' and hollerin'. Been watching us for a week, mostly up in those rocks. Nobody's messed with 'em until now. I bet they haul tail out of here. They done lost one of their big brass. Hee-hee."

It had surprised him as much as it had the officers, as much as his friend Sammie Willis, that Bauer had a serious talent for marksmanship. Once the fight at Vicksburg had settled into the dull routine of a siege, it was the sharpshooters who kept it interesting, trading wickedly accurate strikes into the lines of their enemy, splitting skulls and breaking ribs of careless men who never knew they were being watched from so far away. It was a talent that officers appreciated, as much as they feared it, every man on a horse very aware that, out there, someone might be watching **him.**

Bauer looked now toward the cluster of officers, a Stars and Stripes hanging limp on a flagpole, held by a young aide. They seemed only to be curious, Bauer's display offering a moment's entertainment. He didn't seek that, had only let on about his gift through the paperwork he had gone through, questions about his experience, his talents, whether he could cook or sew or draw maps. Most of the army's training emphasized massed formations, firepower in great quantities. Marksmanship was a skill the army rarely counted on. It had been Lieutenant Crane, the adjutant to Colonel Malloy, who had pushed Bauer to add that detail to any answers the army hoped to hear. Bauer had no idea if marksmanship would help his application to the regulars, or whether it might persuade the Wisconsin officers to keep him close, to refuse his request to enlist in the regular army. But, then, after an agonizing week, the papers had come back with the army's approval, and with that, his orders:

The Army of the United States hereby orders Private Fritz Bauer to report to 18th United States Regulars, 2nd Battalion, Captain Henry Haymond, Commanding. Assignment to Company C, Captain Samuel Willis, Commanding. Orders to be carried out by 1 November, 1863, after which time, Private Fritz Bauer will be considered Absent Without Permission.

He had been overjoyed and terrified. The question of just how and where he was to report had been handled by the adjutants, and for now, Bauer was an unofficial part of the 109th Pennsylvania, part of the Twelfth Army Corps, which, by the rumors that flew through the camps, was about to move toward Chattanooga. All he was doing was hitching a ride.

The crowd around him spread out, men returning

to whatever mundane task was at hand. Some kept their gaze on the far rocks, and Bauer smiled at that. Sure, he thought. Brave men with big talk. But rebs can shoot, whether any of you believe that or not.

He heard hoofbeats now, saw two dozen horsemen galloping out from the far end of the rows of tents, realized they were cavalry themselves, someone's thoughtful notion that if there was a dead rebel officer out there, somebody ought to take a look. I bet that bunch is long gone, he thought. Took their corpse with them. He caught himself, didn't like to think about that. A man. No, it was a rebel, a target. Gray hat, field glasses, gray coat. That's all. It was the same dance Bauer performed often, erasing any image of a man's face, never close enough to see the expression, the look in the eye. There was no purpose to it, no need to think about the target being anything but.

The cluster of officers began to scatter, but a small group rode toward him, the Stars and Stripes coming along. Bauer was still sitting, suddenly realized they were coming straight at **him.** He stood quickly, musket planted by his side, the instinct of training. He focused on the officer leading the way, a huge man on a massive horse, the man's face adorned with the largest beard Bauer had ever seen. Bauer glanced to one side, the sergeant still there, coming to attention, a hard whisper.

"We must be in for it now. He never comes out here."

Bauer responded through closed teeth. "Who?"

"Shut up."

The horsemen were close now, stopped, and the sergeant tossed up a formal salute, Bauer doing the same. He looked past the big man, saw a familiar face, Captain Gimber, the regimental commander. But Gimber stayed back, seemed to know his place.

The older man stayed up on the horse, towering above Bauer, casting a shadow that blocked out the daylight.

"You make a habit of that, Private?"

Bauer ran several responses through his head. What'd I do this time? But there was something deadly serious in the question, not the time for humor.

"I have been known to, sir. Once in a while."

"Where?"

"Vicksburg, mostly, sir. I served Wisconsin regiments since Shiloh. Been in a few scraps."

"Sharpshooter, then?"

"At Vicksburg, yes, sir."

The big man leaned low, held out his hand, pointed to the musket. "Mind if I take a look?"

Bauer reached down, handed it to the man butt-first, saw now the shoulder straps on the man's blue coat, the embroidered star of a brigadier general. The captain spoke now, pointing to Bauer.

"We'd love to keep him, sir. But he's not ours. Just along for the march, at the request of General

McPherson's people last week. I put it in the duty log, sir."

The larger man examined the musket, sighted down the barrel, handed it back to Bauer. "Regular issue. Nothing fancy. Thought you might have had one of those English rifles the rebels are using. Whitworths. I wish we had a pile of 'em, but they're pretty scarce, pretty expensive. Appears you don't require one. Nice shooting, son." He looked at the captain now. "My adjutant has the duty log, Captain. I've got more things to worry about right now." He looked again at Bauer. "I'm General Geary, son. This is my division. I knew you weren't one of ours, from your hat. Regular army, right?"

"Yes, sir. Just enlisted. I was ordered to your unit, to make the march east. Transferred over from the Seventeenth Wisconsin volunteers."

Bauer stopped himself, thought, He doesn't care a whit for your life story. Geary looked out toward the distant rocks.

"Yep. Good shooting, Private." Geary studied the hat. "Eighteenth Regulars, is it?"

"Yes, sir."

"You'll make somebody happy out there. But don't take it for granted. Sharpshooting can be the safest duty in the army. Sit back where it's all cozy, and lay those rebels out one at a time."

"Thank you, sir."

Geary looked down at him, a grim stare. "Not a compliment, son. Most of these boys will never know what it feels like to kill a man, not unless they stick a bayonet through a man's chest. I've seen volleys of a thousand muskets blow through a brigade front, and watched fewer than a dozen men hit. Some say it's instinct, that a man won't purposely aim to hit another man if he can help it. Not sure I believe that. Rather think it's poor training. They don't teach these boys anything about shooting. Where'd they train you to shoot so well?"

"Didn't, sir. It just . . . came to me. Didn't even much hunt when I was a boy."

"Hmm. Well, I'll tell you something about your particular skill, son. Unlike most of these boys here, when **you** hit a man, you know it, you watch him fall, you have time to watch his buddies gather around. You **feel** it, son. At that moment, you're the most alone you'll ever be. You kill a man like that, there's no place to hide it. I hope you can live with it. Some can't." Geary paused, pointed out to the rocks. "Who was that fellow over there?"

"I don't know, sir. Didn't think about it. Maybe an officer."

"Oh, he was a cavalry officer, no doubt. Stood up there in those rocks like he was surveying the whole world. They've been watching us for a while. I sent those horsemen to check out what they might have left behind, maybe find out who they were. But that's not your business, and you best keep it that way. In a few days, that officer's children will find out they lost their daddy. A piece of advice, son. Don't you ever go looking for prizes. Leave that alone. I was at Gettysburg. Somebody just like you killed John Reynolds, maybe the best commander in this army. Real **trophy** that was. But if that reb was smart, he didn't ask who he shot down, didn't have a bunch of boys like these slapping his backside. You start looking for trophies, parading yourself like some kind of hero, you start finding out the names of who you killed, things like that . . . it'll change you. You'll lose that aim, that steady hand. Make you as worthless as the freshest greenhorn here."

Bauer was beginning to dislike this man intensely. Geary sat back in the saddle, still looked at Bauer.

"We're marching out of here pretty quick. They're giving us a job to do. Happy to have a good eye along with us, even if it's only a few days. Keep sharp, son. The rest of you . . . learn from this man. More aim, less caterwauling. You can crow about all the rebels you killed when you go home. Nobody'll believe you anyhow. And they'll be right. Captain, let's ride. No time for this."

Geary turned his horse, the color bearer close behind him, the horses all moving away. Bauer felt the musket heavy in his hands, felt a gloom from Geary's words.

Beside him, the sergeant said, "I guess he knows what he's talking about. Have to, to be a general and all. But there's something about him always struck me . . . strange."

"Maybe I ought not have shot that fellow. Why'd he go and tell me about the man's children?"

Bauer felt the man's hand on his shoulder.

"Leave that alone, dammit. That was just a rebel. An officer to boot. You wanna feel all curled up about that, it's your business. But I was told that's why we're out here. Kill rebels. They sure as hell wanna kill us. Seen that at Gettysburg, too many times. You got a gift, Dutchman. Make good use of it. That'll help out every damn one of us, maybe get us home quicker."

Bauer tried to believe the man, said, "I guess so."

"Hell, yes. The general gave you some good advice. For your sake, I hope he doesn't stick a hot poker through your paperwork and decide to make you a Pennsylvanian. You impressed the hell out of him."

"Well, he impressed me, too. Made me feel awful."

More of the Pennsylvania men were moving through their camps, orders shouted out, the sergeant's platoon commander trotting up, a lieutenant younger than Bauer.

"I heard about your marksmanship, Private. You sure you don't wanna stick with us? Sergeant Burnett here can't hit a barn from inside the damn thing. We could use a good rifle."

"Sorry, sir. I'm just hitching a ride. My enlistment papers are right here."

He tapped his pocket and the lieutenant nodded.

"Yep, I know. We're just your five-thousand-man escort. Sergeant, get your squad up and ready. General Geary's aide just passed along marching orders, and there's already a lot of jabbering about what we're doing. Expected we'd move east, stay on our side of the river. But General Geary says we're crossing over, to the south side. That's gotta be trouble. Strike the tents, be set to march in an hour."

"Yes, sir. Sounds like trouble to me."

The officer walked away quickly, and Bauer absorbed the sergeant's comment. Trouble. Well, sure. That's what generals are good for. He watched the regiment coming alive, more regiments beyond, spread all along the north bank of the riverside town. Nearby, men were scrambling into tents, then back out, carrying backpacks and bedrolls. Bugle calls came now, a group of horsemen moving past, an intense urgency that always gave Bauer goose bumps.

The sergeant stood with his arms crossed, said, "Army's always in a damn hurry. Well, looks like the whole division is making ready to get our feet dirty. You, too, Private Regular Army. Don't worry about the general. He's probably got a lot in his head. His boy's close by, a lieutenant in one of the artillery batteries. I see him hanging around the general's tent every so often. Wouldn't care for that myself. My son's just turned ten, back in Philadelphia. If he was out here with the rest of us, I'd be pretty damn edgy about it. No, sir, wouldn't care for that a'tall."

Bauer stared up toward the rocky hill, saw the blue horsemen spread out across the hillside, some men down, searching for . . . what? A dead man with a pair of field glasses? The gloom had surprised him, something contagious that Geary seemed to carry with him, and Bauer thought of the man's son, serving right under his father's command. I guess that'd make me nervous, too.

The gloom was easing now, Bauer looking at the musket, a flick of his thumb to knock away the spent percussion cap. He felt the energy returning, bolstered by the activity around him. The 109th were veterans, something Bauer could see in their eyes. They knew what was coming, that a march through the rebel countryside wasn't for sightseeing. It's the job, he thought. My job. They know that now. Glad to see that. Just like all those Micks. They appreciated the good aim, made their bets, too, just like these boys. It's my job, after all. Like the sergeant said . . . kill rebels. Too many boys didn't have a chance, went down because some damn rebel was better at killing than they were. That's Sammie's lesson. Don't just learn how to **do** this . . . learn how to **love** it. That reb out there . . . he was just a target. He said it again, a low voice out loud.

"Just a target."

PART TWO

RESOLVE

AND

RESURGENCE

CHAPTER FIFTEEN

BRAGG

The Federal plan created by Baldy Smith came to life just after midnight on October 27. From a landing just above Chattanooga, more than fifty pontoon boats and a ragtag assortment of small transports slipped silently into black water, most carrying twenty-five men each. The orders had been given to the Federal troops only hours before, that their only encumbrance would be their muskets and a fully loaded cartridge box. Once on the river, the current did the work, the boats guided only by oarsmen, ordered to keep the boats as close as possible to their own, northern, side of the river. Silence was essential. For nine miles, the flotilla slipped past camps of the pickets on both sides, the Federal skirmishers hastily ordered into silence, the rebels across from them completely unaware what was moving past them. With extraordinary discipline, the brigade of William B. Hazen, men from Kentucky and Ohio, floated past campfires of rebels in plain view, avoiding any temptation to take a potshot at an unsuspecting enemy. After a gut-twisting journey of nearly three hours, the first of Hazen's men could see large, well-tended fires on their own side of the river, signal fires to tell the oarsmen exactly the point they were to make their landing, straight across the waterway, the gap in the steep riverbank the maps called Brown's Ferry. The landings would be made downriver as well, another quarter mile, the boats to disgorge their passengers with speed and silence, General Smith's agonizing hope that the landings would not be detected until the men were ashore.

At roughly four in the morning, the first of the boats slid into the muddy bank. In short minutes, Hazen's men were up and out of the boats, muskets ready, facing the shock and surprise of the rebels, who had no idea what was happening. Within seconds of the first burst of sound, rebel pickets responded, firing blindly at what was now an obvious attack. The rebels were experienced veterans, Alabamans under the command of William C. Oates, the same man who only months before had assaulted the far left flank of the Union position during the second day's fight at Gettysburg, the hill they now called Little Round Top.

Oates had viewed his position at Brown's Ferry with concern, had asked for reinforcements to bolster the meager forces sent to protect what had once been a well-used river crossing. But Oates had been ignored, and despite his best efforts at a counter-attack, the Confederates along the river were too few. On the Federal side of the river, a second brigade, under General John Turchin, Ohioans and Indianans, waited in the dark silence, close by the landing, knowing only that when the first landings had been completed, the now-empty boats would slip quickly across and transport them as well, adding considerable strength to Hazen's efforts. As the sun rose, the Federal troops pushed inland, establishing a bridgehead on the southern side of the river that the rebels were helpless to stop. With axes and shovels, the Federal troops strengthened their position, pushing up earthworks and felled timber. Immediately Federal engineers worked to lay the pontoon bridge that Smith's sawmill had constructed, the pathway that would bring even more Federal troops directly across the river. Smith's plan had anticipated a heavy rebel effort to shove the Federals back, but that effort never came. Oates, badly wounded, conceded the position, and sent word to his commander, Evander Law, that Brown's Ferry was now in Federal hands. In barely an hour's time, Hazen and Turchin had begun to anchor more than five thousand Federal troops on the southern side of the river.

By late that afternoon, with the Federals well

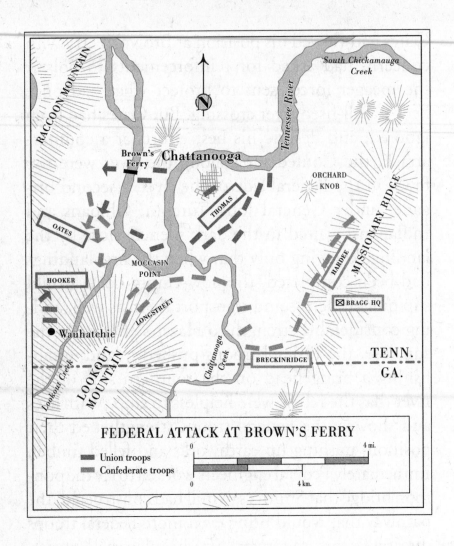

FEDERAL ATTACK AT BROWN'S FERRY

Union troops
Confederate troops

0   4 mi.

0   4 km.

protected by a strong defensive line, it was clear to Ulysses Grant and George Thomas that Baldy Smith's plan had not only been successful, but had come with a minimal cost in casualties. All that remained for the plan to be completed was the arrival of Joe Hooker's divisions, making their march on the southern side of the Tennessee River, pushing up around the southern base of Raccoon Mountain.

LOOKOUT MOUNTAIN—
OCTOBER 28, 1863

Bragg had ridden up the long trail to the peak of the mountain in a red-faced rage. The messages had come down from Longstreet all throughout the day before that the Yankees had come across the river, what Longstreet termed a minor incursion. Bragg had responded with messages of his own, adamant in his orders that Longstreet make every effort to drive the Yankees back, securing Brown's Ferry once more. But Longstreet's response had been muted, what Colonel Brent described as timid. To Bragg it was insubordination, plain and simple. The next morning, with no satisfactory response coming down from Longstreet at all, Bragg made the decision to ride up to the crest of the great peak, to find Longstreet, and issue the orders straight into the man's face. If Longstreet had no interest in fighting this war Bragg's way, Bragg would issue those orders himself, directly to Longstreet's commanders.

"I assure you, this effort by the enemy was only a diversion. I was very clear about that yesterday. It is of little concern."

Bragg rocked on his boot heels, Longstreet's casual arrogance drilling a hole through the searing headache already nesting in his brain. Bragg avoided Longstreet's eyes, stared past him, to the gray sky beyond the rocky peak. He tried to control his temper, but the rage had blossomed all along the annoying ride up the mountain, and Bragg felt an enormous urge to strangle the larger man right on the spot. He knew both staffs were listening to everything being said, Bragg's men in particular anticipating an explosion that one lieutenant had unwisely joked might be heard in Chattanooga. That man had been sent back to Missionary Ridge; Bragg had no patience at all for humor at his own expense.

Below them, far down the face of the sloping rocks, artillery thumped and thundered, streaks of fire launching out toward the Federal batteries at Moccasin Point, those guns answering with fire of their own. But the effect was well away from the crest of the mountain, what Bragg had come to believe was little more than a noisy game played by bored artillerymen. Bragg ignored that, focused all his attention on Longstreet, who turned away from him, staring out, as though watching a scattering of soaring birds. Bragg's fists were tightly clenched, the words coming in a low, hard growl.

"There was a considerable skirmish, so I was told. You did not see fit to investigate?"

Longstreet did not look at him, kept his stare toward Chattanooga, a foggy haze drifting past, obscuring the valley below them.

"It is a diversion. They will come at us here. I believe they will drive up from the south. Already, my

signalmen and the cavalry patrols report a significant Federal force on the march below the river, and
I expect those troops are intending to march south
of this mountain, possibly another push toward the
same battlefield that still holds their blood. Pride,
I suppose. If they are successful in maneuvering
that far south of our position, this mountain will
become useless to us, a trap. If I ignore that, and
commit my troops in a futile effort to address the
enemy's grand show at Brown's Ferry, I will not
have accomplished anything of import, and it will
certainly cost us casualties."

There was little energy in Longstreet's words, a
hint that Longstreet was no happier to be in this
position than Bragg was to have him here. Bragg
had arrived at Longstreet's headquarters fully expecting an argument, but not like this. Longstreet
seemed filled with a hard gloom that was infecting
even his staff.

"General Longstreet, we cannot allow the enemy
to hold a strong position on this side of the river.
All our efforts at a siege . . . to starve him out . . . will
have gone for naught. If we cannot keep control of
this side of the river, we cannot stop his efforts to
resupply. Do you not see that?" Bragg's anger had
wilted, the headache crushing him, new pains in
his stomach now blooming into full force; he had
no fire at all. "I am in command here. I ordered
you to engage the enemy yesterday. To halt their
efforts."

Longstreet continued to look away, his hands clasped behind his back, a small pipe clamped in his mouth. "Their intentions have not yet been made known to us. The cavalry reports that General Hooker has sent at least two divisions south, across the river at Bridgeport. That's all I know. There is no certainty of their destination, but if I was General Hooker, I would march those men south of this mountain and drive right up our backsides. From Chattanooga, this mountain appears formidable, but the slope to the south is far more accessible. Without a strong force guarding the various passes, we cannot hope to hold him away. I do not have strength enough to defend against a significant advance from more than one direction at a time. If I spread my forces thin, the consequences will be considerable. Your orders were received. But you were not **here.** You have not been here at all to my knowledge, to see the disposition of my troops. I accepted the responsibility to protect this position the most effective way possible. Is that not clear to **you**?"

Bragg tried to find the rage again, his mind picking up pieces of what Longstreet was saying. There was logic to the strategy, which drained Bragg even more.

"Why was I not informed of the enemy's movements south of the river?"

Longstreet faced him now, seemed puzzled. "I sent word that I was preparing to defend the passes to the south, anticipating the enemy's advance from that direction. Did you not receive that?"

Bragg rolled the details through his head, was puzzled himself now, said, "I thought it prudent that you defend any place the enemy could attack. But, then, he **did** attack. He has a considerable lodgment now at Brown's Ferry."

Longstreet looked away again. "My message was clear. Brown's Ferry is a diversion."

"My orders were clear as well!"

The outburst blew across the hillside, faces turning, and Bragg took a single step closer to Longstreet, who seemed determined not to notice. Bragg was aware of the faces watching him, struggled to hold himself calm. He lowered his voice, another growl.

"I do not know how General Lee manages his army. But here, you do not choose which orders are acceptable."

Longstreet looked at him, grim, silent eyes, removed his hat, ran a hand through his hair, one hand pulling the pipe from his mouth. Bragg tried to stand taller, the ailments pulling him downward, and Bragg felt the man's strength, the pure stubbornness.

Now it was Longstreet who spoke softly. "General Bragg, there is nothing here that compares to my experiences with General Lee. The general has respect for his subordinates. You do not. If you wish to place yourself in my headquarters, and observe the enemy as I observe him, please do so. I made my decisions based on the most efficient way to employ the forces at my disposal. You may disagree with my decision. But you will not order me to waste an army that is precious to me, as it is precious to General Lee."

Bragg caught the smell of Longstreet's breath, hot and bitter, the pipe jammed again into Longstreet's mouth. Longstreet stared hard at him, waited for a response, and Bragg fought the urge still to lunge at the man, to wrap his fingers around Longstreet's neck, to choke his life away.

"I gave you an order—"

"Sir! General Longstreet! The enemy, sir!"

Bragg forced himself to look that way, Longstreet turning as well. The man was running, pointing to the west, away from the crest of the enormous hill. Longstreet's adjutant intercepted him, a quick harsh word, but the man was animated, called out again, "Sir! The enemy is in force in the valley!"

Longstreet stepped that way, said, "Leave him be, Major. Are there more definite signals from the lookouts? Which direction are they moving?"

"Sir, a considerable force is marching northward, near the base of this here mountain. It appears to be a full division, sir!"

Longstreet looked back at Bragg, and Bragg focused on the soldier, saw the panic on the man's sweating face. Bragg still felt the anger, directed it now toward the soldier.

"I do not endorse such sensational alarms. I wish more evidence than the scattered musings of some signalman."

The man puffed up, and Longstreet's aide said, "Sergeant, you will watch your tongue."

The man was clearly exasperated, said now to Bragg, "Sir! There is more than a signal. If you wish, you can observe the enemy yourself!"

The man turned, as though ready to guide them, and Longstreet said to Bragg, "I suppose we should have a look. If you approve, of course."

They stood on a thick outcropping of rock, the valley to the west of the great mountain curving out far below them, wide and green. Through the floor of the open ground wound a railroad and a roadway, both flanking a narrow stream, Lookout Creek, that flowed directly into the Tennessee. Bragg stared down through his field glasses, Longstreet beside him, doing the same. A cluster of officers had gathered behind them, low talk Bragg ignored. Along the road at the base of the hill he could clearly see the snaking column of blue, driving northward, pushing their way toward the new Federal stronghold at Brown's Ferry. He lowered the glasses, his hands too unsteady, hot frustration, the anger choking away his words. Longstreet kept the glasses to his eyes, said, "Near five thousand. They're moving to join those boys at the river." Longstreet paused, his words now barely audible. "Didn't expect that."

Bragg wrapped his fury around Longstreet's admission, but there was no time now for useless arguments. He tried to focus, more low words from Longstreet.

"Farther down. Another division. Separate. Holding back at that town . . . Wauhatchie. They might still move east, circle behind us."

Bragg swung around sharply to Longstreet. "I believe the enemy has now made his intentions known. Even to **you.** You will attack their line of march as quickly as is practicable, and make use of your entire corps. The enemy is intending to force this position from the west, from the valley right below us! I have no doubt about that. He has already forced open the means to resupply his position in Chattanooga." Bragg paused, tried to see again through the field glasses, a hint of flags, the line of blue still in motion. "Unless you remove those people from this valley . . . they will have the means to resupply. We will have failed to accomplish our goal. They will have broken the siege. You must prevent that."

Bragg turned, his voice fading away. He saw his staff, expectant, some climbing onto horses, saw fear and concern in their faces. He left Longstreet, moved toward a groom holding the reins to his horse, snatched the leather straps from the man's hand. He took a long breath, pulled himself up on the horse. Longstreet was still staring out through the field glasses, a useless show, and Bragg shouted now, no concern for decorum, for any show of respect at all.

"You will carry out my orders! You will employ your entire corps, if necessary!" Bragg paused, thought suddenly of the obvious. "You will also learn why your cavalry did not report this column hours ago!"

He spun the horse, the aides mounting up as well, his color bearer moving in behind him. He spurred the animal hard, moved past Longstreet's staff, others, scattered squads of infantry, a battery of cannon, the men scrambling to salute him. He ignored them all, his stare fixed on the far distant Missionary Ridge. He spoke now, to no one, to everyone, to anyone who heard him.

"He will pay . . . he will suffer for this. I will not have such men. He is overrated in every extreme. His lack of ability . . . his lack of obedience . . . cannot be tolerated."

The words continued, his mind rattling out curses, his staff following down the steep, rocky trail, the road back to his headquarters.

CHAPTER SIXTEEN

BAUER

WAUHATCHIE, TENNESSEE—
OCTOBER 28, 1863

The march had been like so many others, a full day on roads made dusty by the footsteps of a column miles long. Geary's division had moved out from the river crossing at Bridgeport last in line, and already, most of Joe Hooker's newly arrived army was pushing far ahead, aiming for a rendezvous with the growing Federal presence south of the Tennessee River at Brown's Ferry.

The route of march took them past low rolling hills and fat mountains, and Bauer was struck by the beauty of the place, the hillsides green and misty, the road sometimes wrapped in every direction by the lush forests that rose up close enough to hide the sunlight. The hills gave way to bowl-shaped valleys, lush and fertile, with only a scattering of meager farms. The civilians here seemed unaware a war was being fought at all, some coming out to watch the soldiers pass with looks that spoke more of curiosity than hostility. Some were more generous to the men in blue than Bauer had ever seen before, farmers and their families offering barrels of cool water pulled up from deep wells, some with milk cows right along the road, pails of rich milk, a luxury these troops had not enjoyed in a long time. Women appeared, mostly wives and daughters of the families who worked the rugged land, a playful flirtatiousness Bauer had seen before. No matter their obvious charms, the blushing smiles and friendly calls, there was still a tinge of fear in the women that made Bauer uncomfortable. Most of the soldiers had seen these kinds of displays in the past, many long marches through lands where the civilians flocked to the roadsides. But these people had likely never seen a column of soldiers, not like this, thousands of men in a steady stream, all those uniforms and so much weaponry. For all their welcoming greetings, Bauer could see hints of intimidation, a fear of the unknown, that Bauer knew might be justified. There were too many stories in this army about abuse and plunder, the worst in the violations of women, a kind of violence the army handled with ruthless punishment.

Bauer was relieved to hear that these Pennsylvanians didn't carry the blatant hostility toward

civilians he had seen in Mississippi. There the slaveholders inspired a wrath from the troops that surprised him, especially when those feelings infected
him. All throughout the Vicksburg campaign, the
march through the villages and vast plantations,
the slaves had emerged from their fields and home-
steads, flocking gleefully to the blue-clad troops, the
soldiers entertained by salutes and joyful greetings
for "Missuh Lincom's boys." Many of those slaves
had been abandoned by their masters, and so the
Negroes abandoned the plantations that had kept
them captive. They fell into line, following along
behind the soldiers as in a holiday parade. Bauer
had marveled at that, curious about the Negroes,
so many of the Wisconsin men rarely ever seeing
a black man at all. As the Federal column wound
its way through the plantations, the outpouring of
jubilation from the Negroes had added to the morale of the troops who were whipping the rebels at
every turn. The campaign had belonged to Grant,
to be sure, the general's reputation among the politicians now eclipsing every other general in blue.
But it was the soldiers who fought the good fight,
and who, like Bauer now, carried the pride of an
army that had not been defeated. The freed slaves
had been a symbol of that, and some of the troops
had taken the symbolism a step further, putting the
torch to the grand mansions that might still house
the white slaveholders. Bauer had been shocked at
the viciousness from the men around him, until he

had felt it himself. The civilians could be as dangerous as the rebel soldiers, potshots from primitive flintlocks aimed at the passing column, rocks hurled from hidden places. As more slaves sought the sanctuary of the passing army, the tolerance from the soldiers for the grandeur of the plantation homes had turned sour, the response toward any real threat brutal and swift. Bauer had thrown a torch of his own through window glass, had absorbed too much vitriolic spew tossed from behind curtained windows.

But that was Mississippi.

With darkness settling through the green around them, the footsore troops were ordered into camps in a wooded plain near Wauhatchie, a nondescript village nestled in the valley that was flanked now by Raccoon Mountain to the west, and the enormous mass of Lookout Mountain to the east. To the east, closer to the base of the larger mountain, a wide creek flowed northward, flanked by a rail line that extended north and south, Bauer surprised to hear that the state of Georgia was only a few miles below them. As the soldiers pitched their small tents, the people accepted their presence with the same odd gratitude that Bauer had seen all through this part of Tennessee. The faces were smiling, the waves friendly, several older men of the village seeking out the commanders, offering information on the rebels. Whether or not any of that was useful or accurate, Bauer only knew that these people, who

seemed so isolated from the rest of the Confederacy, were genuinely happy that the Federal troops
had chosen their town for their camp.

The tents had been pitched, the officers gathering close to their superiors, orders passed for what
they were expected to do tomorrow. One farmer
in particular had spread alarm that an enormous
mass of rebels was camped close by, not much more
than a mile away, on the far side of Lookout Creek.
As the daylight faded away in the deep trough between the two great hills, some of the men held
tightly to their muskets, fearing that the rumors
were accurate, that the enemy might be slipping
toward them through the deep woods. The others,
like Bauer, knew that a fight in the darkness was
rare, and so the fires blazed high.

The fires rose all through the various regiments,
no shortage of firewood anywhere around them.
Bauer sat cross-legged, chewed on a greasy slab
of dried bacon. He had copied the others, piercing the meat with a stick, holding it over the fire,
the pop and sizzle of the fat spreading a marvelous
odor. Bauer struggled to chew through the tough
meat, the usual routine, caught a glimpse of the
man beside him producing a small silver flask, a
quick sip of what Bauer assumed to be a beverage
more potent than spring water. But the man wasn't
discreet enough for the men around him, who had
no doubt watched that exercise before. Across from
Bauer, through the fire, another man said, "Hey,

Zane. At it again? You still not gonna share? Pretty dang rude, if you ask me."

There was a playfulness to the talk, and Bauer looked at Zane, saw the flask slip away quickly into a pocket.

"Ain't got enough even for me. Ain't even got my lips wet. Mind yourself."

On Bauer's other side, a man nudged Bauer's shoulder.

"He's never without that dang whiskey. Won't never tell us where he gets it. Hey, Zane, you been shinin' some general's boots?"

The man didn't respond, made a show of gnawing on a piece of meat.

The man across from Bauer said, "I bet he's got a whiskey still somewhere's back there. You must be rich. You have your pappy bring you your own wagon? That's it, ain't it? Makes his own brew. I'll find out, sooner or later."

The others joined in, good-natured chatter aimed at the man Bauer studied now, who seemed uneasy, self-conscious as he pretended to struggle with the bacon.

He looked back at Bauer, said, "Hey, Regular Army. You mind yourself. I ain't seen **you** offer nothing to none of us."

Bauer knew he was the outsider, a natural target for taunts and teases. It had been that way through his first weeks in the 17th Wisconsin, the Irishmen only accepting this German after Bauer showed them he could fight. He was curious about these Easterners, saw little difference between their ways and anything he had gone through before. He only knew of Gettysburg from what little the Wisconsin officers had passed along, had a curiosity about that, wondered if what these men had done in Pennsylvania was any different from what Bauer had been through at Shiloh the year before. But there was no talk about that, and Bauer knew enough of veterans not to ask. If they wanted to tell their stories, they would.

"I'm not messing with you, Zane. Don't drink much of nothing stronger than water. Maybe coffee, when we can get it."

The talk seemed to slow, the subject exhausted, and Bauer realized most of the dozen men were staring at him, something he couldn't quite get used to. To one side, a man said, "You think being a regular soldier makes you better'n us?"

It was the kind of question Bauer dreaded, and expected. "Not a bit. But I'm betting that every one of you wishes you were back home right now. Families, children, all that?"

There was a low hum of comments, heads nodding. The man kept his stare on Bauer, an edge of hostility.

"Ain't you? You some kind of outcast? You escape from prison or something?"

Bauer knew the man was picking a fight, aiming

his wrath at the only target presenting itself: the man who wasn't one of them.

"My family's dead. I got no children. No kin. Got a good friend in the regulars. We been through a lot together. Shiloh, Corinth, Vicksburg. That's all. I never thought it'd be like this, but I like soldiering. Don't want to do anything else."

His answer seemed to disarm the man, and beside him, the one he knew as Caldwell said, "Leave him be, Irwin. I know what he's saying, I guess." The man looked at Bauer, heavy, tired eyes, a scruff of a beard. "My little girl passed on a few months ago. A fever took her. Four years old. I ain't been home since before it happened. Can't say I'm itching to go back. But my wife . . . well, a man ain't worth much if he's not there for his woman. She wants more babies. Reckon that's my job to help out. Army lets me go, I'm gone. Nobody waiting for you a'tall?"

Bauer shook his head, stared into the fire. "No wife. Nobody."

Zane said, "Why they call you Dutchman?"

"My family's German. Came over here before I was born. Picked Milwaukee 'cause there was a lot of Germans there."

"Shiloh, huh? You a hero then?"

The words came from the angry man, Irwin. Bauer hesitated, realized he had no reason to hide anything from these men.

"Never been so scared in my life. Rebs come up out of the woods like they were demons. I ran until I gave out. Bunch of us. Took some good officers to gather us back up. It turned out okay. But I'm no hero."

The response seemed to surprise them all, Irwin pointing a knife Bauer's way.

"You do that to my squad, I'll cut you open. No room for cowards in this army. The regulars know you're a coward?"

Caldwell said, "You can shut that up. I seen you at Gettysburg. Crawled behind a damn rock and waited for the storm to pass. And a bunch of us was right there with you. I seen Dutchman shoot, watched him kill a rebel back there day before yesterday. I'll pay heed to **you** when I see you do the same."

Irwin seemed to deflate, aiming his scowl more to the fire than to Bauer. "Hmph. I killed plenty of rebs. Seen the elephant plenty of times."

There was a murmur of laughter, Bauer not in on the joke. Caldwell looked at him, said, "There's no heroes at this fire. But we made the fight. General Geary won't tolerate **timid.** We took our share of musket fire at Chancellorsville, too. Some of these boys were at Cedar Mountain."

The names were familiar but Bauer knew very little of those fights. He stared into the fire, chewing on the last piece of bacon, and after a silent moment, said, "I guess we've all seen rebs. Probably more to come."

There was a mumble of agreement, and Bauer stretched his arms upward, felt a wave of sleepiness. There was a sudden chatter of insects, far out beyond the camps, and Bauer froze, his ears straining to hear, knew it wasn't insects at all. Around him, the men seemed to come awake, sharp glances toward the woods, the road beyond. Voices started now:

"Muskets!"

"Rebs!"

"Hush up! Where they at?"

Their muskets were stacked close by, and already the men were moving, crawling toward them. The drums came now, the long roll, the alarm. Bauer saw the lieutenant running up, bent low.

"Rebels! They're coming!"

There was panic in the man, too much panic, but the musket fire was increasing, still far away, a chattering storm, no sign of the muzzle blasts. The sergeant was there now, handing out muskets from the stack, calling out, "Check your cartridge boxes! Fall into formation!"

The lieutenant was running in a manic scamper among his platoon, called out, "Load muskets! Prepare to receive the enemy!"

The bugles were sounding, a harsh hum of activity all through the wooded camps. Bauer held his musket, went through the routine, energized by the cold in his chest, the feeling he knew too well. He completed the task, placed the percussion cap on the nipple at the musket's breech, the musket now a weapon. His eyes stayed on the trees, darkness broken by the reflected firelight, nothing else to see.

The men began to move, following the officers, swords pointed, other units gathering, the lines forming, facing the sounds of the fight. The order came to halt, the road out to one side, the musket fire coming that way, far to the north. Bauer stood nervously, thought, Night? Darkness? Nobody can fight in the dark. He glanced down the line of men, another line forming up behind, knew to kneel, still nothing to see.

Out on the road, Bauer saw a horseman coming fast from the direction of the fight, an officer riding hard into woods behind them. Beside Bauer, the sergeant said, "He's going to Geary. We'll know pretty quick what's happening."

To one side, the lieutenant called out, "Be prepared to advance! Make ready to receive the enemy!"

The two orders were a contradiction, and Bauer closed his eyes, thought, Too young. Bet he's never done this before. These men are veterans, don't need that kind of panic, not from an officer.

The musket fire stopped now, Bauer, the others straining to hear more. He saw Captain Gimber step out front, as though seeking a closer look, the man staring out with his hands on his hips. There were more horses, from behind them, and Bauer turned with the others, was surprised to see General Geary, a flock of aides, officers stepping out of line to gather closer. Geary halted the horse, stared out down the road, no sounds, and Bauer could see a hard scowl on the man's face, a shake of his head.

The lieutenant kept his place, said aloud, "Come to attention!"

The order was mostly obeyed, others focused more on Geary. Bauer stood, planted the musket by his side, watched the cluster of officers, Gimber walking out to the road, joining the group. Geary looked out toward the men, spoke out loud enough for them to hear.

"You boys did fine. Made ready in good order. Can't say the same for some of the others. There was a skirmish out on the Ferry Road. A handful of rebs tried to do . . . well, whatever rebs do. The Twenty-ninth is posted a half mile out there as pickets, and all I know is that Colonel Rickards came hightailing it down here to tell me all hell was breaking loose. Then, before he could give me the report, **all hell** turned into nothing at all. For all I know, they were shooting at ghosts. There's some old coot lives near these woods, says there's several hundred rebels on the far side of the creek, up thataway. We've also heard that half of Longstreet's corps is breathing down our necks from the base of the big mountain. Not sure if any of that is true. But there's too many Nellies in this bunch. You're all too damn itchy, and as dark as it is now, I don't want any mistakes. Officers, have the men keep close to their muskets, but keep them tight in hand. No firing at anything unless you hear the order. Nobody wanders off, nobody empties his musket, until things calm down."

Bauer looked down again, felt the strength of Geary's order, thought, Guess I like this man a little better today. Nothing wrong with holding on to a loaded musket, when you're in a reb's backyard.

Geary looked upward, seemed to examine the black sky, and Bauer did the same, saw the soft glow of thin clouds drifting past a half-moon. Geary said aloud, "If there's any rebels out and about, they'll probably stay to themselves. The whole Eleventh Corps marched through here today, heading north."

A voice called out, and Geary turned that way, saw men pointing toward the peak of Lookout Mountain. Bauer could see what they saw, flickers of light along the crest, high above them. Gimber moved toward his men, said aloud, "Just rebel signal lights. Get used to it. They're all over the top of that mountain, but no worries for us. They're just jabbering back and forth, showing off how scared they are."

Bauer felt a chill, more nerves than the cold air, didn't care for the thought of rebels looking straight down on him.

Geary said, "Stay close to your fires if you want. But I'd get some sleep if I were you. That's it. Captain, see to your men. Calm them down. There's no damn ghosts out here. Anybody wounded by mistake, it's your responsibility."

Geary nudged the horse, his aides following, was gone quickly, moving along to the next camp, the next regiment, camped farther out in the trees.

The lieutenant was there now, still agitated, moving through his men.

"Back to camp! Pay heed to the general's instructions!"

The men spread out to their own fires, kept their muskets in hand, and Bauer found his place, sat, welcomed the warmth, cradled the musket across his legs. The chatter began again, the men more nervous, Bauer and the rest of them glancing up often to the lights from the rebel camps.

He felt sleep coming, the fire dancing through blurred vision, soaked up a last blanket of warmth. He started to stand up, looked toward his tent, and far out in the trees, a musket fired. Bauer turned that way, nothing to see, felt a stab of annoyance. The words came from Irwin, to one side.

"Some jackass . . ."

More muskets fired now, all from the same place, the muzzle blasts flickering far out in the woods. Around the other fires, men were standing up again, all staring out, the light from the fires blinding, blocking their vision. The musket fire in-

creased now, spreading out to one side, toward the
great mountain, and Bauer felt the cold stirring in
his chest, his fingers curling hard around the musket. Farther away, men were shouting, the camps of
the other units, nearer the village, men close to the
railroad. To one side, Captain Gimber appeared,
stopped, staring out toward the musket fire, then
pulled his sword, held it high, shouted out, "Up,
to formation! Bugler, blow formation! Prepare to
receive the enemy!"

Close to Bauer, a man laughed, Irwin, called out
to the captain, "Hell, it's just ghosts, Capt'n."

The musket ball whistled past Bauer, then another, and he could see specks of fire, the muzzle
blasts scattered out through the far trees. The bugle
sounded, Captain Gimber still waving the sword,
the man calling out, "Prepare to receive the enemy!
He's coming from that way!"

Bauer followed the others, the men moving
forward in good order, most still not believing
what they could all hear in front of them. Behind
him, the voice of the sergeant.

"Kill the fires! Kill the fires! Stomp 'em out! Now!"

The men obeyed, a scramble of dirt and boots,
the flames knocked down. Bauer stumbled, furious
at the darkness, could see more of the muzzle blasts
now, a wide line, flickering through the trees, the
harsh **zip** of the musket balls to one side. Orders
were shouted out from every direction, more mus-

ket fire coming in bursts, volleys fired out of black darkness. He felt a hand on his shoulder, a hard grip on his shirt, loud voice in his ear.

"Form here! Prepare to receive the enemy!"

The men pushed past Bauer, and he followed, falling into line, a bugle call somewhere behind them, more officers pulling their men into formation. The fires were smothered now, the cries and shouts filling the darkness, nonsense and chaos, orders blending into panic. But the line formed, the men in front settling down to one knee, another order, "Advance! Prepare to fire!"

The bugle sounded out the new order, the men up and moving, the lieutenant close in front of them pointing with the sword, pistol in the man's hand. Bauer ignored him, looked for the captain, still struggled to see through the black woods, his eyes not yet clear of the firelight. He blinked, focused forward, furious at the blindness, looked up, finally, could see the tops of trees, a scattering of stars, the clouds still drifting past the moon. All through the woods, voices were rolling through and he felt the sweating grip on the musket, the frantic beating in his chest, looked down, searching the ground in front of him, then out farther through the trees, any kind of movement, anything at all. The officers had command now, the captain to one side, the sergeant up behind him, the orders given, nothing else to do, the line still advancing, slow, steady steps, men slipping forward around the trees, no one firing. And, out in the dark: nothing at all.

They kept to their formation for several minutes, questions coming now, nervous men calling out, Bauer keeping close to the men on either side, the line steady, strong. He thought of Shiloh, the darkness, the panic, men shooting at squirrels, at deer and rabbits, and, sometimes, at one another. Beside him, more questions, rolling anger.

"Who was it? Was it rebs?"

"Hell if I know! Stay ready!"

"Those jackasses in the Twenty-ninth, I bet."

"It's the Twenty-ninth, for sure!"

There was another burst of firing, the volley still to the right, a sharp flash, answered now by their own men, farther down the way. The muskets traded fire again, and Bauer could hear the shouts from officers, one piercing scream from a wounded man. All through that part of the woods, men on both sides were calling out, the rebels rallying their own, pushing forward. But still the Pennsylvanians kept together, the men closest to him with no enemy yet, angry anticipation. Bauer saw the lieutenant, the sword in the air, followed him slowly forward, and now, an obstacle rose up in front of them, the lieutenant calling out, "Fence line!"

Another voice, to one side, Gimber.

"Form here, behind the fence! Good cover! Make ready! No firing until you have a target!"

Bauer put one hand out, felt the heavy timbers, squatted, felt the thick mass of a fence post, steadied himself. He felt the fence rails, leaned the musket up, aiming out, still nothing to see. The captain's words rolled through him. **Good cover.** He glanced to the side, away from the firing, thought, Yeah, good cover. If they don't come up behind us. Or . . . over there, the other side.

All along the fence, the men waited, enduring the fight that pressed against other units, volleys traded back and forth, distant sheets of fire. Bauer kept the musket ready, felt the bayonet hanging at his side, blinked that away, no bayonets, not in the dark. Don't want to be that close to anybody out here. He kept his stare out past the fence line, still no targets, nothing at all but dark woods. He tried to aim, sighted down the barrel, could barely make out the iron sights, thought, Just shoot at 'em. Nothing else we can do. If they come. The musket fire came again, another volley, this time out to the left side. But the men there were ready, a quick order Bauer could hear, the volley returned. Very soon, the firing seemed to scatter, the voices of the rebels calling to their own, officers trying to restore some kind of order. More firing came down to the left, seemed to spread behind them, and Bauer felt a cold stab, looked that way, the men around him doing the same.

"They're flanking us! Make ready!"

The lieutenant was in full panic, and Bauer tried to

ignore that, focused on any kind of light, anything
at all. The fight on the left was scattered, seemed to
spread all through the woods, both directions. He
looked to the front, the anxious shiver blending in
with anger, that the rebels would miss them, take
their fight only to the other units. Damn! We're
here! We're ready! He strained again to see anything
at all, could still see the flicker of fire from single
muskets, but the smoke was rolling through the
trees, obscuring any hint of a target. He kept his
eyes to the front, forced himself to keep ready, tried
not to think what was happening down the way,
if there was a fence, if men were out on the railroad
tracks, if there was any cover at all. The men around
him were mostly silent, as angry and anxious as he
was, some terrified, soft whimpering, the sergeant
barking out close behind them, "Keep still! Stay
ready! They could be coming!"

Bauer saw Irwin in his mind, the big mouth, chip
on the man's shoulder, convinced they were hearing
ghosts. Doesn't sound like ghosts to me, he thought.
Never knew a ghost to shoot a musket. He leaned
hard against the thick fence post, could smell the
smoke from the fight, more scattered firing out to
both sides, thought, Maybe we should be . . . helping out? But the officers were there, moving past
behind them, firm, quiet orders, holding the men
in position. Geary's words suddenly broke through
Bauer's thoughts. **Half of Longstreet's corps.**
That's a bunch, I'm guessing. There's what? Fifteen

hundred of us? He couldn't help feeling respect for Geary, the man who knew what was happening, who knew what they were supposed to do. Bauer thought of the man's words again, **The whole Eleventh Corps marched through here.** That's good, I suppose. But where are those boys now? Right up that road someplace. They gotta be able to hear all this commotion. Maybe. We could use some help.

The blast behind him was sudden, deafening, a burst of terror ripping through him, through the men around him. Out to the front, the shell impacted out past the closest timber, a fiery blast that erupted close, shattering trees, the flash blinding, startling. He fought to see, held the stare, his ears ringing, painful. And now the cannon fired again, the blast ripping past close over his head. Around him, men dropped down, flattened along the fence, the cannon firing again, and Bauer lay flat, the ground shaking beneath him, but the terror was giving way, a surge of relief taking its place. **Ours!** He kept still, waited, one hand on the musket, the other clamped on his ear. The next blast came now, ripping the woods out to the front, and he had to see, to know what was happening, peered up, over the edge of a fence rail, saw the enormous burst of fire, and the silhouettes of men, like so many ghosts, moving straight toward them.

It was nearly 3 A.M. when the fight ended. There had been no success, no failure, both sides fumbling in the dark, Geary's men mostly anchored in two lines, in an L shape, absorbing the surprise shock of nearly equal strength from a brigade of South Carolinians, under the command of Colonel John Bratton. Though Geary's men mostly held their ground, Bratton's men began to gain the momentum, advancing blindly into Geary's supply wagons, threatening to flank the position. As Geary's men began to exhaust their ammunition, Bratton's troops made ready for what Bratton believed would be the final blow, a massed charge that would crush Geary's resistance. But before Bratton could give the order, he received one of his own. The Confederates were ordered to withdraw. Bratton had no choice but to obey, pulling his men northward, across the lone bridge that spanned Lookout Creek. The order had come from Bratton's superior, General Micah Jenkins, who answered to Longstreet.

Farther up the Brown's Ferry Road, the troops of Oliver Howard's Eleventh Corps had indeed heard the eruption of the fight at Wauhatchie. Howard immediately sent a strong force to march southward, to assist whatever crisis had fallen upon John Geary. But Bratton's men were not the only Confederate forces who had ventured out from the base of Lookout Mountain. Howard's troops ran into another brigade of rebels, more of Longstreet's

troops, sent to slice across the road that would keep
Geary's division cut off from the gathering strength
at Brown's Ferry. But the darkness offered no assistance to either side in either place, and by dawn,
like Bratton's men, the rest of the Confederates had
withdrawn from whatever confused contact they
had made. With the daylight on October 29, the
anxious Federal troops could finally see the battle-
ground that showed the effects of Longstreet's night
attack, a fight that had accomplished nothing at all.

They moved through the churned-up ground
searching for anything of value. But Bauer
had found as little as the others, a few canteens tossed aside, cartridge boxes mostly empty,
a bent sword. In the early dawn, the rebels had
pulled most of their wounded away, but scattered
through the broken timber, men still called out,
praying, begging, suffering from wounds inflicted
by an enemy few of them ever saw.

Bauer had returned to his camp with most of
the men of the platoon, those men surveying the
damage to their tents, retrieving bedrolls, sort-
ing through whatever debris the fight had spread
through the camp. The talk was flowing now, anxious fear giving way to pride, to rumor and spouting off, but there was one piece of news that was
definite. For all the advantage of their surprise
assault, driving toward the Federal camps, where

the men in blue had been silhouetted by their own fires, there was one disadvantage Bratton's South Carolinians could not overcome. They had no artillery. In the early morning light, it was clear that the Federal artillery had turned the tide, making the greatest impact on the fight, blasting holes into rebel formations that even the artillerymen could barely see.

Throughout the camps, Bauer shared the gratitude of those around him, hoping to shake the hands of the men who pulled the lanyards, who might have saved the entire division. But it was not to be. The daylight revealed the awful truth, that most of the artillerymen were down. Like the infantry outlined by their campfires, the blasts from the cannon had lit the ground around each gun, offering clear targets for rebel muskets. With each punch of cannon fire, rebel officers had ordered their men to target the gunners, each cannon's eruption offering a momentary glimpse that gave the rebels a perfect field of fire.

As Bauer and the Pennsylvanians absorbed the sadness of the loss of those men who had done the good work, it was their commander who would suffer a tragedy of his own. Geary's son, Lieutenant Edward Geary, had been killed in the act of working his battery. For a fight that seemed to most to have been a useless exercise, the loss of Geary's son cast a pall through the entire unit.

Bauer didn't know the young man, barely knew

any of the men who huddled along the fence with him through two hours of blind terror. But he respected the grief they felt, had gone through that too often himself. It hardly mattered who held the ground, whose troops prevailed. For Geary, and for the men of Joe Hooker's entire force, it seemed that the valley west of Lookout Mountain was now vulnerable to another assault. But Longstreet had made the only effort he seemed willing to attempt. Withdrawing his troops back up to the heights on Lookout Mountain, he could only observe the vast sea of blue that stretched out below him, the forces that had driven up through the valley that now gave the Federal troops in Chattanooga the supply line they desperately needed. The Cracker Line had expanded into something much more, a pathway where the wagons were already rolling, Baldy Smith's beloved straight line, the newly placed pontoon bridges already weighed down by the flow of fresh supplies. Bragg's siege was broken.

CHAPTER SEVENTEEN

BAUER

CHATTANOOGA—
NOVEMBER 1, 1863

The men from Pennsylvania had stayed in their newly captured valley, but for Bauer, it was time to move on. The last leg of his journey took him across the pontoon bridge that would land him in Chattanooga. Where he was to go then was a mystery, something to be cleared up by the provosts who guarded every route that led to the Federal camps.

He had fallen in behind a line of wounded men, a slow, delicate dance over timbers laid flat on a pontoon bridge. There was a pair of stretcher bearers behind him, responding quickly to one of the walking wounded who had collapsed along the way; they gathered the hobbled man in a hammock of dirty canvas. As they moved out onto the rocking bridge, the bearers began chatting about some fistfight, laughing at someone else's misfortune, a casual conversation as though the injured man carried between them was little more than nameless cargo. The stretcher bearers were white, something of a surprise to Bauer, since throughout the most recent campaigns, Negroes had been assigned that job, just as they now served on most of the grave details. Bauer had seen too much of that kind of duty at Shiloh, had naïvely volunteered for work with the shovel, in return for the army's promise of a dose of hard liquor. He recalled that now, dozens of men around him, digging through the soft earth, the shallow ditches that served as a resting place for men who deserved much more. The first rains offered up the futility of the effort, bones and scraps of uniforms protruding from places some farmer might soon reclaim for his crops, a thought that sickened Bauer to his core. The army's reward of liquor had been another lesson Bauer had learned the worst way possible. He knew little of spirits, suffered mightily from the indulgence, heaving out every bit of solid food into a muddy hole, then hauling away a headache that plagued him for two days. In the eighteen months since that horrific fight, Bauer had kept far away from the bottles, even the smell of whiskey turning his stomach. It amazed him that no matter where he went, there were always men who found the means to squirrel away a good supply of the illicit brew.

In the battles since, the grave diggers had been black. No longer did the officers drift through the campsites, trying to cajole or bribe their men out into the fields, shovel in hand. The Negroes were simply ordered to the job, no one daring to complain about the task that someone had decided was too gruesome for white men. At first the black burial details wore blue, came from a regiment of freedmen, but very soon, as the army continued its march through myriad cotton fields and abandoned plantations, many of the laborers came from the ranks of the freed slaves, who seemed to welcome any job that would take them far from their former masters.

The wounded man behind him let out a sudden moan, and Bauer glanced back from instinct, couldn't avoid the brief horror, the cloth of the stretcher stained with a wet patch of dark red. He caught a look from the bearer closest to him, saw a white cloth tied around the man's upper arm, the makeshift insignia he had seen before, as though, without the adornment, the stretcher bearers might otherwise slip away from the sickening duty.

"What's the problem, soldier? You feel like lending a hand? Old Ned here's headed for the hospital. You been in a hospital? Takes a strong man just to go near the place."

"I've been in a hospital."

Bauer turned away, ignored the chuckle from the man, a joke at his expense. But the wounded man called out, a gasping cry, "No. I don't wanna go to no hospital."

"Hey, Ned, you're awake. Can't help it. Doctor says you might lose that leg. But it's a blessing. You'll be going home, that's for sure. Leave this mess for the rest of us."

The chatter continued, and Bauer felt a cold fury, kept his stare to the front, heard the wounded man whimpering now, soft sobs breaking through the jabbering men who carried him. Bauer stepped more quickly, putting distance between them, eased carefully past a man on a single crutch, the bridge bouncing slightly beneath his feet. The man ignored him, focused on keeping his balance, the bridge rocking sideways. Bauer glanced out to the brown water, slow ripples spreading away from the bridge, slowed again, steadied himself, a silent apology to the hobbled man, looked at him, the face of a boy, tears. The boy struggled with the crutch, hopped clumsily, Bauer fighting the urge to help him.

"I'm not gonna lose my leg, am I, sir?"

The childlike voice jolted Bauer, the image coming back to him of a redheaded boy from the 17th Wisconsin. Bauer tried to recall his name, his mind not wanting to see that, a single musket ball through the boy's forehead, the quivering tuft of red hair, the death of a child so dedicated to wearing a man's uniform. Bauer erased the image, hadn't thought of the boy since Vicksburg, wouldn't think of him now. He focused on the young man close behind him.

"No," he said. "Looks good, from here. You're walking okay. Don't worry."

He looked past the boy toward the stretcher bearers, saw a nod toward him from the man up front, no jokes this time, the duty taking over. The stretcher bearer shook his head now, and Bauer followed the man's gaze to the wounded boy's foot, saw the black ooze from the ripped shoe, another gash on the man's calf. Bauer kept his pace slow, in time with the boy. He wanted to reach out, some kind of encouragement, give the boy a hearty pat on the shoulder, but his hand stayed at his side, the other hand gripping the musket.

"You'll be okay. Just . . . get to the hospital."

He had seen this before, heard too many agonizing pleas, had come to understand what so many of the veterans knew, that a quick death was the kindest gift from God, and if Bauer was to die, he hoped desperately for that perfect shot, a rebel's good aim, a musket ball through his head. It was all the inspiration he had needed to perfect that deed on his own. In the camps near the Mississippi, Bauer had practiced, moving the targets out farther, then farther again. He had proven himself at Vicksburg, but those targets were often a hundred yards distant, no real challenge for a man who took his time, who had the knack for relaxing the hands. Very soon he was popping tin plates at two hundred yards, then three, had learned about trajectory and rate of fall, making allowances for sloping ground, or a strong crosswind. Permission for that had come from Willis, allowing Bauer to slip away from the usual field drills, the ridiculous monotony of formations and bugle calls. Musket practice was a luxury for those who professed to be marksmen, and after twenty months in the army, Bauer had come to understand why it attracted him, why it seemed to matter. That lesson had come from Willis as well, and from another officer, a captain who had the gift of the calm hand, the clear eye. Bauer had proven to them he had the skills, what to some was mere trickery, that tin plates were not men, that a long minute's preparation had no meaning in the midst of a firestorm of musket fire. But Bauer believed differently, knew that killing a man was best done the right way, end the man's life before he knows it's happened. Hand him to God, he thought. Here, I've done my duty, now he's Yours. And not in pieces, not like this boy behind me, or the man pouring out his blood in that filthy stretcher.

He looked again to the dark water, saw the splash of some creature, spreading circles, his mind settling there. A fish, probably. Wonder if they eat them around here. Big river, plenty of critters swimming around. Gators, too, probably. Seen enough of those. Snakes, too. No, just think about the fish. Somebody's figured out how to hook a few, for sure. That'd be a heap better than hardtack. Just . . .

don't drink this water. It's as ugly as that stuff in the Mississippi.

He stepped off the bridge, welcomed the solid ground, joined a slow-moving line that ended at the provost officer. Bauer pulled his transfer from his pocket, smoothed the papers, was suddenly in front of a sweating sergeant, the man's round belly pushing toward Bauer, as effective as any roadblock.

"What you doing here, boy?"

Bauer was surprised by the distinct Southern lilt in the man's speech, slid his musket down beside him, held out the papers, saw the cap now, the insignia of Missouri.

"I'm to report—"

"Shut the hell up. You'll report to me, and I'll decide where you go, if'n you go anywheres besides the stockade. Too many spies running through here. Not on my post. You get that, boy?" The question didn't seem to require an answer, and Bauer watched as the man scanned the papers. "This is a pile of horse manure, boy. Never heard of nothing like this. I smell a guttin' coming."

Bauer was suddenly scared of this man, thought again of fish. **Guttin'.** He felt helpless, glanced around, saw passing ambulances, a supply wagon, other provost officers waving them past without hesitation. Bauer sagged, looked at the man's deep frown, said, "Sergeant, it says there I'm to report—"

The man silenced him with a hard glare, leaned close to Bauer's face. "I told you to shut up. I ain't seen any kind of orders like these before. You try to slip past this post, boy, and I'll rip your scalp right off'n your head." The man looked out to the side, waved to a lieutenant, said aloud, "Sir, got a strange one here. This Johnny Reb thinks he can go waltzing right past me, just 'cause he's wearing a blue coat. You might wanna get over this way. Might have cause for a hangin'."

Bauer felt a rising panic, looked at the lieutenant, another older man, serious, thin, gaunt face. He said to the officer, "Sir, please, if you'll look . . . there. I was in the Seventeenth Wisconsin . . ."

The sergeant leaned in close to him again, and Bauer flinched, waited for the inevitable explosion.

"Boy, I'm about to snap your neck in four places. Your bones'll be in that river afore you can holler!"

The lieutenant took the papers from the sergeant, read slowly, and Bauer felt his brain ticking off seconds, the silent word flowing through, please . . . please.

After an agonizing minute, the officer said, "Eighteenth Regulars. First Battalion. All right, Private. Go down that street there, all the way to the end. Turn right, go another three streets. Then left, out into the field. Tents on both sides of the road. Yours will be on the right. Report to the provost officer on duty there. You'll see a headquarters tent, easy to spot. Bigger'n the rest."

The lieutenant moved away now, and Bauer

watched him with breathless relief, turned to the sergeant, saw a wide, toothy smirk.

"Well, now, I guess my lieutenant likes what he sees in you, boy. You must seem awful pretty. No gals hereabouts worth pouncing on. Get outta here."

Bauer didn't hesitate, shouldered his musket, moved out into the path of an ambulance, heard a loud curse, jumped aside. He pushed through the dust, coughed, stood off the dirt street, his heartbeat returning to normal. He looked back toward the fat sergeant, thought of Willis, half the man's size, what Willis would do to the man regardless. Wish I could do that, he thought. Man acts like a scoundrel, just because he can.

Bauer looked out across the street, more streets, alleys and pathways, open ground, and broken storefronts. Well, he thought, you're in Chattanooga. Damn lovely place.

His first impression was no real impression at all, yet another Southern town trampled by the war. He walked now, down the street the lieutenant had directed him, moved past blasted foundations, shattered brick walls. Most of the timbers were gone completely, and Bauer stepped past one smoldering wreck of a house, saw a small flock of civilians, what had to be the citizens of this dismal place, moving slowly through the army that had occupied every part of their lives. Bauer saw the faces, weary and desperate, walking through the men in blue with glances of fear, surrender, hunger. There was a large tent, and Bauer smelled food, something boiling in a large pot, saw the civilians moving that way, noticed tin cups and plates in their hands. He kept walking, thought of the hardtack in his pocket, no appetite now, but that would change. Maybe in the camps . . . they got real food. He was suddenly swallowed, crushed by an odor that curled his face. He made a sound, one hand coming up to his nose, looked to the side, saw a growing bonfire, a heap of carcasses, a mound of dead mules, two men stoking the fire. The men seemed oblivious to the stink around them, one man tossing a split log onto the fire, the wood piercing the gut of a massively swollen animal. Bauer made another sound, quickened his step, saw now out past the bonfire, a corral, a dozen more animals, skeletal beasts with heads hung low. More soldiers were hauling in cloth sacks, spreading corn and grain into a trough, the horses lurching that way, some of them just standing still, too weak to eat. Bauer felt a cold shiver, had not expected this. The wounded men were a part of every fight, but the horses seemed always to be scattered **out there,** mounds of dead flesh far out in the fields, easier to avoid. The burial parties never had to worry about them, the vultures and other scavengers doing that job, the army usually moving on before the smells grew overwhelming. But the smells were there now, and Bauer pushed through it, eyed the street, pulled his brain back to the instructions he had heard from the lieutenant. He had forgotten to count the streets, looked back toward the pontoon bridge, a long block away. He focused on the officer's words, looked the other way, saw a large brick building, a single sign, THE CRUTCH- FIELD HOUSE. It was a surprise, an imposing three- story building that seemed untouched by the war. He was curious, stepped that way, saw a gathering of soldiers, a line of ambulances, and now, beside a row of open windows, a stack of severed limbs. He stopped abruptly, had seen that as well, knew that whatever the Crutchfield House had once been, right now, it was a hospital. He thought of the boy on the bridge, the festering wound, closed his eyes, turned away. He blinked hard, searched his mind for the lieutenant's instructions, gripped the mus- ket, laid it high across his shoulder, turned toward an open street, more soldiers, another scrawny horse, the way the officer had told him to go.

B auer had been directed to the brigade head- quarters, had been jubilant at seeing Willis there, as though his friend was waiting for him. But that illusion was swept away quickly. The show of emotion from his friend had been what he expected, an unsmiling shake of the hand, no display of Willis's affection for him in front of the brass. But Bauer had seen the scolding frown, si- lently questioning why Bauer seemed to need to follow his friend through whatever hell Willis could find. Willis kept his decorum, had formally introduced him to the brigade's commander, Colonel Marshall Moore, Bauer's paperwork handed off to the colonel's adjutant. Bauer had expected more, at least a hearty shake of his shoulders, but Willis was engulfed by the business of the army, maps spread on tables, officers in clean uniforms passing along orders from men high above Colonel Moore. Bauer knew he was out of place, that the meetings went on only because no one seemed to notice him, Willis included. After a crisp salute toward Moore, Willis had motioned Bauer away, then followed him, still no hearty jostling between them, the captain and the private keeping to their place as Willis led him through the camps. In no more than a minute, Willis had taken him to a row of campfires, as familiar to Bauer as the camps of the men he had traveled with, the Pennsylvanians he had now left behind. Willis called the men to attention, but it was not parade drill, the men staying close to the fires, obeying their captain by simply paying attention to what he had to say.

Bauer was nervous, held his musket by his side, saw stacked arms beyond the fire, wondered where they would allow him to add his own to the muskets of the rest. He stood for a long silent moment, waited while the men responded to Willis's call, saw no smile from them, no polite greetings, no friendly camaraderie. They simply watched him, no one speaking, and Willis stepped in front of him.

"New man. Private Bauer. He's a veteran. Believe that. You'll want him along for the ride. I've seen you baboons empty your cartridge boxes at a rebel fifty yards away. Well, you'll want this man to finish the job. Best sharpshooter in the Wisconsin regiments. His fists aren't worth a good damn, so none of you fog brains need to test him. He loses any teeth, I'll come after yours. No time for stupidity."

Bauer saw no change of expression in any of the men. One man spit into the campfire, then turned away, some of the others doing the same. Bauer tried to read the faces, some of the men doing the same to him, but Willis's words seemed to have meaning.

Willis grabbed his arm, said, "This way, Private. I'll show you where you sleep. Tents, we've got plenty. Bedrolls, too. Yours looks like it's been eaten by worms. You carrying any vermin? Any passengers?"

"No, sir. Boiled my uniform back in Bridgeport. The Pennsylvania boys I tagged along with had 'em aplenty."

"Thought you said he was Wisconsin, Captain."

Bauer looked toward the voice, an older man, a corporal, seated in a loose curl of thin legs, burnt red skin, a hat that carried a small round hole.

Willis nudged Bauer. "Answer him."

Bauer tried to add a seriousness to his voice. "Milwaukee, Wisconsin, born and raised. They stuck me in with those Eastern fellows just for the march."

"I heard tell they're soft as a baby's ass, every one of 'em."

Bauer realized he was being challenged, felt Willis watching him.

"That's the way I saw it. I might not have been in as many scraps as you, but I did my piece at Shiloh, Corinth, Vicksburg. On the march with those Pennsylvanians . . . fell into a fight in the valley back over across the river a couple nights ago. Those Pennsylvania fellows . . . well, there was a considerable amount of pee let out when the rebs opened up on us."

He had the man's interest, others eyeing him.

"What about **you**?"

Bauer was in the game now, put a hand on his lower gut.

"Still got mine right here. You got a latrine hereabouts, or you just hold yourself over the fire till it steams out?"

The men laughed, Bauer's ridiculous boast seeming to work. Some of the men went back to their business, the faces looking away, the formal introductions past. The corporal still watched him, a grim smile, looked again to the fire.

"Okay, Captain. If he can shoot as big as he talks,

he'll be fine. You can bed him with me, if you want. Got a space since Garvey went down."

Bauer felt a tug on his sleeve, and Willis said, "Musket over there. That first stack. Then, follow me."

Willis walked away, and Bauer went to the stack of muskets, eased his up carefully, glanced at the other weapons, some of them nearly new, a dark sheen on the barrels. He turned, saw Willis waiting for him, moved that way. He felt a stir in his stomach, realized how nervous he had been. Regulars, he thought.

Willis led him past a row of tents, then turned, pointed. "In there."

Bauer bent low, peered in, saw another man's bedroll, and Willis shoved him from behind, Bauer tumbling face-first onto the soft dirt, the floor of the tent. Bauer spit dust from his mouth, turned, expected Willis's usual scowl, was surprised to see a smile.

"You've not changed a whit. Dumb as an oyster, you know that?" Bauer cleared the dirt from his mouth, and Willis knelt down. "You do know that it's only gonna be a day or so before those boys make you show 'em how to do it."

"Do what?"

"Just how it is that you . . . pee."

Willis laughed again, sat now, his knees up to his chest.

"What the hell were you thinking about? They

toss you out of the Seventeenth Wisconsin, or did you just run away?"

"Glad to see you, too, Sammie." He caught the reaction on Willis's face, had gone through the scolding before, his casual lack of formality. "Sorry. Captain Willis, sir."

"They told me you had signed up for this, that the colonel approved it. So you want to be a regular soldier. You know what that means, Dutchie? It means you'll be expected to **like** this. They've got officers in this unit who went to West Point. That corporal out there? Toughest hombre I've ever seen. I watched him rip a rebel's arm out of his shoulder at Chickamauga. Took the fellow's head off with a knife. The rest? Well, they know how to fight. Been at Stones River, and most everywhere else Buell and Rosecrans decided to put 'em." Willis paused. "What the hell's the matter with you?"

"Nothing. It's different now, that's all. Just not so damn scared anymore. It's a job, Sammie. Captain. Damn."

"It's okay. We're alone. Some of those older gents out there don't pay much mind to rank anyway. They made me prove I was tougher'n nails before they'd pay a bit of attention. Colonel Moore's a good man, they listen to him. He gave me permission to smack any one of 'em if I didn't like the way they looked at me. Only did it once. Broke a fellow's jaw. Big talker. Not so big anymore. Made my point, so now they pay attention. Most of 'em still don't salute, except maybe toward the colonel. The generals? They stay the hell out of here. And woe be to the stupid volunteer who wanders through this camp by mistake. These boys love their reputation, the **legends,** all those tall tales about regulars. It's all bull, but the volunteers don't know that. They think we're over here ripping trees out of the ground with our teeth, gnawing on horse bones. So far, not one cannibal in the bunch, at least so I've been told." Willis laughed again. "And this is where you want to be?"

"Yeah, Sammie."

"They fight like hell, Dutchie. There's no bull about that, I promise you. I'm the tough-assed company commander now, but I tell you what. I used to want to be out front so I could kill the first rebel, lead the way into hellfire all by myself. Still want to, I guess. But these boys . . . only difference between me and them is the rank, the bars on my shoulder. It's like most of these boys hope this war never ends, that we can keep killing rebels, or Mexicans or Indians or whoever else sticks their nose in our business. One day, all those volunteer regiments will toss off their uniforms and run home to their mamas. But these boys will still be out here eating dirt. Like I said, Dutchie. They **like** it."

"That's why you came here, isn't it? You like it, too."

Willis looked down between his knees. "I came over here because this is my home. Figured it out a while back. I'm gonna die a soldier. Only thing that matters to me. I'm gonna kill every rebel who stands up in front of me, until one of 'em gets lucky enough to get me first."

Bauer hesitated, one thought rolling through him. He took a long breath. "What about . . . home, Sammie? What about your boy?"

Willis kept his stare on the ground. "Knew you'd ask me that. She took him. Ran off with some . . . shopkeeper, banker, not even sure. Wrote me not to look for her. Headed to someplace west, California maybe. Might as well be on the moon. I got no son, Dutchie. Maybe best I never seen him. Maybe best she's got a man can give them more than I could."

Bauer felt a cold horror. "My God. How could she. . . ."

Willis jerked his head up, a hard, cold stare Bauer had seen before. "Let it go, Dutchie. It's done. The closest thing I got to a son . . . to family . . . is these boys. And now, **you.** God help me."

There was a hint of humor in Willis's words, and Bauer felt relief, watched his friend for some sign of sadness. But Willis was as stoic as he had always been.

Bauer slipped the backpack off his shoulders, said, "That corporal . . . he sleep here?"

"When he sleeps at all. You heard him. There's a space in here 'cause we lost a man . . . few days ago. Rebel picked him off poking out too far past the picket line. Thought he'd go fight a little bit of the war by himself. No patience for that, no matter how tough these boys think they are. Official word went back to the colonel that he was picked off bathing in the river. Didn't want some high-brass jackass coming in here chewing us out about protocol." Willis paused again, looked hard at Bauer. "You sure this is what you want?"

"I'm here, ain't I? I'll not let you down, Sammie. Not once. I came here to be a soldier, just like you. It feels like I been given a gift. You know that. I'm good at killing a man when he don't even know I'm on this earth. Don't know why it's happened that way. Can't believe God would do that."

"God gave us this war, Dutchie. It's our job to fight it the best way we can. For you, that means blowing a man's brains out. I prefer seeing him up close."

There was grim certainty in Willis's voice, something else Bauer had seen before.

"Look, Captain. I'll kill as many rebels as it takes, as many as you, or some general or President Lincoln, wants me to." He paused. "Last week . . . I killed a reb officer back at Bridgeport. Four hundred yards, maybe. Did it . . . for sport. Impressed the heckfire out of those Pennsylvania boys. Bothered me at first. But those Eastern fellows . . . you shoulda heard them cheering me. Yep, they were impressed. **I** was impressed. Tough shot, took the fellow right off his horse. And ever since then, it's all I can think about. I see wounded men, and it makes me sick. Wounds and chopping up people ain't the best way to end this war. It's gonna take folks who can shoot straight. No matter how scared I get, no matter how many rebels come at us, by God, Sammie, I'm itching to do it again." He paused. "God help me, too, Sammie, but I **do** like it. Just like you."

Willis stood, brushed dirt off his pants. "All right, Private. Bugle sounds at four thirty. There's bacon and coffee. Your tent mate, Corporal Owens, will be up long before that, and if I was you, I'd keep to his good side. So don't roll around in your sleep, and keep your hot wind to yourself." Willis paused, hands on his hips, looked out over the top of the tent. "General Grant's running this army, same as Vicksburg. You wanna kill rebels, I'm pretty sure you'll get your chance. But that doesn't change what I said." Willis bent low, stared at him with a hint of a grin. "You're still as dumb as an oyster."

CHAPTER EIGHTEEN

BAUER

CHATTANOOGA—
NOVEMBER 3, 1863

He followed three other men, the small squad assigned by Willis to find out just what was so exciting about the supposed bounty some of the men were pulling from the murky waters of the Tennessee River. The energy for this particular mission had come from the company's cooks, curious to try their hands at a different fare than what the commissary was providing. Bauer had no problem with the food they had now, ample supplies of ham, beef, dark bread, coffee that actually tasted like coffee. But Willis had heard talk from other commanders, that with so little activity along the front line, especially the wide band of water that separated the two armies, there was no harm in anyone testing out their skills at harvesting a dinner few of these men had enjoyed for many months.

Bauer had no interest in fishing, had rarely done any of that in Wisconsin. There the tales ran tall, his father's friends bragging about the huge hauls they brought in from Lake Michigan, or from the cold-water lakes to the north. There the prize catch was pike, a fish with the kind of bones that impale a child's throat, and so Bauer's mother repeated that lore with enough vigor that his father had given up ever bringing home a fish at all. Bauer had never known any of his childhood friends who had suffered that catastrophic malady, and questions to his mother always produced the same vague response, that it had been some boy somewhere else, a neighbor's friend, some distant cousin of a boy she could never actually name. But the fear had been planted, and Bauer had avoided eating fish most of his life. Now he was on a mission to catch as many as the men could haul, and if they couldn't find the means, the poles and lines and hooks to do the job, they were told to barter with those skilled fishermen who might be interested in sharing. To Bauer, this was the most ridiculous assignment any officer had given him. From the cheerful gleam in Willis's eye, it was obvious to Bauer that Willis felt the same way.

They pushed through a brush line, brief nods to a scattering of skirmishers, men who lay on flat rocks and soft beds of grass, no attempt at disguise, no cover at all. The day was warm and clear, what seemed to be a rarity in this part of the world, and the men along the picket line seemed fully intent on capturing as much of the sun's rays as nature would provide them.

They could see the river now, brown water sliding past, and Bauer's instincts made him cautious, the hard itch spreading through him, that standing in the wide open could only invite trouble. The men in front of him kept moving, down a gentle slope, closer to the water's edge, but Bauer stopped, close enough to the brush that he could make a quick dive into cover. Across the river, Lookout Mountain rose up tall to his right, and to the left was a wide green valley, the low ground that spread out between the mountain and Missionary Ridge. Directly across the river was the mouth of a wide creek, and Bauer froze, the musket pulled in tight to his side. On both banks of that stream were a handful of rebels.

He saw the others who had come with him looking that way, no one speaking, and now a sergeant rose up, said aloud, "Don't go getting all excited about nothing. Any man here fires his musket answers to me. We got us an understanding with those fellows, and I don't need nobody messing that up."

The sergeant settled back down into a grassy bed, his hat down over his eyes. Bauer kept his eyes on the rebels, counted a dozen men, maybe more, none of them paying any attention to the Yankees who spread along this side of the river. He gauged the distance, the river no wider than an easy musket shot, thought, Somebody over here needs to keep a close eye. All it takes is one officer with a burr in his backside, and there's a skirmish. He glanced behind him up the sloping hill, saw men huddled around small fires, no one holding a musket at all. He looked toward the sergeant again, saw the man stretched out flat on his grassy bed, heard a hint of a snore. He still felt uneasy, fought a laugh, thought, Maybe this is the right way to fight a war. Everybody just takes a nap.

He pressed on past the last of the brush, saw more men in blue out to both sides, some right along the water's edge. And every one of them was holding a fishing pole. The scene was idyllic, low, quiet talk, and Bauer looked again toward the rebels, saw the same scene, a scattering of men along their side of the river, their fishing poles extended out over the water.

To one side, another of Willis's men, younger, and the boy Bauer only knew as Hoover. Hoover leaned low behind the man, said, "What kind of fish they got here?"

The man looked back at him, shrugged. "Hell if I know. Some of 'em stink pretty bad. Some eat better than others."

Bauer moved closer, saw the man's bare feet covered in mud, studied the crooked pole, saw a string tied to the far end, dangling loosely in the water.

The line ended at a piece of stick, a makeshift float, which moved with the current, drifting down to the right, the man now raising it out of the water, swinging the line out, dropping it again upstream. Bauer caught a glimpse of the bait, something white dangling from a hook. He moved up beside Hoover, said to the man, "What you using?"

The man looked back at him again, seemed suddenly suspicious. "What's it matter? Family secret."

Bauer saw the man's hat, Missouri, thought of the provost sergeant. They gotta be the most unfriendly bunch in the army. Bauer watched the other three men spreading along the riverbank, joining in beside other fishermen, more men from Missouri. The conversations began now, some of the fishermen bragging about their catch, one man holding up a fish the size of Bauer's forearm. Bauer moved that way, stared at the fish, saw a small cluster of whiskers along its mouth, the gills in motion, the fish still alive. The man looked at him, obviously proud of himself.

"Catfish. So they tell me. River's full of 'em. Carp, and some little pissants, too. They'll all eat better than hardtack." The man eyed Bauer now, suddenly concerned. "You get your own. I caught this fella fair and square."

Bauer backed away, had no idea how to begin.

"I got no pole. Captain just sent us down here, didn't tell us what to bring. Said we could maybe trade you fellows for the right equipment."

"Got none extra. You got nothing I need, anyways."

To one side, a man called out, "Hey! The reb got one. A beauty, looks like."

Bauer followed their gaze across the river, heard a whoop, the rebel holding up the fish, clearly for the benefit of the Yankees. Beside him, the fisherman said, "Dang it all. He does that every blessed day. I catch one, he catches one better."

Bauer couldn't help the question. "Who? You know him?"

"Guess so. Names Goofby, or something like. That whole bunch hails from close by, Tennessee boys. No fair. They growed up fishing in this here place. Looks like I owe that scoundrel another sack of coffee."

There was laughter from the others, one man calling out, "Hey, Herschel, when you gonna learn not to make no wager with a rebel? They probably got a pile of fish stuck in those bushes, and just wait for you to catch something, then drag one out bigger just to make you look stupid."

The man they called Herschel slumped, a low curse.

"Gotta drag the raft out. I'll wait till dark, slip across. Don't need the lieutenant watching that. Unless I get a monster in the next half hour. The contest's over at four. Same every dang day. Well, unless my luck changes, I gotta go steal me some coffee from the mess wagon."

Another man looked back at Bauer, said, "You wanna learn how it's done, don't pay any attention to Herschel. Rebels got these fish trained just so. Those Tennessee boys been mighty accommodating at letting us catch just enough fish that we start thinking we know what we're doing. Rest of us figured out not to waste a bet with 'em. Herschel's not too smart."

Bauer felt the good spirits in the men, looked over at the jubilation of the rebels.

"What do **they** wager?"

"Their fish. Herschel ain't figured that out yet. They done caught all they can eat. They'll toss us one even when this rock brain loses the wager. Guess they figure this river is big enough for all of us."

Bauer pointed to the man's fishing pole. "Can you tell me where we can get . . . those things?"

The man looked at him again, laughed. "Back there in the brush, there's some willows or something close. Cut you one twice as tall as you."

"We got no string, or hooks. Can you spare any?"

"Nope. But if'n you ain't got the tools, you gotta make do. Keep close to the bank and wade out down thataways. Past that dead tree, it's too shallow to fish. But there's plenty of mussels and snails. Just dig in the mud. Bayonet makes it easier."

"What's a mussel?"

"Some kinda slimy thing lives in a shell. Just

one more of God's creatures. But they boil up real good."

The men with Bauer began to move that way, and Bauer followed, still eyeing the rebels. He watched the others now, slipping barefoot into the murky water. Bauer scanned the river, memories of the swamps along the Mississippi, nervous lookouts watching for alligators. But the muddy river flowed past with only the ripples from smaller creatures, what Bauer assumed were fish, swirling tails and flopping fins far out in deeper water. He heard a shout now, "Hey! Got some! Look here!"

Bauer saw a clump of black shells in Hoover's hands, mud dripping away, another man moving out with a cloth sack. The digging continued, the sack filling, and Bauer slipped off his brogans, eased out into the soft mud, the water colder than he expected. He looked into the sack, what seemed to be small, black, oblong rocks. Hoover knelt in the shallow water again, pulled up a thick handful of mud, and Bauer saw a different shell, round and tan, Hoover rinsing it, obvious excitement.

"Look here! Some kinda snail. What you think they taste like?"

Bauer had no appetite for anything covered in mud, said, "Crack it open. Find out."

Hoover sniffed his find, crushed the shell in his hands, picked through the gooey remains of the animal, then slipped it into his mouth, his eyes widening. He ejected it with a loud wet spit.

"Aagh. Ptew. Nasty. Tastes like mud and snot."

Along the riverbank, the men from Missouri were laughing, and one man called out, "You can't eat 'em raw, you brick heads. Fill that sack and haul 'em back to camp. You gotta cook 'em."

Bauer backed away from the men with the sack, said quietly, "Thanks. I'll stick with hardtack."

EAST OF CHATTANOOGA—
NOVEMBER 4, 1863

He was beginning to wonder if the rebels were going to fight at all. The routine was established among the others, and Bauer was now a part, going out on picket duty for a four-hour stretch. He had asked the others, the rest of Willis's men as curious as he was, just what was supposed to happen next. In the camps, the men seemed obsessed with Chickamauga, as though Bauer needed to know what these men had been called upon to do. They had left thirty men on that field, a hundred more wounded or just gone, presumed captured. No one offered a hint to Bauer that any of the men had simply run away, vanishing for reasons Bauer knew well. But now the curse of that fight was past, and the men prepared to do it all again, as they had done since the first year of the war. When they were finally ordered out east of the town to skirmish duty, the expectations ran high that, finally, there would be trouble. But for more than a week now, that duty had been as mundane as sitting idly in the camps, or marching, drilling in their various formations yet again.

He had centered himself in a cluster of brush, just beyond a burned-out barn, sat upright, his back against a soft rotten log, tall grass surrounding him. He was perched just high enough to see out across the flat field in front of him, far enough that anyone standing up would be clearly visible, if the rebels made any effort to push a line of troops his way. To his front rose the heights of Missionary Ridge, what Willis had told him was nearly six miles long, several hundred feet up a steep rocky hillside. Behind him, to his right, stood the eminence of Lookout Mountain, fifteen hundred feet high. High on both hills, the signal flags were clearly visible, the rebels waving their coded messages from one point along the tall ridge to another. Several hundred yards to his front, he could make out the rocks and brush on the slope itself, could see rifle pits and a trench line, cut like a deep scratch halfway up the long ridge. From his vantage point he could see movement on the ridge itself, down the face of the slope, flickers of color, horsemen, traveling along what seemed to be trails and gullies on the face of the slope. At the base of the hill were more rebel works, too low for a clear view, but what Bauer had to believe were stout fortifications. The memories of Vicksburg were fresh in his mind, the great mounds of earth, wide ditches, and wooden stakes, all the impediments to the army's advance. Then it had been a lengthy siege, the Federal commanders making that decision after two disastrous thrusts right into the teeth of the rebels' defenses. Bauer had been surprised to hear that a siege was happening here, but this time the rebels had hemmed in an entire army of blue. He understood now why the few citizens left in Chattanooga were so destitute. The army had been desperate, forced to starvation rations, stripping away everything from the town they could use, every scrap they needed for survival. But that was October. Within the past week, the supplies rolled across the pontoon bridges in massive wagon trains, bringing in every kind of matériel, horses and mules, ammunition, blankets, tents, and, of course, rations. Bauer had heard plenty of talk from the regulars that the rebels had made a ridiculous mistake, that by letting Hooker's divisions shove through the valley west of Lookout Mountain, they had made it easy for the Federal forces to strengthen, to regain their energy, and with that, their confidence. No one Bauer spoke to had compliments for William Rosecrans. At first he had been popular with the men, but the collapse at Chickamauga had soured Willis's men in particular, that they were cursed to follow yet another general whose inept maneuvering only produced disasters, and cost these men serious casualties. From all Bauer could tell, the men respected George Thomas, and word of General Grant's arrival had added that final spark, the impatient urgency to end this thing. The rebels were straight in front of them, and for weeks now, nothing about that had changed. Bauer had no idea what the volunteer regiments thought of that, whether or not they were anxious for another hard scrap. But the regulars had no patience for waiting. They had lost good men in good fights, and every one of them expected to do that again. But if losing men meant a quicker end to the war, that was a trade these men seemed willing to make. As they stood watch over the rebel positions on the distant heights, the question now was: when?

He felt the warmth of the sun, settling low behind him, dark in another hour, fought against sleepiness. No, don't do that. You fall asleep and Sammie'll have you by the tenders. He shifted position, worked the stiffness out of his back, turned, looked over his right shoulder toward Lookout Mountain. The signal flags were active there as well, and Bauer watched them for a long moment, wondered about their messages. What could they be telling each other? Hey, you over there! There's a heap of blue troops down there in the town! He laughed to himself. Every day, it's probably the same message. Or maybe somebody's found out there's better squirrel hunting up on that big rock than over there on the ridge, stupid rebels bragging how many tree rats they shot. He laughed at his own joke, the giddiness of his boredom. Maybe they're waving flags just to convince their officers they got something important to do. Beats marching, beats getting shot at. **Signal corps.** Never really thought about that job. He could see a fleck of color high on the ridge out in front of him, a man standing tall in a leafless tree, the red and white flag shifting position. He guessed the range . . . six hundred yards. No, more. Betcha one of those boys get knocked out of his tree every now and then. Might be fun trying. He glanced down at the musket. Nope. Don't think about that. Sammie'll have you by the tenders for that, too, drawing attention to yourself. And it's uphill a bunch. I'd have to aim twenty feet above the reb's head. He thought of the officer he had dropped at Bridgeport. That signalman would go down the same way . . . never know what hit him, that's for sure. If I hit him at all. No, leave that alone. No need to show off around here. Not yet anyway.

He rolled over to one side, looked again at Lookout Mountain. The highest part of the mountain was imposing, a sheer cliff that extended up across the top third of the heights. It was another of the rare clear days, no fog or mist hiding anything across the entire landscape. The sky overhead was a soft blue, and he rolled to his back again, stared up, the strange clear shapes in his eyes dancing across his vision. It would sure as hell be easy to sleep out here. Maybe that's what we need to do, bring the whole regiment out here. Maybe the whole army. He looked out to the left, a bulging wooded hill, what Willis said was Orchard Knob. Probably rebs there, he thought, watching us. Only high ground across this whole place. Maybe artillery, too. Don't need to get any attention from those boys. And you sure better not let some reb slip up on you. But it's pretty flat ground. No place to hide. He thought of the platoon sergeant, another grim man named Griswold, younger than the corporal, Owens, but just as tough, and like most of the sergeants Bauer had known, a man with the uncanny ability for creative swearing. Yep, you keep to Griswold's good side. Don't need to make enemies in this outfit unless there's a good reason. And I can't think of a single one.

Bauer was quickly learning the men in Willis's company, could see immediately that they had no tolerance for laziness, for shirkers. There were stories about the drumheads, men with shaved heads, forced to march through the entire regiment, and so marched right out of the army, never to return. To the regulars, that kind of shame was the ultimate disgrace. Bauer had heard plenty of talk in the past, knew that the volunteer regiments regarded the regulars with some kind of awe, as though these men carried an aura about them, tougher, rowdier, prone to violence against one another as much as the enemy. Bauer could already see the mythology in that. These men are just soldiers, he thought. Nothing special, except they don't expect to go home anytime soon. They've seen plenty of fights, taken plenty of casualties. Nothing **different** about that. But if the rest of the army thinks they're just a little churned up in the head . . . I guess that's not so bad. We. Not **them. We.**

The 17th Wisconsin had been mostly Irish, and so there was a common bond among those men, habits and family ties. But the men around Bauer now were a mix of every kind of man, vast differences in age, every ethnicity. Corporal Owens seemed to be from someplace near the center of hell, the tent Bauer shared now smelling of burnt cinders and rawhide. But Bauer knew enough of fighting to sense a nasty brand of menace in the man, that when the rebels were close, Owens wouldn't flinch. Another man to stay close to, he thought. Just wish I didn't have to sleep beside him. He has a bad dream, he might strangle me.

He gazed again along the wide ridgeline. The duty was simple. Make sure the rebels on the crest and in their rifle pits stayed there. No surprises. He had done plenty of this before, picket duty. But the flat, grassy plain in front of him was empty, as much as he could tell. To both sides, other men were hidden in the clusters of brush, and he could hear them, low chatter, the occasional laugh. The closest man to him was Brubaker, a short plug of a

man, who rarely had anything to say. Bauer looked
that way, the top of the man's hat barely visible in
a clump of tall grass. No one seemed to care that
he had come from the volunteers, or that he was as
much a veteran as many of them. But Bauer didn't
expect to be ignored, which had turned out to be a
relief. There hadn't been any of the ridiculous challenges, no insistence that he prove his masculinity,
all the foolishness of men who betrayed their own
fears and uncertainty by attacking anyone new. I
guess they took Sammie's word for it, he thought.
Or they just don't care. We get in a fight . . . then
they'll care.

He felt a rumble in his stomach, thought of the
hardtack in his pack, had no appetite for a mouth-
ful of dry dust. He looked to his left, called out,
"Hey, Brubaker."

He waited, saw the hat move slightly, the voice
coming back to him, low, soft. **Careful.**

"Quiet down. What you want?"

"You bring any bacon with you?"

"Nope."

Bauer waited for more, Brubaker now silent. But
the boredom was overwhelming him. Where are
the rebels? They just gonna stay on that big stupid
hill?

He called out again, less volume this time. "Hey,
Brubaker, where you from?"

"New Jersey. Shut up."

Out in front of Brubaker, a voice rolled out

through the grass. "Now, that ain't so dang awful polite, there. Boy's just wantin' some bacon. I'd care for a slab myself, if'n you was willing to swap. Maybe some coffee?"

Bauer's heart leapt in his chest, the musket across his knees grabbed with both hands. He stared ahead, nothing but tall grass, heard another voice, straight out in front of him.

"Aw, you know them bluebellies, Paul. They ain't about to make a decent trade less'n they get all the advantages. Hey, hungry boy! I got some dried corn mush. You got anything I cain't get from home?"

Bauer hesitated, angry at himself now, thought, How close? Thirty yards, maybe. To his left, Brubaker spoke up.

"No time for jabber, Johnnies. We're being relieved pretty quick. The captain says no dealing with you."

"Well, heckfire, Yank. We been holdin' a swap out here right regular. Got me a real nice leather satchel from one of you boys for a pound of tobacco. No need to go and be all **army** on us."

The other rebel spoke now, Bauer straining to see any movement in the grass.

"Now, Paul, you know these lads are regular army. Eighteenth Regiment, First Battalion, Company D. That'd be Captain Willis, Colonel Moore. They say these boys got steel in their backsides. Maybe their front sides, too. Women scared to pieces when these boys march through. Ain't you scared, Paul?"

"Yep. Reckon so. Wonder how they'll stand up to twelve pounds of grapeshot?"

"Reckon that time'll come soon enough."

Bauer understood what the men were doing, the boasting that the rebels knew exactly who they were facing. Their scouts were every bit as efficient as anyone in blue, both sides letting the other know how much information they had.

Bauer waited for more, heard a rustle in the grass behind him, jumped to the side, whipping the musket around, saw the face of Corporal Owens.

"What the hell's ailing you? You weren't sleeping, were you?"

Bauer shook his head. "No. You just . . . surprised me!" He lowered his voice now, pointed out to the front. "There's rebs about thirty yards thataway. Picket line I guess."

Owens slipped up beside him, didn't seem to hear him. "I'm relieving you. Go on back to camp. There's a bucket of something supposed to be chicken. Word came down from Colonel Moore that there's a passel of rebels on the move over in that valley, between the hills. First real marching the rebs have done in a while. Best remember that the next time you're sent out here. Something's up, and if it's coming through here, you better be awake." Owens settled in, his musket across his legs, then leaned closer to Bauer, surprising him, said in a whisper, "Now, Private, let me teach you something." He called out now, "Hey, Paul, that you?"

The response came from in front of Brubaker's perch. "'Tis surely, Randall. Who's the new fella?"

"Wisconsin. Name's Bauer. Edgy chap. Says he can take the eyeball out'n a squirrel at five hundred yards."

"Well, now. We can use us a good squirrel poker back over the river."

"Nope. He's ours, for now. But I'd keep your head down till he gets used to how damn annoying you are."

Bauer tried to hold the laugh inside, but Owens's grim expression never changed. Bauer leaned close, bathed in the man's odd smell, wanted to tease the man, felt utterly foolish for his caution.

"Hell, Corporal, I didn't know you all were friends out here. You shoulda told me. I can bring something to trade, if that'll help."

Owens looked at him, close, eye to eye, said in a soft whisper, "You ain't paying attention, Private Bauer. Let me explain something to you. We're out here making nicely with those boys for one damn good reason. When the game starts, all our 'friends' out there might just pause a wink, that Paul fellow keep his fingers off'n the trigger before he realizes I got my bayonet in his throat."

Bauer sat back, felt the heat in the man's words. Owens settled against the fallen log, pulled his hat low across his brow, said, "Now go on. Git. That chicken'll be gone quick."

Bauer pulled the musket up beside him, crawled

through the matted path in the tall grass, felt suddenly nervous, sweat in his palms. The men around Chattanooga had been behaving as though the war had become **lazy,** long days of nothing to do, nothing to hear but the scattered artillery duels, the gunners on both sides putting up a fireworks display that seemed aimed at no one at all. He looked upward again, the signal flags on Lookout Mountain, rebels sitting high on their perches, no threat, no danger, making no effort even to be an army. But, they're still the enemy. Owens never forgets that, he thought. Sammie, neither. The time's coming, no doubt about it. General Grant's here? They didn't bring him all the way to Chattanooga so we can sit out here and swap tobacco. He glanced back toward Owens, and beyond, out toward the tall grass where the rebel pickets sat, heard more of the talk down the line, more of the pickets still playing the game. He understood now what Owens was saying, what they all seemed to know, that when the **real** game started, these men in blue would move forward together, and those rebels with their bartering and their friendly talk would be the first to die.

CHAPTER NINETEEN

CLEBURNE

NEAR CHICKAMAUGA STATION—
NOVEMBER 4, 1863

The men continued to march well past his camps, a slow, plodding shuffle, no enthusiasm, no spirit at all that would tell anyone that these same men had crushed the enemy at Chickamauga. Cleburne watched intently, had wondered about these men who came from the East, who had broken the enemy's lines so completely at the great fight a month before. He wondered more about their commander, how James Longstreet had marched his troops to Tennessee with expectations of . . . what? Command? Victory? Every general in Bragg's army was well aware that Longstreet had come south with more than a mere chip on his shoulder. His presence had resulted in complete turmoil, had pulled Cleburne into a destructive conspiracy, as it had done to so many others. Longstreet hadn't begun that dissension. Bragg seemed to inspire rebellion among his commanders everywhere he placed his headquarters. But Longstreet had dragged the bitterness out in the open, laid it bare for the army and Jefferson Davis to see. The result thus far had benefited no one, an army held in a sickly paralysis by Bragg's fear of the enemies in his own camp.

The troops marching through the valley below him were moving out toward Tyner's Station, the rail depot near the junction of Chickamauga Creek and the Tennessee River, several miles north of the Federal position at Chattanooga. The only real information Cleburne had about these men had come from Hardee, that Longstreet's corps had been ordered away, to board the trains that would carry them toward Knoxville. Bragg had explained the move to his generals as the most effective way to blunt any threat from Burnside's Federal forces camped now around that city, an essential bit of security to protect the flank that Cleburne held, the northernmost position of Bragg's long line that spread out across Missionary Ridge.

Cleburne watched them from high up the ridgeline, a stand of timber to his left, the drop-off that sloped toward the junction of the two waterways. The men moved past in long lines, no one hurrying them along, no one seeming to care just how long it took for them to fill the cars. The engines had been waiting since dawn, thick black smoke belching out from fat stacks, and Cleburne had counted the cars, then estimated the size of the force Longstreet commanded. It was a puzzle why there seemed to be far too many men for far too few cars. All through the morning, what he had observed seemed clumsy and inefficient, something Cleburne had seen before. So often when Bragg's army was on the move, there were never enough railcars, or the engines to pull them, and now that was more obvious than ever. This will take a ridiculous amount of time, he thought. Moving . . . what? Ten thousand men? Twelve? To what end?

Cleburne's division anchored the far right flank of Bragg's entire position, and so, they were the force closest to the depot at Tyner's Station, on the Georgia and East Tennessee Line, the most direct rail line the Confederates still held that would move a large force toward Knoxville. Already two divisions of Confederate troops and Joe Wheeler's cavalry were maneuvering to confront Burnside's Federals, and Cleburne had studied the maps, had assumed that if Bragg believed a stronger force was needed against Burnside, the most logical maneuver would be for Cleburne's troops to pull out of position on Missionary Ridge and make the short march to Tyner's, where the railcars could be gathered without any threat from the Federal artillery near Chattanooga. To fill the vacancy left by Cleburne, the remaining troops along Missionary Ridge could easily shift to their right, with little sacrifice to the strength Bragg's army held on the heights. But the troops he saw now had marched down from their position on Lookout Mountain, the far end of the Confederate position from where Cleburne stood.

Hardee had left him early that morning, some vague duty involving paperwork, which Hardee wouldn't discuss. But Cleburne began to wonder now, if Hardee had gone to Bragg, another exercise in futility, making yet another effort to convince Bragg that if this army ever had an advantage over the Federal troops in Chattanooga, that advantage was rapidly slipping away.

And now Cleburne saw the color bearer, the telltale staff officers in formation behind their commander. They had gathered around one of Cleburne's outposts, clearly visible, had turned, making the long, slow climb toward where Cleburne sat now. Paperwork be damned, he thought. This is why Hardee left me here. He doesn't want any part of **this.**

The men pushed up the long hill directly toward him, their flag unfamiliar, a handful of aides led by a large hulk of a man who rode slumped over, as though he might tumble forward at any moment. Cleburne recognized Longstreet easily, knew him from the conspiratorial meetings that had brought so much turmoil to Bragg's command. Longstreet was a sour, brooding man, who seemed to enjoy very little, especially the company of the officers who served Bragg. It was very clear to Cleburne, and to everyone else who had taken part in the effort to unseat Bragg, that Longstreet held tightly to his own expertise, believed absolutely that his place was at the head of the table. Cleburne had heard the talk that Longstreet had come to Tennessee expecting full command, and when Bragg resisted that notion, as Bragg certainly would, the animosity between the two men had quickly boiled over into a full-blown feud. Longstreet's stunning heroics at Chickamauga had been a perfectly timed assault against a confused shifting in the Federal lines. Longstreet's men had smashed completely through the Federal center, splitting their position in two. The result was a stampede that swept Rosecrans and his army back to Chattanooga. It was the kind of victory that the newspapers would always embrace, adding one more reason for Bragg to hate the man.

With a dull dread, Cleburne watched him climbing the long hill, searched quickly behind him for any sign that Hardee might rescue him from whatever Longstreet would say to him, or worse, how he would respond.

Longstreet glanced up, no greeting, pushed the horse closer, one hand now rising, holding back the staff. He continued alone, and Cleburne felt the man's eyes on him, probing him, and Cleburne searched his brain for something benign to say, had no talent for meaningless chatter. He couldn't avoid thoughts of Jefferson Davis, extracting from Cleburne what amounted to a pledge of loyalty to Braxton Bragg. Don't bring me into another argument, he thought. I'm just better off keeping my mouth closed.

Longstreet offered a brief smile, halted the horse several yards from Cleburne, as though keeping his distance on purpose.

"Halloo, General. How's things with the Irish these days?"

There was no joy to Longstreet's salute, an odd joke that Cleburne didn't know how to take.

"Can't rightly say, sir. Not many Irish about. Just me, I suppose."

"Then how are things with **you,** General?"

"Watching the enemy. Not much to see in that quarter. I was told to keep a sharp eye out for a retreat northward, but there's no sign of that."

Longstreet nudged the horse closer, as though satisfied Cleburne would actually speak to him.

"No, I'm quite sure you've seen no retreat." Longstreet paused. "These are not good times, Mr. Cleburne. Your commanding general has proven himself to be a master at achieving victories without achieving success. That requires genuine talent. I offer you my sincere regrets. Your commanding general is one of a kind."

Cleburne wouldn't offer any kind of opinion about Bragg, not anymore. He glanced back, his staff gathering, and he focused on Captain Buck, motioned them all away, didn't need any more ears hearing anything Longstreet might say.

"Sir, I do admit to being surprised to see you up this way. I was told by General Hardee that the trains would be embarking this morning. I admit that I was surprised your troops would be the ones to make the journey."

Longstreet leaned forward on his saddle, rubbed a hand through the horse's mane. "Were you now? There should be no surprises left in these parts. If you can dream it, it will happen. The more fantastic your imagination, the more likely your dreams will be realized. My dream was to be free of Braxton Bragg, and yes, miracles do occur. I am taking leave of the Army of Tennessee. I suppose that is a good thing to some. You'll hear talk aplenty, but I assure you, this was not my decision. My men and I are merely following the orders as issued by General Bragg, as approved by the president. They seem to work as a team, you know. Like two oxen, pulling a wheel-less wagon."

Cleburne wasn't completely sure what Longstreet was talking about. "I'm not privy to your orders, sir. Division commanders are not always kept so informed. My job is to manage my brigades, keep 'em sharp, make sure the Yankees don't try to slip out around us . . . or away from us."

"Relax, General. I'm not here to give you an examination. General Hardee is more than capable, and he wouldn't have put you out here on the flank if you weren't up to the task. I would enjoy serving beside General Hardee, should the occasion arise. But that is not a likely happenstance. I've a new task, you know."

"No, sir. Don't really know. Not my place."

Longstreet stared at him hard now. "Bull. You know my men are boarding those trains for Knoxville. Burnside is up there waiting for us, scratching himself with indecision. His way. Could be an opportunity to shove those boys right out of Tennessee. But, you knew that."

"Yes, sir. Suppose I did."

Longstreet moved the horse up beside him, raised his field glasses, scanned across the flat plain toward Chattanooga. "Yep. You're the flank. Good rough ground. Good place to defend. You have the men fit for the task?"

"I believe so, sir."

Longstreet seemed to make a show of using the glasses, passing a silent moment, then he lowered them, turned toward Cleburne. "There's going to be a fight here. You understand that?"

"I try not to make predictions, sir. It's my place to follow General Hardee's orders."

"It's your place to use your men the most efficient way possible to defeat the enemy. Correct?"

"Yes, sir. Certainly."

"One would expect your commanding general to understand that as well."

"Yes, sir."

"Well, now, Mr. Cleburne, let me tell you some-thing you won't enjoy hearing. You see all those men gathering up along those tracks? If this army's headquarters sees fit to provide the necessary rail-cars, we shall embark on a great mission to destroy General Burnside at Knoxville. Flags unfurled, drums a-beating, bugles a-playing. One truly mag-nificent adventure, wouldn't you say?"

"If you say so, sir. I would hope you could return here in short order. If, as you say, there's to be a fight, we'll require all the strength this army can muster."

Longstreet stared at him, shook his head. "You won't be seeing me again, General. We do the job at Knoxville, we'll be marching back to Virginia."

Cleburne was surprised now, a bolt of concern.

"Finish the thought, Mr. Cleburne. Something to add?"

"I had thought . . . your corps would be detached only to deal with the Federals in Knoxville . . . then return here." He paused. "Not sure I understand why we're reducing our strength by your entire corps, in the face of an enemy that is reinforcing. So I've been told, anyway. General Hardee believes that Sherman is coming this way, with more men than you're taking away. I don't question General Bragg's decisions, of course."

Longstreet laughed, but the smile faded quickly. "And that, my good Irish friend, is why you're in a mountain of trouble. Sherman's coming, no doubt about that. Hooker's already over there. My people ran into him right west of the big mountain. Didn't fare well. There was some . . . difficulty with my commanders. Made an attack at night. Not always a good idea. But I allowed it, encouraged it. Surprise can be its own victory. But sometimes, Mr. Cleburne, it's simple mathematics. There were too many of them, and too few of us. Now Hooker has handed Grant control of that whole valley, the rail line west. They'll have no trouble resupplying whatever troops Grant brings in there."

"General Bragg believes they still might retreat, make their base at Nashville, until they can gather the rest of their army together."

Longstreet pulled a small pipe from his pocket, stared at it, seemed to debate lighting it. Cleburne felt a growing urgency to back away from this man, could feel the gloom Longstreet seemed to cast over every conversation. Longstreet kept the pipe unlit, stared out across the great open plain below them.

"Sam Grant's not retreating. Never has, not when it mattered. Bragg should have hit them weeks ago, thrown every artillery shell we had into that town. I suggested a move westward, hit them at Bridgeport, cut their supplies off so far back they'd have no choice but to pull out. Bragg refused, said we didn't have the wagons available, not enough horses or mules. Had another dozen reasons why the plan was wrongheaded. I suppose, if he'd have thought of it himself, we'd be out there right now, executing his 'brilliant' plan. So instead of moving west, I'm taking my men northeast. My mission, as the president explained it, is to ensure that the enemy **there** does us no damage **here.** But Burnside has never damaged much of anything. The problem is not Burnside. It's right out there. Grant will not only damage you, Mr. Cleburne, he'll grind you under his boot heel."

Cleburne saw a different look on Longstreet's face, a hint of a smile.

"You know Grant personally, sir?"

"Thought everyone knew that. You might say we were real close. I stood beside him at his wedding. That sound **close** to you?"

Cleburne was surprised, could see a darkness settling over Longstreet's stare, the man keeping his gaze out toward the town.

"I didn't know that, sir. Your knowledge of General Grant could be very useful in a confrontation, I would think."

Longstreet laughed again, kept his gaze on Chattanooga. "Not in this army. According to those in command, I'm not useful in the least."

Cleburne wondered what kind of memories Longstreet would have of Ulysses Grant. He struggled to fill the silence. "I suppose it's accurate to say, sir, that General Bragg would not have chosen you to stand at **his** wedding."

"Don't try to be clever with me, Mr. Cleburne. Bragg despises me, and for reasons no one in this army can understand, he has the full support of the president. So, together, they have agreed that I can best serve this army by . . . not serving this army. Bragg wants me gone, simple as that. And so he is depleting his strength by one-third, while out there, the enemy is trebling his. I'm not all that expert in mathematics, Mr. Cleburne. But I know poker. You're holding a pair of deuces, staring down the barrel of Grant's four aces." He paused. "President Davis is our own Emperor Nero, fiddling away while Rome burns." He looked at Cleburne now, a tilt of his head. "Risky talk, eh?"

"I can't judge you, sir. I can only wish you well in your campaign at Knoxville, and hope that you return to this army. We will certainly require your strength."

Longstreet shook his head. "You're naïve, Mr. Cleburne. Bragg won a thoroughly satisfying victory when the president authorized him to order me away from here. Reversing that decision, no matter how sound the reason, would give Bragg a defeat. No, whatever happens at Knoxville, my duty will once more be with General Lee. I will not return to this place, unless it is by Lee's command. Bragg will have achieved yet one more 'victory,' and, again, there will be no **success.** And for that, I offer you my condolences."

Longstreet tipped his hat toward Cleburne, rode down toward the crowd of troops still gathering up along the rail line. Cleburne watched him, felt a thick blanket of depression, the effect of Longstreet's demeanor, and his words. A plume of smoke caught his eye, another engine steaming its way up from the south. But there was nothing new to see, nothing he could do to speed along a process that seemed annoyingly slow. He turned his horse, rode up along the crest of the hill, stared out toward a cluster of wooded hills to the north, the river beyond, then down, across the wide plain that led to Chattanooga.

CLEBURNE'S HEADQUARTERS— MISSIONARY RIDGE— NOVEMBER 4, 1863—NIGHT

"You don't think he'll be brought back here?"

Hardee stared at the fire, shook his head. "He explained it quite clearly, Patrick. Bragg wants him gone, and so, he's gone. That happened to me once. Might happen to you one day. Polk's gone. Buckner. Hindman. This army's being managed by the temperament of a very small man."

Cleburne thought of Longstreet's description. **Risky talk.** "He is a strange man, General Longstreet."

Hardee looked at him, took a sip of his coffee. "Why?"

"If my men had been defeated by the enemy in Lookout Valley, as his were, I would be seeking a way to make amends, to turn the tide in our favor. But I heard nothing of protest in his words, or regret. He performed as General Bragg ordered him to, and then . . ."

"And then he did nothing further."

"Yes, sir. He did nothing further. Now he is leaving this place with full expectations that we are doomed, and yet he does not care to assist us. I do not understand him."

Hardee stood, tossed the remnants of his coffee aside. "Doesn't matter a whit, Patrick. We've still got the best ground, and I've got my best division commander on this flank. That's all we can do, all we can think about right now."

"Thank you for the compliment, sir."

"Don't thank me yet. Longstreet's right about one thing. There will be a fight. If not tomorrow, then maybe next week. The rains have slowed, the roads will get better. If I was General Grant, I'd be taking a hard look up this way. We've got the rail line close behind us, and if the enemy rolls up this flank, sweeps us off this ridge, it's open roads all the way to Georgia. Bragg's made his share of errors, no doubt about that. But this might be the worst of all. We're just . . . sitting here."

Cleburne leaned back in his small chair, looked up at Hardee. "Longstreet said we should have attacked the town much sooner."

"I agree."

"You think we should attack him now?"

"That opportunity has slipped away, I'm afraid. Longstreet's correct in his mathematics. We're surely outnumbered, and that's only going to get worse. I suspect Grant will make a strike against Lookout Mountain pretty quick. He's got the numbers to do it, squatting right now in that valley to the west. We've got . . . what? A single division holding that entire rock pile?"

"Then should we not strike at them right now? The longer we wait, the stronger they become. Surely there is some kind of opportunity. A quick surge, move across the plain at night, hit him at dawn, full force, one flank or the other?"

Hardee shook his head. "General Bragg is enjoying himself today, Patrick. He has removed an enormous thorn from his side. These days, that matters more to him than anything he could do to those boys in blue. We'll not move off these hills until Grant forces us to move. And right now, Grant's sitting in a comfortable chair, in front of a hearth fire, eating his evening meal. At some point tonight, he'll inquire of some staff officer just how far off General Sherman might be. The answer to that question will tell Grant when he can plan his next move. Bragg has no plan for attacking anyone. No, Patrick, as long as Braxton Bragg is in command, nothing will change. All we're going to do is wait."

CHAPTER TWENTY

GRANT

CHATTANOOGA—
NOVEMBER 6, 1863

G rant took the paper from Rawlins, even his chief of staff weary of the ceremony.

Grant opened it, said, "Another one?"

"Quite so, sir. There seems to be a surplus of telegraph operators in the capital."

"This is the fifth one this morning. General Halleck is a master of the negative. So much easier for him to say no than yes. But this is different. I'd be amused . . . if this was amusing. Panic is not something I enjoy hearing, certainly not from my superiors, and it seems there is an abundance of panic about Knoxville."

"Do you not think the panic is justified, sir? General Burnside could be facing a serious crisis."

Grant thought of the appropriate response, so

easy to think of the biting insult to a man like Burnside. But he had offered too many opinions about Washington already, knew the staff would gossip about that, no matter his orders that they keep the business of the headquarters locked inside the headquarters.

"Is Mr. Dana about?"

"Yes, sir. He's in the kitchen, last I saw. Shall I retrieve him?"

"That's why I asked."

Rawlins seemed to sense Grant's foul mood, slipped quickly out of the room. Grant stared at the ever-present log fire, the small desk carpeted with papers. Not all of it had come from Halleck. Even now, Grant was dealing with shortages of various supplies, the railcars he had ordered east from Vicksburg and Memphis hung up in a morass of details. Some of that had to do with the rail tracks themselves, so many bridges still out, the rebel cavalry raiders so very good at their jobs. Sherman's progress was slower than Grant expected, and he knew it wasn't Sherman's fault. This is where the next fight will be, he thought. And sure as the dickens Sherman won't miss out on that. He'd rather **his** guns open the charge, all of that grand flag-flying bravado, the first one to go in. But right now, he's too far away for me to wait. He stopped himself, stared at the fire. No, you have no fault with Sherman. There isn't another man in this army you can trust more.

He probed the aching knee, the nagging injury never allowing him any ease in the saddle, the torment of having so many aides still caring for him like some aging matron. He glanced toward a curtained window, the sky darker, thought, Rains again. That's what Smith said. A few days for the ground to dry out, and sure as blazes, there'll be another mud bath. What's wrong with this place, anyway? I expected more from Chattanooga. Beautiful sweep of the river. Some trader probably settled here a hundred years ago, climbed up on Lookout Mountain, and thought he had found God. Now there's scrub and mud and dead horses, and this whole town, if it was ever pretty at all, is a heap of ruins. Hard to win over the people to your cause, when you leave this kind of mess behind you.

"Sir, Mr. Dana."

Rawlins exited quickly, and Dana was there now, all smiles, a short bow.

"Good morning, sir. I see that my superiors in Washington were up early."

Grant was in no mood for Dana's joviality. "Everyone saying the same thing. Burnside's about to be swallowed up. The whole Confederate army is headed toward Knoxville. Just what am I to do about that?"

It was a question Dana wouldn't answer, and Grant knew that, pointed to a chair.

"Sit down. The more you bounce around this room, the more my leg hurts."

Dana eyed the leg. "No better this morning? I had thought by now . . ."

"It's better. It's not fixed. Still hurts me to ride. Just tired of it, that's all. My apologies, Mr. Dana, if I do not seem in festive spirits."

Dana looked at the desk, said, "Is there anything in the secretary's messages I should read?"

"Waste of time."

"That opinion is not a luxury I possess, sir."

Grant couldn't stay angry at Dana, knew that Dana was his ally, especially when it came to any discussion of the predicament the army was in.

"You don't miss General Rosecrans, do you?"

Dana seemed surprised by the question. "Um, well, no. But I assure you, sir, that is no secret around here. I was rather pointed in my reports to Washington. I witnessed many failures of command."

"I'm not accusing you of anything. I see those failures all around me. I have pondered the question since I arrived here. Every day I stand out there on the street and stare at Lookout Mountain, and ask myself how any military commander could back off that hill without being pushed. If only for reconnaissance. Whenever the weather allows, I suspect you can see half the Confederacy from up there. The enemy's artillery is perched all over that place, dueling with our own, and we have every disadvantage. Why didn't Rosecrans hold on to the place? It had to be a defensible position."

"I have no answer to that, sir. I reported the events

of those few days as I saw them. General Rosecrans was not a man in control of himself. I am far more pleased . . . the secretary is far more pleased with General Thomas in that position. And of course, sir, your arrival here has sealed the enemy's fate."

Grant looked down, shook his head. "You trying to be my friend, Mr. Dana? Rather you put your energies to something more positive. Getting General Halleck off of my back would be a good start. Washington is convinced that Lee's entire army is suddenly uprooting itself out of Virginia and marching this way with the speed of the wind. Apparently, General Halleck believes we should be doing the same thing, just waltzing away from Bragg's army and rescuing General Burnside from his desperation. They seem to believe that Knoxville is more important than the possibility of moving toward Atlanta. I do not happen to agree. But if we abandon our position here for the sole purpose of securing Knoxville, Bragg will have regained everything he lost this year. His victory at Chickamauga will actually have meaning. With this army moving away, as Halleck suggests, Bragg will most certainly strike out toward Nashville. It's what I would do, in his place. I do not intend to let that happen."

Dana nodded. "Yes, sir. I have tried to blunt the secretary's concerns. General Halleck does not seek my counsel. It just isn't my place."

Grant bent his legs, tried to stand, Dana up quickly to assist.

"No. Sit down. I need to do this as often as I can. It's the only thing the doctors have told me that I agree with. The longer I sit still, the stiffer it becomes. A few times each day I order myself to make a forced march, even if it's just around this room."

He limped away from the fire, heard Rawlins in the next room, along with the deep voice of George Thomas. Grant heard bits of the conversation, what seemed to be the effort to hush an argument. Grant stopped the slow, hobbled pacing.

"Just wonderful. Everyone's as ornery as I am."

Dana looked toward the doorway, the argument growing more heated, and Grant moved that way, pushed open the door, steadied himself in the opening. Rawlins was facing away from him, face-to-face with Thomas. Thomas looked past Rawlins toward Grant, carried a hard frown, something Grant had grown accustomed to. Rawlins said, "Never mind, General. As I told you, General Grant is in high conference with officials from Washington."

Thomas kept his eye on Grant, a short nod. "How goes your conference, sir?"

Rawlins spun around, silenced by the momentary embarrassment, and Grant said, "In here, please, General. Any such conference should include you. There is considerable agitation in Washington, directed at this command."

Thomas moved slowly past Rawlins, followed Grant into the room. Dana was standing now, the room with only one extra chair. Grant watched

Thomas move toward the chair, saw the pain in the man's face, another common sight. Grant said, "It seems we are both aging badly, General. Perhaps it is why wars are fought by the young."

Grant moved to his perch in front of the fire, Thomas to one side, Dana moving to the corner of the room, eyes on both men. Thomas kept his gaze downward, said, "Every day. Never relief. I'm afraid this ailment shall punish me for a long time."

Grant knew only that Thomas had injured his back, didn't expect such gloom. Grant reached into his pocket, retrieved a cigar, said, "Like one? Should suit you. Supposed to be good Virginia tobacco."

Dana made an audible grunt, and Thomas looked at Grant with a hard stare.

"I never smoke. And it has nothing at all to do with Virginia."

Grant realized his clumsiness now. "Sorry. Didn't mean to suggest anything. I never question your loyalty to our country. I meant no insult to you at all."

Grant felt helpless, Thomas seeming to fill the room with the air of bitterness. Dana stepped forward, nervous now, said, "General Thomas, I am quite certain General Grant did not mean to suggest anything of your loyalty to Virginia. Winfield Scott is a Virginian, as we all know."

Grant saw no change in Thomas, said, "And of course, General Pemberton is a Pennsylvanian. Didn't prevent him from pledging his loyalties to the South. This war has turned our nation upside down. It is a curse."

Thomas looked at him now, a silent moment, Grant feeling completely idiotic, no words to smooth over the awkwardness.

"General Grant, I swore the same oath as you. I obey the same orders as you. I fight the same enemy. I need not prove myself to anyone."

Dana jumped in, seemed eager to smooth the obvious tension. "Absolutely not, sir! General Grant certainly understands that. After all, his father-in-law, Colonel Dent, is in fact a slaveholder!"

Thomas blinked at Grant, a glimmer of surprise, and Grant silenced Dana with a deep frown, thought, Did I ask for your assistance? Dana slipped backward to his corner again, and Grant said, "Yes, well, we all have our crosses to bear. Colonel Dent and I are not especially . . . close. He was not terribly accepting of his daughter marrying a soldier. Ironic, of course, since Colonel Dent is a soldier himself." Grant was running out of energy for this, had no gift for banter. "Look, General. Washington is burying me in telegrams because there is deep concern over General Burnside's vulnerability at Knoxville. Sherman's divisions are still many days away, and I am being ordered to respond to Longstreet's march with the strength at hand. I am preparing orders for you, to strike out to our left flank, a vigorous assault against the enemy's northern flank along the northern portion of Missionary Ridge. The rail line there is close, and Bragg will surely have to respond. He cannot allow us to cut him off from Longstreet. I admit to curiosity why Bragg sent Longstreet away in the first place. It must surely weaken his position here. But General Halleck is more deeply concerned about Burnside than he is our situation here."

"He shouldn't be. Longstreet is still days away from Knoxville. The rail line he's using only goes partway. He will have to move his forces by wagon, or on foot. He will not be ready to make an attack on Knoxville for several days. There could be a better opportunity for us right here. Removing the enemy from Lookout Mountain could be a far simpler task, and could accomplish the same goal."

"Could be. But the War Department has other concerns. We may assume that Knoxville is Longstreet's destination, and we may assume that the absurd rumors of General Lee abandoning Virginia could possibly be accurate. One of General Halleck's dispatches reveals a fear that all of this rebel activity might be the first steps toward a campaign against Nashville, which could open the way to another invasion of Kentucky."

Thomas tilted his head. "You believe that will occur?"

"Nope."

"You believe Lee is coming?"

"Nope."

"But you want Longstreet to turn about and re-turn here?"

"It's not what I **want.** General Halleck is insisting in the strongest terms that we take a significant step toward protecting Burnside. Since I have no inten-tion of uprooting this army and shoving northward, we must convince General Bragg that we are posing a serious threat to his position. Thus will he recall Longstreet. We're estimating Longstreet's strength at fifteen thousand men. For Bragg to order that large a portion of his army away, he must believe Knoxville is some kind of lynchpin to this entire theater. Why else would he weaken himself so pro-foundly, knowing we're growing stronger?"

Thomas seemed unconvinced, and Grant didn't have the energy for a discussion.

"I'm preparing your orders, and will have them to you by this evening."

"I will await them, sir. We can discuss this further at that time, if you don't mind, sir. I would prefer right now to return to my quarters."

Grant had no reason to object, saw the pain in the man's face, Thomas sitting crookedly in the chair.

"You are dismissed, General."

Thomas stood slowly, pulling himself up like an injured bear. "Thank you, sir. I shall be better by tonight. This aggravation flares up occasionally."

Grant nodded, pointed toward the door. "Rest your back, General. Very soon, this army shall re-quire both of us to be in a more agreeable spirit."

Thomas moved slowly out of the room, silence beyond, no commotion at all from Rawlins. Dana moved to the door, closed it, returned to the chair.

"It is disturbing to see the general in such pain. He never finds relief, so it seems." Dana looked at Grant's knee again. "Well, of course, both of you."

"A horse fell on me, Mr. Dana. It's happened before, and no doubt will happen again. Not sure what to make of General Thomas's condition. Only he knows. I just hope he is fit for what must happen now."

"I wouldn't be concerned about your reference to Virginia, sir. I'm certain that General Thomas has endured a great deal of personal agony for that decision. As he noted, sir, he did take an oath to serve. I credit him for his loyalty to his country."

"No argument there." Grant pulled his legs in again, pushed himself out of the chair, Dana knowing to stay away. Grant moved to the mantel, retrieved his hat, planted it on his head, realized he was still holding the unlit cigar. Dana seemed to read him, bent low to the fire, pulled out a narrow piece of wood, a bit of flame at the tip, offered it to Grant. The cigar was lit quickly, the delicious smoke swirling around Grant, Dana retrieving one of his own. Grant watched him for a long second, saw Dana absorbing the smoke around both of them, thought, Good, yes. He held back the thought, the reference to Virginia tobacco. It's one thing to disavow former allegiances. But I can't say I've ever fully trusted a man who says he never smokes.

"Mr. Dana, I wish to ride. Accompany me?"

"Of course, sir."

Dana moved to the door, held it open, waited for Grant to hobble past. Grant heard the usual brief pleasantries between Dana and Rawlins, the nods to other staff officers, a handful of aides spread out in the rooms of the house.

Grant ignored them all, said to no one in particular, "Going for a ride. Inspection. Something."

Rawlins jumped into action, the energy Grant dreaded. "I shall alert the guard, sir. You cannot just go out among the people here without protection."

Grant sagged, didn't look back. "If you insist."

He moved outside, the gray sky low overhead, masking the face of Lookout Mountain. The sounds of artillery thumped out to one side, more of the useless duels that spread across the valley every day. Grant had considered ordering a halt to that, allowing the rebels to expend all the shot and shell they wanted to, while he kept his own supplies well stocked. But the wagons now brought an abundance of ammunition, and trading fire seemed to accomplish something besides entertaining the gunners. With artillery peppering the face of Lookout Mountain, it wasn't likely the rebels were going to make any kind of serious advance from that direction. If the rebels came at all, it would likely be across the flat plain that fed down from Missionary Ridge.

In the wide street, wagons passed, no one paying him any mind, the flag above his headquarters the only hint that the man called Grant was there at all. He enjoyed going unrecognized, never dressed with the pomp of the army's commanding general, and even now, he kept the guards at a distance.

Down the wide street he saw a small group of provost officers, a loud scuffle growing with a crowd of civilians, and he moved out beside the horse, tried to see what was happening.

"Mr. Dana, perhaps you should remain here. The local citizens seemed displeased about something." He turned, saw his aides emerging from the house, responding to the commotion. "Captain Hudson, send a courier to the closest infantry camp. Alert them to a possible problem. Have at least a company of men move this way with haste."

The young man saluted him, moved away quickly. Dana said, "It appears to be mostly women, sir."

Grant girded himself for the inevitable pain, put one foot in the saddle, pulled himself up on the horse with a low grunt. He had a better view of the scene now, more men in blue gathering around the civilians.

"It seems you are correct. I suppose we should have a closer look."

He spurred the horse, regretted now that it was the statuesque Old Jack, the enormous animal that had tumbled him over in New Orleans. Kangaroo was far less recognizable, and he still had no energy for a confrontation that might center on him.

The provosts and the gathering soldiers had seemed to quiet the crowd, one officer standing high on a crate of some kind, commanding attention. Grant rode up closer, annoyed by his own curiosity, and the officer spotted him, a major Grant had seen before. The man seemed relieved to see him.

"Sir! Thank goodness, sir. These women have grievances."

The women seemed to turn toward him in unison, no one seeming impressed with the slouching man in the plain blue coat. One woman stepped toward him now, restrained by a pair of guards, called out to him, "If ye be some kind of commander here, then ye be knowin' how your army has done desecrated our homes! There's not a morsel of grain to be had, the babies are going hungry. The cattle are butchered without any compensation. My own boy, Henry, has been sent away!"

Grant held up his hand to her. "Wait. Your son was sent away? By whom? Where?"

"Not my son, you bluebelly scoundrel. My boy! Your blue devils have set them free, scattered them anywhere they wanted to go! They done left us with no help, nothing to tide us through!"

Dana was close beside him now. "General, I do believe she is referring to her slave."

"Yes, you varmint! If my husband was here, he'd show you how a man stands up for himself. But he's off digging roots, so we can eat!"

Dana seemed to ignite now, nudged his horse ahead of Grant. "So, your husband sends his wife to do his complaining for him? Your slaves have been freed, and you would blame that on this army?"

Grant was surprised by the genuine fury in Dana's voice, moved up again, leaned over to him. "Easy, Mr. Dana. Let's allow the guards to handle this. Major, please have these people return to their homes. If the commissary can spare some grain, corn, flour, anything of the sort, see that the citizens are provided for." Grant looked again at the woman, no change in her hostility. "As for you, madam, I am General Grant. Please return to your husband, and give him my respects, and assure him that he need not gather roots. But he will also make no effort to gather up your slaves. According to the president of the United States, those men are citizens just like yourselves, and shall be regarded as such."

"You shall burn in hell, all of ye!"

Grant saw another platoon of soldiers coming in close, order restored, the women starting to scatter. He looked again at the angry woman, saw the finery of her dress, a gold pin at her throat.

"You might be correct, madam. But we who travel to hell shall have ample company from people like you."

He didn't wait for a response, turned the horse, Dana following him at a slow gallop.

"That was . . . amazing! That woman. Have you ever seen such arrogance?"

Grant stared away, the anger still boiling up, but he kept it in, wouldn't show it to Dana. "Yes, Mr. Dana. There is arrogance aplenty on both sides of this war. You know that better than anyone. I admit to being surprised."

"At me, sir? I regret my outburst, my unseemly behavior. I have no authority here to speak in such a way."

"Not you. Your outrage is admirable. **Her.** A slaveholder. Hadn't given that much thought since I arrived here. In Mississippi, plantations were everywhere. Slaves by the score, by the thousands. Not nearly so many around here. It's the land, I suppose. No need for slave labor in a place that's mostly rocks."

"But so many women. That was a surprise."

"Not so. If her husband was out digging roots, I'm an elephant's toenail. The men stay away, know full well that if they raise an unholy ruckus, we might slap 'em in the stockade. The women can shout out most anything they please, and we'll treat them with a little more decorum. Not sure how long that will last. One of those genteel Southern belles might have had a pistol in her underpinnings. Something like that can turn ugly very quickly."

Dana looked back toward the street, eyes wide. "Never thought of that."

"It's a war, Mr. Dana. Just because they're in dresses doesn't mean they're harmless."

"But . . . what about what she said . . . the food?"

"We'll take care of that. But she's got plenty. I've sympathy for the poor ones, Mr. Dana, the ones we put out of their homes, the ones who get caught in the middle of something they can't help. But she's a leader. You can tell it by her carriage, by her dress, by the way the others shut up and let her talk for 'em. No sympathy for those people. None. That's who started this war. That's who convinced all those others to send their sons off to shoot at us. Now the war's hit her where it hurts. Took away her slaves. That's a really good thing, Mr. Dana, a really good thing. That may be as important as any battle we fight with those boys on those hills. The president's emancipation order freed their slaves, and when we march through this countryside, we're enforcing that. We take away their ability to plant their crops next spring? To grow cotton or tobacco they can sell to whoever's buying, whoever's out there helping them? That's gonna squeeze them hard."

"You mean . . . the British?"

"Maybe. That's not my responsibility, Mr. Dana. My job is to deal with that army up on those hills."

"Hey there! Halloo, gentlemen!"

Grant saw a man jogging slowly toward him, a

civilian, a small box in his hand. Grant glanced back, saw Captain Osband, his cavalry guards there, knew they were never far away. Osband spurred his horse, held a pistol in his hand. Grant looked again at the civilian, the man eyeing the cavalryman, dropping the box, his hands in the air.

"Please, sir! I've no weapon! My name is Horatio Grumbach. I'm a merchant hereabouts."

Osband moved up close to Grant, and Grant said, "It's all right, for now. Let's see what Mr. Grumbach is offering."

The man seemed to know his way was clear, reached down for the box, beaming a salesman's smile.

"Thank you! Yes, indeed." He looked to the captain, who kept the pistol in his hand. "You, too, fine sir! I've only good to offer, only good, I assure you! Allow me to open this case."

Osband said, "Very slowly, sir."

"Ah, yes, of course! No threat here, none! Look! Very valuable! And these can be yours for very little!"

Grant was curious now, Grumbach stepping closer, the box held open.

"What is that? Photographic cards?"

"**Carte de visites,** sir! And the image is not just anyone. This is your rare opportunity to own a likeness of General Grant himself! I cannot make this offer to anyone else. I've only the . . . um . . . three artifacts, taken in the heat of battle!"

Grant looked into the box, said, "May I see one of those?"

"Ah, yes. Examine the merchandise, by all means. Only twenty-five cents each, sir. One quarter of a dollar! A pittance for a fine gentleman such as your friend here." Grant realized the man was motioning to Dana, fought hard to hide his smile. He held up a piece of stiff paper, saw the image of an officer, holding a sword, staring back at him with a cartoonish anger, as though intending something dangerous. Grant glanced down, saw two more in the box, identical, and the man said, "There you have it, sir! General Grant, a vision of heroism!"

Grant smiled, handed the card to Dana. Dana said, "What? Who is this?"

"Why, that's General Grant himself, sir! Notice the fire in the eyes, the sign of a stout heart! The pure image of courage!"

Dana stared wide-eyed, looked at Grant now, and Grant felt the laughter coming, couldn't hold it, the first real laugh he had enjoyed in weeks. Dana seemed to fall into Grant's good humor, smiled, looked at the salesman, said, "Sir, how much for all three?"

"Oh, well now, perhaps fifty cents for the lot. Likenesses of General Grant are extremely hard to come by."

Grant looked toward Osband now, said, "Yes, my good man, they certainly are. Captain Osband, please take this man into custody, and have him arrested for fraud."

Grumbach lost his glad-handing smile, said, "Why, whatever for?"

Grant leaned down, tilted his hat back on his head. "Mr. Dana, would you like to explain?"

"With pleasure, sir. Mr. Grumbach, I wish to introduce to you, in all his glory and with a stout heart and fiery eyes, General Ulysses Grant."

"There. To the right of that pair of trees. Right at the crest."

Dana looked through field glasses of his own, said, "Yes, I see it. You certain, sir?"

"Pretty certain. Some of the scouts go up a whole lot closer than this. Plus, there's deserters. Those fellows always seem eager to impress us with all that they know, how important they are. If they can convince us they have real good information, they know we'll reward them for it. That's one way we confirmed the location of Bragg's headquarters."

"So, that house is Bragg's headquarters?"

"Yep."

"Why don't we shell it, begging your pardon, sir?"

Grant sniffed, tossed the spent cigar to one side, thought, Civilians.

"Too far, for one thing. Too high up for the artillery to get the range. And, the more I think about it, Mr. Dana, the more I'm convinced that the greatest advantage we might have in this fight is the man up there who commands the enemy. We knock Bragg down, they might find someone else who's better. At least, for now, we know what we're facing."

"Do we know, sir, why he sent Longstreet away? Something perhaps you haven't said to General Thomas? If I may be so bold to ask, sir. But you understand. I must report what I can to Secretary Stanton."

"We have scouts, Mr. Dana. But I have yet to find a spy capable enough to sit on Bragg's staff. In time, perhaps."

The name bounced through him now, his old friend, Pete Longstreet. The thought suddenly erupted through his brain. Longstreet is after all . . . Longstreet. Came down here figuring he'd take command, probably with Lee's blessing. But then he runs into another old mule in Braxton Bragg. I'll wager they stood toe-to-toe, like a couple of bantam roosters. But Jefferson Davis has treated Bragg like a favorite son, so that's a fight Longstreet can't win. **Didn't** win. And now, Longstreet is gone. But Halleck insists we can bring him back, just so we can save Burnside. I suppose that's what I have to do.

"Mr. Dana, I should return to my headquarters. It's imperative I complete my orders to General Thomas. I'll provide you a copy, of course, since you're going to find one anyway. Then you may send your report to Washington. I'm tired of this place, Mr. Dana. It's time to move."

CHAPTER TWENTY-ONE

THOMAS

NORTH OF CHATTANOOGA—
NOVEMBER 7, 1863

The order had dug at Thomas like a needle in his aching back. Grant's impatience was obvious, the orders calling for an immediate strike at what was assumed to be Bragg's right flank, the northern reaches of Missionary Ridge. But Thomas had surveyed this ground far longer than Grant, had intended first to assault the rebel position on Lookout Mountain, where Joe Hooker's troops were camped close up to the base of the enormous heights. Thus far, the rebels had made no real forays off his protection on the highest ground, but Thomas could not fathom that Bragg would simply sit still while Grant's army was growing stronger. To Thomas, Bragg's most logical option would be to launch an assault down into Lookout Valley, straight at Hooker, an attempt to crush the supply lines. Thomas had done all he could to convince Hooker to prepare a strong defensive line. To Thomas's dismay, Hooker had fared poorly in preparing any kind of position at all. Earthworks were barely in existence, and the few rifle pits were dug in haphazard patterns, as though Hooker could not conceive he might be in any danger. Thomas had hesitated giving Hooker direct orders, even though the War Department had given Thomas command over his divisions.

Hooker had been contrite about his massive failure at Chancellorsville the spring before and Thomas understood that any general who suffered such a defeat would seek redemption. But Hooker's performance in the valley hadn't done anything to convince Thomas that he was capable of being any more than a subordinate, a corps commander at best. But Hooker still held what Thomas believed was the key to the entire campaign. If Bragg's troops could be swept clear of Lookout Mountain, the Federal forces could then drive farther east, dropping down the east side of the mountain, shoving back behind the rebel left flank on Missionary Ridge, threatening to slice behind Bragg's position, possibly cutting off rebel supply lines. By removing Longstreet's fifteen thousand men, it was simple mathematics that Bragg had weakened his army by a fourth, possibly a third. There was surely an opportunity on Lookout Mountain that Grant would recognize. Thomas had hoped that he could persuade Grant to strike the rebel left. Instead, Grant's orders just added to Thomas's dismay. Grant ordered Thomas to move as many men as possible in as short a time as possible and assault Bragg's right flank, the far northern tip of Missionary Ridge.

Grant was now insisting on a major offensive that would so threaten Bragg's position that he would be forced to recall Longstreet back toward Chattanooga, thus sparing Ambrose Burnside's precarious hold on Knoxville. Whether Burnside was exaggerating his own peril, neither Thomas nor Grant had any idea. Burnside's reputation for leadership or tactical effectiveness was no better than Joe Hooker's. But Thomas respected that Grant was being hounded incessantly from Washington, and that for reasons known only to Henry Halleck, Burnside's precarious position at Knoxville was the greater priority. For Thomas, it was the one saving grace of having Grant as his superior. The avalanche of telegrams coming from the War Department were landing squarely on Grant's desk, not his own.

He rode northward along a wide trail that paralleled the river, a scattering of guards keeping far out in the brush, hidden as much as possible along the river itself. He was joined by Baldy Smith, had wanted Smith's firsthand explanation why an assault on the enemy's northern flanks was any kind of a good idea. With them rode General John Brannan, Thomas's chief of artillery. For most of the past week, Brannan had put his focus south of Chattanooga, anticipating an attack on Lookout Mountain. But Grant's order would require Thomas to haul considerable artillery in the opposite direction, up from the stronghold at Chattanooga, a job that would fall on Brannan.

The horses took them up a low rise, the brush falling away, bare rocks and scrub trees, well above the river. Thomas had followed Smith to a vantage point where the mouth of Chickamauga Creek was visible. He saw it now, feeding into the Tennessee from the far side, and Thomas halted the horse, raised his field glasses, saw a scattering of men along both banks of the smaller creek, a dozen or more rebel pickets.

"They're fishing."

Beside him, Brannan said nervously, "One of them's waving at us. Not certain this is a good idea, sir."

Thomas stared through the field glasses, didn't share Brannan's concern. "No matter, John. No one along this entire river seems to care whether we make a fight at all. This campaign has become one massive holiday, a hundred thousand men gazing across this river at each other as though we've nothing better to do."

He looked toward Smith now, saw the engineer sitting quietly, no field glasses. Smith had been over every part of this ground, and Thomas knew he had probably memorized every tree.

Thomas said, "Well, this is what you proposed. Cross here, hit them straight up that creek, grab that rail depot beyond. Still think it's the right plan?"

Smith rubbed the ragged beard on his chin. "Given this some thought. My apologies, sir, but there are some details here that escaped me before. That one hill across the way, down to the right, those heights with so much timber. It concerns me, sir, that the maps may not be correct."

It was not what Thomas wanted to hear. "Which maps? **These** maps? The ones I'm to rely upon to carry out Grant's orders?"

"Maybe so. I'm wondering . . . if I may ask . . . how many men can be marched up this way by tomorrow?"

Thomas fought the urge to say **none.** He thought a moment.

"It's possible to bring two divisions up here, no more. But that's not the whole problem." He looked at Brannan. "John, do you think you can haul sufficient artillery up here with the draft animals we have now?"

Brannan lowered the glasses, still eyed the rebels, who still eyed him. "The animals are in terrible condition. This kind of march will kill most of them. They haven't grown strong enough yet. We must have replacements, or allow the beasts time to strengthen from additional forage. I don't see how any real strength can be brought here. A few batteries at best."

"Wonderful. I'm to make this assault with almost no artillery."

He stared out for a long moment, dreaded the ride back to the town, knew his back would suffer for it. He felt a wave of black despair, put his hand on the paper in his pocket, Grant's order.

"Baldy, this plan won't work, not with the means we have now. Grant insists we launch this attack tomorrow. I have to tell him it can't be done. I'd like some support for that position."

Smith let out a deep breath. "It was my idea. Not the entire plan, mind you, but I believed we could send some skirmishers across, surprise the enemy, maybe send a larger force in as support, push hard enough and grab the rail depot. At least, we might cut the rail lines, or cut any communications Bragg has with his forces at Knoxville. Still think it's a good plan. Grant wants to jab Bragg hard, agitate him enough to recall Longstreet. I thought it could work." He paused. "How in blazes did I miss those hills? That's not what the map shows, not at all."

Thomas was growing more annoyed. "So, fix the maps. Right now, I don't care how accurate they are. I cannot obey Grant's orders without weakening our position at Chattanooga. We're several miles from the northern limits of our own defensive lines. Bragg's not a complete fool. He sees us move a sizable force up this way, he'll know we're vulnerable in the town. Or worse, he could launch a counterattack just below us right here, cutting off whatever troops we bring up here. We get pinched like that, and then, Longstreet suddenly arrives, we're in serious trouble up here. I'll not have it. We simply need more strength, more numbers."

Smith didn't respond, Thomas angrier by the minute, thought of Grant. Why in blazes aren't you out here? See this for yourself. We're too far removed from the town, from any protection at all. He kept his anger inside, a long silent moment, the cheerful voices of the rebels across the river plainly audible, Federal pickets below responding, their good humor digging into Thomas, more of the same friendly banter that annoyed him everywhere he went. Brannan seemed jumpy still, broke the silence.

"Sir, General Grant will not be pleased with your refusal. You should offer some alternative plan, something the general will find to his liking."

Thomas sniffed, sat back in the saddle, twisted slightly, testing the nagging pain in his back. "Grant believes in this plan, and he is being growled at from Washington. The only alternative I can suggest is that this plan be carried out exactly as he proposes."

Smith said, "What do you mean? At the very least, we would have to delay a day or two."

"Maybe longer than that. But Grant wants this

flank hit and hit hard. I continue to believe that the best strategy is to strike the enemy on the opposite flank, pushing up onto Lookout Mountain. That attack could yield a great deal of fruit. The only pleasing alternative to **this** plan is if, somehow, we can launch both assaults. And for that we will require more troops, more guns, and someone who, from what I've heard, pays little attention to the accuracy of his maps. General Grant will just have to bide his time. There can be no grand assault against this section of Bragg's forces until Sherman arrives."

CHAPTER TWENTY-TWO

GRANT

CHATTANOOGA—
NOVEMBER 8, 1863

He paced about the room, as rapidly as the pain in his leg allowed, hands clasped behind his back. The fire had died down to embers, but Rawlins and the other staff officers knew when to leave Grant alone, and **now** was as good a time as there might ever have been. Grant thought of smoking a cigar, needed the warmth of that, something to clear away the sour taste that rose up as he pondered the impossibility of carrying out his orders. He knew he couldn't display his anger to his staff, that no matter how he felt about his subordinates, as the commanding general, his job seemed to fall more to the role of peacemaker. He knew of others who weren't so discreet, men like Halleck who made no effort to hide their displeasure. The victims of the outbursts might not be the ones most deserving, and Grant knew enough of chain of command to understand that a general might carry ultimate responsibility for some failure, but often, the failure came from a subordinate who just didn't do the job. He had seen too much of that throughout the war, knew that both armies suffered from various failings, that more often, it was the commanding general who endured the disgrace. But to blister any field commander out of hand without knowing every detail was a habit practiced by others, generals for whom Grant held little respect. That description applied to Sherman, certainly, who was legendary for his temper, who would launch artillery shells into the faces of anyone in proximity, even his own staff, when, occasionally, the failure had been Sherman's alone. But Grant's feelings for Sherman were very different, a closeness born of respect and friendship. I suppose, he thought, that a bad temper is not always a bad thing. Sherman knows when he's made a bad mistake, and if he's furious about that, it means he's less likely to repeat the mistake. But today . . . Thomas . . . he sees no mistake. To him, any error of strategy is **mine, my** bad plan, calling on him to do a job he's just not capable of. Or worse, giving him a task he doesn't feel his army can accomplish. Grant heard Thomas's words now, grim and absolute, as though Grant should know better. **Too many difficulties in maneuvering this army, too**

many problems with artillery horses. So, in his mind, it's impossible to carry out my plan, the plan that first came from his own engineer.

It hadn't helped Grant's mood to see Baldy Smith standing alongside Thomas when the refusal came. Grant respected Smith, still would, knew that a good engineer should recognize his errors, and work to correct them. Smith was loyal to Thomas, certainly, another trait Grant had to admire. But, Baldy, he thought, it was **your** idea. You're the one who thought we could charge across that river and slice up Bragg's rail lines, scare the daylights out of every rebel from here to Knoxville, change the entire course of this campaign. Grant stopped pacing, closed his eyes, knew it really wasn't like that. Smith's original plan had suggested a limited expedition across the river, a surprise raid that would grab the rebel pickets, hitting the tracks and the depot with just enough energy to sting Braxton Bragg, convincing him to pull Longstreet back from Knoxville. No, the illusion of some grand campaign up there was all my own. I thought the Army of the Cumberland, and its commander, would be capable of doing something on this ground besides digging ditches, and waiting for winter to arrive. This is worse than Vicksburg.

He hated sieges, the notion that one army could just surround the other until the besieged forces choked to death. If there had been someone else in charge at Vicksburg, someone besides that turncoat

Pennsylvanian Pemberton, our mighty siege there could have blown right back in our faces. I got lucky with that. Washington thinks I'm a hero for it. So does Sherman. And Julia. But in that campaign I had a weak enemy, a man who specializes in uncertainty. Now, what do I have? An enemy who sits up on big fat hills and seems perfectly willing for **me** to do something. All right, Mr. Bragg, I tried. Now what? Is George Thomas just as content as you seem to be to go into winter quarters, so we may begin this conversation again in the spring?

He was pacing again, ignored the stiffness in his knee. Methodical. That's the word, he thought. Thomas is **methodical.** So was Burnside at Fredericksburg, and it bloodied us as badly as any campaign of the war. Lee at Gettysburg . . . the last thing you'd ever say about Bobby Lee is that he's methodical. He got beat to pieces up there, but he did it by moving forward.

Grant grabbed the back of the chair, sat heavily, felt exhausted by his own anger. Good thing I'm alone. My brain's spitting out babble. I don't know what Lee did wrong, and all I know of Burnside is what I'm hearing right now, that he screams for help when he sees a rebel skirmish line. Actually, I'm not hearing anything from Burnside right now.

"Mr. Rawlins!"

He stared at the door, saw it open slowly, the face of Major Babcock.

"Yes, sir? General Rawlins is detained at the moment, sir. May I be of assistance?"

"Is the telegraph to Knoxville still out?"

"Yes, sir. Captain James just returned from the office, said it's silent, no responses at all to our inquiries."

Grant fumed, stared at the dead fire, felt the chill now.

"Send an aide in here to light this thing."

"Yes, sir. Right away."

The door closed, and Grant felt the restlessness, called out again, "Major!"

"Sir?"

"Do we know where Sherman is?"

The man shook his head slowly, as though expecting Grant to erupt. "No, sir. Sorry. I'll try to find out."

"Fine idea."

Babcock was gone again, and in a quick moment, the door opened, one of the couriers carrying a flaming stick, the man going quickly to the hearth, leaning low, stabbing at the remains of the fire. Grant watched the man fiddling with the embers, small remnants of burned logs, a thick blanket of gray ash smothering his efforts. The man seemed more agitated, glanced back at Grant, preparing to apologize, and Grant said, "Son, go get some firewood, and do this right. You're so nervous, you're giving me hives."

The young man stood, left the flaming stick to

die in the ashes, saluted him, said, "Yes, sir. I didn't wish to disturb you, sir. General Rawlins was most insistent. . . ."

"And General Rawlins is not here, correct?"

"Correct, sir."

"Then we'll do things my way. Get some sticks and logs, and light the fire. Understand?"

"Yes, sir. I'll return shortly, sir."

The man seemed to blow out of the room, and Grant folded his arms, shook his head. No, you don't need to put the fear of the Almighty in these men. No call for it. Rawlins does that well enough. But certainly, word has spread through this place that I am prepared to ship the lot of them to the front lines. That's Rawlins, no doubt.

There was an unnecessary knock at the door, two men now appearing, and Grant saw firewood in both men's arms. They seemed to be asking permission to enter, silent fear, and Grant waved them in, said, "Gentlemen, I am not a pit viper. I'm annoyed. I have reason to be, which is not your concern."

The pair moved to the fire, hushed instructions from one man to the other, a soft argument breaking out between them. Grant had no patience for yet one more controversy, pulled himself to his feet.

"When you master the art of lighting that fire, inform General Rawlins, or whoever else is in charge of this headquarters, that I have taken my horse for a walk. And, yes, before Rawlins has an attack of apoplexy, assure him I will have the cavalry guard accompany me."

The rains had returned, a dismal soaking shower that drove cold all through him. He missed the fire already, glanced back, saw smoke curling up from the chimney of the head-quarters, scolded himself for stubbornness. You'll wish you stayed inside, he thought. This whole affair has got you acting like a ten-year-old. Well, if that's the way it is, best not let the staff suffer through that. I need obedience from them, not a spanking from Rawlins. He'd do it, too.

He rode out toward the west, close to the river, Captain Osband's cavalry keeping back a dozen yards. Grant eyed the pontoon bridge, saw a wagon crossing, a handful of horsemen, thought, Excel-lent. It's repaired. Finally. He nudged the horse that way, saw the provosts eyeing him, suddenly aware who he was, Osband moving up, to erase any chance of mistaken identity. But the guards had seen him before, stood back, crisp salutes, which Grant answered limply. He saw the lieutenant in command, an older man, Missouri veteran, a man he had known in St. Louis.

"Good day, Mr. Hallenby. The bridge is sound?"

The man stepped closer, offered a salute, said, "Quite so, sir. The enemy has devised a clever tac-tic of floating enormous logs downstream, which play havoc with the pontoons. The boats are pretty light, sir, no match for a ton of wet timber. We lost six or eight of the boats last night. Just vanished downriver. It's happened a few times now. We've been using the flatboats to get across, but General Smith was through here earlier, had his engineers at work doing the repairs." Grant caught a glance from Hallenby toward his injured leg, knew what was coming. "Sir, perhaps you shouldn't ride across. It's a mite shaky."

"Thank you, Lieutenant. I'll manage. Should I land in the river, it won't require General Smith's engineers to fetch me out." He glanced back toward Osband, saw a smile the man tried to hide. "Captain, let's cross. If Smith's out here, he's somewhere on Moccasin Point. I suppose I should find out what he's doing." He left the rest unsaid, thought of the artillery batteries, heavy siege guns Thomas had been hoping to receive. Grant had seen the wire, a request for the kind of heavy artillery that would batter down walls. Grant hadn't interfered with that, not yet, had expected Thomas to make good use of the thirty-pound Parrott guns against any strong defensive line the rebels might have constructed on the heights. He stopped at the edge of the water, eyed the bridge, thought, Thomas has every intention of placing those batteries out here so he can aim them at that ridiculous mountain. He has no intention at all of wasting his time with my plan. He's not crossing this river up north unless I flat-out order it, or threaten to relieve him. Grant pushed the horse onto the bridge now, the horse doing its best to keep upright, the pontoons swaying, and Grant felt his legs lock tightly against the horse's flanks, a spear of pain jabbing his knee. He glanced at the rain-spattered water to both sides, dreaded the thought that the horse might stumble, yet again. He stared out toward the far side of the river, guards there as well, watching him. Anyone makes a wager on me falling, and I'll put him in a rifle pit. He fought the pain, the horse doing better, the bridge coming to an end, and the horse took him onto solid ground, Grant as relieved as the horse beneath him. He ignored the guards, heard the clop of the cavalrymen behind him, waited for them to complete the crossing, then spurred the horse, rode out away from the river through a muddy bog.

"You intending to smash down that mountain?" Smith seemed miserable on the horse, rainwater flooding down from the bill of his hat. "Sure. We haven't tried that yet. Is that an order, sir?"

There was little humor in Smith's response, and Grant could feel Smith's dark mood, understood immediately.

"What's he expecting here?"

Smith looked at him, said, "I assume you are asking about General Thomas?" Grant didn't respond, and Smith said, "The general is anticipating an assault against those heights at the earliest moment practicable. He has ordered General Howard to make ready to advance in short notice."

Grant caught the name, said, "Howard's under Hooker. So, Thomas is as skeptical of Hooker as I am?"

"I said nothing of the sort, sir. It is General Thomas's desire that we secure the river all the way from Bridgeport to Chattanooga. I do not object to that notion. Unless, of course . . . you do."

Grant understood the awkward position Smith was in. He didn't want that, needed the man's cooperation and expertise.

"Baldy, I want you to carry out the orders you've been given. I've communicated to Washington that we cannot pull Burnside's tail out of the fire as quickly as I had hoped. That's all. No one's neck is in a noose here."

Smith looked at him, a silent nod. Out in front of them, a half-dozen squads of his men were at work with shovels, preparing depressed pits for the big guns. Grant was surprised to see a row of heavy cannon to one side, hidden under a loose mat of cut tree limbs.

"Those are siege guns."

"Yes, sir. If you wish to speak with General Brannan, he's out through those trees, supervising more of these gun pits." Grant said nothing, and Smith said, "Not really necessary, though. He knows what he's doing. He, too, is following orders."

Grant still looked toward the heavy cannon. "When did those pieces arrive? It's not as many as Thomas asked for."

"They came this morning. Not sure how many more are on the way, if any. Not my department, sir. My men spent a good many hours last night repairing the bridges. Damn nuisance, that. Rebel gunners across the way keep trying to land a solid shot square on the pontoons, but they're so far off the mark, I'm guessing they just like to hear the sound of their guns. Those damn floating battering rams are more effective. But, as fast as they can bust up the bridges, we fix 'em. It's a game, that's all. Hell of a way to fight a war."

"I aim to change that."

Smith tilted his head, peered at him from under the hat. "You tried."

"I'll try again. I told Halleck that the best we could do for now was send a small raiding party across upriver, making an attempt to cut the rail line. The enemy does that sort of thing all the time. They have cavalry, we have cavalry. Might as well use it."

"Cutting the rail line is a waste of time. Begging your pardon, sir. They'll have it repaired as quick as we fix these bridges."

"But it sounds good in Washington. **Grant's doing something.** Sometimes that matters to those people more than fighting a battle."

"Not for long. Sooner or later, there's gonna be a fight. I have no idea what Bragg is thinking. It's as though he plans every day around trimming his beard, taking a stroll, maybe he's drilling his men back behind the hills. Other than logs in the river, and random artillery shells, he's not doing a damn thing to cause us any discomfort. The more time passes, the closer we get. I guess you know that. May I ask, sir, when you expect Sherman to arrive?"

Grant watched a handful of men tossing muddy earth out of a wide pit, the rain caving in the sides as quickly as the earth was moved.

"I wanted him here last week. I expect him . . . when he gets here."

"Well, not sure what you intend to do with him. But I can assure you of one thing, General. Down on this end of the line, we're gonna put on a show. Howard's been told, and Hooker before him. Make sure your men can climb a steep damn hill." Smith looked up into the rain, a thick fog obscuring the heights across from Moccasin Point. "Once you give the word, sir, they're heading up there. No idea what they'll find. But if the weather clears, you'll be able to see the whole thing from the town, like watching a show on a big-city stage."

CHATTANOOGA—
NOVEMBER 11, 1863

Grant was annoyed, again. So far, the supply lines between Chattanooga and Bridgeport had been completely free of rebel raiders, and with the return of the rains, the only enemy blocking the way through Lookout Valley was the muddy conditions of the roads. But the wagon trains weren't merely slow. They were few and far between. From his first days in command, Grant's orders had been explicit, helped by the strident wording of John Rawlins, that railcars from Memphis, or anywhere else they could be spared, should be transported as rapidly as possible to assist in the hauling of the crucial supplies. Added to that was his order for the increased use of riverboats, to haul food and supplies from the depot at Stevenson, Alabama. But the boats were as scarce as the railcars. To Grant's enormous frustration, the rebel raiders were having their desired effect, cavalry strikes through northern Mississippi and Alabama requiring constant repairs to the rail lines, raids against smaller ports along the river damaging what few boats could be used. Those boats that did reach Bridgeport were carrying half loads, or even less, empty cargo holds adding to Grant's fury at a supply system that still kept his army stocked day to day. The aggravation Grant felt over the army's seeming paralysis at Chattanooga was the challenge he struggled with every day. Regardless of his disagreements with Thomas, Grant knew that some of that idleness was caused by weather, something not even the commanding general could repair. He continued to believe that defeating Bragg by driving him back into Georgia would solve any supply problems for his army.

CHATTANOOGA—
NOVEMBER 15, 1863

"Anything? Any word?"

Rawlins looked out through the parlor window, the same show he had performed for most of an hour, said, "No, sir. Nothing."

Grant clasped his hands together, stretched them out in front of him, tested the knee, grateful that the pains were finally subsiding. He moved back into his office, pacing more freely now, felt energized, anxious, thought of asking Rawlins to check outside again. But he knew better, knew it would come in time, his attempt at patience waging war with his anticipation.

In the parlor, staff officers continued their work, the usual business of headquarters, sending more angry missives toward the railroad people, the commissary officers, men who seemed as defensive as Grant was aggressive about getting much-needed food to Chattanooga. Word had come that the warehouses at Stevenson were bulging with supplies, another concern, Grant recalling the rebel raid against his enormous supply depot at Holly Springs, Mississippi, just prior to the Vicksburg campaign. That loss had delayed Grant's entire operation, and he couldn't avoid the nagging fear that Stevenson was just another Holly Springs, ripe for some opportunistic rebel cavalryman.

He had a sudden thought, called out to the parlor. "General Rawlins!"

Rawlins peered in, seemed as anxious as Grant was.

"Do we know the whereabouts of Nathan Bedford Forrest?"

Rawlins seemed surprised by the question. "Um . . . no, sir. To the west, pretty certain of that. He might be causing some agitation in Memphis. That's his home, I believe. It's where I would go, were I him."

The image of Rawlins the Cavalry Raider was too much for Grant to absorb. He waved Rawlins away, moved to his chair, sat, slid his hand through the papers on his small desk, read one, familiar, too familiar, reread a dozen times that morning. He tossed it aside, glanced around the room, noticed a portrait of a woman and her dog, the same portrait that had been there since his arrival. Questions bounced through him now, erupting from his nervous energy. What kind of dog is that? Some kind of hound. Well, certainly. They must hunt a good deal around here. The woman . . . homely lass. Her husband probably likes the dog better . . .

"Sir!"

Grant heard the sounds, a commotion of hoof-beats approaching the house. He stood, bumping the desk, papers sliding away to the floor, ignored that, straightened himself, tugged at his coat, felt for the cigars, let that go, then grabbed one again. He held it out, tried to appear calm, his hand too jumpy for the match. He jabbed the cigar back into his pocket, stood straight again, heard the clatter of boots on the wood floor, the loud voice, a hearty salute to Rawlins. And then the man was in the door, the hat off, the red hair, a ratty short beard spread across the rugged face, and, now, a wide grin.

"Hello, Grant. Weather really stinks around here."

Sherman had arrived.

CHAPTER TWENTY-THREE

CLEBURNE

CHATTANOOGA—
NOVEMBER 16, 1863

He had witnessed executions before, this one as solemn as any. Bragg was making an example of deserters, and Cleburne understood, as they all did, that according to the rules of war, it was entirely justified, that a man who refused to stand up and fight was a danger not only to his comrades, but to the entire army. But Cleburne felt more uneasiness than usual, that Bragg was trying to make a point that went far beyond good army discipline. The man was a deserter, to be sure, had slipped down off the heights, seeking whatever comforts could be found in the warm bosom of Yankee camps. But in the dark wetness of the rains, the man had stumbled into his own picket line, and it was the man's misfortune to make his plea straight into the face of an officer, a man Cleburne imagined was suffering deprivations enough of his own. Arrested, the would-be deserter had somehow caught Bragg's attention, a mystery to Cleburne even now why the commanding general would embrace this one man's indiscretion as such a powerful symbol. And it was powerful indeed. More than five hundred men from the man's own division had been called out into the rains to witness the firing squad. Those men would spread the word to thousands more, until every man perched in the wet misery of the Confederate camps would feel the stab of it, one more weapon shoved into their gloom, pushed hard by Braxton Bragg.

Around Cleburne's camp, the men were still suffering from a lack of food and a lack of shelter. Entreaties from all parts of the field had gone through Bragg's office, and Cleburne had received the same response as had every other division commander. It was the Yankees who had refused to engage in a prisoner exchange, and so the Confederate commissary was forced to provide food and shelter for scores of Yankee prisoners. To Cleburne's amazement, Bragg hung on to that excuse, as though the army would simply accept the explanation without doubt. Cleburne didn't know how many prisoners were penned up in Confederate stockades, whether or not those men were even still in Tennessee. But Bragg's explanation had been forcefully spread throughout the army, blame of course laid at the feet of Ulysses Grant. No one dared to ask Bragg just how many prisoners were in Northern hands.

The rock ledge protruded far out from the face of the sloping hillside, a natural shelter from the rain. Cleburne had eyed the place several times, moved there now, his horse left in the care of a groom, a black servant named Billy, whose care for the horses seemed to outweigh any discomfort he might feel standing in the rain.

On his passes through the troop camps, Cleburne had grown increasingly nervous on the horse, the muddy lanes and steep trails offering too many possibilities for a hard tumble out of the saddle. Many months ago, with his elevation to regimental command, he had been given a mount, as appropriate for such a command. The addition of an actual staff, a cluster of officers to do his bidding, was an interesting luxury, but the horse was not. Now, as a division commander, it was not only expected but required that Cleburne make his inspections and tours on the animal's back. What he kept hidden, even from his closest aides, was that he was a poor rider, believed without any doubt that though his command extended over several thousand men, he had no command at all over the beast beneath him. Their relationship was a one-sided agreement, the horse firmly in charge. He had enormous admiration for those Southern officers who seemed to have been born in the saddle, gallant horsemen, skilled cavalrymen, all of them in a kind of partnership with their mounts, mutual affection that produced all those gallant assaults. Cleburne's greatest attachment to his horse now was the hard clamping hold from his legs, the fear that should the horse decide to dump him down the hillside, he would do so for no reason at all.

He had slid beneath the ledge, the rock just above his head. But the ground was not much drier than the trail he had left behind. The rock itself seemed to squeeze out water, dripping on all sides of him, his hat protecting him from one particular stream that seemed aimed directly at anyone who dared to believe this place could be dry.

He shifted himself, more mud, his pants cold, soaked, resigned himself to the discomfort. Down below, men were posted in the rifle pits, and Cleburne saw a steady flow of loose mud drifting past his rock, one of thousands along the face of the hill. They dug pits, he thought, and so, they now have troughs of water in which to sit. Perhaps not. Perhaps they have some kind of cover, like this. Perhaps they have constructed shelters of limbs or brush. He leaned out, tried to see. Yes, and perhaps they will all grow gills, and merely swim out of here when all of this has passed. He folded his arms across his knees, pulled them up tightly to his chest. His sword rested to one side, settling into the mud, and he stared at it for a long moment, thought, My glorious weapon. Slayer of dragons. Excalibur, pulled from a rock, the great hero standing tall, sword high, invincible against his enemies.

He stared out, disgusted with himself. Would you have your men hear such whining? What kind of man wallows in both mud and misery, and considers only himself? Up on that hill behind you, spread out all over this ground, are men who are starving. The Yankees have tents and rations, and they can build fires even in this astounding weather. It's the one part of the vision of Chattanooga we can truly observe. Seas of white tents and smoke from campfires. What am I to do about that? Well, one thing. Go out there and take those tents. Drive the enemy away. Is that not why we're here?

"Sir?"

He looked out toward the edge of his rocky shelter, saw a face, then another. He expected to see his staff officers, knew they would keep close eye on his whereabouts, no matter his momentary escape from the duties of his camps, the need to get down from the horse. Captain Buck was there, always there, a man whose loyalty Cleburne appreciated more than Buck would ever know. But the surprise was in the other man. It was one of Cleburne's brigade commanders, Lucius Polk. Buck was bent low, his hat suddenly falling from his head, rolling down the steep incline, well below the rocky ledge. Cleburne saw the man's dismay, as he saw the salute, and Cleburne pointed down the hill.

"Retrieve your headgear, Captain. No formality is required out here, not on a day like this."

Buck scampered down after the hat, and Cleburne saw Polk staring at him, a glimmer of concern on the man's face.

"Quite sorry to bother you, General, but I've just come from headquarters."

"Sorry, Lucius. I should have sent word to them just where I was going. Didn't know myself until I saw this wonderful piece of shelter. Nature provides, I suppose. Some problem? Major Benham have need of me?"

"Oh, no, sir. I mean . . . **headquarters.** General Bragg sent for a number of us. Didn't know what to expect, still not certain I understand it."

Cleburne felt the tug of concern now. "You still commanding one of my brigades?"

"Well, yes, sir. As far as I can tell." Polk pointed to the muddy area out beside Cleburne. "Um, sir, do you mind?"

Cleburne pulled his sword in closer, said, "By all means. Sorry. There is misery enough for us all without forcing you to stand out there. A warning, though. It's not much drier under here."

"It will suffice, sir."

Polk moved in beside him, and Buck had returned now, the hat covered with a muddy sheen. Cleburne saw the misery on the young man's face, said, "Captain, you may return to camp. Seek some shelter, if you can. I'm certain nothing is happening today. Neither side will be keeping their powder dry, and unless General Bragg orders us to fight this war with rocks and tree limbs, we're staying put."

"Yes, sir. I'll be at the camp if you require. There is a pair of couriers out here still, at your service."

Cleburne glanced around him, the narrow shelter not large enough for more than the two officers. "My apologies to those boys, Captain. Have them seek some shelter beneath their mounts. I doubt I shall require their services, but one never knows."

Buck started to back away, stopped, leaned in again. "Sir, if I may inquire . . . what are you doing under there?"

Cleburne stared out, the rains filling the great valley below him with a heavy mist, nothing visible but the low mounds that rose up halfway to the town.

"Observation, Captain. And now, a conference with General Polk."

"Whatever you say, sir. If I may take my leave . . ."

"Go. I'll not be here much longer. Or, perhaps I will."

Buck was gone now, and Polk sat beside him, adjusted his own sword, said, "All right. You won't tell him. So perhaps you'll tell me. Why is our division commander sitting under a big rock?"

"Easier than riding a horse."

"You think you'll just sit here until the rain stops? That might be three weeks."

"I'm not sure the rains will ever stop, Lucius. And

there's more than one kind of rain. This entire army is awash in bad morale. That execution this morning. Bragg is trying to punch us with his notion that discipline will win out. All we need do is keep our focus, our hatred for the enemy, and that alone will carry us to victory."

"I hate the man, Patrick."

Polk seemed to catch himself, and Cleburne saw the glance toward him, silence now. Cleburne weighed the sentiment, and after a long moment, said, "Haven't heard it expressed quite that way."

"That was not appropriate. My apologies. I should not allow my feelings to take control. My men would not understand such an outburst."

Cleburne looked at Polk, a man five years Cleburne's junior, seeming much younger now. "I believe your men would understand quite well. I would, however, not repeat your choice of words."

Polk looked down between his knees. "I received a letter from my uncle today. The bishop is in Atlanta still, and he is a bitter man, Patrick. I never thought I would see that. Bishop Polk loves life, loves mankind, loves the Almighty. And because of Braxton Bragg, a truly great man sits in exile. That's it. Exile. Why? Because he does not perform? Who among us can claim to be Caesar? Napoleon? Who among our leaders is above reproach? There is a stink here, Patrick. I shall not forgive Bragg. We are being led by a man who has no other goal than to witness our destruction."

Cleburne wasn't surprised by the venom in Polk's words, knew he could not agree, not even with perfect privacy.

"We are suffering, Lucius. There is misery everywhere about us. But we cannot forget why we are here. There is an enemy out there, an enemy who seeks to destroy everything this nation, **your** nation stands for. Yes, I observe the sickness, the lack of spirit, the collapse of our morale, and I feel helpless to change that. I will not deny that. I hear men call out for clean water, and the rains come, and even the rains make them sick."

"It is punishment, Patrick. The Almighty condemns us for following such a man as Bragg."

"Enough of that. One day, you may fight your duel with the commanding general, but right now, you have a responsibility to obey him. Start by obeying me. See to your men. A commander is responsible for his men, yes. But he is responsible **to** them as well. No matter your feelings for General Bragg, you will inspire obedience, and you will show respect for their sacrifice." He paused, suddenly curious. "Why were you summoned to headquarters?"

Polk looked at him, shook his head in raw disgust. "General Bragg is continuing his reorganization of this army. His purge of commanding officers has seemed to abate. Now he is shifting regiments from one brigade to another, without any apparent reason. Florida men are now serving beside Tennessee men, Alabamans with Kentuckians. It is as though he desires that no one in this army should stand by a friend. We must learn to fight alongside strangers. Does that make us a better army, Patrick?"

Cleburne was suddenly concerned. "I was not informed of this. Have any of my regiments been moved? I must know the details."

"No. That's the strange part of this. I was summoned by Bragg's staff just to observe these changes, as though I'm being schooled, taught some lesson."

Cleburne could see it now, more of the chess game. "Learn that lesson, my friend. General Bragg is a student of Napoleon, after all. He is still dividing his enemies. The generals who threatened him have been removed. Now he has turned his attentions to the troops themselves. Divide the Tennesseans, the Kentuckians, split their loyalties so there is no united front against him. It is the only explanation."

"But . . . what of the enemy? The real enemy? You said it yourself, Patrick. Why are we here?"

Cleburne stared out again to the wide plain. "Sherman's out there, you know. The scouts brought word to General Breckinridge. General Hardee spoke of it last evening. They estimate he has close to twenty-five thousand men on the march, which will add considerably to Grant's forces. Everyone in this army is aware what is happening out there. We have been told that this campaign has been halted by the miserable conditions, that for now, this army is paralyzed by the weather. It is apparent the Yankees are not so afflicted."

"It is possible they intend to send Sherman on toward Knoxville, strike our troops there from two sides."

"Possible."

"Are we just to remain here? Have you received any kind of orders? Again, Patrick, why are we here? If we are not to fight, then why do we not withdraw, secure the army in the passes in Georgia, or move the army westward, cut off the Yankees from their bases there? I am losing men every day to sickness, to dysentery. They have no tents, many of them have no coats, no shoes. Winter is coming rapidly. I am losing men every day to desertion. I have officers telling me that their men will not stand guard, that skirmish lines simply . . . vanish. I am hearing that no matter what conditions the Yankees might be suffering, their **starvation** rations are far better than what our commissary insists is a full day's sustenance. The Yankees have coats, and I have platoon commanders telling me that the color of that coat no longer matters. Men will survive any way they can."

The words stung Cleburne, and he held up a hand. "No. Do not speak of that. I cannot know anything of that."

"What do you mean?"

"You ask about orders? I have been ordered to report any deserter we bring back to this camp. The commanding general has chosen not only to wage war against his general officers; he is waging war against our own soldiers, those whose hearts cannot stand up to the hell we are forced to suffer. I will not hear such reports. I will not serve up my men for execution just to satisfy a misguided display of discipline. Do you understand?"

Polk looked at him with surprise. "You have learned lessons, as well."

Cleburne eyed the edge of the rock, the rains still relentless. "I cannot remain here, perched beneath a rock, daydreaming about what might be. Whether or not the commissary or General Bragg can do anything to help my men, I have to make the attempt. Return to your brigade. We should not discuss General Bragg in such a way. Some would call us traitors."

Polk did not move, looked hard at Cleburne. "My uncle, the bishop of Louisiana, has been called that. I have heard General Longstreet called that. General Buckner, General Hindman, and even your friend, General Hardee. And here we sit, you and I. Must we pretend we do not know who the real traitor is?"

Cleburne was angry now, fought the urge to shove Polk away.

"Return to your camp. **Now.** If my horse still waits for me in this absurd weather, I will return to mine. I will send another dispatch to headquarters, requesting in the strongest terms that food and blankets and shoes be brought forward. It is my duty. It is yours. We will not concern ourselves with issues of command we cannot control."

Polk said nothing, slid away from him, moved out into the rain, no salute, disappeared up the trail. Cleburne clenched his fists, knew Polk was his friend, knew that the harsh words would not separate them. He knows this, Cleburne thought. No matter what was done to his uncle's reputation, Lucius Polk is a soldier. No matter how much he professes to . . . hate. No matter how much I might share his feelings, the feelings that are spreading through most of this army, we must obey. It can be no other way. **No other way.**

Cleburne slapped his hat down hard on his head, slid the sword up from its muddy bed, crawled back out into the rain. The horse was there, the groom standing close by, a smile Cleburne ignored. He took the reins, climbed up, the saddle pressing up cold against him, stabbed the horse with his spurs, and rode back up the hill.

CHAPTER TWENTY-FOUR

GRANT

The day after Sherman's arrival, he and Grant had ridden out to the north, to the same overlook where George Thomas had stood beside Baldy Smith. Both of those men came along as well, Smith laying out the geography, explaining just what Sherman might confront. Grant was still holding strongly to the notion that the most effective way to strike the Confederates was on their northern flank, pushing most of Sherman's troops across the Tennessee River, striking the rebel position just below the mouth of Chickamauga Creek. But Sherman would not focus on a pursuit of Longstreet, or interfering with rail or communication lines to Knoxville. The power in numbers that Sherman was bringing gave Grant full confidence that the time had come to strike Bragg's rebels as hard as possible, to put an end to what had become a miserable stalemate.

Thomas still prodded Grant that the primary assault be made against Lookout Mountain, which Thomas insisted would be as much a threat to Bragg's position as Sherman's attack from the north. But Grant kept his faith in one place Thomas did not: Sherman. Grant focused on Sherman's raw optimism, the energy that Grant expected, and right now needed. The reconnaissance of the rebel right flank had shown Grant just what he wanted to see, that from all appearances, the rebels had no expectation at all that Sherman was coming. Earthworks were minimal, most of the rebel forces there seeming to lie back closer to the rail depot off the northern extreme of Missionary Ridge. Sherman had been as enthusiastic as Grant, both men convinced there was no reason to hit the rebels anywhere else. The next step was Grant's: putting the plan to paper.

The attack would commence on November 21, Sherman's main thrust pushing discreetly across the river during the night, a scramble of pontoons and planking that would be assembled as rapidly as the army's engineers could perform the task. Once the bulk of Sherman's troops were on the east side of the river, they would drive hard through what little rebel opposition seemed to be positioned there. The assault would continue with a rolling charge that would put Sherman's men directly onto the northern tip of Missionary Ridge. From there, crushing Bragg's army would be textbook, rolling up the rebel flank southward, until Bragg had no options but to pull back off the ridge completely, or risk annihilation.

On the opposite flank, where Hooker's men craned their necks toward the eminence of Lookout Mountain, there was no real certainty just how much strength the Confederates had positioned there. Grant knew, and Hooker feared, that Bragg might have compensated for Longstreet's absence by bringing up reinforcements, adding to the enormous advantages provided by the mountain itself with a powerful force of artillery and infantry. Hooker's troops had been clearly visible in Lookout Valley for days now, and Grant couldn't fathom that Bragg would just ignore the seriousness of that threat. To test the rebel strength there, and to possibly draw attention away from Sherman's assault on the far end of the position, Grant agreed that Hooker would send his men up the mountain the day before Sherman's crossing. Hooker's efforts would make considerable noise, and even if Hooker failed to drive the enemy off the mountain, Grant believed that Bragg would counter the assault by shifting troops toward the heights, thus potentially weakening the rebel lines along Missionary Ridge. Should Hooker succeed, as Thomas suggested, the loss of Lookout Mountain might force Bragg to withdraw his forces back behind

Chattanooga Creek, the meandering waterway that ran through the lowlands separating the mountain from Missionary Ridge. If Bragg pulled his troops tightly together on the ridge, both his flanks could be vulnerable, opening up the possibility for Grant to thrust to the right of the ridge, possibly cutting Bragg's rail line southward, the vital artery that brought supplies to the rebels from Georgia.

Grant's shaky confidence in Hooker really didn't matter. Grant understood that if Sherman succeeded in driving Bragg's army away from Missionary Ridge, any rebel troops who held tightly to any position on Lookout Mountain would know they were cut off completely. If those rebels didn't surrender, they'd be forced to withdraw southward, directly down the crest of the mountain, pulling them even farther away from Bragg's main body.

In the center, Thomas's Army of the Cumberland held the ground that spread out along the limits of Chattanooga itself, directly facing the bulk of the rebels on Missionary Ridge. Thomas's role would be to offer a noisy demonstration, troop formations marching out in all their glory, in full view of the rebels on the ridge. Grant believed that the show itself would be sufficient, the massed troops sent forward from the Federal lines in a grand display that would force Bragg to keep his rebel army firmly in their works. Creating uncertainty in Bragg's mind was one of Grant's primary goals, forcing Bragg to hold his entire army right where

it was positioned now, keeping Bragg utterly confused as to where the heaviest hammer blow would
come. In Grant's mind, and now, in the plan he put
together, it didn't really matter where Bragg's greatest strength might lie. The primary assault would
be Sherman's, there being no doubt at all in Grant's
mind, or Sherman's, that rolling up the rebel right
flank would decide this campaign once and for all.
Once Bragg had been driven southward, forced to
withdraw completely from Missionary Ridge, the
rest of Grant's army would be in perfect position to
clean up any stragglers Bragg might leave behind.

The day after their scouting mission north of the
town, Sherman left Chattanooga, riding out westward again, to oversee the final advance by his army.

CHATTANOOGA— NOVEMBER 19, 1863

Grant stormed out of his room, saw staff officers
jump in their chairs, wide-eyed.

"Where is he? Any word at all?"

Rawlins motioned to an aide, who read directly
from the telegram Grant had already seen.

"It says, sir . . . 'Arrived at Kelley's Ford. No boat
there. Someone disobeyed my orders to remain. At
Bridgeport now. Army advancing. Rather slow work
crossing the bridge. Will arrive at Chattanooga as
soon as possible.' We have nothing further, sir."

"What is the problem? Why is it taking so long? There is no enemy obstructing his advance."

There was no answer from his staff, and Grant stared out through the windows, a steady drizzle, dark misery from the skies.

"What of the supply trains? Is there some word of that?"

Rawlins shook his head. "The nearest bridge has been repaired. Not sure of the others. It has been most annoying, sir."

Grant stared at Rawlins, had his own feelings about what was annoying him right now. "Keep me informed. Any news! You understand?"

"Certainly, sir."

Grant kept his stare at them, rocked back and forth, the nervous anxiety pulling his stomach inside out. "Do what you must. Just keep me informed. I will not have good men put once more into starvation."

The wagon trains had been kept away from Chattanooga for the past few days, the entire army beginning to suffer again from a lack of rations. It was one more of the ongoing frustrations for Grant, the slow arrival of supplies, made more difficult by the rebels' uncanny success at wrecking the pontoon bridges. But it wasn't just the rebels who played havoc with Federal engineering. The rains had swollen every waterway, and so the Tennessee River was in full roar, and even if the pontoon bridges held, the crossings could be treacherous. But they had not held, the main bridge into Chattanooga smashed by heavily laden rafts sent downriver by the rebels. The lightweight pontoons had been no match for the floating projectiles, nor could they withstand the swirling currents, Grant's engineers scampering downstream in a frustrating attempt to locate and retrieve as many of the small boats as could be found. In the meantime, the flatboats ferried supplies across, but in the harsh current, it was slow going at best. The results were predictable. The food supplies had dwindled, the commissary forced to limit the men to less than a pound of meat per day. Worse for the horses, the forage was disappearing again, the already weakened animals now nearly useless. Grant had seen the reports from Thomas, that the Army of the Cumberland had lost more than ten thousand animals. That number was certain to grow. Grant knew that Sherman was equipped with nearly six thousand animals of his own. If forage was not brought quickly along the supply lines, starving horses would mean paralysis, what Grant had witnessed too often already.

Grant turned abruptly, marched noisily into his room, his eye settling on the dying fire. He felt a furious need to blister an aide for that, spun back around, was surprised to see the door closed behind him. **Rawlins.** Grant forced himself to calm, pounded one hand into the other. You know what is best, he thought, whether I want you to or not. I do not need my staff observing the spectacle of their commanding general screaming like a banshee.

He moved to the fire, reached for the iron poker leaning up against the stone, stabbed at the ashes. The flames responded, and he picked up a log from the wood box nearby, set it into the fire. He added one more, the fire taking hold, the warmth filling him, soothing, and he sat on the floor, close to the fire, stared at the flames. There can be no assault, he thought. Not on my schedule. You cannot fault Sherman. He hates waiting far more than you do. He would make his army **swim** that confounded river, if it would get them here any sooner.

He thought of his wife now, the soft image filling him, drawn by the warmth of the fire. Julia would insist there was some Design in this, some Hand that we cannot understand. But there is no curse upon this army, the Almighty is not casting plagues upon us. Have we not proven that? The greatest accomplishments of this army, the victories that will win this war . . . no matter what kind of success, none of those fights have been simple. How often do campaigns follow what is written on paper? If it was that easy, there would not be a war at all. We could just . . . plan it away.

The memories came now, Sherman, the others, salvaging success from disaster. Shiloh, he thought, such a close thing. We were very nearly crushed. And if that had been the outcome, where would you be now, Grant? What path would this army have taken with Buell in command, or Rosecrans? Burnside, Hooker? Men who lose battles. No mystery about that, I suppose. This war might be over, and not the way the president intended it to be. He thought of Julia, always with the devout blessing, the reliance on the Almighty. With all apologies to you, my dear, I am here by the hand of Lincoln, not the hand of God. He rubbed his chin, blinked at the fire. Or, perhaps they are one and the same. Lincoln would never take credit for his better decisions. But he will most certainly suffer the blame if this goes badly.

Grant turned from the hearth, stood, flexed the knee, almost no pain now, moved into the chair. Thank God she is not here, he thought. This would be an argument she would embrace. Stubborn woman, and I am in a foul way right now. A bad mixture. Yes, my darling wife, every fight has its mysterious ways, the turn of fate, **for the want of a nail.** Wisdom there. Who said that? Shakespeare? No, Ben Franklin perhaps. You have been fortunate, Grant. You haven't lost many **nails.** We defeated a stubborn enemy at Fort Donelson, and it cost us casualties to both the army and navy. Vicksburg . . . it took a slap at my own stubbornness to turn that into a siege. Arrogance. I thought we could just march up close and push the enemy into the river. Sherman thought so, too. Hundreds of men paid the price for our mule-headed decisions. Now, here, we must struggle with rain and mud. Sherman's probably out there at Bridgeport screaming his voice away. Grant imagined that scene, Sherman at the river's edge, launching his epithets into every boat captain's face, every officer who marched his regiment onto a quivering pontoon bridge. There is no defeating nature, he thought. But if Sherman says he'll bring his people up as quickly as possible . . . he will. That's all I need concern myself with. The attack will commence when it can. It's as simple as that.

NOVEMBER 20, 1863

He had not expected to see Thomas, didn't want to see him now. But the man was there, and Grant had a nagging itch that Charles Dana had come along with the general just to see what Grant might do.

The week before, Dana had been sent northward with Grant's staff officer, Charles Wilson, to communicate directly with Ambrose Burnside. That gesture had been made more as an appeasement to the War Department's ongoing panic regarding Knoxville than any real intelligence mission for Grant. With the telegraph lines to Knoxville still down, and the War Department clamoring for information, Grant had decided that the simplest way for Dana to report what was happening was to see it for himself. But Dana returned with news that dug hard at Grant, the one outcome Grant had feared. There had already been several days of fighting there, the rebel forces doing what they could to pin Burnside's army hard into the city. The one enormous distraction that could remove him from Chattanooga was if Burnside was suddenly hemmed into an effective Confederate siege, facing starvation and, ultimately, a crushing defeat. Should Burnside collapse, surrendering his army and the city, the rebels would open up an enormous gash in the Federal hold on Tennessee and Kentucky. Grant knew full well that news of that kind of disaster would cause Henry Halleck to erupt like a volcano, the kind of chaotic response that could cost Grant his command. The best news from Knoxville was that, so far, the rebel efforts had seemed scattered, disorganized, a surprise to Grant. He expected more from his friend Longstreet. Regardless, Grant knew that it was only a matter of time before Longstreet would smooth out whatever problems he was confronting. It only added to Grant's feelings of urgency, that his own plan at Chattanooga be put into motion as quickly as possible. But still, that depended on Sherman. When would his army arrive?

He motioned the two men into the room, Thomas doing the obvious, settling into the lone chair. Grant had observed that behavior more than once, Thomas rarely ever showing Dana even symbolic respect. Dana had seemed to accept that, kept back against the wall, and Grant studied the fire, a futile effort to ignore them both, an effort he knew wouldn't last long.

After a long moment, Thomas said, "General Grant, I regret this intrusion. But there is something of a development here. A courier, under a flag of truce, entered my lines a short while ago. He presented me with . . . this."

Grant glanced at Dana, saw a childlike eagerness, took the paper from Thomas. Grant saw that the wax seal was unbroken.

"You could have examined this yourself, General. It isn't necessary to defer every communication to this headquarters."

"I was not certain of that. I thought it best to err on the side of protocol."

Grant sniffed, didn't respond. He had grown increasingly annoyed with Thomas, even if there seemed to be no good reason why, nothing the man had done beyond preparing his own army for the eventual assault. Grant broke the wax, the paper sliding out into his hand. He was surprised to see the seal of Bragg's Army of Tennessee.

"Well, this is somewhat unexpected." He read for a brief moment, said, "It seems that General

Bragg is making us a generous offer, or rather, an offer generous to the Southern citizens hereabouts. He salutes me in the usual way, and suggests rather pointedly that we remove the noncombatants from this town. The inference is clear. He is warning us of imminent attack." Grant lowered the paper, looked at both men. "Now why on God's earth would he do that?"

Thomas held out his hand. "May I, sir?"

"Absolutely."

Thomas read, and Dana said, "It's nonsense, sir! It's a bluff! The audacity!"

Thomas returned the paper to Grant, who said, "Of course it's a bluff. But there is meaning here. He is attempting to distract us from whatever his true intentions might be."

Thomas stood, took a few paces to the wall, turned slowly, returned, stopped beside his chair. "Knoxville. He's intending to reinforce Longstreet, and wants us to sit still while he does so. He must believe we shall accept this as truth, and hold our position here. In the meantime, he must intend to shift more units northward, adding to his forces now facing Burnside."

Dana seemed to energize, and Grant watched him, thought he might suddenly dart around the room like a housefly. Dana said, "It's devious, no doubt about that! I shall inform Washington of his plans!"

Grant shook his head. "Not yet. We don't know

his plans. If he is sending troops northward, he is weakening himself here even more than he has done already." He looked up at Thomas. "He has not been reinforced from any other direction, has he?"

Thomas shook his head. "No reports of any railcars, no additional troops. The cavalry scouts report that much of his army is in a rather bad way. I do not see how he can launch an effective attack in any quarter, whether here or at Knoxville."

"But he might try. He has the rail line that way. If he can assist Longstreet in a major assault, he must assume it will bring him victory. If Burnside is defeated, he will retreat, which will allow Bragg to return most of his troops back down here." Grant paused. "Or it is possible that Bragg has made the decision to abandon this ground completely. If there is troop movement on the rail lines, it could be a general retreat. That would be . . . extremely unfortunate."

Dana seemed confused, said, "But if he is retreating, it means we have achieved great victory here! We can then secure Burnside's position! The enemy must retreat southward, which means he is not expecting a major assault at Knoxville. If he retreats to the east or north—"

Grant punched a fist into his hand. "If he retreats in any direction, it will mean that all our preparations are worthless. I did not bring Sherman this far just so we can play the role of housecat, chasing a mouse all over this part of the world."

Dana's words seemed to burst out of the man. "Then we must attack him right now! If he is weakened and in the act of retreating, he could be extremely vulnerable!"

Grant glanced at Thomas, saw the man's usual frown, and Grant said, "Mr. Dana, this is why you do not have free access to the telegraph wire without my permission. Most of Sherman's people are still en route, and until he is in place out to our left flank, there will be no attack. As long as we do not know what Bragg's intentions are, we do not know where to attack, or what we are attacking."

Thomas's expression did not change, but there was no critical comment from the man, a gesture Grant appreciated. Dana began to pace now, new thoughts seeming to roll out in a flood of words.

"This could be very bad. Very bad indeed. If the enemy reinforces his army at Knoxville, and we can do nothing to prevent that, it only adds to that crisis. If he is retreating, we must know where. He might not be retreating at all! That message is no doubt a ruse of some sort. I must relate this to the secretary, sir. Even if you do not approve. With all respects, General."

Grant pointed a finger at Dana, silencing him. "I said . . . not yet. There are couriers moving back and forth on various routes from here to Knoxville. If there is a disaster there, we will know of it quite quickly. There is nothing else we can do to assist General Burnside, not while we are facing Bragg's army right here. If Bragg is pulling away, we must know that. That will change . . . everything."

Thomas pointed to the letter in Grant's hand. "Perhaps we should answer those mysteries ourselves, let Bragg show us what he's up to."

Grant saw a flash of energy in Thomas, another surprise.

"What do you propose?"

"Reconnaissance in force." Thomas moved to the wall across from the hearth, a map hung there by Grant's staff. Thomas looked at the map, said slowly, "If I move a large body of troops out toward these low hills in the plain, it may prove valuable. We will first determine if the enemy is still holding that ground with an intent on keeping it. If we remove him, or he removes himself, and we occupy these hills, it will give us a far more practicable observation point from which we may observe Missionary Ridge. If Bragg is moving people away from here, thinning out his lines, we should be able to see that. If he has indeed slipped away, we will know that pretty quickly." Thomas paused. "The next move would of course be up to you."

Grant weighed the man's words, climbed out of the chair, moved to the map. The more prominent of the smaller hills was labeled Orchard Knob, the second called Indian Hill. Grant had observed the hills from the defenses outside Chattanooga, low rises bulging as much as a hundred feet above the plain, the two bare hills connected by a brushy ridge.

The hills sat halfway between Thomas's earthworks at the edge of Chattanooga and the base of Missionary Ridge.

Grant put his finger out to the larger knob. "There are rebels in force there, so I've been told. By you, I believe."

"The rebels sent at least two regiments out there not long after our retreat. General Rosecrans did not see any value to a loss of life in making the effort to hold that ground, since the town gave us the defenses we required. We have since made no efforts in that direction. There just wasn't any good reason. There might be now. We know their skirmish line is still in place. Whether those troops are willing to stand up to an attack will tell us a great deal."

Grant still wasn't convinced. "If Bragg values those hills more than we do, there could be a hard scrap. Just the sort of mess to bring on a general engagement. I don't want that, not yet. Sherman has to move out into position, or be very close to it, before we can show Bragg what we intend."

"Actually, sir, if Bragg is vacating the heights, this is the simplest way of finding out. Our advance will inspire some response. The strength of that response might tell us just who's left on the heights. As for the low hills, advancing twenty thousand men out into that plain will be a display I would enjoy watching myself, were I on Missionary Ridge. I do not believe they will fight to hold those hills.

The alternatives then are that Bragg will sit tight, expecting us perhaps to assault the heights. Or if he is leaving here altogether, he'll be even more noisy about it. Either way, we can take those low hills as a better vantage point than we have now."

"You believe you will require twenty thousand men?"

Thomas shook his head. "I don't know what to believe, sir. That's the point. If we wish to provoke a response, we must provide as much bluster and racket as my men can create. If Bragg is still in force in the ridge, and responds by launching a major attack of his own, we can easily retreat to our defenses here." Thomas stopped, a glance at Dana. "General Grant, I have witnessed an army in retreat. I am here now because of the price General Rosecrans paid for such a move. General Bragg must certainly know that removing himself from our front will cost him his career. I understand your concerns that we have let him slip away. It is my opinion that, beyond the movement of troops toward Knoxville, I don't believe the enemy has gone anywhere. If anything, he is at his weakest, while we are stronger than we have been before."

Grant couldn't help being impressed, saw none of the surliness he had come to expect. "Bragg's career is not the only one that might be in jeopardy. I cannot allow him to retreat, and I cannot allow him to move his forces en masse to Knoxville. General, you may proceed. If he is still in strength on those heights, let us find that out." He studied the map again. "And, I agree with you that grabbing those low hills, with those patches of woodlands, could be most useful. We're running low on firewood."

With crippled pontoon bridges and roads that Sherman described as "ditches of rocks," Sherman's troops struggled to make their way to Chattanooga. To Grant's dismay, Sherman's sluggishness seemed to have come from the arrangement of the march itself. Sherman had ordered each division to march immediately to the front of its own supply and artillery train, the wagons and caissons that required so much extra effort to shove through the muddy misery of the washed-out roads. Each unit coming up behind had to wait for the slow progress of the cumbersome vehicles before they could make progress themselves. When Grant learned of Sherman's dispositions, he responded with an order born of exasperation, a soft scolding to Sherman that was kept quiet even from Grant's own staff. Sherman's men were told to bypass their wagons, the clear priority being to move troops into position as quickly as possible. The supply trains would arrive in time. What mattered most right now were muskets.

As they marched past the numerous Confederate lookouts, Sherman followed another of Grant's instructions, that his army make every effort to be seen by the rebels, a blue-clad parade that would most likely inspire couriers to ride hard from their perches on Lookout Mountain, keeping Bragg informed of Sherman's arrival. But once across Brown's Ferry, Sherman's men would be put into camps far west of the river, in thickets and forest lands where no Confederate might see them. Thus, the seeds of uncertainty could be planted in Bragg's mind just where Sherman was intending to go.

Out in the center, directly in front of Missionary Ridge, Thomas's troops made their preparations for an advance, assembling their formations in full view of the observers on both Lookout Mountain and Missionary Ridge. With Sherman finally settling into his designated camps, Grant gave the order to Thomas to proceed.

It had been two months since the Army of the Cumberland had suffered the bloody disgrace of their retreat from Chickamauga. Now, even if the order called for little more than a reconnaissance in force, Thomas would lead them forward again.

CHAPTER TWENTY-FIVE

BRAGG

NAIL HOUSE,
MISSIONARY RIDGE—
NOVEMBER 23, 1863

The morning had been cool and damp, but finally the sun appeared, a welcome show of light reflecting off the vast pools of mud that blanketed the ridgeline. He walked out from the small house, ignored the blue skies, still felt the impact of his breakfast, some kind of sour meat that he tried not to think about. All along the ridge, his men were going about their routines, which for many included very little to do. Even close to the headquarters there was very little shelter beyond anything the men had been able to improvise, and Bragg had been lenient with them, had not insisted that the commanders put the men through the usual drills, parade ground formations on the flatter ground back to the rear of the ridge. For Bragg himself, observing those exercises had become boring in the extreme. His boredom had turned to outright disgust with some of the regiments, some of them so slovenly in appearance, no one would assume them to be soldiers. To his delight, other units had performed their drills and moved through their formations with crisp precision, a source of pride to their colonels, and of course to Bragg. But there were too many of the others who seemed to go about the maneuvers with purposeful sloppiness, as though they found some kind of perverse satisfaction in taunting him. He couldn't avoid the comparison of those units to bands of unruly children, that no matter how much discipline he tried to force on them, there would always be the stubborn, the rebellious. It bothered Bragg even more that the lack of discipline and deportment was surely a symbol for their disinterest in the Cause they were supposed to be fighting for, the very reason they were facing off against the Yankees. But if they seemed to care not at all for being soldiers, they also continued to show a lack of respect for him. It was the only interpretation that mattered to him, that an army who carried themselves with laziness had contracted that disease from the officers who led them, with no regard for the respect they should be showing to the man at the top. He suspected still that many of the senior officers were participating in secret meetings, what Bragg continued to believe were the conspiracies he could never quite stamp out.

The reassuring letters from Jefferson Davis had come less often, and even those few were less enthusiastic, another stab at Bragg's concern, that somehow even Davis was being turned against him. Bragg pushed the issue, seeking reassurances in letters of his own, and Davis offered the tepid responses that all was well. But Bragg knew that since he had reduced the size of his army at Chattanooga, he might very well be at a numerical disadvantage, and so he tested Davis's endorsement with pleas for additional troops. He had petitioned Joe Johnston as well, had suggested strongly that the Confederate garrison at Mobile be reduced, the manpower much more valuable to the fight certain to come at Chattanooga. Davis had been supportive, if only in spirit, no real promises of any additional troops. Johnston seemed to ignore him altogether, showing an infuriating lack of respect that dug hard at Bragg, one more example of the army's utter disregard for the campaign that Bragg believed might decide the outcome of the entire war. The lukewarm support he was now receiving from Davis forced him to exercise patience, muting the typical fury he would inject into his letters. He felt no great need to put himself into direct confrontation with anyone in Richmond, or any other senior commander outside of his own sphere of control. Victory at Chattanooga would accomplish that far better than any hostile dispatch or bellicose complaint. Time seemed to be on Bragg's side, despite what the cavalry insisted was an enormous buildup of troops under Grant's command. Whether or not the cavalry scouts were accurate in their estimates of Federal strength, the enemy across from Bragg had shown no signs that they were intending any kind of assault, or any kind of significant move to thwart what Bragg still believed was an effective siege. The reports had reached him of renewed shortages in the town, of Federal soldiers desperate for food, no matter the infuriating evidence that Grant's supply lines had been pushed open. For Bragg, there seemed to be more positive news than negative, the constant destruction of the Federal pontoon bridges, and, even better, the obvious loss of enormous numbers of horses and mules. He didn't need cavalry scouts to tell him that the Yankees had suffered that kind of carnage. The putrid smells carried on the breeze had been evidence enough. The estimates of dead draft animals were in the thousands, a satisfying success that convinced Bragg more than ever that his strategy was working, that no matter how many additional troops Grant brought into Chattanooga, the Federal army was still in serious trouble.

As he made his stroll through soggy ground, past filthy men in muddy shelters, he knew he would hear their complaints. There were always complaints, even on those days, like this one, when the good weather returned. He knew the morale of the army had fallen dangerously low, that even the good men were enduring hardships of food, shelter, and adequate clothing. He could not avoid giving attention to that, no matter how unpleasant the task. The dispatches continued to flow, an absurd and useless argument with the commissary offices, first in Atlanta, and then to Richmond, his pleadings for sustenance and shelter for his army. As had happened all during his campaigns in Tennessee, infuriating rumors filtered back to him that the greater percentage of the critical supplies were still being sent northward, the urgent necessity of rebuilding Lee's Army of Northern Virginia, an army that had lost its most significant fight of the war. It dug hard at Bragg's pride that no one in Richmond seemed to acknowledge Lee's inability to defeat the enemy whose leadership was so questionable, while Bragg was faced with a Federal army deep in the heart of the South led by the man whose reputation had seemed to Bragg to have grown far beyond all reason. Of greater concern to Bragg was that Grant's army had dug their way well to the south, threatening rail lines and crucial cities, a far greater threat to the Confederacy than what he saw as Lee's fanciful attempts to find glory in Pennsylvania. But Bragg knew those kinds of sentiments were unwelcome in Richmond, and Bragg could only spew out his anger in letters sent to his greatest ally, his own wife.

He stepped heavily through the mud, his boot heels splashing the brown ooze in every direction. He was angry now, always angry when he thought of Lee, the special treatment Lee received from Richmond. It is politics, he thought. Pure and simple. Perhaps if I was to **lose** a battle, scamper away in a manic retreat from some bloody confrontation with the enemy, then perhaps I would receive the kind of sympathy afforded General Lee. Instead, my greatest flaw is **victory.** And so, my men are abused, neglected, and I am to fight campaigns not only here, but in Knoxville, and must suffer the indignation of trying to manage Lee's own troops, his "favorite son" Longstreet. The man brought a wagonload of vainglory down here, showed only disrespect and disobedience. All right, so if that's how it must be, I have remedied that with a deft hand. Longstreet has his opportunity handed to him with a gracious bow from this headquarters. And still, he complains and lodges his outrageous protests.

Bragg moved past another of the camps, heard the voices, men calling to him, pleadings for even the most basic of foodstuffs. He ignored what he could, heard his aides behind him offering their usual assurances to gathering clusters of men, promises that no one believed. He moved past a scattering of tree stumps, the trees long gone, and he thought now of his horse. Can't even ride through here, he thought. Horse could break a leg. We should at least mark the trails, designate those places where lumber may be cut. It's a complete lack of discipline, of planning, and a complete lack of care for the men. I will not take the blame for that. If they spent their time in more useful pursuits, these kinds of matters could be handled. Instead, they slip away from here at their leisure to prey on civilians, with thieving and vandalism, and God knows what other acts of depravity. Punishment is the only solution, swift and strong. There is little difference between desertion in the ranks, and the abuse of civilians, the very people we are here to protect. He glanced to the side, saw a dozen men gathered around the flickers of a small smoking fire, thought, Where do we find these men? Is it just **my** army that must bear the burden of such moral failure? I am quite certain General Lee receives the cream, the good strong men, stout hearts and devout fiber. I am blessed with the dregs of Southern manhood. And Richmond expects miracles.

He thought of Longstreet again, the constant extension of the nagging hostility he felt toward Lee. For several days, Longstreet had peppered Bragg with desperate calls for reinforcements, and Bragg had read them all with growing disgust. He regards me with no respect at all, he thought. Now he faces an enemy he should crush with ease, a general in Burnside whom he has already defeated handily, and yet now he complains that his army is not adequate to the task. He despises me, and yet he calls upon me for assistance. But his failures at Knoxville will not bloody my hands.

Bragg was suddenly very pleased with himself, stopped, hands on his hips, a gaze out to the north, along the ridgeline, toward the rail station far beyond. Very well, he thought, I have obliged his weaknesses, I have granted him the greatest of favors, and if there is success at Knoxville, those accolades shall rightly fall upon **me.**

The day before, Bragg had finally agreed to add strength to Longstreet's forces by sending two divisions, eleven thousand men, to add to the fifteen thousand Longstreet had marched away from Chattanooga. Even now, Bragg knew those men would be gathering near the rail depot on Chickamauga Creek, starting the journey that would take them partway toward Knoxville. The smaller division, four thousand men, belonged to Simon Buckner, one of the conspirators against Bragg who, despite Bragg's loathing of the man, still remained at hand, a problem Bragg had to accept. Buckner's division had been designated something of an independent unit, one of the odd twists in Jefferson Davis's organization of the army, a compromise Bragg had been forced to swallow during Davis's visit in October. The larger division, seven thousand men, belonged to Patrick Cleburne, a man Bragg still didn't fully understand and certainly didn't trust. Since Cleburne's Arkansas regiments had come east to add to the campaigns in Kentucky and Tennessee, Cleburne had earned enormous respect from Davis, and from the other commanders. Bragg had been assured by Davis that even though Cleburne had signed that damnable petition against him, the Irishman had come around, the president now fully confident that Cleburne embraced a strong loyalty to Bragg, and would perform well in the field. Sending Cleburne to assist Longstreet was an idea that had burst into Bragg's mind like a bolt of blue light, an ingenious way to keep a capable eye on Longstreet's performance, while making certain that Longstreet did in fact return to Chattanooga.

He moved on through the mud, thought of the letter he was composing, anticipating Longstreet's missives to his friends in Richmond. If he fails at Knoxville, Bragg thought, the excuses will flood the War Department. I must be prepared for that, respond to it even before Longstreet spouts out his lies. If there is failure, he alone shall bear the responsibility. I have seen to that, after all. His forces will nearly equal what I have here, and if he cannot complete his task with such men, then he cannot complete any task at all. And who shall be free of blame?

He ran those words through his mind again. Very good. You should write that to Elise, seek her approval. She would insist you tell the president, tell all of them of the sacrifices you make. She would certainly scold you for keeping silent. This is no time for humility, for soft modesty. She will chastise you for allowing them to abuse your reputation. I should have brought her here, an inspiration to the men. Or perhaps she should go to Richmond, make her calls upon the War Department and the president, and give loud voice to my difficulties here. He smiled. I could employ no one better for the task.

He kept his stare out toward Chattanooga, could make out the sea of blue that spread out in neat formations all across the face of the town. Around him, men were doing as he did, focusing their attention on the distant Federal camps. No matter what anyone around him thought of the incredible view of the enemy's army, to Bragg it was simply his target.

His aides were there now, holding men away, the cries still reaching him, but he shut that away, absorbing the marvelous warmth of the sunlight, nearly overhead. Bragg glanced down, saw shadows, his own, dark splotches below the rocks, so very rare for so many days. He tested his ailments, no headache, his stomach finally letting go of the nagging torment from the breakfast. He thought of Elise again. By God, she should see this. She should be up here, admiring what we have done to the enemy. There they stand, performing their daily rituals, consuming their strength and their limited rations in mindless exercise. He looked up toward

Lookout Mountain, could see the signalmen, flags in motion, men doing their jobs. Yes, very good. Keep us informed. I have no desire to make that tedious journey yet again just to learn what my officers should already be telling me.

Down below, he heard shouts, paid no heed to the words. He knew some of the men would cheer him, that on a day like this, when the skies shone blue and the sun relieved their ills, they would understand how much he cared for this army, all that he was giving them, the preparation, the positioning. Yes, you will understand what history will know of you, once this campaign is concluded. You will know of victory.

There were more shouts now, and his staff began to move up beside him, gathering too closely, annoying him. He glanced to the side, was surprised to see Colonel Brent, said, "Why are you out here? Did I not insist you keep close to the headquarters, receive the couriers? I wish to hear reports of the progress of the reinforcements I have ordered to Longstreet. His response to my sudden generosity should be a dispatch worth placing in a picture frame."

"Sir, forgive me, but the signalmen from Lookout Mountain are telling us that the enemy is making preparations for an advance."

Bragg looked out toward Chattanooga, saw more of the distant patches of blue, swelling now, as though flooding out in the plain away from their own defenses. He had seen this before, was irritated with Brent's inexperience.

"Nonsense, Colonel. This break in the infernal rains has encouraged the Yankees to put themselves to work with drilling, occupying their time by practicing what they should already know by heart. It is a lack of effectiveness by their officers."

Brent didn't respond, stared out through field glasses. Bragg felt satisfied he had made his point, and he glanced down the hill, more shouts continuing below, and now, off to the side, more cheers and calls from distant camps.

"What on earth is that caterwauling about?"

Brent lowered the field glasses, pointed out toward the center of the Federal lines, the great formations of blue. The masses continued to swell, pushing out farther from the town, all the pomp of a parade ground display.

"That, sir. It appears to me that they are advancing."

Bragg stared out through his field glasses, saw the flicker of flags, could make out the specks of men on horseback. He scanned the lines, a vast sea, growing larger by the minute. Behind the blue wave came bursts of smoke, and Bragg lowered the glasses, saw the streaks of fire arching up and over the Yankee lines, impacting midway across the plain. In a few seconds, the thunder reached him, dull thumps, more fire from Federal guns, more streaks, plumes of smoke now rising up from the impacting shells in the thickets that spread far out in the plain, between two low hills.

He heard a voice behind him, the man running toward him, out of breath, one of his aides, the words coming in a manic stream, "Sir! The observers on the mountain are saying that the Yankees are advancing to our picket line. The messages say that Yankees are making a fight of it, sir!"

Bragg ignored him, could see a low line of white smoke, waited long seconds, the faint sound of a single chopping blow, the massive volley of musket fire reaching him. Bragg kept his stare to the front, the smoke now rising, obscuring his vision, thought, They're coming. They have waited for the weather to change, and now they are coming. This is . . . wonderful.

"Who's out there? Whose troops are on those small hills?"

Brent stepped away, and Bragg was immediately furious, his question seeming to inspire a debate that spread through his staff. He still watched the smoke, more steady cracks of massed musket fire, heard Brent now.

"Sir, we believe it's Manigault's brigade. Patton Anderson's division."

"How many men, Colonel? Is that also a secret?"

"Don't know, sir. I'll send a courier down that way."

"Anderson's division is all around us, Colonel. It can't be difficult to answer such a simple question."

"I know, sir. I'll take care of it."

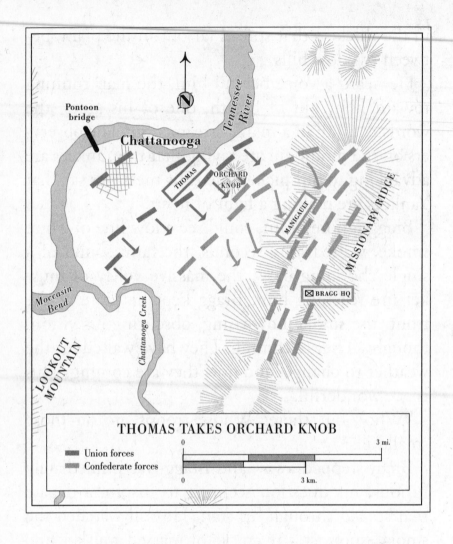

THOMAS TAKES ORCHARD KNOB

Union forces
Confederate forces

0 .... 3 mi.

0 .... 3 km.

Bragg let the field glasses drop against his chest, stared up again toward Lookout Mountain, the signal flags in motion, frightened men communicating the obvious. He felt a rising anger, sensed a stink of incompetence that seemed to swirl around them, men who had no idea what was happening.

He heard a horse approaching, the high-pitched voice of a courier.

"Those men are from Patton Anderson's division, sir. Manigault's brigade has the skirmish duty. General Manigault says he had no more than six hundred men in those far trees. Alabamans, sir. He's sent the order not to make a stand. They'll be falling back, once they receive his order."

"Falling back? Is that how General Manigault intends to fight this war?"

Bragg kept his eyes on the smoke, the rumble of the fight steady, flickers of motion all along the distant woodlands, blasts of fire, more smoke rising.

The courier stayed up on his horse, said, "Sir, General Manigault says there may be fifty thousand Yankees to his front, sir. Several divisions. He has but six hundred men. He is ordering them to withdraw to the rifle pits at the base of the hill."

Bragg kept his stare on the distant hills, the man's report drilling inside him. Fifty thousand?

"General Manigault is a man prone to exaggeration. If his men have more fight in them than their commander, they shall drive the enemy back. Find Anderson. Order him to make the best fight he can. I will not allow retreat, not from such an advantageous position."

"Yes, sir!"

Bragg glanced that way, saw the man ride quickly away, mud splashing high. He looked at Brent now, said, "Order every division commander on this ridge to make ready to receive the enemy. We have glorious ground, and we shall show the enemy their mistake!"

Brent acknowledged him with a salute, and Bragg returned it, saw the others looking at him, saw fear, wide-eyed doubt, all of them watching the great scene in the distance. He turned toward them, facing them, his back to the distant fight, said, "Look at me! All of you! There are not fifty thousand Yankees in the entire state of Tennessee! Do you hear me? General Manigault is showing us his lack of fitness for command! I will deal with him later. For now, do your jobs! Put these troops to their posts. If the enemy intends to assault these heights, we shall cover that ground with his blood!"

They seemed to energize, more of them watching him, men in motion now, moving away, couriers on horseback, spreading out in both directions. He forced a smile, saw Brent returning, his uniform splattered with mud.

"You're a disgrace, Colonel. Do you not have a horse?"

"Sir, with all respects. I have sent word to the division commanders. Their aides are already coming in here, sir, reporting all is in readiness."

"We shall see." Bragg glanced again at Lookout Mountain. "General Hardee is up there, yes?"

"Yes, sir. Last we knew."

"He is wasting his time up there. The enemy is coming right at our center. We require additional artillery, whatever batteries Hardee can move down this way. See to it. And make haste."

"Yes, sir!"

Brent was gone now, and Bragg stood alone, stepped farther out on a rock outcropping, watched the waves of smoke, the bursts of musket fire, thumps of Federal artillery, most of it coming from batteries closer to the town. He focused on what he could see of the Federal troops, the enormous formations spread out to both sides of the low hills. He raised the field glasses, saw Manigault's men streaming back from the woodlands, saw men in blue visible now on the bald hills, their flags waving in the breeze. Bragg yelled the words to himself, We must have all our artillery! Right here! He knew there was time, the range too great still for any kind of precision. He focused on the waves of men coming back toward him, a steady retreat, thought, No, they're following Manigault's orders. Those hills are in the enemy's hands.

The glasses came down again, and he scanned the hillside below him, saw gun crews at their pieces, preparing for any target. Down below, the men were filling their rifle pits, the long trench lines that extended all across the ridge. The firing had nearly stopped now, the smoke clearing, drifting away. He looked down to the right, the far flank out of his view, miles away, thought of Cleburne, the troops he had ordered to Longstreet.

He spun around abruptly, a handful of aides

still there, watching him, said, "Back to the headquarters. We must send word to the rail depot.
Longstreet will make his fight with what he has. I
need those troops right here."

By late afternoon, with the low hills in
their possession, the Federal forces seemed
to halt their advance, content with what
Bragg could only guess was a symbolic victory, a
show of force that Bragg believed had been meant to
frighten his army off the ridge. Manigault's men had
made as much of a fight as their meager numbers
would allow, the 24th and 28th Alabama Regiments
absorbing enormous casualties. By nightfall, they
were back at the base of Missionary Ridge, while
the men in blue seemed content to hunker down
far out in the plain. With thousands of Confederate muskets and their artillery batteries poised for
the assault, the Federal forces held their position. If
there was to be an assault on Missionary Ridge, it
would not be today.

CHAPTER TWENTY-SIX

CLEBURNE

NAIL HOUSE,
MISSIONARY RIDGE—
NOVEMBER 23, 1863

It was still daylight when he had reached Bragg's headquarters. All across the vast ridgeline, he had followed Bragg's courier, trailed by his own Captain Buck. The aide was for guidance, but Buck was there as a helpful bit of assistance, should Cleburne be tossed into some muddy bog by his unruly horse. As he left the rail depot, the calls came, salutes from the men who served him. As he climbed up onto the northern tip of Missionary Ridge, the salutes were less frequent, the men mostly ignoring yet another senior commander who rode past them without any offer to relieve their suffering.

Bragg's messages had been ongoing for more than an hour, repeating the same order, as though

Bragg wasn't certain any one of the couriers could be relied upon to deliver the message without some distraction. But Cleburne had done exactly what Bragg ordered, sending word up the rail line to the various depots to the northeast, ordering the engineers to reverse direction, to bring the railcars and their human cargo back down to Chickamauga Station. Some of his men had yet to board the trains, making Cleburne's job somewhat simpler, and Cleburne reported that to Bragg, his own effort to soothe what seemed to be a heightened level of anxiety at the army's headquarters.

He left the depot in the hands of Lucius Polk, a fortunate piece of chance that Cleburne's most capable brigade commander was still with him at the station. Polk understood the forcefulness of Bragg's order, would press hard for the return of the troops. Whether or not Polk had any use for Braxton Bragg, he would obey Cleburne without fail. Cleburne left the depot with no real timetable for the return of the full two divisions, or understanding of just what Bragg wanted them to do. There was another concern as well: Cleburne had no idea if Longstreet had been informed of the radical change in plans, what would most likely cause an explosion in Longstreet's headquarters. But there had been too many of those already, and Cleburne knew to stay away from that topic with either man, that if Bragg had his reasons for reversing his offer of support for Longstreet, it was Cleburne's job only to find out what that meant for those troops he was authorized to command.

As he pulled up onto the northern edge of Missionary Ridge, most of the Federal assault had ended, but the smoke hung low still in the wide valley, drifting across the two distant hills now in Federal hands. He had seen the last of Manigault's retreat, the pieces of the puzzle coming together in his mind, Bragg's summons making more sense, that the enemy had made a significant move, possibly presaging an attack straight into the center of Bragg's strongest position. He was met outside the Nail House by Colonel Brent, who left him standing alone while Brent announced his arrival. Bragg's thundering voice called him in, very little military decorum to the greeting.

Cleburne stood at Bragg's desk, saw less decorum now, the man seeming scattered, disheveled, his uniform unbuttoned, no hat, sitting with his head down, staring at a makeshift map.

"Sir, I rode as quickly as I could."

Bragg looked up, and Cleburne saw a rough, uneven beard, a harsh anger in the man's expression.

"As well as can be expected, I suppose. Have you recalled your troops? Are they on the march?"

"They have been recalled, sir. General Polk is in command at the depot, and has been ordered to hold the men in readiness as they return. I have received no orders where I am to march them, sir. We await your instructions."

Cleburne saw a narrow squint in Bragg's eyes, as though Bragg was having difficulty seeing him. Bragg seemed to chew on Polk's name, the mention of Cleburne's subordinate hanging between them like a moldy blanket.

"You trust him?"

"By all means, sir. Lucius Polk is most able, in the field and as my subordinate."

"Lucius. The bishop's nephew, correct?"

Cleburne could see Bragg's mind working, staring to one side, as though Bragg were chewing his way through a tough piece of meat.

"Yes, sir. He is a most capable man, sir."

"You said that already. How soon will your men be prepared to march?"

Cleburne was confused, thought, March where? Bragg's head was down again, the man seeming to suffer some kind of twisting pain, and Cleburne leaned low, said, "Are you all right, sir?"

Bragg looked at him abruptly, tried to stand, his legs seeming to give way, settling him back in the chair. He took a deep breath, and Cleburne could feel heat in the man's words.

"No, I am not all right! Not one bit, General! Are your troops prepared to meet the enemy? Are they in the field?"

Cleburne chose his words, spoke slowly. "Sir, my

men have been recalled to Chickamauga Station, per your orders. They were previously under your orders to travel toward Longstreet's command, to reinforce General Longstreet at Knoxville. It was made clear to me, sir, that your instructions had been reversed. As quickly as the men can be returned, they will be gathered up into formation, awaiting your further orders."

"Is it dark outside?"

Cleburne looked to the one small window behind Bragg, a thick canvas curtain drawn closed. "No, sir. The sun is setting, though. Another hour or so."

"Not enough time for them. It's done for today." Bragg looked at Cleburne again, held up the scribble of a map. "They're coming, by God. They've decided it's time, and so, they're coming. The question is where? It has always been the question, has it not? If they come, where will they strike? Every general in this command has offered an opinion on that point. I hear all manner of rumor, mind you. I am forced to fight this campaign with hesitation and uncertainty. My generals toss up their ideas in a maze of conflicting strategy, each one grabbing for the glory in his own part of the field, while I am left to stumble about like some crippled old woman."

Cleburne kept his silence, saw the shakiness in Bragg's hands, could hear it in his voice. Bragg held out the map, and Cleburne took it, saw a crude sketch of the ridge, Lookout Mountain, the town, the river. There was a large arrow scratched in pencil, pointing at the center of Missionary Ridge, a small X where Bragg's headquarters sat.

Bragg stared at the floor to one side of Cleburne, said, "They're coming for me. That's what Grant always intended. Sherman despises me, always did, even back in Louisiana. In Mexico, I was the hero, brevetted so many times, the entire army knew my name. Grant recalls that. So do they all. Longstreet, Thomas, Lee. Even the president knows of my accomplishments there. Of them all, only Jefferson Davis considers me his friend." He focused on Cleburne again. "You weren't there, were you?"

"No, sir. I was still in Ireland."

"Good war, that one. Camaraderie, obedience. Zachary Taylor . . . a man you were happy to fight for, a man you'd follow straight to hell and smile all the way. I wish my wife had met him. General Taylor would have enjoyed that, a woman who speaks her mind."

"Yes, sir. He was elected president, after all."

"How do you know that? They teach you such things in Ireland? Well, of course. Yes, he was president. Died very soon after. Dreadful tragedy for this nation. A man like that could have changed our history. Instead, we have Winfield Scott. A Virginian who kisses the feet of Abraham Lincoln. Disgusting."

Cleburne heard horses outside, voices, but he

kept his eyes on Bragg, wasn't sure what else to do. He still had no idea why he was there.

The boots came in behind him, and Cleburne was surprised to see Hardee, Bragg's Colonel Brent beside him. Hardee seemed just as surprised to see Cleburne, nodded to him, motioned his hand toward Bragg, as though some important business with Cleburne had been interrupted. There was no change to Bragg's permanent scowl and Cleburne felt suddenly like a man caught in the firing line of a duel, wanted to back away, but Hardee nodded toward him again.

"Continue, please."

Cleburne straightened, tried to feel a part of this army's command, as though anything he would say might actually matter to Bragg. "Sir, I rode here as quickly as I could in response to your courier's instructions. Do you have orders for me?"

Bragg looked at Hardee now, nodded slowly, said, "Orders for both of you. General Cleburne, you will march your division to the rear of this ridge, close by this headquarters. You will hold your men in reserve, in preparation of receiving the enemy's attack." Bragg seemed to energize now, pointed to the map in Cleburne's hand. "Look there. I am anticipating the enemy to assault this ridge in the morning, most likely where that arrow is drawn. With your men in place behind those troops already positioned along the ridge, we shall offer General

Grant an unpleasant surprise. General Hardee, you have too many men up on that mountain."

Cleburne looked back toward Hardee, stepped to one side, Hardee moving up close. Hardee gave Cleburne a discreet pat on the back, then said, "If you insist, sir."

"Unnecessary, foolish. The enemy is coming here. If he does not roll up against our center, he will move to the right, and attack us on our flank up toward Chickamauga Creek."

Hardee studied Bragg, his words slow and precise. "Am I to assume you wish me to remove a portion of my troops on Lookout Mountain, and join them with General Cleburne's men in reserve?"

"No! Did you not hear me? They're coming on the right flank! I want you to ride there with all haste, and take command of whoever is out there. You will remove your troops from the mountain, leaving a token defense. The enemy has no reason to attack a big steep rock when they can more easily climb a hill! You are supposed to be the grand master of strategy in this camp, so your acolytes insist. Does this not make sense to you?"

Cleburne flinched slightly, wondered if Hardee would respond to the insult. But Hardee kept his voice low and even.

"I can leave Carter Stevenson's division on the mountain. Walker's division is situated on the low ground along Chattanooga Creek. They can be on the march within minutes."

"Order it done! Move them as quickly as possible to the right flank! General Cleburne, you will leave some force out there as well, guarding against any raid toward the rail depot. We shall be prepared for the enemy's next move with a force that will crush any plan Grant dares to exercise. General Cleburne, you will march your men all night if necessary until they are in position as my reserve. I shall not have our backsides exposed!"

Cleburne waited for more, but Bragg seemed to deflate again, the momentary fire fading away. Hardee said, "If you will excuse me, sir, I will see to carrying out your orders."

"Not yet! One more thing. We shall withdraw the infantry from the rifle pits at the base of this ridge. The artillery as well. Have them pulled back uphill, to strengthen our lines up here."

Hardee said, "Sir, there are no lines up here. The men are encamped in scattered positions."

"Then we shall dig lines! Have the men go to work, and have far more earthworks and trenches prepared across the crest of the ridge. It should have been done weeks ago!"

Hardee responded, his words still controlled. "We shall dig all night long if need be. I shall relocate a full division of my men to the right. General Cleburne shall move into reserve to the rear of this ridge. Those are your orders?"

Bragg stared up at Hardee with the familiar squint. "Is there some confusion?"

"None."

"You both are dismissed. Go about your work, and do it with haste!"

Hardee stepped back, looked at Cleburne, who welcomed the opportunity for an exit. He expected Hardee to move out first, but Hardee waited, extended a hand, making way for Cleburne to pass. Cleburne glanced at Hardee as he moved by, heard the soft words, "With haste, General."

They moved outside, Colonel Brent there, Bragg's staff officer watching as the two generals climbed up in the saddle. Hardee said to Brent, "You have anything to add to your commanding officer's instructions, Colonel?"

Brent shook his head, and Cleburne detected a deep sadness in the man. Hardee called to his staff, who gathered quickly, said to an aide, "Go now to General Walker. Order him to put his men to the march as quickly as he can. He is to immediately vacate the low ground along Chattanooga Creek and march his men along the rear of this ridge, making camp as far northward as he can by daylight. These are General Bragg's orders, do you understand?"

Hardee turned to Cleburne, said, "You best ride hard, get word to your General Polk what our commanding general has in mind."

Cleburne heard a hint of sarcasm, said, "Do you not agree with his orders?"

"Should I disagree? You saw his carefully drawn 'map.' Is there something of a problem with what he anticipates?"

Cleburne shook his head and said, "No, certainly not."

"Then we shall have the men who are now camped along this part of the ridge go to work. Anderson's division. They will spend their evening digging earthworks they should have completed a month ago. I must give credit to General Bragg for understanding what must be done, even if he is somewhat late in doing it. However . . ." Cleburne saw Hardee look toward the west side of the ridge, where the rows of rifle pits down below still held the men who had watched the Yankee assault, who still expected one even now. "We will not withdraw the men from the base of the hill. I will instruct General Anderson to divide his forces, some up along this ridge, some remaining below. It is still a good position. We cannot allow General Bragg's fears to take priority over effective tactics."

Cleburne saw a wagon moving up behind the ridge, the order for shovels already passing to the supply officers nearby. The troops began to move that way, lining up, the shovels handed out, the men guided by their officers to the labor suddenly tossed upon them.

Cleburne felt the familiar nervousness, knew he had been given an important task, that no matter Hardee's sarcasm, it might be critical for Cleburne to bring his men from the depot back to this part of the ridge.

"If you forgive me, General, I should ride back to the depot. I do not know how many have returned, nor how long it will require to assemble them. The general's orders are clear, and I must put my men to the march."

"By all means. It feels good, does it not?"

Cleburne wasn't sure what Hardee meant. "Sir?"

"Doing something. You see that assault today, out there on those hills?"

"No, sir. I was up at the depot."

"Something's happening, Patrick. Grant's run out of patience. And we've run out of time for our holiday."

CHAPTER TWENTY-SEVEN

THOMAS

ORCHARD KNOB—
NOVEMBER 23, 1863

What had begun as a demonstration, an attempt to force the rebels to show their hand, had allowed at least two full divisions of Federal troops to shove forward, halving the distance between their guns and the rebels up on the heights. The response from Missionary Ridge had been muted, adding to the suspicions that most of Bragg's army might have slipped away, but once on the bald hills, Federal observers had a far more precise view of the Confederate position. Even if Bragg kept his men on those heights, conceding the low hills to Thomas's overwhelming force, the rebels were still in place on the ridge. The vantage point on Orchard Knob showed heavily manned rifle pits, artillery emplacements spread all

across the face of the ridge, clearly an army preparing to receive another assault. But the Federal
troops had grabbed a good piece of ground, and
rather than withdraw the men back to their original camps, Thomas ordered them to stay right
where they were.

With the hills swept clean of any lingering enemy
troops, Thomas rode forward, making his own observations from the treeless mound of Orchard
Knob. As his horse climbed up above the plain, he
was already grateful to be outside the miserable en-
virons of Chattanooga. The open ground around
him, the sea of blue troops gathering up into their
newly organized camps, allowed him a sense of accomplishment, a renewed spirit he hadn't felt in
Chattanooga at all.

As the musket fire faded away, Thomas knew his
plan had worked perfectly, a piece of satisfaction he
would keep to himself. He never gloated over a victory, that peculiar show of pride that infected some
of the subordinates, and he also knew there was no
point seeking backslapping approval from Grant.

Thomas had no real reason for his nagging dislike of the man. It was just an instinct, something
he couldn't really explain. Everyone in the Army
of the Cumberland knew that Grant had brought
something to this campaign that Rosecrans never
could, a confident matter-of-factness about his
every intention, and a bullheaded determination to
carry through every plan. There was no panic in

the man, little excitement of any kind that Thomas could see. Despite the casual rumors that flew through the camps, Thomas had almost never seen Grant touch spirits, a glass of wine perhaps before retiring. If there was a single vice that Grant embraced heartily, it was the man's love for his cigars.

Thomas assumed that Grant could be as stubborn as a mule, a trait Thomas knew they shared. But he respected that Grant could be swayed, would allow himself to weigh an alternative plan. But still, there was a tension between the two men. Grant never welcomed him to any of the meetings with a positive handshake, didn't really welcome him at all. When the time came to strike the rebels with the massed power behind so many troops, Thomas fully expected, and believed he had earned, the privilege of leading the way. But Grant had other ideas. The army west of the Appalachians belonged to Grant, and Grant had reached that lofty plateau with Sherman by his side, and Grant would rely on Sherman to carry the greatest weight. Should there be a glorious triumph in this campaign, Thomas had to swallow that Grant would elevate Sherman first, and Thomas perhaps not at all.

Thomas had his difficulties with Joe Hooker as well. Hooker's army had been sent westward as an act of urgency by the War Department, their fear that the Army of the Cumberland was a ripe target for Bragg's jubilant army after their overwhelming success at Chickamauga. Thomas's dislike of the man had less to do with personality, and far more with what Thomas saw as the poor quality of Hooker's leadership. Grant seemed to share those opinions, something Thomas appreciated. Since Hooker's arrival, Thomas had followed Grant's lead, and put considerably more faith in Hooker's immediate subordinate, Oliver Howard. Howard had done no better than his commander at Chancellorsville, but here he seemed in control of his men, moved them with at least an effort toward efficiency. Right now, Howard's ten thousand men were pushing into position primarily as a reserve in support of Sherman, filing out into the plain to Thomas's left. If Sherman succeeded in sweeping Bragg's men off Missionary Ridge, Howard would then be available in support of Thomas, anchoring Thomas's left flank.

And then, Thomas's men achieved a different kind of success. On most days when the weather allowed, observers in many parts of the line could see the Confederate signalmen, flags waving, passing messages from peak to peak. On both sides, the signalmen were taught specific codes, allowing them to keep their messages private from the eyes of the enemy. After weeks of sitting still, observing the same signalmen offering similar messages every hour of every day, the Federal observers had made the breakthrough. The rebel code had been broken.

"Are you certain?"

Thomas fought to breathe through Grant's cigar smoke, nodded. "Quite. Carter Stevenson's division appears to be the sole force holding the mountain. Bragg has withdrawn everyone else, moved them onto the ridge."

Grant pulled the soggy end of the cigar from his mouth, stared at it, what Thomas now understood to be a look of satisfaction.

"And you're certain?"

"Dead certain. They've shifted a number of artillery pieces off the mountain as well. We've picked that up already. They're not responding to our usual idiocy of duels with quite the same vigor. Fewer shells mean fewer guns." He paused. "Bragg has to believe we're going to hit him in the center, and he's making preparations."

Grant stuffed the cigar back in his mouth, tilted his head, looked at Thomas from beneath the low brim of his hat. "You like this, don't you?"

"Is that allowed?"

"Yep, I'll give you that. This demonstration of yours worked as well as we could have hoped." Grant moved toward the entrance of the large tent. "Not as comfortable as that big stone fireplace, but we've got a better view. Just about see the far north end of that ridge. Might actually see Sherman's attack."

Thomas sagged, didn't let it show. But he couldn't just keep silent. "I truly believe that we have the strength right here to drive the rebels off those heights. General Stevenson has signaled to Bragg that he expects us to hit him first, that he feels the far left flank, the mountain, will be our primary point of attack. I must assume that General Stevenson is considerably distressed at being left alone up there."

Grant suddenly stepped away, moved outside the tent, and Thomas followed, annoyed now. He knew Grant wouldn't debate this, not outside, not in front of the men. It was Grant's way of ending the discussion, at least for now.

All around them, the troops were moving up guns, supply wagons, more tents pitched close to the hills, Thomas's headquarters taking shape. The fires were spread out in every direction, the new camps of the army, fresh ground, far removed from the town. Yes, he thought, this was my plan. It should still be my plan. He watched Grant for a long moment, the tip of the cigar glowing orange, Grant seeming to stare off into nothing. Thomas looked upward, the rain in a light spray, the men at the campfires struggling to keep the blazes high. He knew he could do nothing to push the man, Grant seemingly lost in thought, that when Grant was ready to discuss their options, Thomas would know.

The rain had begun again an hour before, and Thomas knew the first to curse Mother Nature would be the supply officers. They all knew that without several days of easy passage for the wagon trains, without fully loaded riverboats coming upstream from the ports in Alabama, the rations for the men would have to be cut again. Grant had been furious at the delays, and just as furious that Sherman's arrival had been so sluggish. It had surprised Thomas that Grant excused that, seemed willing to excuse anything Sherman might do. But Thomas knew that no amount of blame would improve the roads, the trails that had become virtually unusable. Like the pontoon bridges, there was a constant need for repairs, repairs that required too much time. It had cost Sherman the use of one of his own divisions. Those men were trapped south of Brown's Ferry, and Grant had no choice but to place them under command of Joe Hooker.

Thomas felt the rain seeping through his coat, cold down his back, his patience gone. "Sir, might we speak inside?"

Grant turned to him, his hat dripping, seemed to ponder the thought, then pointed the way. Thomas returned to his tent quickly, back into the lingering cloud of smoke.

Grant moved to a small camp chair, bathed himself in another plume of smoke, said, "What do you want to do about Hooker?"

Thomas knew this might be his only opportunity. "Sir, I cannot emphasize this strongly enough. We have been presented with a gift. We know that Bragg has weakened his defenses on Lookout

Mountain, and strengthened his center. Now, we know that General Stevenson is up there in full anticipation that we will attack the mountain. Bragg most certainly disagrees with him, which is why Bragg shifted so much strength elsewhere. I believe we should oblige General Stevenson, and make all the noise we can, convincing him he is correct, that Bragg was wrong to remove so much troop strength from the mountain." Thomas paused. "You agreed to this demonstration today as a means to divert Bragg's attention toward our true goal. I have disagreed with many parts of your plan, but I will obey whatever you instruct me to do. I just ask you to consider that an attack moving uphill out of Lookout Valley, pushing into what should be a meager defense, might serve to confuse Bragg even further, convince him that Stevenson is correct after all, and that we're coming at him from that direction. Bragg might respond by shifting troops back up onto the mountain, thus weakening his center."

"I'm more concerned about Bragg's right. I've not changed my mind. Sherman is going in hard on the enemy's right. I'm through **debating** that with you or anyone else."

"I'm not suggesting otherwise. But you have said yourself that Bragg's uncertainty is a valuable asset to us, certainly to General Sherman as well. Hooker is sitting down there in Lookout Valley with a full division of his own, plus the added strength from Sherman. General Sherman has consented that his

troops be used where you see fit. Hooker's men . . .
all they're doing is guarding the supply routes.
Should we not make use of this, employ those men
to our advantage? And, sir, anything we can do to
lessen Bragg's expectations of an attack on his right
flank will have to aid General Sherman."

He knew he had grabbed Grant's attention, saw
the cigar come out of Grant's mouth, Grant rolling
it over between his fingers.

"A demonstration. No more than that. I don't see
how Hooker or anybody else can push that large a
force up that big rock without taking considerable
fire."

"General Grant, if the reports are accurate, and
you know I believe them to be, there won't be much
enemy fire up there to start with."

Grant stared at him for a long moment, the cigar
plugged back into his mouth, called out, "What
time is it?"

Thomas heard a voice from outside, knew it was
Rawlins.

"Just after eleven, sir."

Thomas said, "He listen in on every council you
have?"

Grant shrugged. "Always has." Grant looked out
toward the darkness beyond the tent, raised his
voice. "Might have to shoot him one day, he hears
one too many secrets."

Thomas realized it was Grant's kind of humor,
heard a low apology from outside the tent. Thomas

thought again of Hooker, said, "We can get a courier to Lookout Valley within an hour. If you will authorize it, I will order him to advance up that mountain at daylight tomorrow, or as quickly as he can put his men into motion. I will not tolerate any debate from **him.** Begging your pardon, sir."

Grant lowered his head. "This is Hooker you're talking about. He doesn't require debate to find a reason why it can't be done, why he has to prepare and inspect and check God knows what."

"I propose, sir, we take that chance. I'll be . . . specific in my order. Something to the effect . . . 'General commanding desires that you make demonstrations early as possible after daybreak on point of Lookout Mountain.' Hard for him to misinterpret that."

"Maybe. I doubt he'll be able to do more than wake up the rebel lookouts. That's a big mountain. Taking that hill completely might require a large-scale assault, open up a general engagement, with our men staring straight up. Can't have that. If the going's easy, fine. If not, make sure he keeps it to a demonstration. That's all."

"That's my intention. Whether we take that mountain altogether, or merely shove Stevenson's troops around a bit, we will make our point. Our goal is to confuse Braxton Bragg."

"And for that, we will depend on Joe Hooker. God help us, General."

"I am hoping, sir, we will depend more on his

soldiers. If those men can make that climb, the rebel position will be in jeopardy." Thomas paused, thought, Be careful here. He knows, after all, how you feel about this. "I am equally concerned about General Sherman."

Grant looked at him, the cigar stuck firmly in one side of his mouth. "Why?"

"Not all of his troops are yet across the river. I know you have ordered him to begin his operations tonight."

"I ordered him to do what he knows he can accomplish. He has given me assurances that, even without his full complement, his advance can begin." Grant looked away, into the dark again. "I have every confidence in him."

Thomas nodded, thought, Yes, and we shall find if that is justified. Some would doubt it.

"He is on unfamiliar ground, sir. It is a dangerous undertaking."

Grant looked at him, the cigar still in place, his words coming through gritted teeth. "He will confront a familiar enemy. And he will cross a river. One more river, in a country full of them." Grant removed the cigar now, a hard stare at Thomas. "I will not repeat this. I have every confidence in him. Are we in agreement?"

Thomas knew he was in a delicate place, a test from Grant that Thomas could not really win.

"I agree that you have confidence in him. I have not yet fought alongside General Sherman. I can only judge what I know. I have confidence in my men. I would assume General Sherman has confidence in his. And, in his commanding officer."

Thomas waited for the question, but Grant didn't ask, and Thomas understood, that whether or not he had any confidence in Grant didn't matter. He had the same task facing him as Sherman did right now. When the enemy stands tall, knock him down.

CHAPTER TWENTY-EIGHT

SHERMAN

NORTH CHICKAMAUGA CREEK—
NOVEMBER 24, 1863

There was more to his shivering anxiousness than the weather. For the past two days, three-fourths of his army, nearly twenty thousand men, had finally made their way past Chattanooga, marching northward to the location chosen for them by Baldy Smith, buried deep in heavy woods just west of the big river. His fourth division had been caught by the destruction of the pontoon bridge at Brown's Ferry, and for now, Sherman had agreed that those men would remain at Lookout Valley, available to assist Hooker's assault on Lookout Mountain. Going into a fight missing a quarter of his strength had given Sherman a hot knot in his stomach, but Grant had waited long enough for this campaign to begin, and Sherman understood that his own indigestion wasn't as important as Grant's. The delays in bringing his troops to Chattanooga had gnawed at Sherman like a bulldog at his backside, and despite Grant's smiling welcome, it was clear to Sherman that Grant's patience was at low ebb. The smiles and friendly conversation had quickly given way to talk of strategy and tactics, and it became clear that Grant was more agitated than Sherman had ever seen him, a show of stern impatience that Sherman knew he had earned. The attack had already been postponed for too many days. It was time to go.

As he moved slowly through the rain, he knew that one column of his men was on the move, a full brigade slipping out through the soggy woodlands, easing closer to this small tributary of the Tennessee River, what the maps showed as North Chickamauga Creek. The mission on this night would be to board pontoon boats, slipping silently down the creek to the Tennessee River, the oarsmen working to catch the current to carry them quickly and silently downstream. The landings would come on both sides of the mouth of South Chickamauga Creek, the men making every effort at pushing ashore without alarming any rebel skirmishers anywhere along the route. The river at that point was nearly a quarter mile across, a dangerous gap between the first men across and any support they might need. The single advantage in such a distance was the rain, which would most certainly deaden any noisy mistakes, a stumble in the boats, a clatter of metal, anything to reveal the presence of the troops. The men had been ordered to load their muskets, but no percussion caps, no chance of an accidental discharge. Even the miserable weather wouldn't hide musket fire, and on this night, there could be no alerting the enemy.

It baffled him still how so many skirmishers could stand ready on each side of the great river, eyeing one another every day for nearly two months, and yet no attempts had been made by either side to punish the other. Downstream, where the sweeping curves wound closer to Chattanooga, the river had narrow places, the men within easy hailing distance, close enough for boats and rafts to paddle across for their bartering, whether the officers approved of that or not. Sherman most definitely did not. He had no tolerance for opposing picket lines who spoke to each other as though perched casually on opposite sides of some country lane, awaiting some parade, all the while tossing bags of sweet treats back and forth like some ridiculous game. If the rebel pickets were out there, on this far north end of Bragg's position, it would be Sherman's job to silence them any way possible. That was not a job for any man who considered those other troops to be his friends.

The enemy had sat on their high ground for far too many weeks, a mystery to Sherman. He had always believed there had to be more to Braxton

Bragg than paralysis, more to the generals who commanded his army, a good army, a victorious army. All along the journey from western Tennessee, he knew that the delays and plodding tediousness of his march could cost him any opportunity to be a part of Grant's campaign. He had disagreed with some of Grant's methods, argued the decisions, had lobbied often for more aggression. It was Sherman's way, shoving forward straight into the enemy's lines and crushing them with a hard fist before there was time for the other fellow to react. To Sherman, preparation took far more time than it was supposed to, gave away any advantage of surprise, and almost always meant that the enemy was just as prepared as you were. The march down along the rail lines in Mississippi and Alabama had driven that home to Sherman every day as they struggled with burned bridges and shattered railroad tracks. Every day of repair gave the enemy a luxury of one more day to rebuild, strengthen, grow fit and strong.

In late September, the news that the rebels were attempting a siege at Chattanooga infuriated him. It didn't require a hard jab from the pen of Henry Halleck to educate Sherman about the potential cost of what Bragg was trying to do. Sherman had seen firsthand what an effective siege could do to any army, the rebel army at Vicksburg forced to stagger into surrender with bare bones and rags on their backs. On the march eastward, that image drove him to raw-tempered fury, the delays from weather and roads holding him back from a mission that might mean the survival of an entire Federal army.

After so many delays, he had expected a thorough blasting from Grant, knew he deserved it. He knew better than to offer excuses for bad roads, knew that there were failings that were his alone. He had no good explanation to offer Grant why he had arranged his divisions in a configuration certain to slow them down. The order that scolded Sherman for his error was more embarrassing to Sherman than he could admit to anyone. But Grant wouldn't push the issue, wouldn't write up the mistake in some report for all the world to see. Sherman had done exactly what Grant expected him to do, had corrected his own error, had finally pushed his men forward far more quickly than their cumbersome supply trains. Sherman had been enormously grateful for Grant's discretion, and Sherman had wondered, if the roles had been reversed, how he might have responded to days of delay from a subordinate who should know better. But Grant was still Grant, had pulled him into the headquarters with the unspoken affection Sherman always hoped to see. Grant seemed to appreciate that what Sherman brought to the fight was far more than numbers. The men who marched behind Sherman knew it, too, saw it in every other encampment they passed.

It had been that way at Bridgeport, throughout Lookout Valley, marching past Joe Hooker's "Easterners," all those officers with polished brass buttons and paper collars, dandies with their shining pistols, their swords housed in clean scabbards. Marching past Hooker's men had given Sherman that wonderful swell of pride, something he shared with his men. His men were dirty, ragged, the officers' uniforms showing the wear of the battlefield. Their buttons carried the grime and tarnish of weather and mud and a bloody struggle, and Sherman never pushed them to "clean it up." This war bore no resemblance to any dress parade, and Hooker's men most certainly caught Sherman's message, even as Sherman himself rode past. He heard the calls, the ridicule tossed his way from the men in white shirts, but the catcalls were soon silenced as word spread of the campaigns these men had fought, the victories they had won. By the time they cleared the valley, making their way across the river, Sherman's troops marched a little straighter, their pace a little quicker. Nearer to Chattanooga, they began moving past the men whose flags carried the word **Cumberland,** and like Hooker's men, it was an army that knew defeat. To the soldiers who tramped their way over the pontoon bridges, that story was told in the eyes of the men they passed, something only another soldier could see. Sherman wouldn't dwell on that, knew that these men around Chattanooga weren't whipped. The devastating defeat at Chickamauga had come from their leadership, a problem that the War Department and Grant himself had seemed to solve. Sherman's men marched out to their wooded camps as confident as their commander that whatever had happened to those **other men** at Chancellorsville or Chickamauga would not be repeated here. Sherman was there to win this fight. If the other parts of this great army were to claim their share of that victory, that would be up to them.

He wasn't sure about George Thomas. Defeat could be contagious, and Thomas had risen up through the ranks under Buell and Rosecrans, men who had shown little of the kind of leadership Grant now displayed. Sherman didn't know either of those men well, knew only what he read in the reports. The campaigns spoke for themselves, and over the past several months, while Grant had crushed his way through Mississippi, while Meade had tossed Lee out of Pennsylvania, these armies in between seemed to stumble about their enemy like a pair of blind bulls. The horns locked once in a while, Stones River, Tullahoma, Perryville, and, of course, the savagery of Chickamauga. But from Sherman's vantage point during the time he made his camps near the Mississippi River, what had passed for campaigns in middle Tennessee and Kentucky had accomplished very little. He knew the clumsiness had extended to both sides, but if George Thomas had learned his methods in service of those generals, what did that say about Thomas now? All Sherman really knew came from the reports that Grant was issuing to Washington and to Sherman himself, why it was so very important that Sherman's people get there in good time. There had been two months of suffering and stagnation around Chattanooga and it made sense to Sherman that Grant might lack confidence in George Thomas. Sherman was completely comfortable with the urgency of Grant's orders, had absolute confidence that any serious problem Thomas could not handle could be solved by his own army.

Sherman rode slowly along the fresh trail, saw the pontoon boats slid up along the bank of the narrow creek, an endless line far out in the darkness. All along the creek, men were scrambling about, making ready, the kind of energy Sherman expected. His guide was a young captain named Farrow, one of Baldy Smith's men, and Sherman kept close to the young man, said in a low voice, "Do we know the whereabouts of Colonel McCook?"

The man pointed ahead. "Should be right up here, sir. According to General Smith, Colonel McCook's done fine work here. Managed the construction of all these here boats."

"How many?"

"One hundred sixteen, sir. At last count. General Smith likes to be precise about that sort of thing. He is duly impressed with Colonel McCook. An Ohio man, I believe."

"Fifty-second Ohio."

"You know the colonel then, sir?"

Sherman scanned the men working around the boats, couldn't help a smile. "More than that. He used to be my law partner."

The captain made a sound, audible surprise. "Begging your pardon, sir, but I didn't know you had a hankering for the law."

Sherman wasn't in the mood for idle chatter, said, "A long time ago. Long ways away. California."

He saw a man step into the road to the front, blocking the way, and now a familiar voice.

"Well, now, we got sightseers coming our way? Whole bunch of horses, I see. Who needs so many men on his staff? Boats are a much more efficient means of travel. Eat less hay, for one."

Sherman halted the horse, said, "I outrank you by about four grades, you know. Watch that big mouth."

"Never bigger, General. Never could compete with your skills as an orator. All that talk, and fists to go with it. Heard you had gone completely insane. Or was that last year?"

Sherman appreciated McCook's joviality, but the rain and the activity around him kept Sherman's good humor away. He reached down, took McCook's hand, a hard shake, felt the rough hide, calluses, a man who worked alongside his men.

"A hundred sixteen? That enough?"

"If I gave you a hundred fifty, would you be any

happier? It's enough, Cump. If you'll allow me, I'll mount up and join you. The men are waiting for your order to launch the first boat."

Sherman felt the nervousness in the men around him, a faint hum of activity, most of it in hushed silence. He leaned closer to the young captain, said, "How far back to Chattanooga?"

"Eight miles or so, sir. You aiming to go back?"

Sherman had no patience for questions, thought, A damn big gap between my boys and Thomas's flank. That's Howard's job. He damn well better be there if we need him.

"I'm not going anywhere, Captain. Let's get the job done."

There was a finality to his words that silenced the captain. He saw McCook riding toward him now, turning his horse to one side, Sherman following. They pushed through a thick line of brush, past cut timber, tall trees that helped shield him from the rain. The ride was short, barely a minute, and he saw the creek again, more of the pontoon boats, a small fleet of flatboats as well.

He said to McCook, "How far out to the Tennessee?"

"Two hundred yards or so. Far enough that no one over there has the slightest notion what's up. Be certain of that, Cump. It's going well enough."

Sherman knew better, that no plan would ever go as smoothly as planned. The construction of the boats had been a secret as carefully guarded as any secret could be in an army this size. The men camped nearby had been kept away from the creek completely, and if the sound of sawmills and carpentry inspired more than idle curiosity, Sherman's provost guards blocked every trail.

He glanced back in the darkness, no telltale signs that more than twenty thousand men were camped in the woods to his rear, no lights, no fires. Good, very good. He looked out toward the big river, thought, How far to the first big rebel camp? Doesn't matter, I guess. We get this job done right, the rebs won't know about it until daylight. And they'll be in a serious fix.

McCook halted on a low rise close to the water, and Sherman saw the single boat, men gathered around it, working in silence, the boat sliding through the mud to the water's edge. He dismounted, said to his closest aides, anonymous in the dark, "Stay here. Don't need to look like a squad of cavalry out here. No telling who might be right across that creek. Take my horse."

"Yes, sir."

He didn't have to watch his staff officer, McCoy, pulling the aides back to the edge of the trees. He walked out over soft mud, McCook following, the young captain as well. To one side, a line of soldiers moved forward, men handpicked for the job by their captain, an Ohioan named Hess. They were halting near the boat, others on board already, oars being moved about, the boat's crew, commanded by another man Smith had suggested. Sherman leaned closer to McCook now, said, "That would be Major Hipp?"

"The same. You've made his acquaintance, I believe."

"Baldy Smith says the major's men know how to row a boat. That makes him the right man for the task at hand."

"Helps that he's from Ohio."

Sherman ignored the joke, was consumed by the tension now. The soldiers began to move forward, and Sherman walked closer to the boat, out in the open, the rain soaking his face, dripping from his hat. He called out in a harsh whisper, "Easy, men. Quiet. Plenty of room for all of you. Boat holds thirty."

He stopped himself, his voice slicing through the cold darkness. The men moved past, and an officer stepped out of the boat, moved close.

"Who might you be, then?"

"Name's Sherman. You Major Hipp?"

"That I am, sir. We'll be on the water in a quick minute. Unless you have other orders, sir."

"No changes, Major. They're all yours."

The men boarded the boat, low talk, some of it aimed toward Sherman. He felt his hands shaking, the cold and the nervousness, felt it rolling all through him. He ached for a cigar, his fists clenching, unclenching, turmoil in his stomach. He wanted to push them into place himself, hurry them along, but the men had been trained well, knew what they were supposed to do. In no more than a minute, the thirty men were settled into the bottom of the boat, the order whispered to the men waiting on-shore. They moved together, pushed the boat out into the creek, and Sherman heard the whispered order, the major from Ohio. The rain coated the creek with a rippling hiss, and Sherman pulled his fists in tight to his stomach, watched as the oars made low splashes through the black water, the boat slipping silently away.

They made the four-mile journey in less than two hours, the boat pulled by the oars and the current, the first boat turning to slip up inside South Chickamauga Creek. The purpose was simple: Disgorge the men where they would likely be behind any rebel skirmishers eyeing the big river. From all the men could tell, the rebel skir-mishers had heard nothing of the landing, no look-outs sounding a warning, no sounds at all. When the thirty men slipped inland, easing toward the enemy outpost at the river's edge, the first of the rebels who heard them coming called out to them, had assumed that the Federal troops were in fact their replacements. In a matter of seconds, the sur-prised rebels were staring into the muzzles of thirty muskets, were gathered up and paraded back to the boat, soon to be hauled away by Major Hipp and a small group of guards. The Federal troops couldn't be completely certain they had captured the entire squad of pickets at the landing point, the nervous talk growing that a single rebel had slipped past them, escaping into the darkness. But so far, the east side of the river stayed quiet, no sign of any rebels in force, of any alarm spreading anywhere along the enemy's side of the river. Sherman's campaign had begun in silence, a perfect piece of maneuver, Major Hipp's boat crossing back to the west side of the river with the stunned cargo of rebels. It was two thirty in the morning.

Fifteen minutes behind the first launch, the other boats had slipped out down the creek, making their way to the river. Sherman paced nervously along the muddy bank of the creek as the boats made their move, four oarsmen each pulling the craft away from the bank until they too caught the flow of the current. With as little fanfare as Major Hipp's single craft, the first two regiments began their journey, men from Illinois and Missouri. Some of those boats made their landing on the north side of South Chickamauga Creek, the majority slipping down below, where the first thirty offered them the signal that all was clear. With no angry reception from any rebels, the men began a different kind of labor, moving inland, shovels in hand, digging in, piling logs and earth, creating a defensive line.

To the cheering delight of Sherman, and the utter surprise of his engineers, the brigade's crossing had been made without any opposition at all, as though no one on the far side of the river was even awake. As the first thousand of Sherman's men completed the work on their defensive position, more men came forward from their camps, lining up along the west side of the river. Quickly the boats were ferried back and forth, each one carrying another load of troops to strengthen their hold on the rebel side. With so little attention from the rebels, Baldy Smith made a daring move, ordering a Federal steamboat, the **Dunbar,** to steam upriver from Chattanooga and pass directly through that part of the river the Federal troops had now secured. The **Dunbar** added its decks to the effort, hundreds of men hauled across the waterway in short minutes. By daybreak, several thousand of Sherman's men had floated across, creating a stout defensive position nearly a mile wide. Following along on a flatboat, even before the first hint of daylight, came their commander.

He watched the engineers as they shifted and paddled the pontoon boats into position. The bridge had reached the near shore, stretching completely across the quarter-mile span, anchored against the current by the **Dunbar.** Already, men and their equipment were making the march across the river, adding to the thousands of men already there.

He kept to the horse now, scanned the water-front, supplies piling high, stacked muskets, the soldiers who would carry them still doing more work with the shovel. With the first hint of day-light, he had moved out through the laboring men, past the cut logs and dugout trenches. He stared up to the wooded hills, a hazy fog blocking most of the view. All he knew of the ground beyond the dark hilly woods was what Baldy Smith had told him, and the maps he had now in his pocket. He yelled silently toward the sun, urging it upward, hoping the dense gray of the clouds would finally thin.

Far up the hill, the scouts had gone out, perching into good hiding places, awaiting the sunlight with one precise mission: Find the rebels. As the army around him continued to swell, the mystery of the peaceful landing confounded him. He stared up toward the shadowy blackness, the tree-lined hills closest to his front, thought, Is no one watching us? No cavalry scout, no skirmish line? Is there no artillery anywhere close enough to disrupt our labor?

So far, the only answer seemed to be that this part of the riverfront held no rebels at all. The few dozen men they had captured had been hauled back to the far side of the river, men who told no tales of vast rebel armies perched up in these hills. That was unexpected, a contradiction to what Sherman had heard in nearly every fight. Rebel prisoners always seemed eager to tell their stories, how the bluebellies would be trampled beneath the magnificent stampede of a glorious rebel army. He had yet to experience anything so dramatic, and his officers had learned how to play on rebel boastfulness to gain useful information. But here, the men Major Hipp had transported back to the west side of the river had nothing to give, no hints that any real force was on the hillsides, hiding in thick woods, no hoards of artillery hidden away, waiting for the signal to hammer the men in blue. Instead the dawn came with an eerie silence, the only sounds the light rain on the dark river, punctuated by the shovels and axes of his men.

He rode closer to the trees above him, saw a line of his skirmishers moving farther up, climbing into thickets, pushing to the crest of the hill. He expected musket fire, waited for it, felt the nervous itch, raised the field glasses, nothing to see, his view blinded by fog and watery lenses.

He turned abruptly, spurred the horse back toward the river, past the men who knew not to cheer. His staff was waiting, a limp flag held high by his color bearer. McCoy was there, seemed anxious, the others just as nervous.

"Sir, anything up there? Haven't heard anything here. The pontoon bridge over the South Chickamauga is completed, just like this one. We're in contact with the regiments in position north of the creek. No sign of the enemy there, either. What do you make of it, sir?"

McCoy's jabbering betrayed his fears, and Sherman fought that himself, the same struggle before every fight. He turned to the misty hill again, had no answers for McCoy.

Another of his officers spoke up now, Dayton, the same high-pitched nervousness.

"Sir, are we certain this is the correct landing area?"

Sherman snapped his head around, pointed out to the north, upriver.

"You see that stream over there? It's the South Chickamauga. If I thought Baldy Smith would send us to some godforsaken mud hole by mistake, I'd tell Grant to shoot him." He knew he was talking nonsense, the tension in his voice betraying the anxiousness he could not show his staff. "Never mind that. We're in the correct location, Colonel. That big damn hill out there is the north end of the Mission Ridge. Bragg's whole damn army is up there somewhere, and it's our job to find them." He paused, shook his head. "I would have thought . . . they'd be waiting for us. Somebody. A single battery, a heavy skirmish line. Maybe . . . with all this maneuvering Grant's been doing, the demonstrations, hell, maybe it's worked better than we ever thought possible. Maybe Bragg's pulled his whole army down to the south; maybe he's really convinced we're gonna hit him in the center. That ought to make Grant happy."

"Yes, sir. That's a good turn of events, surely."

McCoy's voice held a shiver, and Sherman fought that himself, the cold of the rain only making it worse. He looked again to the misty hill, said, "What time is it?"

"Six, sir. Just shy. Never thought it would be this easy, sir."

Sherman kept his stare on the wooded hills. "It never is, Colonel. It never is. But I'm not satisfied by any of this. We're supposed to be leading the way, jamming a bayonet into Bragg's guts. By God, if he's pulled his people away from here . . ."

"Maybe they've withdrawn, sir? Maybe we scared him out of here completely."

Sherman looked toward the voice, Dayton, a cold stare that quieted the man.

"That's about the worst thought imaginable, Colonel. We went to all this trouble so we can whip Bragg, not chase him all over Creation. As soon as all three divisions are across that river, I'm ordering the advance. I didn't come all this way just to build bridges. Our job is to sweep Bragg off that big damn ridge."

"Begging your pardon, sir, but where in blazes are they?"

"Only one way to know that, Colonel. Let's climb that big damn hill."

CHAPTER TWENTY-NINE

BAUER

EAST OF CHATTANOOGA, SOUTH OF ORCHARD KNOB— NOVEMBER 24, 1863

They had moved out to the right flank of the great advance the day before, no one really knowing just what enemy they might confront. The fight had been mostly on their left, the round knobs that protruded from the thick woods, but that fight had been brief, several volleys of musket fire punctuated by their own artillery that burst out back near Chattanooga, what they knew as Fort Wood. For Bauer, the first contact with the enemy had been the sudden emergence of the rebel picket line, half a hundred men responding to the massive parade of Federal troops by firing a brief volley of their own, then scrambling away through the vast fields of tall grass and low brush. The skirmishers had been little more than a brief distraction. What had grabbed Bauer's attention, and that of the men in line around him, was the immense formations of their own troops, long and heavy lines of blue, advancing across the wide-open plain. He had seen massive assaults before, what seemed to be the entire army rolling forward at Vicksburg. But that was a very bad day, the men in blue smacking hard into rebel earthworks, where a well-protected enemy poured out a vicious fire that had punched bloody holes in the Federal advance. This time, there were no earthworks, and no volleys of any significance coming toward them. The only artillery the rebels offered came from the wooded ground near the two bald hills. But even that was brief and ineffective, what seemed to be no more than a single battery, facing off against what Bauer assumed to be four or five divisions. Bauer hadn't even fired his musket.

B auer awoke before the bugle, his habit now, jarred alert by the cold, a sharp breeze that brought the misty rain straight into the tent. He was shivering, pulled hard at the thin blanket, felt wetness everywhere he touched. His knees were up tight against his chest, but there was little room for movement, one knee thumping into the back of his tent mate, the ever angry Corporal Owens.

"Huh? What the hell you want?" Owens sat up abruptly, his head brushing the top of the small tent. "Jesus, it's cold. Rained, too. Dammit anyway. Left my brogans outside."

Bauer had his shoes on still, had heard the rain through much of the night, was surprised Owens hadn't. He looked out across the open ground, the mist visible in the faint gray light, saw men moving past, could see the hats, officers. The bugle blew now, the first call for the battalion to rise, and Owens crawled outside, wrestled with his shoes, low cursing that still impressed Bauer. It was the constant entertainment from Owens, who seemed to create swear words for any occasion, some so profane that Bauer feared the man might be struck down by the hand of God. But Owens continued to blow out his amazing profanity, and Bauer began to wonder if God Himself wasn't impressed by the man's utter originality.

Bauer wasn't as devout as some, had been raised Lutheran by his German parents. He had spent much of his service time around Catholics, the Irishmen of the 17th Wisconsin, even some of the regulars around him now speaking with a hint of an Irish lilt. Many others were Presbyterians, a few Anabaptists, those men seeming to fear the unseen Hand more than most, going into every fight as though God was judging them. Bauer had seen too many horrors to believe God was there at all, that surely the awful things these armies were doing to each other would not please the Almighty one bit. If there was to be punishment, Bauer had come to believe that the war was punishment enough, that if God was truly watching them, He had to be satisfied with the kind of hell the troops had created.

The regulars had chaplains, as did every other unit in the army, but the Sunday services drew fewer than half the men, and whatever guilt Bauer had felt about that had dissolved along with the decorum he had thought would be so much a part of the regular army. There was formality, to be sure, those few officers who demanded the crisp salute. But others, like Willis, seemed to care far more for what these men would be called upon to do, performance in battle meaning more than a neatly fitted uniform. Though the rations had been cut by a third or more, ammunition was plentiful, and, finally, Bauer had been given the opportunity to demonstrate those claims Willis had embarrassed him with. Bauer hadn't disappointed them, shattering glass bottles and rusted mess tins at better than four hundred yards. Just like the Pennsylvanians, the regulars had used Bauer's marksmanship as a cause for wagering, adding pressure to Bauer's steady hand. Even Willis joined into that, often betting a quarter dollar with other officers on Bauer's sharp eye. Willis knew it was a good bet, and Bauer knew as well, that a careful aim was far simpler when the target wasn't shooting back.

He crawled out of the tent behind Owens, saw most of the men up and out, the mist giving way to a hint of daylight, a lighter gray rising over the crest of the great ridge to their front. He stood beside Owens, who stretched, scratching himself, rough hands on his chest, stomach, now down his legs.

"I'll kill you, Wisconsin! You done give me the creepers!"

Bauer took a step away from Owens, was never sure just what this man might do. "Not me. I'm not itching a'tall. Boiled my clothes back in town, all of 'em. They had big pots set up. . . ."

"Don't give me that chicken sludge. I got these things running all over me."

"No, Corporal, really. I'm clean!"

Bauer felt a slight itch on the back of his leg, fought any urge to scratch. Owens continued scratching, and Bauer saw others pointing, a few low laughs. But no one in the company would laugh at Owens for long without paying some kind of brutal price. Owens cursed again, his shirt coming off, scratch marks all across his stomach, every place Owens could reach. Bauer knew what kind of torment lice could bring, had gone through that in the camps outside Vicksburg. The army recognized the misery of that, the best company commanders securing an iron pot or large bucket that could be heated, allowing the men to boil every piece of clothing they had. Bauer had already withstood the indignity of that, standing nearly naked in a line of men, taking his turn at the fire. But the cold rain took away any warmth, and the men scrambled to put on undergarments that quickly turned icy cold. If there was embarrassment from other units nearby, taunts and jeers that came toward the lines of shivering men, those men would be silenced quickly. When the lice swarmed over them, no one was immune. In Willis's company, it seemed to be the men with the biggest mouths who seemed to suffer the affliction before anyone else, a kind of justice Bauer appreciated.

Owens seemed to accept Bauer's claims of innocence, though Bauer still felt the one nagging itch, clamped his jaw, clenched his fists, a hard struggle against the desperate need to scratch. He saw the sergeant now, others gathering, Owens called over, a quick word from the company's first sergeant. Bauer welcomed the brief diversion, responded with a fast grab at his leg, a hard rub against his skin, the itch growing worse, spreading. No! Not again. He watched Owens speaking to the other sergeants, saw one of the lieutenants move close, speaking to them, then another, the platoon commanders. Bauer saw the sergeants scratching themselves as well, and now Willis was there, a glance toward Bauer, who froze, the agony still burning through his pants.

Willis said aloud, "Boil your clothes, all of you. There's a vermin outbreak. Doctor says it's probably this new grass. These little critters are happy to have fresh meat. I guess by now, the reb skirmishers we chased away had gotten stale. I'll not have you going into the fight with one hand twiddling your tenders. Line up over by that tent, where the doctor's standing. Pot's on the fire, and it'll be aboil soon. Then make it quick. We've got work to do."

They moved together, and Bauer could see the doctor now beside the larger tent, a broad smile on the man's face. Always smiling, he thought. How on this earth can a doctor in the army be happy? Most miserable job there is.

"Keep moving, all of you."

Willis walked alongside the forming line, and to one side of Bauer, a voice, the boy, Hoover.

"Hey, Captain, how come officers never get these cootie things?"

Willis stopped, one hand resting on his holster. Bauer knew when Willis was trying to be deadly serious, but Bauer knew better, caught a hint of a smile. He saw Willis glance at him, trying to heighten his ferocity, his voice coming out just a bit deeper than usual.

"Boy, it's like this. A skin critter is just like **you.** He knows full well that if he offends his company commander, he's in for a busted head. Besides, it's hard for those little turd lickers to hold on to a hunk of skin when they've got one hand always saluting."

Hoover seemed to know he was the butt of the joke, the men around him relentless, slapping his back, the good-natured teasing that seemed always to pour out on the youngest men. Willis stood with his hands on both hips now, the men moving past in good order. Just beyond the tent, Bauer could

see the campfire, a roaring blaze, supplied by timber cut the night before. Resting on stout green
logs was a huge iron kettle, steam rising, the men
first in line knowing the routine, already disrobing.
Bauer loosened his pants, began to unbutton his
shirt, moved past Willis, who still watched them
with a grim stare. He caught Bauer's eye now, and
Bauer was surprised there was no smile. Willis's jaw
seemed clamped shut, his fists clenched by his side,
a low curse slipping out, words Bauer could barely
hear. And now, with a quick jerk of his hand, Willis
scratched himself.

It was full daylight now, the rain coming in a
wispy swirl, carried past by a relentless fog, the
entire field cloaked in thick clouds. He knew
a skirmish line had been sent forward, those men a
quarter mile or more to the front, invisible in the
thickets and tall grass. He was grateful to avoid that
today, had no interest in another game of chatter
with any rebels who might be there. Bet those boys
ain't so friendly now, he thought. Everybody was
getting along just dandy, and then we come marching out here and shove the whole army into their
parlors. So now, we're on new ground, and somewhere out there is a bunch of angry rebels. Glad
Sammie let somebody else do that job today. I'd
just like something decent to eat.

The breakfast had been as bad as anything they'd

been given the past few days, moldy crackers, a small sliver of sour bacon. In the wide fields around them, some of the men had taken to chasing rabbits, but those were scarce, and Bauer assumed the rebels had spent many of their long hours on skirmish duty grabbing every rabbit in the area.

In the camps the morning before, they'd been given the typical three-day rations, and just as typical, most of the men devoured their three-day supply within the first hour. It was commonplace now, so many of the men convinced they might not live through the day, or might suffer a wound that would put them in the dreaded hospitals. Bauer had once done that himself, and then suffered for it, an empty backpack and a hollow stomach for two or three days, the memory of that one gorging feast not lasting more than a few hours. He saw men shuffling through their packs now, thought, That's right. You go and gobble down every scrap the army gives you, and then what? We didn't get hit with a single casualty yesterday, and now, every one of those boys who thought the world was gonna end is gonna come looking for grub. And they know I keep mine. Sure as shooting, somebody's gonna find out I got a handful of crackers left over. Best not let anybody see you eating nothing. Some of these boys get a bit ornery when they get hungry. Owens scares the daylights outta me.

The men were packed tightly, close to the fires, and even with the light spray of rain, their clothes were drying out. Wet or not, for now, the vicious curse of the **cooties** was gone. The men were mostly silent, a sure sign of hunger, the chills far worse when a man's stomach was empty. Bauer thought of the hardtack in his backpack, felt suddenly guilty, thought, Yeah, I'll share. But I wish these new fellows would learn that lesson. It ain't never been that **all** of us gets hit. And what good's a full stomach gonna do you if you're dead?

"Private!"

He turned with the others, saw one of the sergeants pointing directly at him.

"Yep, Sarge. Me?"

"You. Captain wants to see you."

The men around him ignored that, so very different from how it had been in the 17th Wisconsin. Then, he had come into the regiment as an officer's "pal," inviting a cascade of ridicule. It bothered Bauer every time, as though the men would think Willis was such a poor platoon commander, he'd show obvious favors to his friend. That had faded, especially when the men learned that Bauer would stand tall in even the worst fights. But that seemed a long time in the past, and Bauer was surprised, and relieved that these men didn't seem to care if Captain Willis was his friend or not. Bauer wasn't really sure why. But he had to believe that Willis had already shown these men he could lead them, and at Chickamauga, he had done just that, in one of the most miserable fights of the war. If the captain had a friend close by, more power to him. He had earned their respect. Friendship was just a bonus.

Bauer followed the sergeant, who stopped now, pointing the way.

"The big tent. Might be your lucky day, Private. They might have coffee."

Bauer had been in officers' tents before, knew they rarely offered any private whatever treat they had for themselves. He moved that way, was surprised to see the company's four lieutenants emerging from the tent, all of them staring up high, back past Bauer. He turned, followed their stares, saw nothing but fog, rain in his eyes. He knew better than to ask, moved by them, stopped at the opening of the tent, heard the familiar voice.

"Get in here. You like standing in the rain?"

Bauer ducked inside, saw Willis sitting on a bedroll, no chairs, no desk. A company commander didn't rank high enough for those kinds of luxuries, and Bauer glanced around, saw a map by Willis's side.

"Well, I'm here, sir. I earn a promotion? It my birthday or something?"

"Don't sass me, Dutchie. No time to play with you. Big doings today. Tomorrow, too. That big show we watched yesterday was only the first act. The brass has plans, and they're not telling me everything. Just that we need to stay close to camp, be ready to move if they need us."

"We moved yesterday, Sammie, and we didn't hardly do anything but take a walk."

"Shut up. Nobody made you smart overnight."

Bauer saw movement behind Willis, jumped in surprise, called out, "Hooey! Sammie, there's a chicken! What's he doing . . . it's a rooster!"

Willis seemed to ignore him, the tall bird moving toward a scrap of something Willis had been eating. The rooster pecked the ground, gobbled up the small morsel, and Willis said, "Meet Henry. Followed me out here, I guess. Had to. Don't think he'd have lasted out here for very long. The rebs would've eaten him for sure. You ever try eating a rooster? Nasty, tough as nails. Soup, maybe, but don't try to roast it over a fire. Actually, nobody at all better be roasting or frying or anything else with Old Henry. I figure he's pretty old. Ugly enough. But he's kind of adopted me."

Bauer felt his mouth hanging open. "Captain Willis, you are telling me that you have a pet rooster?"

Willis feigned offense. "I never said he was a pet. I said he adopted me. Maybe . . . I'm **his** pet. As long as he likes it in this tent, he's coming along. Kinda like the company. He doesn't gripe near as much as you fellows. Can't say he follows orders too well."

Bauer eyed the bird, watched it prance slowly to the back of the tent, disappearing behind Willis's backpack. Bauer stared for a long moment, Willis pretending not to notice, picking up the map, studying, mock seriousness Bauer knew too well.

"Sammie . . . you've gone shaky in the head. I've never seen you care a whit about any animal. You shot a snake, when none of us would go near it. You're saving that bird for a feast, right? Be honest with me, Captain. Nobody's got a pet rooster."

Willis looked up at him now. "You know what I got, Dutchie? In this whole world. You know what I got?"

Bauer knew when Willis was serious, a hint of a threat to his voice.

"You got the army, Sammie. You got me for a friend."

"Nope. I don't **got** the army. They've **got me** for a company commander. I'm in charge of keeping you out of trouble, or putting you right up front of a reb's bayonet. You're my friend, Dutchie, always have been. But I can't think of you that way, not anymore. Every time we run into the enemy, it's my duty to put you out right where you could get killed. I hesitate about that, it makes me a bad officer. No. You're not listening to me. In this whole world, I got nothing else. No family, no home, no treasures squirreled away someplace. Nothing. Except now. Got me a damn rooster. And I'm keeping him as long as he's happy to follow me around and eat hardtack."

Willis returned to the map, and Bauer suddenly realized there was no joke here, that Willis was serious. Bauer felt a stab of pain at Willis's words.

"You are my friend, Sammie. Always have been, when we were both privates. Just 'cause you got bars on your shoulders don't mean we can't be pals."

"Don't get all mushed up, Dutchie. I still like you. You've known me longer than anyone in this army. Been through all kinds of hell, you and me. You even won me some money, too, with that good shooting eye of yours. But out there, around the others, you're just one of the muskets. Hell, you know that already."

"Then why'd you call me in here?"

"Thought you'd like to know what's happening, as much as I can tell you. Pretty good stuff, Dutchie. These boys haven't seen a good fight in a couple months, not since we had to beat tracks away from Chickamauga. But that's about to change. Thought you oughta know. Hell, thought you'd **want** to know."

"You're just telling **me**? You said I was just like the others. Just a musket."

"Dumb as a walnut. Right now, we're not around the others. In here, I even let you call me Sammie. You do that out there . . . well, you know what I'll have to do."

"Where's the fight gonna be? Here?"

"Two walnuts. Of course it's here. We ain't marching to Richmond, Dutchie. You heard any artillery yet?"

Bauer turned his head, listened, a soft hiss of rain, a few voices spread across the soggy ground. "No."

"You will. Pay attention to it."

"Heckfire, Sammie, we hear artillery every blessed day. They drop some on us, we drop some on them. Ain't meant nothing so far."

"You hear me, Private? I'm your company commander. I tell you to listen to artillery, you best listen." Willis glanced at a small pocket watch, snapped it shut. "About now, I'd say."

Bauer waited, the silence broken by the strange clucks from the rooster, Bauer captivated by the bizarre sight, the bird poking his beak down through Willis's blanket. There was a rumble of thunder now, and Willis perked up, stared past Bauer, out through the opening in the tent. The thunder came again, and Bauer knew it was cannon, far in the distance.

"Where's that coming from?"

"Take a look outside. That big damn mountain."

"Heck, Sammie, we been throwing shells up there for weeks. They throw 'em right back." Bauer poked his head out into the heavy mist, thick fog obscuring the heights. "Can't see a blessed thing anyway. Those guns belong to us, or them?"

"Maybe both of us." Willis stood now, moved out to the opening in the tent. The rain had slackened, a thick mist covering the camps, dense fog higher up, the outline of the mountain barely visible. "Game's over, Dutchie. We're putting more than just iron on that big hill today. Up north of here, they tell me that Sherman's crossing the river, but nobody wants to talk about just how he's doing that. If I was a damn general, maybe I'd get to know all the secrets. Doesn't mean I'd tell you. All I know is that this army's not sitting still much longer. Keep an eye on that big damn mountain. I guess General Grant's tired of those rebels waving their damn flags, having the best view. He wants our boys up there doing all that for themselves. General Hooker's got at least a division on the move this morning, climbing up that way, right up outta that valley you marched through. If this confounded weather will clear, we might get a decent look. But we're damn sure gonna hear it. Sounds like the fight's started already. Right on time. Pretty rare for this army."

Bauer stepped out clear of the tent, Willis close beside him. Most of the men were still huddled at the fires, had heard too much cannon fire to pay much attention to what was clearly falling well across the river.

Willis stared up into the fog, said, "Tell you what, Dutchie. I got things to tend to. Colonel wants to see all the company commanders. You go pass the word, tell the boys what's happening. Maybe we'll get a look yet. There's no chance in hell that General Thomas is gonna sit tight and watch while Hooker and Sherman get all the fun. We left that ugly-assed town behind us for a reason, and I bet there's a pile of generals out here somewhere figuring out just what that reason is. Right now, it's somebody else's 'friends' making that climb out there, maybe busting straight into a whole heap of rebels. Tomorrow, it might be mine."

While Sherman's men worked to complete their defenses to the north, his scouts pushing forward to find any sign of rebel troops, Joe Hooker's ten-thousand-man force began their advance against Lookout Mountain. One part of Hooker's strength was to keep low, close to the river, hoping to push through the narrow gap along the river itself, seeking a way to slice into the valley east of the mountain. There, Chattanooga Creek might act as a hard boundary Hooker's men could use to slice the Confederate position in two halves, possibly stranding the rebels who held the ground on the mountain itself. The remainder of Hooker's men would make the climb up the west side of the mountain, until they reached a gently sloping plateau, nearly halfway to the top. Those men included John Geary's brigade, some of those the Pennsylvanians who had been so impressed with Bauer's marksmanship. Masked by the miserable weather, Geary's men and the remaining force under Union general Peter Osterhaus did their best to link up their flanks to form a strong battle line that extended from the base of the mountain to Geary's wide, grassy plateau. Anchoring his right flank against the sheer face of the rock, Geary began a sweep along the plateau, a methodical ad-

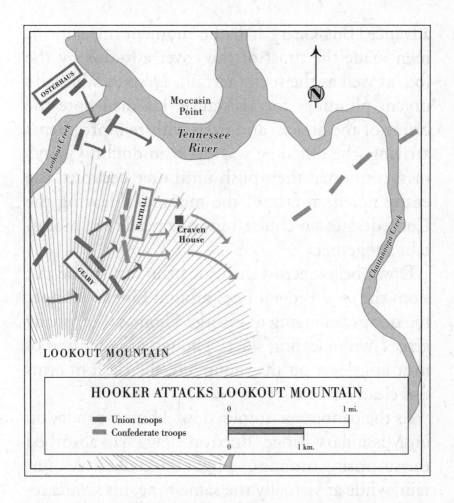

HOOKER ATTACKS LOOKOUT MOUNTAIN

Union troops
Confederate troops

0   1 mi.

0   1 km.

vance through dense fog that soon confronted a brigade of rebels, commanded by General Edward Walthall. Walthall's men held a strong defensive position near a house belonging to a man named Craven, one of the only structures on the mountain's northern face. But Walthall had fewer than fifteen hundred men to hold back Geary's push. Grossly outnumbered, Walthall had no choice but to withdraw, giving ground as slowly as he could, hoping to allow time for reinforcements to stop Geary's advance. But Geary had the momentum, and his men made the most of the cover afforded by the fog, as well as the rocky terrain. Despite Walthall's urgent pleadings for assistance, his men bore the brunt of the attack, and even with reinforcements arriving, the outcome was never in doubt. Geary's men continued their push until they occupied the entire northern face of the mountain, leaving the Confederates no choice but to concede the mountain altogether.

Down below, across the wide plain that spread out from the new Federal lines around Orchard Knob, the troops belonging to George Thomas were finally graced with clearing skies. Though a heavy line of mist hung low on the mountain, the clash of arms was clearly visible.

As the panorama unfolded for Thomas's men, up on Missionary Ridge, Braxton Bragg had absorbed the surprising sounds of a fight on Lookout Mountain, while at virtually the same time, his scouts reported that, to the north, a great mass of troops under Sherman had pushed across the Tennessee River.

CHAPTER THIRTY

CLEBURNE

MISSIONARY RIDGE—
NOVEMBER 24, 1863

The new summons from Bragg had come early that morning, and Cleburne obeyed, had seen a disturbing portrait of a man who seemed to be losing control of his army, and of himself. The orders came with a scattered urgency, couriers moving out in every direction like a flock of wild birds. Through a long night in the misery of the cold rain, Cleburne had followed Bragg's instructions from the day before, had positioned his division along the center of Missionary Ridge, close to Bragg's headquarters, a strong line of support for the men who even now, dug their pits and trenches along the crest of the hill. But with the dawn, something had changed, Bragg ordering Cleburne to shift one of his four brigades far to the north, returning them to the same rail depot where they had boarded the trains days before. Then it was to support Longstreet. Now it was to guard the valuable bridge across Chickamauga Creek against what Bragg had convinced himself was an imminent threat from Federal troops. That report had come to Bragg from lookouts and cavalry scouts upriver, that throughout the night, an enormous force of blue was crossing the river. No one could confirm any numbers, and no one besides Bragg was convinced that those troops were really any threat at all. But Cleburne had followed the order, and early that morning, had sent Lucius Polk's brigade back to the rail depot, ordering them to guard the station as well as the bridge that carried the tracks northward over Chickamauga Creek.

The first hint Cleburne had of any real Federal activity was the distant thunder that rolled down on the army from the heights of Lookout Mountain, Hooker's attack against the very place Bragg had reduced his own strength. Whether or not Bragg was shocked by the sudden flood of fighting from the mountain, Cleburne had reacted by readying his men for the job they were assigned in the first place, preparing to receive a Federal onslaught against the heart of Missionary Ridge. From his vantage point on the ridge, there was little to be seen of the fight that had erupted on Lookout Mountain, the tall mass blanketed by a heavy mist, and layers of fog. The only real signs of the fight came from the high arcing shells of Federal artillery. He had stood in the light rain, his staff caught as he was by the strange beauty of what seemed to be a far distant fireworks display. Cleburne had no idea who was pushing a fight up the mountain, but he was more certain now than he had been the day before that the troops Hardee had been ordered to pull down off the mountain were probably, right now, in the wrong place.

With so little visibility, and so little news coming from Bragg's headquarters, Cleburne had no real certainty just what the enemy was attempting to do. It was possible that General Stevenson had been correct, that Lookout Mountain was the enemy's primary target, but Bragg seemed to believe still that Grant's strategy was far more complicated than that. It was the dirty secret that was no secret at all. The arrival of Sherman's four divisions added to what was already a simple mathematics exercise, that the Federal forces now outnumbered Bragg's army by a wide margin. With Oliver Howard's men crossing the river northward from Lookout Valley, and Sherman's forces seeming to disappear altogether, no one was certain where Grant might strike. But Bragg was convinced, whether Carter Stevenson agreed with him or not, that the burst of fighting on Lookout Mountain was little more than a diversion. The greater vulnerability to Bragg's position was to the north, Bragg convinced that Grant would make every effort to sever the rail lines that led toward Knoxville, a line that intersected with an even more important track that led southeast, what might be the most effective path for either army to move out of Tennessee.

Around Cleburne, some of his own men had followed him to the crest of the ridge, standing alongside troops from other units, men with shovels who stopped their work, staring off toward the rumbles in the distance. Cleburne kept his stare to the front, directly across the plain where the two low hills had fallen into Federal hands, where Grant's forces had pushed forward, closing the distance between the centers of the two armies. There was musket fire down below, far out in the plain, but it was ragged, scattered, skirmishers testing their enemy, exactly the kind of warning he knew to expect if the enemy wanted the men along Cleburne's part of the ridge to stay put. He strained to hear the first sounds of artillery from out front, expected it, knew that most likely Bragg did as well. But the nervous pops from the muskets of the picket line were not increasing, and even in the heavy mist, Cleburne could see no movement by any vast waves of blue troops, no one pressing any assault toward Missionary Ridge.

As the sun rose higher, the fog seemed to settle lower on the mountain, offering some glimmer of what might be happening above. But Cleburne paced nervously for something more, some kind of order that would tell him what the enemy would do next. By now, his faith in Bragg's strategic sense had evaporated, and he stared down the ridge toward the Nail House, thought, He knows little more than I do right here. He must hear that fight, must know what it will mean if the enemy captures the mountain. That's our left flank, after all, the flank of this entire army. If they take those heights, it could give the Yankees a route into Georgia that we cannot block. He stared again to the low hills far out in the plain, glimpses through the fog of Grant's new encampments. No, he thought, Grant will not go around. He will not ignore this army on this ridge while he settles for raids against railroads and telegraph wires.

He turned, looked back to the east, out past the camps of his men, far down the backside of the great ridge. There were farmhouses and narrow roads, small rocky fields cut through with woodlands rolling across smaller hills. Wilderness, he thought. Nothing of value to this ground, no bountiful croplands. The only **value** here is what two armies can do to each other, if one side drives the other completely away, or destroys our ability to fight. He caught himself. **Our.** Is that after all what we are expecting here? A struggle for survival? What chance do we have of destroying Grant's forces? Even Bragg, with all his fantasies, must know that, despite his love of this marvelous ground. Grant surely knows he can punish us from every direction. How much can we defend? And for how long?

The rider came at a gallop, and Cleburne watched

him, saw the familiar face of Hardee's courier. Captain Buck moved up beside him, said, "Looks like somebody's in a hurry, sir. That's Hankins."

"Now we shall find out what is happening. Some word of what is required of us."

"Yes, sir. Appears so."

The rider halted, no smile from a man who usually brought a measure of good cheer. Hankins did not dismount, said, "General Cleburne! General Hardee offers you his respects, and directs you to march your division here positioned, to the far right flank of this ridge."

Cleburne glanced at Lookout Mountain. "The right? Are you certain about that, Lieutenant? The fight appears to be on the left."

Hankins pointed northward, along the crest of the ridge. "There is no mistake, sir. General Bragg has received reports that the enemy has crossed the Tennessee River along both sides of Chickamauga Creek, well beyond our right flank."

Cleburne felt a sickening turn inside, thought of the rail depot, the lone bridge to the north of the great ridge, the single brigade he had sent that way. "How many of the enemy?"

"I do not know, sir. General Hardee is most insistent that you march your entire division that way, with the purpose of protecting our right flank. The general is profoundly concerned that should the enemy make headway along this very ridge, or should he move past our right flank and seek to push in behind us, this army will be considerably disadvantaged. He is most insistent, sir. Are you familiar with that terrain to the north of this ridge, sir?"

"Been there once. If you recall, Lieutenant, I was ordered up that way to the rail depot only two days ago, to put these men on the railcars to Knoxville."

"Yes, of course. The situation is most . . . fluid, sir. General Hardee has ordered Major Poole to the crest of Tunnel Hill, to await your arrival. The major will provide you with details as to your disposition on those heights."

Cleburne looked again at Lookout Mountain, the fog thinning, flashes of fire clearly visible along the face of the hill. He climbed up on his horse, saw Buck, the rest of the staff taking his cue, pulling themselves into the saddle. Hankins seemed impatient, as though he had someplace far more important to be.

"May I report to General Hardee that you have received, and understand, his instructions, sir?"

"By all means, Lieutenant."

"Thank you, sir. I must return to headquarters. The enemy's assault on Lookout Mountain has upset the usual decorum there."

"General Hardee's headquarters?"

"General Bragg's, sir. Forgive my impudence."

Cleburne appreciated the man's sarcasm, understood the kind of "decorum" Bragg seemed to embrace. "Go, Lieutenant. My respects to General Hardee. We will march northward with all haste."

Hankins saluted him, spun the horse around through the muddy ground, moved away quickly. Cleburne motioned to his staff, to mount up, and Cleburne moved to his own horse, patted the wet hair, calming himself as much as the animal. He pulled himself into the saddle, said to Buck, "Get word to each brigade commander to put their men to the march as quickly as possible. This is not the time for dallying."

Mangum said, "Sir, forgive me, but the only fight I hear is . . . that one." He pointed out toward Lookout Mountain. "We're to march the opposite way?"

Cleburne was in no mood for a discussion, even from his former law partner. "I am quite certain there will be further orders. Right now, I am following the only order I have been given. You and Captain Buck will ride with me. Bring two couriers along, and the guard. We shall move out to Tunnel Hill, and see if we can locate Major Poole. Major Benham, you will see to the brigade commanders. Let's go."

Already, men around them were moving away, junior officers taking command of their men, some heading for the stacked muskets, some seeking a last handful of warmth beside low fires. Cleburne spurred the horse gently, wouldn't aggravate the animal, not when he needed to stay upright in the saddle. Buck followed, rode up closest to him, said, "Sir, Mangum is right. The fight is . . . back there."

"We are not ordered to engage in any fight, Captain. We are marching to protect a hill. General Hardee would not create this move on his own. General Bragg has his reasons, and I must believe that he also has an instinct for the inevitable. Unless General Hardee orders me to change position yet again, our mission is to prevent the enemy from sealing off our means of retreat."

Farther to the north, the ridge rose high above deep ravines to both sides, heavily wooded crevasses that laid between the ridge and several smaller hills to the east. Toward the far north end, the ridge dipped lower, then back up to a bald knob, what the local citizens referred to as Tunnel Hill. Beyond the hill, the ground flattened out up toward South Chickamauga Creek, where, farther to the east, the bridge was already being guarded by the brigade of Lucius Polk.

Tunnel Hill itself was mostly hemmed in by thick, wooded ground, but the name came from the passage of the rail line that came north from Chattanooga, passing through the mountain itself, before reaching the depot. The rail line west of the ridge passed through the wide plain where Grant's army now encamped, and all throughout the campaign, that stretch of track was useless for any kind of passage, easily within range of the artillery batteries on either side. East of Tunnel Hill, the tracks offered a vital artery that moved not only toward Knoxville, but made a connection to the Western & Atlantic Railroad, what could provide an avenue of escape for Bragg's entire army.

The guard moved out in front of him, nervous men not accustomed to leading their commander through what seemed to be an empty forest. Cleburne appreciated their vigilance, knew as well as they did that the tall trees down below them could hold an enemy sharpshooter, that a lone general would make for a favored target.

He could see the round knob of Tunnel Hill to the front, halted the men, felt the need for caution. He stared out toward the river, a mile away, but the mist and fog was spread all across that part of the field, the river itself nearly invisible. Someone was sent out here, he thought, maybe men on both sides, peeking up over every ridgeline, a quick glance from behind every tree. And someone convinced the commanding general that the enemy is out here in force. I'd rather see that for myself.

"Let's go. We're supposed to find Major Poole out there somewhere." He pulled out his pocket watch, said aloud, "Just past two o'clock. Plenty of time yet. Dark by, what, Captain? Six thirty or so?"

Buck said, "Yes, sir. The rains will bring it on more quickly."

"The rains will not continue forever, Captain, no

matter if it seems that way. We must assume the enemy is waiting for a bit of sunshine before he reveals just what he's intending to do."

Cleburne looked back toward Lookout Mountain, the haze too thick to see anything at all. He listened for the rumble of that fight, faint echoes, nothing to tell him there was still a fight at all. I suppose, he thought, we should be told something of that by tonight. General Bragg seems to relish parceling his army out into small pieces, expecting, I suppose, that we can each fight our own private war. He kept his thoughts to himself, had no reason to share that kind of dismay to his staff officers.

"Let's move out, gentlemen. Major Poole is no doubt anxious for our arrival."

He kept them to the main trail, glanced toward the river, still little to see, the rain mostly a thick mist now. They rode downward, thickets of dense brush to both sides, the guards eyeing the ground with nervous glances. The trail climbed again, and to the front, the ground cleared, a bare knob, Tunnel Hill. The guards spread out, and Cleburne moved past them, saw the lone officer, his horse off to one side nibbling on a patch of low grass. Cleburne halted the horse, the officers behind him doing the same, and the man seemed desperately relieved to see him, rushed forward, a quick salute.

"General Cleburne! Thank the Almighty you have arrived! I am most pleased to receive your company, sir. I am considerably unprepared to de-

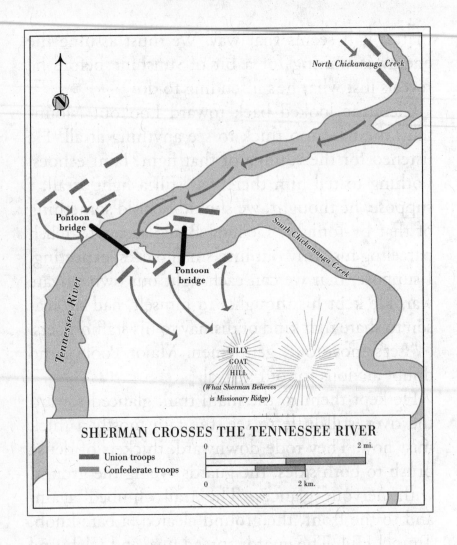

North Chickamauga Creek

Pontoon
bridge

South Chickamauga Creek

Pontoon
bridge

Tennessee River

BILLY
GOAT
HILL
*(What Sherman Believes
is Missionary Ridge)*

SHERMAN CROSSES THE TENNESSEE RIVER

0   2 mi.

Union troops
Confederate troops

0   2 km.

fend this hill by myself. I am reinforced by a half-dozen signalmen out there. Not reassuring, sir."

Cleburne cringed at the announcement of his rank, the sergeant of his guards reacting with an angry grunt. Cleburne dismounted quickly, moved close to the man, said, "Major Poole, it is not in my best interest that you announce to God and anyone else who might hear you, just who I am."

Poole seemed to understand his indiscretion, made a sharp nod, spoke in a whisper, "My apologies, sir. You are quite right. It has been somewhat trying up here, sir. I am only accompanied by a squad of signalmen, who are even now on that far hill to the northwest. I do not care so much for . . . isolation. Not with such enemy as seems to be making their way to this side of the river."

"What enemy? Who? Where are they?"

"Sir, this morning, a company of cavalry under Colonel Grigsby was patrolling near the mouth of Chickamauga Creek, and reported the presence of several brigades of the enemy, forcing a landing on this side of the river. Colonel Grigsby did not have the orders to engage the enemy, and did not believe he had the strength to prevent the crossing. He sent word of this to General Bragg, and withdrew his horsemen so as not to alarm the enemy. Sir, General Hardee urges you in the strongest terms to march your entire division in this direction. You are familiar with this ground, sir? Tunnel Hill?"

"We're standing on it, I believe. I was here once before, when I was ordered to send my division off to another campaign, using the railroad."

"Yes, of course, sir. The railroad. Sir, have you marched a brigade to the bridge?"

Cleburne was surprised how much Poole knew, that clearly Hardee had kept him informed just what Bragg was insisting on.

"Yes, General Polk's brigade should be in position

there now. My orders were to guard the depot and protect the railroad bridge. But who am I guarding against?"

"Sir, it is essential that I convey your orders. Please, if you will follow me . . . ?"

Poole walked away quickly, glancing back impatiently for Cleburne to follow. Cleburne obliged him, the two men moving to the far reaches of the knob, Poole pointing out.

"That's northwest. That hill is called, regrettably, Billy Goat Hill. Foolish names for such places. It's about a half mile from this peak to that one. General Hardee orders you to deploy one brigade on that eminence. You will deploy the remainder of your division along this ridge, securing Tunnel Hill, and the ridgeline to the south. Your left flank shall make contact and attach to the right flank of General Walker's division, as it now sits. Thus you will be extending our main line northward, to include this terrain."

"Major, are you aware that termination of our lines, General Walker's division, is nearly a mile behind us? If I extend my men to attach to that flank, my lines won't be heavy enough to hold back a squad of cavalry. I am assuming that General Hardee feels this ground is extremely valuable, and is under considerable threat. Would it not be wiser if additional troops are shifted northward, in support of my own position covering these hills?"

"Sir, any judgment as to what is **wise** lies with

General Hardee. I was ordered to place your people on these hills."

"Well, Major, I'll have my men up here as quickly as I can march them, and we shall make every disposition to protect this high ground. But you will return now to General Hardee and advise him that I must have support to the south. If the enemy drives below these hills, and strikes this ridge to the south, my entire division will be cut off. I will not have that, Major."

Poole seemed to absorb the situation, said, "Walker's near a mile that way?"

"Very near that, Major. It is a weakness in our position that could offer the enemy an opportunity. Go **now,** Major."

The man seemed to grasp the gravity of what Cleburne was telling him, moved quickly to his horse, a hasty salute, then galloped away southward, the trail Cleburne had just ridden. Cleburne looked to Captain Buck, said, "Go now to General Smith, and make sure word gets to Lowrey and Govan as well. All three brigades are to move as rapidly as possible to this ground. Double time. No complaints, Captain. Get those people up on these hills."

"Yes, sir!"

Buck was up and gone in Poole's tracks, and Cleburne walked to the edge of the hill, leaned out, could see the railroad tracks running toward him, into the gaping maw beneath his feet. Mangum was beside him now, said, "The tunnel could be

very useful. Perhaps an artillery battery? It's a natural rifle pit."

"No. It could end up being a trap. Too easy to
cut off any number of troops from either end. If
the enemy is truly advancing to this position, they
might see the tunnel as a tempting target. That's to
our advantage. One twelve-pounder placed behind
us, at the far end of the tunnel, could fire canister and
sweep the entire opening. No, if we intend to hold
our position on this hill, we must wrap ourselves
around the crest, and force the enemy to come at us
through that dense brush below, between these two
hills. That will definitely slow down any advance
in this direction. I should like to know just who or
how many of the enemy is supposed to be out there
on our side of the river. We should scout Billy Goat
Hill." He paused. "Poole's right. Who names these
places?"

There was a crackling of brush down below, and
Cleburne's guards reacted quickly, a quartet of car-
bines aimed downward. Mangum said, "Sir, I see
them. Our boys!"

Cleburne saw the flicker of clothing, no hint of
blue, said, "Hold fire. Someone's in a bloomin'
hurry."

The men struggled up through the brush, one
man calling out, "Don't be shootin' at us, no how!
We're your'n."

The men completed the climb, three of them collapsing to the bare ground, gasping for breath. One

suddenly recognized he was in the presence of a general, pulled himself to his feet.

"Sir, I was expecting Major Poole. Begging your pardon, sir."

The man snapped up a salute, and Cleburne said, "What's your hurry, soldier?"

"Plenty a' cause, sir. We're signalmen. Been up on that other hill out yonder, taking a gander at what's happening at the river. Fog finally cleared away, and let me tell you, sir, it's a sight. If'n you was to see what we seen, General, you'd knowed why we made hay up here. There's a pile of Yankees out there. Been watching 'em for the past hour now. They been bringing more across the river right regular, but we ain't been able to see much with this nasty weather and all. But there's a big dang boat out middle of the river, and they done built them a bridge clean across, marching troops and wagons all morning, I reckon. But things is changin'. I guess whoever's in charge figures enough's enough. They're coming, sir. Formed up battle lines, and done stepped off, pushing straight toward that there hill we was on. Figured our job was done. Don't need no signals to spell out what's happening." The man looked at Cleburne's staff, the few guards. "Um, forgive me for wonderin', General, but if there's gonna be a scrap out hereabouts, you'll be wantin' to have some muskets to help out."

Cleburne looked out toward the second hill, nothing to see but timber. The rain was still falling, a light mist, hiding any signs of any movement around the other hill. He turned to Mangum, said, "I'd like to know just what we're facing. Maybe we better slip down through this tangle and get a better look."

The signalman put both his hands up. "I wouldn't be doin' none of that, begging your pardon, sir. Only thing you'll find besides Yankees is our signal flags. Left 'em up there. We was in something of a rush, you see. Major Poole'll make us answer for that, if'n he finds out."

"I'm not concerned with flags, Private. How many Yankees?"

"More than two divisions, all told. Once the rain lightened up, we could see nothing but blue all over that river."

Cleburne wiped a wet handkerchief across his face, the rain still a light drizzle. Beside him, Mangum said, "Sir. Drums."

Cleburne looked back, thought of Poole's words, a half mile away. Rugged ground, he thought, but we better get out there first. He looked back at the signalman.

"Tough going through that brush, Private?"

"Quite, sir. Briars and vines to strangle a man. Hole's deeper than it looks, too."

"Good. Your information is most helpful. If I may ask, what's your name?"

"That'd be Henry Smith, sir."

"Indeed? Call that a stroke of fate, Private. Those

drums, that column coming up. That would be another **Smith.** My lead brigade, Jim Smith. Texans.
They'll give us our muskets."

Cleburne's lead brigade was in position facing west, and Smith immediately pushed a
heavy line of his skirmishers out through
the thickets and brambles that led down from the
bald crest of Tunnel Hill. Their mission was to drive
forward as quickly as possible, making a hasty push
through the boggy depths of the ravine that separated Tunnel Hill from the smaller mound of Billy
Goat Hill. If they could establish a defensive position on the smaller hill, the remainder of Smith's
brigade would follow close behind, allowing Cleburne to fulfill Hardee's order. As the skirmishers
made their way forward, the rest of Smith's division
prepared to move out in support. For long, anxious
minutes, Cleburne could only wait and observe,
but his field glasses told the tale. When Smith's
skirmish line pushed up the slopes of Billy Goat
Hill, they were met by a sharp volley from the men
in blue. If this was in fact a race, Cleburne's men
had lost. The Federal troops were already swarming
up across Billy Goat Hill.

Cleburne heard the first clash, expected many
more, stood staring at the distant hill fearing his
men had stumbled into the teeth of Sherman's entire force. But the musket fire did not last, Smith's

skirmishers wisely pulling away. Within minutes, the skirmishers, no more than three hundred men, scrambled back into the protected heights of Tunnel Hill. There was blood, but not what Cleburne feared. The damage came mostly from the briars that ripped the shirts and tore through the skin of the men in their mad dash back to safety. With Smith's men quickly forming a line across the face of Tunnel Hill, Cleburne kept his gaze on the Yankees. He saw a great many men in blue, thought, They will come now. They must know we are only a brigade. But there was no formation, no advancing battle lines. To his amazement, the Yankees seemed more interested in labor. He could see logs hauled up the hillsides, shovels at work. More of them appeared through Cleburne's glasses, far more strength than Cleburne had beside him, but still they kept to their newly acquired ground. And there they remained.

"Line up here! Form out to the right! Circle the crest. Captain Gilley, position Company A, to the northern perimeter, and do what you can to dig in! Be aware of the ground out toward the creek!"

Cleburne stood back, allowed Smith to complete the troop dispositions along the western face of Tunnel Hill. But Cleburne observed carefully, guided the artillery batteries into place, all the while holding away the fear that if his lone division was

to hold the hill, they would certainly have to prepare for the enemy to attempt a sweep around their
far north flank. Even now, he could see Sherman's
men crowding the crest of Billy Goat Hill, still
digging in, more timber hauled into place, what
seemed clearly to be a heavy defensive line. He kept
his gaze on them through wet field glasses, felt a
strange sense of excitement, thought, They're taking too long, too much effort to put up a defense
that I would never attempt to assault. They must
believe we are in serious strength here. And so,
they will wait for their numbers to come forward,
waiting to see if I will begin the attack. Cleburne
was surprised, thought, Sherman is apparently
being . . . cautious. That is not what I have heard of
the man. He thought of Hardee, knew the reports
from the great explosion at Shiloh. There, Hardee's men had burst into Sherman, shoving through
his camps, sweeping Sherman's division away in
a riot of pure terror. And yet, he thought, Sherman found his heart. Found the heart of his men,
pulled them back to the fight. And then, he **won**
that fight. He is a confident man, arrogant perhaps. Surely he expects that we will collapse under
his "valiant assault," that his force cannot be held
away. That is what arrogant men believe. It is what
any good general **must** believe. Then, why did they
stop? The skirmish was only that: a skirmish. They
took a few casualties, but we gave them no reason
to hold back. If they had pressed us, we are only

one brigade. He is . . . what? Many divisions? He must not know that. Or he believes he has done enough for one day. He won his victory. Cleburne looked at his pocket watch. Three thirty. Three more hours of good daylight. Perhaps he wishes to watch his next great triumph in full sunlight. And so he will come tomorrow. And if he keeps to that ground, he will grant us a truly wonderful gift. If he will not use the remainder of this day for good purposes, I shall.

He glanced southward, back down the trail, his lone column snaking their way forward, his other two brigades led into position by Cleburne's staff. He walked forward, stood staring out to the north, toward the creek, thought of Polk, protecting the lone railroad bridge over the Chickamauga, what had to be a mile away. He saw now the trailing end of Missionary Ridge, a narrowing spur of land that bent to the right, extending to the east, closer to the creek, and closer to the position Polk had to be. Beyond, he could see the meanders of the creek, the mist clearing, had a jolt of concern for Polk.

"Sir!"

He turned, saw Mangum pointing to a cluster of men on horseback, riding hard toward him, a flag following behind.

"Yes, good. Just the man I require."

He waited, and they halted near him, one man moving up close. He saw salutes from them all, responded with one of his own, said, "Colonel

Govan, there is mischief in these hills. The enemy has occupied that knob to the northwest, but thus far has shown little inclination to attack us here. That will most certainly change. Bring your men up and attach to the right of General Lowrey." He pointed to the north. "Place your men on that narrow ridge that bends to the right, spreading them as far north as you feel able. That will protect our flank, and extend your brigade toward the creek. General Polk is out there, on the creek itself, and I will not have him left alone. General Lowrey has his lines circling the crest of this hill. This ground is Tunnel Hill."

He saw a nod from Govan.

"Yes, sir. I have consulted the map. But, sir, the orders I received from Captain Buck were to form up to the left of Lowrey, extend back southward along this main ridge."

Cleburne respected Daniel Govan, as much as he respected his other brigade commanders. Govan had come to the army from Arkansas, a kinship Cleburne took seriously. The brigade was composed exclusively of regiments from Arkansas, and Cleburne knew most of their officers by name. He also knew they were prepared for any fight.

"Your orders have changed as of this moment. General Polk's brigade is holding position protecting the railroad bridge along the creek. He is vulnerable, and I order you now to fill the space between this hill and his position. Send a courier to locate him, and inform him of your new orders. I assure you, he will welcome your presence."

"But, sir, there is no one on the ridge to our south. My orders were to fill the gap in that direction, linking up with General Walker's division. If my men move north, that ground will be unoccupied."

Cleburne pointed toward Billy Goat Hill, said, "Look out there, Colonel. I have sent a strong skirmish line down through this brush, and their presence will provide ample alarm should the Yankees attempt the same maneuver. Thus far, the Yankees seem to be more interested in digging in than attacking, as though they are expecting us to dislodge them from that far hill. I have no such intentions. My orders are to prevent the enemy from occupying this very ground, and endangering this army's right flank. I am doing so. You can be of much better service out to the right."

"Sir, General Walker—"

He looked at Govan, put a hand on his shoulder. "Daniel, General Walker knows our position, and I shall inform him of our situation. He can extend his right in this direction, should he feel threatened. But look at the enemy. They're not in force anywhere to our left, not without a lengthy march we can observe clearly. I do not know General Sherman's intentions, but it seems that his gaze is directed right here on Tunnel Hill. If the enemy forces a move to our left, we can change position accordingly. But it is difficult ground below us.

Very difficult. There will be no gallant charge up these hills, not through those thickets."

Govan moved his horse slightly, peering down to the dense ground that separated the two hills.

"This is Shiloh all over again, sir. I pushed my boys through ground like this half the day. Those deep holes, water, mud, thorns. Never saw such tangles. But we pushed through it, sir. That attack was successful, for a while. It could be here. That's Sherman, sir."

"We had **surprise** with us, Daniel. Whatever surprise Sherman brought to this field has been erased. Now, there he sits. And no matter how much more strength he brings across that river, we still have the better ground. If we anchor our flank on the edge of the higher ground, and hold fast to these heights, Sherman's numbers might not matter. Bring 'em up quick, Colonel."

Govan saluted him with a smile Cleburne had seen before. "By your leave, General. We'll teach General Sherman he ought to stay on **his** side of things."

Govan turned, rode away quickly, his staff in tow. The column was close, moving fast, Govan ordering them forward at the double-quick. Cleburne kept the horse to one side, saw familiar faces, caught the cheers, smiling salutes as they passed. He pointed the way, called out, "Be ready, my boys! That's Sherman out there! And he's sure to come."

He hesitated, didn't really know what Sherman's name might mean to some of the men, if their morale would be affected by the man's fiery reputation. But there was no hesitation in the troops passing by him, one man raising his musket, calling out to him, "Got Sherman's musket ball right here, sir!"

Others picked up the chant, and Cleburne saw the fight they carried. He stared out past them, toward Billy Goat Hill, saw flecks of movement, an enormous force of blue spread out down both sides, the work ongoing, earthworks and log walls. He stared out with the field glasses, could see a heavy line of men across the crest of their hill, saw hands in the air, as though someone had called them together, the sound reaching him now, a strangely boisterous cheer.

CHAPTER THIRTY-ONE

GRANT

CHATTANOOGA—
NOVEMBER 24, 1863

With the evening meal concluded, Grant had expected the usual crush of unpleasant visitors, men like the quartermaster, Montgomery Meigs, who would punish Grant with some new tirade about the supply routes. If Meigs didn't torment him, the unpleasantness might come from Thomas, the man's stoic manner seeming to Grant to hide a hostile surliness that had made Grant weary. To Grant it seemed that Thomas only dwelled on the negative, the dispatches focusing on bad news rather than the army's successes. Grant knew that Thomas had earned praise, was worthy of the command he had been given, but something in Thomas's tone seemed to push Grant toward criticism. Throughout the day, Grant had absorbed the sounds that rolled down from Lookout Mountain, but the dispatches from Joe Hooker were few and lacking any real details about the fight. Grant had expected that kind of hesitation from Hooker, knew Thomas dreaded any dealings with the man. Hooker had only grudgingly accepted his subordinate role in this campaign, but neither Thomas nor Grant had any patience for the man's bruised ego. Though Grant shared Thomas's uncertainty about Hooker doing the job, by midafternoon word had come that the rebels had been swept clear of the north face of the mountain, a triumph that Hooker could rightfully claim as his own. But Grant had absorbed too much of Thomas's pessimism about Hooker's abilities, couldn't avoid concerns that Hooker might still make some grievous error, handing the rebels back everything he had gained.

No one was cheered by the weight of the gray skies, unending bouts of rain and fog. But, as Grant received word of Hooker's success, the rains had stopped, the fog lifting, the mist clearing. More riders had come, Hooker trumpeting his victory. By late in the day, Grant could see it for himself, blue troops spread across the plateau, their flags caught by a stiff chilling breeze. The rebels were said to be shoved back completely to the east face of the mountain, Hooker insisting that dense fog had masked the rebel positions, that any further advance on this day could be dangerous. Grant had no way of knowing what the conditions were on that part of the mountain, and for now, he would accept Hooker's version of events. Thomas had agreed with Grant that digging in a strong defensive position along the north face of the mountain was wise, that if there was any attempt by the rebels to take back what they had lost, Hooker should at least be prepared. Grant and Thomas both seemed content to let Hooker enjoy his victory. What might happen tomorrow had much to do with the decisions made by Braxton Bragg.

There had been more dispatches as well, the news throughout the day growing brighter for Grant. From Knoxville had come word of a stalemate in the fighting there, that Burnside was holding Longstreet away with a stubbornness no one expected. Grant was enormously relieved. By holding Longstreet away, if only for a few more days, Burnside had given Grant the opportunity to complete the task at Chattanooga.

The rumors about Bragg's withdrawal had calmed as well. Along the vast sweep of Missionary Ridge, it had become clear that Bragg's troops were still in place, had not made the massive retreat Grant had feared. From their perches east of Orchard Knob, the Federal lookouts confirmed that Bragg's defenses had not changed, with one notable exception. Rather than sending support to the beleaguered Carter Stevenson on Lookout Mountain, Bragg was shifting his forces the other way. Grant had ridden forward to Orchard Knob, and along with Thomas, had observed that movement himself, a column of troops punctuated by flags and wagons, all moving northward. There was only one conclusion to draw: Bragg was responding to the sudden appearance of Sherman on Bragg's side of the Tennessee River.

And then, with Grant pacing anxiously around his headquarters, the word finally came from the most important piece of Grant's puzzle. Not only had Sherman's crossing of the river gone without any major problems for the troops, but he had advanced virtually without opposition, his right flank rolling upward to occupy the northern extremes of Missionary Ridge, while his left flank had marched away from the Tennessee River by keeping close to Chickamauga Creek. Sherman's reports reassured Grant that by the next morning, Sherman would begin the last great shove southward, sweeping away any rebel forces from the creek, all the way to Bragg's headquarters. Once Sherman's attack began, Grant was convinced, Bragg's only alternative would be to vacate the ridge altogether, or risk annihilation. That pursuit would not be the cat-and-mouse game that Grant had feared. Sherman would be moving forward, and Bragg would have little opportunity for any head start that would take him out of danger.

With Sherman's reports, the mood of the headquarters camp had boiled over to a raucous chorus of congratulations. For the first time in this entire campaign, Grant felt a burst of buoyancy, that after so many weeks of gnawing frustration, a victory might be at hand.

He sat on the porch of the house, the cigar warming him, stared up at the flickering lights from the great mountain to the south. There was more musket fire than he expected to hear from scattered picket lines. The wind, he thought. Breezy here, must be blowing a gale up there. The rebels will not try anything significant tonight. But Hooker's colonels had best take that for what it is: a warning. If you haven't finished digging in, finish that tonight.

Dana sat beside him, quiet, composing the letter that Grant knew would go to Washington, possibly tonight. Today's successes would make for good reading at the War Department, and Grant heard the pen scratching, thought, Make it lengthy, Mr. Dana. Give the secretary something to help him sleep.

There had been another rain shower just at dusk, but that had blown through quickly, replaced now by a breezy chill. He pulled the coat more tightly around him, knew Rawlins was close by, no doubt scowling at Grant for breathing in the cold night air, when inside, the stone hearth offered so much comfort. The coat around Grant was just warm enough, and he felt the delicious cold in his lungs,

a brisk contrast to the heat from the cigar. He sa-
vored the taste of the tobacco, rolled it around his
mouth as though chewing on it, the smoke led away
by the steady breeze. He glanced at Dana, thought,
I should offer him the smoke, calm him down a
bit. But no, he rather enjoys all that chirping, telling his stories to Washington with broad flourishes.
A great many flourishes today. Yes, this was one of
those rare things, Grant. A very good day, a very
good fight on two fronts. Pay attention to that.
There will be those **other** days soon enough.

To one side of the house, out in a wide street, several of his staff had built a roaring fire, fueled by the
excess timbers carried to town from the woods near
Orchard Knob. Thomas's gift, he thought. Even
he's in a jovial mood, as much as that's possible.

He watched the aides, who gathered close to the
fire, standing alongside a handful of his cavalry
guards, open hands, the light reflecting off smiling
faces. Men were laughing, glances in Grant's direction, and he turned away from that, knew there
would be jolly talk, a few jokes, possibly at his expense. Give them that, he thought. Just . . . keep
it out of my hearing. And Rawlins. Where is that
man, anyway? No, sit tight. You start looking for
him, and no doubt you'll find him.

He looked up now, above the skeletons of the
homes across the street, held the cigar away, pulled
himself up from the chair.

"Would you look at that."

Dana peered up from his paper, said, "What? The fire? Pretty big."

Grant pointed upward. "There. The stars. It's a clear night. Haven't seen that in a while, not around here."

"My God."

Grant wasn't quite as excited as Dana sounded, but he understood Dana, a man whose emotions could explode all over anyone standing near him.

"They're just stars, Mr. Dana."

"No, sir. Well, yes, but . . . look out there. The mountain. There's a fight."

Grant stared up at the dark hulk of Lookout Mountain, had already seen what Dana saw now, scattered flickers of light, like sparks on a piece of flint.

"Skirmishers, Mr. Dana. Nothing more. Men get brave in the darkness. No doubt the rebels are probing, testing just where we are. Their General Stevenson is a good man, to a point. Faced off against him near Vicksburg, Champion Hill. Whipped him. Today, whipped him again." He paused. "I've changed my mind. He let Joe Hooker whip him. Might be a good man. Maybe not such a good general."

"Sir, I must say, without wishing to sound maudlin . . . but the mountain appears covered with fireflies. It's . . . beautiful to behold."

Grant followed Dana's stare, said, "Every one of those fireflies is a musket ball, Mr. Dana. Not so beautiful if you're the target."

"Well, yes, of course, sir. I don't mean to dismiss the importance of the troops. I have only the deepest respects . . . oh, dear. I have offended the honor of the men."

Grant had heard enough, said, "Mr. Dana, no one is offended. It is rather a sight." Grant stepped down from the porch, walked out to the edge of the house, stared out toward Missionary Ridge. "Look here. Another sight."

Dana stood as well, moved out beside him, said, "Oh. The moon is rising. Full moon." Dana paused, seemed captured by some thought. "General, I must observe, there is something reverential to this, to all of this. The wide-open ground, the campfires of the men spread out beyond the town, the dreariness of this place swept away by the Hand of the Almighty. Perhaps it is a gesture, offered to our success. Who among us does not believe we are doing His work here, yes? So much to observe, so much beauty in the midst of the horror. Think of it, sir. Such conflict of symbolism."

Grant didn't respond, moved back to the porch, sat, lit another cigar, smiled to himself. Dana lingered, staring at the moon, and Grant said, "You should write poetry, Mr. Dana. You have a skill for language. General Halleck could benefit from reading such things."

Dana moved up to the porch, sat again, moved a small lantern, lighting the pad of paper.

"I am just a newspaperman, General. Poetry is

not encouraged." Dana paused. "Do you think it will start up again in the morning? Rebels can't be too happy giving up that mountain. Could try to take it back."

"Could. Doubt they will. All the troop movement we saw today was north, away from that place. Bragg knows he can't hold all this ground with the strength he has now. He might try to hit back at Hooker, but we can probably hold on to the place. Like to ride up there myself, see just what that view is like. Still wonder why Rosecrans didn't understand the value of the heights." He realized Dana was watching him, and Grant knew anything he said might end up on Halleck's desk. "Never mind, Mr. Dana. Our attentions should be aimed at tomorrow. I've told Thomas to keep Hooker in readiness to advance. If the rebels need one more push to get them off that mountain, Hooker needs to take advantage. But I don't expect much from the rebels up there. There's that big creek between the mountain and Mission Ridge. Good defensive line. Bragg'll make use of that. It'll shorten his lines, make it easier for him to defend his left flank. We'll see what Hooker finds in the morning. If the rebels give it to him, Hooker should shove right down that mountain to the creek, and if he's got any fire in his backside, he'll find a way to shove across. I'm more concerned that he pay attention to the troops down here, the right flank that butts up to that creek. That's Palmer's corps, and Hooker needs to keep his people close to Palmer's right. This is no time to be careless. No flanks in the air. For all we know, there's rebel cavalry out there, looking for an opportunity."

"But surely, sir, you believe the enemy is on the run? Bragg cannot withstand too many more days like this one. Victory is certain, wouldn't you say?"

Grant pulled at the cigar, the fire at the tip glowing bright orange. "That's probably what Rosecrans said the day before the fight at Chickamauga. Never take anything for granted, Mr. Dana. Bragg's still dangerous. He's got good men in command of good divisions up there. They can shoot straight, and they've got plenty of bluecoats out here to aim at."

The moonlight was already lighting the streets through the town, a shadow cast by Grant's headquarters. The large fire was dying out, the men moving away, Captain Osband's guards moving to their posts, relieving the others who had kept out in the dark, a vigilance Grant appreciated. He focused on the last two inches of the cigar, saw Dana scratching away on his pad of paper, felt relief at that. Sometimes the man just wants to talk too much. One advantage to having Thomas here, he thought. Doesn't like to jabber all the night through.

The wind picked up again, and Grant pulled the coat tight once more. Cold night tonight, he thought. He glanced up toward Lookout Mountain again. Wonder if Hooker thought of that? I bet when they stepped off, he made them leave their packs behind, their coats. Man climbs a big mountain, he sweats, figures he'll not need anything to keep him warm. Mistake. Hooker's probably still in the valley, nice big fire of his own. Has no idea his men up there are chattering their teeth together. Maybe worse for the rebels. Never saw so many bare feet, or maybe that's just the ones we grab. But nobody's lighting big campfires up there with so many skirmishers about. Nothing poetic about that.

It was close to midnight, and he had dismissed most of the staff, kept a handful of aides nearby. He stood staring at the stone hearth, the last few logs crumbling into embers. Thomas stood in the doorway, and behind him, Rawlins seemed to wait, as though wondering if Grant would toss the man out of his headquarters.

"Might as well come in."

"Thank you, sir. My staff is preparing for bed, I see yours is mostly in their quarters. I just thought I would confirm your orders for the morning."

Grant avoided looking at him, kept his eyes on the fading fire. "Why? Something unclear?"

"Not at all."

Thomas moved inside the room, and Grant pondered another cigar, felt too weary for that now. Thomas sat on the small chair with a heavy grunt, seemed to adjust himself, struggling as he always did with the discomfort in his back.

"Are you ill, General?"

"Certainly not, sir. I'll manage. Getting used to it. No choice, really. Could be worse, you know. Oliver Howard's got one arm. Can't imagine that."

Grant knew that Howard had come into camp earlier that evening, a surprise to Grant, since Howard was protecting Thomas's left flank, had positioned his men exactly where Grant ordered, acting as a valuable reserve for Sherman should events to the north go badly.

"Not sure I wouldn't have ordered Howard to ride back up there. He should be with his men."

Thomas nodded. "Told him that. He's pretty adamant that he's not really doing anything helpful where he is. Seems to believe you and I have sat him on a shelf, keeping him out of the fight. He'd rather have been leading the way on Lookout Mountain. Insists he's pretty useless behind Sherman. He did leave one of his colonels in command up there." Thomas paused. "I get the impression he is not terribly impressed with General Sherman."

"After today? How can anyone not be impressed with the accomplishments of today?"

Thomas twisted to the side, stretching. "If Sherman's report is accurate, Howard's right. His troops won't be required. Likely, I won't need his support, either. I hope Sherman's appraisal of his position is sound."

Grant couldn't ignore the flicker of doubt in Thomas's words. "Why wouldn't Sherman's report be accurate?"

"Would never suggest that, sir. But those maps Baldy has . . . they're no good. He knows that, and I recall Sherman hearing that. Baldy says he didn't have time to prepare new ones."

Grant had a flicker of annoyance, thought, You would plant that seed in me? You would inflict your doubts about Sherman on me? Grant looked again to the fire, measured his words, kept his voice as calm as he could. "I have no reason to doubt General Sherman. He says his troops have advanced to the railroad tunnel and are preparing to move along the creek and down the ridge in the morning. Nothing complicated about that."

Thomas scratched his forehead, seemed to hesitate. "I mean no disrespect to General Sherman. But we know how badly chopped up that ground is. We know Bragg sent a number of troops up that way. Surely Bragg knows what Sherman's trying to do. Forgive me for saying so, General, but I've learned that confidence does not ensure success. I offer my congratulations to anyone who succeeds, but only when the campaign has concluded. This campaign has not concluded."

Grant was too tired to entertain Thomas's pessimism. "General Thomas, your orders were made clear, were they not?"

Thomas hesitated, seemed to understand he had

trod into a sensitive place. "Yes, sir. We will maintain readiness until we are called upon."

Grant didn't want the tension between them yet again, looked at Thomas, saw a flash of pain in the man's face, another slight twisting in the chair.

"I disagree with you on that, General. I offer my congratulations to you and your men for the exceptional work taking Orchard Knob. I am grateful for your efforts. Your men will be of service again when called upon, and that could be at any moment. This war cannot be fought by any of us alone. This strategy is my own, and since General Bragg has obliged us by holding his army along that ridge, this plan shall be employed as I intended."

Thomas pulled himself painfully to his feet. "I understand completely, sir. I do hope that General Bragg does not use this beautiful moonlit night to withdraw from that ridge. He suffered a serious defeat today on the mountain. There are no doubt commanders in his camp who believe he should withdraw his army to a more formidable position. He surely understands how badly outnumbered he is."

"I don't have any idea what Bragg understands. Except . . . he knows for certain that your army occupies this enormous swath of ground directly to his front. He cannot maneuver anywhere without expecting you to respond. My job, General, is to create a situation he cannot respond to effectively. That is why Sherman will punish his right flank tomorrow morning. Should Bragg respond to that by weakening his center in any substantial way, you must be prepared to take advantage."

"I am prepared, sir."

"Thank you. Good night, General."

Thomas left without speaking, and Grant felt a nervous stirring, couldn't keep the anger away. He reached for another cigar, fumbled with the matches, the small flame flickering, the cigar lit. He tossed the matchbox aside, felt his heart beating heavily, was fully awake now, stared at the embers. He thought of Baldy Smith, the image of perfection, efficiency. Baldy said the maps were wrong. Sherman knows that. He would not go into a fight without knowing the ground he has to cross. The ground he **did** cross. I am far more concerned that Hooker will do something incredibly stupid up on that mountain, give away his success.

Grant turned, paced across the small room. Give Thomas some benefit, he thought. Perhaps he is carrying more weight on his back than I appreciate. His men lost a fight at Chickamauga that could be one of the worst defeats of the war, certainly the worst defeat suffered by the Army of the Cumberland. He has to answer for that, and so he has been ordered to keep his army in line, while others on both his flanks carry the campaign. That is my doing, those are my orders. I cannot worry about the weight on anyone else's back. If we are successful, the weight will be lifted from us all. It is but one fight, after all. One campaign. There will be others, and if Thomas believes he must fight for some kind of personal honor, he will have his chance. If it does not happen, if this war ends too quickly for that . . . am I to care?

He tossed the cigar into the hearth, scolded himself for his sour mood. Get some sleep, Grant. You will need your wits tomorrow. And by tomorrow evening, we shall know a good deal more about Bragg's army, and what kind of fight they can make. We shall accomplish our goals, or we shall suffer mistakes. I care not a whit for any man who believes his own "honor" matters as much as the blood of the men who will make this fight.

CHAPTER THIRTY-TWO

CLEBURNE

TUNNEL HILL—
NOVEMBER 24, 1863

Hardee had come late that afternoon, and Cleburne had made it very clear just how vulnerable he was, that the gap between his own division and Walker's, down the ridge, meant that any defense between them would be so thin as to be virtually useless. Hardee had responded as Cleburne hoped, had authorized Cleburne to shift even more of his strength to the northern tip of Missionary Ridge, promising to march other troops from the south to fill in the open ground behind Cleburne's left flank.

Hardee also brought him the news he dreaded, but it was no surprise. Lookout Mountain was now mostly in Federal hands. Cleburne knew that the loss of the army's left flank was a defeat Bragg would have to take seriously, that the way could now be open for Yankee troops to swarm all down through the valley that divided the mountain from Missionary Ridge. As darkness came, Cleburne stayed up close to the summit of Tunnel Hill, sent aides probing southward, testing whether Hardee had fulfilled his promise, or if Bragg had reacted to the loss of the mountain by issuing a completely different order. The more Cleburne pondered that, the more convinced he became that, with Sherman's overwhelming numbers to Cleburne's front, the best decision Bragg could make would be to withdraw completely from the ridge, pulling back to a new strongpoint somewhere to the south and east, perhaps back toward the same ground along Chickamauga Creek where the brutal fight had taken place in September.

He had stayed in the saddle well after dark, moving slowly among the men, ensuring that the officers were putting their troops where he expected them to be, the dispositions Hardee had heartily approved. Along the face of Tunnel Hill, Yankee artillery shells pounded and thumped at random, the sight of Cleburne's troops digging in too tempting for Sherman's gunners to ignore.

As Cleburne rode along the narrowing spur to the north, he chewed on a hard piece of stale bread, a remnant in the bottom of his pocket of a better meal the day before. But the men around him were eating nothing at all, their attention focused on the labor of constructing some kind of defensive line against the attack Cleburne knew was coming. The shelling came mostly on the larger hill itself, his men taking advantage of the relative calm farther down along the spur, many of them hidden by tufts of thick brush. The ridge here was no great barrier, nothing like Lookout Mountain, and the farther north he went, the closer he was to the dense, thorny brush, only a slight rise above the ravine Sherman's men would have to push through. The ground was still a challenge for any troops who faced harrowing musket fire, small comfort for Cleburne as he glanced out toward the mass of troops camped now on and around Billy Goat Hill. He thought of Shiloh, the ground just as nasty, brutal fighting against Yankees who, on that ground, had the advantage of shooting downward. But the Confederates there pushed on through, fought the vines as they fought the Yankees, and when they made the last few feet of their climb, it was the Yankees who had broken. It was all the more reason to expect the withdrawal order from Bragg, that this position, no matter the thickets and high ground, would be only a temporary stronghold.

He climbed back toward the crest of the ridge, kept the horse along the backside, avoiding the chance encounter with exploding shrapnel. He saw the speck of light, moved that way, halted the horse, dropped down, felt immediate relief of standing on hard ground. The staff had gathered close around a single lantern, hidden down in a thicket well behind any view from Billy Goat Hill. Cleburne moved close, said to Buck, "Show me the map again."

Buck complied, unrolled the rough paper, and Cleburne knelt low, the light spreading across the sketchy pencil lines. He stared at the one detail he already knew, the winding sweep of the creek to his north and east.

"Sherman should send a good many men by that route. It is far simpler than pushing his people right up to this long ridge. He must know we are here, preparing. If he has no other information, he can hear the axes. That should tell him everything. He may not know how limited our strength is here, but he will know we are making ready for whatever he brings us. If I was in Mr. Sherman's boots, I would keep most of my people closer to the creek, push farther across our north end, forcing us to extend our lines. We are already extended like a blooming fishhook. If Sherman can drive his men through Polk's position, there is little to stop him from moving around behind this ridge completely."

He looked up at the faces, saw the cavalry scout, Kingman, a rugged, filthy man Cleburne respected. Kingman had a talent for crawling through whatever kind of ground lay between the lines, could recite the list of units he saw if Cleburne required it. Right now, Cleburne required only the most basic facts.

"Do we know their strength, Major? Are they still bringing people across the river?"

Kingman was staring at the map, shook his head slowly. "He has three divisions between us and the river right now. Supplies are coming across the pontoons, a few wagons, but they're being careful with their long bridge. We attempted to ram it with a makeshift raft, but they've run ropes or something across the river just above the bridge, catching anything we float down." Kingman pointed to the map, where the creek entered the river. "They put up a pontoon bridge across the creek, not too far off the river. They've got people on both sides of the creek, and that bridge links them together. Guess their engineers are smarter than we thought."

Cleburne focused again on the map. "It isn't about **smart,** Major. It's about mathematics. If the enemy stays to the creek, he will run straight into Polk, and one brigade will not stop even a single division, no matter who is 'smarter.'"

Mangum stood to one side, pointed out over the crest of the hill. "Sir, there's a considerable force right out there. Must be a hundred campfires out to both sides of Billy Goat Hill, and those are just the ones we can see. I didn't study General Hardee's book or anything, and I don't know if it's 'smarter' for Sherman to try to drive right past us along the creek. But I'd be wagering that **those** folks out there are making ready to come right up here."

Cleburne stood. "Extinguish the light."

The aides obeyed, the darkness complete, Cleburne staring into the woods below, trying to regain his vision. He was surprised now by the glow off the treetops, and to the right, toward the far end of the ridge, in the tops of distant trees, the white orb of the full moon. He walked out away from the others, heard the footsteps behind him, knew it would be Buck keeping close to him. He looked up toward the crest of Tunnel Hill, and between the impacts from Sherman's artillery, he could hear the axes, shovels, the low voices of the officers, the work ongoing. Buck walked up beside him, stared at the full moon, rising higher, clearing the tree line to the southeast.

Cleburne said, "Bragg has to be admiring this just like we are. There's opportunity here."

"Sir? Not sure—"

"Clear skies, full moon. Captain, send another courier down toward General Walker's camp. If Bragg sent orders up this way, his aide might have been waylaid by a good bottle of spirits. Might be lost in the woods, for all I know. Walker would know if anyone's out here trying to find me."

"Sir, we have two couriers at General Walker's camp right now. They know to ride quick if there's cause."

Cleburne clenched his fists, rubbed a hand down his face. "There's a fine cause, Captain. We should be using this marvelous moonlight to pull this army off this ridge." He walked to the crest of the hill, stopped just shy, the flashes from a single artillery shell coming down right across from him.

"Damn nuisance, that. Keep your head down, Captain."

Down to one side, he could see the silhouettes of men working, lit by the glow from the moon. Another shell impacted, down to the left, farther down the face of the hill, a man's cry piercing the air. Cleburne clapped his hands together, a gesture of utter frustration. "This is complete insanity. I'm not waiting any longer."

He moved up onto the ridge, stared out at Billy Goat Hill, the vast sea of campfires that Mangum had mentioned. He saw an officer approaching, knew it was Smith, who said, "Sir! Best keep back of the ridgeline!"

"I know where I'm supposed to be, General. I'm riding down to General Polk's position and ordering the artillery pulled away across the creek. If Sherman's going to have a picnic against us tomorrow, at least we can protect some of the guns."

"Sir, what of the batteries here? Except for the face of the hill, we've positioned them in good—"

"Yes, yes. Fine. You shall keep your batteries in place along this hill until I order otherwise. But prepare them for movement. Captain Buck?"

Buck hurried toward him, ducking low, another blast coming down below the ridge. "Sir?"

"I cannot rely on the skills of some courier. You will ride to General Bragg's headquarters and seek a direct response. I must know what is happening, what determination has been made for the disposition of this army. If General Bragg has decided that we should fight on this ground, I must know that so we may place the artillery accordingly. But if we are to retreat, I will not sacrifice my guns, nor my men in useless delays. Go now!"

Buck did not hesitate, ran quickly down the backside of the ridge. Cleburne listened for the hoofbeats of Buck's horse, had a sudden thought. Maybe they've gone already. Maybe Bragg's pulled them off this hill, and just left us up here. Like . . . he forgot. That damned paper I signed. This is how he will punish me.

Cleburne moved out to the edge of the hill, smelled the stinking odor of sulfur from the Yankee shells, watched a red streak arcing toward him from the base of the far hill, falling toward the face of the hill below him. He ignored that, felt a tug on his arm, Smith.

"Sir, you must withdraw."

Cleburne pulled his arm from the man's grasp, stared at the distant fires, then down into the dark abyss below him, the thickets not yet lit by the moon. If we are to be sacrificed, he thought, there will be a very good reason for it. If General Bragg is consumed by the defeat we suffered on Lookout Mountain, so be it. If it is my calling to fight this war alone, then I will obey. But Bragg cannot be allowed to forget that this army has **two** flanks.

He had grown furious waiting for Buck to return.

The shelling had continued, still along the face of the larger hill, and Cleburne had taken Smith's advice, left the horse behind, keeping himself out of sight of any Yankee observer. He walked with angry steps, cursed Buck's tardiness, his boots thumping hard into soft ground. He passed behind the newly dug entrenchments, one piece of satisfaction, that most of that work was now completed. All around him, exhausted men were reclining on the bare ground, a few of them with the remnants of thin blankets, fewer still with anything to eat. He had already spoken with each of the brigade commanders, giving special attention to Polk, the farthest away. Cleburne still expected the order to retreat, but Buck had been gone far longer than it would require a man to make that ride, and Cleburne wondered if there was confusion at Bragg's headquarters, if Bragg was even to be found. Cleburne fumed to himself, kept the aides away, would not risk some indiscreet insult to Irving Buck. This is not his fault, he thought, not at all. He could be dead, for God's sake.

He halted his march, stared ahead. Stop that nonsense. If Buck is delayed, there is a reason. He would not do what Bragg is doing, and simply leave me out here . . . in the dark. He glanced up, eyed the moon, now straight overhead, so bright that the stars were wiped away. It is a perfect opportunity, he thought. How can Bragg just leave these men with no word, no instructions as to what is expected of us?

He turned, walked over to the backside of Tunnel Hill, heard soft voices, men huddled together in their fresh earthworks, shielded from the stiff breeze. The artillery thumped against the far side of the hill, the blasts muffled by the ground. He wanted to climb up once more, to stare at the fires around Billy Goat Hill. But there were hoofbeats now, and he turned abruptly toward the trail leading south. The horseman climbed the rise, dismounted, headed straight for Cleburne. It was Buck.

"Sir! I rode as quickly as I could!"

"It's been three hours! Is your horse lame, Captain?"

Cleburne pulled at his anger, scolded himself silently. Buck stood straight, said, "Sir, I have orders from General Hardee. The general wishes me to tell you directly, sir, that we shall fight on this ground. It is certain that this position will be heavily attacked, and we must be prepared."

Cleburne stared at Buck's face, hidden by the shadow of his hat. "Those words came from General Hardee directly?"

"Yes, sir."

Cleburne put his hands on his hips, let out a long breath, saw his aides moving closer, responding to Buck's message. Cleburne turned to them, said, "Go now to General Polk. Instruct him to recall his artillery, and any of the other batteries I ordered to safety. Instruct the brigade commanders to meet with me here. We must place the guns where they can be most useful. If General Bragg will not make the best use of this moonlight, I shall use it to whatever advantage we have. We shall complete the fortifications any way possible, using such time and the moonlight as we now have."

The men moved away, each one knowing the commander he would seek. Cleburne turned again to Buck, who seemed to anticipate the question, and Buck said, "Sir, my apologies for such delay. It was not a pleasant situation, sir. I was made to remain outside of General Bragg's headquarters while he and General Breckinridge and General Hardee argued about this very decision. I did not intend to overhear that which was improper. . . ."

"What did they say?"

Buck lowered his voice. "General Bragg was insistent that this army, as presently situated, holds ground that no force on God's earth can overrun. There was some agreement with that from General Breckinridge. General Breckinridge was mighty upset about the defeat on Lookout Mountain. He insists we must have our revenge, sir."

"He would have us fight for . . . revenge? What did Hardee say?"

"General Hardee insisted in the most vigorous terms, sir, that this army should withdraw. But his view was not subscribed to."

Cleburne absorbed that, thought, He wrote the book on this subject. Perhaps the others should take the time to read it. Buck leaned in closer, said, "Sir, General Hardee was granted permission to march additional troops to our assistance. General Stevenson's division, specifically. They should be moving this way even now."

"Stevenson? Did Stevenson not suffer mightily today on Lookout Mountain?"

"I wouldn't know about that, sir. But General Hardee is sending him up to support our left."

The questions burst through Cleburne's mind. How did Stevenson withdraw his entire force from Lookout Mountain? Was his defeat so profoundly complete that he ordered a full retreat? Is no one holding a line on those heights at all? How many men is he marching . . . here? He knew Buck wouldn't have the answers to any of that, thought, It's likely that even Stevenson doesn't know his casualty counts, his effective strength. But he will obey, and he will march what remains of his division this way. Thank you, General Hardee.

He heard horses approaching quickly up the trail, looked out past Buck, saw a cluster of riders, a familiar silhouette, and Buck said, "Hooee, sir. That's—"

"General Hardee."

It was just past midnight, no one on either side settling in for any sleep. The shelling from Sherman's guns continued, nearly all of it still aimed at the western face of Tunnel Hill, keeping Cleburne's men there down in their holes. The two commanders rode out along the spur, kept their horses back off the crest, moving slowly past Cleburne's earthworks, which now extended more than a mile. Hardee had kept his staff at a distance behind them, as much for safety as for the privacy of his words with Cleburne. In the moonlight, both men understood that a careful lookout might still spot a gathering of horsemen, that a single artillery shell might do more damage to this end of the line than even Bragg would prefer.

"He's dangerous to himself. I believe that. Worse, he's dangerous to this army."

Cleburne felt a sickening dismay at Hardee's words, said, "I had hoped we would be made dangerous to the enemy."

"We are. If Bragg will allow us to manage this fight the way we ought to. He insists we can maintain our hold on this ridgeline with little more than a regiment of skirmishers. I rather believe he enjoys saying that. And so, he has convinced himself it is true."

"You know it isn't."

"Of course it isn't. It's utter foolishness. Bravado for the benefit of Richmond newspapers. Breckinridge supports him for the same reason. If his name is to be shouted about, let it be for his bravery, not for retreat."

"We shall give them a good thumping here, sir."

"I know. I've seen your dispositions. Your placement of artillery is good, most effective positioning."

Cleburne said nothing, wouldn't tell Hardee he had nearly ordered most of the big guns to begin their retreat across the creek, without knowing for certain that order would ever come.

The rumble from Sherman's cannon thumped mostly behind them, out against the face of the hill, and Cleburne turned, said, "Makes it a mite difficult to place a battery at the tunnel. Ought to have at least something heavy above the tunnel itself. Nuisance, those Yankee gunners."

Hardee stopped the horse, stared upward, and Cleburne pulled on the reins, heard Hardee say, "I'll be damned. Never seen one so clearly."

Cleburne looked upward, saw the arcing shadow cutting across the face of the moon, realized the light had dimmed all around them. To both sides, the men were up from their earthworks, calling out, a hum of excitement through the lines. Hardee said, "It's gonna be full, complete. Just look at that. You ever see an eclipse?"

Cleburne stared up, could see the slight shift in the shadow, the face of the moon blanketed ever so slowly. "It's gonna cover up the whole thing?"

Hardee chuckled. "Looks like it."

He was smiling at Cleburne now, wouldn't embarrass the man, and Cleburne watched the spectacle, more of his men calling out, pointing upward. He looked back toward the sudden silence now, said, "The guns . . . Sherman's stopped shelling us."

Hardee was still chuckling. "For now. Might be a good time to move your battery into position at the tunnel. This won't last too very long. The shadow will slip off the other way, just like it never happened."

Cleburne felt an uneasiness, a memory of very long ago, a small boy, a priest, angry warnings to the townspeople. He stared up, his eyes fixed, said, "I heard it was a sign . . . bad things to come. God's warning."

Hardee seemed surprised. "Some believe that. I believe it's an eclipse of the moon. The earth getting in between the sun and the moon. A shadow. Amazing sight, that's all."

Cleburne kept his eyes skyward, heard nervous talk around him, some of the men standing in the open, watching the event with awe, nervous chatter, and one man, close by, quiet urgency in the man's voice, soft words Cleburne could barely hear. He was praying.

PART THREE

REDEMPTION

AND

REGRET

CHAPTER THIRTY-THREE

SHERMAN

NEAR BILLY GOAT HILL— NOVEMBER 25, 1863

For the first time in days, the dawn came without the misty rains, the hillsides and thickets slowly revealed by a fast-rising sun. Sherman had been up early, his usual routine, had used the brisk cold air to energize him as he rode through the camps of his men. The bugles had sounded early as well, and already the men were up and into formation, word passing through their officers that on this day, there would be no delays. The men he passed already had their muskets, orders going through the lines to load, to prepare, and Sherman thought briefly of breakfast, whether any of these men had time to fortify themselves with the meager rations they carried. Most of the supply wagons remained on the far side of the

Tennessee River, a precaution in the event of disaster. But Sherman had every confidence that in this campaign, there would be no disaster. When the enemy had been crushed, the wagons would come soon enough, the men around him now sure to enjoy a meal laced with the raw satisfaction that comes from victory.

He had moved out first to the left, closer to Chickamauga Creek. Most of the troops who had been positioned north of the creek had crossed southward on the smaller of the pontoon bridges, adding to the strength that Sherman could feel around him. The horses he heard were mostly artillery batteries, moving closer to the enemy's positions, what the scouts had told him were pockets of infantry, scattered guns along the hilly ridge to their front. He knew of the rail line to the east, cared little for making an assault only to punch artillery shells through railcars. His orders from Grant had told Sherman what he already knew, that his primary goal, the goal for this entire army, was to drive the rebels off the great long ridge, and if they did not withdraw, he would crush them.

He had heard the reports of Hooker's victory the day before, had barely heard the thumps that peppered the face of Lookout Mountain. He never thought there was much purpose to Hooker's advance, beyond the diversion meant to pull the enemy's troops in that direction, possibly weakening the position that Sherman would attack. Sherman believed with absolute certainty that Hooker's success had been the product of luck, that even with the help of Sherman's own division, Hooker's men had stumbled up and over rocky cliffs to find a woefully undermanned enemy, troops who had no expectation of any blue wave suddenly pushing into their mountain perch. Sherman cared little for Hooker at all, a man best known for failure, believed he had been sent to Tennessee as a panicky afterthought by Henry Halleck. Yes, he thought, you are a dashing, handsome man who draws camp followers like insects to honey. If you focused more on fighting, and less on drunken debauchery, you might not have been sent to this wasteland in the first place. But after yesterday, there will be newspaper headlines, no doubt about that. Sherman couldn't help feeling the disgust for the newspapermen who were flocking around Hooker now, like so many mosquitoes. He is most certainly dancing merrily across his mountain meadows, Sherman thought, chirping like the morning's songbirds about his great victory. Fine, General. Enjoy that while you can. But let us see if you can offer General Grant more than a single day's glory.

Sherman was less dismissive of Oliver Howard, Hooker's subordinate. Howard had brought a full division to camp just behind Sherman's right flank, would act as a reserve, should Sherman require it. Sherman couldn't object to that at all, knew it was Grant's textbook precautions. Grant had placed

Sherman at the point of the spear, and whatever else Grant ordered behind Sherman was only sound strategy. But Sherman's success the day before had given him the confidence that Howard would not be needed at all. If Howard's men saw any action, it would come in the aftermath of Sherman's victorious sweep down Missionary Ridge, a mop-up perhaps of the rebel stragglers Sherman had passed by, once Bragg's army had been destroyed.

He pushed the horse past a cluster of timber, heard men talking, a campfire suddenly doused, someone aware the commanding general was riding past. He acknowledged that with a quick glance, saw an officer standing beside a horse, the man holding a salute. Sherman returned it, couldn't see the man's face, could just make out the colors, Illinois. He moved quickly past, saw more troops filling a narrow grassy field, more colors, more horses.

Sherman knew that Grant had ordered Hooker to press forward again, testing the rebel strength that remained on Lookout Mountain. It was still part of Grant's strategy, creating confusion in Bragg's camps about just where he should defend. The maps showed a wide creek east of the mountain, the last barrier to an advance against the south end of Missionary Ridge, the opposite flank from where Sherman was now. If the mountain was wholly in Federal hands, the next line of battle for Hooker would certainly be the creek. Sherman had no idea what Hooker would do, and for now, he didn't

care. That was miles away, and if Hooker was successful in driving down off the mountain, pushing
straight into the base of Missionary Ridge, or even
past it, Sherman knew it would be only because
the rebels were more focused on Sherman. Bragg
knows the greater threat is here, he thought. And I
am quite sure he relishes thoughts of busting me in
the mouth.

There were too many memories of Louisiana,
long before the war, the two men familiar acquain-
tances, though no one would describe them as
friends. He never cared for me, Sherman thought,
seemed always to be fearful of me, as though every
opinion was an insult, every conversation some
hidden assault on his honor. What was he fighting
against? No one there particularly liked the man,
but no one challenged him to a duel. He seemed
to expect that, as though he suffered through every
day in some struggle all his own, a duel with himself. Well, today, we shall bring that to pass. If he
ever believed I was a challenge to his honor, to his
dignity, today, I will prove him correct.

Grant's final order had come to Sherman very
late, after midnight, responding to Sherman's reports of glowing success the day before. Sherman
was ordered to launch his primary assault early,
against whatever rebel forces were in front of him.
The daylight had not yet spread across the ground
his men would cross, and he stared impatiently to
the east, knew it would come very soon. He knew

that Grant would be waiting, expecting to hear the first thunder from Sherman's guns.

Sherman kept the horse moving, couldn't help a wave of nervousness, glanced out to several batteries placed with a perfect field of fire toward where the rebels seemed to be the day before. He wasn't entirely certain just where they were positioned now, had been told by Grant that Bragg had responded to his surprising presence by marching a column of troops northward up the ridge. It matters very little, he thought. Unless Bragg has sent his entire army to mass together on this part of the ridge-line, he cannot hold us away. And if he weakens his center, then he merely opens the door for Thomas's people to waltz straight up to the face of the ridge. No, Bragg is caught in a hard squeeze, and it makes very little difference whom he marched up this way. Once we step off, they will not stop us. It simply isn't possible.

He watched a formation of men moving into line, their officers aware he was watching them, crisp precision, self-conscious looks his way. He held his cigar tightly in his teeth, gripped the leather straps, felt the nervous churning inside. It was this way before every fight, what had once been a kind of sickening terror, that any order he gave would be a grievous error, that men would die because he made a mistake. That kind of fear had been with him since the first fight at Bull Run, far worse then, but still it followed him, a struggle he tried to hide from his staff, from any of his officers. The torment angered him, and he tried to keep his thoughts **out there,** aiming his impatient wrath at someone else, some show of sluggishness that would give Sherman an excuse for blistering a man who might not always deserve it.

He spurred the horse again, moved up a low incline, the daylight expanding his vision. He continued to climb, seeking a better vantage point, the horse splashing along a muddy trail, a narrow path through tall thin trees. The staff was strung out behind him, and he ignored them, had no need for orders, for couriers. That would come soon, when that first order went out to his division commanders, those few words that carried such weight, that would put this enormous force into motion. The horse carried him out onto clear ground now, the rocky crest of a bald hill. He pulled the reins, stopping the horse, studied the ground. The sky was lighter still, and he was puzzled to see a taller hill to the front, silhouetted by the glow of the rising sun. He glanced around, the hill he was on falling away in all directions. He could see it plainly now, a rocky knob, his men manning batteries down both sides, smoldering remains of campfires spreading out to both sides. There was brush in vast thickets, a flat plain spreading out to his right. The anxiety in his brain tightened, fueled by questions. The staff had caught up to him, kept back, other officers on the hill watching him, as though expecting orders.

He kept his stare on the far ridge, felt overwhelmed by a sudden burst of uncertainty, questions he did not want to ask. But the fear had anchored inside him, a voice in his brain he couldn't ignore, that something was very wrong, that the ground was not what he expected it to be.

The butt of the cigar was chewed to mush, and he spit it out, glanced around again, the artillery batteries making ready, officers calling out orders. He looked back toward the staff, felt a cold pit in his stomach, searched the faces, his voice coming out in an unexpected shout.

"McCoy!"

The man rode forward, and Sherman pointed out to the far ridgeline.

"What ridge is that? What hill?"

McCoy didn't respond, and Sherman felt the familiar fury growling through him.

"I asked you, Captain, what ground is that?"

"I don't know, sir. Begging your pardon."

"What ground is **this**?"

"We were informed by the scouts that this was Missionary Ridge, sir."

"What scouts?"

"Not certain of that, sir. I assumed you had been given a report by the cavalry last evening. Perhaps the skirmishers reported. There are the maps—"

"The maps show nothing like this. This ground is not where it is supposed to be."

He silenced himself, clamped his jaw shut, knew

how ridiculous he sounded. McCoy looked back to the other aides, as though seeking help, and Sherman spurred the horse again, moved out across the crest of the open hill, past another battery, saw an officer, sword in hand, guiding his men into formation. Sherman stopped again, could make out the man's face, young, familiar.

"Major, what do you call this ground?"

The man saluted him, and Sherman returned it out of reflex, the man responding with a shout. "Sir, we call this Tennessee! Tonight it will be Federal ground once more!"

Sherman ignored the mindless boasting, dug his spurs into the horse's flanks, moved on past, his temper flooding through him. He rode downhill now, saw more troops in line, avoided their officers, didn't need the annoyance of more glad-handing patriotism. He stared out again to the wooded hill before him, looked back to the left, saw another smaller hill, the ground cut and uneven. But his eyes centered on the larger bulge out in front of him, another bare knob, ground that his artillery had targeted throughout the night, what the observers insisted was an enemy laboring at their defenses.

"Why is there a valley between these hills?"

McCoy was there again, the others, no one answering him, but there was no answer he wanted to hear.

He saw movement on the far ridge, the dawn

expanding with a soft pink glow above that larger hill, silhouettes of men in motion. He raised his field glasses, felt a cold paralysis, his eyes scanning, absorbing the details, clearer by the minute. The ridge extended to the left, seemed to fade downward, the face of the hill specked with artillery batteries, rifle pits.

McCoy said, "We do know that the creek is up to the left, sir. Is that what you were asking?"

Sherman felt sick, a haze of blurriness in his eyes. He ignored McCoy, knew exactly where the creek was, kept his eyes on the tallest mound, another bald hill, like this one, could see with perfect clarity, just below the crest of the tallest hill, the mouth of a railroad tunnel.

"It seems, Captain, that I have misinterpreted our position. My dispatch to General Grant last evening might have been somewhat inaccurate. The rains yesterday . . . there was no way to be certain." He raised his field glasses again, focused first on the tunnel, could see rebel batteries spread out to both sides, movement, men, rifle pits, earthworks, cut logs, the growing daylight revealing rows of musket.

McCoy was still there, the man's words coming with high nervousness. "Sir, there's a good bit of distance between us and the enemy. We do not appear to be on Missionary Ridge."

Sherman wanted to strike the man, slap him with his sword, held the fury inside, the ice in his chest expanding, a quivering in his hands. He felt the worst of it now, the terrifying fog in his brain, clouding his thoughts, his reason, his courage. He closed his eyes, felt suddenly like crying, fought that, a silent screaming struggle, his heart pounding. The image of yesterday came to him, the rain and fog and mist that hid so much of the terrain, that drew him into a trap of overconfidence, a trap of his own making. There was talk behind him, the staff offering opinions, advice, worthless sounds his brain tossed away.

He opened his eyes, blinked through the blurriness, his mind alive with curses, fury at his own weakness. He tried to turn it outward, aim it elsewhere, said in a low voice, "Damn the fog, damn this miserable weather, this miserable place. Damn Baldy Smith and his maps, damn the enemy for knowing his own ground better than we do. Damn my own arrogance for believing I can do anything Grant requires of me."

Grant. The thought brought him back to a sharp moment, the image of the small, quiet man, the subtle smile, the warm handshake. He took a deep, cold breath, tried to calm the hard thumping in his chest. McCoy had backed away, seemed to understand what Sherman was doing, and Sherman turned to him, forced calm into his words.

"It appears our estimates of our position are in error. Our orders are to dislodge the enemy from Missionary Ridge, and crush his right flank. We will carry out those orders. It just appears that there

is a bit more territory to cover than I had first believed." He paused, forced the words out through
a clenched jaw. "Captain, it is time. Send word to
the commanders that they may proceed as ordered,
make every effort to cross this ground, and when
possible, confront the enemy."

The first wave pushed through a storm of
rebel artillery, and when they reached the
base of the ridge, they were struck hard by
rebel musket fire. Many of the men stumbled into
a surprise, what seemed to be good fortune, a line
of abandoned earthworks. But the rebels who had
been there had withdrawn up the hill above them,
allowing the Federal troops to gather close to the
hill, but not much closer to their enemy. And then
the crossfire from rebel muskets along the ridgeline
poured down through them, artillery to both sides
rolling shot and shell into the men who had nothing but brush to protect them. Within minutes, the
wave collapsed, many of the troops falling back to
their original position.

Out to the right flank, the more open ground,
those men met with the same fate, absorbing rebel
fire for too long across too much open space, most
of that from a vicious crossfire that kept them far
back of the rebel works. Though the morning was
clear and cold, fog still lingered, drifting through
the valleys between the rugged hills, adding to the

doubts of the men who drove forward, just what kind of enemy, how much strength they were confronting.

He sat high on the horse, strained to see through the smoke, cursed the new layer of fog that masked most of the rebel position. The musket fire was continuous, the waves of artillery adding to a chaotic blend of sounds that took away any detail, any kind of organization. For the first hour, the reports had come to him, a parade of couriers each with the same plea from their commanders, desperate calls for support, for reinforcements, that the ground took away any advantage they might have in numbers. The casualties were many and everywhere, officers, men he knew well, others, pulled back out of the brush, off the open ground. But many more still lay in the open, the rebels taking careful aim, punching down every man in blue who made the effort to help the wounded.

He moved the horse to different vantage points, none better than the last, kept his mind focused on whatever help he could provide, shifting troops to assist those in the worst part of the fight. The staff was doing their job as well, working with the couriers, passing along the orders that would maneuver the regiments and brigades where they were most needed. Through it all, the sounds and smells of the fight drove into him, sweeping away the fears, his quiet terror. But he could not lie to himself, and now, even worse, he knew he could not lie to Grant, that his errors from the night before could not be repeated. There was no victory, no progress in securing the larger hill, the ridgeline, and by 8 A.M., new reports reached him that the enemy was bringing more troops up along the ridge from the south, strengthening their defensive position. With a hard stare back toward Chattanooga, Sherman knew he had no option. Ignoring the assault to his pride, he sent word to Grant. There was still no accurate estimate of the strength he was facing on the northern end of Missionary Ridge, how his numbers compared to what the rebels had on their good ground. But there was help, if he required it. The message went back to Chattanooga with the kind of urgency Sherman had rarely employed in any note to Grant. He needed reinforcements. It was time for Oliver Howard to move up on Sherman's right flank.

With the addition of Howard's division, somewhere in Sherman's mind, the calculations flowed past, that no matter the fog and smoke and confusion of the fight, he would now have thirty thousand troops on his end of the line. The attacks thus far had been disjointed, heavy skirmish lines testing the ground, the enemy's defenses, the expectation that the enemy would give way, or would simply be overrun by vastly greater numbers. As the sun rose higher, Sherman understood that his confidence had been misplaced. So far, Sherman had yet to drive the enemy anywhere. For two long hours, Sherman moved back and forth among his commanders, furious at everyone, more furious at himself. For another two hours, the fight mostly stalled, Sherman's men pulling back, regrouping, bloodied officers struggling to pull their men back together.

At eleven in the morning, Howard's troops reached Sherman's lines, their commander reporting personally to Sherman. As the new formations came together, Sherman knew that somewhere close to Chattanooga, Grant was watching, waiting for the results they had all expected, waiting to hear of Sherman's certain triumph. It was all the inspiration Sherman required to push away the fear, the paralysis, the doubts. With his men regrouped, their lines re-formed, the officers prepared, and the artillery poised to protect the men, Sherman gave the order. It was time to try again.

CHAPTER THIRTY-FOUR

CLEBURNE

TUNNEL HILL—
NOVEMBER 25, 1863

The first wave had been a beautiful sight, massed lines of blue that stretched out past both flanks of Cleburne's position on Tunnel Hill. The first clash of fire had been glorious and brutally destructive to the Yankees, Cleburne's artillery doing the most effective work, a storm of canister that wiped great gaps through the men in blue, pinning them down, keeping them off the hillside in any kind of useful strength. The confusion among the advancing Yankees had been absolute, the men crawling forward through the brush and thickets, and when they were too close for the artillery to find them, the fiery sheets of musket fire from the men in Cleburne's earthworks proved just as deadly. The men in blue had no alterna-

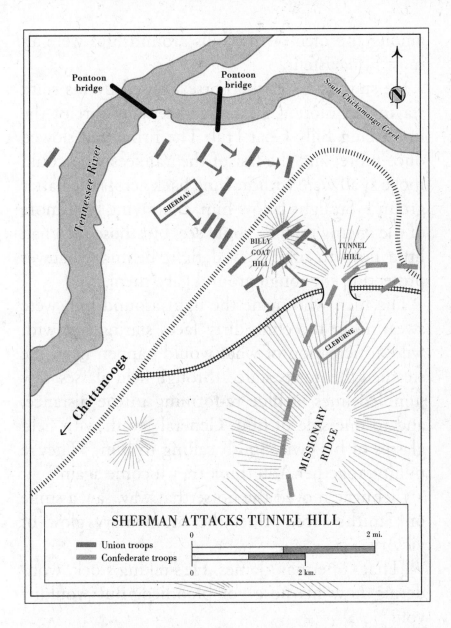

SHERMAN ATTACKS TUNNEL HILL

Union troops
Confederate troops

0   2 mi.

0   2 km.

tive but retreat, and as they pulled away, Cleburne
could see what they left behind, the valley between
the two hills flecked with dead and wounded. From
his own men, the cheers went out, and Cleburne
had seen it for himself, that the casualty counts

among the men on the hills around him were al-most nonexistent.

He stayed up on the horse, chased by his staff, staying in motion all along the main part of the line facing Billy Goat Hill. The firing had slowed once more, and the last of the Yankees who could move at all were withdrawing back across the flatter ground. Straight below him, the ravine held more of the enemy than he could see, but those men had little fight to offer, stayed tight behind whatever protection the rough ground gave them.

The men who made the fight around him were sweating in the chill, dirty faces staring out with wild anticipation of what would happen next. He steadied the horse, stared through field glasses, saw jumbled lines of blue re-forming in the distance, and to one side of him, General Smith with field glasses of his own, Smith calling to him, "They're pulling together. You think they'll come again?"

Cleburne moved the horse that way, saw a smile on Smith's face, pride, the momentary glow of victory.

"That's Sherman, James. He's taking stock, won-dering how his nose got bloodied. But wouldn't you?"

"Sir?"

"Wouldn't you come again? Look at them. The scouts said three divisions. From the flags we can see, there's at least that many. That assault wasn't very strong, a brigade, maybe more. They're holding back, feeling us out, a test to see how many muskets we've got."

Smith kept the smile. "I suppose, sir, we passed that test."

Cleburne kept his stare on the distant knob, could see men on horseback standing in the open, saw the flap of the flag, thought, Yes, general, I see you as well. Did we surprise you? Did you expect us to disappear from these heights? Our retreat last night might still have been the correct decision. But we're past that now, past worrying about whose strategy is better, who's making mistakes.

Bragg had surprised him yet again, had made a brief inspection along the lines just at dawn, approving the positioning of Cleburne's men. There had been no opportunity for any kind of discussion about withdrawing, Bragg sweeping past him with a cursory glance at the lines, the defensive works. And just as quickly as he rumbled up the trail, Bragg had disappeared again, back toward his headquarters. But Hardee had come as well, seemed to wait for Bragg to clear out of the way. Hardee did more than glance, rode deliberately through the cut logs, acknowledging the men with praise for their efforts, drawing the kind of salutes Cleburne expected. But Hardee had moved away as well, and in his path had come reinforcements, the commanders farther down the ridgeline shifting position, peeling off regiments that could be spared, adding to Cleburne's strength.

He kept the stare through the field glasses, could see the men in blue flowing through distant brush, men on horseback, the reflection off muskets, swords, bayonets.

"General, they're forming up, or will be very soon. Keep your men tight together, make every effort to fill in any gaps. And instruct them to aim downward."

He didn't wait for a response, felt foolish giving James Smith the kind of orders any green lieutenant should understand. But Cleburne couldn't avoid the anxiousness, the raw excitement of feeling the enemy so close, the pressure, the brute force of so many guns driving hard right toward the center of his lines.

He spurred the horse, always a risky thing to do, the animal leaping forward, Cleburne holding himself steady in the saddle. He gripped hard with his legs, rode out closer to the nearest battery, saw the commander there, Shannon, the man watching him come, a crisp salute. Cleburne returned it from reflex, said, "Well, Lieutenant, have the Mississippians been able to hit anything this morning?"

It was the ongoing game, the rivalry between the Arkansans and the men from the delta country, and the hard look on Shannon's face betrayed a fierceness that made Cleburne regret the jest.

"We've taken their measure, sir. We're prepared for more. Lost a couple of good men, but we'll make do. Plenty of canister. All four Napoleons have hit their mark more than once. Short range, mostly."

Cleburne took Shannon's words with the same gravity the man offered them. The Mississippi battery was positioned in close support of Smith's brigade of infantry, and down the line another battery was dug in, centered right above the mouth of the railroad tunnel. Cleburne pulled the horse's reins, said to Shannon, "Fire as low as you can, Lieutenant. That's a steep hill."

He felt suddenly useless, like a strutting martinet, had no reason to give any good artilleryman advice. But Shannon saluted again, said, "We'll make you proud of us, sir. We'll give them our best."

He saw the pride in the young man's face, heard the confidence in his words. He nodded, no smile, felt a strange burst of fear that Shannon might not survive this fight.

"Keep yourself low as well, Lieutenant. No carelessness."

"These guns shall be protected, sir. They don't take kindly to Yankee hands. They'll not leave this hill without my orders, sir."

It's not the guns I'm thinking of, Lieutenant.

He kept the words inside, no time for a show of sentiment, spurred the horse again, moving past a line of cut trees, men settling behind, checking their muskets, sergeants and officers giving the familiar commands. He rode closer to the second battery, Arkansans commanded by a young lieutenant he knew well, Tom Key. Key was sighting one of his six guns, his gunners calling out Cleburne's presence. Key looked up toward him, then back to the gun, and Cleburne avoided any kind of joviality, knew Key took his work very seriously, far more than some rivalry with any other battery.

"How is it, Lieutenant? The crews holding up?"

Key looked at him with a glimmer of hostility, and Cleburne knew it wasn't aimed toward him.

"We killed a pile of 'em, sir. Lost four men. Jake Masters, for one. Neighbor of mine. We'll make them pay for that. I see 'em forming up out past that hillside. They want this tunnel like it's some prize."

"They won't get it, Lieutenant."

"No, sir. And they'll die tryin'."

Cleburne watched Key move to another of his guns, low talk with the crews, cold efficiency. Cleburne didn't wait for a salute, moved back up to the crest of the hill, saw Buck there, the others, couriers riding up. Mangum rode out to meet him.

"Sir! By Jesus I wish you wouldn't ride out there so close to the front. Not on that blamed horse, anyway. You're makin' a mighty fine target."

Cleburne ignored Mangum's concern, had heard it before, the lawyer not yet the warrior. Cleburne kept his focus on the couriers, messages delivered to Buck, who looked toward him now.

"Nothing urgent, sir. The troops all down the line have closed up, pulled in tight, expecting the

Yankees to come anytime. There's not as much happening down to the right, on the spur of the hill.
Colonel Govan's expecting the Yankees to maybe
move his way. He's ready."

Cleburne looked at his watch, nearly eleven.
Sherman. A whole day still in front of him. He's
not going anywhere else.

"Captain, send word to each brigade commander
to be prepared. I suspect they are, but let them know
I'm paying attention to every part of the lines. So
far, the fight looks to be right here, so I'll keep to
this part of the line."

"Yes, sir."

Cleburne felt his breathing, hard and quick, felt
cramps in his legs from gripping the horse, tried to
relax that, clearing away the talk, the messages, the
concerns. For one long moment he kept his eyes
on Billy Goat Hill, felt a strange pressure, a great
weight pushing against him. This is what it means
to be in the middle of it all, he thought. This is
what it means to **hold on.**

At Chickamauga, Cleburne's men had spent the
greater part of that fight moving forward. This was
very different. He thought of Bragg, his love of this
ridge, the grand position on good high ground. He
could be right after all. But it's not over. And Sherman won't waste time. We bloodied his nose, yes.
But just maybe . . . he **likes** it that way.

The assault began just as before, but the numbers in the blue lines were much deeper, a far stronger push than Cleburne had seen earlier. Once more, Sherman's advance overlapped the most prominent bulge along Tunnel Hill, and once more the artillery did the greater part of the work.

Cleburne kept to the horse, rode slowly through dense smoke, fought the coughing, the tears in his eyes from the spent powder. The thunder was continuous, bright flashes from the two closest batteries, pouring sprays of shrapnel into targets Cleburne couldn't see. To the left, the flatter ground, he saw the blue formations pushing up to the base of the hill, the Mississippians aiming their twelve-pounders that way. The blasts from the four Napoleons seemed to rupture the blue masses, formations breaking down. But still they came, and Cleburne felt the first wave of panic, rode that way, knew the ridgeline farther to his left was manned by the men who had marched most of the night, Carter Stevenson's men. He saw Buck, waved him close, shouted through the din of cannon fire, "Go now, to the left. Find General Stevenson, or his nearest brigade commander. We must have additional support closer to the left. The enemy is in strength there!"

Buck nodded, silent, the quick salute, rode quickly away. Cleburne watched the blue lines advancing, some of those men hidden by the thickets, some stopping to fire muskets, aiming at targets farther up the hill, men well protected behind their logs. Mangum was calling him again, the same urgency, "Sir! You must not present yourself this way!"

Cleburne ignored him again, saw uneven rows of Yankees moving up closer to the tall hill, most of them disappearing out of his view, huddling close to the base, some of them close to the rail-road tunnel itself. The musket fire roared to life, some of the men in their works farther down the hill. The artillery slowed now, fewer targets, the Yankees too close below them. But the troops were seeking targets of their own, solid volleys now re-placed by scattered shots, men taking careful aim, the Yankees with nowhere else to go. The infantry officers were screaming out orders, and Cleburne moved closer to the line along the forward crest of the hill, saw Smith's men rising up, aiming down-ward, then dropping back, reloading. The Yankees were returning fire, a sharp whistle of musket balls flowing up past Cleburne, most of it harmless, the lead balls arcing far past him, over the crest of the hill. He moved closer to the works, had to see it for himself, saw the officers watching him, call-ing their orders out with more volume, respond-ing to the new bursts of firing from below. The men stood as they fired, took their aim at steep angles, and he saw an officer waving to him, a lieutenant.

"Sir!" the lieutenant exclaimed. "They're right

below us! No more than fifty yards! We've got 'em penned up, sir!"

The man suddenly tumbled backward, his hat flung to one side, facedown into brush. Cleburne absorbed the shock of that, Mangum close behind him again, saying, "Sir! Back here! You must withdraw!"

Cleburne ignored him still, moved past the fallen officer, guided the horse downward, a narrow trail, keeping a tight grip on the reins, the horse obeying with careful steps. Men were noticing him now, surprised looks, brief cheers from blackened faces, the dark eyes watching him. But there was no time for celebrating, the men pulled around by their officers, muskets reloaded, men standing, aiming downward, firing, reloading again. The air was alive with the buzzing and cracking, more of the high whistles, the quick zips and pops of lead against logs, against stone. The batteries opened up again, the blasts pouring out straight across where Cleburne sat, the horse reacting with a hop, jerking backward. Cleburne kept his knees tight, a hard grip on the reins, No, stay here! I will see! Another officer called to him, the man's voice obliterated by the sounds of his own muskets, but Cleburne saw past the works now, a cluster of blue, the men lying flat in a bowl of thick grass, no more than twenty yards away.

He heard a sound behind him, was surprised to see another horse, Smith, the man with a pistol in

one hand, and Smith said, "Sir! They're withdrawing on my right! With your permission, sir, I shall
order a pursuit!"

Cleburne looked down the hill where Smith
pointed, saw the men up, ready, watching him,
watching their own general.

"Yes! Go!"

Smith was away quickly, and in less than a minute, the men were up and over their own earthworks, pouring out down the hill with a terrifying
scream, more of them stumbling along the steep
slope than any kind of organized advance. He
moved the horse that way, saw Smith dismount,
pistol and sword, following close behind his men.
Cleburne felt the raw, cold thrill, the screams of the
men like a thousand banshees, a child's nightmares
long forgotten, the terror now striking toward the
enemy, sent by his hand. He drew his own sword,
raised it high, called out, no sounds but the musket
fire, the artillery, the rebel yell.

Within a half hour, Smith had pulled his
men back to their defenses, breathless
and delirious, more of the backslapping
pride, some with hearty laughter through their
gasping breaths. Others kept the grim stare, what
Cleburne knew well, the men who ignored small
victories, who tended first to their muskets, tightening the bayonets, checking cartridge boxes. The

sounds of the fight had drifted away to scattered volleys, a hard skirmish far to the right, well beyond where he could see. Others were taking their aim farther down the hill, and he saw that now, men in blue in the open ground, some crawling, men with lighter wounds. But there was no cover, no terrain to hide them, and so, the men on the hillside took their time, made the careful aim, the single shots that dropped the wounded man flat into the grass.

He turned away from that, thought, No, not proper. Save it for the men who can hurt you. But he wouldn't hold them back, wouldn't temper the lust for the fight, the hatred for the Yankees.

He moved the horse back up the hill, had to know what was happening farther down the line, out on the spur to the east. But the firing that way had been light, a surprise, no real attempt by Sherman to drive past his right flank. He pulled the horse up to the crest, caught a cool breath of clear air, coughed out the smoke, saw Buck, who saluted him, said, "Sir! I spoke with General Hardee! He was down to the left, keeping a good eye on the lines there."

Cleburne was suddenly concerned. "Does he wish to see me? Is there a problem?"

"Oh, no, sir. Not that he said. The enemy is keeping their assault up this way."

Cleburne looked down that way, southward, saw a column of troops moving up at the double-quick, their flag, Kentucky. Buck smiled now, pointed.

"Those would be General Lewis's brigade, sir. Gen

eral Hardee ordered them to march up here. General Lewis is to make himself known to you upon his arrival. Uh . . . right now, sir."

Cleburne turned the horse, saw a dapper man, a wide, perfect hat, followed by four aides and the color bearer.

"General Cleburne, I believe! General Joseph Lewis, sir. It is a pleasure to make your acquaintance. I am told you might require my men up this way. I am at your disposal, sir."

Cleburne offered a hand, and the man seemed surprised, took it with a smile, and Cleburne said, "Thank you. Your assistance is appreciated."

"My, a gentleman to boot. Forgive me, sir. I've heard tales of the Irish fighting man. You give lie to the image, sir."

Cleburne wasn't sure what the man meant, realized it was most likely a compliment. "Not sure about the other Irishmen in this army, General, but I intend to kill Yankees until the job is complete. Does that strike you as acceptable?"

"Oh, my, yes! Good one! Allow me to help, sir. Where should I place my men?"

Cleburne saw the column still moving up the slope of the hill, pointed behind the crest. "For now, put them in a reserve just off the knob here. We can expect another assault."

"Are you certain, sir? Your men have done exemplary work driving the enemy away. Mighty fine effort, if I do say."

Cleburne detected a hint of politics in the man's tone, pointed again. "Right back there, General. When they come again, we'll see where they hit us."

"By your leave, sir!"

The orders went out quickly, the Kentuckians following, lining up just back of the crest. Cleburne turned, saw Buck pointing toward the front side of the hill, saw Lieutenant Key waving frantically toward him. Cleburne spun the horse around, had no more time for Lewis's pleasantries, pushed the horse up close to Key, who said, "Sir! We must have support to the right. The enemy came within twenty paces of my guns. We cannot depress the angle once they're on the face of the hill. We're losing crew as quick as we can fire. I had men roll rocks down on them, anything we could find. If we lose these guns, sir, they could advance right over the hill."

Cleburne looked back the other way, toward the Mississippi battery. "Return to your guns. I'll have your support."

He motioned to Buck, said, "Go to Lieutenant Shannon, order him to move two of his guns out to the right of the Arkansas battery. We must have better crossfire across this hill. Send a courier to Douglas's battery, order them to expend more fire downward. No wasting ammunition seeing how far they can shoot."

Buck was gone, and Cleburne saw a satisfied glare from Key, who saluted him, moved quickly back over the edge of the hill.

More couriers were coming in, Mangum, the others intercepting them, and Cleburne moved that way, said, "Is there any difficulty? Are there weaknesses we must confront?"

The couriers deferred to Mangum, who said, "Sir, the lines are holding well. The Yankees are not putting any strong force to the far right. Colonel Govan is secure in his position. He requests, sir, that we send more of the enemy his way."

He looked at Govan's courier, saw a hint of a smile.

"Return to Colonel Govan, corporal. Offer him my respects and tell him that if he desires to meet the enemy, we shall do our best to arrange that. Perhaps when they're in our stockades. But advise the colonel that it is wise to temper one's wishes. There are still a great many Yankees out there."

The man wiped away the smile, saluted, was gone up along the ridgeline.

Cleburne moved again toward the front crest of the hill, smoke lingering in the deep valley beneath him.

"They coming again, sir?"

He looked back at Mangum, felt energized by the question. "Of course they are, Lieutenant. That's still Sherman, and as I told Govan's courier, he's got a good many men to throw against us."

"Then we'll keep killing them, sir!"

Cleburne knew the joke had come first from him,

but the words didn't settle well, Cleburne avoiding Mangum's smile. He stared out toward the flat ground to the left of Billy Goat Hill, thought of the wounded Yankees, the potshots taken by his men against targets who had no place to hide. Those Yankees did their duty, he thought. A wounded man is no threat. I must speak with General Smith about that.

"Sir! The Yankees are forming again!"

Cleburne looked out over the low ground, raised field glasses, saw the blue coming together, men on horses, more colors. He heard hoofbeats now, saw a pair of artillery pieces changing position, moving out to the right, past the mouth of the tunnel, his orders to Shannon carried out.

Mangum moved closer to him, said in a low voice, "Dang it all, Patrick. If I have to rope you like a bull, I'll do it. You got no need to be riding out right in the middle of the storm! You're just **making yourself a bloomin' target.**"

Cleburne caught the tease, Mangum's words coming with an Irish brogue.

"I've got a job to do, Lieutenant. Stay close to me. The enemy has surely learned a few things about our position. We have to be prepared to make changes, shift troops as need be. He most certainly has the advantage in numbers, but we have a compact line."

Mangum seemed resigned to the task at hand, said, "Well, at least duck your head once in a while."

"I'll follow your example."

Mangum nodded with a smile. "Plenty of that, sir."

They came in heavy lines once more, Cleburne's artillery blasting enormous gaps in the blue formations, closed by men who knew just where they were supposed to go. Once more, Sherman's men moved up to hug the base of the hills, then drove up, close to Cleburne's earthworks. The artillery continued to do their good work, the crossfire sweeping the brushy hillsides with searing storms of scrap iron, the canister that ripped through the brush and the men who sought any kind of cover. The assault collapsed as quickly as the one before, the Yankees pulling back once more, leaving the brush and the open ground littered with dead and the screaming wounded.

By one o'clock, Cleburne's men were low on ammunition, staring out toward an enemy that showed no signs of pulling away. Cleburne rode again along his lines, encouraging the officers to send men down the slopes to retrieve cartridges and the muskets made to fire them. Within minutes of their last withdrawal, Sherman's men were up, in line again, and again, they pushed forward.

He did as before, the horse pushing along a narrow path just above the earthworks that held the enemy back from the crest of Tunnel Hill. The sounds had become a continuous deafening roar, the flashes of fire blinding, the smoke pouring out in a fog around him. Cleburne could see by the direction of the Yankee musket fire that one lesson had been learned well. As the men reached the base of the hill, they seemed to focus more toward the batteries, taking aim at the men who worked the big guns.

He moved again toward Key's battery, saw men falling, half of Key's gun crews shot down, but the guns still fired. Key was shouting out to the men to one side of him, infantry, Arkansans, and Cleburne knew what Key required, spurred the horse that way, called out, echoing Key's own plea.

"Soldiers! Man these guns! Keep up the fire!"

The barrels of the twelve-pounders pointed down as steeply as possible, but Cleburne could see now, it wasn't steep enough. The troops added their hands to assist, but Cleburne saw the blue just below, the Yankees climbing in a desperate scramble straight at the gun pits. He called out, others doing the same, muskets pointing nearly straight down, but the men who stood were targets for the enemy farther down, and men began to drop back now, blood on faces, chests. Cleburne felt the helplessness again, his hand gripping the pistol, drawing it from the holster. Close in front of him, his men were firing

at Yankees from only yards away, the men still coming up the hill, closer still, the smoke masking the
confusion. The musket fire slowed, and Cleburne
saw men in blue coming up over the log wall, met
by the men with bayonets, many more using their
muskets as clubs. The struggle seemed to roll toward
him, a dozen Yankees inside the earthworks, more
coming over the logs. He aimed the pistol, didn't
fire, men massed together, shouts, an officer with a
pistol of his own, point-blank fire into a man's face.
The club came down now, crushing the man to the
ground, others taking his place, the blue surge still
coming up over the logs. The horse jerked beneath
him, and Cleburne tried to steady it, kept the pistol
in his hand, no aim, the animal bouncing. He saw
Mangum now, the reins snatched from Cleburne's
hands, the horse turning about, pulled along, up
the trail. Cleburne struck out with his hand, jabbing Mangum away, fumbled for the reins, had
to see, turned, the fight in the earthworks ongoing, knives and clubs and fists and screaming men.
There was a blast of musket fire now, straight back
behind him, a storm of smoke blowing past him,
blinding, the men descending the hill, driving closer
to the works. He saw them now, the Kentuckians,
the reserve, another volley from a hundred muskets, the enemy still up on the logs punched away
in a flaming blast. The few men in blue still in
the works were losing the fight now, too few, too
much exhaustion. Cleburne's men had taken con-

trol, the few Yankees still standing pulled backward, prisoners, some of those with bloody wounds. Cleburne watched his men coming together, the Kentuckians keeping their position, making ready for another volley. But there were no targets. The few Yankees who had made it up and over the defenses were down, dead or gripped by hard hands. The men below the works had done what each of Sherman's advances had done. It was the Yankee officers who understood the hopelessness, the power they faced above them, the strength Cleburne had put in their path. And so the orders went out, the bugles sounding, the men in blue pulled back off Tunnel Hill, called once more to retreat.

By midafternoon, Sherman's men had mounted a half-dozen assaults, most directed toward the eminence of Tunnel Hill. The forces under Sherman's command numbered more than thirty thousand troops. On the hill, facing them, Cleburne had made the fight with barely a fifth of that number. And Cleburne still held the hill.

CHAPTER THIRTY-FIVE

THOMAS

ORCHARD KNOB—
NOVEMBER 25, 1863

With the discovery that the rebels had indeed pulled completely off Lookout Mountain, the order had gone out to Joe Hooker early that morning to push onward, down and across Chattanooga Creek, making every effort to drive Bragg's army so severely that Hooker might be able to establish a Federal force along the southern base of Missionary Ridge. Thomas gave the order as instructed by Grant, and without any hint from Grant, Thomas knew in his heart that neither of them expected Hooker to complete the task.

Sherman's attack had launched as planned, at first light, and Thomas had stood on the bare hilltop, staring out northward toward the hard rumble of artillery. For the first two hours, there had been nothing to see, the drifting fog masking the ridge from view, and Thomas had stood beside Grant wondering if Grant truly believed Sherman's fight would decide this thing. Thomas had no reasons to doubt Sherman's planning, or his fire, had no reason to question the accuracy of his reports to Grant. It was far more to do with Thomas's own pride, that quiet sense of accomplishment Grant had refused to give him. If Thomas had been stained by failure, any failure, he could have accepted his dismissal of the Army of the Cumberland. But in this campaign, Thomas had done nothing at all to drain faith away from his abilities. His command of Hooker's forces had been precise and perfunctory. The assault on Lookout Mountain had been wildly successful, which surprised both Grant and Thomas. But the plan had been Thomas's alone. If there was credit to be tossed around Hooker's camp for the accomplishment of those men, Thomas couldn't avoid feeling that some of that praise should go his way as well.

He'd never admit that, of course, wouldn't even say that to his own staff, not even to his friend Alfred Hough. But he nursed that bruise inside, trying to understand Grant's reasoning, why the Army of the Cumberland would spread out as the center of Grant's position, only to sit and watch while others did the work.

He understood tactics, and whether or not he cared for Sherman's personality, or his methods,

Thomas could not fault Grant's plan to hammer Bragg's flanks. If either flank collapsed, the route would be open for a crushing blow all across Bragg's defenses, heights or not. Attacking Lookout Mountain had paved the way for Hooker to push his people across Rossville Gap, a major artery for escape, should Bragg attempt to withdraw that way. Sherman's assault could accomplish exactly the same thing to the north. But Thomas understood why Grant put more faith in Sherman than either of them did in Hooker. Sweeping the enemy off Lookout Mountain improved the possibilities of an assault on that end of Missionary Ridge. But crushing Bragg's right flank would squeeze the center from both directions, and could so jeopardize the rebel army's route of escape that the entire campaign could end with Bragg's wholesale surrender. Thomas had grudgingly conceded that the mathematics still made sense, even if Thomas's men sat idly by. None of the Federal commanders knew just what kind of strength Bragg had on the ridge. But Grant's army had more than doubled since his arrival, and every indication was that Bragg's army had been cut in half.

He studied his own camps, the vast sea of canvas around him, many of those men doing what he did now, observing, listening for the sounds of the fight to the north. Even with no advance of their own, they were an imposing force, and Thomas had wondered what the sight of so much blue had done to the minds of the men who hunkered down all along the crest of Missionary Ridge. The rebel deserters brought in wild stories, utterly contradictory, some claiming that Bragg had fled the area completely, others with grandiose tales of enormous numbers of reinforcements arriving, claims that half of Lee's army in Virginia had suddenly appeared to strengthen Bragg's lines. Thomas knew better than to trust the word of any deserter, any prisoner. He respected Grant for that same bit of wisdom. But Washington was reacting to every rumor, most of that still fueled by their fears for the survival of Ambrose Burnside. He respected Grant for that as well, that Grant would not be bowed by Halleck's ranting, would regard the War Department's missives as **advice,** suggestions to be followed if the situation allowed it. Thomas had seen Rosecrans crumble under that same kind of pressure, so much uncertainty in Washington, which of course was fed by uncertainty from Rosecrans. But Grant had none of that, seemed to be **certain** to a fault. His plan was **the plan.** There might be changes, amendments, but in the end, Grant would not entertain councils of war as the means for making his decisions. From what Thomas could see of Grant, it was grim confidence, but Thomas had to admit that he shared the trait he saw in Grant, what some, including his friend Hough, called stubbornness.

Grant stood beside him, Rawlins close behind, Thomas's own staff handling the
flood of dispatches, most of those passing back and forth to the south. The other senior
commanders from Thomas's army were spread out
along the crest of Orchard Knob, some in idle conversation with their subordinates, some just waiting for something to do.

Grant smoked his usual cigar, rocked on his heels
slightly, stared out toward Sherman's fight, plainly
audible now. The thunder of the artillery had
come in waves, as though the attacks were shifting ground, an ebb and flow that seemed clearly to
disturb Grant. He heard the call from Lieutenant
Ramsey, turned, saw the paper in the man's hand, a
courier trailing behind.

"What is it now?"

Ramsey handed Thomas the note without speaking, and Thomas stared at the paper with aching dismay. He has time to write notes? Well, yes, that would
be Hooker's way. Trust no one but your own pen.

Grant was looking his way now, said, "What's he
say? They make it across the creek?"

Thomas reread the scribbled words with a silent
growl, wanted to rip the paper in two, but he knew
Grant was watching his reaction, held the heat
inside. "He says the enemy has burned the most
usable bridge across the creek."

"Is that a surprise? That's why we have engineers.
Build another one."

Thomas folded the paper, returned it to his aide. "He is. Says it might require three hours or more. He does not seem to be concerned."

Thomas looked toward the valley where Hooker's troops were supposed to be, waited for some kind of explosion from Grant. Grant said, "He received your orders this morning. I assume he understands just what an **order** is. Why in blazes did it take him so long to advance? From what we heard, there isn't a single rebel soldier on that whole mountain."

Thomas stared ahead, Missionary Ridge a mile to the front. "He followed the order the way he has followed every order I've given him. I have not served with the man before, but it seems apparent that he arranges all his details in precise order before he moves. I admit, General, to some frustration."

Grant still looked at him, and Thomas glanced toward him, saw a frown, the cigar clamped hard in Grant's mouth. Grant said, "He ran like a rabbit at Chancellorsville. Shows he can get up and **move** when he has to. It's an acquired skill, the rapid retreat." Grant paused. "No offense to your army, Mr. Thomas."

Thomas felt the knife wound from Grant's comment, had heard too much of that since Chickamauga. "Changes have been made, sir. What happened two months ago shall not be repeated. No one knows that more than you."

Grant seemed uncomfortable, as though he had pricked a sore wound. "Yes, quite right. I meant no disrespect. Your men have admiration for you, your leadership. Well earned."

Thomas said nothing, thought, Not so well earned that we're given anything to do.

He stared out to the south again, the open plain where his army sat with their muskets. There had been plans to have at least three full divisions march out, a hard demonstration for the benefit of the rebel front, perhaps a nudge against the rebel skirmishers, shoving them back to the rifle pits that Bragg had positioned just out from the base of the ridge. But Grant had changed his mind about that, the order canceled the night before, once again his unbridled faith in Sherman overriding any other suggestion Thomas could make.

From some of the field officers, word had filtered toward him that there was grousing in the ranks, many of the soldiers and their officers expecting that the capture of Orchard Knob was just the first step in their inevitable assault against the center of the ridge. To the veterans of Chickamauga, who still carried the shame of such a complete defeat, that kind of assault would offer the opportunity for perfect redemption. None of that had any impact on Grant, that particular tactic dismissed outright, and Thomas was quietly grateful. No matter the sentiment of his men, Thomas knew that a massed assault against Bragg's strongest point would be precisely what Bragg was hoping for, his entire defense designed for that very move.

Grant's alternative against Bragg's flanks was sound strategy, opening up the possibility that either flank would be turned completely. Thomas looked again toward the sounds from Sherman's fight, couldn't help thinking of the chaotic Federal stampede away from Chickamauga. If Bragg's army was swept away so completely, he thought, it would be sweet revenge indeed. But the men who should be making that attack, who deserve to have their pride and their reputations restored . . . are sitting still.

It was afternoon, and Grant had walked back behind the knob, seeking lunch from the lone commissary wagon parked nearby. Thomas stayed up on the highest part of the hill, along with most of his generals, kept his gaze on the ridge to his front. For most of the late morning, rebel troops could be seen moving along the ridge, most of them shifting toward Bragg's right flank. Sherman's fight had changed very little, beyond the strange message Grant had received, the request for Howard's troops to be brought forward. Thomas had been surprised by the request, the tone from the courier suggesting an urgency that Grant certainly didn't expect. Howard's men had moved out that way, partially exposing Thomas's flank to the north of Orchard Knob. Grant had remedied that possible weakness by shifting another division from John Palmer's Fourteenth Corps, under Absalom

Baird. But no one on Missionary Ridge seemed to be reacting to any of that at all. What movement of the rebels Thomas could see was a flow of rebels and guns to his left, what he would expect with the volume of fire coming from Sherman. But neither Thomas nor his observers could confirm if Bragg had weakened his center. The field glasses showed without doubt that Bragg's men along the center of the ridge were still in force, still waiting, watching Thomas's army. Thomas had to believe that a full-on frontal assault against that position could, even now, cost far more casualties than he was willing to lose.

For the past hour, the fog across the plain had moved off, the skies blue and bright, a harsh, chilling breeze buffeting Thomas from behind. Grant was moving back up the hill, and Thomas heard Rawlins.

"Sir, you must do something! Order more troops that way! General Hooker should be reprimanded, most certainly!"

"Calm yourself, General. Matters are in hand. Battles do not fight themselves in short minutes."

"Yes, but we should have heard more positive results from General Sherman. I admit to some concern."

Thomas watched the scene, Grant climbing up with his usual deliberate plod, Rawlins flitting about him like an angry stork. They reached the crest of the hill, Grant still chewing on something, and Rawlins silenced himself, understood decorum around the other senior commanders. Thomas hid a smile, knew his own staff was back behind him, that there would be teasing about Rawlins. For now, Hough, Ramsey, the others were receiving the couriers, would continue to do exactly that unless he called upon them. He actually liked Rawlins, knew the man was exceptional at his job, the kind of hovering presence Grant seemed to need, whether Grant agreed with that or not. Thomas couldn't help thinking of the two men as an old married couple, Grant the stern-faced husband, as Rawlins jabbed and poked him with questions and details.

Grant moved up beside Thomas now, said, "Saw General Hunter back there. Man knows how to fill a dinner plate. Crusty, disagreeable fellow. Rather good at his job, though. Knows how to tell a joke. Hates card playing. I had to hold him in check on that one. An inspector general doesn't need to legislate morals, and the men seem to like it. I admit, I did outlaw card playing in Mississippi. We were on the march, no time for much else." Grant paused, and Thomas looked at him, surprised at Grant's unusual chattiness. Grant seemed suddenly uncomfortable, a nervous twitchiness, seemed self-conscious about Thomas actually listening to him. "There is some decent beef at the wagon, and the bread's not bad. Take a walk back there, if you wish." Thomas hadn't felt hungry since breakfast, the cold drilling into him, and he pulled the coat tighter, saw Grant doing the same. Grant said, "Good day for a coat. Cold's better than the rain. Fog finally gone."

Thomas could feel some kind of uneasiness in Grant's babbling conversation, so completely unlike Grant. He glanced back to his staff, four aides, standing with Lieutenant Ramsey, Ramsey responding to his look by moving forward. Thomas held up his hand, said, "Go eat something. Not much to be concerned with right now."

Ramsey nodded, a quick, short bow, turned, motioning for the others. Thomas was surprised to hear a loud grunt from Grant, who said, "What in blazes? Look there."

Thomas saw Grant raising the field glasses, other officers across the hill doing the same. Thomas looked through his own, scanned the sloping hills to the north, some of the details hidden by the rough terrain. But one detail was very plain, made more clear by the bright sun. Thomas knew what he was seeing, kept it inside, let the observation come from Grant.

"Those troops . . . they're retreating. I cannot understand this. Is he being defeated? What in blazes has Sherman been doing up there?"

Thomas stared silently, knew Grant's description was accurate. The word crossed through his mind. **Stampede.** He turned to the south, scanned the far reaches of Missionary Ridge, searching for some signs that Hooker's men had made their way across the creek, might have shoved up to the southernmost ground near the ridge. Grant said the word, as Thomas thought it.

"Nothing. Hooker's still fooling around trying to build a bridge. We should have sent him to Burnside, let the two of them trip over each other's feet."

Thomas held a blast of anger inside, thought of Hooker. I would have you removed for this. Defeat is one thing. Useless delay is another. Grant turned again toward Sherman's fight, Thomas as well. He could see a haze of smoke drifting up across the ridge, felt a cold stirring in his stomach. The artillery fire was falling away, but the men in blue could clearly be seen, gathering back along the flatter plain away from the ridge. Grant said, "What time is it?"

Rawlins was there, always. "Three ten, sir."

"General Thomas, I see General Granger there. Summon his division commanders. Those are the men whose camps are nearest this position, yes?"

Thomas knew the other generals were there, keeping close to Orchard Knob. He motioned to Hough, the others, the aides responding with a quick jog toward Granger. Grant was impatient now, slapped his hands against his heavy coat.

"This is unacceptable. Sherman has sent no word of any collapse. He's going to shove his people up that hill until no one's left. He should. No excuses."

Thomas saw Granger leading his two closest generals, Wood and Sheridan, and behind them, Richard Johnson, who commanded the division farthest to the south. All four were on horseback, moving quickly, followed by Thomas's aides.

Gordon Granger had endeared himself to Thomas by his performance at Chickamauga, adding strength to Thomas's final stand, allowing the rest of Rosecrans's army to escape annihilation. But Granger carried a chip on his shoulder, had thought himself capable of a senior command, an opinion not shared by the War Department. From early 1862, he had commanded the Army of Kentucky, but with the fights expanding down through Tennessee, the War Department merged his command with Rosecrans's Army of the Cumberland, a move Granger took to be an obvious slap against his abilities. Instead of the independent command of an army, Granger now had to accept a subordinate position as a corps commander. Thomas had never been impressed with Granger's efficiency, wasn't sure if Grant felt the same way. But his men were the closest at hand, and, along with Johnson's division, would be the ones most capable of putting their troops into position, should Grant actually order an attack.

Tom Wood was a small, wiry man, straight-backed, carrying the look of the dashing cavalier. Like Granger, Wood was another of the veterans of Mexico, was an obvious choice for a command position at the start of the war. The only real stain on Wood's reputation had come at Chickamauga, through no fault of his own. It was Rosecrans's order to Wood to relocate his division that had opened a yawning gap in the Federal lines, allowing Longstreet's rebels to crush straight through the entire position. But Wood had kept his command, not even Rosecrans making the excuse that any of that disaster was Wood's fault.

Phil Sheridan was by far the youngest of the group, not much beyond thirty years old. Like Wood, Sheridan was a small, tightly wound man, who had built an excellent reputation for field command under both Rosecrans and Don Carlos Buell. It had surprised Thomas that Sheridan had been close friends with Sherman early in the war, and along the way, had endeared himself to Henry Halleck, no easy feat.

Richard Johnson was known as much for his outsized handlebar mustache as he was for good leadership in the field, a man beloved by his troops for his appearance as well as his sturdiness under fire. Like Granger, Johnson had been with Thomas at Chickamauga, and though he served a different corps commander than Granger, by chance his positioning in line had put him on the right flank of Thomas's position, with Johnson's right resting against a loop on Chattanooga Creek.

All four men were West Pointers, all had impatient, energized troops, who seemed even now to be reacting to the summoning of their generals with a scattering of cheers.

Grant watched with Thomas, the men dismounting, and Grant said, "Last evening, I reversed my order for your men to advance in demonstration against that ridge." Thomas saw the men glancing back and forth between him and Grant, and Grant seemed to hesitate, as though trying to recall just how much he knew of these men. Grant spoke first to Wood, didn't seem to care that Granger outranked him, and Thomas had no reason to object. He had more faith in Wood than he had in Granger. Perhaps Grant felt the same way.

After a long moment Grant said, "General Wood, it seems that General Sherman is having a difficult time. I think that if you were to advance your divisions and carry the enemy's rifle pits along the base of the ridge, it would threaten Bragg's center, so that he might feel the urgency of removing troops from his right flank. This could assist General Sherman's efforts. Do you agree?"

Wood looked at Granger, then Thomas, as though seeking permission to speak for the others. Thomas nodded, and Wood said, "Perhaps it will work out that way, sir. If you order it, we shall try it. I believe we can carry those entrenchments without any serious difficulty."

Thomas felt a stab of nervousness, said, "Sir, we will be exposing a considerable number of good men to murderous fire. Once they move out across that open ground, the enemy's artillery will play heavily on their ranks."

Grant pulled the cigar from his mouth, glanced at the others, then said to Thomas, "Right now, rebel artillery is playing heavily on Sherman. Wouldn't you agree? We can sit on our perches here and watch that, or we can do something about it. If these gentlemen agree, I prefer the latter course."

There was no room for argument in Grant's expression, and Thomas knew the order had to be given. The others spoke to one another, Grant paying more attention to them, the details of what he expected them to do. Thomas pulled himself back, his mind working on the plan. He knew Grant had made a mistake reversing the order that would have sent these men forward at first light. But that kind of discussion was useless, would only damage the strange air of tension he felt with Grant now.

He waited for a silent moment, said, "There will be casualties. Gentlemen, I expect you to advance your ranks with alacrity. Do what is required to convince Bragg we're coming with all hell right through his center."

He looked at Sheridan, saw the man shifting his feet nervously, a hard stare toward the ground. The others were absorbing what Grant was telling them to do, all of them as aware as Thomas what the cost might be. Granger seemed the most energized, eager, as though engulfed by a sudden wave of childlike excitement.

Thomas pointed toward him, said, "You will remain here, close to this command. General Wood, General Sheridan, General Johnson . . . it is essential that you be alert to what you might encounter. The enemy will most certainly not come down off those heights to engage you. They will rely on artillery and muskets. Stay close to your troops, but do not expose yourself needlessly."

Thomas looked back out toward the far ridge, toward Sherman's attack, thought of Grant's words, **Assist General Sherman's efforts.** That is, he thought, what we are here for. Perhaps we shall allow Sherman to have his success. He looked at the four, Granger speaking to his aides, a groom moving off with his horse. Sheridan and Johnson walked slowly toward their own horses, both men staring silently out toward the ridge. Wood was still looking at Grant, but the questions were past, the decision made, the order given.

Thomas said, "General Granger, tell the others; we shall fire six guns in quick succession from Fort Wood. That will be the signal to step off. No straggling, no one holds back. Do the job, capture and hold those rifle pits at the base of the hill. The order shall be sent if it is determined the men should remain there, or return back to their camps."

Wood moved away, brief words with the other three, and Thomas looked at Grant, saw him staring out toward Sherman yet again. Thomas said, "We shall do what we can to **assist** him, sir."

Grant looked back at him, a brief glance. "Yes,

well, see it through. There shall be no celebration in Bragg's headquarters. Not on this day."

Thomas turned away, saw the flags gathering, the staffs of the generals moving out to pass along the orders. He glanced again to the pass east of Lookout Mountain. Still nothing from Hooker, he thought. No word, no sign, no fight. And, probably, no bridge. So, we shall make our demonstration, and if we perform our duty well enough, General Sherman shall have his victory.

CHAPTER THIRTY-SIX

BAUER

SOUTH OF ORCHARD KNOB— NOVEMBER 25, 1863

His first thought had been to kill the rooster. He had been awakened by the crowing at three that morning, the men around Bauer cursing aloud in the direction of Willis's tent. Beside him, Corporal Owens had sat up with a violent start, waking Bauer by frantically searching for whatever invisible demon was driving the strange noise into Owens's head, and threatening to dig for it straight through Bauer's guts. As the men lost any ability to sleep, the explanation became clear, their logic taking over for the jolt from the amazingly loud cackle from the bird. It was Owens who had gone out into the darkness, calling out Willis's name, and Bauer suddenly feared for his friend, wondered if Owens respected a captain's bars more than he demanded his full allotment of sleep.

As Bauer huddled in the tent, avoiding the sharp chill of the breezy dawn, Willis's rooster had finally quieted, though not before waking the entire battalion of regulars, and from the loud curses beyond the tents, it was likely that the 11th Michigan, camped nearby, was no more pleased with "Henry" than the men around Bauer.

In the cold silence that finally settled over the camps, it was only a few short minutes before the bugle came. If the rooster had miscalculated the timing of reveille, the bugler had one advantage: He knew how to read a timepiece.

The morning had drifted upon them with patches of fog, but the cold winds soon swept that out toward the east, obscuring the shadowy hulk of Missionary Ridge. As they had done on so many days before, the men peered out from their tents into a dreary dawn, dreading whatever new misery would descend upon them from the skies, and Bauer shared the surprise with the men around him that, in fact, on this day, the sky was blue.

The campfires were welcomed with hand-rubbing enthusiasm, pots of coffee appearing from someplace Bauer knew never to ask. But the coffee actually tasted like the precious fuel he recalled from distant memories, as though some commissary officer had discovered the miraculous, a spring of crystal-clean water, then brewed the mixture using something very close to actual coffee. That was unusual enough, what many of the regular soldiers called unique, as though somewhere, somebody was actually paying attention to the care of the men. But then the wonder changed to awe, the breakfast arriving in wagons that produced odors these men had not enjoyed for many weeks. The cooked bacon seemed reasonably fresh, a miracle in itself, and the bread showed only the first traces of blue and green mold. Bauer reveled in the feast, though when the meal was past, the boxes of hardtack appeared. It was another usual routine, the men cursing the commissaries once again, Bauer wise enough to draw his share, perhaps a bit more. Around the campfires the talk began, the wariest of veterans suggesting that a bountiful breakfast could mean either of two things: The army was staying put in these camps for a while yet, or, more likely, they were about to move. And when the army gave you a meal, there had to be a price attached. If they were moving, it was most likely straight into a fight.

The clues to that were many. The advance to capture Orchard Knob had been a maneuver that seemed only to improve their position, putting them closer to the enemy. It had worked. The attack along the heights on Lookout Mountain had been another purposeful assault, and from all the men had heard, that fight was successful as well. But no real information came to the men about just what had happened on the mountain. As always, rumors drifted by, and then their speculation had been whisked away by the official version of reality.

As the fog cleared, the prominent stone face of Lookout Mountain had loomed over their right flank like some monument, flecked with canvas tents and men in blue. By midmorning, someone fortunate enough to carry field glasses had called out, sending word in every direction. More field glasses went up, scanning the great mass of the mountain, the glasses passed around, the men allowed to see it for themselves. Bauer had been among the last, the surprise and the enthusiastic clamor toward the mountain now explained. Like the others, he could make out the unmistakable flutter of the flag, the speck of color that no one could mistake for anything but the Stars and Stripes. The flag had been mounted on the tallest peak of Lookout Mountain, caught by the brisk winds in a full glorious display. Word had been passed officially down to Willis, who had passed it on to his company. The rebels were gone completely from the great rock, and it had been the men of the 8th Kentucky who had made the vigorous climb to the summit. Now those men stood proudly around their flag, hoping someone, or everyone, down below was watching. Even if the private soldiers around Bauer didn't know the details, just what had happened months before from someplace called Chancellorsville, for today, no one who heard the fight rolling over Lookout Mountain had anything bad to say about the men who made that climb, who fought in dense fog, what the quartermaster, Montgomery Meigs, would describe as **the battle above the clouds.**

The euphoria over the planting of the flag had soon been overshadowed by rumblings from the far end of the line, what seemed to be miles to the north. The men knew what the sounds meant, and with every wave of artillery fire that drifted toward them, Bauer had done what many of the men were doing now, moving out from the comfort of the campfire to stare northward, trying to find out for themselves what no officer would tell them. As each new assault began, the men halted their card playing, their chatter, the various games involving knives and glass marbles. The mystery was made more curious by their blindness. For most of the morning, the smoke had mixed with the last of the hazy fog, but by midmorning, the bright sun showed the smoke itself, thin clouds that drifted up and over the ridgeline far away, too far for Bauer to see details at all. As always, the rumors sprouted quickly, word passing around the fires with convincing authority that Bragg had launched an attack around the northern flank, others insisting the attack was Sherman's, some claiming that Burnside had come down from Knoxville, or even that Longstreet's rebels had returned, assaulting the army's left flank with a bloody vengeance. Bauer tried to ignore all the talk, as had many of the regulars who had heard so much of this jabber before. If there was anything important enough to affect these men, that word would come soon enough. Bauer had settled close to a fire, talked into playing a wagering card game, had lost most of a month's pay in a game of chance he really didn't understand. He left the game to taunts from the other players, understood that his boredom had caused an outbreak of personal stupidity.

No orders had come that morning at all, and the men were already talking of a midday meal, if the army was to be so generous one more time. Bauer felt restless, the cold in his toes and fingers putting him into motion, a brisk walk through the camp, past the stacked muskets, more campfires, all the mundane rituals in the camp performed by the men who, yet again, had little to do. He expected field drills, but Colonel Moore was one of those who seemed to understand that what had been drilled into these men hadn't been erased by a few weeks' time, that putting the men into formations and marching them all over the grassy fields just meant they'd be hungrier by the day's end. Instead, they were allowed their leisure, some of the men filling their day in exhibitions of various talents, singing songs, one man with a ragged fiddle, another helping out the concert with a stringed instrument captured from a rebel, what someone called a banjo.

Bauer had grown tired of bad voices and poor attempts at music, kept his wandering around the limits of their camp. Along one boundary, he stood facing the camps of the next unit, the men from Michigan, and beyond them, another battalion of regulars, the 15th. He was curious about those men, if they shared the rough edges he saw among the 18th, no one really talking much about any competition between the soldiers who had set themselves apart from the volunteers. Like Bauer, most of the men in the 18th Regulars seemed bored. The fight on the mountain had energized them all, and the mysterious artillery assaults to the north seemed to pull at them, adding to the boredom with an annoying sense that someone else was having a good go at the enemy, while these boys played cards.

He moved past more of the muskets, a supply wagon, saw a teamster up on the wagon slicing slivers off a stick with a knife large enough for the kind of fight Bauer never wanted to see. He stepped past the wagon, caught the unmistakable odor of cooking, thought, Dinner indeed. The commissary's got something going on. Just hope it's not officers only. Fellows like Corporal Owens don't take well to that kind of thing. Man scares me. That's sure as the dickens why Willis stuck me in the same tent with him. Sure, Sammie, make sure I get nightmares, just so you can hear about them.

He looked out toward the larger tent, saw a small herd of horses, a color bearer sitting upright, holding tightly to the Stars and Stripes. Bauer was surprised, moved that way, saw an enormous man standing tall, watching him come, and the man held out his hand.

"What do you want, soldier?"

Bauer looked past the man, saw a pair of officers standing close to Willis's tent, minding the horses.

"Just came to see the captain."

"Why? You have a problem, you go see your platoon officer."

Bauer thought of the only explanation he could offer, kept the words to himself. Well, you grouchy skull cracker, the captain's not really an officer. He's my friend. No, he thought, best let that go. He studied the man's size, a head taller than Bauer, arms like curved logs, a face that leaked cruelty. I bet he's never laughed once in his whole life.

From Willis's tent, three men suddenly appeared, and Bauer watched them with wide-eyed wonder, said aloud, "Brass. What're they doing with Sammie?"

The guard ignored him, moved off that way, and Bauer waited, watched as they all mounted the horses. Willis emerged from the tent, saluted the men with stiff-backed respect, something Bauer had never seen. Willis seemed to wait as the horses shifted into formation, the guard glancing back out toward Bauer, then past, scanning the tents, searching for . . . what? He's a bodyguard, for certain. For who?

The men rode off now, the color bearer bringing up the rear, and Bauer realized it was the second Stars and Stripes he had seen that day. That's big brass, he thought. Damn it all, Sammie, what did you do?

The horsemen were out on the flattened trail now, moving toward the camp of the Michigan men, and Bauer took advantage, moved toward Willis with quick steps. Willis saw him, his shoulders returning to their familiar droop, Willis always seeming to crouch slightly, as though ready to throw a fist.

"Hey, Sammie, what's happening? You get in trouble? I saw Colonel Moore. Who were the other fellows?"

Willis motioned him with a discreet wave of the hand, backed into the tent. Bauer knew when to be quiet, followed, Willis's tent perfumed with cigar and pipe smoke. Willis waited for him to get inside, peered out past, as though looking for eavesdroppers.

"We'll be calling formation in a minute. No wasting time. You might as well know, since you're the nosiest man in this outfit."

"Naw. It's just 'cause I know you'll tell me secrets, before you tell anybody else."

"Keep that to yourself, you stump brain."

"So, who's the brass?"

"General Johnson's aide, Major Hawke. The general's sending staff out to every company, issuing us orders."

"Wowee, Sammie. That fellow had a guard with him. Tough-looking brute. He didn't like me coming round, for sure. I never seen you talking to so much brass since you become an officer. That's pretty impressive."

"Not that impressive. Hell, Dutchie, you done met General Grant."

That was a piece of pride Bauer carried since Vicksburg. There had been an opportunity for him to show off his marksmanship by taking down another rebel officer. But this time, the shot had been witnessed by Grant himself. Grant's presence had been pure chance, fortunate timing for Bauer, but Bauer made no effort to stop the embellishment of the story that soon flowed through the camp of the regiment, that Grant had actually come to see Bauer on purpose.

"Wait a minute, Sammie. A general's adjutant makes a big show of coming to see you?"

"They're sending word out to every company. I guess they're making sure we keep our brains unscrambled."

"You yankin' on me again? Dang it, you been promoted again?"

"Yeah, that's it. General Thomas is stepping aside. Picked my name out of a hat to run the whole damn Army of the Cumberland. Now listen, beef brain. We're lining up pretty quick, moving out against that ridgeline. We're supposed to hit the rebels hard enough to take their earthworks along the base of the ridge. If we can make it that far without getting blown to bits by their artillery, we hunker down in their works and wait for the order to pull back. If the rebs don't like the looks of us sitting so close to 'em, they might withdraw, pull out of here completely. They do that, we might get to climb that ridgeline, see what the view's like. But that's for another day. Barely enough daylight left to make it to the first line of reb sharpshooters."

Bauer soaked up the explanation, could see the seriousness in Willis's face. Bauer shook his head. "Makes no sense. You telling me we risk getting killed crossing all that open ground just so we can chase the rebs away, and then just sit out there waiting for the generals to figure out what's happening next?"

"One more reason you're not an officer. What we're doing is called a **demonstration.** That's why the general's staff is giving out the order to every company commander. They're worried we'll either fall down too quick, or that we'll keep fighting after dark, when it's all over up north."

"Up north . . . where? Kentucky?"

"A whole damn bag of walnuts has more brains than you. You been listening to that fight all morning, up to the left flank. That's Sherman, and he's having a tough go. General Grant wants us to help him out. Maybe we should just send **you.**"

"You mean, we're gonna help out Sherman by doing a **pretend** attack?"

"I didn't say we won't fight. There'll be reb skirmishers out there, for certain, and they'll put up
a scrap. Not sure what else we'll find. Our orders
are to scare the devil out of the rebs in front of
us. Look, Dutchie, it's not my job to explain every
damn thing, and it's not your job to figure things
out. Just do what you're told." Willis strapped on
his pistol. "Let's go. I gotta pass along these orders
to the company. The long roll's gonna sound in
about ten minutes."

Bauer looked around the tent now, was suddenly curious. "Hey, Sammie, where's Henry?
Your rooster. Boy, he really riled up the camp this
morning."

Willis moved out past him, the word coming in a
low growl. "Dinner."

The drums brought them together, the lines
forming up two deep. Bauer hated the
drums, had wondered why the army used
them, had heard the steady beats in every fight
he had seen, rumbling through the ranks of both
sides. If there was supposed to be inspiration from
that, strength from the steady rhythm, Bauer had
already learned that the rebels took as much from
that as the men in blue. It just tells 'em you're coming, he thought.

He stood upright, the musket on his shoulder, the
others in their standard formation out to both sides

of him. Out front the 15th Regulars had fallen in, would lead the way, some of the men around Bauer griping about that already. Bauer had never felt any particular honor in being the first man to be a target, but he also understood that if those men took it hard, were swept down, he would see it all, would know exactly what might happen next.

An officer moved out front, the beardless face of Lieutenant Jasper, a man younger than Bauer. Down to one side, he could see Willis, sword in hand, a hard glare toward the men, no particular glance at Bauer. Doing his job, he thought. Does it better than anybody in this army, I'll bet. And we're going in right with him. No better place I'd rather be.

He wasn't completely sure of that, said it to himself again, trying to find strength, to erase the hammering thunder in his chest, the cold, quivering fear of what this formation meant. He kept his eyes on Willis, heard the lieutenant shout out something, the usual clamor for straight lines, no gaps, everyone moving together. He glanced around, realized Owens was right behind him, and Bauer nodded, unsmiling, saw no acknowledgment from Owens. Bauer turned, heard the sergeant yelling out, repeating most of what the lieutenant had already said, his words a harsh bellow that drowned out the drums. The talking was done now, the men silent, the lieutenant facing forward, sword in hand, Willis doing the same, a breathless minute. Bauer stared out to the men in front of them, a hundred-yard gap, horsemen, a flag, a solid blue line. The first line.

From far behind them, back to the left, Bauer heard the hard thump of a cannon, then another, another, six in all. He knew not to look, nothing to see, but there was meaning there, and now, out to the front, a bugle sounded. The men of the 15th began to move, the singular motion of marching legs, pushing out through the grass. Bauer waited for the command, closed his eyes, thought of the bugler, the least popular man in camp, stealer of sleep, messenger of mindless formations. The notes came now, distinct, clear, Willis raising the sword, others down the line doing the same, the lines stretching a half mile to the left, many fewer to the right. The flank. We're the flank.

The words flowed through him, meaningless distraction, his legs moving now, by themselves, his brain no part of the drill. He moved in perfect unison with the men on either side of him, felt the presence of Owens behind him, could smell the man, too familiar. He stepped to the rhythm of the drums, the bolt of clarity through his brain. That's why they use drums. It had never occurred to him before, and now, more nonsensical jabber rolled through his thoughts, more distractions. He glanced up, saw a huge bird circling above, and beyond, one wispy cloud, heard now the calls of the young lieutenant, the words every man in these lines had heard before, hoped that when this day was past, they would survive to hear those words again.

The first skirmishers had been swept away well to the front, a few chattering shots that seemed very far away. The men of the 15th had not paused, kept up their advance without firing, no volleys necessary. Bauer marched in the footsteps of those men, trampled grass, scrub brush, the occasional tree. He kept his eyes to the front, but his brain was alive with questions, meaningless talk, the fear inside him swelling into terror, his flickering courage held in place by the sheer bulk of the men around him.

The ground rose slightly, then dropped back down, more trampled footsteps, and Bauer saw the telltale signs of skirmishers, flattened bare ground, logs piled up, brush gathered for disguise. There were cast-aside backpacks, canteens, used cartridge boxes, scraps of a man's time spent staring out toward the enemy who stared back. Trading tobacco, he thought. Stupid. Never do that. One man decides to make his war personal, and while you carry out your little sack of coffee, all smiles and happy handshakes, he bushwhacks you, cuts your throat. Not me. Just . . . don't like those fellows.

He passed a row of shallow entrenchments, dug like an afterthought, no real protection. The same cast-off equipment was there as well, signs of men who were long gone. They skedaddled, he thought. Heard us coming . . . hell, they **saw** us coming. No place to hide out here. Don't need drums to tell nobody nothing. He glanced down, caught his legs in motion with the man beside him, the boy, Hoover. There was no talk, Bauer keeping his thoughts silent, glanced at the boy, thought, You scared? Bet you're scared to hell. Or maybe you're too fresh, too dumb. Anybody's done this before knows exactly why he ought to be running like hell the other way. Can't do that. Sammie would kill me. Owens would kill me. Worse, they'd hate me for it.

The first artillery shell came overhead now, a harsh whistle that impacted somewhere behind. He focused on the ridgeline, as though seeing it for the first time. Puffs of smoke popped out all across the top, and more, halfway down. He could see the firing from the rebels all down the long ridge, drifting smoke, the faint chatter, and, now, more thunder, blasts of fire from well up the hill, the balls arcing downward, heavy thumps, one shell erupting with a fiery blast between the two formations. More shells fell to the left, where most of the men were advancing, solid shot tumbling past, tossing up the soft earth. The firing blew past him, a sharp zip past his head, more, some impacting the dirt in front of him. The musket balls were mostly spent, but there was death in the sounds, and he saw the line in front staggering. The officers came to life now, shouts and orders, the men keeping their lines tight, the 15th shifting position, closing up the gaps torn through their formation. In seconds he saw the men who had been struck down, blue and red, white faces staring up, men calling out, agony, suffering, and no stopping to help. He kept up the march, heard the whistle and zip again, a volley from far out front, smoke rising well beyond the front lines. The gaps in the lines in front of him were wider now, but still the men of the 15th kept together, pushing forward, Bauer and the men around him following.

He watched as more of the men to the front fell away, the sounds growing, a steady roar of musket fire, smoke rising in a vast cloud all across the ridgeline, smoke everywhere, the crest high above coming alive, as though on fire. The 15th suddenly stopped, more men collapsing, but they answered, firing a volley of their own, then rose up again, still moving forward. Bauer watched with shaking hands, the thunder of his heartbeats, shouts of the officers reaching him, the lieutenant close by, voice like a girl, and he looked out to the side, saw Willis, steady steps, sword high, no stopping, no pause. Bauer passed more wounded, one man shot through his forehead, his eyes wide, staring up with surprise. Bauer had seen that before, couldn't ignore it, felt the tug of sickness, but Owens was still behind him, the frightening push Bauer felt in his mind, no stopping, no hesitating. The ridgeline seemed alive, thick lines of smoke from muskets up the slope, the hillside bathed in thin fog now, the cannon fire blowing through with fiery bursts. To one side, the ground erupted, a blinding flash, deafening thunder, dirt sprayed over him, men ducking, but no one halted, the sergeants screaming at them, needlessly, the men knowing what to do.

The musket fire was much closer now, and Bauer saw the first line enveloped in smoke, firing their own volleys, and now a horseman rode past, close to Bauer, a hard yell at Willis, the man riding on, orders to more of the officers. Willis turned toward him for the first time, a flash of recognition, and Bauer saw the fire, the look he had seen at Shiloh, at Vicksburg, in every fight Willis could make. His voice broke through the din in front of them.

"To the double-quick! Forward!"

The men responded, other companies down the line doing the same. Bauer ran into a wave of smoke, fought to breathe, was past it now, saw the ridge, steep and tall, saw men scrambling to climb up, some of them shot down. There was a deep earthwork spread out to both sides, a hundred yards or more from the base of the hill, the men of the 15th settling in, seeking some kind of protection. Bauer jumped down, saw men he didn't know, wide-eyed terror, grim fury, red eyes, tears. The earthworks filled now, heavy with blue, and Willis was there, screaming at them, pointing the sword up the hill. The men responded with their muskets, the men on the hillside tumbling back-ward, some just collapsing, caught by rocks and rubble and brush. Bauer stared for a long moment, a charge up the great hill, but it was no charge at all. It was escape. The men were rebels.

CHAPTER THIRTY-SEVEN

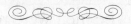

BAUER

BASE OF MISSIONARY RIDGE—
NOVEMBER 25, 1863

He was deafened by the blasts from the artillery, the rebels on the ridgeline above him dropping shells in a high arc, the only way to impact anyone so close to the ridge. But far out to either side, rebel artillery had the angle, could fire in a flatter trajectory, those shells sweeping close to parallel with the trenches now holding the blue troops.

Around Bauer, the men pulled themselves as low into cover as possible, but the earthworks and log walls had been built to face outward, toward Chattanooga. The parapets and ditches that faced the hillside were low, flimsy, and Bauer could see, from his spot in line, that the base of the hill was nearly two hundred yards away. That span was mostly flat, grassy ground that offered little or no cover. Some of the men had dared to rush out that way, seeking the protection of anything they could find, a rock, tree stump, a cluster of brush. But the officers screamed them back, the orders barely heard above the amazing din of the ongoing fire from the heights above them.

Across the way, Federal guns had responded to the barrage of rebel artillery fire, the shells streaking past, impacting with rock-crushing blasts high up on the face of the hill. The rebels responded, but their targets were human, and very close, and so their fire continued downward, the vicious attempt to swat away the vast wave of Federal troops who now filled their own earthworks.

Bauer curled into a ball, his back against the dirt wall, the stacked logs to his front. The smacks of lead seemed aimed into the logs themselves, the rebels high above taking aim at any movement they could find. But the artillery was far worse, the shells overtaking any threat from the muskets. He pulled his head down between his arms, tried to hear more than the blistering screams from canister, sprays of dirt and rock blown over him, more shrapnel whistling past from fiery shells bursting high overhead. He kept his knees in tight, eyes closed against the smoke and splattering dirt, felt numb, the terrifying helplessness of where he was. One shell burst just behind him, hot metal tumbling, bouncing overhead, thick smoke, searing heat. He glanced to the side, saw other men doing just what he was, some of those men carrying wounds, struck by the shrapnel, by bits of metal from the canister or the lucky shot from a rebel musket. There were shouted orders, but no words he could hear, just the roar of the big guns, the shelling in no kind of pattern, no rhythm, the guns seeming to erupt over them from every part of the ridge, more shells coming in from their own guns a mile away. In the works, the men who dared to move at all were crawling, some seeking a deeper hole, but the rebels had dug their trench with care, uniform depth, a good solid stack of logs facing outward. There were transverse trenches, but not many, the defensive line not so well constructed as to hold away a major assault. I guess we were a major assault, he thought. Had to look pretty damn impressive coming at them from way across that open ground. So they ran. Maybe not so many of 'em down here this low. If they'd have been thick in this ditch, they could have busted us up real good. If they'd have had cannon down here, it might have been a whole lot worse. But doesn't much matter now. Here we are. The question rose up inside of him, the orders Willis had told him about. Take these lines, and then wait to see what happens next. This is all about some other fight, up the other way? Sherman? What's he doing, anyway? If we're just out "demonstrating," what else are we supposed to do? I ain't demonstrating a damn thing but keeping my head down.

Down to one side, an officer sat curled up as he was, no orders, no attempt to rally the men for anything more than what they were doing, seeking shelter any way they could. He saw other men, lying flat just outside the log wall, more desperation, but the artillery shells were finding them as well, the air blasts spraying hot iron into those men more easily than the men in the trench. A horse rode past, just out from the logs, a surprise, and Bauer wanted to rise up, to see, knew better than to try. More horses thundered past, some of those moving out away from the works, back the way they came, and Bauer could see through the openings in the logs that the horses had no riders. He felt a jab at that, thought, Officers on horses . . . never seemed very damn smart. Or maybe, they just dismounted, drove the horses away. Damn kind of 'em. Especially if they're not dead.

Another shell tumbled in heavily to one side, impacting down into the line, ripping through the huddled men, then erupting in a blast of fire and flesh. Bauer closed his eyes again, the thoughts driven away by a sudden wave of panic. He kept his head down, the words coming out in a hard shout few could hear.

"What are we supposed to do? We can't just stay here!"

Others took up the cry, the men beside him, strangers mostly, one man yelling out, "We gotta get the hell out of this place!"

Hell. Bauer was struck by the word, the place. Yep. This has to be close. He heard splattering against the wood, musket balls ripping close past his head, a volley fired from high above. He looked again through the gaps in the logs, could see across the flat ground they had come from, wondered if another line of troops was moving up in support, that wonderful sense of strength, reinforcements, salvation. Somebody else for the rebels to shoot at. But the ground to their rear was churned up, smoking, few men but the wounded, no stretcher bearers yet with the courage to wander out into wide-open spaces. He felt cramps in his legs, forced himself to roll over, his face pushed against the dirt, and officers were shouting now, an order barely above the sound from a pair of shells coming down close behind him.

"Get up! Get to the hill! Find cover there!"

"To hell with you!"

The words came next to him, echoed in Bauer's own head, others responding, some picking up the call, the men understanding there was no safety here, no real protection. Another shell tumbled into the trench, a hissing fuse, a man screaming, pushing back with his feet, a desperate scramble to get away. Bauer covered his head with his arms, useless effort, the fuse going silent, the shell not exploding. Another man rolled over, hoisted the shell up, rolled it out past the logs, then dropped back down, and just as suddenly, the shell erupted, logs tossed up on one end, smoke and fire, hard shrieks from the men close by.

Another order came, another officer, a different direction, "Up! Get to the ridge! Climb! Let's go! Rebs are way up the hill, pulling back!"

Bauer knew Willis's voice, couldn't ignore that, had to see, to know what Willis was telling them to do, had to see himself if the rebels had truly gone. He removed his hat, healthy precaution, jabbed his head up a few inches, a quick scan of the ground toward the ridge, saw a handful of bodies, wounded men, others not moving at all, not all of them in blue. He felt a hard grab on his back, surprising, terrifying, heard the words yelled into his ear.

"Get up! Move to the hill! Get up! Find cover!"

It was Willis.

He watched Willis slide past him, grabbing at the men, the shouts continuing, the heavy impact of his voice pulling the men together, muskets drawn up, men preparing to move. The men closest to Bauer were from the 15th, strangers, but Willis affected them as well, a voice of authority everyone seemed to need. Bauer watched him, saw Willis pull his pistol, standing upright in the trench, pointing out toward the hill. He was gone now, a quick climbing leap upward, still shouting, and Bauer rose up, saw Willis running hard, falling now against the slope, heavy brush above him. Others followed, climbing up, some hesitating, others bursting up and away, faster now, more of the men understanding that this cover was no cover at all. Bauer gripped the musket hard, couldn't watch Willis in the open, wouldn't see what might happen. But the air ruptured close overhead, the shell blowing straight into the logs, a shattering blast that tore a wide opening, the ground behind him suddenly open, clear. He rolled over, stared that way, **back,** ignored the wounded, looked out toward small stands of trees, the slight rolling ground, the trampled grass from the feet of a thousand regulars, the men who had taken the enemy's works, and now suffered for it. He felt the quivering in his chest, the ice in his fingers, searing heat on his face, a fire to one side, the logs starting to burn. He didn't move, kept his eyes on the open ground, felt suffocated by the raw terror pouring from his brain, no thoughts but one. **Run!**

He started to move that way, **back,** out of the earthworks, the convenient hole blown in the logs, saw the tree line far out in the plain, safety, sanctuary. He heard more shouts, a high-pitched yell, saw men down the trench from him rising up, climbing, pawing their way out through the embankments, some crawling, then up, running. But they were moving **forward,** obeying Willis and their own officers, scrambling out toward the steep slope, toward the fire from the enemy. Bauer tried to move, his legs frozen, icy paralysis, his eyes still caught by the ground behind him, farther from the shelling. He fought against the terror in his brain, struggling to move, cursing against his own fears, the word rolling into him now, a voice in his brain, a voice from every fight, the worst curse of all, one part of him turning inward, the single word drilling into him. **Coward.**

The tears came now, his fingers cramped around the musket, the hard breathing, his heart racing. He watched more of the men crawl up, gone, the trench still holding men who hesitated, who sat frozen as he was, consumed by the fear, the awful terror. He heard orders again, shouts from an officer, saw Captain Haymond, the battalion commander, out behind the logs, trying to rally the men who stayed behind. Bauer curled his knees up tightly again, sobbing now, but the ice broke free in his brain, and he thought of Willis, had a sudden vision, clarity, knew that Willis would die, that Bauer would never see him again. But Willis was out there, had gone . . . where? I can't let him know, I can't let him ever see this. **Coward.**

He rolled over again, on his knees, pushed the hat down hard on his head, moved the musket out on the dirt, pulled himself up. The flat ground was littered with bodies, bloody stains, torn pieces of men ripped by canister. He climbed up, stood for a long second, the musket balls zipping past, more blasts from artillery coming down behind the trench line. He saw the men in motion now, spots of blue, some pausing, hugging the ground on the hillside, then crawling upward, some of those men running uphill, hunched over, making their way along paths,

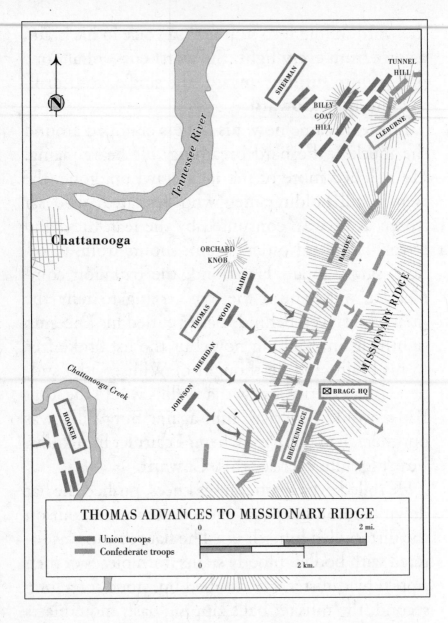

THOMAS ADVANCES TO MISSIONARY RIDGE

Union troops
Confederate troops

0   2 mi.

0   2 km.

shoving through brush. He searched for Willis, but there were too many, and he saw now, all across the ridge, out to the left, as far as he could see, a half mile, men doing the same, swarms of blue ants, all of them moving up the hill. He gripped the musket to his chest, looked up toward the top of the ridge, hundreds of feet, the smoke blowing out in a dirty cloud. The artillery was firing steadily, the blasts still aimed downward, sideways, along the hill, the gunners sweeping men away, men too slow to find cover. Bauer stared at that for a long second, heard a musket ball sing past his ear, another, impacting at his feet. He took a deep breath, fought through the paralysis, no thoughts of the ground out behind him, of leaving these men. He moved one leg, then the other, the slope so far away, two hundred endless yards, dirt thrown up, another whistle past him, musket fire from above, and he saw the backs of men, all of them climbing, pushing up into rocks and thickets and he began to run.

The first hundred feet up the hillside was thick with cut timber where the rebels had taken down trees, the logs used to build their fortifications. Now the treetops and limbs made a brushy tangle, the men struggling through. But there was one great advantage to the obstacle. The brush gave cover, hiding the men from the gunners above. The artillerymen didn't seek perfect targets, knew only to sweep the hillside as closely as the aim of the big guns would allow. Those men kept up their fire mostly to the side, the slope just below them far too steep to allow the artillery to aim downward. But out to both flanks, the gunners along the crest turned their artillery to the side as much as the ground would allow. In the brushy thickets below, whatever cover the men in blue could find was no barrier to the canister and exploding shells, the sloping ground ripped, the brushy limbs shattered into splintering projectiles.

Bauer kept flat, his legs pushing against loose dirt and rocks, any kind of foothold. Gradually he made his way upward, followed the churned-up dirt, the small gaps in the brush where men had gone before him. The effort was agonizing, his legs exhausted, burning in his lungs from the strain and the smoke. But above him and out to both sides, many more men were doing the same, no talk, their voices silenced by the effort, by the ongoing fire, the blasts and musket fire still sweeping through them. Bauer grabbed a fat limb, pushed the brush away, saw now, the ground above the brush line was open, dotted with crags and rocks, cut with small ravines, slices in the earth. There were rifle pits above, rebels standing, the quick firing of the musket, then down, reloading. The new earthworks were nearly halfway up the slope, piled dirt and logs that extended in both directions as far as he could see. He saw the heads peering up, quick shots, bursts of smoke from the barrels of a hundred muskets. Around him, men were returning fire, most of that useless, impacting straight into the dirt that protected the rebels. Bauer watched one man right above him, the rebel slow moving, a **target,** the man's musket coming up, aiming, but Bauer was in no place to make a shot, and he rolled to one side, the sound of the man's musket erased by so many others. He lay still, fought for air, wiped dirt from his eyes, could see men in blue now on every side of him, some coming up from below, many more up above, still moving up the hill. Most of those men were finding cover, filling every hole, sliding up behind every rock. Bauer glanced up toward the rebel works again, fifty yards above him, angry at himself, no way to take aim without standing upright. Not now, he thought. Let's get someplace better than this. He took a breath, spit dust from his mouth, dug his feet into the soft dirt, lunged upward, his feet slipping, then grabbing, a hard struggle for a few feet higher. He wouldn't stop, pushed harder, his feet catching rock, better traction, saw flashes from above, the rebels making their effort, but the men in blue were closing the distance, some of them waiting for opportunity, for the rebel to show himself, the hard crack close by Bauer, a rebel falling over the dirt, another rising up beside him, suddenly punched backward.

He kept pushing himself higher, felt the hot breath of wind, canister blowing past him, peppering the hillside below him, pushing him farther, faster, his eyes in a mad search for any safe place. The shouts were more audible now, men calling out from the good cover, bringing others in with them, the men stacking up, banding together. Bauer pushed against a small rock, anchored in the dirt, the boost pushing him farther up, a flat, narrow shelf, big rocks above him, men in a thick line around him. He fell in among them, no one cursing him, the men shoving aside, making space. He tried to shrink himself, to give room, but it was nearly impossible, the men crushed together in what seemed to be a haven, heavy cover. He was on his side, slid the musket upward, still no place to aim, heard the talk now, the men huddled together, sharing their fear, their fury. Bauer tried to see faces, saw mostly hats, men of the 15th, and his own, no one asking for officers, no officer seeking order. The musket fire from close above seemed to slow, men down below Bauer taking aim, picking targets. He felt the eagerness at that, his job, his talent, but not now. Now, what? He looked around, finally an officer, the man standing out to one side, Captain Haymond, then hunkering down, doing his job, searching for the next move, the best route they should take. Men were crawling past, just below, some with eyes of desperate fear, others seeking friends, offering names, units, as though any company commander would care just what boulder his men had called their own.

Close beside him, the stink of sweat and blood, a wound on a man's arm, the blood staining Bauer's coat, and Bauer grabbed the man's shoulder, said, "Hey! You're wounded. Let me stuff a handkerchief into that."

Bauer pulled himself up, saw now, it was the boy, Hoover, saw teary-eyed fear, and Hoover said, "I'm killed! They done killed me!"

"No, they just shot you. Just your arm. Here, hold this tight."

Hoover grabbed at Bauer's hand, wild animal eyes, and Bauer pushed the boy's hand onto the cloth, knew it was all he could do. Beside the boy, a man Bauer didn't know, a handful of others, men from the 15th, a few from the 18th. The faces showed every emotion, fear and anger, exhaustion, relief, men finding their strength, and now Bauer heard the familiar voice, the growling curse, Willis, crawling along just below them.

"Get your fat bottoms out of this hole and climb! There's better cover above. The damn rebs can't shoot straight down. The higher you go, the easer it'll be. You don't wanna take my word for it, the colonel's up there right now."

"Captain!"

Bauer looked toward the voice, down the slope, saw one of the colonel's aides, Lieutenant Moyer, the man crawling up the hill in a panic, pushing through the loose rocks like a deranged spider. Moyer was in good cover now, out of breath, seemed desperately relieved to find Willis, or any officer. He fought to catch his breath, his words coming in short bursts.

"Captain! You have to withdraw these men. They've gone too far!"

Willis didn't respond, stared at the man with a look Bauer knew well. Around Bauer, other men answered, "Too far? It ain't far enough!"

"We made it halfway up this hill!"

Willis reached down, grabbed the lieutenant's collar, pulled him up the hill, a hard hiss into the man's face. "These men have **fought** their way up this hill. If we'd have stayed down there, we'd all be dead. Who in hell thinks we done the wrong thing? Some fat general back there eating his dinner? Colonel Moore is right up above us, in those rocks. You gonna crawl up there and tell him it's time to go home?"

The lieutenant seemed ready to cry, said, "Captain, it's orders. Down below. General Johnson's aide. We were supposed to take the rifle pits down below, and hold there, waiting for orders. You're not supposed to be up here at all! There's more rifle pits not too far above us. You can see 'em plain from down below. The rebs are there in force, and they're hitting our boys good. Same all the way down this ridgeline. Hell, the general says half the army's gone too far up this hill!"

Willis glanced at Bauer now, as though seeing him for the first time. "You hear that, Dutchie? We disobeyed orders by staying alive." Willis looked out to the others, all eyes on him, more men out to the side, more rocks, more cover, other officers trying to hear through the showers of artillery fire. Willis looked up, raised his head slightly, then down, smiled.

"You're right about one thing. There's rebs not thirty yards up the hill. They gotta be sitting in their own pee, knowing we're up this close. Lieutenant, I don't know anything about General Johnson, other than that hairy thing on his face he's always playing with. But these men followed me out of that pit down there because they didn't want to die sitting still. Now I don't aim to die running backward. That's what you're telling us to do."

Men responded now, agreeing with Willis. The lieutenant seemed desperate, staring at Willis, what seemed like an agonizing effort to be understood.

"Captain, all I know is what the general is telling his aides. We're not supposed to climb this here mountain. The orders are for these men to withdraw back to the rebel works at the base of the ridge."

There was a burst of musket fire down to the left, more from above, volleys both ways, and Bauer peered up, saw a dozen men in blue rising up, climbing quickly through rocks, one man falling, tumbling backward. Now others did the same, farther away, shouts and screams. Willis looked that way, then turned to the aide.

"Lieutenant, you can go back to General Johnson's aide and tell him the fight's up this hill. We push those rebs just a little more, and they'll haul it out of those rifle pits, and make their way to the top, just like those boys did down below. The higher we go, the better it is for us. You tell the general that if our artillery back there wants to keep up their little show for our benefit, they might aim a little high."

"Captain . . . please. I was told . . ."

Over from Bauer, a deep, thunderous voice, and Bauer looked that way, knew the growl of Corporal Owens.

"Look here. I signed up to kill rebels. Indians. Mexicans. Hell, I don't rightly care. But right now it's rebels. And they're not too far up this hill. Sounds like the place I wanna be. If'n you don't mind, Captain, I'd rather follow you up this damn hill than run away from a fight 'cause of this bloomer-wearin' mama squawler, and whatever general he thinks is so damn smart. Running away ain't never won a fight."

Willis didn't smile, said, "There you go, Lieu-tenant. I don't care for being called names by none such as this fellow. He wants me to lead him up this hill, that's what I'm gonna do. With all my respects to General Johnson, and his aide. You can tell the general, or anyone else back there who's paying mind to what we're doing, this is a fight we're aim-ing to **win.**"

Willis scanned the men closest to him, more agreements, men making ready to move once more. Bauer sat up, saw more men down to the left climb-ing out of cover, pushing their fight higher, smoke and musket fire engulfing them as they moved up-ward. All around him, the men began to shout, and

Bauer saw others pointing, waving toward them to rise up, to keep moving upward.

Willis responded, his head up over the rocks, said aloud, "They're running! The rebs are running! Let's help 'em. If you haven't fixed bayonets, do it now! Get up! Climb the damn hill! Get to those next earthworks!"

Willis pulled himself up over the rocks, the others following. Bauer waited for the space, rolled over, pulled his bayonet from his belt, tugged it tightly to the musket. He stood, put one foot higher on the slope, then climbed, stepping alongside the others, many more above. He ducked from the whistling canister, blowing past, too high, fought through smoke and dust, the men crowding together, the rebel rifle pits just above him. There were logs there as well, and Bauer saw beyond, above, those men pulling out, muskets dropped, pushing their way uphill. He looked out to the side, stopped, frozen by the stunning view of the enormous blue wave spread all along the ridge. The advance was flowing up the hill all down the slope, Johnson's division, beyond, Sheridan's division, and many more Bauer couldn't see. The rebel artillery fire still came, ripping through the men, clouds of billowing smoke, adding to the musket fire that sought them out, panicked firing by the rebels still holding to the pits along the hillside. But those men were few, most of the rebels doing what their men down below had already done, pulling away, their numbers too few to hold back this enormous wave, the rebels desperate to find the safety at the crest of the hill. Bauer took aim now, finally, leveled the musket at a man staggering up the hill, a dozen yards above him. But another man fired first, the rebel rolling over, sliding back down, Bauer stung by rage, disappointment. He looked for the rival, saw Owens, the big dirty man, a smile through clenched yellow teeth. Owens looked at him now, still smiling, nodded toward him, pointed a crooked finger toward the crest of the hill.

CHAPTER THIRTY-EIGHT

THOMAS

ORCHARD KNOB—
NOVEMBER 25, 1863—4:30 P.M.

The advance of the army had been spectacular, the view from Orchard Knob offering a clear panorama of the attack. Thomas had watched in awe, the crisp cold adding to the nervousness inside him he tried to hide from the men around him. Like Thomas, the others had stood in reverent silence as the thick lines of blue infantry pushed first through the dense thickets, the stands of trees, and then, with nearly perfect symmetry, had rolled forward across the final half mile of open ground. But the enemy had watched the same scene, had responded as Thomas knew they would. From their vantage point on the knob, the observers had estimated that the rebels had placed as many as fifty cannon in various positions along the center of Missionary Ridge, and with the blue troops in clear view, every one of those guns had started its work.

As the flashes of fire blew down off the heights, Federal guns had begun their efforts to assist the advance, those gunners already knowing the range, the practice they had engaged in for the past several days. What had once annoyed Thomas, those useless duels that did nothing but consume ammunition, now became purposeful and precise. The rebel cannon responded to the batteries close to Orchard Knob, but more often, their muzzles were aimed at the oncoming infantry. Thomas had seen that kind of assault before, could never just accept that artillery fire was one of the usual hazards for men who had only their legs to propel them. In every fight, he had watched his men moving closer to the enemy with the same twisting dread, each blast burrowing through the lines of blue hitting him somewhere inside. It was the same today, that final race to the rebel rifle pits staggered by the waves of shelling, and then, the musket fire from those rebels brave enough to make a stand at the foot of the ridge. The couriers had come then, uncertain, nervous men, asking for orders, for clarity of what they had already been told. It had infuriated Thomas that the same men who had stood before Grant were now showing such uncertainty, or that each man seemed to regard the assault in a different way. The complaints came as well, fears that the attack was doomed to disaster, that with so much firepower raining down on them from the heights, even the rifle pits were a challenge the men could not overcome. For nearly an hour, Thomas had stood close beside Grant, fielding the doubts, the pessimism, the confusion, had responded to the couriers and staff officers by repeating the command they had been given already: Grab the first line, capture the rebels there, and wait for instructions.

Grant had grown furious at the confusion, and Thomas knew the anger was directed at him. It was logical, in its own way, Thomas being the senior commander on the field. But Thomas also knew he was being scrutinized by civilian eyes, too many for comfort. The newspapermen had come forward, men like Sylvanus Cadwallader, who seemed to trail behind Grant like an overeager puppy. Charles Dana was there as well, no surprise, Dana sure to record any possibility of disaster in his next wire to the War Department. Thomas had grown to dislike Dana intensely, had wondered for some time now if Dana would ever care to send Secretary Stanton a dispatch that contained **good** news.

The staffs were there as well, no harm in that, Grant's aides as useful as Thomas's in fielding the steady stream of riders from out front. Thomas had expected Granger to keep close, especially since it was the corps commander's two divisions who held the center point of the entire advance. But Granger had slipped away, and Thomas had learned that

Granger's love of artillery had superseded his care for his own generals. Granger had occupied himself with ranging the guns of an Indiana battery, inserting himself into a job far more suited to the men who stood to the side, helpless to object. Whether or not Granger's gunners appreciated the intrusion, Thomas knew Grant was not happy at all. The comments had come with pointed subtlety, Grant agreeing with Thomas that a corps commander had better things to do in the middle of a fight than play with cannons. With Grant's displeasure reinforcing his own, Thomas had ordered Granger to return to the peak of Orchard Knob, Granger told in precise terms that his guns were already in capable hands.

As the troops pressed closer to the rebel positions, the smoke had risen, obscuring most of the details, beyond glimpses of disorganization in the lines. It was to be expected, the men advancing at different speeds, depending on the punishment each regiment was absorbing. But the smoke continued to rise, enveloping the ridge itself, adding considerably to Thomas's anxiety. He stared through field glasses, a dozen more pairs spread out across the knob, eyes fixed on anything that would tell the commanders just what was happening.

Beside him, Grant chewed furiously on a cigar, then shouted to a nearby aide, "Have we heard any more? Is Sherman succeeding?"

The aide responded in a low voice, as though no

one else should know just what Sherman might be doing. "I'm not certain, sir. No word has yet come since your last order, at three o'clock. Shall I send another rider up that way?"

Grant seemed to growl, the cigar moving, shifting in his tightening jaw. "He will not keep me in the dark. There is nothing to be seen that way except smoke, and I must believe that he is carrying the fight." Grant turned to Thomas, who knew the man's anger would flow his way. "What is happening out here? I will not tolerate failure on such a scale, General."

Thomas felt the stab of Grant's question, gritted his teeth before answering. "I know all that you know, sir. We have all kept to this same position. You have heard the couriers. The men have pushed hard against the rebel works. If there is anything significant in that, either for the good or the bad, I trust we shall be told soon enough."

Grant stared through the glasses, said nothing, and Thomas glanced toward Granger, who had watched the brief conversation. Granger shook his head, no comfort to Thomas, and Granger raised his glasses again, said, "Oh. My word. I see troops on the hillside. A great many troops."

Thomas aimed his stare that way, caught the slight clearing in the smoke, saw what Granger saw, men in blue spreading upward. They stared in silence for a long minute, the smoke clearing again, more of the ridge visible, the blue pushing upward in wide swaths, most of the advance far past the place they were ordered to hold. Thomas absorbed the sight, felt his nervousness increasing, heard low mumbling from Grant, and now Grant lowered the glasses, said, "General Thomas, who gave that order? Who ordered those troops to climb that ridge?"

Thomas felt sick, a burst of fear that he was witnessing another disaster, one of his own making. "I don't know. I did not."

He turned to Granger, who still stared out through the glasses, and Thomas gathered himself, put authority into his voice, as much for Grant's benefit as his own.

"General Granger, did you order your divisions to assault the ridge?"

Granger kept the glasses at his eyes. "No. Not me. No such orders were given. But I tell you this, sir. When those boys get their dander up, no force in hell can stop them."

Thomas winced, didn't need a dose of boastfulness. He looked at Grant, who rocked the field glasses in his hand, and Grant then looked toward Granger, said, "I will not have this. Someone will pay dearly for this. Attacking that hill was not in my orders."

Grant turned away, raised the field glasses again, and Thomas stood between the two men, felt the heat from Grant, saw a sheepish expression from Granger. Granger said nothing, the silence settling over them all.

Thomas looked again toward the ridge, flashes of fire, waves of smoke, the surge of blue seeming to spread upward, higher still. He thought of the generals, the ones he knew well, Wood and Sheridan, the center of the assault, couldn't fathom these men would so blatantly disregard their orders, risking their careers, and the lives of their men. He closed his eyes, looked downward, heard nothing more from Grant, no one around them offering a word, the staffs kept silent by the anticipation of a slaughter, the fear silencing even the chattiness of the newspapermen. Thomas opened his eyes, kept his gaze to the ground, let out a breath. God help us, he thought. God help them. I didn't want this command, I didn't expect ever to order so many men to such a potential disaster. But . . . here we are, and when this is over, the responsibility will be mine alone.

He twisted slightly, trying to relieve the dull aching in his back. Beside him, Granger said, "Will you look at that. . . ."

The words came with enthusiasm, something Thomas didn't expect. Grant held his silence, and Thomas raised the glasses again, stared into vast clouds of smoke, caught glimpses of blue, a clearing now, solid blue mass, realized with a sudden bolt that he was looking at the crest of the hill. He saw it now, unmistakable, the hard flutter of a flag, what seemed to be the Stars and Stripes. He strained to see, wouldn't accept that image, not yet, wouldn't allow himself to feel anything but the awful nagging fear that the assault was still rolling over into a catastrophe.

Behind him, a cheer went up, one of the staff, and Thomas winced again, no, there can be no such certainty, no wishful thinking. He strained to see, scanned the crest of the ridgeline, another clearing through the smoke, saw it again, a different place, saw another flag, surrounded by a mass of blue spreading out along the top of the hill. The hope came now, a burst of optimism, and he held it inside, couldn't be certain of anything, not yet, not until word came from the commanders. Beside him, Grant grunted, then said, "It appears, General, that some of your boys made it to the top."

CHAPTER THIRTY-NINE

BRAGG

OUTSIDE THE NAIL HOUSE—
MISSIONARY RIDGE—
NOVEMBER 25, 1863—3:00 P.M.

He had been out to the right flank twice that morning, couldn't help being impressed with the fight Cleburne was making to hold Sherman away from Tunnel Hill. The effort from the Yankees there gave Bragg enormous satisfaction that he had been right all along, that Grant's army would not just march into the center of his strongest lines, would instead punch in on the flanks. But Bragg's attention had been too focused on the right, a mistake he grudgingly accepted. The loss of Lookout Mountain had rattled him severely, which he tried to keep to himself, not giving any of his commanders the ammunition to use against him for what someone in Richmond might call an oversight. But the insistence by Hardee that the loss of the mountain called for a full-out withdrawal made no sense to Bragg at all. There was still the ridgeline, so many miles of undulating, difficult ground, where the men on top had every advantage. Bragg could already sense that Grant had conceded that strength, evidenced by a complete lack of Federal aggressiveness across the center of Missionary Ridge. All Grant seemed willing to do was march out in grand parades, while Federal artillery scattered shells along the ridge in a haphazard game of target practice.

Breckinridge continued to support Bragg's decisions, and Bragg suspected it was the politician doing what politicians did best: Offend no one, make friends. Bragg had no use for friends now at all, only expected Breckinridge to do the job, anchoring the left of the army on the marvelous ground Bragg had provided for him. He knew that Hardee had very little respect for Breckinridge as a field commander, but right now that didn't matter. Hardee had all his attention focused on Bragg's right, including Cleburne's stout efforts on Tunnel Hill. Breckinridge held the left half of Bragg's entire position now, those troops holding the ground that ran southward from Hardee's left flank, near the center of Missionary Ridge, then downward to the deep valley that separated Lookout Mountain from the southern tip of the ridge.

Bragg had been forced to accept the complete retreat from Lookout Mountain, would reserve harsh judgment for that failure for another time. But pulling off the mountain had shortened the Confederate lines, the one silver lining on a very dark cloud, made more shining by the opposition on the left flank. That morning, the Yankees had done just what Bragg had expected, had driven down from Lookout Mountain, Joe Hooker's men slogging into the marshy ground near Chattanooga Creek with no means of getting across without considerable effort. Facing them, Breckinridge had posted a minimal force, all that could be spared, what was now of little concern to Bragg. The most important fight was northward, Cleburne proving to Bragg that his tenacity was more than a match for what was supposed to be the fierce and unstoppable willpower of William T. Sherman.

With Hooker bogged down at the creek, and Cleburne deflecting every assault from Sherman, Bragg had returned to his headquarters with the full confidence that the clear skies and bracing chill were a positive omen for his army. As he rode along the crest of Missionary Ridge, Bragg sought to share his energetic optimism with his men, offering up encouraging words, spreading confidence, hoping to hear the cheers that would inspire him as much as it would them. But the officers seemed to hold their men down in a deep gloom, as though discouraging them from making any kind of show of congratu-

lations for Bragg's perfect strategy. It was custom-
ary for troops to cheer their commanding general,
but the reception he had received was anything but
glorious. In Bragg's mind, there could be but one
cause: seeds of hostility toward him, planted by
their officers. It infuriated him, but the impact of
scattered Yankee artillery held his attention away
from thoughts of punishment. The brigade and division commanders moved along through their own
troops as he did, but Bragg had no need for councils, received no welcoming gestures, very few signs
of outright respect. Instead, the men who owed
Bragg their very survival seemed more interested in
nervous observations of what lay out to their front,
the wide-open ground around Orchard Knob, as
though none of Bragg's successes on the flank deserved any recognition at all.

The staff kept mostly close to the Nail House,
the duties of the headquarters, more arguments
with the supply people, dismissive denials from
Richmond for more reinforcements. Little word
had come from Longstreet, as though his fight at
Knoxville were taking place a continent away. If
Longstreet was sending any news to Richmond,
that news died there, no one seeming to care if
Bragg was given any real information at all. It was
one more reason for Bragg to congratulate himself,
that by sending Longstreet away, he had indeed rid
his army of a disease. Hardee's insistence on withdrawal from the ridge, the outrageous notion of a

full-out retreat, was one more sign to Bragg that few in his command had the best interests of the army at heart. The advice and suggestions and councils still seemed designed to injure Bragg's reputation with Richmond, laying blame for failure squarely at his feet. Withdrawing from such a strong position, even if his army might be outnumbered, would be the kind of failure that even Jefferson Davis could not ignore. Bragg had ridden through Hardee's headquarters knowing the feelings against him, that Hardee's plan for disgracing Bragg had not been implemented, not this time. Today's success seemed to fill the air. If the men who held the center of his line refused to offer those glad tidings to him, even now, Bragg forced himself to ignore that. He knew better. These men would find soon enough that a crushing defeat of Sherman's army would change everything across the way, that Grant would suffer a blow that would likely cause the Federal army to reexamine their entire campaign. Bragg held tightly to the confidence that Grant might yet withdraw, convinced that any further bloodletting against Bragg's invulnerable positions might cost Grant his command. That no one else seemed to share that kind of optimism dug hard at Bragg's sense of satisfaction. It was one more reason for Bragg to keep a sharp eye on the men who professed obedience to his command, even as they pretended not to notice just how successful this army had been.

NEAR THE NAIL HOUSE—
MISSIONARY RIDGE—
NOVEMBER 25, 1863—5:00 P.M.

The appearance of the massive Federal advance emerging from the woods and thickets had been extraordinary, Bragg stung into silence by the sheer beauty of it. The formations of blue had rolled toward him with martial precision, the Federal artillery still throwing their shells against Missionary Ridge as though saluting their own parade with a rousing fireworks display. But very soon, the formations had pushed far closer than Bragg expected, and his own artillery began their work, smashing into the perfect lines with shot and shell, the smoke hiding the chaos that he knew was engulfing the Yankees, even as they kept up their advance. He rode out to one vantage point after another, small peaks along the ridge where he could see clearly, and the scale of the advance had become apparent. The Federal lines seemed to expand nearly two miles wide, the observers sending word through his staff that four divisions, possibly twenty-five thousand men, were pressing their advance straight into the teeth of his defenses. The first wave of musket fire from down below had exhilarated him, though the smoke hid most of the effects the volleys had against the enemy's formations. But for the first time, the men around him took up his own cheer, that the enemy seemed eager to slaughter themselves against his guns, as though Grant was committing an act of mass suicide. There was a horror to that, even to Bragg, especially when the enemy troops emerged from the last of the thickets and woodlands, rolling forward across a half mile of wide-open ground. Bragg watched as the blue lines absorbed a stunning volume of punishment from every Confederate battery along that part of the ridge. But on they came, with almost no answering fire from the Yankee muskets, as though holding to a single-minded goal to reach the foot of the slope, no matter the horrific cost.

What Bragg saw then crushed his exuberance. Instead of holding to their position in the rifle pits along the base of the ridge, his men withdrew, a mad, desperate scramble up the hill, some of them making their climb driven by the kind of terror he had seen in fights before. His staff had reacted by pressing the officers for explanations, bringing nothing but conflicting reports. Some of the commanders had ordered their men not to hold that ground, that if pressed, they should immediately withdraw to the heights. Others had been instructed to stay put, but when the men holding their position observed so many others pulling away, the piecemeal retreat exploded into infectious panic. By the time Bragg could sort out the confusion, too many of his men had fled the flat ground, those works now firmly in the hands of the men in blue. Bragg could only point to Hardee as the source of the chaos.

Most of the regiments along the center of the ridge had been divided, half their strength sent down along the base of the ridge, the rest either holding a thin line midway up, or put into hastily dug works along the crest of the hill. Even Breckinridge had been concerned that the army's lines were too thin, that keeping the men together in a heavy line seemed a far wiser course, the most effective way to combat what even Bragg accepted to be Grant's superior numbers. But Hardee had insisted that dividing the men was the most effective defense, what Bragg now believed to be one more treasonous display of inept tactics.

With Bragg's troops flowing up the hill in a panicked scramble for safety, Bragg moved again along the lines of the men who held the top of the crest, calling to them to hold the enemy back, to assist the good work of the artillery. It was only then that Bragg saw that the men had dug their entrenchments along the topmost part of the crest, with no field of fire downward. Any man who attempted to shoot down the slope would have to expose himself in the wide open, an easy target for Yankee muskets farther down the hill.

His men continued to pour up the hill toward him in a stumbling, exhausted mob, collapsing on the first level ground they reached. He dug the spurs hard into the horse, kept moving along the ridge, seeking answers, seeking anyone who knew why this was happening at all.

The crest of the ridgeline wasn't level; there were dips and valleys that made coherence difficult for the units whose flanks were supposed to be tied together. The width of the ridge varied as well, and from the placement of the artillery, he could see that little care had been given to defending the ridge itself from a direct Federal assault. The guns were mostly in the wide open, the crews working around them through smoke and heat, many of those men already down, swept away by Federal artillery far across the way. The earthworks held the men who had not yet joined the fight, bristling rows of bayonets, muskets at the ready, but those men were now confronted by the waves of survivors from down below, struggling, exhausted men who had lost the will or the ability to offer any kind of fight. He watched the men tumbling into cover, many rejoining their own units, the regiments divided by placing so much of their strength in the defensive lines now held by the Yankees, what Bragg screamed to himself was Hardee's great error. He watched in horror as so much of his army crawled and staggered past him, weaponless, some with small wounds, some injured from the climb itself. He looked around frantically, saw junior officers screaming out orders, making the effort to gather their men, but in his mind, he saw only the face of Hardee, the only face that mattered to him now. He fingered the pistol in his belt, thought, If you were here, now, if you could see what you have caused, I would kill you.

His brain fought through a fog, the chaos around him driving through his thoughts. He stared northward, thought of Cleburne, the good fight, but that was miles away, the sounds of any fight on Tunnel Hill erased by the thunderous eruptions around him now, incoming Federal shells impacting all across the ridgeline, keeping his men down in their cover. Along the front edge of the ridge, his own guns kept up their fire, some aimed out toward the distant flashes from Yankee guns, but many more were turning, the barrels pointing downward, the artillerymen improvising as much as they could to spread fire on the hillside itself.

He jabbed his spurs hard into the horse's flank, pushed through clouds of smoke from the big guns, heard more shouts of his officers, the men rallying their troops, what was becoming a futile attempt to keep the fugitives from running completely across and over the ridge. Many of the men who had made the climb were regaining their wind, and as quickly as they could rise, they continued their mad dash backward, shoving men aside as they dropped down through their own trench works, then back up and out, across the top of the ridge, only to vanish down the east side of the hill. Bragg jerked the horse to a halt, saw an officer with a sword high, the man imploring his men to stop, to add their strength to the others in the trenches. But there was little strength in those men at all, most of them without muskets. Bragg saw riders coming toward him, couriers, ignored them, spurred the horse again, moved farther to the north, down a slight draw, then back up, more trenches, more exposed artillery. He saw a man on horseback, the colors, rode that way, still fighting the smoke.

Bragg reined up, saw one of the brigade commanders, Arthur Manigault, the South Carolinian, shouted out as the horse bucked beneath him, "What is the meaning of this? Can you not stop these renegades?"

Manigault looked at him with a hard glare of disgust, said, "Sir, this position is intact. But there are enemy soldiers up on the ridge down to the right. A brigade of Mississippians has broken. We will make every attempt to hold here, and by the grace of God, the men are giving them a fight. But the earthworks, sir—"

"I know nothing of earthworks! I know of heart and courage! Do your men possess neither?"

Manigault pointed down the ridgeline, and Bragg could see blue now, a cluster of men on the next mound along the crest, a sharp fight at very close range.

"There! You see! Others will stand tall! What of your men?"

"General Bragg, my men are facing the enemy

from works that were dug down the face of the hill. I will not argue this with you, sir. I have done all I could to convince the engineers that their placement of the trenches was incorrect. I ordered my own brigade to dig their trenches farther down the face of the hill, giving them a line of fire. Look out to both flanks, sir! Look! The works were placed too high, on the crest of the ridge. They can fire no volleys until the enemy has reached the crest!"

"Bah! I see Yankees twenty paces below those far rocks. They must be pressed back, driven away!"

"By whom, sir? The artillery cannot make that shot. I have instructed Captain Dent's battery to direct his fire as close as possible to the hill, but there is no means to provide cover for his men. His crews are being shot down before they can fire."

"Then send your men over those rocks and drive the enemy away with the bayonet! Must you be told?"

Bragg spurred the horse again, had no patience for hesitation, for men with excuses. He saw more officers, screaming efforts at pulling their men together, driving a line directly along the ridge. He saw Patton Anderson, Manigault's division commander, and he moved that way, felt the aching need for a bullwhip, thought, I would whip them right here, show their men how to stand tall!

Anderson saw him coming, pointed down the hill, a hard shout, "Sir! The enemy is in cover down below these rocks. This is not a safe place for you!"

"Then why are you not advancing on their position, if they are so close? I will have your command!"

Anderson seemed to fight for control, holding his temper, and Bragg felt his own heat rising, would welcome an outright act of insubordination, reached for his sword, would slice this man from his saddle. A courier arrived now, riding hard with one of Bragg's staff officers, the courier reining the horse, in full panic, screaming at him, "Sir! The enemy has broken over the crest near your headquarters!"

Bragg looked that way, too much smoke, men running, some forming up a line far across the next rise, facing south. Anderson pointed that way, toward the far end of Breckinridge's position, said, "Sir! We must turn the lines to the flank. We must advance where the enemy has broken through!"

Bragg felt a wave of confusion, the smoke obliterating any sign of organization. "Then do what you must to protect your flanks!"

"Sir, there are no flanks. The enemy is already on the crest to the north. We are fighting in three directions!"

Bragg spun the horse, saw a ragged group of Yankees suddenly rising up along the far side of the ridge, men aiming muskets, seeking targets. Bragg ignored Anderson, pushed the horse once more, rode hard to the rear of the ridge, the crest there barely a hundred yards wide. There Manigault's men were forming up into a new line, and Bragg rode through them, heard the volley behind him, muskets fighting muskets. The smoke was still in thick, stinking clouds, and he drove the horse farther, down an incline, large rocks to his right, saw blue on the rocks, men struggling to climb over, musket fire to his left, the men driven back. He jerked his head around, fought to see whose men they were, thought, Yes, now we shall see! There is one warrior up here, one man among us who understands his duty!

He saw his officers now, some on foot, moving their men into line, turning them to face down the ridge, and Bragg pointed toward the larger rocks, swarming now with Yankees, a hard shout, "Here! Bring them here!"

"Sir! This way! The enemy has broken through!"

Bragg saw it now, another cluster of blue surging up over the ridgeline, pushing straight for the freshly dug trenches, a burst of musket fire blowing into them, cutting them down, halting their advance. Bragg felt a jolt of excitement. Yes! That's it, boys! Now, the bayonet! He rode that way, would see it up close, would watch his men destroy the enemy, would see the terror on the faces of the men in blue.

"Fire again! Another volley!"

His voice was drowned out by the echoing artillery fire, the thunderous blasts thrown out across the crest, the shells coming in from far out in the plain. He heard it again, the same infuriating plea, "Sir! This is no place for you! The enemy has broken through on both sides of us!"

He turned, saw his own staff officers, fear in their faces, would not hear their cowardice. "Do we know where General Breckinridge is? His men are giving way! There shall be punishment for this! Find him, bring him to me!"

He saw a helplessness on the officer's face, ignored that, faced the nearest breakthrough, more men in blue rolling up toward him. Manigault was there again, directing artillery to swing about, firing straight along the ridgeline. Bragg spurred again, rode to the east side of the ridge, the ground falling away, saw men running down the hill, **his** men, making their escape from the enemy. More men were running past him, and he waved his sword in the air, called out to them, "Stop! Fight here! Form a line! Prepare to fire!"

The men ignored him, some pushing into his horse with blind panic as they ran past. He felt a sickening weakness, utter impotence, saw Manigault again, would exact punishment, and Manigault shouted toward him, "Sir! We are making a stand! Colonel Pressley is holding his men together!"

"Pressley? Who is that?"

"Tenth South Carolina, sir! The Twenty-eighth, Colonel Butler, is doing well down the hill there!"

Bragg felt his anger blunted, could not find fault with Manigault now, searched for another bit of fury, pointed back down the hill to the east.

"Who are those men? They are running away!"

"Deas's brigade, sir. They have broken."

"I will find Deas, then. I will have his command. This is not excusable, not at all!"

Manigault stared at him silently, turned his horse, moved again to his men. Another volley of musket fire erupted, Manigault's men staggering back, more Yankees rolling up the hill toward them. Bragg jerked the horse's head to one side, dug his spurs in, the animal lurching forward, and Bragg kept the name in his head, **Deas.** I will have Breckinridge remove him, once I settle these matters. I will not have such officers in my command. **Never.**

He rode back toward his headquarters now, remembered the courier's panic, saw a gathering of blue moving around the house, more of them far down the ridge. In every direction, there were more of his officers, vain attempts to rally fleeing troops, more of his men running from their protection, straight toward him, toward the backside of the ridge. They must see me, he thought, they will obey my orders!

He dismounted, stood tall with his sword high, waved the blade above his head. "Rally with me here! We shall drive them off!"

Men looked at him as they passed, and he was shocked to see smiles, one man laughing out loud, others with the unstoppable fear, tears and raw panic. He tried the call again, "Hold with me here! Do not disgrace yourselves. Do not disgrace your country! I am your general! Fight with me!"

His voice left him, the energy draining away. More men were watching him as they passed, an officer, calling out to him, "Leave here, sir! The enemy is close to both sides! You must withdraw!"

"We must fight! Do not disgrace your families!"

But the energy was gone, and he lowered the sword, felt a sudden jerk around his waist, was picked up off the ground, a booming voice in his ear, "And here's your mule! Yessir, Old Bragg, **he's hell on retreat!**"

The man dropped him now, Bragg falling to one knee, pulled himself up, saw others laughing out loud, still moving away from him. The Yankees were closer now, their lines coming together, more organized, spreading out through the batteries, some of them swinging the guns around, others firing muskets into the backs of his men.

"Sir! This way!"

Bragg saw the horse, another officer, one of his own, saw his colors, the color bearer staying close. Bragg started to speak, caught the look on the young man's face, had never noticed him before, clean-shaven, terrified eyes, another aide there now, with Bragg's horse.

"Sir! We must leave this place!"

Bragg stared out to the front again, the rocky ledge, the ground falling away, a swarm of blue still climbing up, moving his way, scattered firing, a hard thump of artillery, more horsemen, officers, pulling their men back. He still held the sword, pointed it slowly out, toward the gathering lines of the enemy, felt a single spark of defiance. I will not allow this. I will fight you myself. But there was a hand on his shoulder, pulling him, the horse's reins put into his hand, the voices of the aides reaching him.

"Sir! We must go! Now!"

He struggled to climb the horse, swung his leg over, searched out to both flanks, expected to see lines of his men advancing, the counterattack, driving the bluebellies off the ridge. More smoke drifted past, hiding the fight, but even the clearings were darkening, and he looked upward, the daylight nearly gone. He slid the sword back into its scabbard, looked again along the ridge, the good high ground, the strong perfect lines of his army, broken, shattered by . . . what? He ran names through his mind, would have them charged, thought, There will be inquiries. There will be consequences!

He ignored the hand pulling his horse, looked out to the west, saw silhouettes along the rocks, more of the Yankees crawling, rising up, rushing forward, blue-coated officers calling out, bringing their men together. Bragg ignored the movement of the horse, the helping hands from his aides, his mind drifting away, absorbing the terrible dream. He tried to focus his eyes, looked past the enemy troops, stared now at the last glow of sunlight settling down onto the hills far to the west, out beyond Chattanooga.

CHAPTER FORTY

BAUER

MISSIONARY RIDGE—
NOVEMBER 25, 1863—5:30 P.M.

As they climbed higher, the cannon fire had slowed, the rebel gunners forced to seek targets they could actually reach, farther down the hill. Some targeted the wounded men who lay spread out across the open slope, or those who still sought the protection in the rebel rifle pits at the base of the hill. Closer to the crest, the men around Bauer had suffered only the impact of the musket fire that came from those few rebels who dared to step out closer to the slope. But those men didn't survive long. The soldiers around Bauer took advantage of the pause in their climb, resting weary legs, regaining their wind, and with their composure came marksmanship. It was the first time today Bauer had fired at any target, and he was accurate now as he had been so many times before. The men around him barely noticed, too tired, struggling to hug the good cover. But Willis had watched him, and Bauer caught that crack in Willis's sternness, a brief smile as Bauer took down a rebel from two hundred yards, the instinct for reloading automatic, and then a new target, even farther away.

No matter the safety from the steep ledges above them, the orders began to flow up the hill, senior officers making the climb, joining their men, the men who should never have been there at all. There was little word about that now, no one talking about orders or a demonstration. If the men didn't really know what they had accomplished, their officers did, the entire chain of command realizing that what their men had done was far more effective and far less costly than anyone on Orchard Knob had predicted.

Willis passed the word, as it was passed to him, that the men hunkered down so close to the crest could not simply stay there. They all knew the next order, the next piece of the attack, and so, with fresher legs, they surged up and over the rocks, up through the narrow defiles, feet digging into the steepest slopes. Just behind them, the officers could not avoid the dread, that their senior commanders might still be right, that allowing these men to climb the slope had simply been part of a rebel plan. Colonel Moore had passed through his men, other officers as well, cautioning them to expect a counterattack, that surely, the rebels were waiting, that massed musket fire could greet their surge over the top. With Moore giving the order, the first few pushed up, Willis leading them, as he always led them, and Bauer had hesitated for a long second, the inevitable struggle brief and angry. But climb he did, pushing himself up the last few yards of the slope only a few feet behind Willis.

Once they had climbed over the last of the rocks, the first wave of men had bolted quickly forward, no real resistance in front of them. Bauer had been as surprised as the officers who held back, peering over the rocks, that the rebels had seemed to pull away almost immediately. On the flatter ground, Bauer pushed forward through his exhaustion, fought the cramping in his legs, the sharp pains in his rib cage finally dropping him down to his knees. But the men around him kept moving, and very quickly, Bauer was up with them. Almost immediately, he could see what remained of the rebel works along the crest of the ridge, logs scattered in haphazard patterns, shallow ditches, the occasional shovel lying among the scattered muskets, backpacks, and every other piece of clothing and equipment the rebels had abandoned. The artillery fire from far behind him had done little damage on the crest itself, and what seemed to be broken-down defenses were in fact works that had never been completed. But damage was everywhere, most of it human, coming from the muskets of the men who rolled up across the crest of the hill, the pursuit of the rebels they had driven away. The dead and wounded lay spread out over much of the crest, men from both sides.

In short minutes, the men had driven up onto the tallest peak of the crest, had sought out cover in the trench works, the next safe place that presented itself. Once more, the rebels had dug the holes and laid the logs. And as had happened down below, the snakelike trenches were now filled with the men in blue.

They walked in time to a silent drummer, the same kind of formation that had crossed the wide plain now out behind them. Bauer heard the musket balls fly past, but the enemy had mostly pulled away, few men still up on the ridge itself. The rebels he could see had gathered to face the Federal troops in small bunches, pulled together by those officers who still kept control, and Bauer saw Willis point the sword, the young lieutenant there to pass along the instructions. There were more Federal units to both sides, advancing as Willis's men advanced, slow, deliberate, still the expectation that the deadly reception would greet them at any time. Bauer stared ahead to the far slope, memories of Shiloh coming to him again, the sudden rise of a vast rebel horde, coming up from hidden places in the low ground, as though rising from the earth itself. But the slope on the backside of the ridge was mostly empty, a swath of ground that showed only debris and destruction, and the bodies left behind.

Behind him, he heard Colonel Moore, on foot, pushing them onward, still the hint of caution.

"Watch for it, boys! They're up here! Route step!"

It was an unnecessary order, Bauer as cautious as every man in the line, even Willis jerking his head to the side, then back again, waiting for the inevitable surprise.

"Halt here!"

Bauer was surprised, but he obeyed the order, saw Willis staring back at the colonel, a silent protest, waiting for something more. Bauer turned slightly, could see Moore speaking to another officer, more officers gathering. Far out to the left, Bauer heard a burst of musket fire, saw the smoke blowing over the next rise, much more beyond. The sounds of a spreading fight were reaching them now and for the first time since they had made the crest, there was artillery fire. Bauer kept his eyes that way, felt the jittery stirring in his gut, men around him with low comments, Willis now moving across in front of them, moving up close to the gathering of officers. Bauer knew the look, Willis with little patience for discussion.

Moore shouted to them now, "Halt here! Rest on your muskets! We're awaiting orders!"

Bauer watched Willis, saw clenched fists, a crisp, obedient spin back toward his men. Willis repeated the colonel's order, the men responding quickly, gratefully, most just dropping down where they stood. Bauer sat heavily, matted grass beneath him, a rebel canteen lying close, one of the men reaching for it, and Bauer suddenly realized how thirsty he was. The man sampled the contents, too much of a sample, others protesting, the growling voice of Owens, "Give me that damn thing! You ain't alone up here, boy. Pass it along."

The man grudgingly agreed, handed the canteen to the next man beside him, small swigs of whatever it held, the canteen passed down the line. Bauer looked at Owens, the permanently dirty face, the frightening stare, and Bauer thought, Smart man, that fellow. Owens wants anything I got, he can have it.

The canteen was emptied quickly, Bauer still without, and he tapped his own, knew it had been empty since he had been pinned down on the slope. He looked at the musket, saw the bayonet still affixed, most of the others the same. Willis was talking to Moore now, another officer there, the hat with the insignia of the 15th. Bauer saw more of those men pulled into formation down to the right. For the first time, he noticed the far right of the ridge, saw it drop away, a wide green valley beyond. But the sounds from the left grabbed his attention, a new burst of fire, a volley from more men than

Bauer had around him now. The sound seemed to trigger a response from the colonel, and Moore shouted to them, "Eighteenth! Up, to arms! Right wheel! Fall in beside the Fifteenth! Fix bayonets!"

Willis moved with deliberate steps, took his place to Bauer's right, and the order came, the lieutenant in front raising his sword, the high childlike shout that inspired jokes at the young man's expense.

"Let's go, boys! Somebody needs our help!"

The line formed quickly, few gripes, some men repeating the lieutenant's order in low mocking voices. But Bauer watched the fight, smoke in a thin cloud masking the view, the sounds still rolling toward them, echoing through the uneven ground. Bauer felt the cold in his chest, could never escape that, moved in rhythm with the men beside him. They marched past another row of rebel works, more debris, shovels, muskets, some of the men searching discreetly for canteens. The hill sloped downward slightly, and Bauer looked out to the left, realized they were marching straight along the ridge. To his left was the amazing panorama of Chattanooga, the wide ground they had crossed, the thickets and bald knobs where Willis said the brass had been, where Grant himself had no doubt watched the assault.

Bauer felt a surge of excitement, said aloud, "We're up here! All these weeks, and now, we're up on top!"

Beside him, a man responded, "Pretty place. No

wonder they liked it up here. You can see all the way to home."

"Eyes front! The enemy is just over the hill!"

The voice belonged to Willis, and Bauer stared ahead, saw only smoke on the next rise, the men moving farther downhill, pants legs snagged by low thickets of briars. Willis called out again, "Make ready! Climb together, no straggling!"

Bauer could smell the smoke now, a thick haze passing overhead, no gazing out to the open ground. The talk began now, the nervous chatter, men swearing, praying, eagerness, terror, the slow march up the hill taking them straight into the smoke.

Men were coming toward them now, their own, an officer, a color bearer, the man holding a pistol, a handful of soldiers, walking wounded. There were more wounded now, scattered beneath the brush, some lying flat, stretcher bearers bringing more off the hill. Bauer tried not to look, wouldn't see the wounds, not yet, not with the fight so close. The lines were halted now, the young lieutenant obeying a command Bauer didn't hear, the boyish face showing fear of his own, holding the sword up above his head, facing them, looking back toward the officers. Bauer stopped, felt the energy of the men beside him, behind him, the halt only delaying what they knew was coming. He strained to hear their talk, but the roar of firing swept away the voices, the officer pointing back up the hill, animated, Moore listening, nodding, looking now to his men. The other company commanders had moved up close, Willis as well, and Bauer saw Moore still listening, thought, That fellow's brass, for sure. Outranks the colonel. Telling us what to do. I guess . . . somebody has to. Moore spoke to the company commanders now, and Bauer saw Willis give a short, quick nod. Willis looked back at his own men, seemed to count them, measuring what was left of his company. More companies had moved in beside them, behind them, and Bauer felt a wave of relief at the added strength, saw several hundred men pushing forward, crowding along the crest. Willis was still scanning the men, his eyes catching Bauer's, no emotion, no acknowledgment, and Willis turned, pointed his sword to the front, and once more, they began to walk.

He coughed through the smoke, felt the burning in his eyes, saw flashes of fire to one side, screams of the wounded coming from every direction. The first man he had seen was a rebel, part of a dozen men kneeling, an officer standing beside them, but that man went down with the first volley, most of the rebels down as well. But across from them, the bald hill showed more men in blue, the rebels between them, and the volleys grew quiet, the fight closing up between men who used the bayonet, who grappled and clubbed and struck out with fists. The line had

come apart, the men not following Willis or anyone else now. The rebels came at them, men alone,
men in pairs, in small bands. The fight seemed to
explode in front of Bauer in waves of shouting, the
only other sounds the cracking of bone, the thump
and smack of muskets across skulls. Bauer held
back, had never fought hand to hand, was engulfed
by terror, a quick desperate glance at the cap on the
musket, still loaded. But the weapon seemed useless, too many men in blue, the best tool the bayonet, training few took seriously. He kept pushing
forward with the men close beside him, sharing the
fear, the horrific sight, a man's head split open by a
sword, another punched down by a pistol shot to
his face. He stood in silence, felt very alone, a spec-
tator, heard men shouting every kind of word. The
fight spread closer to him, men wrestling, falling to
the ground, a rebel with an enormous knife. To one
side, a flash of blue, and Bauer saw the man leap
into the fight, the bayonet into the rebel's back,
the knife tucked into a belt, ghastly souvenir, or a
weapon still to be used. The man swung around, as
though searching for another target, and Bauer saw
the face now, the raw animal madness, the big man,
black eyes. It was Owens. Owens caught his eye,
yelled something to him, waved to him, threatening
him with the bloody bayonet, and Bauer felt more
afraid of Owens now than anyone around him. He
stepped forward, others doing the same, a line of
rebels suddenly coming out of the smoke, moving

at them from the side. Bauer heard the first terrifying scream, saw the man's mouth open, the single voice, others with him joining the chorus. The man pushed a bayonet in front of him, pointed at another man close beside Bauer, and Bauer felt the iciness again, cold and frozen. The rebel lunged forward, the bayonet knocked away, the men locking together, a hard fist finding jaw, the soldier collapsing, the rebel down on him, more fists, and now the other rebels were there, choosing their targets, a sword flashing, the fire from a pistol. Bauer saw one man come straight toward him, looking at him, cold hate, their eyes locked, as though no one else was there. The man slowed, and Bauer saw a smile now, the man holding a musket back like a club, a step closer, and now the high-pitched shout. Bauer tried to step aside, stumbled, nowhere to go, too many men pushing back at him, and he held the bayonet out straight, waited for the blow, his musket firing, magnificent surprise, a blast of smoke and fire into the man's chest, the rebel collapsing at Bauer's feet. But there were more now, all around him, another man in front of him, the glaze of hate in the man's eyes, a bayonet, pointed at Bauer's face, the man jumping forward, and Bauer slapped at the man's musket with his own, both weapons knocked away, the man still coming, fists up, and Bauer raised his hands, felt a crushing blow to his jaw, another, the man on top of him, hands at Bauer's throat. He grabbed the man's arms, pulled in a desperate struggle, the rebel's fingers digging into his neck, crushing strength. Bauer fought to breathe, raw panic, and now the man jerked to one side, rolling off him, the hands gone. Bauer fought to get air, gasping, felt men tumbling across his legs, another fight, but he saw the face now, his savior, looking down at him, a bloody sword in the man's hand.

"Get your ass up! Grab your bayonet! We're not done here!"

It was Willis.

Willis moved away now, blending into the mass of fighting, bodies moving around Bauer still, men down under his feet, blood in muddy pools. The shouts seemed to change, orders, pulling men up, and Bauer saw now, there were fewer rebels, a hundred or more in a rapid retreat, moving away. Willis was there, still the sword, looked at him with a gleaming smile, and Bauer saw blood on Willis's hands, a wound in his shirt. Willis was watching him still, let out a hard shout, no words, nonsensical, the fire emerging from the man's heart. The rebels who could had withdrawn, and Willis waved the sword, orders now, the men responding, some rising up, rebels at their feet, some of the rebels still with a fight to give, the men making quick work of anyone who tried. Bauer kept his eyes on Willis, thought of the stern lesson, **no such thing as friends,** this from the man who so loves . . . **this.** You saved me, Sammie. He wanted to say the words, but Willis was on to the next duty, orders coming to find muskets, to reload, make ready for another drive by the rebels, or some order that would turn the push the other way. Bauer searched for a musket, picked one up, bent bayonet, but it was Union, and he pushed a shaking hand into his cartridge box, retrieved a load, still shaking as he reloaded the weapon. Willis was looking away now, raised his sword toward the retreating rebels, a taunt, something Bauer had not heard before. Another officer was there now, the young lieutenant, the young man's face a bloody smear, and he moved out close to Willis, reached for Willis's shoulder, then dropped to his knees, rolled to one side. Bauer moved quickly, others, offers of help, and Bauer saw one eye gone, blood pouring out in a small river from the young man's mouth. A hand had him, pulling him up, and Bauer saw the face of Owens.

"Leave him be. He gave his piece." Owens looked at Bauer, the yellow toothy smile. "Good fighting, eh? Gave 'em all they needed. Looks like they're forming up on that hill over there."

Bauer looked that way, saw Willis in front, staring out, others coming together, the formation organizing once more. Moore was there now, and Bauer felt relief at that. Other officers moved through the men, a quick check of the wounded, some of those men able to stand, to move off the hill, some crawling to tend to the others. Moore was shouting out orders, putting the men into line, and Bauer focused on him, the musket in one hand, hanging down beside him. He felt swallowed by exhaustion, his brain protesting, no energy for a fight, too many thoughts, the bloody memories drifting through his brain. **Hand to hand.** We can't do this again, not like that. We need help . . . reinforcements.

Moore was talking to Willis now, and another captain, the colonel pointing out toward another hill down the ridgeline, then back, to where the rebels had run. Bauer's head was clearing and he saw the wide-open ground to the backside of the ridge, the rebels pulling together, making their stand on a smaller hilltop. Bauer looked down into darkening brush, saw a wide slope, the ground off the ridge rolling, small hills and thickets. The daylight was nearly gone, and he heard commotion, looked toward the officers, saw what seemed to be an argument, another officer there now. From behind he heard horses, another surprise, another officer, older man, more horses, color bearers. The argument was expanding, but the man on the horse quieted them, his words reaching Bauer.

"Stand down, Colonel. This is all for today. We're to make camp along this ridge. General Sheridan is down to our left, and he is pushing the enemy farther back, but they're holding to some artillery still, and it's a risky affair."

Moore spoke up, pointed toward the rebels, still visible on the next hill to the rear, gathering, as though watching the scene. "Sir, the enemy is in retreat. We can press them!"

"Yes, we **have** pressed them, Colonel. We're holding this ridgeline, and they're whipped. Have your men patrol this stretch of the ridge. Gather up weapons, anything useful. There are some rebel batteries still farther up the ridge, might be ripe for the taking. No campfires, but we'll try to find rations."

Moore seemed resigned to the orders, and Bauer watched Willis, saw raw anger toward the officer, but Moore pulled him away, a hard word Bauer couldn't hear. Willis moved back toward Bauer, slid his sword into the scabbard at his side, drew the pistol, began to reload with jerking motions.

"Damn them all. It's getting dark, so we go to sleep. The enemy's right out there, and if we give them a shove, they'll be ours."

"You saved my ass, Sammie."

"Shut up. Might not happen again."

Beside Bauer, Owens had moved up, said, "Look there. We can go get us a reb cannon. Maybe a whole battery."

Bauer looked that way, the hill that held the rebels, saw men in motion, the darkness hiding them, heard the crack of a musket close by, another, men not accepting that the fight was past. Bauer felt the urge, knelt, aimed the musket, and Willis jerked it up, said aloud, "No more! Save it for the morning. . . ."

The flash erupted on the distant hill, the sharp screaming whistle blowing right past Bauer, the

hot wind, a burst of fire out behind. He felt a searing punch in his leg, screamed, fell back, twisting
agony, looked up at Willis, the pain still ripping
through him. Willis kept his stare out toward the
enemy, then turned slowly, looking down at him,
smiling eyes, bending over. Willis put a hand out
toward him, and Bauer saw now, Willis's arm was
gone, a spray of blood from a hole in his neck. His
hand came down, fingers reaching toward Bauer
still. Bauer fought to move, to grab the hand, but
Willis turned away, tumbled down heavily on the
ground close beside him. Bauer heard screaming,
his own voice, the name of his friend. Men were
there now, hands on him, pulling him, his own
hands trying to grab for Willis, touching only dirt,
ripping through briars, wet and bloody. But there
was nothing to hold, nothing there at all, and he
stared up into dark treetops, skeletons against the
night sky, the stars blurred by the tears in his eyes.

CHAPTER FORTY-ONE

CLEBURNE

TUNNEL HILL—
NOVEMBER 25, 1863—5:00 P.M.

The Yankees had pulled away, punched back once more by the hard defense Cleburne put in their way. The latest assault had come just after three, and just as before, Sherman's troops had driven hard straight into men who would not give ground. The assaults had gone both ways, counterattacks, some led by Cleburne himself, some by officers he had never met. Hardee had done as much as Cleburne could have hoped, had sent additional troops northward both to lengthen and strengthen what Cleburne had on the ridgeline. Throughout the last hours of daylight, little had changed except the casualty counts, both sides badly bruised. But Cleburne knew that Sherman had suffered a far greater cost, the ground out in front of Tunnel Hill littered with the bodies of his men.

· Late in the day, as Sherman's forces pulled back once again, Cleburne continued to maneuver, shifting units into weaker places, bringing up caissons to resupply the big guns. He had no reason to expect Sherman would just sit tight, to concede that Cleburne had won the day. But with daylight beginning to fade, the men around him showed more confidence, the men breaking into cheers, a soldier's instincts that his enemy had given all he could. Cleburne still feared there would be another wave, had to expect that with Sherman's overwhelming numbers, the Yankees would come again. Even with the darkness filling every low place, Cleburne kept tall in the saddle, scanning the distant hills and thickets for some sign of movement, the first signs that Sherman was determined to accomplish in the darkness what they could not achieve throughout the day.

To his right, a single gun fired, a flash of light, the ball streaking red out toward Billy Goat Hill. He jumped at that, nervous still, wondered if those men had seen something threatening, if an observer had spotted movement through the brush below. But the blast was followed now by more cheers, and he kept his eyes that way, could make out hats in the air, realized now, it was the day's final salute. The ammunition is almost gone, he thought, and I should scold them for wasting powder. But they are entitled to a celebration. They did extraordinary work today, and no one should forget that. Certainly not me.

He leaned heavily on the nose of the saddle, stared out with tired eyes, saw the first campfires springing up far out in the Yankee lines, no real effort to mask them, as though Sherman was sending a message, that there was precious little in Cleburne's caissons to interrupt a Yankee dinner, even Cleburne's sharpshooters with mostly empty cartridge boxes. In that, he thought, Sherman is correct. There will be no bombardments, no careless aim toward the enemy's camps. Cleburne thought of Sherman now, had seen him on the far hill several times throughout the day. What is he feeling? Is he beaten? Will he skulk away in the night, conceding this ground? No. That's not how he came to be here, not why Grant has come to rely on him. He was sent up here to break this flank, and if he had been successful, there might not have been any chance for this army to stop him at all. Certainly, he knows that. So, tomorrow, he will try again.

The idea broke through his weariness, and he thought of the ammunition train, far back behind Chickamauga Creek. There must be wagons sent forward, he thought. Bragg will see to it. Even he knows what we have done here today, and he will be prepared for what could happen tomorrow. Hardee will not let him ignore us.

He moved the horse to the side, rode slowly along the front edge of the hill, could hear men down below, the artillerymen seeing to their guns, the troops repairing and strengthening the logs and earthen walls that had served them so well. They are surely more tired than I am, he thought. They require rations. I will see to that immediately. He turned, saw staff officers gathering behind, thought, Their work is not yet done.

"Captain Buck, here please."

He could see the weariness in Buck's eyes, the man riding the horse slowly his way. He's done his share today, Cleburne thought. More than his share. His and mine. They all have. Something else I will not forget.

"Sir?"

"We must send word to General Hardee. We have great needs out here. Rations and ammunition."

Behind Buck, he heard the hoofbeats, saw the shadowy figure moving up quickly. Buck said, "Courier. That's Hardee's man, Newell."

Cleburne felt a calm satisfaction, thought, Hardee wishes to know how we fared. This shall be a delight.

Newell reined up the horse, saluted, said, "Sir! General Hardee offers his respects, and orders you to take any troops you can afford to remove from your lines, and march them with all haste to the south. The enemy has assaulted the center of our position with considerable strength. General Hardee insists in the strongest terms that you provide any forces not now engaged."

Cleburne stared at the man, saw nervousness, the man breathing heavily, and Cleburne said, "Repeat that, Sergeant. The enemy has done what, exactly?"

"Sir, did you not hear the artillery? The enemy assaulted the center of the ridge with substantial force. General Breckinridge is in considerable difficulty. General Hardee orders you to march those troops you can spare, and have them support his forces as quickly as they can be put to the march."

He saw exasperation on the man's face, knew Hardee would not waste anyone's time with this kind of urgency unless it was necessary.

"We heard nothing of any fight, Sergeant. We had noise enough right here. Very well, return to General Hardee, and advise him that I will lead those men myself. At present, there is no fighting on this front, and thus far, the enemy is making no preparations to strike us again this evening."

"Yes, sir. If I may return to the general, sir."

"Yes, of course. You are dismissed."

Newell spun the horse, was gone quickly, and Cleburne saw Buck, uncertainty, questions rising up in his own mind.

"What do you make of it, sir?"

Cleburne looked out southward through the treetops. "What I make of it, Captain, is that we are expected to move with haste. Let's do so. Send word to General Cumming's brigade. He is on our left flank. I will go directly to General Maney, and instruct him to fall in behind Cumming's men. This is unexpected, to be sure. But we can pose our questions to General Hardee later."

The columns fell in quickly, and Cleburne pushed out to the front, expected to hear some distinct signs that the fight was ongoing. He heard thumps of artillery, but not many, and no musket fire at all, the ground too undulating for the sounds to carry beyond the next hill. He crested a rise, saw low drifting smoke far out to the east, behind the ridge, and along the crest, scattered troops, no organization, most of the men drifting east, away from any fight. He felt a stab of caution, thought of Hardee. He would not panic. He would not send a courier who panicked. But I hear nothing of any general engagement.

He glanced up, darkness very soon, felt comforted by the tramping of so many feet behind him. Cumming was back close to the head of his column, even more comforting. He knew little of Alfred Cumming but what he had seen today, and the Georgians had done as well as any unit in Cleburne's lines. A West Pointer, he thought, a veteran. I must thank him for his service today. I would gladly serve with him again. That's Hardee's doing, certainly, sending good men to help us.

Out ahead of him, a dozen guards crept forward, a caution taken by Cumming that Cleburne appreciated. He thought of his pocket watch, tired fingers fumbling with his coat, his attention caught now by a rider coming toward him. He saw the guards jump out into the trail, intercepting the man, heard the manic high-pitched voice, the rider pointing toward him. Cleburne pushed the horse forward, heard the horseman pleading to be let through. The guards stood aside now, one man speaking out.

"Sir! Says he's from General Hardee."

"He is, soldier. Sergeant Newell, you have another dispatch for me?"

Newell seemed desperately relieved, saluted Cleburne, said, "Sir! It is most urgent, sir! Your orders have changed. The enemy has overrun the ridge in several places. General Breckinridge's forces have been cut off from this end of the line, and are thought to be in some confusion, sir."

Cleburne stared at the man, looked past him, could still hear scattered thumps of distant artillery. "Is this from General Hardee himself?"

"I just left him, sir. It is most urgent. General Hardee has formed a line astride this ridge, a half mile or so ahead, attempting to hold back the enemy from this direction."

"What are my orders? I have two brigades in this column. What does the general wish me to do?"

"Sir, General Hardee can best explain himself. It

is most distressing, sir. A terrible turn. If you wish to follow me, I will take you to the general."

"By all means. Let's move, Sergeant."

He left the two brigades behind, followed the courier in a hard gallop through the dimming light, relied on the horse not to tumble him out of the saddle. There was clear panic in the sergeant's voice, but he rode with skill, pulling out far ahead of Cleburne, then slowing, allowing Cleburne to catch up. It was a humiliating exercise, but Cleburne focused more on the trail, scattered troops, cracks of musket fire to the front. And now, a cluster of horsemen, a limp flag, and Hardee.

Cleburne fought to steady the horse, focused on Hardee, who offered no formal greeting, pushed his horse out from the others, said, "The ridge has broken. The enemy has taken strong positions all across what was our lines to the south."

Cleburne let the words flow through him, felt a numbing shock, waves of disbelief. Hardee seemed to wait for a response, then said, "General Cleburne, did you not hear me? We are in a dire situation to the south. Your efforts holding the right flank were the only success we had today."

Cleburne sat upright in the saddle now, his weariness pushed aside. "How did this occur, sir? We were most strong in the center."

"The enemy drove four divisions into Breckinridge's lines and my far left flank. They made breakthroughs at several points, and now have reinforced. They are in strength along the crest of the ridge. Bragg's headquarters is in enemy hands, and Bragg has retreated back toward Chickamauga Station."

Hardee seemed out of breath, and Cleburne looked out across the ridge, saw troops in motion, flags, men on horseback, the soldiers lined up not to face the great open plain, but down, toward the south.

He looked again at Hardee, almost expected a smile, as though this news was someone's bizarre attempt at humor. But he knew Hardee well enough, could see the despair on the man's face. Cleburne could not stop the words, the question.

"What happened? How did they break us?"

"Their army defeated ours, General. What more must you be told?"

There was no patience in Hardee's voice, and Cleburne said, "I have two brigades up the trail behind me. They held the position, sir. We did good work on the flank. Sherman could still attempt another assault tonight, but I have yet seen no sign of that."

"That hardly matters now, General. Walthall's and Brown's brigade have formed a good line across the ridge. We anticipated the enemy pushing up this way, but they seemed to welcome the end of this day as much as we have. Grant seems content with what he has accomplished, and I do not expect any further attacks until morning." He paused. "What you will do now is protect this army from its utter destruction. Bragg is hoping to with-draw as many of the troops off the ridge as can be gathered up, and pull them to the rail depot, where they can be marched to the south. There are fugi-tives from our lines for miles, I'm certain of that. I am placing you in command of the three divi-sions on your flank. Once I am fully satisfied the enemy has halted his efforts, we shall begin an im-mediate withdrawal to the east, across the creek. I will attempt to find General Bragg at Chickamauga Station."

"The army is to withdraw? To the trains?"

"The enemy has forced our withdrawal, Patrick. I have no idea what remains of this army, how many commanders can rally their men, or if we are in any kind of condition to make another fight. If there are trains, more the better. If not, we must march the men south along the rail line. Bragg has but one duty now, to salvage what he can of the army. Is General Polk still holding the bridge to the northeast?"

Polk. Cleburne hadn't thought of Lucius Polk in a while now, that brigade seeing almost no fire from Sherman's troops.

"Yes, sir. Polk's brigade is fresh."

"Keep them at that bridge. That's your route of escape."

The word rattled Cleburne, and he couldn't just accept that as a command. "Sir, forgive me, but are you completely certain this is necessary? My troops have held back a substantial force of the enemy. Sherman's dead and wounded are thick on that ground down below us. To ask these men to abandon their position, after such a fight . . ."

"I am not **asking** anything, General. I am **ordering** you to save what remains of this army. It is no more complicated than that." Hardee stopped, let out a long breath, and Cleburne could feel the man's anguish, felt it himself. "Patrick, this day has been a disaster for us all. We do not yet know what remains of our troops, our regiments, any organization at all, beyond your forces to the north. Bragg sent a courier here, ordering the army to rendezvous at the station, and prepare for withdrawal southward. Whether or not anyone will be there to follow him . . . well, we shall see. Our greatest hope right now is that the enemy is content to celebrate in our camps, and keep to this ridge until morning. We have no such luxury. As soon as you can put your men into motion, you will withdraw from your position along this ridge and march them across Chickamauga Creek. Salvage what equipment and guns you believe practicable. There is no time to waste."

Hardee was looking down, and Cleburne heard the emotion in his voice. Cleburne waited for more, but Hardee was silent, had said all he needed to say. Cleburne leaned closer to him, said in a low voice, "We can bring my troops down this way, drive the enemy off the ridge. We are very strong. Three divisions. You said it yourself."

"And what of Sherman? He'll be on your backsides before you fire the first musket. It is done, Patrick. You have your orders."

Cleburne couldn't just ride away, so much uncertainty, so many questions. He had never seen Hardee engulfed in so much despair. "Sir, where will **you** go?"

"The men are receiving orders now. I will lead what remains of these troops to a place of safety. That is my duty, Patrick. Right now, it's the only duty."

Cleburne still burned with questions, and Hardee looked at him, a grim stare, seemed to read him.

"Patrick, we have been outmanned, we have been outmaneuvered, and today we were outgeneraled. There is but one choice. Much of that is left to you. You will do what you must. There is nothing left of any defensible positions to the south. I do not wish to see this entire army ground to dust. Your command is the only organized force remaining in strength. You must protect our withdrawal."

It was after ten o'clock, the orders already issued to his brigade commanders, others, the men Cleburne barely knew. But the duty now was clear to them all. They crossed the bridge in good order, led by the men who had led them in the most difficult fight of their lives. There was grousing, complaints, questions for the officers. But the briefest of instructions held the answer, and no one in Cleburne's force could argue with the perfect logic that their impervious defensive lines had been shattered, that any troops remaining up on Tunnel Hill would most certainly be cut off from any chance of escape. And so, throughout the night they marched, fording an icy stream, pushing on toward the good roads, the rail line, adding to Bragg's retreat into Georgia.

Once his men had crossed Chickamauga Creek, the bridge had been burned, but Cleburne already knew that no enemy was in pursuit. He allowed his men to rest, an hour's sleep, then roused them again at two thirty in the morning, continuing the march. Along the way, another courier reached him, a surprising message from Bragg, clear instructions from a man who rarely seemed **clear** at all. Cleburne's troops were still to be the army's rear guard, would march as rapidly as possible to a point of strength some fifteen miles to the southeast, Ringgold Gap, where the road and rail line sliced through a deep and narrow pass. There Cleburne's men would make every effort to hold off any pursuit by the Yankees until the fugitives of Bragg's command could be brought together. The order added one phrase Cleburne hoped never to see. He was to hold the gap **at all costs.**

As he left the crest of Tunnel Hill, Cleburne could not just pull away from Sherman without taking the right kind of precautions. Mark Lowrey's brigade was the last to leave the hill, holding the lines just above the mouth of the tunnel that Cleburne had fought so tenaciously to hold. Lowrey was ordered to drive down the hill, shoving Sherman's picket lines away, preventing any casual observation of the withdrawal. It was sound tactics, preventing the enemy from knowing just when Cleburne's troops had pulled away, just which direction they would march. But to Cleburne, it was a symbol, a final act of defiance. There was no escaping the utter despair for what had occurred, the entire army forced to give up the best ground Cleburne had ever seen, brought to complete collapse by the better efforts of a superior enemy. But on Tunnel Hill, it had been very different. While Lowrey's men drove the Yankees away, Cleburne kept his gaze on the scattered musket fire, what was little more than a brief skirmish that drove the enemy's pickets away. The emotions were unstoppable, the fury, the crushing sadness, the hopelessness of what might happen now. He couldn't help thinking of Bragg, the others, if there had been generals in this fight who would continue to lead this army, if there was yet some new disaster awaiting them. With Lowrey's mission completed, Cleburne watched as they pulled back, climbing once more over the crest, joining the rest of Cleburne's forces beyond the protection of the creek. As they moved past him, Cleburne tried not to hear their cries, their anger, their cheers of well-earned satisfaction. He kept his eyes on the distant campfires, the dark mound of Billy Goat Hill, thought only of Sherman, the enormous numbers of blue troops sent his way, so many assaults over so many hours. He wondered if he would ever meet the man, would have the opportunity to ask him directly if he would admit what had happened here. I would truly like to know that, he thought. No matter the enormous breadth of Grant's victory, you made your best efforts to crush the men I put in your way, and you did not succeed. No, I would ask him, push him more than that. No matter what else your army accomplished on this day, I would compel you, **force** you to admit it to these men, that out here, on this one day, across this rolling, wooded ground, you were thoroughly beaten.

CHAPTER FORTY-TWO

SHERMAN

RINGGOLD, GEORGIA— NOVEMBER 27, 1863

The debris was everywhere, some of it human, rebel stragglers who seemed almost eager for captivity. But much more could be seen from the rapid retreat of Bragg's army, and Sherman knew, that as his men were advancing, they fought the temptation to sift through the massive amount of equipment the rebels could not or chose not to carry. There had been skirmishes along the way, the town of Graysville hotly contested for brief minutes, the Federal troops surprised to stumble straight into a rebel camp, desperately tired men on both sides. But the rebels seemed unwilling to make a stand against the inevitable, the numbers too few to hold the men in blue back for more than a brief time.

He had been ordered by Grant to push hard against Bragg's retreat, had marched his men back away from Billy Goat Hill, moving across Chickamauga Creek on the small pontoon bridge his men had laid days before, then circling around to the north of the creek. Sherman hoped for speed, to cut off a mass of rebels before they could slip through the mountain passes, but the movement of his own men was as plodding and cumbersome as the ragged army they pursued. The lesson learned on Missionary Ridge had been learned first by Sherman, that assuming the rebels would just fall away in the face of a stout charge could cost far more casualties than Grant would find acceptable, and Sherman pushed his men with far more caution now than he had against Tunnel Hill.

To Sherman's surprise, and certainly to Grant's, the rebels had moved away far more quickly than any disorganized force could be expected to travel. The retreat was so efficient that Sherman could not avoid the first of several surprises when he reached the town of Ringgold. The deserters had offered great tales of woe, a starving rebel army, men forced to eat the leather on their shoes. But along the route of Sherman's pursuit, he had ridden often toward rising columns of black smoke, warehouses engulfed in flames, put to the torch by rebel soldiers who had no wagons and no time to haul away the supplies. In some places, the warehouses seemed bursting with rations, sacks of corn and flour, even meat, the distinct odor flowing through the smoke, the hypnotic smells that captured the attention of his own men. Sherman had passed the destruction in wonder, had seen too many Confederate troops with gaunt faces, men who seemed for all the world to be starving. Yet their supply depots had been abundant, and Sherman could only wonder if the rebels he had seen had been denied sustenance by some grotesque inefficiency that seemed to suit the personality of Braxton Bragg.

At Ringgold, there had been word of a fight, much more than a simple skirmish. The name had rattled Sherman, as it had infuriated him at Tunnel Hill. Patrick Cleburne had held off the Federal pursuit, allowing the rebels to escape. It seemed hardly to matter that along the way, they had left behind enough matériel to wage some new campaign for some time to come. But those goods that survived the torch were now in Federal hands, and if the rebels were to make another strong effort at driving Grant's army away, they would have to find supplies from another source.

Days before, when he crossed into Chattanooga from the valley west of Lookout Mountain, Sherman had left one division behind, commanded by the German, Peter Osterhaus. Osterhaus had then been half of the assault that swept the rebels off of the mountain, and since, had kept his troops alongside the rest of the men who answered to Joe Hooker. Sherman had expected to rendezvous with Osterhaus at Ringgold, adding that division once more to the Army of Tennessee, filling the gaps in Sherman's command that had come from the vicious fight at Tunnel Hill. But Hooker had pushed Osterhaus to the vanguard of his pursuit of Bragg's army, and clearly had expectations of his own. Hooker still seemed to operate beneath the black cloud of low expectations, and despite Grant's concerns that Bragg's army might yet be dangerous, Hooker expected nothing of the sort. The Federal troops knew they had been victorious, and Hooker, who expected trumpeting headlines for his conquest of Lookout Mountain, seemed intent on securing his place in the gallant accounts of this campaign. His delays in crossing Chattanooga Creek had seemed to drain away the glory he felt he had earned on the mountain, word reaching him that both Thomas and Grant were severely disappointed by Hooker's sluggishness. Hooker had been left completely out of the army's enormous success in driving the enemy away from Missionary Ridge. By all accounts, Hooker seemed eager to erase that stain, and so he drove his men in a rapid pursuit of what he believed to be a gang of terrified fugitives.

At Ringgold Gap, an overeager Joe Hooker sent Osterhaus's division forward in pursuit of what Hooker thought was the trailing end of the rebel retreat. Instead, Ringgold Gap provided an opportunity for Patrick Cleburne to bloody another Federal nose. Moving quickly forward without the benefit of artillery, Hooker's drive was ambushed by Cleburne's far inferior numbers, the gap itself offering good cover, masking Cleburne's own artillery, a stunning and bloody surprise to the lead elements of Osterhaus's division. For several hours, Cleburne's forces punched hard at any effort by Hooker to drive them away, costing Hooker another heavy toll in casualties. When Cleburne did finally withdraw, it was only because he chose to, after receiving word from Bragg that the army was safely to the south. If Hooker had hoped this campaign would elevate his reputation in Washington, and throughout the army, Sherman knew that Grant would offer little praise for his haphazard and costly search for glory. For Sherman, the worst part of Hooker's blunder had been the loss of so many of Sherman's own, the ground in front of Ringgold Gap spread with the bodies of too many men.

Sherman saw the horsemen, moved that way, his staff in tow. The smoke still boiled up from the warehouses along the road, more of the rebel supplies now reduced to smoldering ruins. Throughout the small town, blue-clad soldiers worked through the ash piles. The smells struck him, burnt corn, or the pungent odor of burning flour. Men were slinging sacks of whatever remained over their shoulders, some with the prize of slabs of bacon.

Officers saluted him as he passed, but Sherman ignored most of that, had been in the saddle too long today. He searched through the various flags, saw the larger Stars and Stripes, felt relieved, knew he would find answers to the myriad questions, and even better, would find out just what Grant wanted him to do. He focused on the larger cluster of horsemen, saw civilians among them, the ever-present Charles Dana, others, the newspaper reporters who clamored about the generals like fleas on a house pet. He dreaded that, had learned that lesson long ago, that those men, despite their broad smiles and glad-handing, were not his friends. He saw a pair of them to one side of the gathering officers, men pointing out toward the ridgeline a half mile way, smoke still drifting above the trees, the last signs of Hooker's absurd fight. Sherman searched the officers for the least conspicuous man in the bunch. He saw him now, an automatic smile, marveling once more at Grant's utter lack of military decorum. The uniform was plain and dull, Grant seeming to blend into any gathering of officers as the man least likely to be in command. It was the same now, Grant sitting slouched in the saddle, the plain coat, the hat pulled low, as though shading himself from everyone around him.

Grant saw him, raised the brim of the hat, and

Sherman saw the briefest of smiles from Grant, the slow nod, the cigar offered up in a brief salute. Sherman closed the gap between them, could feel the staff hanging back.

"Good afternoon, Grant. I had hoped we'd put Bragg's army in a bag."

Grant pulled away from the others, and Sherman saw Dana watching, knew Dana would come along. It was Grant's logic, that including Dana in any conversation now meant that the reports going to Washington would carry Grant's approval. Sherman knew to guard his words, and Grant moved closer to him, waited for Dana to come up with him, said, "Afternoon, Sherman. Pleasant day. The enemy's burned enough supplies to last them for months. Curious."

"Not curious at all. They didn't have time to grab everything they had back here. Left a mess of artillery and wagons near Graysville. Some of the guns are in good condition, too. We'll make use of that." Sherman looked at Dana now, said, "I would hope you're telling the War Department that they've got something to celebrate."

Grant glared at him, and Sherman wasn't sure why. Harmless enough question, he thought. Grant said, "He didn't have to. Told them myself. Rather enjoy crowing about a victory once and again."

Dana raised his hat, a salute of his own, said, "I've told them as well, sir. Marvelous experience, watching that final assault. Like a painting, a work of art, the army assembled in such martial perfection. Quite sure the enemy saw that for what it was. Destiny. Yes, that's it. Destiny. They could not hope to hold their position in the face of such overwhelming superiority."

Grant was looking at Sherman, no expression, but Sherman felt the message, had received it too often before. Keep your mouth shut. Dana seemed eager for something back from Sherman, and he forced a smile, said, "Yes, wonderful. Washington should hear some good news occasionally."

Grant kept his eyes on Sherman, said, "Mr. Dana, if you will allow us a brief moment."

"By all means, sir. I understand. Permit me to join the others, then."

Grant gave a quick wave of his hand, all the permission Dana required. They were alone now, and Sherman turned the horse, stared out toward the scavenging soldiers, said, "Heard about Osterhaus. Which regiments got hit the worst?"

Grant let out a breath. "Thirteenth Illinois took it badly. Missouri boys, too. The Seventeenth, Twenty-ninth, Thirty-first. Made a devil of a fight. But Cleburne set it up just right. Perfect ambush."

Sherman felt a burn. "You sure it was Cleburne?"

Grant tilted his head, held the cigar in his hand. "Matter?"

Sherman stared ahead, fought to keep his voice

calm. Yes, by damned. It matters to me. I'll whip that man yet. The thoughts were held tightly, and Sherman shrugged. "Suppose not."

"Hooker's taking it hard. Knows he really messed things up. He'll probably stay away from you for a while. Not in his nature to apologize for getting his boys killed. In this case, **your** boys."

Sherman tried to feel something kind for Hooker, thought of the man's smug handsomeness, couldn't help but dislike him, even from before the war. "I'll stay away from him. I assume he's going back to . . . wherever he came from."

"Not sure yet. Up to Halleck."

"I'll talk to Osterhaus. He's gotta be pretty ripped up by this."

"Did already. But, he's yours, so, yep. I'd do that."

Sherman felt a hesitation from Grant, something digging through Sherman he didn't enjoy.

"You have something to say to me, by damned, say it."

Grant pulled at the cigar, stared away, watching the soldiers. "Like what?"

"Like Cleburne fought one hell of a fight. Like I should have taken that ridge. Like you put me up on that flank to win this thing."

Grant still didn't look at him. "We won this thing. That's what the War Department will care about. Shame they got away, though. Cavalry says Bragg's headed for Dalton. They'll likely resupply, refit, wait for us to come after them. Can't yet."

Sherman wanted to say more about his fight, about Cleburne, could feel a numbing cold in Grant's words. He glanced to the side, no one close. "It was a hell of a fight, Grant. Made one bad mistake, relying on the maps. That ground was cut up, hills and woods. Damnedest place to try to move. Enemy had the good ground, dug in strong. Lost some good men. Maybe too many."

"Maybe. That's more than Hooker will say."

Sherman stared at Grant, who avoided his eyes. He ached for something more from Grant, a scorching blast, the kind of response Sherman would put out himself. But he knew it wasn't Grant's way. He glanced down at the dusty ground beneath them, felt the chill of a cold wind.

Grant said, "Thomas's people did something I'd never thought I'd see. Disobeyed orders and made themselves heroes. I wouldn't say this to Washington, but I'd rather they not do that."

Sherman absorbed the obvious, that the newspapers would latch on to Thomas more than anyone else. He rolled that over in his mind, shrugged. "Dana was there. Saw it for what it was. A real spectacle. If he'd have been up on my end of things . . . well, might not go well for me."

Grant looked at him now. "He wasn't on your end. And he told Washington what they needed to hear, which was the truth. Thomas broke through, sent Bragg scurrying off into the woods. Any reason he shouldn't get credit for that? Man saved the army at Chickamauga, so everyone keeps telling me. His star's rising, no doubt. He'll keep command of the Army of the Cumberland, for certain."

"And the Army of Tennessee?"

"You resigning?"

Sherman was stunned at the question. "Hell no. Um . . . should I?"

Grant looked at him again, a brief smile. "Not while I'm your superior. Besides, got a job for you. Once Bragg was whipped, I ordered Granger to move it quick up to Knoxville. You want to get a rise out of the War Department, have them think we forgot about Burnside. It seems General Granger didn't like the assignment. Dallied about, took his time putting his men together. Not sure what he has against Burnside, but I changed his orders, told him to stay put in Chattanooga. I need you to march up to Knoxville, as quick as you can get moving. Burnside collapses, and none of this will matter. Halleck's been on me from the beginning to take care of Knoxville, and now that we're not so **distracted** by things around here, they're squalling again."

Sherman slumped, had no use for Burnside at all. "I had hoped my men would get some rest."

"It's winter. Go up there and kick Longstreet in the backside, and they'll get all the rest they need. And Washington will be mighty grateful for your good work."

It was rare sarcasm from Grant, but Sherman

knew he was being given a gift, that Grant was offering him a way to move past what had happened to him at Tunnel Hill. He looked out toward the gap, the smoke fading, men and wagons moving back from the ground where the fight had been, wounded men hauled to makeshift hospitals, the houses in Ringgold now fulfilling a service that their residents never expected to see.

"Hope I run into that fellow again."

"Who?"

"General Cleburne."

"It's not your personal war, Sherman. You go help Burnside. The rest will follow in time."

Sherman heard meaning in Grant's words. "You have a plan? You do, don't you? You already know what we're going to do next."

"Don't you?"

Sherman kept his stare on the distant gap in the hills, felt Grant's eyes. "Well, since I have my orders, my first priority will be to march my men toward Knoxville. After that, I suppose there's one place left to go."

"Knoxville first. Clean up things there. Let Burnside go back to Washington for his parade."

Sherman waited for more, and Grant smiled at him again, held out a cigar.

"Then, we'll talk about Atlanta."

AFTERWORD

I have on several occasions been repulsed and driven back when taking part in an attack, but never before or since have I been one of a routed army, where panic seemed to seize upon all, and all order, obedience and discipline were for the time forgotten and disregarded.

—GENERAL ARTHUR MANIGAULT, CSA

In very many cases, Jefferson Davis's assessments of his generals were so poor as to be ultimately ruinous. As the war progressed unsatisfactorily, Davis's decisions about his generals, and stubborn pride in sustaining them, perhaps contributed the most to the ultimate defeat of the Confederacy.

—HISTORIAN WILEY SWORD

We had the advantage in position and ought to have whipped them. We will never have another such opportunity of completely destroying the Yankee army.

—CAPTAIN JAMES L. COOPER, CSA

This battle has driven a big nail into the coffin of the Confederacy.

—ULYSSES S. GRANT

On November 29, Sherman begins his march toward Knoxville, his troops destroying the railroad along the way, preventing any possibility that Longstreet might yet return to assist Bragg's defeated army. Sherman is told that Burnside's desperate plea for aid comes not only from the threat by Longstreet's assaults, but by the effectiveness of Longstreet's siege of the city, which has reduced supplies, especially rations, to starvation levels. When Sherman arrives in Knoxville, he is stunned, and annoyed, to discover that, days before, Burnside has defeated Longstreet's army, driving the rebels away, that Longstreet has withdrawn completely from his siege of the city, retreating eastward toward Virginia. In addition, Burnside welcomes Sherman by offering an elaborate feast, giving lie to the claims of imminent starvation that Burnside has used to gather support for his plight. Disgusted, Sherman withdraws his army back toward Chattanooga.

For the first time in the war, the Confederate forces hold no significant position anywhere in the state of Tennessee.

In the east, Lee's Army of Northern Virginia is still recovering from their crushing defeat at Gettysburg, and the Federal War Department looks to the new year by anticipating what could become a last-gasp campaign by Lee to preserve his army. But if any significant offensive is to be carried out, it will naturally involve George Meade's Army of the Potomac. Few in Washington have confidence that Meade has the aggressiveness to drive southward, that no matter Meade's victory at Gettysburg, Lee is still a dangerous foe. A frustrated Abraham Lincoln has grown weary with the parade of sluggish or inept commanders in the East, and the meteoric rise in the reputation of Ulysses Grant inspires Lincoln to make a radical change in the Federal army's hierarchy. In March 1864, Grant is rewarded for his successes in the West with a promotion to lieutenant general, a rank previously held by only two men: George Washington and Winfield Scott. Grant is called to Washington, and meets with Lincoln, who pointedly gives Grant responsibility for the entire Federal army, with the assurances that, as long as Grant is aggressive in his pursuit of the enemy, no one in Washington will interfere. Grant is impressed by Lincoln's candor, and accepts the promise that he will be free to conduct the war his way. Ironically, with the promotion, he now outranks his nemesis, Henry Halleck, who remains in Washington as a titular chief of staff.

To no one's surprise, Grant names William T. Sherman as his successor in command of the armies in the West. While Grant plans for the spring offensive in the East, the pursuit and destruction of Lee's army, Sherman plans the campaign designed to drive a hard wedge into Georgia, with the goal of capturing the critical rail and supply hub of Atlanta.

Since the conquest of Vicksburg, in July 1863, the Federal army and navy maintain uncontested control of the Mississippi River, which severs the Confederacy in two. Richmond is helpless to support those troops west of the river (the Trans-Mississippi Department), while the Confederate government reluctantly accepts, even if their president does not, that the enormously valuable natural and human resources from Texas, Louisiana, and Arkansas are simply lost. Between the river and the inevitable pursuit of Lee in Virginia lies the dwindling hopes for supply and reinforcement for the battered Confederate armies. The Confederate hierarchy understands the value of Atlanta as well, and with winter settling upon both armies, preparations are made for the defense of the city, the Confederate command keeping alive a faint optimism that Sherman's army can be destroyed. Both sides are well aware that Grant's pursuit of Lee is of critical importance to the survival of the Confederate government in Richmond. But if Sherman conquers Georgia, the

Confederacy will be divided once again, what will most likely end the war.

THOSE WHO WORE GRAY

BRAXTON BRAGG

Arrives at his new base of command in Dalton, Georgia, on November 27. Still eager to place blame for every failure, Bragg issues a note to his senior commanders, requesting lists of names of those officers who were found wanting during the campaign, writing to Joseph Johnston, "The disastrous panic . . . is unexplainable." But explain he does, in a letter to Jefferson Davis, in which he accuses General John Breckinridge of continuous drunkenness, labels General Benjamin Cheatham "dangerous," and requests "an investigation into the causes of the defeat." No formal inquiry is convened.

Despite nurturing his own blamelessness, Bragg understands the inevitable, and on November 28, in a gesture that Bragg concedes is entirely appropriate, he writes to Davis, formally accepts responsibility for the disaster at Chattanooga, and asks to be relieved of command. This request has gone to Richmond before, but to Bragg's surprise, this time Jefferson Davis does not stand in his corner. On November 30, Adjutant General Samuel Cooper replies to Bragg, "Your request to be relieved has been submitted to the president, who . . . directs me to notify you that you are relieved from command." Bragg is shocked by the speed with which Davis accepts his resignation, considers it a form of betrayal, a Bragg hallmark.

He leaves the army on December 2, joins his wife, Elise, at Warm Springs, Georgia, where he spends the winter months in angry reflections on the various injustices inflicted upon him. His wife, as always, is his greatest advocate, insisting that the president must certainly be aware "that only [Bragg] alone can repair this great disaster." Davis does not agree, and appoints William Hardee as Bragg's successor. Hardee accepts only reluctantly, but by year's end relinquishes the command to his superior, Joseph Johnston.

In the months following his removal, Bragg continues to insist that he is the victim of a conspiracy, writing in a letter to a friend, "The whole clamor against me was by a few individuals of rank and their immediate partisans, who were actuated by . . . ambition and revenge."

But Bragg has his supporters, and in February 1864, when he petitions for service ("any service") in the army, Davis appoints him to the informal post of military adviser to the president, allegedly placing Bragg in command of "the conduct of military operations in the armies of the Confederacy." The appointment pleases those in the army who still support Bragg, but infuriates

much of official Richmond, and a great number
of Southern civilians, who fill newspapers with
vitriolic editorials. But the position is symbolic
at best, Davis making the appointment as a
flicker of loyalty to his friend. General William
Mackall, Bragg's former chief of staff, acknowl-
edges this when he writes, "Bragg . . . is in honorable exile."

Bragg is allowed to return to the field in late
1864, when he commands the garrison at Wilm-
ington, North Carolina, and then as a corps commander under Joseph Johnston in the war's final
campaign in North Carolina. He is blamed for
defeat once more, after the fall of Fort Fisher, on
the Atlantic coast, and accomplishes no real success
against Sherman's advancing army.

At the war's end, Bragg joins the fugitive Jefferson Davis in South Carolina, and like Davis, is
captured by Federal troops in Georgia on May 9,
1865. Unlike Davis, Bragg is paroled by Federal
authorities. He moves to New Orleans, where his
skills as an engineer land him the lucrative position
as chief of that city's water utilities. But Bragg still
demonstrates a remarkable talent for making enemies, and when forced to resign that position, he
considers leaving the country, when he is offered
a military command by the government of Egypt.
Though tempted, Bragg will not make such a radical change, and he relocates instead to Mobile,
Alabama, and then, in 1874, to Galveston, Texas,

where he serves as chief engineer for the Gulf, Colorado & Santa Fe Railway.

Always the unreconstructed Confederate, Bragg resists any relationship with anyone who wore blue, and writes viciously negative commentaries for the Southern Historical Society Papers, continuing the mostly one-sided feuds with anyone in either army who opposed him.

He dies in Galveston in 1876, at age fifty-nine, and is buried in Magnolia Cemetery in Mobile.

In a perfect display of the contradictions that surround Bragg and his career, Confederate general Arthur Manigault, whose troops anchor the ill-fated center of Missionary Ridge, writes in his memoirs,

> I have always regarded him as one of the best organizers of an army and disciplinarians that I have ever met with, and he possessed many of the qualities essential to a commander. I think that the army, under his command, was in a higher state of efficiency . . . than ever before or after. He was not, however, a great general. He made many mistakes . . . was always overmatched in numbers, and when pitted against Grant, his inferiority was too evident. His campaign . . . after the victory at Chickamauga, showed great deficiency both as a tactician and strategist. The least said about

it, the better. . . . Personally, I learned to like him.

In contrast, a Richmond newspaper offers in its editorial, "An army of asses led by a lion is better than an army of lions led by an ass."

Referring to President Davis's loyalty to Bragg, and to other officers who were elevated in rank by their friendship to Davis rather than any skills on the battlefield, Ulysses Grant writes in his memoirs, "Mr. Davis had an exalted opinion of his own military genius. On several occasions during the war he came to the relief of the Union army by reason of his superior military genius."

PATRICK CLEBURNE

Cleburne and his division are recognized for their extraordinary defense of Tunnel Hill, and the successful defense at Ringgold Gap, with an Official Resolution of Thanks from the Confederate Congress, and the "Stonewall of the West" becomes one of the Confederacy's brightest stars. Many in the Confederate high command, including William Hardee and Robert E. Lee, consider him the finest field commander in the Army of Tennessee.

He spends the winter in a defensive posture near Dalton, Georgia, anticipating another Federal campaign. But the Federal army around Chattanooga and Ringgold makes good use of the winter for the same refit and rest so desperately needed by the

Confederates. Cleburne's division does not see combat until May 8, 1864, when he is attacked at Mill Creek Gap, just outside Dalton. The fight begins a campaign that will push both armies toward the city of Atlanta. The fights that take place throughout the next few weeks are bloody and in some cases, indecisive. But the Confederate commander, Joseph Johnston, adopts a strategy of tactical retreat in a way that infuriates Richmond, where it is believed that Johnston has conceded too much open ground to Sherman's forces without exacting the proper toll in blood. In July 1864, Jefferson Davis's frustrations with Johnston's lack of success against Sherman's army come to a head, and Johnston is relieved. He is replaced by John Bell Hood.

The change does not improve Confederate fortunes. Cleburne is elevated to corps command, but under Hood, his skillful handling of troops does not measure up to what Cleburne had accomplished the year before. By September, Hood loses the battles for Atlanta, and thus he loses the city. Unable to dislodge Sherman's forces from their new strongholds, Hood attempts to pull Sherman away by attacking Sherman's supply lines northward into Tennessee. But Sherman remains in Atlanta, and to counteract Hood's "invasion" of Tennessee, George Thomas is given command of the enormous Federal forces positioned at Nashville. Despite grossly inferior numbers, and questionable tactics, Hood drives northward in a fanciful effort to recapture Nashville.

Cleburne, who has never found favor with Hood, returns to division command. On November 30, 1864, during the Battle of Franklin, Tennessee, Cleburne loses two horses to enemy fire, and thus leads his troops against the staunch Federal defenses on foot. He is shot through the heart and dies immediately. He is thirty-six years old.

Cleburne's legacy spreads far beyond the battlefield. During the winter camps in 1863–64, Cleburne authors what he believes is a significant solution to the South's shortage of manpower. With the same passion that he exhibits in the field, Cleburne insists that the South possesses an enormous untapped resource, and proposes that the slaves be freed, in return for their service in the Confederate army. To stunned officers who question this principle, Cleburne responds "they could be induced to fight as gallantly as the Yankees." He argues vociferously that any costs involved in ending slavery would be offset by the enormous triumph of independence. "As between the loss of independence and the loss of slavery, we assume that every patriot will freely give up the . . . Negro slave rather than be a slave himself." It is a lofty ideal, but not one that finds a receptive audience in Richmond, nor throughout most of the army, including a response from General William Bate that Cleburne's notions are "hideous and objectionable . . . the serpent of abolitionism." To salvage Cleburne's well-earned reputation, the proposal is quietly put aside, and he is allowed to continue his military career.

His premature death is marked by an additional tragedy. In January 1864, Cleburne attends the wedding of his commander, William Hardee, during which Cleburne is introduced to Sue Tarleton. The two become utterly infatuated with each other and within short weeks, they are engaged. But the duties of the army prevent the luxury of a wedding, and upon learning of Cleburne's death, Sue goes into mourning for more than a year. Though she marries another Confederate officer three years later, her health never recovers, and she dies in 1868, at age twenty-eight.

After a fund-raising effort by many, including his former staff officer and law partner, Learned Mangum, a monument is created, and Cleburne is memorialized at the Evergreen Cemetery in Helena, Arkansas. Confederate general George Gordon eulogizes Cleburne with these words: "A truer patriot or knightlier soldier never fought and never died. Valor never lost a braver son or freedom a nobler champion. He loved his country, its soldiers, its banners, its battleflags, its sovereignty, its independence. For these he fought, for these he fell."

General William Hardee writes, "He was an Irishman by birth, a Southerner by adoption . . . a lawyer by profession, a soldier in the British army by accident, and a soldier in the Southern armies from patriotism and conviction of duty in his manhood."

Historian Craig L. Symonds writes, "Cleburne was an emotional man who felt the pull of patriotic sentiment and romantic love as well as the burden of duty. In their name, he sought—and found—glory on the battlefield."

ARTHUR MANIGAULT

One of the officers who serves Pierre Beauregard during the war's first conflict at Fort Sumter, South Carolina, Manigault serves capably in most of the major commands throughout Tennessee and Kentucky. He continues to lead troops in the battles for Atlanta, and accompanies John Bell Hood on Hood's invasion of Tennessee. He is severely wounded at the Battle of Franklin, which forces his resignation from the army. He returns to his native South Carolina, attempts to reenter civilian life as a planter on his beloved rice plantation, and dies from the aftereffects of his wound in 1886. He is sixty-one. His memoir, **A Carolinian Goes to War,** is not published until 1983, and is an exceptional firsthand account of the struggle for Missionary Ridge.

THOSE WHO WORE BLUE

FRITZ "DUTCHIE" BAUER

Bauer survives the horrific wound received on Missionary Ridge, but loses his right leg. Despite Bauer's passion for life as a soldier, the wound, and the death of his closest friend, Sammie Willis, drain away Bauer's desire for service. After his surgery in the army's hospital in Chattanooga and a lengthy recovery in Nashville, he returns to the only other home he knows, the city of Milwaukee.

With no talent for his deceased father's sausage-making business, Bauer searches for any kind of work that allows for his disability, and finally lands a job as a newspaper reporter. At a gathering of Civil War veterans in 1869, he meets Hanna Rose, who writes for a war veterans' journal in Chicago. They correspond for two years before Bauer builds the courage to propose. They are married in Chicago in 1871, and she bears him four children, including a son he names Samuel Willis Bauer. Three of his children reach adulthood, with direct descendants who survive to this day, including four veterans of the military.

Bauer lives until 1904, and dies of pneumonia at age sixty-two. Hanna lives another twenty-four years, and dies at age eighty-four.

GEORGE THOMAS

After his army's astounding success on Missionary Ridge, Thomas accepts the subordinate position to Sherman's elevated command, and accompanies Sherman's forces toward Atlanta. He serves Sherman well, but the two men can never be called friends, both recognizing their wildly differing personalities. Moreover, Thomas technically outranks Sherman, though Grant's appointment of Sherman erases the distinction. It is the second time that Thomas finds himself subordinate to an officer he outranks (the first being Rosecrans).

In July 1864, Thomas's army decisively defeats John Bell Hood at the Battle of Peachtree Creek, which opens the door to Sherman's conquest of the city of Atlanta. But Thomas's penchant for attention to detail causes conflicts with Sherman, who, after capturing Atlanta writes to Henry Halleck, "I ought to have reaped larger fruits of victory, but a part of my army is too slow." Halleck's response is diplomatic: "Thomas is a noble old war-horse. It is true that he is slow, but he is always sure."

Responding to Hood's invasion of Tennessee, Thomas arrives at Nashville on October 3, 1864, and immediately supervises the strengthening of Federal outposts and supply depots from Chattanooga northward. Though Ulysses Grant and most of official Washington expect Thomas to meet Hood's challenge with a bold, aggressive stroke, Thomas prefers to strengthen his fortifications and encourages Hood to destroy himself. While tactically sound, the contrast with Sherman once again casts Thomas in an unfavorable light and gives fuel to his many critics. But Thomas's efforts bear fruit when his troops crush Hood's assault at Franklin, Tennessee. Again Grant has expectations that Thomas will finish the task and destroy what remains of Hood's army before Hood escapes southward. When Hood refuses to retreat, Thomas reassures Washington that he intends to attack the stubborn and outmanned enemy, but Thomas injures his reputation by informing Halleck, "If I can perfect my arrangements, I shall move. . . ." The choice of words adds more fuel to the fires against him. Grant is aware that Thomas's army outnumbers Hood's by a substantial margin. Yet Thomas seems to have an instinct for his adversary, and instead of pursuing what should have been a Confederate retreat, Thomas fortifies Nashville into an invincible citadel. On December 6, 1864, an exasperated Grant orders Thomas to "attack Hood at once, and wait no longer." The war of words heats up further, as Thomas attempts to explain his delays as an effort to protect his flanks, and put sufficient cavalry forces into the saddle, countering what he believes to be Hood's only real chance for success. Grant's frustrations with what he continues to see as Thomas's reluctance to act results in a letter to Henry Halleck two days later, insisting that "if Thomas has not struck yet, he ought to be ordered to hand over his command."

The criticism of Thomas grows, spreading to the pen of Secretary of War Stanton, who tells Grant, "Thomas seems unwilling to attack because it is hazardous, as if all war was anything but hazardous." Grant responds on December 9 by drafting an order to Henry Halleck instructing Thomas to turn his command over to General John Schofield, a Thomas subordinate. But Halleck is not one to hurry paperwork, and the order is not yet official when Thomas finally orders the attack. On December 15, Hood's army is outnumbered two to one, and is utterly routed. Despite criticism of Thomas's methods or attention to detail, his strategy is completely successful, and the Confederate threat to Tennessee is wiped away. What remains of Hood's army withdraws into Mississippi, and Hood's military career is terminated by Jefferson Davis.

But accolades for the victory are delayed. Instead of allowing Thomas's victorious army to rest in winter quarters, Grant immediately orders Thomas to resume campaigning southward, hoping to eliminate remaining Confederate strongholds in Mississippi and Alabama.

In spring 1865, as the war concludes, Thomas commands occupied Confederate territory in the states west and south of the Appalachians, what is known as the Department of the Cumberland.

In 1869, Thomas is assigned to command the

Military Division of the Pacific, and moves to San Francisco. But his service there is brief. He dies in 1870, at age fifty-three, and is buried in Troy, New York. He is still considered a traitor to the Confederacy by his family, and none of his Southern relatives attend the funeral. But the list of those who attend his memorial service includes (now president) Ulysses Grant, and Generals Sherman, Meade, Sheridan, Rosecrans, and Hooker, among many others.

It is an ongoing debate whether Thomas was grotesquely mistreated by both Grant and Sherman, both of whom condemn Thomas in their memoirs. Thomas does not live to counter the attacks on his character, though in subsequent years, a great many others, including Charles Dana and (later president) James Garfield, are effusive in their praise for Thomas as a commander. There is no confusion about the loyalty of his own troops, who vehemently defend his campaigning style. The United States Congress agrees, and even before the war's end, in early March 1865, Thomas is presented with a formal resolution of thanks. Later that year, the state of Tennessee recognizes him with the issuance of a gold medal.

One consistency to Thomas's character is a lack of self-promotion, which in the end is likely responsible for his being overlooked by history. Unlike Sherman and Grant, Thomas does not write memoirs, and instead burns his private papers, saying "my private life is my own, and I will not have it hawked about in print for the amusement of the curious." He dislikes public speaking, is no orator in any sense, and does not seek the accolades that come to him after the war, including an attempt by some to draft him as a candidate for president in 1867. In 1868, he refuses his nomination to the rank of lieutenant general, believing that his services "do not rank so high a compliment."

To this day, Thomas has both detractors and admirers, and his early death, compared to so many of his contemporaries, has likely erased a reputation that deserves far greater mention.

With unexpected graciousness, General in Chief Sherman officially announces Thomas's death to the army: "In battle he never wavered, he never sought advancement of rank or honor at the expense of anyone. Whatever he earned of these were his own and no one disputes his fame. General Thomas was the very impersonation of honesty, integrity and honor . . . the beau ideal of the soldier and gentleman. The old Army of the Cumberland . . . will weep for him many tears of grief."

Historian Bruce Catton responds to Thomas's critics with even more enthusiasm: "What a general could do, Thomas did. No more dependable soldier for a moment of crisis existed on the North American continent . . . there was nothing slow about Thomas, nor was he primarily defensive. Grant was wrong."

The controversy is best summed up by historian Benson Bobrick: "Either Thomas was overcautious and deliberate . . . or quite simply, the greatest Union general of the war."

But this story continues. From Atlanta to the last struggles for the Confederacy in the Carolinas, the Federal army, led now by William T. Sherman, must confront the last stand of the Confederates and Joseph Johnston, in a campaign that tears and burns through the beleaguered lands and fading light of Southern hopes. It is a story to come . . .

ABOUT THE AUTHOR

JEFF SHAARA is the **New York Times** bestselling author of **A Chain of Thunder, A Blaze of Glory, The Final Storm, No Less Than Victory, The Steel Wave, The Rising Tide, To the Last Man, The Glorious Cause, Rise to Rebellion,** and **Gone for Soldiers,** as well as **Gods and Generals** and **The Last Full Measure**—two novels that complete the Civil War trilogy that began with his father's Pulitzer Prize–winning classic, **The Killer Angels.** Shaara was born into a family of Italian immigrants in New Brunswick, New Jersey. He grew up in Tallahassee, Florida, and graduated from Florida State University. He lives in Gettysburg.

LIKE WHAT YOU'VE READ?

If you enjoyed this large print edition of
THE SMOKE AT DAWN,
here are a few of Jeff Shaara's latest bestsellers
also available in large print.

A Chain of Thunder
(paperback)
978-0-307-99088-4
($28.00/$34.00C)

A Blaze of Glory
(paperback)
978-0-307-99064-8
($28.00/$34.00C)

The Final Storm
(paperback)
978-0-7393-7820-5
($28.00/$33.00C)

The Steel Wave
(paperback)
978-0-7393-2784-5
($29.95/$34.00C)

Large print books are available wherever books
are sold and at many local libraries.

All prices are subject to change. Check with your
local retailer for current pricing and availability.
For more information on these and other large print titles,
visit www.randomhouse.com/largeprint.